School Story

D. B., D. C., T. C., G. D., T. D., B. S., & N. R.
know the truth of it.

SCHOOL STORY

Iain Mackenzie-Blair

Copyright © Iain Mackenzie-Blair 2005
First published in 2005 by Three Cats Press
Aultgrishan
Wester Ross, IV21 2DZ
email: tcp@bcd3.wanadoo.co.uk

Distributed by Gazelle Book Services Limited
Hightown, White Cross Mills, South Rd, Lancaster, England LA1 4XS

The right of Iain Mackenzie-Blair to be identified as the author of the work has been asserted herein in accordance with the Copyright, Designs and Patents Act 1988.

All rights reserved. This book is sold subject to the condition that it shall not, by way of trade or otherwise, be lent, resold, hired out or otherwise circulated without the publisher's prior consent in any form of binding or cover other than that in which it is published and without a similar condition including this condition being imposed on the subsequent purchaser.

British Library Cataloguing in Publication Data
A catalogue record for this book is available from the British Library

All of the characters in this book are fictitious and any resemblance to actual people, living or dead, is purely imaginary.

ISBN 0-9547630-1-7

Typeset by Amolibros, Milverton, Somerset
This book production has been managed by Amolibros
Printed and bound by Advance Book Printing, Oxford, UK

One

1941-1942 Drift   1

Two

1942-1945 Blood   161

Three

1945-1946 Fall   327

1941-1942

Drift

> *Though this child's drift*
>
> *Seems by a divíne doom chánnelled*
>
> Gerard Manley Hopkins
> '*The Bugler's First Communion*'

Chapter One

'Angus? Baker? Dermott-Powell? Ellerman? Mawsom? Notting? Snider? Good. Look sharp and let the man from Winters' photograph your Election...'

Almost without realising it, I have begun to tell the story I vowed I would never tell at all; a story I have avoided telling for a lifetime. It has always lain there waiting – lurking; during the past months it has thrust itself forward, at first merely nagging, but now insistent.

Perhaps you will not be able to believe what I have to say, holding it instead to be mere fiction – the work of a not very pleasant imagination. If only you could be right; I would prefer that, because if you cannot believe it then maybe I shall be able to persuade myself it never really happened at all and that what I am about to write is the figment of a mind distorted by age.

The photograph is real enough. It shows our 'Election' – the seven of us who were shepherded in Great Quad that autumn afternoon. Every intake into Ansell's was known as an 'Election' because we laid claim to being the original Ansell's Hall, where all Queensmen (as Scholars are still termed) had been housed until the latter part of the nineteenth century. After that, in the wake of other more searching reforms recommended by the Clarendon Commission, they were distributed amongst all the 'Houses' that then comprised the School. Already, for more than a hundred years, it had chosen subtly to hold aloof from nearby Cranchester by affecting to pronounce the School 'Ca'aster' out of deference to an early nineteenth-century Master whose antiquarian speculations suggested that the small market town had once been the site of a Roman fort.

On the desk in front of me, sharp and bright as if it had been taken yesterday:

Angus. Guileless, eager, freckled face and sensitive mouth. You can clearly see in his well-groomed dark hair, that curious flash of congenitally premature silver which he could never disguise even by the dint of most careful brushing.

Baker. Square face, horn-rimmed glasses, straight hair cut slightly too short so that there was a border of pale skin between it and the holiday tan. Baker was almost plump then. I remember, on the first night, when he leaned his hands on the table, the small rolls of flesh at the wrist.

Mawsom looks straight into the camera as though, although frightened, he is determined not to show it. His clothes are neat. His features are neat too, but his eyebrows are curiously arched over his grey eyes and they give the effect of being in a permanent state of questioning surprise.

Notting. Small for his age, but big-boned and solidly built, with short blunt fingers and a fringe of mousy hair which, even in the photograph shows signs of the endless battle he waged to make it succumb to the parting that was *de rigueur* at Ansell's.

Snider is beside him, considerably taller than anyone else, almost willowy, with dark straight hair and deep-set eyes. The photograph does not show his hands which are behind his back, so you cannot see the long, slender fingers. Snider had the most perfect half-moons above the cuticle that I had ever seen. His were the hands of a musician, but he was not a musician, in fact he was tone deaf. However, in Biology practicals he undertook dissection with a precision and delicacy that was quite exceptional.

Dermott-Powell. The most delicately formed of the group, with rather secret eyes, wide lips and even teeth, features which must have been perfectly set off by the wide collar and scarlet cassock of the famous cathedral where he had been Head Chorister. The black and white print cannot show the way his auburn hair gleamed in sun.

Even at that first meeting, when we were all more or less subdued and apprehensive, he exuded a sort of sparkle that was exciting and disturbing at the same time. We sensed that there was something which set him apart from the rest of us; as though he had crossed some threshold of which the rest of us were totally unaware. It was not until many years later, that I recognised what none of us then, at the age of thirteen, could have defined.

I had attended a lecture on Caravaggio. The hall was sparsely occupied for it was a cold November afternoon and I was already regretting my decision, when a slide of a youthful John the Baptist was projected onto the screen. In the sensual prettiness of the artist's beggar-boy model, I first recognised for what it was, the knowing ambivalence which I now detect in the Dermott-Powell looking out at me from the photograph.

However, it is, of course, Ellerman who dominates the group. Even after all these years, he comes across as a magnetically beautiful boy with a quality quite different from the cherubic good looks of Dermott-Powell and many other children of similar age. Despite the Cranchester uniform, Ellerman still seems elegantly proportioned. He looks just as Public School boys are meant to look. In fact he looks as, at the time, we felt *we* were expected to look. Fair springy hair, not quite curly or ostentatious, carefully parted; genuinely smiling lips; blue eyes; an open intelligent face. On that first day, I remember, he seemed to glow with stored sunlight for his appearance was enhanced by the fact that his skin had been tanned to a golden colour by an outdoor holiday to which tennis, cricket, sailing, swimming had all contributed. So must Ganymede have looked among his contemporaries.

There are half a dozen other photographs, each one quite unfaded because, from the time I left Ansell's until this afternoon, I had never taken them from this large brown envelope of thin 'utility' paper. Ellerman never lost his outstanding good looks. He developed, painlessly it seemed, from being a beautiful child into a strikingly handsome young man. He suffered none of the usual adolescent ugliness and skin rash so common at fifteen and sixteen. Here is another, later, photograph. Notting, drawn and thin-faced, almost sullen, dark hollows beneath his eyes. Mawsom and Angus have lost their open attractiveness. Baker looks like a concentration-camp guard and Snider seems almost emaciated, but Ellerman looks superb.

In the last, Ellerman is very much Head of House; from the moment of first meeting it was obvious that he was the archetypal 'Golden Boy'. It came as no surprise to discover that he was a superlative natural games-player. I think that our whole Election was so conventional, so seduced by the schoolboy *cliché* that it would have been astonishing had he not been a fine sportsman. There is one other photograph, a snapshot in a worn, much re-addressed envelope.

ii

When I walked through Lodge that first time it was the conclusion of a two-day journey. Small for my age, I was timid, apprehensive and terrified by a vast congregation of boys, all of whom were taller, stronger, more purposeful and far more confident than I.

Although it has never struck me before, I realise I must have been considerably younger too; it occurs to me now that I spent every birthday on the train returning to Cranchester for the Spring half.

It had been boat, sleeper and an overnight stay in London with a godfather I did not recognise, a big kindly man who had been at Ansell's with my father. On the following day I boarded the Cranchester train, awed and impressed by the fact that it was even pulled by a locomotive bearing the name of the school.

I sat for more than three hours in a corner seat and throughout the whole of that time I spoke not one word. Nor was any word addressed to me. Yet I was wearing school dress with an Ansell's tie and every single passenger on the train, boy and adult, was in some way connected with Cranchester.

Five other boys in the compartment ignored me completely, although they talked animatedly amongst themselves. One, daringly, smoked a cigarette out of the window whilst his companions pulled down the blinds on the corridor side. I might just as well have been the Invisible Man and I cannot remember that I ever recognised any of them again, so little did I regard their faces.

I was in limbo.

Subsequently I remember treating new boys in the same insensitive way. On one occasion I had been asked to look out for a distant relation – cousin or second cousin unable to get a place in Ansell's so had to make do with Jonquil's or Pettifer's, I cannot remember which. I glimpsed him at the London terminal, recognising his distinctive red hair and I deliberately walked in another direction. Twelve hours later we came face to face crossing Great Quad.

'Oh! Hello. I think I caught a glimpse of you at the station yesterday,' he said, the relief clear in his voice. 'I was going to say "hello" then, but lost sight of you in the crush.'

I knew just how he felt, but I remember replying, 'Just as well you didn't. It's not "on" to talk with "frogs" until they've been through Lodge.' In Ansell's new boys were never called 'frogs' – a tradition respected even by the other Houses.

I was at the time all of fifteen and I doubt he was as many months younger. I gave him no more than a nod for the rest of that Half and, as he was not an Ansell's Man, I don't think we ever exchanged a word thereafter.

'Ca'aster' education began the moment you set foot on your first school train. It took you over and it never let go, even after your final Half when, convinced that as of right, the world was your oyster, you stepped from a school train for the last time.

Characteristically, that moment too was governed by tradition, for no Castonian might wear his Old Castonian tie until his feet had touched the platform of the London terminal. I recall only one case where this custom was flouted and, as a dare, the tie was donned during the course of that final journey. Despite a subsequent career which has been both impeccable and distinguished, I have never seen the name of the culprit on a Castonian Association List. Possibly he never asked to be restored, but it would not surprise me in the slightest to learn that his offence was considered too heinous to be absolved, despite the fact that on the List are names of several Castonians who have been imprisoned and one who was lucky to escape hanging for a particularly notorious crime just after the war. Presumably, though criminal, they had never offended against Cranchester's exclusive and idiosyncratic code.

Ansell's had, in addition, its own code which was even more individual, idiosyncratic and persuasively chauvinistic; for example our Toast on 'Tassel Night' was 'Ansell's and the School'; in every other House 'the School' came first. It engendered such an intoxicating ethos that within twelve hours of our arrival at the age of thirteen, we thought of ourselves as 'Ansell's Men' first and Castonians a long way second.

iii

I have been at considerable pains to obscure the true identity of Ansell's and Cranchester, however diligently records of the top dozen Public Schools might be perused; I have changed all names completely. So should there be, by chance, somewhere in existence a Division List, or school roll, which includes an Angus, an Ellerman, a Dermott-Powell, then quite certainly it is the wrong school and the coincidence would be far more worthy of report than the 'discovery' itself. The real Ellerman for instance, has none of those letters in his name, though he does now have a title.

I reveal that Cranchester is one of the top dozen schools, because it is important that no one shall be tempted to dismiss the story as something that could only happen at a latter-day Dotheboys Hall, peopled by unsophisticated boys and low-calibre masters. On the contrary, Cranchester is very well known, even to those who have never been there. The distinctive Old Castonian tie often appears on television when notable men in politics, commerce, or public life are interviewed and writers of plays frequently invoke it to characterise certain stereotypes.

The saddest casualty of the necessity to conceal the identity of the real Cranchester has been the abandonment, for obvious reasons, of its unique, evocative and hallowed 'language'. Nonetheless it would be impossible to convey what happened without invoking the atmosphere of a community cocooned far more effectively by its own language and customs than by any encircling wall. To resolve this problem, I have borrowed appropriate phrases, words and slang from several other schools. If therefore you feel a surge of excitement as you identify a phrase, and think 'Good Heavens! It must be...', naming your own school, then beware, for I have left unchanged only those words which the real 'Cranchester' has in common with other similar establishments.

Although many Castonians may not recognise their school, Ansell's Men will recognise their 'House', despite its change of name, because I have altered none of the internal geography, none of the customs. However, unless they have been far more successful than I in expunging the past, I do not expect that those of our Election will wish to identify themselves.

I, certainly, am now hardly identifiable as one of the seven small boys gazing out from the photograph on the desk in front of me. Nevertheless, I discover that even after all these years, when some of those who were central to the story are no longer living, I still lack courage enough to identify myself unequivocally. Furthermore, even were the seven of us brought together again, I believe I could and would, dissemble convincingly enough to keep the others uncertain of authorship and preserve my anonymity.

Why then, you may ask with justifiable impatience, do I bother at all? Why expect any reader to take an interest in events which took place long ago, concerning people whose names have been altered, who attended a school which has been thoroughly disguised and written by an anonymous author? Why go to such exceptional lengths to conceal identities and still feel it is worth relating the story?

I cannot offer you a satisfactory explanation, because I am not sure that I really have one. I can only say that, despite those vigorous assurances to myself and all my vows that I would never relate these events, in my heart of hearts I always knew there would come a time when the necessity to tell the story would push everything else from me. That moment has arrived. Like the Ancient Mariner, I must now tell somebody – because until I have finished I shall be able to do nothing else.

Three specific events jogged my hand. Coincidences? Perhaps. Each in itself was insignificant, even trifling. Three months ago. I was driving through the West Country in glorious summer weather, with the roof of the car open. I checked on an appointment, to discover that, for reasons outside my control, it had been cancelled. I had not long returned from a lengthy and dusty sojourn in the United States and, because I unexpectedly had half a day to spare, I decided to take my time about returning to London. Abandoning the main road, I dawdled through tangles of deep lanes and villages with attractive, unlikely, names. Then I decided, on a whim, to stay overnight at one of those small country pubs where, against all expectation, they provide outstanding food.

The following morning, after a leisurely breakfast, I began, with genuine reluctance, to make my way back to the motorway. I had been paying only casual attention to the map when all of a sudden (Chance? Fate?) I found myself driving up wide, sleepy Market Street in Cranchester.

The old, almost forgotten, choking panic overcame me. I stopped the car. Until that moment I had not registered that I was anywhere near the school. I felt beads of perspiration round my eyes, my heart pounded.

Eventually, when I had recovered, I got out – to find myself facing Winters, the photographer. I crossed the road to Crandall's, a coffee-shop with bow windows and dim interior. It was still the same. Small wooden booths with chintz curtains ranged down the back of the shop from a communal 'front parlour' with wooden tables and chairs. Even the respectable middle-aged lady who approached for an order seemed timeless.

I was fifteen again, in stiff collar, black jacket, striped trousers and much-polished shoes, feeling rather emancipated to be able to sit there and order coffee. Crandall's was out of bounds to Ansell's Men in their first two years, unless accompanied by someone senior, or a relation. As far as I know it was no regulation of, nor reflection on, Crandall's. It was just one of the many hierarchical privileges which threaded our lives like veins and arteries.

I sat sipping coffee, toying with a cherry bun I did not want, procrastinating – pretending to myself that I might still ignore the dusty road at the end of Market Street, with its signpost to the exquisite little church of St Peter and St Paul on the left; to 'Cranchester School' straight ahead.

Can I really have been so completely unaware that I was so close to Cranchester? Had I been subconsciously pretending I didn't know where I was, but daring to test myself? Certainly I was not conscious of such an intention, otherwise I could not have felt so much at ease the previous evening and at breakfast. Or, after all those years of shutting out, had I been drawn back by some ineluctable force born of a deeply buried desire for absolution, a subconscious need to exorcise, once and for all, the ghosts which still haunted me however much I wanted to suppress them?

Fifteen minutes later I was walking through Lodge, vaguely recognising the fit, elderly head porter in his dark green uniform with its gold buttons. I heard myself asking if I could look round. Even then I was, I suppose, unconsciously obscuring my connection, because Old Castonians simply walk through Lodge with a casual 'Good Morning', confident that Cranchester is still theirs and that they deserve to be recognised.

'Of course, sir, it's the Half.'

'Half' is the Cranchester word for 'Term'; a Cranchester school year consists of three 'Halfs' – never 'halves'. However, it also means the break in the middle of the morning moreover, even more confusingly '*the* Half' means the half-term exeat.

He emerged from his glass-fronted cubby-hole, offering a simplified map of the school on a board with a handle. 'Visitors find this useful. We're standing here, sir, where the red dot is. Buildings available to visitors are outlined in green, sir. You can drop this back when you return.'

'Thank you very much.'

'I expect you'll be from the States, sir,' he offered in his West Country burr. 'We've lots of visitors from America these days.'

'Clever of you to guess, I thought I'd managed to eliminate my accent,' I added, playing up to his mistake on the spur of the moment.

'I can always tell, sir. I worked with the Americans during the war for a bit. Until I was wounded.'

I remembered him then. Sergeant Major Starlight; he arrived late in the war and was, at that stage, far the youngest member of the ground-staff. He had, then, a curious pallor and a pronounced limp. We were told that he had been awarded the Military Medal in Italy.

I had never been back to the school since the early morning I left so ignominiously; never replied to, or even opened, the trickle of notices, appeals and invitations that pursue a Castonian across the world throughout his life, but it was only at the moment of confirming, implicitly, Starlight's mistaken view that I was an American visitor, that I was aware how much

I did not want him, or anyone else, to know that I was a Castonian. In fact, I suppose I was safe enough without resorting to becoming an 'American'. No porter would dream that any Castonian might decline to claim his birthright! However, at that same moment, I also knew that, had boys and masters been around, I should have turned tail and hurried to my car parked on the great sweep of gravel.

※

I abandoned the cool shadows of Lodge and, as I came into the sun, was once again the apprehensive boy I had been on that first occasion so many years before. Great Quad is the most magnificent part of the Foundation, its huge honey-coloured flagstones once paved the refectory of a noble monastery dissolved by Henry VIII. Cranchester School spreads out from it like a small village. It is enclosed on three sides by the original academic buildings which had, as the School flourished and expanded, been gradually supplemented by incorporating the scattering of dwellings and little farms of the small hamlet which had originally sprung up in the protection of the monastery

Like so much else connected with Cranchester, its boundaries are singular. There is no gate, despite the implications of 'Lodge', nor are there any walls, because the founder died with spectacular nobility on the battlefield before he had fulfilled his intention 'to bilde the gretest Scole in the Realme'. Bounds are therefore known only to Castonians and consist of a field here ('Meadow'), a hedge there ('Hawthorn'), a footpath ('Parsons'), a stream ('Splash') and even an enormous ancient oak, known perversely as 'Acorn'. Typically, we at Ansell's rejoiced at the fact that our fag door ('Door') was the boundary in that particular direction. It meant that the House (which lay on the far side of 'Door) was technically 'out of bounds' and thus, some argued, beyond jurisdiction of the High Master – a claim never tested in The Digger's time!

A Castonian with permission for 'Leave Out' showed his 'Leave Slip' at Lodge and, on his return, handed it in, from where it eventually found its way back to the Housemaster. If he had no Leave Slip, or could not be bothered to get one, he walked across the fields, taking care not to get caught. The wooden box marked 'Leave Slips' is still in evidence, so presumably the custom continues.

As I paused, heat glancing down from the surrounding buildings and beating up from the ancient flagstones, I very clearly remember saying aloud to myself, 'I shall not visit Ansell's,' but knowing, even as I said it, that I would be unable to prevent myself. However, once more attempting to maintain the fiction that I had willpower enough to be my own master, I deliberately turned into the lobby of Old Library, a handsome sixteenth-century building, housing a fine collection of early printed books and an official 'Antiquarian Archivist' to look after them.

Doors to some of the Division Rooms were unlocked and I was struck by the light airy colours — one even had a blue ceiling — overhead projectors, posters, pictures, tables with melamine tops and comfortable plastic chairs. One room remained as I remembered them all. There were the heavy oak-and-iron double desks; a high dais with steps below a wall-length blackboard, still carried the massive master's desk. Decoration here was unchanged, the lower half of the walls deep chocolate and the upper half coffee-coloured, both darkening with age. Light bulbs under glass shades (white underside, green topside) hung suspended with that peculiarly naked appearance on long flex from a high, discoloured, ceiling. There were three tattered maps by the board. One showed **The Classical World,** another, **The Modern World,** glowed with great areas of British Empire pink. The third was a **Physical Map of the World**. The room smelled of dust, chalk, old paper and dry decay. The lintel above the door read 'Dr Larchfield', in cracked and yellowing letters.

Larchfield joined the Common Room during my last Half, slight of stature and looking younger than most of the Praefaectors. Except for the fact that he had seemed so very youthful I could remember nothing of him at all.

Then, inevitably, before I knew it, I found myself on the familiar path and, surrendering to the inevitable, opened Door. Originally, Ansell's had been a fine Georgian house replacing an earlier Jacobean farmhouse destroyed by fire. A large rectangular three-storey building had been grafted onto the back of it in the nineteenth century in order to accommodate some fifty boys. From the front where the Housemaster lived, it still looked the elegant little mansion it had once been.

At the centre of the addition, at the back, lies a rectangular space open to the sky. We called it 'Yard' and it gave rise to 'Yard Fives' ('YF' for short), a game peculiar to Ansell's, the main object of which was to strike a fives-ball so that it bounced off one of the many pipes and window ledges to disadvantage your opponent. Hitting windows (which were numerous) incurred penalty points; a broken window meant 'three-up', however senior. We were so expert that I can remember only one broken window in the whole time I was there.

Yard looked exactly as I remembered first seeing it, incredibly dusty, with a few blades of grey grass at the edge. To each side of me were familiar battered blue-painted doors. I turned the handle on the right – I never remember it being locked. The familiar claustrophobia engulfed me at once; my stomach tightened to that unforgettable tang of lineament, stale sweat and dampness which always characterised 'Big Change'.

I passed instead through the door on the left to be greeted by a different but equally familiar smell – dry, dusty, tinged by an indefinable odour of long-finished cooking.

Immediately to my right and behind my back were the worn stairs to 'Big Dorm', with their iron banister. Ahead, in the dim light, my eyes picked out the flimsy doors of 'Little Studies' which lined 'Corridor' and, at the far end, the much heavier door into 'Libe'.

That was unlocked too. Sun poured in through windows with heavy bars on the outside. The tiny 'Cells' projecting from the walls, like spokes on a rectangular wheel, seemed unchanged, although perhaps a bit more battered. At the centre of the room was 'Long School', complete with 'Cranton's Throne' and, at the far end, the familiar shabby wooden lockers.

A Time Machine?

Even the chairs looked the same; the benches on each side of Long School certainly were. The familiar vast fireplace, with its brass-topped fireguard glinting in the light, gaped like a cavernous mouth. I moved the length of Libe in a dream and on through the door at the far end into 'Din. Room'.

Nothing had changed there either. High Table on its discreet dais; four other long tables polished and shining, flanked by polished and shining benches; at the end of each table, farthest from High Table, four carvers with high backs and arms. The heavy wooden chairs at High Table are probably museum pieces (tradition has it that they belonged to the Founder) each one distinguished by some piece of individual design and the hierarchy of Praefaectors was thus reflected by the chair each occupied. The Housemaster's chair, at the centre, with a higher back, is undecorated except for an exquisitely carved coat of arms which seemed to surmount The Digger's head like a dark crown.

Praefaectors and Housemaster all sat on one side of High Table, overlooking the assembled House. Visitors sat either end; except for one occasion I never recall Praefaectors being displaced. On rare occasions, when there were more than two visitors, the extra guests were seated opposite the Praefaectors with their backs to the rest of us.

Behind High Table, I could see the names of previous Housemasters, each ungilded set of initials and dates meticulously carved into the dark panelling at the end of the incumbent's reign. We had to learn them by heart: 'Jonah; Elwell; Livingstone; Gunther; Rawison; Wrighton; Rigwell; Holden-Smith; Dulverton; Winsell; Seymour', and now, of course, Jowling and his successors. Going closer, as well as 'D.I.G. Jowling, 1921-1947, I could make out, A. St. J. Winderton, 1947-1961; J. Le P. Orme 1961-1970'. I realised I would have known who was the present Housemaster had I ever read the copies of **The Castonian** which I always binned unopened. Had I not known what I did, I would never have noticed how subtly the date after The Digger's name had been altered, so expertly had the extraneous carving been filled; even the grain matched.

The Digger!

Suddenly, silently, hardly seeming to have aged at all, he was there before me, daunting as ever in his black MA gown, long flapping, sleeves with their half-moon cut-outs. Over six-foot, broad-shouldered, quietly well-tailored, bottom waistcoat-button undone. (He always turned back his right cuff when at his desk, something we secretly envied; our own war-time austerity suits had no cuff-buttons.) Immaculate shirt-cuffs gathered by discreetly embossed gold links. His shirt was always crisp and fresh. Who, I wonder, laundered them daily for him? (Our had to last a week, even ten days in the darkest days of the war and our twice-a-week, ill-starched collars became limp and grubby within hours.) Curiously, I can't recall the tie he was wearing, but I do remember that it was only for Confirmation Classes he ever donned a clerical collar – and then so thin that it showed like a mere cord.

Strong hands, despite almost delicate, ring-less, fingers, still powerful enough to beat any racquets player in the School: legendary hands which had struck six sixes in one over at Lords, winning that famous Varsity Match.

Neatly barbered wavy black hair (no hint of grey yet?). His clean-shaven jaw-line chiselled as if by wholesome plain living and reticent physical self-confidence: no incipient jowl, heightened colour, or any other sign of over-indulgence. White, even, teeth; firm but not cruel mouth and straight brows above disconcertingly shrewd grey-blue eyes.

Those eyes. Their uncompromising gaze – stern, unbending, luminous apparently with straightforward decency and their expectation of the highest standards of integrity – penetrating your very soul. Once and once only, in sheer terror had I dared meet it with a lie. Now I knew he was about to tax me with my craven dishonesty. Momentary paralysis before I stepped hesitantly forward and offered my hand.

Twenty-five years dead, he vanished.

Ghosts.

Back in the present I found my half-outstretched hand trembling violently.

Below, over a fireplace complete with fire-screen incorporating the Cranchester coat of arms, on a broad over-mantel, two glass cases – one at either end. Each contains a cap. It is the same cap – dark maroon, with thin blue piping at the peak; one has a 'Tassel' of gold and the other of silver. Football and Cricket caps vanished at the outbreak of war when Cranchester magnanimously responded to the national emergency by suspending a rule which had decreed 'no Castonian may go bareheaded'. However, in Ansell's the much-coveted Tassels continued to be awarded. Evidently they still are.

Between the two cases, on a little stand, is a dark, oak board with a worn crest of Sir Thomas Cranton, the Elizabethan soldier-poet who died of his wounds with such elegance. His quaint 'Grace Before Meat' is carved on the board and Head of House read it out at the beginning of every meal; at the end he reads the companion piece, 'Grace After Meat'.

Ansell's Men who have been Tasselled – gold for Football and silver for Cricket – and, on the long wall opposite High Table, the names of Praefaectors in black (red for Head of House). I found my own name. It came as a shock to see how many more had been added; it was the first time I had ever been genuinely conscious of my age. Ellerman's name is there – in red, silver and gold.

M.R.E. Ellerman

I see him in the mind's eye. An elegant figure, seemingly never muddy, wearing those Cranchester shorts which appear to be slightly wider at the pocket than the waist (thus accentuating the taper of the legs) and the blue-banded maroon jersey sidestepping, without apparent haste, an onrush threatening to engulf him, before setting off on that characteristic run with its deceptive half-swerve and astonishing acceleration. Tasselled for both Football and Cricket in his first year; Head of House; Captain of Cranchester Football; Captain of Cranchester Cricket; Captain of the School.

Next to the door to 'Private' (as the Housemaster's quarters were known) a narrow oak shelf on which stand nine silver tankards, each one slightly different and at least two centuries old. 'Praefaectors Pots' were used daily at High Table. There were pewter or silver tankards enough for every boy in the House on special occasions, each one contributed by an Ansell's Man of the past whose name is inscribed on his donation. I had my hand out to lift down the Pot I had once used when I heard, or imagined I could hear, a noise in the adjoining kitchen. I left like a thief, hastening back into Libe, down Corridor and, without thinking, up the stairs.

The door to Big Dorm stood open. There had been no structural alteration at all. It still seemed to accommodate about forty boys; at the far end, the small fireplace and, to its right, the door into 'Tosher'. On each side of a wide central gangway bed-spaces still separated by wooden partitions which did not go up to the ceilings and which, because of an imagined kinship with loose-boxes, were called 'Mangers'.

But there were differences. The partitions were now white-painted, with beams and ceilings in imaginative light blue. The beds themselves (they seemed to me the identical iron frames) were cheerful with tartan blankets and even duvets instead of the uniform red top-blanket I remembered so well. There were the same narrow stone-mullioned windows, one to each Manger, only now they boasted bright curtains, each individually chosen it seemed, and the heavy curtains at the end of the Mangers were varied and welcoming, no longer the dull brown hangings which provided our only privacy. On most partition walls were large posters. I felt reassured, thankful that time had, not after all, stopped still, and closed the door gently.

Outside, in the gloom once again, I could feel the chipped wall behind me; I knew that to my left lay the stairs and the passage to 'Upper Studies', but most acutely I was aware of the door now directly in front of me across the little landing, although I was willing myself not to look at it. To no avail. As if mesmerised, I moved forward and felt again in my fingers the dints in the familiar fluted brass door knob as they turned it. Then I was standing again in the threshold of 'Big Study'.

Big Study!

The window looking out onto the chestnut tree was closed, so the room was stifling, musty in the hot sun. Two or three books lay on the bottom shelf next to the fireplace, as though left in haste only moments before. Even the dowdy, rubbed, velvet curtains look the same as those which had been hanging there on my first day in Ansell's. The battered carver with wooden arms occupied its customary position, as did the huge old Bible, now even looser in its battered cover by the look of it. Memory ran finger of coldness up my spine.

Ghosts.

I shut the door quickly, but with quiet restraint and hastened to the stairs. I hurried down, out into the sun and then actually ran along the shadowy passage until I was 'safe' again in the heat and light of Great

Quad. For the second time that morning I could feel my heart pounding and I knew that blood had drained from my face.

I did not feel up to facing the cheerful and obliging Starlight at once, so turned into Chapel with its faint smell of incense (although incense was never allowed at Cranchester). Somebody was playing the organ. I could not see who, for the organ loft is high and lost in gloom. 'Jesu Joy of Man's Desiring'. It was played delicately, almost abstractedly, lingering on some of the high notes as I had so often heard it at evening Chapel. Simultaneously a phrase of Mendelssohn's music came back into my mind; the recollection was so strong that, for a fleeting second, I was certain that my ears actually caught the words – *I waited for the Lord.*

There came a discreet cough at my elbow. For that instant, choking panic once more; lost in the past, I was a new boy again until, swept by an immense relief, reality flooded back and I knew that we had never met before. In the diffused light of Chapel he evidently noticed nothing amiss in my hesitation. He must have been about fifteen and I realised how timeless were the faces of all Castonians.

'May I help you, sir?'

'Was that you playing?' Did I accentuate my American accent?

'Not very good, I'm afraid,' he said with an endearingly deprecating smile. 'It's just that I love playing the organ.'

'It sounded all right to me. The Porter said you were all on holiday.'

'We are. I live here because my Father's a Housemaster. That is,' he continued in polite deference to a Transatlantic visitor who might find the concept incomprehensible, 'He's one of fifteen masters who look after boarding houses. I'm a day-boy in a different House. He teaches Modern Languages, but,' he hesitated and then continued reverting to his attractive half-confidential manner, 'actually, I'm not much good at Modern Languages.'

'Nor am I!' I said it to be companionable because, in fact, I've become quite an able linguist. We moved outside into the sun.

'I don't suppose you've anything quite like this lot in America,' he said lightly but half-apologetically. 'But it's quite fun. Nowadays. Better than it was when my father was here. At least,' he added as an afterthought,

'It *sounds* a lot better from what he tells me.' Then after a pause, 'But he didn't seem to mind.'

Just in time I stopped myself from asking the sort of question which would have betrayed my own Castonian origins.

At Lodge I handed back the map-board together with a five-pound note.

'It must be a richly rewarding experience to go to school in buildings as historical as these,' I said, knowing that I was perhaps overdoing the admiring American visitor.

'Thank you, sir. That's most generous of you. Yes, sir, the young gentlemen are very fortunate indeed.'

Still 'young gentlemen'! We also had been 'young gentlemen' to Old Stubbington, even when he handed out a 'Pink Slip', with its ominous invitation – *The High Master requests the presence of...* – reserved for matters too serious to be disciplined by the Housemaster. Pink Slips were rare in my day; perhaps have now vanished altogether. Once upon a time they had signified a formal birching, the cost of the birch being noted on the slip by the head porter and sent to the victim's father with the end-of-Half bill.

'I met a very civil young fellow,' I said, 'playing the organ in the chapel. I gather he lives here.'

'Quite correct, sir. His father's one of the Housemasters.'

'That's all right!' I put in, seeing that Starlight was intending to embark on an explanation, 'He told me what Housemasters do.'

'Well, sir, his father's in a House called Ansell's.'

Of course! I ought to have expected one more coincidence, ought to have known it would concern Ansell's. Thanking my stars I had not bumped into the boy's father during my surreptitious visit to the House, I said graciously, 'Well, please tell his father, from me, that his son's a credit to, er, Cranchester.'

It was Starlight's reply that put me to flight.

'Of course I will, sir. A very nice young gentleman is Mr Ashton's son.'

Ghosts.

Chapter Two

'My name's Ashton and I'm your Nanny because I'm senior man of the previous election. In future when "List" is read, you answer "Present", followed by the name of whoever's reading List. So when Maunder reads "Curfew" tonight, you say "Present, Maunder." Don't forget. And speak up.'

It seemed impossible that the thin, tall, boy with straight fair hair, parted with engineering precision, looking cool and confident could be older than himself by only ten or twelve months. The mile-long trek from the station had been exhausting, there were no seats in the few taxis for 'frogs'. They had walked the hot, dust-thick road carrying leaden overnight cases, not daring even to speak amongst themselves, shuffling along in silence, ignorance and trepidation. The dark arch of Lodge had provided only a brief moment of relief.

Now he could feel heat pushing up from the great yellow stones into the soles of his shoes and down from the walls and windows of the buildings that surrounded the great quadrangle.

'Come on, we go this way.' A small crocodile began to move. 'Angus, buck up.' He woke with a start from his daydream. 'Ansell's is some way from the other houses and in a different direction. We prefer it that way. And Ansell's Men never get lost.'

The heat from the stone was as great as if a fiery throat were swallowing him without trace. They passed a chapel and plunged suddenly into a narrow passage between windowless walls as fiercely dark as formerly it had been bright. Patches of green, damp, moss were evidence of the fact that the sun never reached in there, but the shadowy alley seemed even more oppressive than the heat.

He felt his stomach lurch then tighten and the tension moving up till it began to constrict his chest. Between his teeth and closed lips he prayed. 'Please God. Not now.' He could feel beads of sweat under his hair on his forehead. The doctors had said he would be all right, but he began to feel the panic breathlessness which he remembered so vividly from that first terrifying attack when he was so much younger. 'Please God, not now. Not today of all days. And I *will* say my prayers.'

'I say Angus, you'll have to get a move on with your unpacking. Trunks go down to the cellars tomorrow, but I'll show you round now, all of you. You only get one tour, so you'd better remember. Ansell's Men don't ask their way around after the first day.' They moved off along the gangway between the Mangers. Heads turned and looked up as they passed. Angus thought, 'You move up Big Dormitory towards the fireplace as you become more senior.' There was a larger space by the fireplace with half a dozen hard chairs. By the door to the right Ashton said, 'This is "Tosher".' It opened onto a tiled floor and, on the left, was a line of lavatories. To the right, double doors with glass led into a washroom with white tiled walls. 'Through there,' Ashton pointed to the end of the row of lavatories, 'is "Private". It leads straight to Digger's rooms and he sometimes comes through that way at night. It's a fire escape too. Those are the Toshes – there at the far end on the right. Don't use more than six inches of water! There's a war on.' They moved back down the dormitory arid onto the landing.

'This is Big Study;' Ashton knocked respectfully on a door to the right. After a moment and no reply, Ashton opened the door. After the long, warm holiday and with closed windows, it smelt musty. 'You'd better come in. This is where you'll come when you get beaten.'

'That's *if* we get beaten, Ashton.' Dermott-Powell said in a joking voice.

Ashton, unsmiling, looked straight at him and said nothing, but pulled out an old wooden chair with arms polished from wear. 'You're told to get over "The Chair". This is it. Do it this way.' He demonstrated matter-of-factly: 'You'd better all try it. I get it, if you don't know what to do.'

Angus felt the choking sensation coming upon him again. Ashton continued unemotionally, 'I don't suppose it's much different from being beaten at your private school – except that if you don't get over The Chair the right way you get an extra cut and if you spout you get more. You'd better all try.' Sheepishly they did so. Notting trying to make a sort of joke of it, Ellerman nonchalant. Angus did as he was told quickly, trying not to think and, afterwards, putting the whole thing from his mind.

'Remember this, in the first ten days, if *you* make any mistakes, *I'm* the one who has to "tighten-up",' Ashton said.

Dermott-Powell said archly, 'It puts you in our power, doesn't it?' It was not received as a joke. There was a pause.

'We don't behave that way in Ansell's. You'd better leave that sort of thing at your private school.'

Snider asked quietly, 'Who has authority to beat us?'

'In Ansell's, only Praefaectors. And in your first three Halfs, or at least until there's another Election, you can only be beaten by the Praefaector for whom you're "Warmer". I'll explain about that in a minute.'

Ellerman said, 'My father said that there's a Praefaectors' beating?'

'It's only happened once since I've been in Ansell's. Usually for something like showing *side* and that sort of thing.'

Baker took off his glasses. 'What happens, Ashton?'

'A card is put up in Corridor and you come in here after Curfew. And you tighten-up to all the Monitors.'

After a long silence. Mawsom said, '*All* the Monitors! How many are there?'

'Six, but it's usually only one from each. Well, two from the Head of House. Seven, well eight in your case. You could of course get three more if you spout.'

'Does everyone tighten-up all the time?' Angus said in a thin voice.

Ashton stared. 'Good Lord no! Where do you think you are? And I ought to say that no Praefaector can give more than six cuts for one offence. Most are one or two. There have been Ansell's Men who've never had to tighten-up,' he said, before adding, 'So I've been told.'

'I say, Ashton, what happens if a Praefaector gives six and you spout?'

'You still can't be given more. Unless it's a Praefaectors' and even then it's a maximum of twelve, but nobody's ever had that many.'

'What if it's a mistake?' Snider said. 'I mean, say you've got blamed for something you didn't do?'

'It's too bad, but they always ask you first whether you've anything to say. And according to the school rules you can always appeal to Digger – that is to the Housemaster. Newton did that. He was the Election above ours.' Ashton sounded disapproving.

'Why?' Snider persisted.

'Head of House said he was to get three for cutting a Colts' practice and Newton said he'd been told to stay inside by Matron because he had a bad throat.'

'So the Housemaster let him off?' Snider said.

'Well, yes, Digger refused to let Head of House beat him. Then gave him twelve himself and told him that the Head of House knew what he was doing and he didn't like snivellers. Newton's people removed him about a Half later. He wasn't really an Ansell's Man. Sort of chap you find in Jonquil's or Henderson's. Come on, you'd better look downstairs.'

'What's a "Warmer"? You said you'd tell us.'

'Oh yes. Well there are seven of you so you'll all be Warmers – stands for 'bed-Warmer'. The Junior Election provide bed-Warmers for the Praefaectors. After Digger's been round at Curfew, you have to get off round to the Studies upstairs beyond Tosher with beds. Not the Little Studies out there – they don't have beds. You simply get in the Praefaector's bed and get it warm for him. When he comes in and is ready for bed you get out and go back to your own.'

'Which'll be very cold,' Baker said.

'But you can always stay in your own bed and get *Warmed* in Big Study,' Ellerman completed.

'You're learning, Ellerman. By the way, you Warm the bed in the Big Dorm when your Praefaector's on duty there. Come on. Downstairs now.'

Dermott-Powell said, 'Are there any other punishments? Except tightening-up, I mean?'

'Not really, not in Ansell's...well, there's writing out List several times, but that's a bit feeble. Only somebody like Singleton would ever use that. Actually,' he went on, 'in Ansell's, you either get a blasting – that's being told off pretty fiercely, or have to tighten-up. It's much better than lines and detentions like some of the other Houses because it's soon over. Mostly Ansell's men do as they're told. I've only ever been called to Big Study about a dozen times and I've been here a year.'

Ellerman said, 'What for?'

'Oh! My own fault. A couple of times I was very tired and simply fell asleep before Digger came round, so I never Warmed Maunder's bed. He let me off twice. I had to go to Big Study the third time. That was before he was Head of House. I got it for the same thing each of my first three Halves. You get one cut the first time you forget, two the second time and so on.' They were ranged on the stairs, listening. 'Come on, we must get round, but you start with a clean sheet each Half, so it's pretty fair really.'

As they went down the stairs Angus said hesitantly to Mawsom, 'Have you, well, ever been beaten?'

'Got it for the slightest thing at my Private School. The head said it made a man of you. He always asked you to choose which cane he should use. What about you?'

'No. Never.'

As if seeing Angus for the first time, Mawsom said, 'Oh! I see.'

Unnoticed, Notting behind them had overheard. He said, 'Sounds as if you've got a whole new experience ahead of you, Angus. Or should I say *behind* you.'

Mawsom said, 'Shut up, Notting.' He turned back to Angus: 'It'll probably not happen to you here then. Anyway,' he added comfortingly, 'it's not all that bad. As Ashton says, it's soon over!' Angus looked at him. 'You scared?' They were at the back. 'Sorry, I shouldn't have asked that.'

'You won't tell the others?'

'Of course not.'

'Thanks.'

They had all arrived at the bottom of the stairs and they moved into a dark passage with doors leading into tiny studies which just had barely room for a desk, two chairs, a bookcase and a small fireplace. 'This is "Corridor",' Ashton explained. 'All Ansell's Men are expected to know what's on the notice-boards and sometimes Praefaectors ask you to see if you've bothered.' He turned. 'These are called Little Studies for pretty obvious reasons and they're used by the next most senior, under the Praefaectors. Incidentally, Big Study is Praefaectors only, but as I told you, nobody sleeps in Little Studies. If a Little Study wants someone to fag for him, do his fire and so on, he can ask anyone except a Warmer, but he must pay you at the end of term. It's a pound,' Ashton added cheerfully, 'and you get a lot of perks because you can usually use his study when he's not there. I've been asked by Daly who lives here,' and he pushed a door of one of the rooms, as they moved on towards the double door at the end of Corridor.

'This is Library. We call it "Libe".'

A large handsome room panelled in wood. Ranged from each of the long walls were a series of small stalls or cubicles, divided by dark wooden partitions. Each partition supported a flat wooden desk top about twenty inches wide Above the desk was a narrow ledge with beading, evidently for pens and pencils. To the right of the desk, attached to the panelled wall was a wooden cupboard about two feet high with a door, divided inside by two shelves. Each had on it a hasp for a modest padlock. There was a hard wooden chair. The other side of the partition provided the rear 'wall' of the adjoining cubicle.

'They're called "Cells", from the monks,' Ashton explained, 'not prisons.'

They all laughed, more from relief and relaxing of tension than anything else. It almost physically lightened the oppression that had been weighing on them since Big Study. Might it be possible to survive, Angus thought to himself and, catching Mawsom's eye, raised his eyebrows in a half-smile. He knew from the response that Mawsom had been thinking much the same.

They examined the Cells. There was the ubiquitous unshaded bulb on a long flex and a window, or part of a window, for each Cell along the outer wall and a black-out shutter. On the inner wall, which evidently gave onto Yard, there were only three or four windows for seven or eight

Cells. Ellerman noted them with evident satisfaction; the six-foot by four-foot space enclosed by the partitions seemed positive luxury, despite its shabbiness.

Ashton said, 'You lot don't get a Cell yet.' He indicated the long, polished table in the central space. 'The new Election is on "Long School".' There were two benches each side. It looked as though it would perhaps seat twelve. 'The Praefaector taking Evening School sits there.' Ashton indicated the elaborate carved and much repaired chair at one end. 'And the senior man in your Election sits there.' There was a plain wooden chair at the other end. 'The Praefaector's chair belonged to the Founder, that's why it looks so old. It's called "Cranton's Throne". And if you're caught sitting in it you get a Praefaectors'.'

They trooped down to the end of the room, where a clock and seven or eight silver cups stood on the broad mantel above the fireplace. On each side were wooden lockers. 'These lockers are for your stuff – when you're on Long School.'

Dermott-Powell ran his hand along the shiny brass rail at the top of a substantial fireguard screwed to the panelling at each end of the gaping void.

'Junior Election lights the fire and now, because of the War, you have to clear it before School in the morning. You have to go inside.'

'I bet it's hot when it's burning,' Notting said.

'If you're wise you won't go too near it when it's alight until you're senior. Only ten people are allowed round the fire at any one time. That means the ten most senior in the room. It's up to you to keep count, because nobody will tell you and the first thing you'll know is when you're told to go to Big Study after Curfew.' Ashton dropped his voice confidentially; 'Actually it's only one cut if you're caught, so sometimes it's worth the chance when it's really cold. Of course only a Praefaector can send you up, so mostly there's a big crowd and as long as somebody keeps an eye on the door it's pretty safe.'

He opened a door in the panelling. 'This is "Din. Room".' They walked in almost on tiptoe, never to forget their first view. The tables were laid and the shining surfaces, the glasses and cutlery in the last sun from the high window in the west wall, made it look a bit like a church.

'Listen carefully. Here's your table.' He led them to the table nearest the kitchen door. 'There'll be a Little Study sitting at that end. On the wall there are the names of Tassels – Gold for Football, Silver for Cricket, and the names of the Housemasters are carved there. You have to know them by heart. It's not only your Election on this table, in fact, I'm on it too.' He turned round. 'At those meals when the Housemaster's here – that's for breakfast and lunch and sometimes for supper – the Housemaster sits in that chair on the dais there in the middle, with the Praefaectors on each side of him.'

'What happens at supper?' Baker enquired.

'When he's not there? Well, all weekdays the Praefaectors have dinner after everyone else has gone. They sit up there and you serve them.'

Ellerman said, 'What, all of us?'

'Yes. One behind each chair. Like a footman. Only Ansell's still does it like that!'

Angus asked rather hesitantly, 'What are the rest of Ansell's doing?'

'In the middle of Evening School there's a break and it's free time. That's when the Praefaectors have dinner.'

'How long?'

'Usually thirty minutes. It ends whenever they finish. The Praefaector in Libe rings the bell for us to continue. It sounds worse than it is. It's quite fun actually because the Praefaectors make jokes and forget we're there and there's often leftovers if you have time to eat them before the second half of Evening School. Is there anyone who has any other question?' There was a small silence.

'What's Curfew?'

'Oh yes. That's at the end of Evening School. Usually about nine-fifteen. Everyone comes into Libe and you stand there in List order with hands folded. The Head of House fetches the Housemaster. The Duty Praefaector reads List. Remember what I said about answering? The Junior Praefaector reads a piece from the New Testament and the Housemaster says a prayer. He then shakes the hand of all the Praefaectors, says "Goodnight, Ansell's" and we all say, "Goodnight, sir." Like that, very crisply, not a sort of drone. Then he goes back to Private and if there are any announcements Head of House makes them. Anything else?'

There was so much information that they were all silent. Then Dermott-Powell burst out, 'I say, Ashton, is it true that we have to go to Tosher absolutely starkers? That's what our Master of Choristers told me.'

'Actually, thanks for reminding me. Yes. Nobody in Big Dormitory may wear pyjamas, or dressing-gown, or a towel to Tosher until he has permission from Head of House to "cover-up".'

Snider said, 'How do we get permission?'

'You won't. Not yet. Armitage hasn't ever had permission and he's in the Fifth form; rather bad luck on him.'

'Have you got permission, Ashton?'

There was a small pause. 'Actually, no.'

'But how can we get permission?' Snider insisted.

'You can cover-up if you're Tasselled for Football or Cricket. Martin of our Election was Tasselled in his second Half. Otherwise you don't get permission till you've got enough hair down here.'

Baker went very pink, and looked at his feet. Angus assumed he had mistaken the gesture because he had never supposed anyone might have hair where Ashton indicated. Further explanation was cut short because a bell rang somewhere. 'Supper,' Ashton said, brightening visibly. 'I'll show you Big Change afterwards.'

Din. Room was busy and bustling, but just after they entered an absolute silence fell. D I G Jowling was an imposing figure. It was rumoured that, before the war, he refused to tour Australia for England because it would take him away from Ansell's. His name still has a university record against it in Wisden.

His height was accentuated by the dais; they had never, ever, seen such a powerful, frightening person. He spoke courteously, but with quietly chilling authority, as soon as Grace after Meat had been said: 'The new Election will please present themselves at my study in exactly half an hour. Ashton, I shall rely on you to see that they are all present on time.'

Ashton, standing very straight, said, 'Yes, sir.' The Housemaster disappeared through his door in a dark swirl of gown, carrying his mortarboard.

'Whuh!' It was Dermott-Powell.

Ashton said, 'He's all right, but if he asks you to do something, you have to look him straight in the eye and speak up loudly. I've never been up to him for a row or a beating, or anything, and I don't want to. So for Heaven's sake never get sent to him by your Div Pro — that's your form master. Teaching beaks don't beat, they send them to the Housemaster. Or the High Master if it's very serious.'

'Does that happen often, I mean the High Master?' Notting asked.

'It hasn't happened since I've been here. And I don't think anyone, even Maunder, can remember when it did. I think The Digger would probably kill anyone who got sent to the High Master!'

Mawsom said, 'I'm not surprised.'

'Remember this, all of you. If you're in real trouble with a beak or anything, ask Maunder if you can go and see Digger. He'll move the earth to make sure an Ansell's Man is treated properly, but'—he dropped his voice and said with emphasis, 'don't ever tell anything but the absolute truth. If you do, he may stick up for you outside, but he'll thrash the daylights out of you back here.' Ashton stopped. There was silence. Then, dropping his voice, 'You saw that big chap who was sitting over there, the one with very black hair?' They nodded. 'That's Barling. Last year he was dropped from the Third Fifteen. He went to see Digger. He said he didn't know why and that the beak running it had simply told the captain of the side that Barling shouldn't be chosen. Well, Digger raised hell and Barling played. And they won. Actually Barling scored twice, but that evening The Digger called Barling through and asked him why he had not told him the real reason he'd been dropped was that he had questioned a referee's decision in a practice.'

'And?' Ellerman urged.

'The Digger gave Barling twelve up. Just before List. Then he sent Barling in immediately ahead of him. We could all see that Barling had been spouting.'

'But he's in the Sixth isn't he?' Ellerman sounded aghast.

'He was in the Fifth then. I don't think that anyone could take twelve from Digger dry-eyed if he meant them to spout. You know he batted twice for England while he was at Cambridge? Scored sixty-two and seventy-five mainly in boundaries. Well, think of tightening-up to that! Come on, I'll show you Change.' He led them out into Corridor and across the arch to the other double doors they had noticed on arrival. 'This is Big Change.'

It was a large room with shabby wooden benches fixed to the floor and numbered hooks and pegs, already crepuscular, gloomy, redolent of lineament, mouldering football boots and steamy dampness. 'Through there is "Big Plunge".'

They viewed, without enthusiasm, the big tiled room with duckboards round a bath some four feet deep and over fifteen feet square. 'Every Ansell's Man has to Plunge after every game. Or...'

'Or you have to tighten-up!' Dermott-Powell cut in irrepressibly, almost flippantly. 'All right, Ashton, how many?'

'Three,' Ashton snapped. 'And if you go on like that, Dermott-Powell, you'll find you get half-a-dozen-up for putting on *side*. Even in your first ten days they'll tan your arse for *that*.'

'I'm sorry, Ashton.' Dermott-Powell looked becomingly penitent, 'I was just trying to cheer us all up. So far it seems you have to tighten-up for everything. Even breathing.' He was only slightly self-conscious in his use of the unfamiliar Ansell's language.

'I've told you already, it sound's worse than it is. And I can tell you, you'll soon realise it's better to be in Ansell's than any of the other slacker Houses. Really! If you show a bit of common sense you'll probably not even forget to go and Warm a bed,' he grinned cheerfully. ' "Small Change" is through there and, beyond that, "Little Plunge". You can only use that if you're a Praefaector, or a Tassel. It gets hotter water and doesn't stink of rotting socks like Big Change.' He looked at the clock. 'Come on, time to go and meet The Digger.' They followed him out and back to Din. Room and stopped at the door through which the Housemaster had vanished.

'You knock at half-past *exactly*. There's a second door just inside and you knock there too. Then he'll say "Come" and you're in. Go on, Angus, you're first alphabetically.' Angus hesitantly stepped forward, heart thudding and dry-lipped. The clock chimed.

'Go on,' Ashton said urgently. 'He won't eat you. At least not unless you're late.'

Angus knocked. He opened the first door. He knocked again.

'Come.' They went in and stood in alphabetical order.

The carpet was deep-pile and red. One wall was entirely covered by shelves of leather-bound books and another, shorter, wall held more modern-looking volumes. The curtains, of a red matching the carpet, still undrawn, were held back by a red cord. Over the fireplace, a large gold clock ticked majestically and above it, on each side, were two cricket bats which seemed to have their blades signed. In between was a single stump. There was no fire, but the fireplace was surrounded by a leather bench-seat also in red, supported on polished brass rods bedded in the substantial, immaculately-blacked, steel fender.

Jowling himself sat imposingly behind his desk from which shone a carefully shaded brass-mounted light He still wore his gown. There were two crystal ink-wells and a spotless blotter at the centre of which was a single sheet of paper which, they could see, held their names.

'I welcome you all as Ansell's Men,' he began, putting his fingers together at the tips. 'I have given each of you a place in my House. It is now up to you to justify that place. I remember your father, Ellerman. He was here when I came into Ansell's. A fine games player. And yours too, Angus. They were both Praefaectors before they left, although at that time the House was not what it has since become. Dermott-Powell, I have had a letter from Mr Prinsep who was, as you know an Ansell's Man and indeed Head of House, although before my time. He says you have a fine voice and I hope we shall hear it in Chapel.'

Dermott-Powell said, 'Yes, sir,' in the tone of one used to accepting-compliments about his skill.

'What I am now going to say is this. It is quite simply Ansell's is the best House in Cranchester. I have made it that way and it will stay that way. If you do anything to bring Ansell's into disrepute, you will be dealt with most severely. And let me say here and now that, although fortunately very rarely, there have indeed been occasions when I have not hesitated to rid Ansell's of those who were a credit neither to themselves or us. However, I am sure that your Election will bring distinction. You, Ellerman are a fine footballer and cricketer I believe. You, Snider, have an excellent brain, I gather, and Mawsom, you, I know, are a promising mathematician, but you must remember that everything you do will reflect not merely on yourselves, but also on Ansell's. Because we are the best House, we do things our own way. Or perhaps it is because we do things our own way that we *are* the best House. In the first place no Ansell's Man may join the Scouts (which the High Master has, in his wisdom, decreed is an alternative to the OTC). Until you are old enough to become Cadets you will act as batmen for Ansell's Under Officers and NCOs. Secondly, no Ansell's Man is Confirmed until he is at least in his second year. I trust that none of you is Confirmed? Ah! You, Dermott-Powell? Yes, well I can see that, at the Cathedral, you would be an exception.

'Third point. You are all growing up. You may from time to time experience certain, ah, feelings and become aware of certain bodily phenomena which might cause you concern. You will *never* on any account discuss these with Castonians from other Houses, amongst yourselves, or even with other Ansell's Men – other than Praefaectors from who you'll get sound advice. And of course I can and will reassure you if you have any problems or doubts they cannot resolve. Do not forget that.

'Finally, and this is very important, I never "make up" a Praefaector unless I am sure of him and his moral judgement. In consequence, I know I can trust my Praefaectors implicitly – I only wish I could say the same for Praefaectors in other parts of the School – it means that you can trust the Ansell's Praefaectors implicitly too. I trust their judgement and particularly I trust them fully in matters of discipline. Naturally, if you feel that you are the victim of some unfairness at the hands of a Praefaector, you have the right, as have all Castonians, to appeal to your Housemaster. Nevertheless, I have to say that I cannot easily recall the last time that such an appeal was justified. I must stress that the reason I trust the judgement of my Praefaectors is because I trust my own judgement when I make them up. Are there any questions?'

He stood up, evidently expecting none. 'You will shake hands with me twice in here. Once, as now, on your arrival in Ansell's and are using that door. And once on your last day, when you leave the House for good, when you go out by that door – and by which you'd re-enter should you visit as me an Old Castonian—' He indicated a door at the far end of the room. He stood beside the door into Din. Room. 'Come forward, Angus. I imagine that although educated privately you do know how to shake hands.' It was evidently meant to be a joke to put him at ease, but it almost rooted him to the spot.

'Good evening, sir.'

'On this occasion and when you leave you say, "Good evening, Mr Jowling."'

Angus swallowed. 'Good evening, Mr Jowling.' Almost adding 'Sir', he shook hands and escaped through the second door.

Eventually the others joined him. Even Dermott-Powell was a little shaken: 'I say, I thought he was going to have me unconfirmed, or something!'

Ashton appeared through the door of Libe.

'Quite an experience?'

Mawsom said, 'I hope I never have to go there...for any reason.'

'Upstairs to Big Dorm, it's getting late.' Ashton ushered them on. When they reached Big Dorm it was in darkness. 'You're too late for Tosher,' Ashton said. 'You'll have to stink.' He vanished.

'Mawsom?'

'Yes?' They were whispering.

'We've only been here six hours.'

'I know.'

'I don't think I can manage if...if as much as this happens.' He found the tightness again gripping his chest.

'Perhaps it won't be as bad.'

'Do you really think so?'

There was silence.

'I don't think I can spend a whole day in this terrible place.'

'Yes, you can, Angus. Everyone does. Goodnight.'

'Mawsom? Do you think we're going to be friends?'

'What a funny thing to say.'

'Well...'

'I won't tell anyone else what you say, if that's what you mean.'

It was exactly what he meant. 'Thanks. Goodnight, Mawsom.'

He heard Mawsom draw the curtain at the end of his Manger, before he began undressing slowly in the pitch dark, trying to find the chair on which to place his clothes. It was a long time before he felt sleepy and then, as he was dozing off, he remembered his prayers and his promise. He climbed from the bed and knelt on the floor. He could feel the uneven grooves and knots pressing into his knees. It seemed very cold and he felt shrivelled inside his large, new, stiff pyjamas. When he climbed back into bed, it felt cold, almost damp and it was another half hour before he dropped uneasily into an exhausted slumber

ii

Angus woke early and stayed unmoving until there were other sounds of stirring. He got up. Dermott-Powell appeared at the end of his bed, 'You coming to Tosher?' He carried his towel and Angus sensed he wanted a companion for his first walk up Big Dorm.

When they got back, Baker still in pyjamas said, 'You back already then?'

'Yes,' Angus said, surprised that Baker was still dawdling in his pyjamas.

Dermott-Powell said, 'What's the matter, Baker? Don't you want us to see what you've got?'

Baker flushed. 'It's not *that*.' But it clearly was exactly *that*.

'Hurry up, Baker, you'll be late for List.' That was Ashton.

Reluctantly Baker stripped and, pink with embarrassment, trotted off flat-footed. As he was by now virtually the last, most of the Mangers were occupied by half-clad boys and he returned, his face fiery red.

'You're a bit fat, Baker,' Ellerman observed casually.

'*SHUT UP!*' Baker turned such a face of passionate fury on Ellerman that Angus realised that it was the plumpness his nakedness revealed, as much as his prudery, which so embarrassed Baker.

A bell rang and boys began to leave Big Dorm.

✻

Despite Angus' anxiety, Sunday was as empty of activity as the previous day had been full of it. Apart from Chapel, the new Election men were left to themselves. The hours stretched ahead and the emptiness was unnerving. Nobody at all took any notice of them. Everyone else seemed busy.

Ashton said, 'You just find your way around today,' and hardly came near them again until the evening.

As they sat disconsolately at Long School during an otherwise empty afternoon Snider said, 'It's just as if we don't exist.'

'Well we don't, until we've been Inspected by the Praefaectors.'

'That's what my Father said.' Ellerman spoke confidently.

They were just preparing to go to bed, when Ashton appeared, a towel over his shoulder, but otherwise completely naked. 'If you've not yet been to Tosher, you're too late. You've got to be in Big Study for "Inspection" in about two minutes. Get into pyjamas He disappeared and reappeared almost at once, tying his pyjama cord, hair no longer tousled from washing but parted into its customary precision.'

'What's "Inspection"?'

'Nothing much. Just the Praefaector inspecting you. I'm the one who has to worry in case I've not Nannied you properly.'

They stood at the door of Big Study in pyjamas which, for all except Snider, flopped on their limbs in tribute to cautious use of clothing coupons and allowance for growth. Ashton knocked.

'Come.'

'Go on,' Ashton said in a rather tense voice. He stayed outside.

Apprehensively, shuffling in an attempt to keep the loose slippers on their toes, they went in. The curtains had been drawn and the fire lit. The Praefaectors lounged back in a mixture of battered armchairs ranged round the table, but some way back from it. They looked so grown up. They must be Masters! Couldn't be mere boys!

'I'm Maunder, as you know,' the tall man with the slicked-back crinkly, fair hair said. 'Ashton should have told you that. This is where you come when you're to be beaten with this... . It's called a switch. He waved a thin, dark cane which had a silver band at the handle and made them jump by thwacking it on the table. He looked at Ellerman. 'Did Ashton tell you what to do? Come on, speak up.'

Ellerman said, 'Yes, Maunder.'

'Well go on! Show us!'

Ellerman placed himself across the arms of The Chair.

'Your hands are in the wrong place.'

'Sorry, Maunder!' He extended his arms and grasped the round rung which tied the front and back legs of The Chair.

'Didn't Ashton tell you to tighten your arse?' It was obviously, something Ashton had omitted.

Ellerman said, 'Yes, sorry, Maunder, I forgot.'

'Well do it now. Remember that in Ansell's it's "beating" or "tightening-up" – "caning" is for oiks.'

Ellerman shuffled his feet forward.

'Okay That's better.' Maunder stroked his switch over the tight contour of Ellerman's pyjamas. 'And remember all of you, if ever we have to tell you to tighten your arse, then it's one cut extra.'

'Yes, Maunder.' A cowed chorus.

'Right, get up. What do you do after you've been beaten, before you go?'

'Shake your hand, say, "Thank you, Maunder."'

'Any exceptions?'

'After a Praefaectors'. I just shake your hand.'

'You, Dermott-Powell, anything else?'

'Er, no. That is, yes, Maunder. If we cr...that is if we spout we get two extra cuts.'

'Okay. You can come in, Ashton.'

The door opened and Ashton entered looking a little pale. Listening through the door, he had realised that he had omitted some part of the instructions and he tried to signal by a grateful look his thanks to Ellerman for coming to his rescue. Maunder said casually, 'If you hadn't got it right we'd have had to give a demonstration, wouldn't we, Ashton?'

'Yes, Maunder.'

'So,' he said turning to them, 'whichever one of you is Nanny to the next election ought to remember he'll have to tighten-up for the mistakes made by any of his charges during the first ten days. Okay, Ashton, cut along now.'

'Yes, Maunder. Thank you, Maunder.' Ashton opened the door and left without a backward glance.

'Now,' Maunder said again bringing switch sharply on the table with a noise that made them all jump, 'Inspection. Ellerman, get up there on the table. No, you ass, take off your pyjamas first! Do you think we're inspecting Vyella patterns?'

Ellerman climbed onto the table and stood in the pool of light. 'You stand there, on the Bible, that's to make sure you tell us the truth. Now turn round. We all want to see what you've got. I say! Where do you spend your summer?'

'Cornwall, Maunder.'

'Don't you wear bathers?'

Ellerman's golden tan covered his whole body. 'We have our own beach under the cliffs, nobody else can get there.'

'Do you know what we call this at Ansell's?' With the tip of his switch, Maunder lifted Ellerman's penis.

'No, Maunder.'

'It's your tassel.'

'Yes, Maunder.'

'Do you know why it's called that?'

There was a silence. Eventually Ellerman said, 'Not really, Maunder, but on the farm in Cornwall our stockman always refers to the bull's tassel…'

'That's quite good, Ellerman. In fact, nobody's quite sure why we use that name at Ansell's, but you could be right. Do you know what I mean by "permission to cover-up"?'

'Yes, Maunder. Ashton said…'

'Ashton said what?'

'That we could get permission to cover-up if we had hair round our tassel…'

'And have you?'

'A bit, Maunder, it's quite hard to see.'

'We're not proposing to use a bloody magnifying glass on you, Ellerman. We have to see it at twenty paces.' The other Praefaectors laughed.

'No, Maunder.'

'Okay, you can get down.'

Ellerman stood hesitating.

'And for God's sake put your pyjamas back on. You may have a beautiful arse, but we've seen enough of it for tonight.'

Ellerman stepped down onto the floor, his knees suddenly weak and, as he tried to tie his pyjama cord, he found his hand shaking so much that he could hardly manage the bow.

'Mawsom.'

After Ellerman's handsome athletic proportions, Mawsom seemed almost puny.

'And have you any hair, Mawsom?'

'I don't think so, Maunder. I...'

'You...what?'

'I've never looked.'

One of the Praefaectors put in, 'Just as well, you'd strain your eyes!' There was another general laugh.

'Baker.'

There was silence as Baker heaved himself up on the table, balancing precariously on the great Bible.

'Are you trying to hold your belly in?'

'Yes, Maunder.'

'Well don't bother, it's too fat and you'll need to get fit.' Maunder prodded him with the switch. 'You could do with less in the belly and more in the tassel. Yours is bloody pathetic.'

Baker flushed to the roots of his hair.

Snider's head almost touched the light.

'How old are you, Snider?'

'Thirteen last month, Maunder.' He was clearly deeply embarrassed by the scrutiny of his nakedness and there was a suspicious gleam in his eyes.

'Mawsom. Come over here. What do you see there?' Maunder pointed with his switch.

'It looks like hair, Maunder.'

Angus, astonished, could clearly see from where he stood, black hair curling over a scrotum and penis which, to his eyes seemed disproportionately large, despite Snider's height. Snider stood, pale with embarrassment.

One of the Praefaectors said, 'At least his balls have dropped.' A remark which meant nothing to Angus, but raised an amused 'hear, hear' from another Praefaector.

Speaking so quietly that he could hardly be heard, Snider said, 'Does that mean I have permission to cover-up, please, Maunder?'

Maunder paused and said conversationally, 'You're circumcised, Snider? Are you Jewish?'

'No—' Snider looked defiantly at his fingers, '—but my grandfather was. Does it matter?'

'It just means you can't cover-up yet awhile because you lot always have an unfair advantage. You always grow hair before the rest of us, but you can get down now.' There was no animosity at all in Maunder's voice. Dermott-Powell stepped out of his pyjamas onto The Chair, lightly onto the table and almost delicately onto the Bible, his auburn head glowing darkly red under the light. After a moment Maunder said, with some edge, 'Have you done this before? Do you enjoy doing it?'

Expertly avoiding the first question, Dermott-Powell said, 'I don't mind.' He paused. 'I say, Maunder, may I have permission—?'

'Turn round.' There was a pause. 'Has your voice broken?'

'Well, Maunder, I think it's going to soon. I have got some...'

'Nothing like enough,' Maunder said with finality. 'And by the way, you'll need to exert more self-control now you're at Ansell's.'

'I'm sorry, Maunder. It always begins to stick out if I'm in a warm room,' and with no embarrassment at his partial erection, Dermott-Powell jumped down and began to put on his pyjama jacket.

'*I'm* not Jewish, Maunder. They said I 'ad to 'ave it done or I wouldn't be able to...' Notting ran out of words under Maunder's disdainful gaze.

'Is that why yours is so much bigger than Baker's?'

'I don't...'

'Or do you have it out on Night Exercises?'

The euphemistic Cranchester slang, with its allusion to OTC training, baffled Angus.

'Oh *no*, Maunder.' Then, realising the implication of such instantaneous denial, looking at his feet and blushing scarlet, 'I...I...I mean, I don't know what you mean, Maunder.'

'So...we...should...hope. Your Private was a day school?'

'Yes, Maunder.'

'Day schools are for oiks.'

'Yes, Maunder.'
'Oiks drop their aitches.'
'Yes, Maunder.'
'No Ansell's Man *ever* drops his aitches.'
'Yes, Maunder...I mean no, Maunder...I mean of course, Maunder.'
'Oh, get down, Notting.'
'Angus.'

His heart had been thudding and he had feared the tightness in his chest might return, but by the time he heard his name he felt quite calm. However, he had never been in the slightest embarrassed by nakedness – his own or that of others. Snider's obvious discomfort puzzled him, as had Baker's that morning. It was of no concern to him that they had to walk down Big Dormitory to Tosher stark naked. In fact, it saved the bother of getting pyjama trousers wet at the ankles. Sometimes he did not bother at home and, now, if they insisted on it as one of Ansell's customs, it did not seem to matter very much. On the other hand, Maunder's bland assumption that he would at some stage inevitably be beaten, frightened him very much indeed. Whilst Maunder had talked and Ellerman had been demonstrating across The Chair, he had been choking for breath. He had told Mawsom no lie. He had never been struck, let alone beaten. He tried to banish the black thought to the back of his mind until he realised Maunder was surveying him, unaware that his childish body was the source of some amusement.

'You're about as badly off as Baker in the tassel department,' Maunder said touching him lightly with the switch.

A tall dark Praefaector with sleek dark hair said languidly, with a smile which Angus could not fathom, to his companions, 'Oh by the way, Angus, how often do you masturbate?'

There was the same stifled laugh from the Praefaectors.

'Oh, only ten or twelve times, I'm afraid.'

Although the room was already quiet, his words brought a complete, astonished silence. Each of the Praefaectors seemed to be holding his breath. Maunder said carefully, 'Do you mean each week? Or each month?' The Monitor with dark hair sniggered. The slightly anxious expression on Angus' face cleared.

'Oh no! More than that! Twenty times each mouthful Miss Criven told us, but that's...'

The rest was drowned in a great shout of laughter. Although thoroughly mystified, the release of tension was infectious and Angus found himself laughing. It was some minutes before Maunder could speak.

'God, Angus, you'll probably be the death of Ansell's! I suggest you get a dictionary. I think the word *you* need is masticate.' Still laughing, Maunder patted the calf of his leg with the switch. 'Go on, get down now, before you give us all a heart attack.'

Clad in pyjamas once again, Angus heard Maunder say, 'You might as well all know that if any of you do masturbate, you'll have me to deal with. It'll be a Praefaectors' at least, probably The Digger too. It's a disgusting habit and just needs a bit of self-control. It ruins your fitness for football. Ansell's is the fittest House in Cranchester and it's going to stay that way.' He paused. 'There's one more thing. Warming? Has Ashton told you about that?'

They nodded.

'Well then, you know that you always go and Warm our beds and stay there until we come. Remember, a cold bed for us means a warm arse for you.'

There was a chorus of 'Yes, Maunder.'

'Right. Ellerman you're my Warmer. And don't forget. It's in Big Dorm this week.'

'No, I won't forget, Maunder.'

'Dermott-Powell, you're with Tarrant.' The tall, dark-haired Praefaector gave Dermott-Powell a long, speculative look.

'Baker, you go to Crewe,' and a small Praefaector said quietly, 'That's me.'

'Snider. You're with Robinson.' Robinson was as unlike Snider as it was possible to be. Red-haired, broad-shouldered with enormous hands and biceps, he was the mainstay of the Cranchester forwards that season.

'Notting, you're with Crowder.' He, evidently, was the stocky, tough-looking boy with, unusually at Cranchester, still the trace of a northern accent.

'Mawsom, you look after Wilder's warmth.' Wilder, who had been almost hidden in the shadows at the back, stood up. He was like an older version of Mawsom himself, with intelligent eyes and head.

'Lastly, Angus. You're with Singleton. He's Junior Praefaector. You'll be all right with him because his father's a clergyman and he'll be able to make sure you don't do it even once a week.' The final baffling remark was greeted by a loud laugh from most of the Praefaectors, although Singleton did not join in. 'You can all cut along now.'

They trooped out into the dim corridor. Mawsom said, 'What did it mean? Masturbate?'

Dermott-Powell gestured with a half-closed hand, 'You know!' Then flushed slightly, realising he had betrayed himself.

Baker looked quickly down at his feet and Notting said, 'Oh!' started to say something else and then closed his mouth.

Ellerman said quickly, 'We'll get cold.'

Mawsom muttered, 'I see,' in a tone of voice which might have meant he did not see at all. Nor had Dermott-Powell's half-stifled gesture meant anything to Angus, but conscious of the fact that he had made some gaffe in Big Study, he said in a bright, open voice, 'Oh *that*!' which caused Dermott-Powell to look at him sharply!

They reached their Mangers in the darkened dormitory. Mawsom whispered, 'I say, Angus, did you really understand what Dermott-Powell meant?'

Angus hesitated, he was by nature and instinct, truthful. He said eventually, 'Actually no. Haven't the faintest. Did you?'

'I'm not sure. Goodnight, Angus.'

At breakfast Mawsom said to Angus, 'I see Dermott-Powell's Senior Man of our Election.'

'How did you know?'

'There's a notice in Corridor.'

The card, signed by Maunder read: '*Dermott-Powell; Ellerman; Notting; Mawsom; Snider; Baker; Angus.*'

Baker said loudly, 'At my school seniority always went in alphabetical order. That would've meant you, Angus.'

'I'm glad it's not. I wouldn't have wanted the job of Nannying the next Election. I wouldn't be much good.' The thought of doing what Ashton had undertaken made him momentarily breathless. 'But I wonder how it's decided.'

Mawsom had joined them, together with Notting, and said, 'It's probably on entrance results.'

'Dermott-Powell! I bet he didn't do very well,' Notting refuted in a sneering voice.

In the event it was Snider who asked Ashton that night. 'Oh List. That was done after Inspection last night.'

With a sudden enlightenment, Dermott-Powell said, 'You mean who'd got most hair?'

Ashton nodded, 'The most *mature*.'

Mawsom said, 'Then it should be Snider.'

Notting cut in with, 'It couldn't be Snider because he's a bloody Yid.'

'I had a Jewish grandfather.' Snider spoke with great dignity.

Ashton said, 'Notting, it doesn't matter whether he's a Zulu. We don't have any of that stuff here. An Ansell's Man is an Ansell's Man. We're not against Jews like Pettifer's, or Oliphant's, so you'd better get it right, Notting. And we ever don't talk of "bloody Yids" either.'

Notting shut up.

'In that case, why not Snider?' Mawsom asked. 'He's hairier than any of us?'

Ashton was momentarily silent. Then he said, 'I'm not sure when you put it like that. Lots of hair doesn't count if you're well, not quite English.'

'But I *am* English,' Snider said determinedly.

'Well Maunder obviously thinks you're not English *enough*,' Ashton said with finality, washing his hands of the argument. 'You could always take it up with him, I suppose.' They knew from his tone that he did not offer that as a serious suggestion.

iii

In Big Dorm, on the tenth day after their arrival, Notting said, 'Oh Ashton, I'm very sorry but Crowder wants to see you in Big Study after Curfew.'

'Me? Why?' He had taken one of his two allowed hot baths for the week and was rubbing his head briskly. There was a pause. 'I expect it's because I forgot to Warm his bed last night. I'm sorry.'

Ashton put the towel down. 'But I reminded you. I reminded all of you.'

'I'm sorry, Ashton,' Notting spoke in an uninflected voice. 'I simply forgot. I was very tired. *After the football.*'

Ashton went away and returning clad in pyjamas, he said quietly, 'I shouldn't forget again tonight. It's your own look-out now. Crowder is the best racquets player in the school and has a wrist like nobody's business.'

He returned about three minutes later, a little pale but obviously recovering. He said to the Election gathered at Notting's Manger, 'This is what you'll all be in for from tomorrow if you don't do your stuff.' He slid down his pyjamas with an off-hand shrug. Two distinct and obviously painful weals made Angus swallow hard and turn away.

Ellerman said, 'Not bad, Ashton, but you should have seen what the Headmaster at my Private could do. Whooh!'

Fully recovered, Ashton said, in a bad imitation of the Northern accent, 'For Notting forgetting to Warm my bed and one more because you've not been Nannying properly.'

Notting said waspishly, 'I've said I'm sorry, Ashton. If you think I did it just because of that knock-on...' And stopped.

Ashton turned and looked hard at him. Then he said, 'That never occurred to me. Because if an Ansell's Man did that sort of thing to me, I'd boot his arse round Big Dormitory until it was black and blue. What's more, the rest of Ansell's would help.' He went back to his bed.

Dermott-Powell said, 'Did you really forget, Notting?'

'Of course I did.'

'Well, you were jolly silent. It'd be pretty beastly if you were getting your own back.'

'*You* pointed out he was in our power for the first ten days,' Notting said.

'That was a joke!'

Angus who had been looking at Notting throughout said aloud, without meaning to, 'Actually Notting, that knock-on.... You looked...'

'Guilty as hell!' Snider cut in quietly.

'Shut up, you bloody Yid,' Notting spat. 'Ashton deserved anything that was coming to him. If you must know it *wasn't* a knock-on. I ought to know.'

They had all, except for Angus, been involved in the game. Ellerman said, 'I was inside and gave you the pass and thought it was a knock-on.'

Mawsom added, 'Considering Ashton was only told to referee at the last minute, he actually did jolly well. I mean he was up with the play.'

Notting said, 'If it hadn't been for that, I'd've gone over for a try and we'd've won.'

'But it was only a run-about! Not even a real practice,' Snider said wonderingly.

'If you've got to play, you might as well win,' Notting persisted doggedly.

Angus, unaware of his danger said, 'I'm not absolutely sure what a "knock-on" is, Notting, but just now you looked as if you knew Ellerman was right.'

Notting turned on him and said with venom, 'What do you know about it, you little Scottish *cunt*?' The word shocked the others into silence, although it meant nothing to Angus, but the tone frightened him.

'Notting? I must've imagined you used a word I'm sure you didn't use? Because at Ansell's we don't use oik language. If you had, I'd be giving you six-up in Big Study. I came in to remind you to Warm for me. You've let Ashton down once already.' The faint Northern accent behind them spoke quietly into the silence which had followed Notting's outburst.

Notting went away very demurely with a 'Yes, Crowder.'

Crowder gave them all a searching look. He said, 'I meant what I said. We don't use that sort of language here.'

In all the years that followed, neither Angus nor the others ever heard it in Ansell's again. After he had gone, Snider said, 'I wonder how long Crowder was behind us. How much he overheard?'

'Not enough!' Mawsom answered.

'Notting's a bit of a worm. You never disagree with the referee,' Ellerman said somewhat complacently.

'I reckon somebody should tell somebody!' Dermott-Powell burst out indignantly.

Ellerman looked at him pityingly and said languidly 'You don't do that sort of thing, either, Dermott. You're not still Choirmaster's Choice at your bloody cathedral.' It was such an unexpected and unnecessarily cruel remark that for an instant Dermott-Powell looked as if he might burst into tears. Privately Angus rather sympathised with Dermott-Powell, but said nothing.

'We'll all get two-up if we're not careful,' Baker reminded them. They scuttled off.

Angus had barely time to slide between the sheets when Singleton came in; he hoped the bed was warm enough. When Singleton was ready he got out and went to the door. 'Goodnight, Singleton.'

Singleton said pleasantly, 'I must say I'd rather have a hot-water bottle than you, Angus. Do you live at the North Pole?' Did that mean you had to tighten-up if the bed wasn't warm enough? 'Goodnight, Angus.'

❋

The following evening, before Curfew, Crowder stopped him. 'Tell Notting to be in Big Study after Curfew, please, Angus.' When Notting heard, he turned down the corner of his lips. 'If you've been...' he began, to Angus' alarm.

'Of course he hasn't, Notting. I saw Crowder stop him and ask him to tell you.'

With a thumping heart Notting went to Big Study and knocked.

'Come in...Notting? Do you know why you're here?'

'Was it about the word you thought I said that I really didn't...'

'As a matter of fact you did, Notting. I heard it quite plainly, but let that go. Only don't bother to lie.'

'No, Crowder.'

'While we're on the subject, Snider's an Ansell's Man like you: it does not matter whether his father is Jewish or Hindu. I heard it all because I'd been behind you for some time. As a matter of fact Snider is Christian.'

Notting said nothing. There was a pause.

'You deliberately got Ashton into trouble.'

Too quickly Notting said, 'I didn't.'

'*Don't lie,* Notting! You deliberately "forgot" my bed because you knew Ashton was your Nanny for ten days.'

'Well, it never was a knock-on.' Belligerent.

'I don't care whether it was or not. Ashton was referee and doing his job. He thought it was. Do you understand?'

'I suppose so, Crowder.'

'You only *suppose* so. I'm sorry the matter is so difficult for you to understand. I *suppose* you do know what this is?' There was silence. 'Well, what is it?'

'It's a switch, Crowder.'

'Do you know what it's for?'

'Yes, Crowder.'

'Well, tell me.'

'It's to beat people.'

'It's to tan the arse of a vindictive, lying little oik who should never be at Ansell's. What's it for?'

'It's to tan the arse of a vindictive lying little oik who should never be at Ansell's.'

'And who is this vindictive little oik, do you *suppose?*'

Silence.

'And who, Notting, do you *suppose,* is this vindictive little oik?'

'Me, Crowder. Me. Notting.'

'I gave Ashton two and I shall pass them on to you. Does that seem fair?'

'I suppose so,' sullenly.

'Oh in that case. If you only *suppose* so, let's add one more. Is that fair now?'

'Yes, Crowder.'

'Get across The Chair.'

Notting, now cold and frightened, truculence quite vanished, did as he was told.

'Tighten your arse, Notting. That's two more.'

There were five, quick and extremely painful.

'Get up, Notting.' He got up.

'Do you know why I gave you the extra one?'

'No, Crowder.'

'Because,' Crowder said with an intensity absent from his voice until then, 'I'm not allowed to give you seven more to make up the round dozen, Notting, you little worm. And if you ever do anything like this again, you'll tighten-up for the six of us. Is that understood, Notting?' Crowder's Northern vowels were very pronounced.

'Yes, Crowder.'

'Haven't you forgotten something?'

'Oh, Thank you, Crowder.' He held out his hand.

Crowder appeared not to notice it. Instead he said with an air of infinite distaste, 'I shan't need a Warmer tonight and you'll need to go to Tosher again. You seem to have wet yourself, Notting. You'd better cut along before you stain the rug. Big Study isn't the kindergarten.'

Notting fled.

Self-conscious in Tosher the following morning, Notting found that, with one exception, he was accorded none of the sympathy which Big Dorm had shown Ashton. The exception was Ashton himself, who came over and said with obvious sincerity, 'I'm really sorry about that, Notting. It must have bloody well hurt!'

Notting could not say, 'Thanks, Ashton.' Unable to restrain himself, he muttered, 'It *wasn't* a knock-on.' Ashton, like Notting, was stark naked, but with a quaint, rather touching dignity, he turned and quietly walked away. Notting felt a fleeting impulse to rush after him and apologise, but stubbornly he said again to himself, 'Well, *IT WASN'T!*' by which time Ashton had disappeared into Big Dorm. When Notting reached his Manger he found that the rest of the Election had, unusually for them, gone down for Morning List rather early and that he was alone at his end of Big Dorm.

Chapter Three

Early in October, Crewe found Baker copying a Latin Prose from a printed crib. At Curfew, after The Digger had gone, Maunder said, 'Baker will be beaten tonight for using a crib. If it hadn't been his first Half, it'd have been a Praefaectors'. I don't have to remind the rest of you that Ansell's Men *never* use a crib. It's forbidden at Cranchester and it's even more forbidden at Ansell's. You're bloody lucky, Baker, that Crewe discovered it before your Div Pro. Then it would have been a matter for the High Master.'

Baker stood there fatly, scarlet with shame.

That night, after Curfew, he was left severely to himself, except by Snider who was waiting for him when he came out of Big Study.

'I'm sorry, Baker.'

Baker looked about him pathetically and muttered, 'We always used 'em at my Private, but you'd better not be seen talking to me just now.'

Snider said shortly, 'You've been punished.' Deliberately he walked up to Big Dorm with Baker and his humanity shamed Angus for his own attitude towards Baker.

'I'd've died if that had been me at Curfew,' he ventured timidly as a sort of apology.

'I almost did, but thanks.'

So it was that Snider's example encouraged all of the Election, each one in his own way, to restore their relationship with Baker. Even Ashton came across: 'Bad luck, Baker.' He added, 'But if you don't get a move on you'll all have to tighten-up for not Warming.

❊

The following day, after lunch, Dermott-Powell came up to Angus. 'By the way, you and I are to sing in Chapel.'

'Solo?'

'Well, duet. Ever done it before?'

'No.' He could feel tension in his chest, but he was not much frightened. He had never sung in public before, but the discovery that he had a 'voice' had, strangely, for all his timidity, not worried or embarrassed him. It surprised, but pleased him to find that he could so easily follow the music and memorise a tune without effort. 'In Chapel? What is it?'

'Mendelssohn. I've sung it before in the Cathedral. "I waited for the Lord" – that's what it's called.'

'Why me?'

'You've got a very good voice. Better than mine ever was. I mean it,' he added with a professional frankness.

Angus coloured slightly. 'What about you?'

'Mine's not really up to it any longer.'

'Why not?'

'Because the voice changes,' Dermott-Powell said shortly. 'Anyhow, you'll have to manage the top line and I'll have to cheat it a bit.'

Snider, who had come up said, 'What's up? Big Study after Curfew?'

'Dermott-Powell and I are to sing in Chapel,' Angus said.

Dermott-Powell added, 'By the way, I gather Mawsom got two-up in Big Study last night.' He rubbed the seat of his trousers with an exaggerated grimace.

Snider said, 'You wait! It damn well hurts!'

'*I* don't forget to Warm,' Dermott-Powell said smugly.

After lunch Mawsom said, 'I'm doing Marathon. What about you?' Marathon was the name by which the six-and-a-half-mile cross-country course was known.

'Do you know the route?'

'Of course. Come on, I'll show you.'

It was a magnificent autumn afternoon. The leaves had turned red in an early frost and there had been no wind to take them from the branches of the trees. Day after day they had fallen; quietly and crisply and, for the first stage of Marathon, the crunch of leaves beneath their gym-shoes prevented conversation. Then they were clear of the leaves and, as they trotted on, they chatted in a desultory fashion. Mawsom asked, 'What's Singleton like? You know, Warming for him?'

'He's all right. Nice really.'

'The other Praefaectors think he's a bit...well, wet.'

Angus ran on. 'He's all right. He's not like the others.'

'You've not had to tighten-up to him yet.'

'No!'

'They say he doesn't beat?'

Angus said, 'P'rhaps I haven't done anything to deserve it.'

'I got two up. Last night. You heard?'

'I'm sorry.'

'Didn't hurt. Well, not much. I think Wilder just made the excuse. He said that I didn't make the bed warm enough! But he'd told me earlier in the week that Maunder felt the Praefaectors were going too easy on us.'

Angus shivered slightly. 'I don't think Singleton would do it for that reason. Anyway Dermott-Powell hasn't. Nor Ellerman, of course.'

With an odd timbre, Mawsom said, 'Ellerman's not the sort who gets beaten. Not by Maunder.' There was in his voice both envy and acceptance.

'You mean because he's too good at games?'

They had come to the highest point on the run. The Downs sloped away on all sides. Mawsom leaned against a battered gate, its rungs worn by hundreds of Castonian feet scrambling over it. Known as 'Roman Gate', it was the turn in Marathon and, for about four hundred yards, the route lay along an overgrown track which, reputedly, marked the remains of a stretch of Roman road. Mawsom said, 'You get back pretty late from Warming sometimes. Last night?'

Angus looked at him in a slightly guilty manner. 'Oh, did I?'

'Ellerman's noticed too. What do you get up to?' Angus wondered whether he dared tell him. It would be breaking a confidence and Singleton had said it was illegal. He certainly would not want Ellerman to know.

'All right, you needn't tell me if you don't want to, but I shan't tell anyone.'

'I'll think about it on the way back.' Mawsom's questions made him reflective.

※

After the first week, the evenings had become assuring, almost comforting. Singleton entering with his quiet 'Hello, young Angus. Still freezing my bed?' Singleton undressing, carefully folding everything and putting it in its place. Singleton brushing his hair and saying, 'Thanks, Angus and goodnight,' before Angus scurried back to Big Dorm in the dark.

Yet, now, there was more to it than that. His first timorous worry about whether he would Warm the bed enough, or whether Singleton would tell him to go to Big Study, had gradually been replaced by the realisation that, somehow, in Singleton's room, it was as if they were not at Ansell's at all. Singleton himself never introduced Cranchester, or Ansell's, into the conversation. A chance remark revealed the fact that they both were fond of dogs. After much hesitation he had shown Singleton a poor snapshot.

'Golden Labrador-ish,' Singleton said. 'Like Sheba, that's our dog at home.' He gave back the picture.

'I wish he were here!'

Singleton was silent, then, 'Perhaps Ansell's wouldn't be much fun for a dog!' Was it possible he implied that a dog would be too sensible to come to Ansell's? The idea that Singleton could say anything so blasphemous about Ansell's seemed itself blasphemous. Singleton went on, 'I find it best not to mix up home and Ansell's.'

'I know!' He felt his eyes prick with tears.

'Sorry, Angus, didn't mean to upset you.'

'Y—y—you didn't, Singleton. It just that I thought...' He was conscious that the stammer which had always embarrassed him at times of emotional crisis had once more betrayed him.

'You cold?' Singleton said suddenly, as if to change the subject.

'A bit.' Even in bed he was cold. Ansell's always seemed cold.

'Don't give me away, Angus, I'm going to light a fire. I've got a secret hoard of coal and fir cones.' Singleton lifted the shabby rug and, with a little juggling, removed a half floor-board. From the bed, Angus focussed a torch with a new battery. Singleton pushed in his arm and, after some scrabbling, drew out half a dozen lumps of coal and about a dozen fir cones. Quickly and carefully he lit it; bright crackling cones illuminated the room and caught the coal.

'Come on, Angus. Come and get warm!'

In truth, the warmth was illusory but, crouching by the grate, they could feel real heat on hands and face. Hunched over the small fireplace, dressing-gowns pulled tight about them, the shared experience engendered the warmth of a special intimacy. Eventually the heat began to die, but they squatted on in companionable silence.

'I say, Singleton. I could collect cones, if you wanted. For your secret hoard. Or wood?'

Singleton said, 'We're not supposed to light a fire. War effort! But I brought the coal from home. It's not the School's.' Then, suddenly, 'You'd better get back to Big Dorm, or they'll think…' he paused, 'they might think…that I've…murdered you…or something.'

Angus laughed, although fleetingly aware that somehow 'murder' was not what the other had been about to say. 'But…yes, of course…you can always add some cones…. For the next fire.'

So Singleton's room began to symbolise something more than warmth and comfort, although in truth it would have struck few outsiders as comfortable. A single forty-watt bulb beneath the usual green and white glass shade suspended from the lofty ceiling on a long length of frayed flex; dingy, marked walls; floorboards, warped and uneven with gaps between them, smoothed white in some places by successions of bare feet. The worn rug in front of the fireplace had a threadbare patch in the middle that was on the verge of becoming a hole. A darkly varnished chest of drawers with one of its knob-feet missing supported by an extremely ancient, battered copy of Kennedy *Latin Primer* conventionally defaced into *Eat **ing** **Prime** Beef*.

Above a solid desk, chipped, inked and scored by past users, were three bookshelves stretching from wall to window frame. For an Ansell's Man, Singleton was bookish; the shelves were crammed and there was another row of books on top of the desk. In addition, above the fireplace on the black iron over-mantle, were another four volumes which seemed to be especial favourites, one or another of them often lay open on the bed or desk: a well-thumbed *New Testament*; *The Selected Poems of Alfred, Lord Tennyson*; *An Anthology of Poetry 1830-1930*. The fourth was so worn that he'd had to wait until, one evening before Singleton arrived, greatly daring, he took it down and, recognising the pictures, exclaimed aloud in astonishment, 'Winnie the Pooh – in *Latin?*' before becoming aware that he was no longer alone. He turned, book in hand. Singleton stood, hands on hips, surveying him with an amused expression.

'Oh, I'm sorry, Singleton, I didn't mean...'

'You're very welcome to look, but why not look and Warm at the same time?'

'Oh! I'd forgotten all about...Warming, I...' He was appalled.

'Don't worry, I've come up early, so you wouldn't have made much difference yet. In fact, Angus, I think you probably make the bed colder. That is a joke,' he concluded, noting Angus' stricken expression.

Replacing the book, Angus slid between cold, almost clammy, sheets. As he unknotted his tie, Singleton said kindly, 'You know, Angus, you mustn't let Ansell's frighten you.'

'No, Singleton.'

They both knew he was unconvinced.

During the course of the following days, Angus unobtrusively collected dry fir cones, until there were too many for the secret hiding place and they completely filled the small grate. Singleton said, 'Good lord! We'd better have another burn-up.'

The second, bigger, fire burned for quite a long time and seemed to warm the whole room. Angus continued avidly collect cones and kindling, so the fires became a regular event. It was in this way that Singleton's study became a welcome oasis in the impersonal desert of Cranchester and Ansell's; Singleton ceased to be a remote senior boy in a hierarchy of boys. He became a sympathetic, friendly adult who could be trusted. It was the only thing that made much else bearable. It was also the reason he could not easily discuss Singleton in the context of Wilder's treatment of Mawsom.

They reached the last part of Marathon, where a shallow ford intersected the River Crann. He said, 'Mawsom, do you promise you'll not tell anyone? About me and Singleton I mean. About what we do when I'm Warming.' They had stopped at the water's edge. Speculatively Mawsom looked at him and said quietly, 'It's all right, Angus, you don't have to say, but if you *really* want to tell me, I'll not say anything to anyone else.'

Taking a deep breath, Angus said, 'Well, we light a fire!'

'You do *what*?' Sheer disbelief made Mawsom widen his eyes.

Mistaking his tone for one of censure, Angus hurried on, 'I know, I know. It's not really allowed, because of the war, but it's not *really* illegal either, because Singleton brought coal from home.'

Somehow, as he told Mawsom, out there in the fading afternoon light, fires in Singleton's room seemed not so much illegal, but trivial, silly, even childish. He was momentarily ashamed and especially glad Notting was not nearby, 'I say, Mawsom, you won't say anything – to the others? Ellerman? Notting?'

'No, of course not!' Mawsom laughed. 'Well, I'd never have guessed *that*,' in a tone which momentarily caused Angus to wonder what he had guessed. 'You sound like a pair of Boy Scouts.' Had Notting said the same words they would have seemed cruel, but Mawsom sounded amused, even pleased. His initial astonishment had been occasioned by the fleeting supposition that Angus was lying, but almost immediately the patent guilelessness banished the notion. Yes, with Angus and Singleton, it *would* be something as mundanely 'illegal' as a fir-cone fire! He felt protectively older than Angus; much, much older than he had been at the beginning of the Half.

After they had plunged in Big Change and climbed back into school clothes, Mawsom said with a grin and hissed with mock secrecy, 'Psst! You'd better take these!' He thrust three fir cones into Angus' hand.

That evening, Singleton in an academic, almost scientific, way, experimented to see if there was enough heat to make toast. It was not an unqualified success, although, as he chewed his tough and smoky half, it somehow sealed a bond between himself and the older boy, or so it seemed to Angus. Singleton too recognised that the warmth of the fire was symbolic, rather than physical and he divined that their relationship had altered. Later in bed, after Angus had gone, he knew he would not want Maunder to know about the shared fires; he felt he had compromised himself for reasons he was unwilling to analyse. The resulting twinges of guilt were to make him more distant on the next few evenings, re-awakening, for a time, Angus' fears and uncertainties. However, it did not last long. Within ten days it was necessary to have another fire, for Singleton, despite his misgivings, had neither the heart nor, if truth were told, the inclination to forbid Angus to collect kindling.

Late though it was when he reached Big Dorm, Angus found Snider and Ellerman whispering outside on the landing. Ellerman said, 'Heard about Dermott-Powell?'

'What about him?'

'Tarrant gave him six-up. Bloody hard too! You could hear it in Big Dorm.'

'What for?' He could feel the chill, but not of cold, and the constriction of his throat.

'Can't you guess?'

He looked at, them blankly.

Snider said humorously, 'No, Angus, I suppose *you* couldn't.' He turned to the others, 'I reckon Dermott-Powell was simply unlucky. It might have been any one of us.' He looked meaningfully across at Ellerman. 'Except Angus of course.' There was the sound of steps. 'That'll be Wilder!' They scuttled inside.

Too tired to puzzle over Dermott-Powell's fate, Angus fell into a deep, dreamless sleep. He awoke with a start about two hours later, aware that somebody was in his Manger. In the moonlight he could make out Dermott-Powell.

'You awake, Angus?' came a tense whisper.

'I am now.'

Dermott-Powell slid into bed beside him. 'You're warm as toast!'

Dermott-Powell was cold, shivering. In the silvery light Angus could see the marks of tears on his cheeks like the trail of snails.

'The others said you had to tighten-up for Tarrant?'

'Yes. Six. Nearly cut me in half. He enjoys beating people.'

'What for? Not Warming?' The sleepiness had gone. He was a little breathless again.

'Didn't the others tell you?'

'Not really. Anyhow I didn't understand.'

'No, I suppose not.' There was a silence. Then, heartfelt, 'God, you're so lucky, Angus!' Unexpectedly Dermott-Powell put an arm round his shoulders, held on to him and said with genuine desperation in his voice, 'There must be something wrong with me! Sometimes I can't...can't help it, however much I try. I just can't stop myself. And tonight Tarrant came in and caught me.'

Angus sensed that Dermott-Powell was crying again. Not knowing what else to say, he gave expression to his own fears. 'It must have hurt a lot.'

'It's not that. It's this place. This *bloody* place! Ansell's!' There was loathing and terror in Dermott-Powell's voice. 'I know that I shan't last out here, you know...'

'You're shivering again.'

Dermott-Powell pushed himself down into the bed. 'Do you really not know why Tarrant beat me?'

'No.' Angus yawned heavily.

'You remember what Maunder said? At the beginning of Half?'

'Mmmm. Sort of...didn't...' He drifted into untroubled sleep with the other's now warm, comforting, body beside him.

Dermott-Powell lay for some time, looking up at the marked ceiling in the moonlight. Eventually, calmer and warmer, he got carefully out of the bed. Looking down at Angus, sound asleep in the shaft of moonlight, he felt decades older. Shaking his head, he breathed a sort of laugh. It was not derision, but his inadvertent tribute to an innocence which, reluctantly, in his heart of hearts he envied, although he knew he would have mocked it in public.

ii

After breakfast on the last Tuesday in November, Notting came up to Ellerman where he was putting his books together in Library and said with a flat voice, 'Did you know your name's up in Corridor, Ellerman?'

'In Corridor,' he said turning white. 'It can't be. You're having me on.'

'No,' Notting said. 'I wouldn't have you on like that. Your name's up.' With leaden legs Ellerman turned into Corridor. A Praefaectors' beating! What had he done? Or not done? There was a group of boys noisily gathered round the Head of House section. As he came up, they made way for him and somebody said, 'Bloody well done, Ellerman!'

At the bottom of the list of the Fifteen for the House Match against Jonquil's, was *M.R.E. Ellerman w/3* – Cranchester code for 'Wing three-quarter'. Behind him he heard Notting say, 'I told you your name was on the board.' He added provocatively, 'But our golden boy thought he was going to have to tighten-up, didn't he? What've you been up to, Ellerman?' There was a hint of knowing spite behind the envy in Notting's voice.

Ashton said, 'Well you'd know all about that, wouldn't you, Notting?' so pointedly that Notting snapped his mouth shut like a trap. 'Bloody good for you, Ellerman.'

Ellerman said with warmth, 'Thanks very much, Ashton. They've probably put me in by mistake.'

'Oh no,' Ashton said, 'you deserve it. Everyone says so. Good luck. By the way, you'll be the youngest Ansell's Man ever to play for the House,' he added, turning away before they could see his own disappointment at not being chosen himself.

After Ashton had gone, Mawsom said, 'He's very decent, Ashton I mean. It was between you and him, you know.'

'Yes, I know. It's bad luck for him, but neither of us would have had a chance if it hadn't been for all the injuries.'

Singleton, who had come up unobserved, said over their shoulders, 'Remember Chapel. The bell will be starting in about two minutes.

Congratulations, Ellerman. Do you know the last Ansell's Man to play in his first term?'

Ellerman shook his head.' No, Singleton.' He had not realised that it was as unusual as all that.

'It was Maunder. He also came in because of an injury. They Tasselled him in his first term too. Our Election felt no end bucked.'

Divisions that morning seemed to flow over Ellerman. He was not nervous, he never was. He was buoyed up, almost intoxicated with the expectation. One or two from other Houses in his Division had heard and congratulated or teased him. Seymour, from Jonquil's, said, 'I wouldn't want to be you, Ellerman. Don't forget "Crusher".'

'Crusher' Cruttwell was large, strong and extremely fit. He had led the Cranchester pack for a season and a half. The previous week, against Marlborough, he had scored one try, literally carrying two of his opponents on his back for the final few yards. Earlier in the season, an inexperienced full-back, from a lesser school, who had gallantly but foolishly tackled him on the line, had been taken off to Nurs'ry badly concussed. Cruttwell was not rough, nor unfair, just very strong, although he needed time to get up speed. Ellerman had overheard Maunder discussing tactics the night before during Praefaectors' Dinner. 'Never let him get away, that's the answer,' Maunder had remarked. 'We'll have two Ansell's Men on him.'

'I thought that'd make you change your mind,' Seymour goaded. 'We've got Lightman too.' Lightman was the Cranchester full-back that season, an elegant and intelligent player, with a safe pair of hands, a splendid kick and the reputation for having missed only one tackle in his life. 'So it's hard luck for Ansell's, but I'll tell our lot to keep the score down to double figures as it's your first match, Ellerman,' Seymour added with a laugh. Then with a change of tone, 'Actually, Ellerman, you've done jolly well. Everyone knows Ansell's are hard to beat. However, when we wipe the floor with you I might even cheer for you personally…as they carry off your coffin!' He skipped out of the way to avoid Ellerman's expected lunge.

There was some truth in it. Ellerman had been there unnoticed in the crowd, behind Tarrant talking to Crowder after breakfast, as they looked at the notice-board in Corridor. 'Ellerman? Cruttwell will kill him!'

'He's bloody good. I've seen him.' That was Crowder. 'I know he is pretty small, but...'

'Well, he's certainly *pretty*!' Ellerman shrank back out of sight in the doorway of Little Studies.

'Come off it. Maunder's not like that!'

'We're *all* like that!'

'But seriously, Maunder's right. If we play him outside, nobody'll take much note of him as a serious threat and all he's got to do is take a pass or two and make a pass or two.'

Tarrant said, with heavy ambiguity, 'Perhaps Maunder hopes Jonquil's will "make a pass or two" at Ellerman and then we'll get through and score while they're still licking their lips.'

'You're impossible, Tarrant! Anyhow, nobody suggests he'll score or anything.'

'Except with Maunder?'

Crowder laughed. 'God, don't you ever think of anything else?'

'Which of us does think of anything else in this monastic set-up? Except Singleton of course and he's a bloody monk already!'

'Was, you mean! Haven't you noticed how he treats Angus?' Ellerman, pretending to put books away, understood both tone and implication.

Tarrant said, 'No, but seriously, Ellerman's so small compared with us. Jonquil's'll murder him.'

'Perhaps, you're right, but we must have somebody.'

'Everyone will want to have Ellerman.'

'Ashton's bigger.'

'Tries hard, but not much talent.' There came Tarrant's laugh. '*Football*, talent I mean.'

At lunch, Snider said, 'Too nervous to eat, Ellerman?'

Ellerman considered. 'No,' he replied at last, 'no *side*.' (The Cranchester word for anything from impertinence to boasting had come back into vogue.) He continued, 'But I don't think I'm ever nervous before a match. Just excited.... Like waiting for the starting-pistol in a race.'

✻

The match against Jonquil's was to be played on 'Old Fifteen', a pitch in the middle of the School, surrounded by Houses and other buildings. It always attracted strollers because it was the most central at Cranchester and had originally been the First Fifteen pitch, whence its name. However, the increasing encroachment of buildings and paths made it progressively unsuitable until finally it had been decided that there was too little grass outside the minimal playing area to make it entirely safe for First XV matches. Nonetheless, it was the favourite and there was always competition to use it; Old Castonians always preferred it for their matches against the School.

A grey afternoon had gathered up a wind which kept acquiring strength and bluster. It had rained for some days. The grass was very green, but after a few minutes play it began to churn up in the middle. Virtually the whole of Ansell's and Jonquil's were present from the first whistle and other spectators joined. It was evidently to be a hard, dogged struggle dominated by forward play. The leather grew slimy; neither three-quarter line could make much use of the ball, as it slipped from their fingers, or skidded off the ground in a confusing bounce. Lightman was impenetrable. Coolly and calmly, he picked up every loose ball as though it had been a dry spring day. He kicked with marvellous elegance and precision, even, it seemed, knowing what the wind was going to do. The forwards ground away, but Tarrant and Bartlett stuck to Cruttwell like burrs. He was never able to get going on the treacherous surface. To the new Election, coldly watching on the sideline, the match was a considerable disappointment. Ellerman hardly touched the ball through the whole of the first half, although what he did do let nobody down; a useful short kick into touch, a sweet pass back to Maunder in the centre, who was smothered by Lightman anticipating the entire move.

At half-time covered, panting and with mud, Tarrant said, 'What wouldn't I give for a half-time lemon.'

'There's a war-r-r-r on,' rasped somebody else, imitating the voice of a popular radio comedian.

Maunder said, 'Listen, Ansell's. We're doing well. They expected to have scored now and we've kept 'em out. They've got the wind next half. Keep awake. If we're lucky, I reckon we might get one chance, and one only, but if we can take it, I think we take the match.'

The whistle blew.

The chance came about twenty-five minutes into the second half. Like so many chances on the football field, it arose from a tactical situation which seemed hardly propitious. Forward play had grown even more dogged and grinding since the interval. Light was fading and it seemed much colder. Spectators had begun to thin out, for it was clear that Jonquil's were the better side and that, at most, Ansell's might hold them to a pointless draw. Ellerman was feeling cold. The ball had not reached him once since the half-time restart.

A scrum was given; the muddied figures locked and strained a little way out from the touch. Maunder signalled him to stay right out on the line on the blind side. He clasped his fingers under his arms to warm them and began to move forward on his toes as the greasy ball, put in for the third time by Jonquil's scrum half, vanished from sight until, with a desperate effort, Bartlett hooked it away from his opposite number.

Wilder, a competent but not outstanding scrum-half, picked it up and flung out to his right, which was perhaps the best pass he would ever make in his life. It seemed to the spectators that the wet ball spurted out with the velocity of a shell. Somebody called, 'Fine pass!' Both sides slightly relaxed for the inevitable throw-in, or knock-on. They had not reckoned on Ellerman. Already running, he took the ball with his right arm as it passed across his body and scooped it securely to his side, seemingly just as it was about to go into touch. Those who were dawdling away, turned back at the moment of silence.

'Oh, well taken, Ansell's!'

It was the highlight of an afternoon of dull but determined football. Maunder had justified his decision to 'blood' so new and small a player. They waited philosophically for the ensuing tangle as Ellerman was tackled, glad to have witnessed the few seconds which had proved him already to be a future player of class.

Ellerman, speeding forward, did not intend to be caught if he could help it. He heard Maunder coming up behind him, say quietly, authoritatively, 'I'm here when you want me, Ellerman,' not instructing him, but backing him up. Ahead was Gardener, a very useful inside, who represented Cranchester Colts. Gardener heard Maunder too and positioned himself so that he could either tackle Ellerman and knock him over the line, or smother Maunder as he received a pass. Ellerman moved the ball into both hands, ready to give it to Maunder who was running slightly behind him out on his left. With an economic movement he drew the ball slightly back to the right and swung it easily across his pivoting body, removing his right hand as he began to let it go. A classic textbook pass.

Then, at the last moment, just as his left hand was at full stretch, with an intuitive skill which never can be taught, he scooped the ball back to the left-hand side of his body, swaying a little to the right all in the same movement, just inside the white line. Maunder, certain the pass was on its way, had his hands out ready to receive it; Gardener, poised to smother the pass, could not prevent himself from cannoning into Maunder.

There was an electric silence. Then an astonished, piercing, solitary voice shouted out, '*A DUMMY!* He's sold them a bloody dummy!' Then the one voice was drowned by great laugh and a cry of 'Ansell's! Ansell's!' Of course it could not last, but nevertheless they wanted it to end in the try which, in the best sort of school story, it would have deserved. However everyone knew that Lightman would expertly snuff out such an entertainingly cheeky move. He came across, calmly, very fast. For an eighteen-year-old he was perhaps slight but, even so, his size and speed made Ellerman seem incredibly fragile. Ellerman had accelerated too but, with an inward sigh, the spectators hunched in their coats saw the younger boy, possibly exalted by his successful dummy, lose concentration and drift towards the centre of the field, inadvertently shortening the distance between himself and Lightman.

'Ansell's! Ansell's! An-n-n-**sells**!' Ellerman could hear the shouts. He could hear Maunder, recovered, call urgently 'No! Go right! Go for the *FLAG*!'

If he went for the flag, he might just possibly make it, but Lightman was older, longer in leg, heavier, more experienced. If there were a tackle at the corner he, Ellerman, would certainly be carried into touch. Instead he swung slightly, but quite deliberately, towards the centre of the field and into the path of the oncoming full-back. Maunder shouted as if in anguish, '*NO*! Ellerman! *GO RIGHT.*' At that instant, on their twenty five, Ellerman perceived the gleam of satisfaction in Lightman's face.

The crowd groaned aloud in sympathy and frustration as, in response to their groan and Maunder's instruction and, although now too late, the smaller boy seemed to change his mind. In that hesitation he appeared momentarily even to have lost the edge of his pace. Another communal sigh. So near! Nevertheless such a gallant attempt negated criticism, they could not blame him.

One or two began to clap.

Ellerman angled back towards the corner-flag and the touchline, seeming tardily to obey Maunder's despairing bellow. At that instant, exactly as Ellerman anticipated, Lightman committed himself. In mid-stride, Ellerman took a half-pace with his left foot, pressed hard with his right, followed it by another left step. Back once more on his original tack, he simply lengthened his stride and accelerated. Realising he had been bluffed, Lightman miraculously retained balance, but Ellerman had melted from his reach.

It all happened so quickly, that at first it seemed to the watchers as if Ellerman had run straight into Lightman's arms; they sensed, rather than saw, the double-footed jink. Then they saw Lightman half on one knee, with Ellerman still up and going towards midfield. The lone voice screamed frenziedly, '*BLOOD-Y MARRRR-VELLOUS ANSELL'S!*' This time it was not followed by shouts and cheers, but continuous, respectful clapping like that accorded to an established soloist at a concert. Ellerman, alone of the players to retain a pristine cleanness, touched the ball almost demurely between the posts as if in acknowledgement of the applause.

Angus, a little apart on the touchline and far less knowledgeable about the game than most other spectators, was awed by the evident mastery which had somehow communicated itself to him. It was a game he loathed, but he found that, perhaps because of the cold wind, or for some other reason, he had tears in his eyes. He didn't know he was not alone.

Ellerman brought back the ball for the kick. Maunder said, 'Well run, Ellerman.' He received other similarly quietly fervent comments as he loped, head modestly down, back to his place on the wing. Inside, he felt a burning exultation, because he knew for certain that nobody else at Ansell's could have done it. Maunder converted, placing the ball firmly between the posts. The tremendous cheer which arose, causing rooks to rise in impatience, had in reality, nothing to do with the relatively easy kick. It was a tribute to a young player who had awed them into silence – doing for the first time at Cranchester what would one day make him idol of the Calcutta Cup.

As they restarted, Maunder said, 'Hold on! They'll counter-attack like a Panzer division. We must hold on, there's only about twelve minutes.' Jonquil's did counter-attack. Again and again, but the ball would not come free. The minutes trickled past.

'Jonquil's Jonquil's.'

'Ansell's! Ansell's.'

With about five minutes to go, Ansell's were under severe pressure between their own twenty-five and the half-way line. Again Ellerman was on the blind side. Again the ball went in. It was messily heeled. Jonquil's scrum half fumbled it and it bounced to Cruttwell. He stopped, turned, saw Ellerman's slight figure as the only obstacle and began his slowly accelerating, lumbering, run.

Maunder shouted very clearly, 'Yours, Ellerman.'

Ellerman knew exactly what Cruttwell was thinking. He saw fifteen stone, gathering speed and he was afraid. Nevertheless he positioned himself well, forcing the other towards the line. Then Cruttwell was up to him and there came the precise moment for the tackle. Ellerman did not want to do it but knew he must be seen to try. So a fraction of pace too late, he threw himself with convincing desperation, although he knew it would now be to no avail. To the watching spectators it seemed bad luck; a gallant attempt. They could not blame him. Cruttwell's heel grazed his cheek and Ellerman found himself trampled on by pursuing forwards. He felt his ankle go as a careless boot trod on it.

Grinling, Ansell's full-back, renowned more for his courage than his skill, flung himself desperately in a high awkward smother tackle at the line. Everyone heard his collar-bone crack as he crashed to the ground under his opponent, who triumphantly grounded, the ball just inside the corner flag.

'Jonquil's! Jonquil's! Jonnnn-quil's!'

Grinling was helped away, clasping his arm, supported by friends, but they all turned to watch the kick. Ellerman standing with his throbbing ankle, tried to persuade himself that he could not have prevented the tackle although he knew he was deluding himself. He tried to dispel the knowledge that, had he done so, Grinling would not have been mangled. He found Ashton and Angus and one or two others near him on the line.

Ashton said, 'Bloody bad luck, but you did all you could to stop that brute! He's bloody lethal, Ellerman. That's the third man he's crushed this season.'

Bartlett came over, 'Sorry, Ellerman. He just tore himself away from me. Like a bloody Samson. You were jolly plucky to have a go.'

It was a long kick and a difficult one, but Jonquil's had Lightman. He went right back almost to the half way line to give himself the right angle. Ellerman heard Tarrant whisper, 'He's relying on the wind to help.'

Lightman stepped carefully back from the ball, counting his paces. The referee had looked at his watch and would obviously be blowing up as soon as the kick was concluded. Lightman dabbed a finger on his tongue, held it briefly in the breeze and gave a satisfied half-nod. There was absolute silence except for the wind. Ellerman was now standing with the team behind the Ansell's line, close to Maunder and Wilder. From between the posts, they watched Lightman place his fingers carefully straight down by his sides, rise on his toes and then, accelerating a little, as he trotted with elegant ease towards the ball as it was put down by the holder, pointing forwards. He struck it hard and sweetly, precisely on the spot he had previously dried with his sleeve. It rose in a marvellously graceful swoop, its torpedo shape cutting cleanly through the air.

'What a bloody marvellous kick!' Bartlett whispered. Why whisper, Ellerman thought? 'But at least we've drawn.'

The ball came on between the Ansell's posts straight and true. Then there came an indefinable difference. The fitful, fickle, wind, lulled a moment; the ball seemed to hang there like the finger of an old man on a cloud he had seen somewhere in a picture, an old man leaning to touch the outstretched, but almost lifeless, finger of a younger, lesser figure. Almost as quickly as the wind had dropped it strengthened again. However in that critical half-second the ball had swung slightly. Ever so gently, the ball dabbed at the very top of the slender post. Without forward motion it dropped, scraped the bar – and fell back onto the field of play, almost at Ellerman's feet, where it then rolled back over the line. Maunder put his hand on it. The linesman signalling no score. A whistle blew and the referee's voice could be heard, clear and precise, saying, 'No Side.'

Maunder said, 'Well done, Ansell's. Well played indeed!'

Ellerman's heart leaped. His moment of cowardice had not mattered after all. The wind had decided in his favour! They had won! Even the gods were on his side. They always were! He had got away with it.

※

After he returned from Tosher and was climbing into pyjamas, Mawsom said, 'I say Ellerman, Maunder's in Big Study and would like to see you!'

'Is he going to beat you Ellerman?' Dermott-Powell teased.

'Shouldn't think so. What for?'

Snider said, 'It'll be about the match, I should think. Probably to tell you you're getting Tasselled on Saturday.'

'Not for one match,' Ellerman said modestly, but he knew it not unlikely.

He knocked at the door of Big Study.

'Come in.'

With a slight lurch of heart he entered. 'You wanted to see me, Maunder?'

'Yes, Ellerman. About the match this afternoon.'

'Oh.'

'You know that was a bloody marvellous try.'

'Thank you, Maunder. Bit of luck.'

'The pass was luck, but the rest was you. You sold the dummy. And you jinked Lightman. That's only about the second time he's ever missed a tackle. I say, have you hurt your ankle?'

'Bruised I think, Maunder, just at the end of the match.'

'Bad luck. Do you know how you do that sort of double-footed business?'

'Not really, Maunder. I've just seem to be able to do it. I see somebody coming and it just sort of happens.'

'Great stuff.'

'Thank you, Maunder.'

He felt the interview was at an end and turned to go with a light heart.

'One other thing before you go, Ellerman.'

'Yes, Maunder?'

'Get over The Chair.'

'What?' Unnerved by the sudden, unexpected change in the tone of the interview, he swallowed, not believing his ears.

'I said get over The Chair, Ellerman. I think you demonstrated the method on first day of Half.'

'Yes, Maunder.'

'I hope you have not forgotten.'

'No, Maunder.'

He tightened-up, shuffling his foot up to the bar. Four hard, stinging cuts made him bite his lip.

'Get up, Ellerman.'

He found himself looking into Maunder's penetrating gaze.

'You know what that was for?'

'No, Maunder...'

Maunder waited without moving his eyes.

'Not really...I...' Then Ellerman dropped his eyes.

'Well?'

'Was it for missing that tackle?'

'No, not for *missing* it. You funked it. Had you persisted in telling me you didn't know why you were tightening-up, then you'd have had three tomorrow...for lying to me today.'

'Yes, Maunder.'

'Look me in the eye, Ellerman.'

Reluctantly he did so.

'Do you know who was the best player out there this afternoon?'

'Lightman? You, Maunder!'

'Lightman and I were second best.' There was a pause. 'You were the best player on the field. I don't tell you to flatter you. It's a fact. If you wish to, you'll play for England once this bloody war's over.'

'Thank you, Maunder.'

'But if you ever cut a tackle again, you'll not play for Ansell's, no matter how good you are.'

'No, Maunder.'

'Nor how pretty you are.'

Ellerman blushed.

'At least, not while I'm here.'

'I understand, Maunder.'

'I'm a good enough footballer, Ellerman, to know that somebody who could make the run you made this afternoon would never be able to come in even a fraction late with a tackle, unless he wanted to. I'm right, aren't I?'

'I thought nobody'd notice.'

'Nobody else did! You saw what happened to Grinling?'

'Yes.'

'An early tackle on that lumbering oaf would have stopped that, wouldn't it?'

'I suppose so, Maunder.'

'Suppose?'

'I'm *sure*, Maunder.'

'So am I. Remember, Ellerman, Ansell's isn't the place for cowards or liars – and you've almost lied to me this evening – in fact, I find that the one is usually the other.'

Ellerman had never before been so completely dressed down; never so completely 'found out'. The fact that, like the rest of the Election, he hero-worshipped Maunder made it ten times worse. Bitterly ashamed and now close to tears, he said in a low voice, 'Yes, Maunder. I'm sorry. It'll never happen again.'

'It had better not. You can cut along now. You needn't do any Warming tonight.'

'Thank you, Maunder.'

Formally they shook hands. Maunder said casually as he turned for the door, 'Oh one other thing. If it hadn't been for that tackle, you'd have been Tasselled on Saturday.'

Disappointment almost destroyed him. He didn't dare turn round.

'So if anyone says it's only to preserve my own record, we shall both have to hold our peace, won't we? Or tell the truth?'

Ellerman nodded, unable to speak. He moved towards the door.

Thankfully in the dark of Big Dormitory he slipped to his Manger. Snider whispered, 'Was it about the match?'

'Yes!'

'Did he congratulate you on the try?'

A pause, then, 'Yes.'

'You'll get Tasselled on Saturday. All Ansell's think so.'

'Good Lord no! What, break Maunder's record for one game and one try?' The implication was out of his mouth before he could stop himself.

'Goodnight, Ellerman. It was *Bloody Mar-vellous*,' Snider said, emphasising the Cranchester phrase.

Ellerman lay awake in the dark. Funk? Liar? The four cuts did not matter. Immediately painful perhaps, but soon over. He had been beaten previously, but always for something 'respectable', something to which he could have cheerfully admit; something of which his contemporaries would have approved and for which he might even be admired – breaking bounds, owning up to a smashed window. Early on, at his Private, he had realised that talent on the games field, open charm of manner and, as Maunder had shrewdly, if brutally, pointed out, his good looks encouraged authority to absolve him of complicity in any offence reflecting dishonesty or untruthfulness. He had not really lied to Snider! Maunder had talked about the match, but he did not want anyone to know he had been beaten, or, more particularly, why! He would tell nobody.

Tosher!

He was wide awake again. They would all see in the morning. Every morning. And in Big Change. Every single person in Ansell's would know by breakfast. What could he do? Illness! He could spin his bad ankle out for at least a week. That would at least keep him out of Big Change. Then he had another idea. Nobody would notice if he missed Tosher in the evening and, if he got up really early in the morning, he'd be back and dressed by the time the others were up and about.

It proved to be a successful plan.

iii

'What happens on Tassel Night?'

Ashton said, 'Oh, well there are speeches. And we get Cider. I expect Ellerman will be Tasselled.'

Angus said, 'A sort of party?'

'Sort of. Except that the new Election have to sing. You won't mind that, Angus.'

'Sing what?' Baker said, alarmed.

'It's very easy. Goes to the tune of "Ten Green Bottles". Almost the same words too.'

Baker looked doubtful. 'Do we all sing it?'

'Oh yes. It's a sort of joke.'

'And *afterwards?*' Dermott-Powell asked with a curious lift of voice.

Ashton returned Dermott-Powell's quizzical gaze. He said evenly, 'You'll find out soon enough. I must cut along now.'

'What do you mean by *afterwards*, Dermott-Powell?'

'Nothing really...just something I was told.' Then hastily, with a grotesque mockery of a German accent, 'I haf bin svorn to secrecy!'

Ellerman looked momentarily uncomfortable but Mawsom added, 'Zis iss Funff speaking,' and the reference to ***ITMA*** sparked off a round of laughter.

※

Tassel Night was quite a formal occasion. The Digger was there and the food, despite wartime exigencies, was more plentiful and decorative than usual. There was an air too of a Christmas Dinner about it, with the pudding and some tired decorations which had been put up. On each table was a stone jug of cider and, outside in the kitchen, a barrel from which the jug could be refilled.

Angus found it sweetly rough, biting the back of his throat. There were pieces (of apple?) floating and it was quite unlike the clear bottled liquid he had been occasionally allowed at home. After two or three swallows, he felt slightly light-headed and imagined he might be sickening for something, but that cleared with the food. However, one pewter mug-full sufficed for the entire evening. Others drank far more and the level of noise and chatter rose.

Towards the end, The Digger stood up. Silence fell as if switched on. 'It is my pleasant duty to propose the health of my Praefaectors. We have, in Ansell's, always been fortunate in those who have taken responsibility. In expressing my thanks, I am, I know, expressing your gratitude to Maunder and the other Praefaectors.

'Although of course I'm prejudiced, I know that Ansell's is the best House at Cranchester. And it's that way because of the Praefaectors who uphold our standards, my standards and yours. This Half we have done well to succeed in the football. As you all know we are still in competition for the Final next Half, because we beat Jonquil's by dint of a fine try scored by the youngest Ansell's Man ever to play for the House side in my time.' There was a cheer.

Dermott-Powell whispered, 'Told you, Ellerman. You're bound to get Tasselled.'

Digger held up a hand and continued: 'Winning a Final doesn't make a House a good House of course, but it may be opportune to remind you that we have been in the Lent Half of the Competition for the last ten years. And the last time we were knocked out of it before Christmas, we won the Plate competition with a score that has never been equalled since!' He paused. 'On behalf of the best House, I give you the best Praefaectors!' The House rose. Only the Praefaectors sat. 'The Praefaectors!'

There was a great cheer. Then Maunder stood up. 'Thank you, sir. I give the toast Ansell's – and the School!'

Another cheer and everyone was on his feet. They sat down. Digger said, 'Now Gentlemen, I shall leave you. I know that Maunder wishes to address you. It will leave him more scope if I am not here!' It was a joke he made each time. He vanished through the door to Private.

Somebody called out, 'Come on, Maunder!'

Maunder banged for silence. 'I've not much to say. Except that The Digger's right. There's only one House at Cranchester worth a button.'

Several voices called, 'Hear! Hear!' 'We're the fittest.' 'We look after each other.'

'And I can tell you, I'd rather be Head of Ansell's than Captain of the School!'

There was a great cheer. The relaxing of tension which was apparent as the Half drew to an end, the food and most of all the strength of the cider, seemed to make Maunder's sentiments everyone's sentiments for, like all successful orators, he knew his audience and knew the mood of the moment. 'We may not win the Football Cup, but the other's'll bloody well know that we're there! More cheering. 'Anyhow, tonight we're Tasselling Grinling.'

Great cheers.

Grinling, his shoulder still in a sling from his attempt to stop Cruttwell hobbled forward. Maunder had lifted the glass cover from the Tasselled football cap and he put it on Grinling's head. Then, removing it and replacing it, he handed over a coveted golden Tassel.

More cheers.

'And Eckersley.' Eckersley, a tall prop forward in his final year came forward sheepishly. The ceremony was repeated. There were more cheers. Maunder said, 'They're the only Tassels this Half.' Ansell's, who had been expecting Ellerman to be called, were momentarily silent as Maunder went on quickly. 'Now it's time for the new Election to sing to us!' Immediately, the raucous cheers and laughter were renewed. A bench from Long School was brought to the dais.

'I bet Maunder didn't want you to equal his own record – Tasselled in his first Half,' Notting muttered. Ellerman was saved from commenting by being called to the front.

The seven of them stood on the bench.

Tarrant said, 'You have to stand on one leg!'

Maunder said, 'Now sing. You first, Ellerman. *Seven Green Ansell's Men, standing on a wall*...Go on...'

'Seven Green Ansell's Men, standing on a wall!'

'Seven Green Ansell's Men standing on a wall!

'And if one Green Ansell's Man, should accidentally fall...'

'There'd be **Six** Green Ansell's Men standing on the wall...' the whole of Ansell's bellowed in chorus, as they let fly with screwed-up paper, bread, apple cores, so that, overbalancing, Ellerman fell off to a great cheer.

Maunder called, 'Okay, Ellerman, you can join Ansell's now. So it continued with Five Green Ansell's Men; Four; Three. Each time the chorus was accompanied by a shower of missiles, although as the song progressed down List, there was less and less ammunition available. Mawsom was hit above the eye by a hard crust.

'One Green Ansell's Man, standing on the wall!'

'One Green Ansell's Man standing on the wall!'

'And if one Green Ansell's Man should accidentally fall...'

'There'd be *NO* GREEN ANSELL'S MEN standing on the wall,' came the deafening final shout.

By now the rain of missiles was puny compared with that which had greeted Ellerman, so Angus, inevitably last, found he could avoid them easily so that when it abated he was still standing one-footed on the bench.

Maunder said in an exhausted hoarse laugh, 'It seems that we've still got one green Ansell's Man after all.' A remark greeted with a raucous cheers and garbled shouts which Angus could not interpret.

It was time for Curfew.

※

He was almost asleep in Singleton's bed when Singleton arrived and said, as though infected by end of Half conviviality, 'If we make a fire, I've collected some chestnuts and we could roast them.' He seemed tense. Angus, although sleepy, was intrigued. The fire easily caught and the coal glowed satisfactorily. However, the chestnuts took a long time to cook and in his heart of hearts he would have preferred to be in bed, asleep.

'I hear you and Dermott-Powell are Singing in Chapel tomorrow at Evensong. Nervous?'

Angus yawned, 'Tired! But I expect I will be nervous.'

'You don't sound it. I'd be petrified.'

'No!' Angus said. 'I don't feel like that. Singing doesn't seem bother me. It didn't tonight, but I expect it'll be different tomorrow.'

The chestnuts were unexpectedly good.

'Like Christmas,' Angus said. 'Except it doesn't seem much like Christmas time at...'

'At Ansell's?'

'I was going to say at Cranchester. There haven't even been any Carols or anything yet.'

Singleton said, 'Never is till the last week.' He noticed Angus yawning again: 'Do you want to get back to Big Dorm?'

'But your bed'll be cold again by now.'

'Doesn't matter, off you go.'

It seemed to Angus that perhaps Singleton did not really want him to go. He said, 'Thanks for the chestnuts. You know...'

'Yes?'

'Tonight was really good. The supper I mean. Bad luck on Ellerman, not getting Tasselled, but it was good fun. Even the singing! I'm glad I wasn't first!'

Singleton said in a detached way, 'You'll need some sleep if you're singing tomorrow.' He paused. 'I'm looking forward to hearing you.'

'And Dermott-Powell! He's done it before. In the Cathedral.'

'And Dermott-Powell. Of course,' Singleton agreed.

'G'night, Singleton.'

'Goodnight, young Angus.' He stood looking out of the window for some time after Angus had gone.

Back in Big Dorm Angus looked in to see if Mawsom were awake, but he had not yet returned from Warming. So he slipped into a cold bed, and fell asleep, almost immediately.

iv

As soon as he awoke, he remembered that he was to sing. For the first time he felt fear in the pit of his stomach. Sunday morning always meant later rising, but after Tassel Night, there seemed to be an air of *ennui*, almost lassitude, which invested everyone, like a communal hangover which, in a way it was; even at breakfast there was little chatter.

Afterwards, Mawsom, a discolouring bruise above his eye, came up to him. 'What did you think of last night?' he said quietly.

'Good fun. I suppose I was lucky with the singing, I was last! I saw you get hit pretty hard with that crust. Did it hurt?'

Mawsom said, 'I didn't mean that, I meant afterwards...later on?' He looked enquiringly at Angus.

Angus dropped his voice, 'Singleton and I roasted some chestnuts. Like at Christmas! They were jolly good.'

Mawsom said flatly almost with exasperation, 'I expect they were.'

'You weren't back when I came in. I'd've told you then. Did you and Wilder do anything?' and as a new thought occurred to him he added, 'You haven't told him about Singleton's fire.'

'Of course I haven't told him! And *we* didn't roast chestnuts!' Mawsom said abruptly and vanished.

'What's up with Mawsom?' It was Dermott-Powell who had joined them unobserved.

'I don't think he enjoyed Tassel Night very much.'

'Oh?'

'Yes, he got hit in the eye with a crust!'

'Oh. Did he?' Dermott-Powell seemed as chirpy as Mawsom had seemed brusque.

'I thought it was great fun. What about you?'

Dermott-Powell looked at him sharply and said, 'Yes. As a matter or fact, I thought it was fun too. Ansell's is more fun than I thought! Then after a long pause, changing the subject, 'Nervous about this evening?'

'I wasn't, until this morning. Now I can feel my chest is tight.'

Dermott-Powell smiled: 'Here's a tip. Before you come in – your first entry – give yourself time to take at least three, very deep breaths. It always works with me. Don't forget we've got to be at Chapel half an hour early.'

※

The rest of Sunday passed with its customary slowness but, at last, they were sitting in the choir stalls. Dermott-Powell whispered to Angus, 'I think there are one or two notes I'm not going to make. You'll have to cover for me if that happens and we're both singing. Don't let it put you off.'

The last stragglers were scuttling into seats. Dim lighting took the expression out of most of the faces. As Angus looked along the back rows on the opposite side, he could see in the semi-dark, Singleton gazing straight ahead. At the front, he could see Ellerman; by chance a light was near him and he seemed to glow, whilst everyone else was in shadow.

He was relieved to find that, with the black firm notes of the music on the page before him, his hesitation and nervousness had vanished. It was odd, he thought, the rest of them saying they'd 'never be able to stand up and sing' in Chapel. Yet they were not afraid of other things, as he was – Big Study, tightening-up, for instance. None of them knew how completely the thought of that petrified him. He felt his breathing quicken, so turned his thoughts elsewhere. Baker, for instance, still after all these weeks was embarrassed to walk naked down Big Dorm! As if anyone even noticed him! He could not understand that.

The service began. Lesson. Psalm. Lesson. At last they came to the Anthem: the choir stood, he and Dermott-Powell slightly apart. Remembering Dermott-Powell's advice, he drew three long, deep breaths, but he knew he did not need them. He watched the music as the choir sang, he then heard Dermott-Powell. Then it was time for him. Perfectly on time, absolutely in pitch, he sang,

'I waited for the Lord. And he heard my complaint.'

As if two separate people, singer and auditor, he listened to his notes lose themselves in the tracery of the ceiling high above and knew with a great certainty that it was right and that the tone was true. He felt that he was in charge of the music – that his instinct and the music were complementing each other. With a flash of insight, the detached part of him thought, 'It must have felt like this for Ellerman out there on Old Fifteen, scoring that try!' He could detect the very faint roughness that had begun to mar the purity of Dermott-Powell's high notes, but Dermott-Powell was experienced enough to give them less volume and so the two voices twined and interlinked in Mendelssohn's elegiac music until, it seemed to Angus, that he was not at Cranchester, or anywhere entirely on earth. The choir, inspired by the perfection of the two soloists, achieved a pitch of expression and tone which could never have been rehearsed.

'I waited for the Lord. And he heard my complaint.'

The congregation, cold and, before supper, even hungry, anticipating with boredom, a sermon, began to take notice. The fine notes seemed to pierce each one of them sitting there, impelling spontaneous stillness.

Singleton sat transfixed. Looking down the aisle in the almost unlit chapel, he could see, dimly, the choir. Dermott-Powell's head shone more like a red aura than hair, glowing in the light of the lamp he shared with Angus. Singleton could also see that, Angus, smaller, more fragile, was, like Dermott-Powell evidently no longer using the music, but singing from memory, with such feeling and spontaneity, that he felt almost suffocated by emotion. He had to shield his face with his hand so that nobody should guess tears had sprung unbidden to his eyes. When it ended there was a long moment of utter silence before listeners and singers came out of their trance and were once more the impatient school congregation waiting to be bored.

Coming out of Chapel, Dermott-Powell said, 'You know you were very good in there, don't you?'

Angus was silent.

'Come on, Angus, no *side*, I mean it.'

'Thanks. You too.'

Dermott-Powell shook his head. 'No. You held it. You took it; I know what I'm talking about.'

Angus said, 'We did it together. It was your tip about breathing.'

Dermott-Powell seemed about to say something, but instead smiled and after a bit said, 'You're an extraordinary chap, Angus. Most of the time you look so scared that you'd have a fit if anyone said boo! Yet in Chapel there, you never batted an eyelid. You didn't need my breathing exercise.'

In Great Quad they were stopped by the High Master. 'You are Dermott-Powell? And you are Angus?'

'Yes, sir,' in chorus.

'We have never before had that Mendelssohn sung at Cranchester. Am I to think that Ansell's will be supplying the School with singers as well as sportsmen now?'

They divined it to be a joke. 'Thank you very much, sir.'

The High Master said gravely, 'Thank you both.'

Dermott-Powell shivered a bit. 'I didn't think he knew who I was.'

'Nor me.'

On the way back to Ansell's, several other figures, virtually anonymous in the dark, said, 'Well sung,' One was a Master with a severe limp who had arrived that Half. He said, 'That was very beautiful and very musical.' As his figure vanished in the dark, Dermott-Powell muttered, 'That's Craigie. He got an MC in Crete. Nearly died of wounds.'

At the end of List, The Digger said, 'It pleased me very much to hear the Anthem sung so splendidly tonight. And sung by two Ansell's Men.' As they left Ashton said, 'That's the first time in a year he's spoken after List! But the singing was bloody *mar*-vellous!'

He was again very tired. Singleton came in later than usual and Angus was almost asleep by the time the door opened. 'Didn't realise that you and Dermott-Powell could sing like that. Bloody marvellous.' He had never heard Singleton swear before and the words, even though taken for granted throughout Cranchester, seemed to sit uncomfortably on his lips.

Angus sat up and swung his legs over the side of the bed. Singleton threw off his dressing-gown and sat beside him. 'Bloody mar-vellous.' With an affectionate gesture which he tried to disguise at the last minute by making it boisterous, Singleton put his left arm round Angus' shoulder, so that Angus who was about to stand up overbalanced half into the other's lap. Apologetic, but not embarrassed, sure of Singleton's affability and relaxed by the insidious end-of-Half camaraderie, through his thin pyjamas Angus was conscious of the warmth of Singleton's body and the beating of his heart. It was so unexpectedly reassuring, so different from the remoteness which Ansell's epitomised that, to his chagrin he felt his eyes begin to prick and he was glad that Singleton could not see his face.

He felt Singleton place a hand lightly on the flat of his stomach, where the pyjamas gaped. Because it was such an intimate, comforting gesture, and also perhaps because of the emotional demands the solo had made upon him, tears actually brimmed his eyes. Trying to stop them rolling down his cheek he bit his lip and pushed his head back till it came against Singleton's shoulder. He heard Singleton say softly, perhaps only to himself, 'You really don't know, do you?'

Puzzled but still fearing to trust the steadiness of his voice, Angus put his own right hand on top of Singleton's, finger for finger, as if measuring its smallness against Singleton's hand, where it lay warm and reassuring on the smooth skin of his belly. They did not move for a full minute. It allowed him time enough to recover his equanimity and ask lightly, 'Don't know what, Singleton?'

Singleton said, again as if to himself, 'You just don't know...' Then louder, 'Well...what effect you have.'

'Oh! My singing you mean!' He was relieved he did understand after all.

Very carefully, Singleton withdrew his hand and said with gentle intensity, 'I suppose that's part of it.' He paused, 'And the singing *was* bloody mar-vellous. Thought you were going to crack the roof.' He stopped. Angus did not move, He felt happier and less frightened than at any time since he had arrived at Ansell's.

'You'd better be getting back. You'll get cold.'

'Goodnight, Singleton.'

With great gentleness, Singleton took hold of his left ear lobe with finger and thumb so that Angus had to face him. Thankfully, the threatening tears had receded.

'Goodnight, young Angus.'

Still standing between Singleton's knees he half-turned towards the door.

'Angus?'

He turned back again. It was light as day in the full moonlight. He wondered what else Singleton had to say, but Singleton briefly and unexpectedly pushed his fingers through Angus' hair, ruffling it slightly. 'Off you go,' and Angus heard him say under his breath, '...or we'll both regret it.'

Regret what?

Puzzled, he paused irresolute for the moment. Singleton looked curiously forlorn, sitting in the moonlight on the bed's edge. The small study seemed so personal, so domestic, so welcoming and so unlike Ansell's, that for an instant he had the impulse to kiss Singleton 'Goodnight', as he still kissed his father or grandfather goodnight at home. Almost as soon as the thought occurred, he was again oppressed by Ansell's, Conscious that Ansell's was not home nor ever could be and that Singleton and the other Praefaectors would find such a 'goodnight' utterly out of place, he said quickly, 'Goodnight, Singleton, and thanks!' before scuttling, back to Big Dormitory.

It was very late, but Ellerman was still awake and Angus had the impression that he was not long back himself. He came over in the dark and whispered, 'Angus? You're late.'

'Singleton didn't come in from Big Study for ages. Then he went on about the singing.'

'What did he say? Come on! It's not *side* – after all I've asked you.'

'He liked it. Actually, he said it was "bloody marvellous".'

'Fancy! Aunty Singleton swearing!'

'I know!'

'Well, the singing was pretty decent,' Ellerman allowed. 'Everyone says so.' Angus knew he meant everyone in Ansell's. Others. did not really count.

'What else did he say?'

'Nothing really. Oh he said there was something or other which I didn't understand.'

Ellerman said, 'My dear old Angus, there's quite a lot *you* don't understand.' There was a pause. 'Did you do anything?' Ellerman seemed almost artificially casual. What luck they had not lit the fire! 'Or did he?'

'What? No.' Angus was puzzled. 'Oh well, he pinched my ear. A sort of joke.'

'Joke?'

'It wasn't meant to hurt. Like this,' he squeezed Ellerman's ear in the dark.

'He's very nice, you know, friendly.'

'I'm sure he is,' Ellerman said in a voice which Angus could not interpret. 'I'm sure he's nice to *you*.' There was a long pause. Then, 'You really don't understand – do you?'

'You're almost as bad as Singleton,' Angus said with a flare of impatience.

'And you're too good to be true! You and Singleton make a pair,' Ellerman said with a half-laugh and went back to his own Manger.

As he climbed into bed, Angus felt a twitch of annoyance. Now Ellerman! What was there to *understand*? Except that Singleton was much nicer than he had ever supposed a Praefaector could be! Perhaps the others were like that too? Even Tarrant? He could not believe that! He slid into total and untroubled sleep.

Singleton gazed out of the open window into moonlight, breathing cold air. He felt like a mountaineer who has just negotiated one terrible precipice and fears the next. There had, thank God, been nothing really heinous in his conduct. He inhaled deeply as if to draw the purifying rawness into the depth of his being. Angus, it was clear, had sensed nothing amiss; however, he could not disguise from himself his own inclinations; some of them had been more than questionable. Angus' response had been one of almost culpable naivety and he knew it was only because Angus had, so demonstrably, felt no guilt at all that he, Singleton, could attempt to dispel his own. Dimly, he began to perceive that only Angus' complete absence of sexual awareness had enabled him to rein in that side of his own nature which, during the years at Ansell's, he had struggled, not always with success, to constrain; a side of himself to which, in the previous half-hour, he might have succumbed so easily, so completely, and, he recognised with another flutter of panic, so willingly.

✻

In Tosher, on the last full morning of the Half, Mawsom noticed faded evidence of Ellerman's encounter with Maunder in Big Study. 'I didn't know you'd had to tighten-up for Maunder.'

'Oh that! It was nothing. Hardly noticed it!'

'So even you forgot to Warm!' (Ellerman's efficiency in Warming had become something of a legend.)

With great daring, Ellerman said through his toothbrush, in a bright playful voice, 'Me? Of course not. I got this for playing football – instead of a Tassel!'

'In that case,' Mawsom said, 'I expect Angus'll have to tighten-up for singing!'

Notting turned to Angus at the next basin: 'You do realise you're now the only one of the Election who hasn't had his arse well and truly tanned? He hummed provokingly, *One green Ansell's Man **still** standing on the wall!* The implication aroused one or two chuckles, but went completely over Angus' head.

Angus wished they would not go on about tightening-up; as the days to end of Half had passed, his anxiety had increased rather than diminished and it was not until he stepped from train in London that the lurking dread of having to tighten-up really lifted.

Chapter Four

The train drew into Cranchester station as the first flakes of snow drifted idly down from a sky the colour of bright lead and by the time they had walked to Lodge it already lay shoe deep. There were few 'frogs' and none for Ansell's, so they still remained Junior Election. Angus, already cold beneath his coat, trudged between Snider and Mawsom, his feet damp inside his shoes and his heart as heavy as the sky which had darkened almost to night. They hardly exchanged a word. Great Quad was crisscrossed by footprints which seemed like dark scores and the track to Ansell's was already trodden to ice. The air was oppressive, damply cold. He shivered again as they came, inevitably, to the familiar chipped paint.

Mawsom said, unnecessarily, 'Back again.'

'At least we'll be warmer inside,' Snider muttered as they pushed open Door with their cases; beyond them, Yard was an unbroken white sheet. It was not warmer inside. If anything it was colder, with the accumulated coldness of the unheated holiday. The fire in Libe had not been lighted; the three antiquated iron radiators served by the hot-water system, reactivated only that afternoon, were barely warm.

A cold clamminess seeped from floor, from the walls and hung in the air. It was as if the interior, somehow, deliberately sought to epitomise the depressing end-of-the-holiday mood. In Big Dorm there was little conversation even amongst the most senior. Daylight had almost gone. The few dim light bulbs served merely to accentuate the surrounding gloom, seeming almost to wear a halo in the damp air.

Ellerman came across: 'Have you heard about Singleton?'

Angus turned. 'No? What is it?'

'He's leaving at the end of the Half.'

'How do you know?'

'I was in Maunder's compartment in the train. I heard him tell Maunder.'

Angus, Snider and Mawsom had shared a compartment with four other Castonians of their own age from Pettifer's, but the two groups had ignored the presence of each other. Angus said nothing. He had not seen Singleton. The news added further chill to the cold blackness.

❋

He was lying on his back staring up through the dimness when Singleton came in that night.

'Singleton? I say, Ellerman says this is your last Half?'

'Accepted for "potential officer" training last vac. And I heard at Christmas that I've got a place at my father's old Oxford College, but I'm not "going up" until after the war's over.' He laughed: 'Must do my bit.' There was a pause. 'Of course if the war goes on for another four or five years, we could both end up at Oxford at the same time.'

'Yes, I suppose so.'

After another pause Singleton, changing the subject said, with forced cheerfulness, 'Look, let's light a fire. I've brought some more coal from home.'

Angus sat up. 'Did you? So did I! I'll bring it along tomorrow and put it in the store.' He spoke with more animation.

As if it too had absorbed the chilly dampness, the pyramid of wood and coal took a long time to light, but eventually it caught and flared cheerfully. The heat not only pushed back the coldness but, as gradually the comfortable familiarity of the previous Half was taken up again, it seemed also to alleviate the depression that was threatening to engulf Angus. The holiday was another country. He said, 'It doesn't seem possible that we weren't here last night. It's as though we've never been away.'

'I used to feel like that.'

'I wish you weren't going.'

'You'll be all right.' There was another silence. 'Make sure it's a Half to remember. Enjoy it. Shall you sing in Chapel again?'

'Yes. The Anthem at the end of the month. Dermott-Powell says his voice's "gone".'

'I'm not surprised!'

'Did you really used to wish you weren't coming back after the holiday?'

'Always. Until today, actually. Now it's the last time I'm coming back, I find I'm quite sorry.'

'It seems so much worse than the last time...I mean last time we didn't know what it was going to be like,' Angus ended lamely.

Singleton looked across at him through the light of the fire. 'Are you tired?'

'Mmmm. A bit.'

'You'd better be going back to bed. You had a long journey?'

'Yes, there was a raid somewhere. We all had to get out at Crewe. It was three o'clock in the morning! But your bed's still very cold.'

'Doesn't matter. Not tonight. Anyhow, there's hardly enough of you to make much difference this weather. And unless you learn to wear your dressing-gown properly, you'll catch pneumonia or something and end up in Nurs'ry.' Singleton pulled Angus' gaping lapels, tugging the front together under the cord. It was another moment, like those in the previous Half, which seemed to have nothing to do with Cranchester or Ansell's. It betrayed him into saying, before he could stop himself, 'Anyway seeing you again has cheered me up!' Recovering, he gently propelled Angus towards the door: 'Off you go!'

'Goodnight, Singleton.'

When he had gone, Singleton continued to sit by the dying fire until the surrounding cold bit into his back. In his cold bed, he lay awake for a long time, as he always did on the first night of a new Half. He was aware of conflicting emotions. Part of him could hardly bear the thought of leaving; Angus seemed so vulnerable. He could, he knew, have deferred his call-up until July. At the same time, another part of him was relieved. He knew he trod a precarious path; his relationship with Angus must inevitably become more testing. He remembered almost guiltily the comment he had unintentionally made to Angus that evening. He was also aware that the context of Ansell's, in some insidious way, encouraged him subtly to evade the scruples which, until now, he believed, his staunchest allies.

Ellerman was still awake. 'Angus?'

'Yes?' in a whisper. He slipped behind the curtains of Ellerman's Manger.

'Did Singleton say anything about leaving?'

'He's got a place at Oxford, but he's not going up until after the war. He's going into the army first.'

'He would! Are you cold?'

'Yes. Very.'

'Get in here with me. We'll warm each other.'

'I'm very tired. I'll probably fall asleep and never get up.'

There was a pause in the dark. 'Okay. Goodnight.'

His own bed was so cold that the sheets felt almost moist. For half an hour he was unable to entice sleep to overtake him. Eventually, teeth chattering, he got up and put on a jersey, some games' socks and his dressing-gown and got back into bed again. Within five minutes he dropped into exhausted slumber, from which he woke late and with difficulty the following morning. Dermott-Powell was shaking him.

'Everyone's been to Tosher, Angus!'

'Thanks!' He got up and stripped. Cold air bit his skin.

※

Snow had fallen all night and lay thick on the window ledges and snow continued to fall. It did not come dramatically, in a great storm, but trickled on, day after day, from a dead sky. The air was very, very, cold; the snow hard, gritty. As the novelty wore off, snow battles, which had enlivened the first days of the Half, died away; they seemed a poor replacement for the games which could not happen. Each day after breakfast, the Junior Election were set to clear Yard, so that Yard Fives could take place. Maunder organised runs. They were long and bleak; the hard crust of snow which had frozen overnight chipped and chapped the skin. Angus found his ankles bleeding; Baker's grew so bad that he was eventually forbidden to run by the School doctor. Water in Big Change was rarely more than lukewarm; towels never dry.

The whole school grew irritable, frustrated by cold discomfort, cheerless war-time food and dammed-up energy. In Ansell's, always more highly charged than other Houses, it seemed to foster suppressed mutual hostility. Ansell's Men had to tighten-up for trivialities which, at other times, would have merited no more than a warning and, unusually for Ansell's, it was resented for days. Ironically, in view of the thick snow, Angus learned his solo was to be 'Sheep may safely graze'.

ii

The film was shown on the last Saturday of January. It had been provided by a wealthy benefactress of Cranchester, who lived in a large country house not far away. She was elderly, widowed, childless and influential enough to persuade the High Master that the film would be edifying for Castonians.

This is itself was remarkable; his antipathy to any sort of 'kinema' was proverbial. However, the title innocuous enough to persuade him that it would be morally harmless, was ambiguous enough to encourage the school in the belief that it was a thriller of a similar title which had recently been released. That ensured a large audience.

Nevertheless it became clear after the first ten minutes that it was, in truth, a Hollywood saga of unsurpassed sentimentality. Set at the end of the previous century, its complex plot involved true love, mistaken marriage, early death and an almost-forfeited inheritance. Two major stars managed to conceal any merit or genuine emotion that may have resided in the script, behind rapid, stilted, dialogue and clipped accents. Far more damaging, they utterly failed to cope with competition from the child star whose curly hair, melting eyes and angelic demeanour had reduced the matrons of two continents to copious tears.

His effect on the Castonian audience however, was very different. Despite a certain restiveness, the School remained in a state of guarded, if restrained, politeness until a tear-jerking scene in which the helpless ward (consigned by his crooked, unfeeling, guardian to a boarding school of unremitting harshness) sang *Ave Maria* in the school chapel so movingly that even the unbendingly stern clergyman-headmaster dedicated to never-spoiling-the-child-by-sparing-the-rod, furtively dabbed his eye. After this, there were subdued, but increasingly unmistakable, Castonian murmurs of approval at each new misfortune which befell the tear-jerking little hero.

However, even these comments remained relatively decorous until the climax of the film where, having rescued the most persistent and cruellest of his boy tormentors from a flooded river, the child star lay at death's door with pneumonia, motionless in a sparsely furnished garret to which he had been banished (vigorous Castonian cheers!) most unjustly, tended by the only person at the school to have shown him any sympathy. She was an amply proportioned negress who sat mopping his brow and clasping the small fevered hand lying wanly on the sheets. During an ominously dramatic pause in the syrupy background music, eyes brimming, she murmured in a low, throaty voice, 'Wid dat heavenly voice o' yours, ah always noo you wasn' long fer this worl (SIGH) mah Angel Chile.'

It was received with stunned incredulity. Then, the momentary silence which preceded a fresh surge of gospel-choir music, was broken by a beautifully modulated, well-bred voice from the back, pronouncing each word quietly but very distinctly.

'And about bloody time too!'

An explosion of laughter erupted all over the hall, dissolving the last remaining restraint which had governed the audience until then.

The final ten minutes of the film were accompanied by other shouted comments which sought to emulate the success of the first, an increasing number of which reflected ways the child star's prettiness might be rewarded were he a Castonian. Encouraged by the anonymity of semi-darkness these inevitably sought to surpass each other in ribaldry and bawdiness. At times the noise was so raucous that even the triumphant music on the soundtrack was drowned, and it obliterated entirely the unlikely dialogue that purported to unravel the final twists of an improbable plot.

This would have been regarded as a serious disciplinary matter but for two fortunate circumstances. At the last moment the benefactress had been unwell and was therefore unable to attend herself, thus the High

Master had, thankfully, been able to excuse himself from attendance at a function which would have given him no pleasure.

The second piece of good fortune lay in the fact that the Master charged with ensuring that the audience (excused from the usual Saturday evening academic preparation) behaved with decorum, was a man of long experience, who had been living quietly in retirement until the outbreak of war recalled him to the School at which he had taught for forty years. Luckily, the film had virtually ended; as the cast-list appeared, he briskly switched on the lights and began to play *God Save The King* very loudly on an elderly out-of-tune upright piano, causing Castonians to stand in silence just before the situation escalated into riot. He was also experienced enough to understand that in certain circumstances, the fewer words spoken the better and therefore said nothing.

After Chapel the following evening, the High Master enquired cautiously, 'Ah, Begley, I imagine that I may write to our benefactress and say that Saturday's film was enjoyed by the school? Could I say it was both entertaining and instructive?'

With his hands clasped behind him, gown billowing in the lazily falling snow, Begley, a notably shrewd Housemaster in his time, answered in even tones, 'Indeed yes, High Master. Quite apart from its impeccable moral message, I fancy the School found it, shall I say, more entertaining than it might have reasonably anticipated.'

In Big Dorm Mawsom said quietly, 'Bloody *mar*-vellous, your solo in the Anthem to-night.'

'Thanks, but I almost missed the top note. It's hard to sing when it's cold.

Notting overheard the exchange. On the spur of the moment, with the unnerving inspiration of the born bully, he said raspingly, 'Wid dat Heavenly voice o' yours, ah always noo you wasn't long for this worl', mah Angel Chile.' He was gratified by the roar of laughter.

'Shut *UP*, Notting!'

Unaccustomed heat in Angus' voice told Notting that he had found an Achille's heel. Within the week virtually everyone in Ansell's was referring to him as 'AC'; the fact that they were also his initials, reversed, made it even more appropriate.

※

About a week later Notting was summoned to Big Study for the fifth time. On his return to Big Dorm he cannoned into Angus. He said viciously, 'You needn't look so bloody smug, Angus! If Singleton wasn't so pathetic, you'd be getting your arse tanned too.'

'I wasn't looking smug. I'm just sorry...'

Notting, still smarting, spat out, 'I don't want you to be sorry for me. *I* want you to be sorry for yourself, Angel Arse!'

'Don't call me that!'

'Why not? Has Aunty Singleton ever given you so much as one-up?'

Dermott-Powell had come up unnoticed: 'I don't suppose Angus forgets his Warming duties.'

'*I DIDNT FORGET!*' Notting almost shouted. 'Crowder just decided it wasn't warm enough. It's this bloody weather. I'd been there thirty minutes.' He was already regaining control of himself. 'And what's more, four-up hurts a damn sight more in this bloody weather, especially when Crowder really lets fly. What about you last night?'

Philosophically Dermott-Powell said, 'I only got two-up. Tarrant was in a bad mood. He told me so afterwards.'

Snider joined them: 'I don't see that we should grudge AC his luck.'

'We're all envious of you being Singleton's Warmer, AC,' Mawsom added kindly.

'I'm not envious!' Ellerman said. He was sitting on the end of Angus' bed. 'I agree with Notting, Aunty Singleton is pathetic.'

They moved off, but Mawsom hung back.

'What's up? You look fed up.' He waited and suddenly added, 'You don't mean to say Singleton's told you to go along to Big Study after all?'

'No, of course not!' Even as he said it, he knew the 'of course' was revealing. 'There's nothing.'

'Must be something.'

'Well, if you must know, I wish everyone wouldn't keep on with this AC business.'

'Is that all? It's only a joke! You've got a lot to learn yet, AC.'

Singleton was a little later than usual. When he was almost ready for bed he said, 'What's up, AC? Not very chatty tonight.'

'Nothing much.' He started for the door as Singleton got into bed.

'Come on, tell me.'

'Well, it's just that everyone goes on calling me AC...and things.'

'Me included?'

'That's different. I don't mind you.'

'I'll try to remember you don't like it, but I expect I'll forget sometimes. It's quite a good sign, in a way. He paused, 'A sign that you belong. It's only meant as a joke.'

'That's what Mawsom said.'

'If you take my advice you'll not let on you dislike it. Otherwise people will do it to annoy. Works best if you can sort of, play up to it.' Singleton paused and continued in a slightly lower tone, 'There are worse nicknames. As a matter of fact I don't care for mine. I expect you've heard it.'

Angus nodded, glad that he had himself never used it.

'But I know that I oughtn't to show it.' Singleton stopped, then said in a lighter tone, 'It was bad luck they showed the film just before your solo, best try and make a joke of it if you can.'

Snow stopped falling early in February, but it continued to lie. Occasionally the surface melted a little in the sun and then froze hard again when the sun vanished. Classrooms seemed to grow even colder than the Houses; food congealed as it left the kitchens.

There was no wind, but the cold crept in from every possible crevice and keyhole. At night, it was impossible to keep warm unless dressing-gowns and jerseys were worn in bed. As if to complement the bleak hostility of the weather Maunder decreed such remedies to be unacceptable and unhealthy.

On the evening of St Valentine's Day, the Praefaectors made an unexpected inspection after lights out; fifteen members of Ansell's were beaten. Baker, given six-up for wearing gloves and two pairs of socks in bed, was the picture of misery, though the beating was only a marginal contributor to that. His plumpness chapped and chilblained more easily and more dramatically than anyone else; an ugly red sore had developed round his mouth.

'If you don't go and Warm for Crewe you'll probably get another six-up,' Dermott-Powell said to him the following night.

'I don't have to. Crewe said not.'

'Why's that?'

There came an uncertain pause. 'He said I was "probably bloody infectious",' Baker muttered in a low voice.

Snider said, 'Rot! It's just chilblains and things.'

'I know, but I don't care. In this bloody place you get your arse tanned for the slightest thing. And the food's rotten.' Baker got into his bed, defiantly wearing his socks and pulled the covers over his head.

Dermott-Powell turned and, noticing Angus, said in a light tone of voice, 'If you don't get yourself two-up from Singleton soon, AC, you'll probably get yourself stabbed in the back!'

'He's scared of getting even one-up,' Notting jeered.

Angus said nothing, but was conscious of the tension.

'The whole system is barbaric anyhow,' Snider continued finally.

'When you're a Praefaector, Snider, I bet you'll do it.'

Snider said quickly, and with an unexpected edge to his voice, 'Yes. I expect I shall, Notting. Because you and I always do what everyone else does, but at least I hope I shan't *enjoy* doing it.' It was uncharacteristically heated for Snider.

'I was just joking.' Deprived of one victim, he turned back on Angus to whom he spoke with menacing silkiness, 'If Singleton did have to tan your arse, AC,' he paused with skilful timing, before adding with a spurt of savage coarseness, 'I bet he'd kiss it better.'

It was very cold indeed in Tosher the next morning. Dermott-Powell said, 'You mustn't mind Notting.'

'I try not to.'

'He's got to go to Big Study again tonight.'

'What for?'

'Chucking soap at Baker just now, before you came in. It missed. Hit Crewe's mug full of hot shaving-water and smashed it.'

Angus was appalled. 'Crowder'll kill him!'

'Not really! Crowder doesn't like Crewe very much. He's only giving Notting one-up. That's what he said. It's a sort of insult to Crewe that it's not worth more. Crewe looked livid He actually went white. If we weren't still Junior Election, and Crewe were doing the beating...'

Dermott-Powell left hanging in the air the implication that, were Crewe to administer the beating, Notting would be lucky to escape with his life.

Angus shivered. It was not merely the cold air.

On the way down to breakfast Angus found himself behind Notting. He said, 'I'm sorry about what happened this morning,' cautiously in case of retaliation.

Notting said, carelessly, over his shoulder, 'It was worth it to see Crewe's face.' Then he turned and realised that it was Angus who had spoken. 'Not the sort of thing Angel Chile would ever do of course!'

Snider, beside them, said quickly, 'It's bad luck. Isn't it your sixth time, Notting?'

Notting's face darkened; he said, 'Yes. Must be a record even for Ansell's. We're not even halfway through the first half of the Half.'

Angus was grateful for Snider's well-meant intervention, but Notting's tone had had none of its familiar spitefulness. He had sounded bitter certainly, but also somehow despairing and Angus found that more unnerving than the vicious crudity of the outburst the previous evening.

Warming Singleton's bed that night, Angus was almost overwhelmed by desperation. When Singleton eventually climbed into bed, he said, 'You really aren't a very good hot-water bottle, Christopher.' It was his usual joke. Angus was already at the door.

He replied in a tight, clipped voice, 'Would I'uv got two-up, if I'd forgotten to Warm, Singleton?'

Raising himself on one elbow, disturbed by the timbre in Angus' voice, Singleton asked quietly, '*Did* you nearly forget?' From the way Singleton's response avoided the question, Angus knew that it would be as unthinkable for Singleton to beat him, as it would be for him genuinely to forget.

Later, in his own bed, Angus gazed up into the dark. Fragmented thoughts tumbled themselves together in his sleepily confused mind.

Questions, although scarcely formulated, floated to momentary clarity. Did others resent him Warming for Singleton? Why? What about Ellerman and Maunder? Or Dermott-Powell and Tarrant? Or any of the others? If Singleton beat him, would they then leave him alone? Could he summon up courage to force Singleton's hand? Was it possible that, as well as all its other tyrannies, Ansell's expected him to provoke a punishment that he feared almost to the point of suffocation? And which, he divined, Singleton – whom he admired and who, he was sure, liked him – would be loath to administer? These notions were so fleeting that they dissolved almost as soon as they formed; by the following morning no conscious memory of them remained at all.

iii

Still the cold weather did not break. Angus was hurrying out of Din Room when Singleton stopped him: 'I say, AC, I've left a pile of books in my study. Be a good chap and get 'em for me, please.'

It *was* a nuisance. Two questions, part of his Maths preparation, remained unanswered. There was just time to complete them before Chapel. 'Of course, Singleton.' He was conscious that Baker and Notting were behind him. They followed him up the stairs.

'*Please* get my books for me, mah Angel Chile,' Baker said in a mocking syrupy throaty voice.

'Of course, Singleton. *Anything* for *you*, Singleton,' Notting added in a falsetto.

'You two can bloody well shut up.'

'Ooh! Fancy Angel Arse swearing!'

Notting added, 'Aunty won't like that, Angel Arse.' Angus swung round at the top of the stairs and, to his own surprise, let fly with his fists, catching Baker on the nose and Notting on the ear with inexpert and harmless blows. As he ran down the corridor to Singleton's room he heard Tarrant say, 'What's all this now?' and Notting answer cheerfully, 'Sorry, Tarrant, we were just talking to AC.' But the incident upset him. It was the first time he could remember that he had ever attempted to strike anyone.

They had both vanished when he returned, laden with books, but they could not be far away. Singleton was waiting in Corridor.

'Oh thanks, AC, Very decent of you.' He was making for Libe door and the unfinished Maths, when Singleton spoke again. 'Oh damn, the Lexicon's not here. It must be on the table in Big Study; it's got my name in. Do you mind getting that too, AC?'

Angus, with his hand on the door, conscious of precious minutes wasted, heard Notting's voice in the distance and, appalled, heard his own voice say, 'Yes, Singleton, actually I *do* mind.' It came out of him without him meaning to. The tone too was unintended, heated and harsh as if he were responding still to Notting or Baker. On Singleton's face a look of utter astonishment and Angus, panic-stricken, began to add, 'Singleton, I didn't mean that. Of course I'll go,' but his throat closed up after 'Singleton, I…'

Before he had recovered another voice cut in, 'We don't care very much for *side* in Ansell's.'

He had not noticed the other figure in the gloom. 'Yes, Maunder…I'm sorry, Singleton…sorry, Maunder, I didn't mean…'

Maunder said in the same icy voice, 'You were told to get the Lexicon. Get it now. I mean At Once.'

Angus sped off, his legs literally trembling.

When he returned they were both still there. Singleton looked if anything whiter than Angus. Angus handed him the book. 'Here's the Lexicon, Singleton, I'm sorry.'

Singleton began, 'That's all right, Angus,' but Maunder said, 'If you're in Choir, Angus, don't you have to be in Chapel five minutes early?'

'Yes, Maunder!'

He hurried off still trembling. Apologetically, he tried to find Singleton's eye in Chapel, but Singleton studiously avoided him. Suppose he was sacked as Singleton's Warmer and had to Warm for Crowder! Or Tarrant! He could feel the constriction in his chest and he sang not one word. In the back of his mind he knew that Singleton would have to give him at least four-up. The fact that Maunder had heard his stupid rudeness made that inevitable. The constriction in his chest seemed suffocating. He closed his eyes, but the suffocation grew worse. He seemed to stop breathing.

He tried to face up to his own particular terror. He had no doubt he deserved it. If only he had not said aloud what momentary impatience caused him to think. If only he had not allowed Notting and Baker to goad him into losing his temper. He remembered the look on Singleton's face. If only a beating *could* make amends. He gritted his teeth. He'd apologise to Singleton anyhow, not to get out of the punishment, but because he was sorry – really sorry. He would do it that evening. After Big Study. He had to convince Singleton that he had not intended to show side. Then Singleton might still keep him on as Warmer.

The chance to apologise was the most important thing. Without Singleton's amiable, friendly conversations in the evenings, life at Ansell's would be impossible for him. As for the loathsome beating, at least Ansell's custom decreed that none of the other Praefaectors would be present.

The rest of the day went badly too. He was given one hundred lines of Virgil to copy out, for day-dreaming in Latin. The last teaching of the day was Maths and his inadequate preparation found him out. The Div Pro, a quiet man with the steady eye of the fierce disciplinarian, said, 'Angus. This is inadequate. I should send you to show this to your Housemaster, but as you are not usually an offender I will instead set five problems for you to solve by Saturday.'

Walking back to lunch in Ansell's, Mawsom said, 'I'm sorry, AC. You seem to have had a bad morning.'

'You don't know how bad!'

'What do you mean?'

'I showed Singleton *side* this morning,' he explained.

'What on earth came over you? But since it's Singleton I doubt he'll tan your arse.'

'He'll have to. Maunder overheard!'

'Oh dear! Well, at least it isn't Maunder himself! Or Tarrant!'

Angus said, 'The worst part of it is that I like Singleton. I mean I just don't know what came over me.'

'Well, it'll probably be only three-up. Maybe two for a first offence.'

Angus said, 'Thanks.' And as they came to the doors of Ansell's he even managed to say lightly, 'There'll be no green bottles after tonight!'

Mawsom said, 'You'd not have been able to take it like that last Half.'

Inside himself, Angus knew that he was still unable to take it 'like that'.

※

He was settling at Long School for evening preparation when Dermott-Powell and Ellerman came up to him. 'AC? Do you know you've got to go to Big Study after Curfew?'

'Yes.' He felt his heart beating and his chest tighten. 'Yes, I know. I gave *side* to Singleton this morning.'

Dermott-Powell stared at him. 'You did what, AC? Singleton! My God what's coming over our Angel Child?'

'Don't call me that!'

Baker, with unaccustomed shrewdness, said, 'Was it after this morning? Is that why you did it?' He turned to the others. 'After we'd all been going on at him, he lashed out. Isn't that right, Angus?'

Angus kept his lips closed.

Ellerman said, 'Is it true that you've never been beaten before?'

'You must have been,' Dermott-Powell put in. 'At your Private.'

Breathing with difficulty, Angus said, 'I didn't go to a Private. We had a governess and then a tutor.'

Even Notting looked a little chastened. 'Well I'm sorry if what Baker and I said made you show *side* to Singleton.'

'It was a sort of accident. I was in an awful mood,' Angus muttered. 'I wanted to say I was busy and that I'd get something for him later. I meant it to be a question, but it didn't come out like that.'

'Singleton wouldn't want to beat anyone, least of all *you*,' Dermott-Powell said with an emphasis and a particular quietness which escaped no one except Angus.

'Maunder was there too, only I hadn't seen him.'

'Bad luck!' Dermott-Powell said. 'Well, that explains it,' he added almost to himself.

'Explains what?'

With sudden understanding, Mawsom said gently, 'I say, AC, haven't you been out in Corridor?'

He looked at their faces. Getting up from Long School he walked quickly to the door. Glancing back, he saw they had not moved. He walked along Corridor and a small knot of boys faded away as he came up to them. In the space marked by blue tape and titled Head of House, was a white card and written in a neat hand:

Angus will be beaten by the Praefaectors after Curfew for showing 'side'.
A.E. Maunder

His heart stood still. It had to be a dream. A nightmare. He closed his eyes. When he opened them the card was still there. What could he do? He would go, run away. There must be some unimaginable mistake. A bell rang. Automatically he turned back to Libe, moved back to his seat and sat down. Mawsom touched the back of his hand as if to offer comfort. 'I'm so sorry, AC.'

Despair flared. He whispered fiercely, 'If you hadn't all gone on and on calling me AC it would never have happened. What's the use of saying sorry?'

Although Angus had been often apprehensive and sometimes genuinely frightened in Ansell's, he had never before experienced sheer terror. The hands of the clock moved with infinite slowness. The paper in front of him remained blank. He was surprised to find that he did not cry as he had feared, but the deadening terror brought back his asthmatic tightness of chest.

At last it came to an end. Then there was Curfew. He answered his name mechanically. There was a pause for a moment before the Praefaectors went out. Singleton, as Junior Monitor, said in a barely recognisable voice, 'Angus will report to Big Study at nine forty-five.' Ansell's dispersed in a subdued hush. The fact that there was to be a Praefaectors' beating cowed the whole House.

If the time before Curfew had dragged, now it sped past. Nobody tried to say much to him in Big Dorm or in Tosher. He got slowly into his pyjamas.

Ashton appeared. 'I have to take you along. You don't need that dressing-gown.'

They went out of the door and Angus automatically turned to close it.

'It's left open. So's the door of Big Study. Praefaectors' beatings used to take place in Libe with everyone there once upon a time. Now they can only hear it,' Ashton whispered.

They stood in the doorway of Big Study. The table had been pushed back and Angus could feel himself shaking; he clenched his hand.

Ashton said, 'Angus is present,' and left him.

They stood in a curiously unmoving group, each with his switch. Singleton avoided his eye.

'Good evening, Angus.'

'Good evening, Maunder.'

It was all so calm. He thought, 'Perhaps it's a joke.'

'Please come in, Angus. Do you understand why you're here?'

'Yes, Maunder.'

'Tell us then.'

'I...I showed *side* when Singleton asked me to fetch a book for him.' He was astonished that he was able to speak without his voice faltering.

'I would say you absolutely refused to obey a direct order given by the Junior Praefaector. What do you say to that?'

'Please, Maunder, it wasn't meant to sound like that. I just meant to ask him if I could go a little later.'

'What I heard was not a request, Angus. It was disobedience. And you're going to be beaten for it.'

He swallowed with difficulty. 'Yes, Maunder.'

Maunder's voice hardened: 'We don't think much of an Ansell's Man who tries to wriggle out of it.'

'No, Maunder.'

'I'm told that you've never had your arse tanned. Is that correct?' The cold voice made the word 'arse' sound almost brutal.

'Yes, Maunder.' A whisper. He had not thought it was possible to feel so ashamed.

'Well you're certainly going to remember the first time, aren't you?'

'Yes...' Rising tears which had to be choked back They did not seem people he knew at all. They were huge, menacing totally implacable. He was at the mercy of forces over which he could never have any control.

'Yes, *what!*'

'Yes...' he swallowed '...Maunder.' Even he could hardly hear his voice.

'What you've got to understand, Angus, is this. You may have the voice of an angel. You may have managed to squirm out of trouble so far, but that doesn't entitle you, or anyone else in Ansell's for that matter, to talk back to a Praefaector. Do you understand what I'm saying?'

'Yes, Maunder, but really I...'

'*But really* nothing! You really are a bloody disgrace to Ansell's, aren't you? I seem to remember you can't even run a touch-line without making a mess of it.'

'No, Maunder.'

'Speak up!'

'No. Maunder.'

'Do you know how many you're going to get?'

'Seven?' his lip trembled. '...Maunder?'

'Yes and I'm not sure why it isn't a dozen. The first and last come from me, Angus, and I'll make bloody certain you know it. If you spout you get another three. Understand?'

Unable to speak from misery and terror, Angus nodded. With a new surge of anguish he thought for one terrible moment that his bowels and bladder were going to loosen.

'Get over The Chair.'

What if he had forgotten how? What if he refused? They might kill him! Nothing seemed unlikely. He tried to recall Ashton's detailed instruction, acutely conscious of the cold arm of The Chair where it touched the naked flesh at the gap in his pyjamas. His chest, tight, suffocatingly breathless, was across the other arm; he clenched his hands round the bottom rung and waited.

With a feeling of total despair he heard Tarrant say smoothly, 'Angus! Tighten that arse.' Two more! It wouldn't GO any tighter, his feet were already wedged hard under the other bar. There was a small silence. He saw Maunder's shadow on the carpet. There came a whirring sound, he braced himself. Nothing! Then a second. Nothing!!! So it *was* a joke after all! He felt weak with relief. He did not hear the third whirring sound.

Searing, scalding pain so shocked him that the involuntary cry of agony and terror could not force itself past his constricted throat. The second cut also took him by surprise and he choked. The third he expected. It was much worse. He had stopped trying to breathe; spots danced before his eyes.

Please God, not again!

Four.

God! Please listen!

Five.

'You now, Singleton.' He heard Maunder's voice, but was in such pain and emotional turmoil that he hardly noticed the cut when it came. God did not exist! There was a pause. Had he miscounted? Then came the whirr again and pain which cut the breath out of him for the seventh time. He heard Maunder grunt through his teeth with the effort.

'Two more for not tightening-up!' A pause.

Maunder said, 'No, Tarrant, I think not. He's had enough. It's only his second Half.' Was there a touch of sympathy in Maunder's voice; as if he was inclined to question the punishment now it had been executed?

'You can get up, Angus.'

He straightened up, looking straight ahead. He was in shock: passionate tears of shame, humiliation and genuine repentance were damned behind an unnatural, traumatic impassivity. He said in a flat voice which he did not recognise as his own, 'Thank you, Maunder.' Very politely they shook hands. With what might have been the slightest gesture of distaste, Maunder dropped his switch on to the table. He said in a quiet, even voice, 'Cut along now, Angus.' It was difficult to believe this was the same person who had, only minutes before, terrified him. He left, still rigid with delayed shock and pent-up emotional stress. He overheard Maunder say, in the same quiet matter-of-fact tone, 'That wouldn't have been necessary if you'd been doing your job, Singleton. If you ever let Angus or anyone else show you *side* again, I'll let The Digger know we don't need you as a Praefaector.'

The door closed behind him.

In the dark open doorway of Big Dorm several indistinct figures stood. Ellerman whispered, 'We thought they'd cut you in half. I'm sorry about what we said.' Angus stood as if in a trance. He could feel tears beginning to moisten his cheeks, but he made no sound at all.

Mawsom crept out into the dim corridor light: 'You were unlucky. It's just that Singleton's never beaten anyone and Maunder doesn't want Ansell's Praefaectors like that lot in Jonquil's.'

Dermott-Powell joined them; touching his arm comfortingly, he whispered, 'What about Singleton's bed?'

He had forgotten!

He did not want them to see the tears. He reached the small room and flung himself face down on Singleton's bed. Shortly afterwards, the door opened and Singleton stood outlined in the faint light from the corridor. Angus did not move.

Ill at ease, surprised, Singleton said hesitantly, embarrassed, 'Oh! Angus!' There was a pause. 'I didn't expect...I mean it's all right if you don't bother tonight, Angus.'

Singleton's voice triggered suppressed emotion and guilt within Angus. Exacerbated by his frantic but now fruitless efforts to keep silent, it took possession of him entirely. 'Singleton, I'm sorry...I didn't mean...p-please don't...don't...' He lifted his head, tasting salt on his lips, quite unable to get the words out because of the convulsive sobs which incapacitated him as the last ineffectual remnants of self slipped away. He got up from the bed and stood like a suppliant. 'Oh please, Singleton don't tt-tell them I'm li-like this...I-i-i don't want to go to Big Study again.' Tears cascaded down his face. He did not care if Singleton saw it.

Singleton was shocked into dumbness. Misinterpreting his silence as refusal, but without realising quite what he was doing, Angus was kneeling, hands clasped, as if in church.

'Please, please, Singleton, p-*pup-PLEASE!*' His long-cured stammer had returned and the fact that he was trying to whisper made it much worse, grotesque.

Appalled by the hysterical figure before him, Singleton said in low-voiced desperation, 'Get up! Please, get up, Angus.' He had no idea how to cope. If Maunder came past! Or, God forbid, The Digger! '*GET UP, ANGUS!*' he whispered roughly, hoarse with his own panic. He put his hands beneath Angus' arms and brought him forcibly to his feet.

'Of *course* I won't say anything to anyone, but *you must stop*. Please. I won't say anything. I never would've.' With his foot he pushed the door, securing them from any prying eyes and cutting off the dim light from the corridor, save for a small amount that came from the glass fanlight, but the hiccupping sobs continued uncontrollably.

Now affected himself, Singleton said unsteadily, 'Come on. *Really*, I won't say anything. Of course I won't. I *promise*.' He hugged the little boy tightly, realising instinctively perhaps that only physical assurance could communicate across such tempestuous distress. Angus' heart thumped wildly against him and sobs shook the child's entire body. He could find nothing to say except, 'There! There!' again and again, moving his hand soothingly over the thin, shaking shoulder blades and flexing ribs. Minutes passed. Gradually the intensity of the sobs began to abate and, as they did so, Singleton became uncomfortably aware that his own body was beginning to respond, sexually, of its own volition.

Guiltily, almost brusquely, he tried to push Angus from him, but the boy clutched at his jacket as if it were a lifeline. Singleton tried to prise open the clutching fingers. '*Angus!* Angus, *Let go*!' He felt panic rising. What if somebody heard them and opened the door? 'Let go! *Please* Christopher!' It was the use of his Christian name that finally reached Angus in his misery. He released Singleton's lapels. 'Ttha-thank you Singleton. Th-thanks. I'd better go.'

'You can't possibly go in this state! Everyone'd know.' Singleton, helplessly, did not quite know what to suggest. He paused and then, unintentionally, half-changing the subject, he blurted out, 'What on earth got into you this morning?'

The question did not seem out of place to Angus. 'I-I didn't mean t-to sound li-like that. I tt-tried to tell M-maunder, but he wouldn't listen.'

'I was there. I know, but you ought to have known better! It was almost as if you *wanted* to get punished.'

Angus said nothing.

'Was that it?' Singleton had sudden insight. 'Your Election?'

'Angel Chile.' Angus forced the hateful phrase through his teeth with such despair in his voice that Singleton was again at loss for a reply. 'That's what they call me. I *told you*.' Another convulsion of sobs overwhelmed the younger boy. 'And…and…Angel *Arse*.'

'Angus, listen.' He took him by the shoulder.

'I'm lull-listening, Singleton.'

'You must always be your own man. Always. Listen to the rest, yes, but don't take too much notice. You must make up your own mind.'

He could tell the advice meant very little to the bedraggled and demoralised figure. 'I say! Are you all right?' Angus had begun to shiver violently. 'I'm-m c-cold.' His teeth were actually chattering.

'Lie down. Oh! On your front if you like.' Singleton pulled a blanket over him. There was a pause.

'It hurt...a lot...' He hardly recognised the brittle voice. Tears welled up again, but not so volcanically. 'I-I-I did didn't think anything c-could hurt so much. Bbbut it wasn't jjjust that. It was all of yyou. Standing there as if you'd never seen me before. Then Tarrant...I thought.... It seemed it might go on for ever.' How could he explain? A hiccup became a choke.

For the first time in his life, Singleton was pierced by overwhelming compassion and, for the first time, he experienced the inevitable sense of isolation it confers. He perceived, for an instant, how far, in all but the most superficial ways, he had already journeyed in that one evening, from Cranchester and Ansell's. However, like Angus, he could not articulate what he felt and, at first, could not even find words with which to frame a reply. Eventually he managed to say distantly, almost as if only to himself, 'I know what you mean. At least I think I know.' Despite the inadequacy of the words and his own emotional chaos, Angus sensed from the tone and from the desolation which seemed, somehow, to embrace them both, that Singleton really did understand what he himself could not properly explain because he could not fully comprehend. Then after another pause, as if by an effort of will, Singleton drew them back to the immediate situation which governed them both. He said flatly, confidentially, 'I don't really agree with tightening-up.'

'M-m-my Election said it was your first time.' He was much calmer. 'I'm sorry I made it happen, Singleton, if you didn't want it.'

Horrified at the implication, Singleton said quickly, 'You don't think it was my idea, do you? *Do* you, Christopher?'

'Oh nno, Singleton.'

Singleton said dully, under his breath, 'I ought to have stopped it happening.' He paused: 'Warmer now?'

'Yes. Much. Thanks.' Best of all, the tears had stopped. Anxiety returned to his voice, 'You really won't tell anyone about...'

'I promised I wouldn't. Don't worry. Still hurts?'

Umm, but not so much.' He put his hand behind him and with a lift of panic in his voice, 'Singleton! I think there's blood.'

'Just a moment. I've a bicycle lamp somewhere.' The beam flicked on in the darkness. 'Don't worry. It happens sometimes if you've got a tender arse.' Trying to lighten the atmosphere, he continued, 'Did to me once. Yes. I think you might be cut. If you want a proper look you'll have to use the mirror.'

In the yellow light of the bicycle lamp seven marks showed angry and red, but blue bruising had already begun to blur the sharp outlines. In a couple of places the skin had slightly broken. Singleton said more calmly than he felt, 'Listen Angus – Christopher – I've got some stuff for my eyes. Boracic water. You could bathe it with that. I've got some ointment too, somewhere. After a few moments Angus felt him sit on the bed and a refreshingly damp padded handkerchief was pressed into his fingers. He stood up, painfully, leaning forward a little. It stung. 'Am I in the right place?'

'A bit to the right.'

'I can't see properly, even with the mirror and the torch. Singleton? Could you do it for me?' Without any inhibition and without waiting for a reply, like a very small child Angus folded himself across Singleton's knees as he sat on the bed.

After a moment Singleton said, uncertainly, 'Well, if you like.' He sought to ignore the possibility that he might again be prey to the conflicting impulses which had already frightened him that evening. With an attempt to keep his fears at bay he said with forced jocularity, 'You'd better not let anyone know. I mean, people'd think it a bit of a joke a Praefaector...well...patching up the arse of somebody he'd just beaten.' It came awkwardly off his tongue with an unconvincing half-laugh.

'I expect they would.' Angus made an equally unsuccessful effort to turn it into a joke but his voice was still uncertain and he hiccupped again. All he knew for certain was that he felt an enormous gratitude for the fact that Singleton was still friendly after his showing *side* that morning.

The soothing, competent, first aid that was being administered, also reassured him.

'What about this ointment stuff? It may sting a bit?'

'I don't mind, Singleton. Thanks.'

Singleton dipped his fingers into the jar and very gently applied the salve to the marked skin. Then, with a quick movement, he drew back his hand as if bitten. He could feel the raised weals! He had not anticipated that. He felt physically nauseated – conscious-stricken at such incontrovertible evidence of the vulnerability of the slight body pressing its warmth on his knees. He thought, 'I'll not have any part of it next time. Next time, if there is a next time before I leave Ansell's. I'll resign as Praefaector.'

Would he really ever have the nerve to do something as dramatic and unheard of as that? But perhaps what he said would encourage Angus, in his turn as Praefaector. Angus might even be Head of House one day. The thoughts raced through his head so vigorously and vividly that he said aloud, 'Promise *you* won't do it?' forgetting until he had spoken that Angus was totally ignorant of the context, but, as Singleton immediately comprehended, Angus never doubted that the words referred to his catastrophic show of *side* that morning. He said fervently with another shaky attempt at a laugh, 'Not again, you bet!' The younger boy's unquestioning acceptance that he had merited the punishment meted out depressed Singleton almost more than anything else. He felt ashamed of himself, ashamed of Ansell's.

Angus stood up. He was calmer. Singleton put his hand lightly on Angus' shoulders: 'Better?'

The pain was still there, but it no longer mattered; nothing had changed between himself and Singleton. That was what mattered. Or rather, something had changed. Inexplicably, He knew their relationship was tighter now, more important to him and, he sensed, more important to Singleton. If there were words to express what he felt he could not find them. All he could find to say was, 'Thank you, Singleton. For being so decent about...everything.' Then, quite unselfconsciously, Angus put his arms tightly round Singleton, kissed him sexlessly on the cheek and vanished swiftly through the door. It was so unexpected and fleeting that the following morning Singleton was unable to convince himself that it had ever happened at all.

After Angus disappeared, Singleton sat without moving, relieved to find himself untroubled by the inclinations which, a little earlier, he had once again feared might overwhelm him. With surprise, he suddenly murmured aloud, 'He's too young!' With dawning enlightenment, 'He shouldn't be here yet.' Then something else occurred to him. Should people like Angus ever be here at all? Should he, Singleton, be there? Should any of them?

For the second time in his life and the second time that evening, Singleton felt a shadow of doubt about Ansell's. Had he himself been like Angus five years before? Surely not? Like Notting? Or Mawsom? Certainly not like the golden Ellerman. Nor Dermott-Powell for that matter! His initial feeling of astonishment was replaced by an unexpected twinge of alarm, for, in his own mind's eye, of himself at that age he could find no picture at all.

※

Angus woke earlier than anyone else and the shadow of the previous day's events swept over him. He moved onto his side, wincing. ' So it's true,' he thought miserably. 'All those jokes about not being able to sit down for a week.' The thought of walking naked to Tosher made his heart lurch. Everyone would laugh! Then, why not go now before the others were up? The seniors never got up earlier than necessary. He took his towel, slipped off his pyjamas. It never occurred to him to cheat. On bare feet he walked past the curtained Mangers. There was slight snoring from Ashton's. He looked at his watch. Twenty-four hours ago he had been still asleep and the whole business had been in the future, his uncharacteristic bad temper, his belligerence at Singleton's unremarkable request. There was still time to have a bath. It was too early for him to be accused of using up hot water, because that was turned on later. He knew the water would be tepid. Quietly he turned the tap, it was warm enough. He didn't want it too warm.

He measured the regulation six inches with the battered ruler tied to the bath tap. In Jonquil's they had painted thin red lines on the baths, a pale twitchy boy in his Division had told him that. If you took more and Praefaectors, or Housemaster caught you, then you had to tighten-up there and then ('bare-arsed' Marquand-Johnson had assured him in hushed tones) for 'spoiling the war effort'. It was true that once or twice in the week, The Digger would push open a bathroom door and inquire courteously, 'Have you only six inches, Angus?' (Or Ashton, or whoever it was.) And you would say, 'Yes,' and he would go. On the whole, Ansell's Men told the truth. Baker, inevitably, had lied. Crewe had given him three-up in Big Study for having too much water and three more for 'lying to the Housemaster'.

Angus lowered himself carefully into the bath. Once the stinging sensation subsided, he let his full weight down, feeling the bruises against the hard enamel. He splashed himself with the tepid water, stood up and, letting the water out, experimentally dried himself carefully. Then he went back into the washroom to do his teeth. Hearing noises of others stirring, he braced himself against the public commentary to come, wishing he had omitted the bath and got back into his cubicle and his clothes before the others awoke.

He looked in one of the long mirrors. No blood now! The frightening redness already seemed less than he remembered from the previous night, but the bruising was an ugly blue and there was a hint of the yellowing to come.

Eldridge, a gregarious Tassel, came in whistling, clad in a rakishly draped towel, and grinned at the sight of the smaller boy cautiously examining himself. Before Angus could turn round, Eldridge said, 'Let's see! Whew. Bad luck! It's quite a rainbow arse we've got today, isn't it!' He pressed his fist playfully onto Angus' collar-bone. 'Still hurt?'

Angus said, 'A bit.'

'Spout?'

Angus said nothing and the older boy said quietly, kindly, 'In Big Study, I mean?'

'No, I didn't spout in Big Study,' Angus said responding with a small grin.

'Bloody good, AC, you'll be a true Ansell's Man yet!' Angus felt the compliment wash over and then blossom inside him, filling him with unexpected warmth.

Tarrant, wearing his dressing-gown, entered. Angus felt his heart thump. Tarrant would undoubtedly remember about him not tightening-up properly and the two he had not been given, but Tarrant said encouragingly, 'Good Morning, Angus!' As it was customary for the junior to offer greeting first, Tarrant obviously wanted to put him at ease. Amazed, he said with a slight stutter, 'G-good morning, Tarrant.'

Maunder hopped in from one of the bathrooms, holding his left foot and looking at a discoloured toenail. Leaning on Angus as if he were a human crutch, he said,

'Hello! Flogger Tarrant admiring his handiwork?'

Less than twelve hours ago they had terrified him, yet now they could refer to it as a sort of joke Had it all been play-acting? He looked from Tarrant to Maunder. Then he said cautiously, 'Good Morning, Maunder. I'm very sorry...'

Maunder cut in immediately, '*No*, AC. It's all over. Forgotten. A clean sheet.' With a familiar, almost affectionate gesture, he tugged the white patch of Angus' damp hair and said quietly, 'They'll soon fade! In spite of what I said to you, I'd told the Praefaectors to go easy.' Then, 'You took it well. You'll do.'

'Thank you, Maunder.' Ridiculously, he felt as if he had been given a medal.

He walked back to his Manger as if on air. There was no laughing at his expense. The only comments were sympathetic – even from those who had never spoken to him before. It was as if somehow, in some way, they were thanking him, thinking it might just as easily have been themselves. Somebody sang out, 'No green bottles hanging on the wall,' which raised a good-natured laugh. He thought, Ansell's all over. You can never tell. In a way it was the unpredictability which was most frightening.

His own Election made respectful noises when they saw the damage. Snider looked almost green. 'I think it was beastly,' he said vehemently. 'If I'd been Angus, I'd probably have run away.'

'Then you wouldn't have been allowed back to Ansell's,' Notting said. Snider's look indicated that he would not wish to come back.

As Angus was putting on his socks, Dermott-Powell sat on the bed beside him, and put an arm round his shoulder. He had just come back from Tosher and was looking pink. He said, 'Tarrant gave me some chocolate. He says he's in training. I'll leave some under your pillow. It's American. And,' he added, 'Maunder's never having another Praefaectors' whilst he's Head of House. So you're a sort of martyr.'

'Thanks, that's nice to know,' Angus replied wryly, 'but I don't recommend it.'

※

In the afternoon, walking back from Bunner, Mawsom said, 'You looked awful last night. You were back in Big Dorm very late. Did Singleton go on at you?'

'Singleton? No! Of course not! Actually, he was very decent. Otherwise I think I might have run away. Like Snider said.' They walked in silence for a while. Then he added, 'He doesn't agree about tightening-up. It's as if they were punishing him too.'

'I know,' said Mawsom. 'I don't think I agree with it.'

'We'll stop it when we're Praefaectors!'

Mawsom looked at him: 'Will we? There isn't much else you can do as a Praefaector.'

'Mawsom, if I tell you something, you won't tell anyone will you? Ellerman? Notting?'

'Not if you don't want me to.'

'I did spout last night. A lot. Not in Big Study. Afterwards.'

'I'm not surprised. I noticed when you ran off to Singleton. Did he see? Or was he late?'

'That's what I mean about him being so decent. I just couldn't stop. It was awful. I went on and on. It was like being ill. If I'd done that in Big Study...'

Mawsom said comfortingly, 'Probably because it was the first time. It happened like that at my Private School. The first time.' There was a slight pause: 'Me included. I howled.' Then, 'You can't believe anyone would *really* want to hurt you. Then they do.'

Angus said, 'I had to tell somebody.' After a short silence, he added cheerfully, 'Maunder was very decent to me this morning. So was Tarrant. Maunder said he'd told the Praefaectors to go easy.'

'That's what Wilder said.'

'I'm glad he did.'

'But, Wilder told me, they didn't go easy.'

'To teach me a lesson?' Angus shivered. 'It certainly did teach me a lesson.'

'Not you. Singleton.'

Angus said quietly, 'Two of the cuts bled.'

'Tarrant and Robinson,' Mawsom deduced. 'You've heard that Maunder's not allowing another Praefaectors'?'

Back in Ansell's he was once again aware that in some indefinable way the whole atmosphere had changed. He felt euphoric, almost in ecstasy. To think that, when he had woken up in the morning, he had imagined he would be in disgrace – possibly even 'in Coventry', but as the day had worn on he had realised that it was just the opposite. He was now accepted by Ansell's in an almost affectionate way, which even his singing had never brought about; overnight he had achieved an integration as complete and enthusiastic as that earned by Ellerman with his skill on the football field.

With a flicker of surprise Angus realised also that he no longer resented being called AC, nor even Notting's coarser derivative. Obscurely, he perceived it rather as conferring honourable distinction – a unique status accorded him by Ansell's. Perhaps, it came to him in a flash of insight, they felt grateful that he had in some way served as scapegoat for them all.

Ellerman hurried across, eyes bright with news he intended to share. 'I say AC, guess what? Maunder reckons we'll be playing rugger by the end of the week. Have you noticed? It's really begun to thaw at last.'

iv

At moments when his mind was not fully occupied, Singleton's impending departure filled Angus with heaviness of heart. During the last weeks, they lit a fire almost every evening. Once or twice he must have been very late back to Big Dorm, but, if anyone noticed at all, they ignored it. Only Dermott-Powell made any reference and the hostility which had preceded his Praefaectors' had vanished so completely that it was difficult to believe it had ever existed. Possibly the burst of spring-like weather relieved the tension as much as anything else. Angus felt more content, less anxious than at any time since he had come to Ansell's; had it not been for the pressing knowledge that Singleton would not be there for the Summer Half, he would have called himself happy.

Because of the snow and because it was such a short Half, the Sevens ended on Tassel Night which was also the last night. After the speeches, for Ansell's had won the competition, and a song or two from the new Tassels, they broke up noisily. Once again Angus wondered at his own Election. Although, as a new Tassel, Ellerman was understandably effervescent, Dermott-Powell was equally ebullient; Snider and Notting and Baker had been nudging each other and grinning as various Praefaectors made speeches. Mawsom, however, seemed sombre, almost guiltily uncommunicative. On the stairs, Angus said to him, 'You okay, Mawsom?'

Mawsom merely nodded and gave him a long look. Then eventually he said, 'Well anyway, it's home tomorrow!' With sinking heart Angus remembered it was Singleton's final night.

Slowly he went along for the last time. Singleton was already there, putting items in a trunk and an overnight case, the familiar study looked very bare and shockingly shabby. There was not even a light shade.

'Hello, young Christopher.'

The imminence of the holidays, the use of his Christian name, the fact that it was the last time, the rough cider, and a determination to seem cheerful, encouraged him to retort with a pert familiarity he did not feel, 'Hello, Old Singleton!' Immediately he was appalled at what he had done.

'Any more of that and I'll tan your arse.'

'You wouldn't!' It came out before he realised Singleton was joking, but the momentary terror had been real enough.

'Well, perhaps only a dozen-up, as it's my last night,' Singleton said with mock severity. They both knew that the mutual banter was a way of avoiding saying 'goodbye'. 'Anyhow, you hop into that bed and see whether, at long last, you can Warm it whilst I finish off. Forlornly, he watched Singleton pack his remaining possessions. The four books above the fireplace were left to last. As he took them up, he turned to Angus and said, 'Would you like to have one of these?'

'Oh, but I couldn't! You've always said those are your favourites.'

'I'd like you to have one of them.'

'Only if you're sure, Singleton.'

'I am quite sure.' He held out the books, 'Choose one.' Angus did not know quite what to do. He thought of *Winnie ille Pu* but something held him back. What if he happened to choose the very book which Singleton liked most? The one he really didn't want to give away? Singleton was still waiting.

Angus said, 'You decide, Singleton, I bet the one you choose'll be the one that I'd like best.'

Singleton sat on the end of the bed. With a wry shake of the head, he murmured absently to himself, 'Mannerly-hearted...' then aloud, 'I ought to have guessed!'

'Guessed what, Singleton?'

Singleton unscrewed the cap from a fat black fountain pen: 'This'll explain, it's from a poem in the anthology...' He turned away, ostensibly in order to rest the volume on the over-mantle, his normally quiet voice momentarily muffled, oddly hesitant. Partly because of this and partly because he was overwhelmed by misery, conscious once again that it was their last evening, Angus pulled himself together only just in time to hear Singleton saying, '...a gracious answer.'

There seemed no appropriate response but fortunately Singleton seemed not to notice and, after a brief pause, concluded, 'The poet went to Balliol, where I'm going after the war. Then he became a Roman Catholic priest.'

Ought he to ask Singleton if he too was going to become a priest? He decided against it; instead he took the book and looked at the still damp inscription:

for A. C. – Best Wishes from C.S. (Lent Half 1942)

and a quotation

'Father, what <u>you</u> buy me I like best'

Right at the top was written in another hand, 'From your Father, on your birthday, with love 1940'. Somebody else, probably Singleton himself, had lightly pencilled 'C. Singleton, Ansell's'.

'I know you don't go much for poetry at the moment, but I daresay that'll change. Anyhow, look up the poem before then.... One day when you've got a spare moment.' He understood that Singleton did not wish him to look up the poem there and then.

'You always said this book was your particular favourite?'

Singleton turned his attention suddenly back to the almost packed trunk. Rapidly, in a tone Angus could not fathom, he rattled off, 'Well, one always wants one's favourite things to be well looked after.'

'Oh I will!' Conscious that he was being paid a compliment, although he could not quite understand it, Angus added warmly, 'Thanks, Singleton, it's very decent of you!'

Singleton stuffed away the final oddments, at the same time getting into his pyjamas and, finally, brushing his hair. That was always the last thing he did at night. Angus began to get up, but Singleton sat beside him on the bed and, as Maunder had done, gently pulled the recalcitrant tuft of white hair. After a moment he said, 'You'll be all right? Next Half?'

Angus said dutifully, 'Oh yes thanks, Singleton.' It was not true and so he amended it by adding, 'I think so.' Then after a while, 'I wish you weren't going.' With a change of voice he said, 'Dawes is to come in here. I'm carrying on as his Warmer.'

Singleton said, 'Yes, I heard,' with an abruptness that Angus neither recognised nor understood. There came another pause.

'I wish I didn't hate being beaten.'

'Everyone hates it.'

'But not as much as I do.' Singleton knew how Angus felt and that he was naively sounding him out about Dawes, He also knew Dawes. He said nothing.

'Singleton. That night, across The Chair...I felt.... He drew a deep breath. 'I felt really frightened, not just ashamed of being there like that, but I thought you'd all always remember...' He spoke so quickly and frantically that he ran out of breath. It was the first time since the beating that either of them had mentioned it but he felt Singleton had to know his cowardice.

Taking his shoulders, Singleton said quietly but firmly, 'Of course you were! So would I have been! But that was all over weeks ago. Everybody's forgotten – except you. I suppose that's the sort of chap you are. Probably always will be,' he said mentally making it into a hope. 'To be honest I think it suits you, but now – forget about that Praefaectors'.'

Having got the small confession off his chest, Angus suddenly felt very tired. His eyes took in also the dingy little study which, even with its dim naked bulb, seemed so domestic. Forgetting he was not in his own bed, he said, 'Mmmm. Goo'night, Singleton,' and fell fast asleep.

Singleton knew that on the last night of the Half, let alone on Tassel Night, few would notice and none question Angus' absence from Big Dorm. In addition he knew that, as a leaving Praefaector, even if he were in a far more explicitly compromising situation, the blindest of eyes would be turned. However, it was not because of the assurance that virtually any licence would be allowed him his last night which put him at ease, but because, for the first time, he was quite certain that he could trust own emotions.

On the pillow lay the tousled hair, delicately closed lids and slightly parted lips of every sleeping child. He felt, as he had felt increasingly while his final weeks whispered away, an affection, aching in its intensity but now without sexual desire. He yearned for the impossible that Christopher Angus could be his – his brother, his son – it did not matter as long as he had some control over his destiny. He knew that, were it so, he would not leave him there at Ansell's for anything in the world. The knowledge that he himself would not be there the following Half caused his eyes to blur. He touched the hair of the sleeper who did not stir. Then he rose quietly, turned off the light and eased himself gently between the sheets. Carefully he put his arm round the slumbering boy beside him; slowly, chastely he too drifted into sleep.

✳

He awoke very early and slipped away to Tosher. When he returned and switched on the light, Angus was sleeping almost exactly as he had been the previous night, except that he had one half-closed hand up on the pillow near his face. Without making a sound, Singleton packed pyjamas and dressing-gown. Angus slumbered on in childish, death-like totality. Light from the March dawn caught the grey patch in his hair. Eventually, packing complete, Singleton roused the sleeper by taking an ear lobe between finger and thumb and squeezing it gently.

Angus awoke slowly but then, recollecting where he was, sat up suddenly. He really did rub his eyes, Singleton noted, amused at the truth of the *cliché*. 'Oh Singleton I *am* sorry. It must be jolly late.'

'Actually it's jolly *early*,' Singleton nodded to the window. 'In fact it's tomorrow morning,' he teased.

'Oh no!' Angus, jaw literally dropping in dismay, was indeed comic.

'Very early. In fact, that's dawn. Don't worry. I let you fall asleep. Nobody'll notice or, if they do, it's the sort of day nobody'll mind! Did you sleep well?'

'Like a log.' Then, in sudden concern, 'What about you?'

'Me too.'

Angus registered the untucked sheets. 'You must have been jolly quiet getting up.'

'You were jolly fast asleep.'

'I suppose I'd better get back now.'

'Probably a good idea.'

'Shall I see you before I go, Singleton? To say cheerio?'

'Possibly, but last morning's a real scrum as you know, specially if you're leaving.'

'And I've still got lots of packing. Boots and socks and things.'

'You'd better buck up with that. So in case we don't have a chance to say it again, goodbye, Angus…Christopher.'

'Goodbye, Singleton…and good luck in the army. I expect they'll make you a general right away and Ansell's will be famous.' Then dropping the jokey tone, he said, holding the book, 'Thanks again…for being so decent about…things.'

There seemed nobody up in Big Dorm. His bed, littered with bits of packing looked as if it had been hit by a bomb, or as if he had himself risen early. He shovelled some last things in a trunk. Catching sight of his letter case, he took it out of the trunk, looked inside and then placed it in his overnight case. Slipping off his pyjamas he put them in his overnight case too. Then he wandered up to Tosher, dawdling with his teeth and washing.

He was still there when Notting appeared. Even on the last morning, Notting had lost none of his gift for pithy spite. He said, 'Has Aunty Singleton kissed his Angel Arse goodbye then?'

Totally unaffected by the sneering tone (unaware of its darker implications) Angus said, with saccharine sweetness, 'If by that, you mean have I said goodbye to Singleton, yes, I have.' He waited until he was almost out of the door, before turning back and adding with an exaggerated attempt to imitate Notting's plebeian twang, 'I certainly have...Notty-Botty!' and whisked away as Notting's irate face flannel slapped on the swinging double door.

※

There was still a good deal of time before breakfast on this last morning. The book Singleton had given him lay on his overnight case. It was true he did not read much poetry. He looked again at the inscription written in Singleton's firm hand. Could he find the poem? Dimly he remembered Singleton's saying it was called something like 'The Answer', no, 'A something Answer'. There was no such poem in the index. He turned the pages. He was about to put the book down when he struck the right page. It seemed fairly impenetrable.

The Handsome Heart:
at a Gracious Answer

'But tell me, child, your choice; what shall I buy
You?— 'Father, what you buy me I like best.'
With the sweetest air that said, still plied and pressed,
He swung to his first poised purport of reply.

What the heart is! which, like carriers let fly—
Doff darkness, homing nature knows the rest—
To its own fine function, wild and self-instressed,
Falls light as ten years long taught how to and why.

Mannerly-hearted! more than handsome face—
Beauty's bearing or muse of mounting vein,
All, in this case, bathed in high hallowing grace...

Of heaven what boon to buy you, boy, or gain
Not granted! – Only...On that path you pace
Run all your race, O brace sterner that strain!

He read it through a second time, lingering over the line Singleton had inscribed and which he now found lightly underlined, *Father, what you buy me, I like best*. He remembered Singleton telling him that the poet was a priest. Perhaps that accounted for 'Father', but he did not fully understand the poem, nor did he then realise that there were notes at the back which might have enlightened him. He read it again in the early sunshine and spotted the line which completed some words he'd thought had heard Singleton mutter, *Mannerly hearted, more than handsome face*. Despite faulty comprehension, Angus sensed the poet's delicate affection for...? For whom? He was quite incapable of putting his intuition into words, nor did it occur to him to draw any parallel although Singleton had pencilled *?A.C.!!!* against this stanza (which Angus found particularly incomprehensible). All he knew, with a warm pleasurable certainty, was that the quotation inscribed on the flyleaf was a wholly affectionate compliment – some sort of declaration?

✻

When Singleton returned to fetch his overnight case, he found a slightly dog-eared envelope addressed to General Singelton. Angus, he realised, had never before had cause actually to write his name. As he opened it, a snapshot fell out and half a Cranchester 'punishment sheet'. He read, 'Caesar...Caesar...Ceser BLAST and DAM and BLARST' followed by scribble. He turned it over and found, in the same rather neat schoolboy hand;

> Dear Singelton,
> Found this in my writting case. Thought you might like it so you can recognise me when you come back for the Match next Half, if you've forgotten me!!! Thanks again for being so descent about last night and heaps of other times.
>
> Love
>   from
>   Christopher (AC!)

The snapshot, evidently taken in the summer before Angus' arrival at Ansell's, showed that he had grown very little since. It was not a good picture – half another person and the whole of a rather woolly-looking dog, in a vague mountainy place – were all a little blurred. Angus himself was sharply in focus, the snap had caught him getting his breath back, leaning slightly forward, hands spread on the flat of his stomach as if he had just climbed a hill. There were the same freckles and rather eager eyes; a bit like those of the dog, Singleton thought. The sensitive mouth was obviously laughing at being caught by the photographer. His hair was awry and the silvery streak showed distinctly. He wore an aertex open-necked shirt, sandals, knee-length stockings and a battered, faded-looking kilt. Singleton had never consciously associated Angus with a Scottish background until that moment – and yet it explained so much. He turned the photograph over.

> 'Last year – on Skye. The dog's called <u>Hairy</u> Lauder and that's half my cousin, Rory. I'm the one in the kilt! <u>Don't</u> EVER tell anyone in Ansell's about the kilt!!!!!!!'

Tears he had restrained with difficulty the previous night came, again unbidden, to Singleton's eyes; he went to the window and looked out for a long five minutes. Then, envelope and contents in his wallet, he lost himself amongst the hundreds of Castonians making their way to the London train.

Chapter Five

As if to make up for the snow, sun burst upon Cranchester on the first day of the new Half and bathed it in heat for week after week. They spent so much time outside on the newly mown cricket fields and watching matches beneath the chestnut trees that it seemed as if Ansell's had somehow lost its hold. Dawes had done something to his leg in the holiday – poisoned it, or broken it – and was away for a long time. It left Angus in a state of particular freedom and the fact he did not have to Warm for anyone else made Singleton's absence less noticeable.

In the event Dawes returned two days before Tassel Night, which it was customary to hold early in the Summer Half.

'There's lots of other events like Match Night and Field Day,' Ashton explained, 'so it's always early.'

On Angus' first appearance, Dawes said, 'Damn good thing for you it's hot weather, you don't get the bed very warm. You'll be tightening-up for me quite a lot if you don't manage better than that. Did you ever have to tighten-up for Singleton?'

'No, Dawes, but he said I wasn't a very good Warmer!'

The second night Angus went as early as he could and was relieved when Dawes said nothing at all. The little room had lost all its friendliness.

On Tassel Night, as usual, the cider made him a little muzzy. Angus walked up the stairs in a slight haze. Dermott-Powell said with his attractive grin, 'This'll be the first Tassel Night since Singleton left, won't it, Angus?' And, when Angus nodded, added, 'Have fun with Dawes! Or was Singleton a dark horse?'

Puzzled but too fuzzy to disentangle it, Angus said, 'Actually I'm a bit tired. G'ni'ght, D-P.' He fell sound asleep the moment he touched Dawes' pillow. It must have been well over an hour later that Dawes arrived and began to undress. Angus woke with a start and began to get up. Dawes said, 'You must be still half asleep. It's Tassel Night. Forgotten?'

The springs gave as, to his surprise, Dawes, naked pulled back the sheets and got on the bed beside him. Like most small boys, Angus had shown momentary curiosity about his own occasional tumescence. Now, awed by the impressive size of an adult erection, he was amazed by its almost comic ungainliness which must, he thought, suppressing a desire to giggle, be sometimes very inconvenient if it happened as unpredictably as his own childish stiffenings.

'Hey! Don't drop off again. Not till we've finished.' There was a pause. Dawes whispered urgently, 'Come *on*, Angus, tassel me.'

Angus' evident ignorance of what was expected of him eventually communicated itself to Dawes: 'Surely Singleton.... Oh no, I suppose bloody Aunty Singleton never did...'

Sleepily, Angus asked, 'Never did what?' There was a momentary pause.

'Bloody Aunty Singleton!' Dawes took hold of Angus' hand and, with thick, almost brutal expectation, in his voice, muttered, 'I suppose you *do* know what this is...?'

※

Sitting in the sun, watching cricket the following afternoon, Mawsom was not very communicative and the obvious topics of conversation were exhausted after a few minutes. Angus said, as if suddenly remembering something, 'A jolly funny thing happened last night. You know Dawes? Well, he got me to sort of hold him...' Then, assuming Mawsom's silence to be non-comprehension, 'His tassel I mean,' adding with a giggle, 'It was enormous, Mawsom! I had to do this,' he gestured, 'till suddenly,' he giggled, 'it, well, sort of burst!'

Mawsom looked quickly round. There was nobody very near; he seemed to find a lot of interest in an earwig. Without looking up he hissed very distinctly, but *sotto voce*, 'For God's sake, Angus, *SHUT UP*. Don't *do* that! *And keep your voice down*! What else do you expect on Tassel Night?'

He took in Angus' genuine incomprehension 'You must know Tassel Night's always like that, AC.'

'You mean *every* Tassel Night? Last Half as well?'

'Yes. Of course.'

Angus stared in disbelief.

'Obviously it didn't happen with Singleton, otherwise you'd have known ages ago.'

'When did *you* find out?'

Mawsom looked back at the earwig. 'Our first Half of course.'

'Ellerman? Baker? Notting too?' Mawsom nodded.

'You all knew and never told me?' Had he been less fearful of them being overheard and less embarrassed, Mawsom might have found Angus' indignation funny. 'Even Snider? Dermott-Powell?' Angus sounded incredulous.

'*Especially* Dermott-Powell, I think *he* knew before he came to Ansell's. Don't you remember that first night outside Big Study? After you'd caused such a big laugh?'

Angus searched his memory, but could only remember the incident vaguely. In some alarm he began, 'When Maunder said we mustn't m...' He could not remember the word.

Mawsom leaned across on his elbow and said quietly, 'The word was "masturbate". That's when you do it to yourself, AC. Tassel Night's different.'

'Oh! I see!' Angus was relieved, although he had not really supposed that Dawes, or any other Praefaector, would break the rules. So you do it to Wilder?'

'*Keep your voice down*!' Mawsom looked back at the earwig again.

'But *do* you?'

'Of course.'

Angus thought, 'Why won't Mawsom look at me?' He said with a trace of petulance, 'Well, if everyone does it, I can't see why we need to whisper. Anyway, actually,' he confided speculatively, 'I can't see what Dawes and people see in it. I suppose that's why Singleton never bothered. And it's a bit messy.' After a silence he said with renewed interest, 'I say do you like it? Does Wilder do it to you?'

Mawsom turned fiercely on him, 'For Christ's sake *SHUT UP*!'

'Oh! It's just that Dawes said he would if I wanted.' He could see Mawsom had turned crimson behind the ears. Setting his jaw determinedly he glanced at the pitch. The fielders were going in to tea. He spoke out ahead of himself. 'Listen, Angus...Dawes should never've suggested it. It's for Tassels and Praefaectors only. If Dawes had done it to you, you might've got another Praefaectors'. Even been sacked.'

A little pale, Angus said, 'I didn't know! Anyway, nothing happened because Dawes said I wasn't ready. You know, all stiff...'

They were the only figures left on the field. Mawsom muttered, 'Well, you know now! Wilder says it's only necessary for senior men in the teams and Praefaectors and so on, because, when you're older you build up this special energy. but if you do it to yourself you won't be fit. And,' Mawsom concluded, evidently quoting Wilder, 'there aren't any girls.'

Angus could not understand how girls came into it, but said obligingly, 'Oh, I *see*.'

They lay on the grass without speaking for some time. Then Mawsom said tentatively, 'I say, AC, don't you think it's disgusting?'

'What?'

'You know, tasselling!'

'Disgusting?' Angus was genuinely surprised for it had not occurred to him. He thought briefly. 'No! Just silly. Bit of a waste of time. And messy, like I said.'

'Some people might say it's wrong. A sin.'

'People in Ansell's?'

There was a hesitation. 'People outside. Masters.' Another silence. 'I thought it was. At first. Till Wilder explained about fitness.'

'Oh?'

'The headmaster of my Private said...well he...sort of hinted, but I couldn't understand what he meant till I got to Ansell's.'

Another thought struck Angus, 'Ellerman and Maunder?'

'Oh yes!'

Angus said enquiringly, 'Ellerman's a Tassel now, so it'll he all right for Maunder to do it to Ellerman?'

'Yes.'

'In that case it must be all right. Maunder wouldn't allow it to happen if it were wrong. Look at what he said about...the other thing because it *is* wrong.' Mawsom realised with astonishment that Angus spoke with the utter conviction of clear conscience as, almost idly, as if an afterthought, he added, 'I say Mawsom, do you ever get like that? All stiff I mean?' There was no reply, once again. Mawsom was looking at the ground. 'Mawsom? Mawsom, do you?'

Mawsom looked up from the blade of grass at which he had been staring hard. He said brutally, '*SHUT UP*! Do you want everyone in the world to hear? You're so innocent you're a bloody menace, AC.' Then he added, after a pause, in a more conciliatory tone, 'Of course I do. Sometimes. Everybody does. Except you, course, AC.' It seemed to Angus as if Mawsom were almost apologising. Then in a confidential rush Mawsom said, 'Actually, quite often. Quite a lot, as a matter of fact. It happens all...' He was on the verge of saying more, but swamped by self-consciousness, he ended lamely, 'It happens to everyone.'

Angus threw himself on his back and chewed grass up at the sky. 'Not me. I'm never like that. Well, only a bit in the bath sometimes. But not,' he ended with another giggle, 'like Dawes!' Then, with a momentary touch of anxiety, 'I say, Mawsom, do you think there's anything wrong with me? I mean Dawes' tassel is so much bigger than mine...huge...'

Not for the first time in his company Mawsom felt at least a generation older than Angus. 'Of course there's nothing wrong with you.' He paused, 'One day it'll just happen.' He added half to himself, 'You're jolly lucky!' Then louder he said, 'I can't make you out. You're scared stiff of being beaten, but these other things never seem to bother you, AC?'

Angus said nothing for a bit, then, 'You know my father's in the desert? Well, when I was coming to Ansell's, he wrote me a letter. A jolly long one. I couldn't really understand all of it, but there was one bit he underlined. He said, "God gave you your body. You should never be ashamed of it. If you are, then you know something's going wrong."'

'I never thought of it like that,' Mawsom said.

'Things like going to Tosher've never bothered me,' Angus observed.

Mawsom said, 'I wish I had a father who wrote like that. I say, what's up?' for Angus had begun to giggle.

'Snider told me that he was hoping Maunder'd let him cover-up.'

'Well, he's as hairy as a gorilla.'

'I know, but I've just thought that since he doesn't like having to walk to Tosher, perhaps God *didn't* give him *his* body.' Mawsom laughed too and, guiltily, Angus realised he might have been Notting speaking; it was the first time he could remember having made an unkind remark at the expense of somebody else. So, in a mood of repentance, he jumped up and said, 'I'm going to Bunner, Coming? I'll pay.'

However, their conversation had roused Mawsom sexually; embarrassed, he did not get to his feet at once.

'Come *on*, Mawsom! Anyhow, there's not another Tassel Night till next Half!'

'There's the Old Ansell's Match and Ashton says it's just another Tassel Night really.'

'Oh that'll be all right. It says on the list that Singleton's playing,' Angus retorted. '*Come on*, or I'll go without you.'

They arrived back at Ansell's after eating rather stodgy wartime cake in Bunner and came face to face with Notting.

'You really have got it cushy, AC!'

'What do you mean?'

'Haven't you heard? Dawes' leg's blown up again. He's got to sleep and eat in Nurs'ry.'

Secretly Angus felt relieved, but he said neutrally, 'What bad luck on him.'

As he went on down Corridor, he overheard Notting joke, 'One Tassel Night with AC and you're a hospital case!' and then laugh brayingly. Angus wondered if Mawsom found it amusing too.

ii

The day of the Old Ansell's matches was as clear and hot. School stopped after the first two teaching periods. Angus hurried back to Ansell's and bumped into Notting.

'Has Angel Arse found his Auntie yet?'

He ignored the taunt but, hastily dumping books, walked out quickly and back to Lodge. There was no sign of Singleton. He felt faintly disappointed and resigned himself to waiting.

'Hello, AC.' The voice took him by surprise. He turned and realised that the figure he had noted in the distance must have been Singleton after all. He looked so very different in uniform, taller, somehow, slimmer and, beneath his beret, surprisingly, so much younger than he had held him in memory.

'You can still recognise me without the photograph?'

'I think so.' Singleton felt buoyed up. Throughout the long journey from Catterick, he had several times found himself hoping that Angus would be the first person he'd see. 'Absolutely the same. Taller?'

Angus nodded. 'A little.'

'Better than shrinking.'

Despite the friendliness, there was still restraint, which did not vanish until Singleton had changed into flannels. Khaki seemed to distance him somehow, as if emphasising that he no longer belonged to Cranchester any more.

'Maunder said you're all to have our beds, but I bagged your old room for you, as Dawes is in Nurs'ry.' They walked towards the cricket. 'I wouldn't have minded sleeping on the floor of course.' He grinned, 'Especially to give a bed to one of our gallant soldiers.' Angus felt elated. He had banked on Singleton's visit more than he had dared admit to himself. 'I say, Singleton, you looked pretty special in uniform. What are the white things on the lapels and behind the badge?'

Singleton said, 'Officer Cadet! Second Lieutenant Singleton, 17/21st Lancers, by the autumn if all goes well.'

'General Singleton by the end of the war!'

'Of course!'

'What about that stick – the leather-covered one? Is it a switch for beating soldiers?'

'It's for swank...called a swagger-stick really. They don't beat soldiers nowadays. By the way, we call them troopers in the cavalry.'

'Cavalry! Horses?'

'Mechanised now. Tanks, armoured cars...'

The day passed in undemanding cricket. Angus scored with meticulous neatness beneath the great chestnut tree. He was relieved by Dermott-Powell and Mawsom from time to time. There was little drama, except for a fine athletic catch by Ellerman and a century from Maunder. Singleton took two wickets. Ansell's beat Old Ansell's by fifteen runs which livened up the last hour.

A certain reorganising of Din. Room meant that the Old Ansell's Men could eat with the House, but the non-players left before the end. Preparation in Libe was interrupted by singing and laughter. The Digger did not appear for Curfew, nor did the Praefaectors except for Maunder. He said meaningfully, 'They're Old Ansell's Men and we make them welcome if that's what they want.'

There was a certain amount of speculation in Big Dorm when they went to bed. Dermott-Powell said, 'It's just another Tassel Night.'

'How do you know?' It was Notting. 'Who told you?'

'I was told by an Old Ansell's Man.'

Baker added, 'Ashton says that somebody in his Election was given a five-pound tip last year.'

'Who was that?' Ellerman said.

'Ashton wouldn't say.'

Dermott-Powell said positively, 'It was Carter.'

'How do you know?'

'Tarrant told me.'

Angus left them quietly and went along to the familiar room. It felt like old times, except for the patchwork cover that Dawes had provided. Without quite knowing why, he pulled it from the bed and stuffed it in a drawer till the room looked identical to the last time he had been there with Singleton on the final night of the previous Half.

Eventually Singleton appeared. 'I'm glad to see you've not forgotten to Warm! How long's Dawes been in Nurs'ry?'

'He didn't come back from home for ages. Now his leg's gone wrong again.'

'Was he here on Tassel Night?'

'Oh yes! He came back just before.' The as if something had suddenly dawned on him, 'Oh, it's all right, Singleton, Dawes showed me what to do.' The cheerful frankness told Singleton that the younger boy felt no guilt at all. 'When you get into bed I'll show you if you like.'

'Do you want to?'

'Of course. If you want. But,' he added with a touch of naive confidentiality, 'Dawes said I wasn't very good...' It was, Singleton thought, as if he were confessing ineptitude at cricket. A sudden thought caused Angus to say, 'I say, Mawsom says some people think it's wrong. Do you think it wrong, Singleton?'

'What do you think, AC? That's what's important.' He was conscious that he had turned the question.

'I can't see what's in it, what all the fuss is about. Anyway, Maunder allows Tassel Night so it must be all right.'

'Things look different when you've left Ansell's.'

'What about when you were Junior Election?'

'I dare say I thought rather like you.' Even as he said it, he knew he had never experienced Angus' unblemished conscience. 'But then, later on.... You know, Christopher, most of us are a bit like...Dawes, even if we don't like to admit it,' he stumbled.

Angus, although sleepily glad that Singleton was not Dawes, wondered impatiently why everyone kept going on about tasselling; wanting it to happen, yet talking about it only in hushed tones. Now, even Singleton was speaking softly. It didn't matter anyway. To change the subject he muttered indistinctly, 'You remember that time I was in such a state?'

'Um-huh.

'I don't know what I'd've done that night without you.'

'Still thinking of that?' Singleton said quietly.

'I haven't had to tighten-up since.'

'Good for you.'

'But I don't think I'll ever forget it, even when I'm old.'

Singleton said, 'Some people would say that's the purpose of Praefaectors' beatings, AC,' in a tone of voice which indicated he was not one of them.

There was silence.

'Anyway, thanks, Singleton.' He caught hold of Singleton's hand as if he intended to shake it on a bargain finally concluded, gave a small sigh and fell fast asleep.

✳

It was dawn when Angus awoke. Singleton, also awake, was sprawled in the battered armchair by the window. 'I say, I'm sorry, Singleton! I've done it again like last Half. Don't tell Maunder! He said we were to give you our beds even if we had to sleep on the floor ourselves.'

'Not many sleep on the floor on Match Night,' Singleton said wryly. 'I know. This is my fifth! Anyhow, this chair's better than the floor. Now I must dress and go. If I don't get the first train, I shan't get back to camp before tomorrow.'

'I'll come to the station with you!'

'No need. You get back to sleep.'

'I'd like to walk to the station. It's another fine day.'

'I'd not bother about Tosher till you get back then.' Singleton began to put on the component parts of his cadet's uniform.

They crept downstairs and through a silent arch and silent Lodge.

'Stubbington never minds on these Match mornings. You tell him you were carrying a bag for "Mr Singleton" when you come back.'

'Oh. I'm sorry!' He put his hand out for the cricket bag Singleton carried.

'That wasn't meant as a hint! But take one handle if you like.'

They walked on down a green-banked road which was heavy with dew and smelt of early summer. Evidently there was something on Angus' mind. Finally he said, 'About last night. I really do know what to do, now.' He had awoken troubled that he had failed and disappointed Singleton. Or, worse that Singleton supposed him incompetent? He could remember almost nothing of Singleton's halting attempt at explanation.

They stopped at a worn stile beside a field of wheat. It was still green. Beads of shining moisture hung on the whiskers of the ears. The squat tower of the little church of St Peter and St Paul, with its tiny pointed steeple, showed against the sky of another cloudless day. It was still not six o'clock, yet the air was warm. There was no breath of wind. Singleton heaved the bag onto the lower step and sat astride the wooden bar. Unbidden Angus did the same and they sat opposite each other without speaking for some seconds.

Singleton hoped that what he had attempted to say the previous evening had somehow sorted itself out in his mind. The stillness of the morning and the fact that they were there, encapsulated between the high summer hedges, gave him a confidence which had failed him before. He said quietly, 'Christopher, I'm very fond of you. You must know that.' His sincerity had nothing of sentimentality about it.

Without embarrassment, Angus looked straight at him. 'Oh yes, me too! I expect that's why I'm so glad you came for the match.'

'Well, what I think I was trying to say to you last night is that part of me – the Dawes bit of me so to speak – is the bit of me I don't like at all. It scares me. I can't control it. In Junior Election I just did what everyone else did.'

From a sympathetic urge to soften what he divined from Singleton's tone to be a confession, Angus added encouragingly, 'Like me? Even though it seemed a bit silly?' Drawing a deep breath, Singleton continued as if he had not heard, 'After a bit…after a bit…' There was a long pause. 'I…I probably looked forward to it as much as anyone for a long time.'

'I was the only one who didn't know about Tassel Nights,' Angus said after a pause and without emphasis, but perhaps with a hint of reproach.

'I expect you were.'

'I'd rather it had been you than Dawes. Actually.' The breathtaking innocence which lay behind such disarming frankness almost undid Singleton.

'Thanks!' His attempt to lighten the tone did not work. 'It's not really what I mean. Listen, Christopher…. About last night. It wouldn't have been the end of the world, but I thought…that is…I thought that if we don't meet again…for a long time…I don't want to be remembered simply as…as somebody you tasselled one Match night,' he ended rapidly.

'I wouldn't remember *you*, like *that*, Singleton!'

The genuine indignation in Angus' voice pricked his conscience. So he said gently, 'How will you remember Dawes?' He knew it was unfair, a debating point.

'That's *totally* different!'

'I'd rather it remained totally different but, much more important, Christopher,' he took Angus' shoulder in the familiar and reassuring gesture and said with an almost disturbing intensity, 'it is not the way *I* want to remember *you*.'

Angus knew it was a compliment; even so he could not help exclaiming with a ruefulness that was not entirely jokey, 'Angel Chile?'

Singleton paused and then said, 'Well, perhaps that's better than being a *fallen* Angel Chile.' He squeezed Angus' ear lobe as he had done on the last morning of the previous Half and said lightly, 'Time my batman carried my bag to catch that train.'

It was far too early for the ancient, remaining porter to be present. In the bright air, filled with birdsong, they stood alone on the platform. A grubby train boiled laboriously into sight. It was almost entirely empty, like a train going from nowhere into nowhere, Angus thought inconsequentially. Singleton got into a First Class compartment. He said, laughing, 'Officer Cadets must not mix with the common soldiery.'

Heavily, the train dragged itself away. Singleton waved from the window until a bend shut the platform from sight. For no obvious reason, Angus was reminded of the moment in Singleton's study the previous Half, when he had so impulsively kissed him 'goodnight'. It was a measure of the imperceptible change which Ansell's had wrought in him that even fleeting remembrance of the incident now embarrassed him as the act itself had never done at the time. He turned abruptly from the vanishing train and walked quickly through the station entrance to disguise his discomfort.

Had Singleton known he would have been saddened; he wanted to believe that Angus, and others like him, were able to change Ansell's rather than be changed by it. Sitting on a worn velvet seat, facing oval sepia photographs of fading seaside promenades, now almost certainly barbwired against invasion, he turned over in his mind what he had said to Angus astride the stile. As he did so, he realised that, despite all his intentions, he had never really answered Angus' question of the previous night. '*Do you think it wrong, Singleton?*' Or had he deliberately avoided it?

Angus too reflected on what Singleton had said. He reached the stile and perched again on the top bar. What had Singleton tried to say? Was it a warning? He had been glad to see Singleton, but Singleton was no longer part of Ansell's, while he, Angus, was. Nevertheless, he knew that somewhere amongst all the words that had confused him, Singleton had been offering advice, trying to help.

Sliding down, he began to trot along the centre of the still-deserted lane towards Lodge. Lifted in spirit by the splendid morning, he said affectionately, aloud, 'Good old Auntie Singleton,' unaware that it was the first time he had ever used the phrase. In the clear summer air it did not seem a betrayal.

iii

Field Day was a big event, involving Cranchester and three other schools. It was Snider who broke the unexpected news. 'We're not needed. I mean apart from getting kit ready for the Praefaectors. There'll not be any teaching!'

Notting had joined them: 'We're allowed the day off! We're being given packed lunch and have to be away from Cranchester till six o'clock. There's a notice in Corridor.' Mawsom and Snider were already reading it.

Ellerman said, 'We'll be part of the OTC next year, so we'd better make the most of this!'

Angus was talking to Dermott-Powell under the chestnut tree as they watched a House match against Jonquil's the following day; when Mawsom came up to them. 'I've found a map. It's a bit old.' He showed them the date – 1898. 'It was with those second-hand books in Bunner. Why don't the three of us go on an expedition?'

'Where to?'

'Well, this doesn't quite show Cranchester – it's just at the edge of the map, but it shows Avebury.'

Dermott-Powell blew on a piece of grass trapped between his cupped hands. It made a satisfactory and rather owl-like musical note. 'I've heard about Avebury. In fact I think I've been there. It's prehistoric or something. Then witches used it, we were once told that by the Dean.'

Angus said, 'I'll not be able to get that far. I've no bicycle.'

'You could borrow one,' Mawsom encouraged, but they all knew that bicycles would be at a premium. Then he added thoughtfully, 'Or you could go by bus. I'm sure there *is* one to Avebury, or nearly, and meet us.'

Dermott-Powell said, 'Dawes has got a bicycle. He can't use it with his leg. You're his Warmer, why not ask him? He's only in Nurs'ry at nights now.'

Scandalised, Angus said, 'I couldn't ask him. He's a *Praefaector!*'

'I know, but he'd probably lend it, if you asked.'

Angus was unconvinced. 'I'll catch the bus and meet you there.'

The following afternoon Dermott-Powell found Angus in Big Change and said cheerfully, 'It's all right. I've got the bike for you. I told you Dawes wouldn't mind.'

You mean *you* asked him if *I* could borrow *his* bike!' He was astonished at Dermott-Powell's temerity.

Dermott-Powell smiled triumphantly, 'Not exactly. You can borrow mine. I let Dawes think I hadn't got one, so he lent his to me.'

Angus, impressed, was not sure what to say. 'Thanks,' he managed at last. 'The bus would have been a bit of a drag because it takes two hours to Avebury; it goes through all the small villages. I'd never have dared ask Dawes.'

'I'm good at asking for things,' Dermott-Powell said simply.

✻

Field Day began very early, with breakfast for all at six o'clock. Heavy army lorries lined up outside Lodge to transport the OTC, after an impressive muster parade in Great Quad.

'It looks quite like a real army.'

'We'll be in it next Half.'

Baker said morosely, 'I hear it's not as much fun as it looks.' He suffered a good deal in the heat as well as the cold. His face had peeled several times but still looked red, and he sweated unpleasantly despite frantic (and illegal) bathing. They ambled back to Ansell's to collect a packet of sandwiches and an apple and to put on 'Change'. It was not yet eight o'clock and they were already quite hungry again. Baker ate his sandwiches and put the apple in his pocket. 'I'm going to spend all morning finding a place to get lunch and all afternoon sleeping it off,' he said fatly. He was never short of pocket money and had chosen to spend the day in his own company.

Mawsom said, 'I didn't see Dermott-Powell at breakfast.'

'Perhaps he overslept?'

In Big Dorm Dermott-Powell was sitting in bed. He said, 'I'm afraid I can't come with you. I've got a bad headache and the Flanders' Mare says I'm not to leave Ansell's today. In fact I'm not even to get up until she's taken my temperature again.' 'Flanders' Mare' was the unflattering nickname by which the Ansell's Matron was unofficially known by all (except the Junior Election who traditionally had to tighten-up for *side* if heard using it).

Mawsom said, 'Bad luck, today of all days.'

'Yes. It is rather. Good luck for you though.'

'How do you mean?' Angus asked.

'Well you've got some extra sandwiches. They're always stingy on these occasions.'

As they went downstairs Mawsom said, 'Dermott-Powell didn't look very ill.'

'No, not really, but it's not as if it's an ordinary day. I mean what's the point in faking on a day when there are no Divisions?'

'That's true. I say, should we give his food to Baker?'

'Nor likely! Anyhow everyone else seems to have gone.'

They wheeled their bicycles through Lodge. It seemed as if they were the last inhabitants on earth, for there was nobody else in sight at all. They freewheeled down the slight slope of gravel, still marked by the army vehicles. Mawsom said, 'You know, it'll be better, just two of us.'

Mist still lay in the valley but, as the road rose, the sun grew very much warmer and the air heavy with the scent of grass and hedgerow. It seemed all uphill. It was about eleven o'clock that they flopped on the high verge. Despite the fact that it was a main road, there was little traffic except army convoys which passed by at intervals, keeping to some predefined speed. Their heavy-treaded tyres made a characteristic whirr on the warm tarred surface. Lying on his back Mawsom said, 'Avebury's not far. Next turning on the left.'

Angus was studying the map. 'What's a "barrow" exactly? It a sort of burial mound, isn't it?'

'Ancient Britons, you know, Druids and all that,' Mawsom said inaccurately.

'Have you ever seen one? A barrow I mean!'

'I'm not sure. Why?'

'There's one near here. Marked on the map. "Long Barrow". On the Downs behind West Kennet.'

'Let's see.' Mawsom took the map. 'Yes, we could easily go and look. It might be fun.'

It took them some time to discover exactly where it lay, for the map was no longer accurate as far as the roads were concerned. In the end they had to ask an elderly countryman scything the verge below a hedgerow.

'Up theere. A'top the downs. Yer can't mistake it, looks like a sleeping dog.' He went back to his scything.

'Father Time,' Mawsom said as they set off again, 'except he's not old enough and no beard.'

They left their cycles by the roadside under the hedge and followed an ill-defined path that led them over a shaky bridge across a small clear river. 'I think it must be the Crann,' Angus remarked, looking at the map. Across the river, the path was almost indistinguishable for it lay across flinty, newly turned downland earth, ploughed for the first time in history as part of the war effort. An early cutting of hay had already encouraged new growth and, although they stuck to the fence, the grass was already calf-high. It had grown very hot. At last they topped the ridge. The last few feet had been quite steep. There was nothing much to see except a mound and two or three almost-buried boulders.

'We must've taken the wrong path.'

'No. Father Time pointed it out.'

What a swizz!'

Mawsom was looking around him, then he laughed.

'What's the matter?'

'We're standing on it!'

'*On* the *barrow*!'

'Yes, look.'

Sure enough, they were on a sort of mound which rose up some feet from the surrounding ridge but, in context was, little more than a pimple.

Angus said, 'It doesn't look much like a dog. Even a *sleeping* dog!'

They scrambled down the side and stood a few feet off.

'I suppose,' Mawsom admitted grudgingly, 'that it is, sort of, like a sleeping dog. You know, nose on the ground and higher at the back.'

'More like a dog waiting for you to throw a stick!'

'What's that?'

'That' turned out to be a shabby post with an almost faded notice. They could just make out the words *Ancient Monument*.

'The notice looks as though it's been here as long as the barrow.'

They climbed up again. Angus said, 'It's not as exciting as I thought.'

'No, but I wonder what's underneath?'

'Remains of a battle perhaps?'

'Maybe a king's been buried here.'

'With a crown and jewels!'

Mawsom said, 'I've got an uncle who was an archaeologist before the war. Used to dig up ancient sites. Bones and things. Abroad somewhere. Palestine I think.'

Angus looked down at his feet as though trying to pierce the flower-speckled turf. 'I wouldn't mind doing that. Especially in this weather.'

'It's too hot. I'm taking my shirt off. Nobody'll ever see.' He pulled off the striped rugger jersey which, with thick blue games shorts and grey stockings, constituted 'cycling Change' at Cranchester. Angus followed suit. For some time they lay throwing spears of grass at each other. High overhead a plane left a delicate vapour trail.

'Spitfire!'

'Hurricane!'

It was much too far away to be heard, let alone identified. Angus closed his eyes. The sun burned his skin. Flies and insects buzzed on their business. He felt a tickling on his nostril.

'Pack it in, Mawsom!' He brushed his face with his hand.

'Pack what in?'

'Tickling me with grass.'

'I'm not.'

Angus sat up. 'I'm itching all over.'

'Me too. It's the grass.'

'No it isn't. *ANTS*.'

'*Ants*!' Mawsom stood up quickly, brushing his face and body with his hand.

Angus said, 'Well at least *an* ant. I'm sure they're in my hair.'

'There's one on your neck.' Mawsom plucked it off. 'Let's get back to the bikes.'

'And the sandwiches.'

Trailing their jerseys in the air, they half ran, half walked back down the hill. Before they got to the bridge, they stopped and looked at the river.

'This would make a good bathing place.'

There were smooth white crystal pebbles and the clear chalk stream flowed into a large pool floored by silvery sand and surrounded by trees.

Mawsom said, 'Somebody might object.'

'I don't see why. There's nobody about. I mean it's not as if it's public.'

'I was thinking of the fishing.'

Angus had already peeled off the grey stockings. Stepping from the heavy serge shorts which were still too large, he walked into the water. 'Just the thing to get rid of ants.' He ducked his head and splashed at Mawsom. 'Come on.'

The glistening water was too enticing to resist. In a minute or so he had joined Angus in the pool although it was hardly deep or wide enough to swim more than a few strokes.

'I say, Angus! We've no towels.'

'I'm going to use my jersey.' Angus was floating, the whiteness of his body contrasting vividly in the water with the tan on his arms and legs. 'Anyhow the sun'll dry us.'

They fooled about, splashing, for some time. The contrast between them was striking. Mawsom had grown considerably and even begun to fill out. Beside him, Angus was immature, a child still. They paused in their attempts to chop water at each other and Angus said, 'I say, Mawsom, you'll soon be getting permission to cover-up.'

Mawsom said, 'Possibly!' Then after a pause, 'Angus, let's make a pact.'

'How do you mean?'

'Not to say anything about Ansell's, or Cranchester, all day. At least till we get back.'

Angus looked thoughtfully at Mawsom across the pool, 'All right. If you like.'

'It's just that I don't want to think about Ansell's here. It's too good a place...'

Suddenly perceptive, Angus said, 'Too good a place to spoil, you mean? Like home! Or the holidays.'

'You feel it too?'

'Singleton said never to mix home and Ansell's.'

'Did he?'

'Tell you what. The first one of us to mention anything to do with Cranchester from now on has to buy the other toasted teacakes in Bunner.'

'Okay We'd better be getting out. I say, who's that?' Neither of them had noticed the figure on the bank with a fringe of beard and straggling grey hair.

Mawsom said, *sotto voce*, 'I told you somebody'd object.'

'He doesn't seem to be objecting. In fact he looks about a hundred years old. This really *is* Father Time,' Angus whispered back.

Wading across, Mawsom said, 'I'm very sorry if we've done any harm to the fishing.'

'Not much fishing theere.' The old man was as unembarrassed by their nakedness as Angus, who climbed out, shook himself like a spaniel, and began to dab experimentally with his jersey-towel.

'I bathed theere, when I weere your age. And me broother. Jest like the twoeryew. Brothers?'

'Friends,' Angus said politely.

'We use'ter run up ter the oold burial in the sun to dry. Noaw plough then. Jest the grass.'

Angus said, 'We've already been there, this was on our way back.'

The old man grinned knowingly, 'Should be in school.' He laughed deep inside, 'But a day like this's not for any schoolroom! Me an' my broother thought th' same. Though we knowed it'ud be the stick next day, but it weere always worth et.'

Mawsom said, 'We've got...a sort of holiday.' He did not intend to break the bargain he had just made with Angus by explaining details of Field Day.

'Ar? That's what we called it when nosey ol' varmints like me interfeered.' He chuckled again and coughed. He leaned on a high walking stick which came almost to his chin, sucking a scarred pipe made of some gnarled wood and regarded them in silence. His face was so lined that it looked like crumpled tissue paper; he seemed to be staring through and beyond them. 'I wish I could still'erv joined you in there, boys. It's a long time back.' He began to move off.

Mawsom struggled to pull shorts over his still damp body. As he slowly passed them, the old man stopped again and took Angus fiercely by the elbow: 'You enjoy these days, boy! *Whatever* they say. You just enjoy days like this; we're not young lads forever.' Angus saw that he had very blue eyes, not like those of his own grandfather, cloudy and dull, but bright and piercing like those of a young man. They would have been unnerving if they had not been so kind. 'They may not tell you that, boy.' He paused again, whether for effect or to take a breath, Angus could not tell. 'We're all tears for those as die young, over there.' He waved vaguely to the south. 'But'—he paused again—''tisn't much fun being old.' Another breath, 'You'll remember that?' The face was anxious.

'Yes...sir?'

The old man raised his bushed eyebrows and laughed his breathless laugh. 'Sir? Yer'll be the furrrst to call me that.' He moved on slowly out of sight. Angus stood motionless watching him, until Mawsom said, 'Do you think he was dotty? What an odd thing to say. About being old, I mean.'

Angus struggled to pull on a stocking, gave up and tied his shoes barelegged. 'Yes, I suppose it was, but I don't think he was mad.'

'Nor do I really! It seemed as if he was giving the advice to you. As though I wasn't here,' Mawsom added. As they were about to set off: 'It's funny to think of him bathing here once. At our age. Did you see his skin? All those creases?'

Do you suppose we'll be like it one day?' I've never really thought about it before,' Angus said thoughtfully.

Mawsom, equally pensive, answered obliquely, 'I say, Angus, if he really was a hundred, he'd've been bathing here at the time of the Indian Mutiny.' History was his special interest. Then, briskly changing the subject, 'I'm not putting on my jersey till we reach the bikes so that it can dry off a little.'

They ate lunch in the shade of a small copse. 'I reckon this is another barrow,' Angus said as they stood up to go.

'It's all covered in trees. Why do you think so?'

Angus held out his hand. In the palm there was a fragment of rough reddish pottery. 'Ancient Britons,' he said lightly. 'I found it in that rabbit hole. I expect it leads to the treasure.'

'It looks pretty old,' Mawsom admitted. 'Come on. Let's get on to Avebury.'

The clock struck one as they came through a cluster of houses situated within concentric circles of banks and standing stones. It was very quiet. Whether it was his imagination, or fact, Angus did not know, but the grass seemed greener and somehow, although there was not a cloud in the sky, it seemed as if it were darker too, inside the circle. An elderly black and white cat dozed on the wall of a sleeping pub. Further along, the small primary school stood with doors and windows open. Faintly in the air was a smell of cooking.

'It's as if it's under a spell.'

'Perhaps everyone's been taken away suddenly,' Angus said. 'Like the *Marie Celeste*!'

Scent from the flowers in a dozen gardens hung in the air. It was very, very hot. There was no wind. In the middle of the road, outside the church they stood holding their bicycles. There was nothing stirring at all.

'It's…quite spooky really,' Mawsom said.

As he spoke there came another sound. Heavy and purring, it made them turn. A dusty country bus lumbered into view and stopped outside the pub. They watched a small crowd, mostly women, get off carrying bags. Two or three came down the road towards them.

'That's the bus I'd've come on if I hadn't a bike,' Angus said, just in time avoiding mention of Dermott-Powell.

Brought to life by the sound of the bus, the rest of Avebury began to show itself. Even the cat woke up and stretched; as they returned along the one street it was vigorously grooming itself, oblivious of all else. Eventually they came to the post office. It seemed deserted. A sign in the window said *Teas. Lemonade.* They went inside. It was quite dark. No one answered the bell which had tingled as they pushed the door. Mawsom became absorbed in a small, very battered little pamphlet on a table. The words **DO NOT REMOVE** were written in heavy lead pencil on each of the pages. He said, 'It's quite true about the witches. According to this booklet, various bishops tried to have the stones destroyed because they were used in witchcraft. After a man got killed trying to topple them, nobody would touch them.'

A small, rather anxious woman approached through a back door, dusting flour from her hands. 'I'm afraid I can't sell that book. It's all we've got. They aren't printing any more. Can't get the paper, but you're welcome to read it.'

Mawsom apologised, 'Sorry!' It had occurred to neither of them to offer to buy it.'

Angus said, 'The notice in the window said Lemonade…?'

'You're lucky! Delivery this morning.' It was red and very fizzy. They had to buy the whole bottle, but she lent them two glasses. The label announced garishly **TIZER – the AppeTIZER,** and made them belch very satisfactorily. They had difficulty finishing it off, but it seemed a pity to waste it. The postmistress emerged again from the back.

'Two growing lads like you'll know what to do with these. You don't look as if they feed you properly,' she remarked to Angus, 'or perhaps the big one there eats your share.' These were two jam tarts, still warm from the oven.

'We used to get a lot of visitors before the war,' she said. 'I did teas then.' She added, 'No! No!' for Angus suddenly thought it was a hint that they should pay for the tarts. 'These are a present for you and your friend. Come back when they've done this Hitler in the eye. You can have a proper tea then – and pay for it.'

Angus said, 'In the book it says there's a big mound which might be Viking.'

'Oh that'll be Silbury. You can't miss it. It's just like a sandcastle made with a giant bucket – you know flat at the top. There's a path to it just beyond the stones. That way.' She took them to the door and pointed.

They ate the tarts sitting on the wall of the pub; the black and white cat graciously accepted crumbs of pastry. At last Mawsom said, 'Now for Silbury. I've found it on the map and it's right by the main road, on our way back. They followed the road out past the stones and the banks. 'I wonder how they got them here. They're massive,' Mawsom pondered.

'Don't know why, but I'm quite glad to leave. Imagine living with all these things round you. I suppose it's meant to be very nice...but with the stones and the banks...'

Standing up on his pedals Mawsom added, 'And the witches!' He was not altogether joking; he also felt that the sun outside the village was somehow more welcoming. They had to push their bicycles most of the way along the footpath, when they reached it, for it was largely overgrown. Silbury Hill loomed ahead. It was very impressive. They left the cycles at the bottom and began to climb its steep, grassy sides. In the hot afternoon sun, they both panted for breath and, almost in unison, flung off their shirts again, before lying in the shallow bowl at the top.

'That's a convoy passing,' Mawsom said as they heard the regular beat of engines seemingly in another world. 'Do you think the war will end soon?'

'Do you think there really is a Viking king buried beneath this?' Angus countered.

'Wouldn't be surprised.'

'Didn't they bury their kings in ships?'

'There's plenty of room for a ship beneath this.'

'I wonder if anyone'll dig it up one day. Your uncle?'

'I think,' Mawsom said, 'that somebody ages ago did try to find out. I once heard a master say something about it at my Private when he knew I was going to Cranchester.'

'I've won the bet!'

'Damn'nblast! So you have! Still let's start again. Double or quits?'

'Double or quits! I say, I suppose when you're as old as Father Time this morning, you can't get up to places like this.'

'Perhaps that's what he meant. Enjoy things whilst you can.'

'I can't imagine a time when I wouldn't be able to get up here, I mean unless I was in a wheelchair or something.'

'Or had your legs shot off in the war.'

'I suppose that's what's so beastly about war. It makes you like the old man, although you're still young.'

'You're very serious today. Anything wrong?'

'Not really. I haven't heard from my father for ages. He's fighting in the Desert.'

'Probably a letter waiting for you when you get back. Nothing could possibly spoil a day like this.'

Angus rolled onto his stomach: 'Ooch!' He pulled out the leaf of a small thistly plant and examined some red marks on his skin. 'I expect you're right. My father always says it's the bad news which travels fast. Is your father...?' He stopped, pulled up by Ansell's code, which frowned on asking about families.

Mawsom said, 'I haven't seen my father since I was six. I live with my mother. And grandparents.'

'I'm sorry!'

'Doesn't matter. It wasn't much fun when he was there.'

'Mawsom? Oughtn't we to be starting back. It seems quite late.'

The ride back seemed hillier and dustier than it had been in the morning. They were passed by three great convoys. It was so hot they cycled without shirts. The last of the convoys was filled with troops. As the final truck passed them at a sedate speed, they were riding the bicycles up a hill, standing heavily first on one pedal then another. A wag in battledress called out to Angus, 'Keep it up, Tarzan!'

They rested at the top. Mawsom began to put his shirt back on.

'Somebody might see us.' He meant somebody from Cranchester. They freewheeled down and after a mile or so were in Market Street. A clock said five to six.

'What timing!' Somehow the environment of the school had already closed in on them again. As they passed the little road to Cranchester Church, Angus said, 'You know, Mawsom, being at Avebury was a bit like being back at Cranchester.'

'Yes, I thought that too. It's been a good day.' He paused. 'But we've never really been away from Ansell's, have we?'

Angus knew what he meant. 'Do you think we'll ever get away from Ansell's?'

※

As Mawsom had predicted, Angus found a letter from his father awaiting him on Long School when they hurried into Din Room. Anticipation of reading it afterwards and hunger blunted him to the tension which seemed to invest the whole building. He said to Ellerman, 'We had a great day! What about you?'

'It was all right.'

'Dermott-Powell lent me his bike.' He looked round. There was no sign of him.

Ellerman said in a low voice, 'Haven't you heard? Dermott-Powell's gone!'

'Gone?' He thought of The Nurs'ry. 'Oh, he must be quite ill after all then. He told me the Flanders' Mare sent him back to bed.'

'That's where The Digger found him!' The tone was odd.

'Oh! Is it infectious?'

Notting on the other side of him said, 'Well, it was for Dawes!'

Snider leaned across and said quietly, but patiently, 'He and Dawes were sacked. They were driven to the station for the four-five this afternoon.'

'Sacked! Whatever for?'

'I told you. The Digger found them in bed...together.'

'Dermott-Powell? He gazed uncomprehending. 'With Dawes? He caught a glance from Mawsom: an inkling of enlightenment flickered.

At that moment The Digger came through his door and called for silence; There was an elaborate hush, broken only by a senior boy called Bartlett accidentally clattering his knife.

'Before you go,' The Digger said, 'it has been my most unhappy duty today to ask the High Master to expel Dawes and Dermott-Powell. I discovered them behaving in a quite degrading manner, which disgraces them, their families, the School and, worst still, all of us at Ansell's. You should all know that anyone sent away for such unmentionable offences may never become an Old Castonian. I am having their names inked from the present Ansell's list. I request you to do the same with your copies.' He coughed. 'I have only once before had to take action of this sort. It was in my second year as Housemaster, since when I had long supposed this sort of promiscuous beastliness to be a thing of the past. I suppose we can take a fragment of comfort from the fact that Dawes came to us from a different school, abroad. He did not spend his formative junior years in Ansell's and Dermott-Powell was of the most recent Election and, it seems, he may have been corrupted before he arrived here, but that is no comfort. Needless to say, were I to hear of any other similar conduct, I shall not hesitate to take the same action. One further thing. Although I cannot imagine that any Ansell's Man should wish to communicate with either Dawes or Dermott-Powell, I do specifically forbid any communication from this address.' He turned and went through the door.

In the awed hush that followed, Maunder stood up. 'Listen, Ansell's, it's a pretty bloody thing to happen and The Digger's no end upset. No wonder. So just remember I'll tan the arse off anyone who so much as mentions anything to anyone outside Ansell's. The School's bound to know something, but they'll learn nothing very definite unless we tell 'em. We keep it in the family. Right? We get it right for next Half. And remember what The Digger said – neither Dawes nor Dermott-Powell were really Ansell's Men, but we are!'

They drifted out into the warm evening. Because it was Field Day, there was no Evening School and they were free until Curfew. As if by unspoken consent the whole Election had found its way into the ruined, overgrown walled garden that belonged to Ansell's. It felt as if they were all tarnished.

Ellerman said, 'Dermott-Powell was just a tart.'

The term puzzled Angus, although fleetingly reminded of the kindness of the lady at Avebury, the tone was unmistakably condemnatory. He recalled Dermott's numerous kindnesses. He said, mildly, incorrectly reading the mood of the others, 'Well, I thought he was quite nice. Good fun.'

'Oh he was "good fun" all right!' Ellerman said savagely. 'Did you see him on the night of the Old Ansell's Match?'

Angus shook his head.

Unexpectedly Snider spoke, 'Was he any worse than you on Match Night?'

Ellerman flushed darkly.

'Or me? Or any of us?'

Notting said with his customary spite, 'Dermott-Powell gave Jarndyce a royal welcome. He really enjoyed it.'

'Didn't you enjoy it, Notting?' Snider asked quietly. 'Didn't you?' Notting opened his mouth but no words came. 'We all did if we're honest. I'm not excluding myself. It might have been one of us rather than Dermott-Powell on that train with Dawes.'

Mawsom looked covertly to Angus who, although still uncertain as to exactly what had happened, felt for the first time a pang of guilt. Might it have been himself in the train with Dawes? Is that what Mawsom meant? Snider had from the first been taller than the rest of them, but he seemed now much, much older too. He said in the same persistent logical tone, 'What about Tassel Night?'

Ellerman said indignantly, 'Tassel Night's different. So's Match Night.'

'*Why* is it different? How can something be okay one moment and get you sacked the next?'

There was silence.

Mawsom said diffidently, 'Maunder wouldn't allow Tassel Night if...' Angus recognised his own argument.

Ellerman came in quickly, 'That's quite right. Maunder wouldn't allow it.'

'Then why's it wrong on Field Day for Dawes and Dermott-Powell?' Snider persisted.

'Tassel Night's a sort of…sort of special,' Ellerman said with an inspired flash of imagination. 'It could be like **No Smoking** – you know, on trains – only the other way round. I mean it's not wrong to smoke on a train – except in a non-smoker.'

'I can't really answer that,' Snider said after some thought, 'but I'm sure it's the wrong sort of argument. 'Anyhow, it was bad luck that Dermott-Powell had a headache.'

'Dermott-Powell didn't have a headache! He was faking. He was planning to get the day off, but he didn't say why. I saw him talking with Dawes last evening. I've told you, he was just a little tart,' Ellerman concluded.

'Well, you should know, Ellerman. He was in your Manger the night before last,' Snider said pointedly without raising his voice.

Ellerman stood scarlet and speechless. 'Or you, Notting, after last week. What about you, Baker, did *you* tell him to push off?' There came no denials. 'I didn't, nor did Mawsom. I should think AC is about the only one who hasn't had the slightest notion of what's been going on. Nobody said anything, so Snider continued, 'What I mean is that we're all responsible for Dermott-Powell. It's not just Dawes. It's everyone in Ansell's. It's no good Ellerman saying he's a tart. If he is, then most of Ansell's helped to make him one. What's more, if he'd told The Digger everything he knew, you wouldn't all be feeling so goody-goody now.'

Shamefaced they began to break up, but Baker who had not spoken till then stopped them. He said, 'Anyhow Snider, you're quite wrong. It wasn't like Tassel Night.'

'What do you mean?'

'They didn't get sacked just for tasselling!'

'The Digger said…'

'No he didn't.' Baker paused, determined, 'It wasn't for just tasselling…most of us know perfectly well that Dawes and Dermott-Powell were…'

Notting spat, '*SHUT UP* Baker!'

'Well, Snider's wrong!'

'How am I wrong?'

Baker looked at Notting pudgily defiant, but a bit scared. 'You just *are*. Anyhow, if you want to know any more you'd better ask Ellerman, or Notting – they've had more to do with Dermott-Powell than me.'

He walked off through the dusk.

Ellerman said, 'Baker doesn't know what he's talking about,' in a tone which dared somebody to challenge him. Notting, looking white, said nothing at all. 'Anyway, does anyone really think The Digger would approve of Tassel Night, whatever Maunder says?' It was a question that would never have occurred to Angus.

He found an envelope tucked deep under his pillow.

Dear AC,
You'll have heard by now what happened. It's lucky I didn't tell everything I know. I bet one or two Ansell's Men will be uneasy tonight. Most of the House! I wish I'd come with you and Mawsom today. Keep the bike. Hope the singing goes well. Perhaps we'll meet again one day. You're the only Ansell's Man I'd ever want to meet again. Don't let them get you down.

Love from
Edward Sean Dermott-Powell.

Curiously touched, he remembered Dermott-Powell's kindness, contrasting it with the priggish distaste the rest of his Election now displayed. He recalled Dermott-Powell's late-night visit very vividly; the way he had held on to him; his conviction that he could not 'last' at Ansell's; his desperate confession…of what? Was that what had found him out? Anyway, what exactly had he done with Dawes? He felt momentarily uneasy as he remembered Mawsom's look. What did Baker and Ellerman and Notting know about it that Snider didn't? It occurred to him that the animated gossip about Dawes and Dermott-Powell, which had occupied them all since his return, had effectively blurred the remembrance of an otherwise marvellous day. It was almost as if Ansell's was revenging itself on him for daring to exclude it from his thoughts for a few hours.

It was not the only retaliation. Unintentionally, he came across the volume of poems. He realised that he had hardly opened it all this Half! He felt that somehow he had let Singleton down. To quell a twinge of guilt he opened it at the now familiar page, but experienced a frisson of embarrassment. Quickly he put it away. He did not want to be found reading it, nor for the inscription to be read by others, even by Mawsom. Above all, he now felt faintly ashamed of the pencilled *AC*, which had, only last Half, given him such pleasure.

iv

The expulsion of Dawes and Dermott-Powell not only exploded the rhythm of Ansell's, but also upset morale. The usual end-of-term exuberance was missing. Instead, there was once again a brittle tension which affected everyone: they failed to win the House Match which would have put them in the final and the fact that they had fallen to Jonquil's made Maunder and the other Praefaectors unpredictably irascible. Several people had to tighten-up in the space of the following few days, although till then there had been singularly little beating.

About a fortnight before the end of the Half, as Angus was dropping off to sleep, for no reason he could understand, he thought of Dermott-Powell and Dawes. Also, and again for no apparent reason, he recalled Dermott-Powell standing on the table at their Inspection, though he had never remembered it before. At the same time he became aware his own tassel was stiffening so rapidly that he had to move to be comfortable. Drowsily he remembered his enquiry to Mawsom as to whether there was something wrong with him and was glad at the evidence that there was not. Dawes would not have been able to say he was not ready tonight! Experimentally he stroked himself as he had been encouraged to stroke Dawes.

The half-dream faded; he wondered why he should have thought of either of them at all. His own body resumed more manageable proportions and as he drifted away to sleep he imagined momentary moistness. Two nights later the same images occurred again and the same sequence of events. It happened the next night and the next. By the last week of the Half he had accepted it as a part of his pre-sleep ritual.

On the last Monday morning of the Half, he awoke very early indeed. It was just light. He woke completely, with a sense of panic and foreboding. Somehow, in his sleep, all sorts of pieces had slotted together, as though belonging to a jigsaw. He remembered again, but not with total clarity, the embarrassment of Baker and Ellerman as they had stood outside Big Study after Inspection and understood for the first time the significance of Dermott-Powell's explicit gesture. Above all he heard again Maunder's warning. Try as he would, he could not remember the word, but those who did it would have Maunder 'to deal with'. He remembered Mawsom saying 'that's when you do it to yourself' and that 'it ruined physical fitness'. He, Angus, was doing it every night. Maunder would be sure to know as soon as he looked at him. For about forty minutes he lay actually shivering. He whispered aloud, 'Please God, don't let Maunder notice and I promise I'll never do it again. Never, ever. And I'll always sing the "Amen" in Chapel,' he added to clinch the bargain.

Tosher!

Everyone would know. Especially Maunder. His prayer was already too late. For a further five minutes he lay afraid even to look at himself. Eventually, finding no mark of Cain, the relief was so great that it made him tremble again. He thought, if I go to Tosher immediately, I'll be quite safe. Nobody will see. He got up. It was still very early, but a few Ansell's Men were already about.

He came face to face with Maunder himself, towelling vigorously after an early bath. He was tempted to turn and run, but Maunder said cheerfully in an end-of-Half way, 'Good morning, AC, I see you still need hair restorer before you can ask to cover-up.' Angus knew it was a joke. For two nights afterwards he managed to keep his promise to God without difficulty. He had to renew it the following night and the next. Maunder, it seemed, noticed nothing and when the urge once again overtook him and defeated him, he capitulated with the thought, 'Well the world hasn't come to an end!' and amended his prayer 'to *try* never to do it again'.

By the last night he had begun to relax. He had conquered the habit that Maunder so fiercely condemned; he had kept his bargain with God on five successive nights. He had won the battle! It was very hot, so he had packed his pyjamas in his overnight case and lay on top of the sheets, allowing the cool air from the window to bathe him. He became aware that somebody was standing in his Manger.

'You awake?' Ellerman spoke in a whisper. 'It's all right, Maunder and Tarrant are with The Digger.' (Tarrant's elevation to succeed Maunder as Head of House had not been universally welcomed in Ansell's.) Before Angus fully realised what was happening, Ellerman was on the bed beside him. Ellerman too was naked. 'Come on, AC, after all I am a Tassel, don't forget.'

'It's not Tassel Night.'

'If you'd been Warmer to anyone but Singleton, you'd know that the last night of Half is just another Tassel Night!'

All right then.' Angus was not as disinterested as he might have been a fortnight before and, remembering how he had been tutored to fondle Dawes' circumcised enormity (with which Ellerman's slender hardness contrasted invitingly) he heard him expel his breath in a gasp of satisfaction. Then with a shock of pleasurable surprise he felt Ellerman begin to explore his own thigh.

'I'm not a Tassel, Ellerman!' He knew it to be only a token protest which he willed Ellerman to ignore.

'So what? Who takes much notice of that!'

Angus thought, 'I wonder if Mawsom lied?' but, his own excitement now matching Ellerman's, he whispered, 'All right! I don't suppose it'll be the end of the world!'

Then Ellerman touched Angus' own tumescence. At that instant he understood immediately and completely what Dawes and the others 'saw in it'. His pelvis arched of its own volition, thrusting him stiff, urgent, ever more insistent into the slow rhythm of Ellerman's obviously experienced fingers. He perceived, intuitively, that he was on the verge of an experience of such intoxicating promise that nothing afterwards would ever seem quite the same again. An involuntary shiver of anticipatory delight closed his eyes, as he surrendered himself to sensations that ravished him utterly.

And the world ended.

'Big study Now! Both of you.'

Naked mutual ecstasy revealed Maunder's quiet voice behind the torchlight.

✳

The door with its ribbed and dented handle stood wide open. Maunder had evidently gone for the other Praefaectors. Attempting a nonchalance which his stark nakedness ought to have rendered hilarious in any other context, Ellerman said through chattering teeth, 'Chilly for sum-mm-mer.'

Angus was also trembling violently. His sexual excitement, like Ellerman's had completely vanished. In a voice choked high with sheer terror, he said, 'Dawes and Dermott-Powell were...'

Ellerman turned on him with extraordinary anger. 'Shut up, you pathetic little v-virgin,' he stuttered through still-chattering teeth. Tears were not far away from either of them. Angus wondered miserably what virgins had to worry about. They were safely in the Bible. 'Dawes and Dermott-Powell were doing something else! Everyone in Ansell's knows that. Except you of course,' Ellerman hissed with unsuppressed scorn. 'Dermott was a bloody little tart!' Ellerman literally spat the final word.

Maunder entered. He was by himself. So it was not to be a Praefaectors' after all! Angus found his hands sweating. Maunder closed the door.

'Over The Chair, AC.'

Still trembling violently Angus did as he was told. Was it possible that somehow the atmosphere had changed?

'Tighten that arse, Angus!'

He felt Maunder run the switch encouragingly round the contour of his 'arse'. He knew that they must get a dozen-up. He felt bitterly ashamed but, at the same time he realised with astonishment, his shame had almost nothing to do with being found *in flagrante* as Maunder had found them. No, he was ashamed at having been so craven and terrified on that previous occasion in Big Study, cringing at the memory of the way he had spouted in front of Singleton afterwards.

He braced himself, certain he would not spout. Nevertheless, as a precaution, he bit his lip. The first stroke cut him, momentarily painful, but bearable.

He braced, again.

And again.

And...nothing? In disbelief he heard Maunder say, 'You've got a very presentable little arse, Angus, but you'd better remove it unless you're volunteering for Ellerman's share!'

Only three!

He stood up slowly. Maunder had almost sounded as if he were amused.

'Now let me have *your* arse over The Chair, Ellerman.' Quite definitely something in the atmosphere had changed, imperceptibly, but quite definitely. Ellerman felt it too. He caught Angus' glance and gave a quick raise of the eyebrows – almost a wink? As he arranged himself, he made obvious the fact that he was ensuring his tassel was comfortably below the arm. There was now a very particular element of impertinence in Ellerman's demeanour which Angus could not identify although, fleetingly, he recalled Dermott-Powell. However, the contrast between Ellerman's present undignified situation and his god-like grace and elegance on the football field almost caused Angus to smile.

Maunder quickly, economically, delivered three more cuts on Ellerman's dutifully tight, but undeniably provocative, buttocks, perhaps a little harder than for Angus. Even so they were distinctly casual.

'Get up, Ellerman. I suppose you both realise that if it hadn't been my last night and that I've already handed over to Tarrant, I'd've had the Praefaectors give each of you at least a dozen-up?' Then unexpectedly he laughed and added, lightly, 'I do believe, Ellerman, that you're the only Ansell's Man who can show *side* with his arse!'

Taken by surprise, Angus had difficulty in suppressing a giggle. Maunder looked at them both. He was *grinning*! 'You're a pair of randy little swine!' He lobbed the switch out of the open window and laughed. Angus' jaw literally dropped. It was as if Maunder had taken off the mask that had been a necessity of office until that moment. The two culprits stood side by side with stinging buttocks but singing hearts.

They sensed that, on this occasion, for some arcane reason, the offence did not really count. It was almost as if Maunder were pleased with them. Angus felt that he and Ellerman and Maunder were part of a cosy conspiracy which made them all equals, as if he were at last 'inside' – belonging to some exclusive club from which he had, until then, been excluded. Or had he excluded himself?

'You can tell Tarrant where to find the switch if he asks,' Maunder said, still laughing, and pretended to dust his hands. 'Turn round.' Obediently they did so. 'Ah! Two professionally tanned arses. I see I haven't yet lost the old skill. The marks don't overlap. Remember that, when you're Praefaectors.' Maunder spoke in the matter-of-fact tone of a master-craftsman explaining his mystery.

Ellerman, Angus noticed, was beginning to regain some of his sexual excitement; obscurely, he was aware that Maunder had noticed too. Maunder slapped them both playfully – a joke that was not entirely painless in the circumstances – and walked round in front of them. 'Anyhow, tomorrow morning you'll be able to claim to be the proud possessors of the Last Two Arses Tanned by Eliot Maunder.' So that was what the 'E' stood for!

Then Ellerman overstepped the mark. He held out his hand and, imitating Maunder's own bantering tone, said, 'Oh! Thank very much for the privilege, Maunder!'

He had presumed too much, crossed an undefined line. Maunder's eyes hooded a fraction at the over-familiarity; cosy conspiracy vanished, the mask was back on. He did not let Ellerman's hand go, but held his eye for a moment. Then he moved his gaze coolly, deliberately, down the younger boy's body to stare, with infinite hauteur, at the partial erection. Ellerman dropped eyes and head in humiliation. Maunder released his hand; almost as if with a flicker of distaste, he said, with elegant and disarming politeness, 'Goodnight, Ellerman. And goodbye,' before adding in the same tone of exquisitely gentle courtesy, 'Oh by the way, Ellerman, don't forget that, even in Ansell's, a pretty little games player can easily become a tiresome little tart.'

Ellerman's whole body flamed scarlet. Suddenly, ignominiously, he fled.

Angus, far more timid by nature, took no chances. He said, courteously, 'Thank you, Maunder and goodbye.' For a moment he wondered whether Maunder might say, 'I'm surprised at you, AC,' or something of the sort and experienced a fleeting pang of regret when Maunder did not. The handshake was firm enough. 'Goodnight, Angus.' However, Angus was not to get off scot-free; courteously, 'You prefer telling the truth don't you?'

'I...I...I suppose so, Maunder.' He was puzzled.

'Then I don't imagine that you'll want to join in family bathing for a week or so – unless you want to tell your people why you got your arse tanned on the last night of the Half.' Angus felt himself blushing. Then smiling, 'It isn't really so awful, is it, Angus? Tightening-up, I mean.'

'Not really.' With a rush of confidentiality he said, 'I'm sorry I was such...an ass last time...at the Praefaectors', I mean.'

'Were you?' Maunder's disconcertingly direct gaze discomfited him. 'And now? What are you now, AC?' Again Angus was baffled. Maunder had lost him and he was beginning to feel cold, but Maunder answered his own question. 'A *fallen* angel child perhaps?'

Because he did not know what to do, Angus half laughed and shrugged his shoulders. 'I suppose so, Maunder,' although Maunder's joke reminded him uncomfortably of Singleton's comment on their early-morning walk to the station after the Old Ansell's Match. He was glad to escape.

Ellerman gave no sign of being awake when Angus returned, although there was not time for him to have gone to sleep. He knew that Maunder's final comment had hurt Ellerman more deeply than a dozen cuts. Angus lay face down on his own bed and felt his pulse move slower. It was only minutes since he had lain there with Ellerman. The sheets, he fancied, were still warm. He felt his pulse slowing. He was swept by relief that it was all over – the shattering moment not ten minutes before when Maunder had spoken from the darkness, the Half, the whole of that year. Experimentally he touched himself gingerly; there were no marks despite a tingling sensation.

He pondered that curious moment of intimacy which had embraced all three of them in Big Study, when Maunder had tossed the switch through the window. He thought he understood why Maunder had resented Ellerman's presumption and found his sympathy lay entirely with Maunder.

Above all, he was exalted. Tightening-up no longer terrified him! Tightening-up meant nothing! Nothing at all! It was merely a penalty in a game with curious and complicated rules. Sometimes it mattered and sometimes it was merely a convention, to fulfil the formalities. He felt no fear, no shame, instead he felt almost privileged to have been allowed to participate! The certainty that he had miraculously overcome his craven fear of tightening-up elevated his spirits almost to intoxication.

Nevertheless, he could not entirely push Maunder's final remark from his mind. Despite his buoyancy of spirit, he was uneasily aware that, deep down, he regretted Maunder's words. However hard he tried, he could not disguise from himself the core of his regret; 'fallen angel child' – Maunder had chanced upon Singleton's phrase, giving it a quite different emphasis and, in his heart of hearts, he had to admit Maunder was justified in doing so. Suddenly, vividly, there came to him again the memory of his shameful, childish behaviour in front of Singleton after the Praefaectors' the previous Half, even in the dark it made him wince and close his eyes against the recollection. In an attempt to ward off this uncomfortable embarrassment, he sought for a different track on which to turn his mind.

What exactly was the 'something else' which had precipitated the expulsion of Dawes and Dermott-Powell? He would ask Ellerman. Quick as thought, tumescence returned, hardening to the irresistible sensuousness which, under Ellerman's practised ministration, had taken him far beyond anything engendered by his own naive experimentation. All at once he knew that what he really wanted was Ellerman's exciting nakedness beside him, even if it meant Maunder discovering them again for, at that moment, the addictive pleasure extinguished any flicker of guilt and seemed to be worth any retribution.

Anyway, was not his stinging arse – and how he relished the coarseness on his tongue, as he consciously abandoned his fastidious refusal to use the word even in his imagination – proof enough that he was 'in credit' so to speak? It was, he intuitively perceived, much more than a receipt acknowledging punishment administered for an offence committed. Perhaps it was his perception of Maunder's ambivalence which enabled him to divine with great inner certainty that it was not only the first instalment of his subscription as a fully paid-up Ansell's Man; it was also, he realised with fearful but delightful anticipation, payment on account for pleasures yet to come.

1942-1945

Blood

To what serves mortal beauty | —dangerous; does set dancing blood—

Gerard Manley Hopkins
To What serves Mortal Beauty?

Chapter Six

The rest is predictable enough. Not perhaps the detail, but the general direction. And the end of it all.

Osmosis.

Thirteen years old, on the lowest rung of a fiercely hierarchical adolescent community, cut off from parents for twelve weeks, a world where the king is a child – absorbing the ethos every minute of every hour of every day. How anomalous, that parents who can afford it, send their sons to be expensively educated by the sons of other parents like themselves: teachers, housemasters, headmaster are largely irrelevant.

So it was with us, growing up in that enclosed wartime world where there were few young men amongst the ageing staff. Each Half, Cranchester swallowed us. What happened in the classroom was peripheral; Ansell's educated us.

True, we grew taller, older, more experienced but, on the whole, we became what you would have expected. What you would have predicted. We never changed from the people we were already becoming that first year. Ellerman's sporting brilliance for instance; nobody was surprised that he had his first County trial when he was only sixteen. Admittedly, who would have prophesied in his first year that Angus would be the second of our Election to be Tasselled? Nonetheless, we all, even Angus, became the people we were educating ourselves to be; the people Ansell's was making us. The seeds were sown. What followed was therefore so inevitable that I can now put my pen down.

'*What?*' comes an incredulous voice, '*Do you mean to say that you think you've finished? That this was the reason for your fears? Your guilt? Ridiculous!*

Granted, it is hardly an elevating tale – not the jolly world of Billy Bunter's Greyfriars' chums. However, you tell us nothing new. We've all been through it. Or read about it. Furtive (and not so furtive) grubby experimental sex amongst adolescent boys cooped up together is nothing unusual. Come on! Initiation, hero-worship, 'beating and buggery': in the cold perspective of time, it's not so very shocking. Surely these experiences, deplorable no doubt but not entirely uncommon, at thirteen cannot account for such trauma a lifetime later? There must be something else. What are you hiding? What have you not told us? What really happened?'

'I've told you quite enough,' I hear myself reply. 'That is all you need to know. You've read what happened to us in our first year. If you understood Maunder's revealing gesture that July night at the end of the Half, nothing more than your imagination is required to project forward and to predict how it must surely end.'

And I meant it. I really did not intend to go on. That is where I stopped, believing I could write *finis*, hoping I had said enough, confessed enough, was now free of my albatross, and my burden lightened, if not completely lifted. I wanted absolution. I wanted desperately to be able to believe that I had no responsibility for what followed. I wanted to believe that what happened subsequently had never really happened at all. Or would, at worst, no longer rouse more than shadowy unease like faded memories of a childish nightmare and that my precipitous flight from Porter Starlight that summer afternoon forty years later was a ridiculous over-reaction.

✻

Was it Fate determined me to remain in London over the weekend? On Sunday morning, an autumn sun invitingly warm, I went for a breath of air. Although it had not been my intention, I turned into Camden Market and loitered for an instant by a barrow laden down with scruffy books. Was it pre-ordained, or merely chance that I flipped open one of the few hardback volumes, a book which until that moment I never knew existed? *Their Prime of Life*; privately published at The Wykeham Press in 1956;

author A H Trelawney Ross, Housemaster at Sherborne from 1914 (when a chronic medical condition prevented him volunteering for the front) until 1946. I bought it for 5p.

What pricked me on to confront my self-deception is where he says his main reason for writing the book *is to show future generations what Public Schools, as we know them, stood for* and that *the purpose, basis and origin of the book is a picture of life in a Public School derived from one House...as in a country the family is the most important unit, so at school it is the House where boys live together and learn to develop ideals of service and loyalty.*

Oh yes, we certainly were loyal to the ideals of Ansell's. I find no difficulty at all in believing that, had the Third Reich invaded Britain, Ansell's would obstinately have persisted in its own idiosyncratic philosophy quite unperturbed. It was, however, my surprise and dismay when I found myself undecided as to whether I deplored or secretly admired Trelawney-Ross's breathtaking arrogance, which determined me to continue and perhaps complete my own picture of *life in a Public School derived from one House* and, like Trelawney Ross, *show future generations* the road down which its ideals and loyalty led us. Perhaps, in finally confronting our responsibility for everything that happened, I shall at last be able to exorcise demons which have haunted a lifetime.

No. That will not do. No more evasion. *I* must face up to *my* responsibility, to my part in precipitating the terrible climax and to acknowledge that, although not alone in maintaining such a long silence, I too, cravenly condoned the shameful aftermath by my cowardice in saying nothing at the time.

ii

His new Manger had a window. Rain dropped heavily from a ragged, sullen sky, tearing leaves from the great chestnut tree and scattering them in a sodden mushy brown carpet. The bedraggled column emerged from Passage led by an immaculate Ellerman with an umbrella he made no attempt to share. Angus heard Mawsom say, 'Well at least we're not Junior Election any longer.'

'*At least.*'

'Cheer up!'

'Do you feel very cheery?'

'Not really.' There came a pause. 'I say, AC, did you think about last year? When you were at home?' Angus did not reply and Mawsom went on partly to himself, 'I mean...it didn't seem real. But now we're back here, it's as if the holiday was the unreal bit.'

Angus looked across at him but said nothing.

Autumn Half closed over the memory of the summer holiday, blotting it out as if it had never happened. It had been like that from the moment he stepped through the barrier to the Cranchester train; familiar terror had taken his chest and throat as soon as he had seen the familiar scarves and ties. Now, back in Ansell's, it was as if they had never been away; Summer Half and Autumn Half had become one long continuum. Snider joined them, taller than ever. 'They ought to have waited for the taxis to return to the station,' he nodded to the last of the dripping crocodile below them. 'They look pretty wet!'

Mawsom said, 'If it'd been us, we wouldn't have dared.'

Notting called out in an unexpectedly deep voice, 'They look pretty *wet* in every sense.'

'Didn't we all?'

'Ellerman didn't.'

The newcomers had by this time appeared in the doorway to Big Dorm and they heard Ellerman tell them to look for their Mangers.

'Do you think we should say "Hullo", or something?'

'Did anyone say it to us?'

Angus looked down the gloomy barn of a room. In his old Manger there was a very thin, studious-looking boy with gold-wire glasses, gazing forlornly at the windowless cubicle.

Ellerman came up to them. 'I'm glad it wasn't raining when we got here last year! Do you know Winters couldn't even take the photographs. First time ever.'

Outside, the rain had become torrential.

'I say, AC, you haven't grown very much. The new Election are all taller than you!'

'I expect they are.'

'Anyhow I'm looking forward to not being Junior Election, aren't you?'

Angus nodded.

Snider said, 'I'm glad I'm not their Nanny anyhow.'

'I don't mind. There are advantages – privileges.'

'Such as?'

'I don't have to do any fagging. Except in Big Study. *And* I can go in there and make toast when nobody's there.'

Angus said, 'Ashton kept quiet about that.'

'Oh it didn't happen last year. Maunder abolished it. But Tarrant's brought it back. He said I can use his Study too.'

Snider said, 'You'll still have to tighten-up for him if they make any mistakes in the first ten days.'

'So what? I reckon we'll all be tightening-up pretty often this Half. Tarrant thinks Maunder let things get too slack. He says that our Election's a damn disgrace. I expect he means Dermott-Powell.' Ellerman went back to his charges.

Mawsom said, 'I found this downstairs.' It was a postcard addressed *C. Angus and the Election. Good Luck. ESD-P* On the other side was a poor reproduction of Botticelli's *Venus*.

'He shouldn't have written!'

Angus said, 'Whatever he's done, he was…a kind person.' Mawsom gave him a sideways look which went unnoticed. 'I say, Mawsom, do you know he told me, in our first Half, that he didn't think he'd last?'

'Well, I wouldn't want to be sacked.'

'Nor me!'

'After all,' Mawsom added, 'Cranchester's a damn good school and Ansell's is the best House. That lot from Pettifer's were jealous of us. You could tell.'

He had come across Mawsom by chance whilst trying to find a seat on the Cranchester train and they had been early enough to be able to take their pick, exchanging fragments of conversation as the train filled and, as if by mutual unspoken consent, avoiding attracting any other Ansell's Men to their particular compartment. Eventually, two obvious newcomers to the school had occupied the other corner until they were turfed out by five older Castonians from Pettifer's who wanted to sit together.

After the train got under way a tall boy with fiery hair said to them, 'You're Ansell's Men, aren't you?' Mawsom nodded. 'Why was Dawes sacked?' The others grinned.

One of them said, 'We heard he was caught in bed with that chap who sang in the choir. What exactly were they up to?' in a tone of voice suggesting he very well knew. The others laughed knowingly. In the ensuing silence he went on, 'On Field Day, wasn't it? Night ops?'

'We're not to talk about it!'

The boy with the red hair persisted: 'Is it true that The Digger caught them?'

After further silence one of the others said, in a tone of mild exasperation, 'For God's sake why so tight-arsed about it? Why make such a fuss about keeping quiet?'

Red-hair said, 'You're all such a pious bloody lot in Ansell's, I'm surprised any of you knows where his arse *is*.' There was a great guffaw.

After that they ignored Mawsom and Angus, spending the rest of the journey playing cards, smoking cigarettes wrapped in black paper and discussing the betting possibilities from a list which they found in a pink newspaper.

Angus said, 'Well, we didn't give anything away.'

'Did we know anything to give away?' In a desultory way they began to unpack. Just before Curfew, Ellerman came with a message that Tarrant wanted to see the whole of their Election in Big Study 'about pulling our socks up'. Angus could not calm himself enough to stop his heart pounding.

In a way Ellerman was right. Tarrant said, 'Your Election was a bloody disgrace last year. So, this year, you can damn well make up for it.' He looked at them fiercely. 'Angus, did you get a postcard from that tart Dermott-Powell?'

'Yes, Tarrant!'

'The Housemaster said nobody was to communicate with him.'

'Please, Tarrant, I didn't. We didn't. It just arrived.'

'It was addressed to you.'

Snider said, 'And all our Election. It just said, "Good Luck".'

'Well, I'm not having cards from Dermott-Powell coming to Ansell's. Do you understand?'

They said in chorus, 'No, Tarrant.'

'Next time it will be six-up.'

'Yes, Tarrant.' There was a communal air of relief.

'So this time it'll only be two. You're first. Get over The Chair, Angus. It's three for you as it was your name.'

They took him by surprise it was so unexpected, but it was over so quickly that, almost before they realised, they were standing, squirming, in line again.

'Thank you, Tarrant,' in chorus again.

Outside Ellerman said, 'Didn't hurt much, but I reckon we're all going to have stinging arses this Half. Even you, AC.'

At his Manger, Mawsom whispered, 'You okay, Angus?'

'Yes, thanks.'

'I just remembered the last time you had to tighten-up.'

Angus knew he meant the Praefaectors' beating and reddened in the darkness. Mawsom had not guessed about Maunder finding himself and Ellerman.... He paused before saying, 'Thanks. I was pathetic last year.' Conscious that he did not sound very gracious and, knowing that Mawsom had intended to help, he added, with a burst of his old frankness, 'I don't agree with Ellerman! It *does* hurt!'

He heard Mawsom laugh softly. 'Just a bit. Soon wears off. I bet Tarrant'll've gone easy on Ellerman.'

It certainly had hurt. He could feel three distinct weals; however, he was conscious mainly of an elevation of spirits. His shameful fear of being beaten had not returned as he had dreaded. It had been exorcised on that final night of the previous Half. Although he could not stop his heart from pounding at the thought of Big Study, he now knew for certain what he had first suspected that night; tightening-up was part of a game – a bizarre version of snakes and ladders. Tarrant's punishment was over and done with. The fact that it had been spectacularly undeserved on this occasion did not matter. In fact, somehow it made it seem an unavoidable stroke of fate, like toothache, or the onset of measles, and not a punishment at all. Moreover, he was warmed by the thought that all of them – himself, Ellerman, Mawsom and the rest – had been in the same boat. It was the price of being an Ansell's Man. It occurred to him too that on other occasions he might, perhaps just as arbitrarily, escape a punishment he genuinely deserved.

It was as well for Angus that he had managed to overcome his fear of tightening-up, for Tarrant was a man with a mission. On the twelfth day after their arrival each of the new Election received two-up, to dispel any incipient slackness. A week later, the entire Colts side tightened-up to the Praefaectors' for failing to win against Jonquil's.

Baker said, 'We got a bloody draw. It's not as if we lost!'

Ellerman retorted, 'We should've thrashed them. That's why you lot got thrashed!' As Captain, he had been exempted by Tarrant; this would might been a source of further aggravation, but Ellerman had played with spectacular flair and courage, scoring the equaliser in the last minute of the game. Angus was linesman. He had not been exempt.

They won their next game by forty-nine points to nil. Snider was beaten for missing a tackle and Angus for making a bad line decision. After two stinging blows Tarrant said, 'Was it in our favour or theirs, Angus?'

'Ours please, Tarrant.'

There were two more savage cuts. 'You can get up, Angus. And don't think next time that your incompetence'll go unnoticed because you give unfair decisions in Ansell's favour. We win according to the rules.'

'Yes, Tarrant. Thank you, Tarrant.'

The following night, at Curfew, Tarrant said succinctly, 'Ansell's is going to win everything winnable this Half.' They knew he meant on the football field. 'If you lose you'll each get a dozen-up, even if it takes me all night to thrash you. If anyone ever funks a tackle, it'll be a Praefaectors'.'

Five days later Baker was given four-up for conceding a penalty in front of goal. They had won the game by twenty-three points. Just before lights were turned out, Snider came across to where Angus and Mawsom were commiserating with Baker.

'I like the French Revolution. The reign of terror.'

Ellerman joined them: 'You have to admit it works. Things had got pretty slack under Maunder.'

Angus said, 'I thought you liked Maunder.'

Colouring slightly, Ellerman muttered, 'Perhaps he was too easy-going at the end.'

Snider said, 'Was he? I heard you had to tighten-up to him on the last night of the Half.'

'Who said that?'

'Isn't it true?'

'Nobody tightens up on the last night.'

'Not what I heard,' Snider said unemotionally.

The following afternoon on the way down to the match Ellerman caught Angus up. 'Did you tell Snider about last Half?'

'Of course not!'

'How did Snider know then?'

'I don't know. He might have been awake.'

'I suppose so. You'll not say anything to the others?'

Angus said nothing.

'Good man!' Ellerman squeezed his arm. 'And, for God's sake, do a good job on the line this afternoon. Tarrant says that you don't know your arse from your elbow and that if you bog it you'll get six-up.'

Angus said distinctly, 'He won't know if *I* do bog it, unless *you* tell him.'

Ellerman stopped and looked him in the eye with amused admiration. 'My dear old AC! If it were anyone else, I'd say you were making terms! Well! Well!'

Angus stayed silent.

'Anyhow,' Ellerman went on, 'provided you don't make such a hash that Pettifer's complain, I can assure you that your incompetence will never be mentioned!'

Angus said, 'In that case, nor will what Maunder called you the last night of the Summer Half.'

By midway through the Half, Ansell's were heading the Colts' League and Ellerman had been 'Trialled'. In November he made his debut for the Cranchester XV against a northern school, long regarded as arch-rivals. The match took place alternate years at each school and, because of the two-day journeying, was regarded as a tough blood match. In that company, Ellerman looked diminutive and even fragile, although he had been placed out on the wing, away from the savage rucking of the forwards. Six minutes from the end he scored the deciding try with a carbon copy of the deceptive jinking run which had won Ansell's the House match almost exactly one year before. On his second outing, again in front of a home crowd, he scored a brilliant and versatile hat-trick, came off the field through a tunnel of players in the long-established tradition, to be 'Capped' by the Captain of the XV – a ceremony almost as heady as a coronation, which in a way it was.

At Curfew, Tarrant congratulated Ellerman publicly and added, 'You might all like to know that Ellerman's beaten Maunder's record as the youngest Castonian ever to be Capped for the Fifteen!' Ellerman accepted congratulations with becoming modesty; it was a tribute to his personality that almost nobody grudged him his success.

When Notting said acidly, 'Trust Tarrant to make a fuss of you, Ellerman,' Snider, who took notoriously little interest in sporting success retorted sharply, 'It is a *record*, Notting! Anyhow, you're so jealous of Ellerman that you can't even say "Well done".'

Notting, red in the face, turned away without replying.

Tassel Night came some ten days before the end of the Half. Mawsom said on the way back from Tosher, 'I wonder what the new Election will think by tomorrow morning?'

'They'll get used to it. Like us. Even AC doesn't mind!' That was Notting.

Angus said, 'What happens now we're not Warmers?'

Notting said, 'We have to be asked if a Tassel wants us.'

'Ellerman's a Tassel?'

'Tarrant's asked Ellerman.'

'What's happened to Jeffrey?' Jeffrey was Tarrant's Warmer.

'He's in Nurs'ry.'

'What's wrong?'

Notting said coarsely, 'Too much Tarrant, probably!' Jeffrey's long-lashed good looks and sleepy smile had been the subject of a good deal of comment inside and outside Ansell's.

Snider said, 'He's got mumps or something.'

Notting giggled and said, 'Hope Tarrant's had them.'

Ashton was Tasselled. All the new Election were knocked off their perch under the hail of bread crusts. In Tosher Angus said, 'Well done, Ashton. Bloody marv-ellous.' He used the Ansell's phrase without noticing it.

'Thanks, AC.' Then, after a brief pause added quietly, 'Shall I see you?' It was the accepted phrase.

'If you like, Ashton.'

When the lights were turned off he went to Ashton's Manger and slipped behind the heavy curtain. The sheets were quite chilly and they lay motionless. After a minute or so, Ashton said almost diffidently, 'Come on, Angus.'

Ashton, however, was no Dawes and was not even as stimulated as Angus himself. He shifted closer to Ashton, but it was clear that, unlike Ellerman, Ashton had no intention of reciprocating, because he said meaningfully, 'I heard that you and Ellerman got a dozen-up from Maunder on his last night for being disgusting.'

Angus said nothing.

'Is it true?'

'What do you think?'

'I think you both deserved it. You're not even a Tassel and it wasn't even Tassel Night.'

Ashton's pomposity stung Angus and with a new instinct for retaliation, he said, 'You're not really "ready", are you, Ashton?' He used Dawes' phrase because he guessed Ashton would not like it.

'What do you mean?'

'What I said. You're not "ready"!'

'*You're* not any good! Aunty Singleton's fault I suppose!'

There was a silence. His own erection had quite vanished. He said deliberately, 'Can I go, Ashton?' There came no reply. 'As you're not "ready".'

'If you like!'

As he got out of the bed, Ashton caught his arm, 'You won't tell anyone? Promise?'

'Tell them what?'

'About me...not being ready.'

He could tell from Ashton's voice that he was frightened. 'Why should I, Ashton?'

Fearful of Tarrant's reign of terror and of Maunder's dire warning the year before, Angus had managed almost entirely to repress the habit which had begun to overtake him the previous Summer Half. He had lapsed only once or twice during the holiday, each time renewing his vows to the Almighty.

Eight days previously, Baker had received a Praefaectors'; the card in the corridor read: *For disgusting and immoral behaviour.* He had been caught *in flagrante* by Tarrant. However, the unsatisfactory episode with Ashton now rekindled Angus and the welcome-unwelcome urge returned, all the more fiercely it seemed after his self-imposed abstinence. Back in his own bed, ineffectually repressed memories of the previous Half sprang into his mind with disturbing clarity. Not for the first time he was overtaken by remembrance of the last night, but never so intensely as now. It seduced him utterly.

A delicious helplessness overwhelmed languid compliance as he succumbed to intimations of an ensuing climax, unimaginable because never before experienced, of such intensity that he surrendered unrepentantly. Suddenly, quite without warning, the expected, enjoyable sensations which had become so familiar were swept aside by uncontrollable surges so exquisite that they galvanised his body seemingly of their own volition without restraint until, all at once, gripped by the familiar, choking, panic he felt himself emptying emotionally and, unthinkably and, far more appalling, physically as well.

Eventually the involuntary spasms of his first-ever complete orgasm receded, leaving him exhausted, terrified and revolted by the incontrovertible evidence of his guilt. Tarrant was right! Baker deserved his Praefaectors'! Baker was disgusting! 'It' was disgusting! He was disgusting.

He vowed to God that he would never, ever, let 'it' happen again. By frenzied repetition of his prayer, he strove frantically to blot out his intuitive realisation that, however sincerely he might promise never again to succumb, the truth was that he doubted he would ever have the willpower to resist those exquisite surges. Even as he prayed, he found he was hardening again and now with such urgency that his shaky resolution crumbled immediately. And then, after that, after more prayers, unbelievably, it all happened again.

Early next morning, he awoke, still exhausted, to discover sticky proof that sleep had afforded him no sanctuary. Guiltily, he muttered the now customary prayer only to confirm its inefficacy, discovering, with horrified disbelief that, quickly as his brain formulated them, the very words themselves re-awakened desire so urgently that even getting up quickly did not abate it. Rolling soiled pyjamas in his towel, he slipped along to Tosher, filled the bath full of cold water and made himself lie in it till his teeth chattered. Whether it was an act of contrition or a cleansing he would not have been able to say. Perhaps it was both.

He towelled himself vigorously; yes, there was definitely hair, although not yet enough to cover-up. Then, as a glow of warmth returned to his body, panic choked him once again because he felt, before he saw unmistakably in the long, peeling mirror, tumescence begin to re-assert itself and, with it, an almost irresistible temptation to revisit the bliss of those addictive surges. Something was terribly wrong with him! He must visit Nurs'ry! He must see the School doctor! He was seriously, even terminally, ill!

Desperate to avoid the knowing eye of others – especially Tarrant, who would surely detect his guilt – he ran back to his Manger. Now he understood Baker's daily ordeal: for the first time in his life he was embarrassed by his own nakedness.

Ashton was sitting conspiratorially on Angus' bed. 'Remember! You've given your word!'

'I know!' He spoke sharply, anxious for Ashton to leave.

Then Ashton said, quietly, in a different tone, 'If anything gets out, Tarrant will know about you.'

'What do you mean, Ashton?' He could not sound calm.

'Maunder was right, masturbation's disgusting. And it makes you unfit.'

'Ashton, I ...'

Ashton pointed to the damp bundle. 'I suppose your pyjamas fell in the bath by accident? Or was it a wet dream?' Ashton paused and Angus could not look at him. 'Anyhow, don't worry, AC, I won't say anything.' With elaborate casualness he added, 'About last night. I was just very tired after the match. That was all. Not your fault.'

'I shan't say anything, Ashton. I promise.'

✻

The last days of the Half were clouded by fear. Fear of the consequences, were Ashton's failure somehow to become known, fear of giving in to the newly revealed, exciting but shameful, side of his nature which he could scarcely control and which, when inevitably overmastered into the surrender he secretly invited, he knew he did not really wish to control. Fear of having to confront the shameful truth about his degradation on those occasions, now increasingly rare, when he was fleetingly revisited by flashes of the unflinching integrity, which had, formerly, characterised him in his own eyes and those of the rest of his Election.

Although, ostensibly, others had found his guileless, often inconvenient, transparency risible, he sensed that they also envied him. It was as if their amused affection, encapsulated in their adoption of the nickname AC, also signified an unconscious nostalgic longing for a world which, intuitively, they perceived they could never enter again. 'AC', once so loathed, had become a source of quiet pride to him and, with absolute astonishment, he realised that what he feared most of all was no longer meriting his right to the very *cachet* which had so embarrassed him scarcely a year ago.

Mawsom said, 'I say, AC, are you okay? You've been looking very grim.'

'I'm singing on Sunday. *Solo...*'

'That never worried you before.'

'I don't think I'm good enough any longer. My voice is going.'

'It happens to us all. Even you, AC.'

In the event the solo went all right, despite a slight harshness which had not been there before. He had had to squeeze his throat to get the top notes in a way which was almost painful. As he left Chapel, Craigie, the master with the slight limp, who had spoken to him after his triumphant debut with Dermott-Powell, said kindly, 'Well sung! I expect you'll be with the Altos or Tenors next Half, Angus.'

'Thank you, sir.' He wondered if he really wanted to continue with the choir.

On the last full day, Notting said, 'Have you seen the notice in Corridor?' They were on their way to a late Division. Panic seized him. 'Don't worry, AC. It's not a Praefaectors' for you!' Did Notting know? Had Ashton said something? But it was evident Notting knew nothing because he went on, 'Bartlett's been made a Praefaector!'

Mawsom said, 'Not surprising!'

'Who'll be his Warmer? There's nobody left in the new Election.' He paused for effect. 'I just wonder who it'll be.' It was clear that everyone but Angus knew the answer.

Guilelessly he asked, 'Who?'

Baker said kindly, 'I don't think you're in our world, AC. Who do you think?'

Angus said flatly, 'Me I suppose. I'm Junior.' The words were greeted with a great deal of laughter.

Later in the evening, just after Curfew, Mawsom said, 'Did you really think Bartlett would ask you?'

'Why not?'

'In Ansell's a Warmer from any except the Junior Election has to be paid It's a fiver each Half.'

Angus was impressed. 'Wouldn't mind a fiver!'

'Not a chance. It's bound to be Ellerman.'

'Oh?'

'Don't you notice anything?'

'About Ellerman and Bartlett?'

'Who else!
'I don't seem to notice very much.'
'Never a truer word!'
'Well he's always talking with him, but since Bartlett's Captain of Ansell's XV and Ellerman's Captain of Colts I can see why...'

Mawsom said patiently, 'Never mind, AC, You're probably too good for us all! Anyhow you can take it from me that Bartlett won't require your services.'

In the event it turned out that Mawsom was not entirely accurate.

iii

During Sevens Final in the Lent Half, Ellerman pulled a hamstring muscle scoring the last of his seventy-two personal points in the tournament. He was in Nurs'ry for Tassel Night. As they left the Din Room, Bartlett said, 'Shall I see you, Angus?'

'If you like, Bartlett.' He had been wondering, unenthusiastically whether Ashton would ask him and felt almost flattered that Bartlett saw him as a substitute for the wounded Adonis. Notting nudged him: 'Is our AC a bit of a dark horse?' He grinned knowingly.

Bartlett was an Ellerman who had not quite come out right. He had arrived as a spectacularly good-looking member of his Election with outstanding ability on the games field, although without Ellerman's genius. He had grown into a handsome and personable young man whose magnificent physique and graceful limbs turned heads. However, at the same time his features had broadened and somehow lost the sensitivity and fineness which had distinguished him as a small boy. Instead there was an almost coarse voluptuousness about his nose and mouth.

When he opened the study door, Bartlett was already there, naked and aroused. He said, 'Well for a start you'll not need those pyjamas, Angus.'

It was at once clear that the fact Angus was not a Tassel had been either forgotten or ignored. However, as Bartlett moved his hands over his belly, Angus found that, despite familiar initial excitement and anticipation, he also felt a twinge of fear. It was not like it had been with Ellerman. In a thick, almost unrecognisable voice, Bartlett said, 'You were Dawes' Warmer, weren't you?'

'Yes Bartlett.' Again the twinge of apprehension.

Then he felt Bartlett turn away from him muttering in the same heavy voice, 'We don't want to spoil things yet, do we?' But after a minute or two he again drew Angus fiercely towards him again. Running his hands between Angus' thighs, he said with a quiet intensity, which was almost alarming, 'You've got a nice little arse, Angus, you *have* got a nice little arse. No wonder old Aunty S wanted it to himself!'

He felt Bartlett's hands cup his buttocks and then, with a start, Bartlett's lips against his neck and cheek, kissing. His shoulders against Bartlett's chest, the strong fingers holding him securely at the top of his thighs, slid beneath him, touching, exploring as familiarly as Ellerman had done. He had immediately responded involuntarily to the other's hardness, stiffening instantly to a now familiar tenderness under Bartlett's experienced caress. He could feel his own heart thumping, but whether it was because of this alone, or whether it was due to the mystery which, he inferred, lay ahead, he did not know. Every bit as massively erect as Dawes, Bartlett was worrying apart his legs and buttocks. Trying to *enter* him? Half of him was intent on resolving the almost guessable implications of these unusual, but exciting attentions at the same time, as another part of him urged him to free himself.

Bartlett said throatily, 'You're enjoying this, AC. I bet Aunty Singleton didn't realise you were such a randy little tart! However, let's keep your tight little arse for later and you're not coming all over the place just yet.'

Although he did not understand the unfamiliar term, he sensed Bartlett knew very well that he had brought Angus to the point where, at any moment now, he would no longer be able to restrain the already almost uncontrollable surges and inevitable ejaculation. To his relief, just in time, he was pulled to the position Ansell's convention decreed, facing Bartlett's chest. Angus reached down to stroke him, as Dawes had shown him, but found himself being pushed firmly down the older boy's body until he could feel coarse hair pressing, first his chest, then his lips.

Whether it was Bartlett's pubic wiriness, the awakening of his dormant self-respect, fear of something so dark and menacing, or a combination of all three, some subconscious instinct for salvation invested him with a flash of enlightenment recalled Baker's words *'They didn't get sacked just for tasselling!'*

'You *have* got a pretty little mouth, AC, haven't you?' Bartlett muttered thickly. 'So go on, kiss me. AC. Pretend it's a lollipop.' Bartlett's swollen flesh sought his lips. Instantly revolted, Angus' own arousal shrivelled, as if a switch had been thrown. What was he, Angus, doing? Why was he here?

'I don't feel very well,' he lied desperately. 'I'm very sorry, Bartlett, I think I've eaten too much.' Despite Bartlett's evident unwillingness to release him, he pushed himself away. 'I think I'm going to be sick.'

That broke whatever spell may have remained. After a brief silence, Bartlett, still very obviously aroused, ostentatiously took in Angus' detumescence. Scarcely containing his anger, voice still unattractively thickened by lust, Bartlett whispered savagely, 'God, that's all we need! Aunty Singleton's bloody little Angel Arse puking over everything!' He shoved Angus away with a gesture of petulant disgust as violent as the genuine disgust Angus now felt for himself.

'May I go then, Bartlett?' There was no reply. 'To…to Tosher?'

'Don't bother to come back!'

In the dark, clutching his pyjamas to him, he slipped through the study door, heart pounding as if it would burst. He was unable to rationalise, or dissect, the precise nature of his fear. It had been instinctive. After all, in the end nothing much had actually *happened*. Nothing at all. He did not even really understand very clearly what it was he had thought was going to happen. Or was he afraid even to dare to imagine what the outcome might have been?

However, he understood only too well how his own hectic sensuality, which had been indulging so often these days, had very nearly betrayed him into a way so dark that, instinct told him, there might have been no turning back.

He shivered, but not from cold. He had narrowly escaped from he knew not exactly what, but something which, he sensed, was too degrading to contemplate. Had he been on the verge of induction into those evasively unspecified practices with which Dawes was deemed to have depraved Dermott-Powell?

His pulse was no longer racing. The mere thought of arousal disgusted him. Silently, he prayed that he had banished his treacherous sensuality once and for all. Silently, in Tosher, he bathed his face, scrubbing his lips with the strong soap he found there and put on his pyjamas. Passing very quietly towards his Manger he heard Mawsom's whisper.

'Have you been with Bartlett?'

'Yes.'

'Better not let Ellerman know!'

He lay awake for a long time. 'I'll have nothing more to do with Tassel Night!' Even as he said it he suspected he was deluding himself for, now his terror and revulsion had abated, a treacherous worm of curiosity deep inside regretted he had not stayed to discover what Bartlett had intended. However, it was only a spark of lust, quenched almost at once by the unnerving overall relief that flooded through him.

Some quirk of memory projected into his mind a gloomy engraving in his grandfather's house that had terrified him as a small child. A small, fair, long-haired, ringletted boy, dressed cavalier fashion, stood fearfully in the sunlight at the edge of a dark forest; the gnarled trunks seemed to suggest writhing demonic animals. Deep within in the black depths beyond he, like the boy, knew there lurked some formless, evil. There was no title except what was obviously a quotation: '*Within the navel of this hideous wood*'. He had never forgotten the words because he had been puzzled by the absence of anything to do with ships.

Ellerman came out of Nurs'ry and was back in Ansell's for Curfew on the Sunday. On the Monday afternoon he came up to Angus before the OTC parade and said with a rather elaborate casualness, 'Did you see Bartlett on Tassel Night?'

'Yes.' He wondered what Bartlett had said.

Ellerman probed with a curious carefulness, 'I don't expect he remembered you weren't a Tassel.' Angus kept silent and Ellerman continued in a spiteful tone reminiscent of Notting, 'Well, I hope you both enjoyed it.'

It provoked Angus into a more vigorous response than he intended. 'I didn't enjoy it at all. I don't think *I* was what he expected.'

Without moving his eyes from Angus' face, Ellerman said 'What do you mean by that?'

Angus recognised his mistake. 'I don't mean that he would've expected it from you, Ellerman.' He blundered on, 'I didn't feel very well. I was jolly glad to go.'

'Oh?'

'He wanted...wanted me to sort of...do...things.... To kiss...'

Ellerman interrupted quickly in a curiously edged voice, 'Oh *did* he!' and walked off very quickly.

Angus drew breath. He still would not have been able to explain to Ellerman exactly what he had meant by the indefinable 'things'.

Two days later he was alone in Libe when Bartlett came in.

'Angus, would you get my Virgil for me from Big Study?' Angus cursed beneath his breath but remembering his previous protest and its consequence he went immediately. The book was not in evidence. As he turned towards the door Bartlett himself entered.

'I want to talk to you, Angus.' Bartlett looked white with anger.

Angus was very frightened: 'Talk to me, Bartlett?'

'What the hell have you been telling Ellerman?'

'Ellerman?' His heart was thumping and he could feel his heart pounding.

'Yes, ELLERMAN – Your own Election! What have you said?'

'Said?'

Bartlett grabbed his jacket and spat with furious pent-up energy. 'Yes. *Said*. Don't keep repeating what I say. What did you *tell* him? About Tassel Night?' He shook Angus.

Still trembling, although Bartlett had released him. Angus stuttered 'I...I said that...' He drew a deep, trembling breath, 'I didn't want...to...kiss...and...'

'What else did you say?'

'Nothing else, Bartlett.' Bartlett's obvious fury made his own voice unsteady as he waited for Bartlett to tell him to tighten-up. He could feel tears of terror forming at the back of his eyes.

'You don't think that me kissing you meant anything, do you, you farting little prig?' The scorn in Bartlett's voice was electric.

'N-n-no, Bartlett.' He could not work out the implication of Bartlett's rhetorical question.

'You-are-a-farting-pissing-little-prig.' Bartlett dropped each word distinctly.

He said nothing.

'What are you, Angus?'

'A farting pissing little prig, Bartlett.' He would have said, or done, anything to bring the interview to an end.

'For Christ's sake, why can't you keep your mouth shut?'

'I'm sorry, Bartlett.'

'You were Dawes' Warmer?'

Angus nodded miserably.

'You remember what happened to him and to Dermott-Powell?'

He nodded again.

'Do you want the same thing to happen to you?'

'No, Bartlett.' He no longer understood anything.

'Well if you go on broadcasting rumours, you *will* be.'

What had Ellerman said?

'Now just you listen, Angel Arse. If you say *anything* more about this, *anything at all*, I shall—' dropping his voice '—I shall kill you.' Bartlett looked as if he meant it.

'I won't, Bartlett, I promise. I don't know what Ellerman told you...'

'I don't know what you told him. But it meant *nothing*.'

'No, Bartlett.'

'I got pissed on cider.'

'Yes, Bartlett.'

'Do you know what you're going to do now?' Bartlett turned towards the table.

So he was to tighten-up after all. Here and now? 'Shall I get across The Chair, Bartlett?'

'Swear on this.' Bartlett held out the great battered Bible.

'But Bartlett...'

'If you don't, I'll make sure you tighten-up every day for the rest of this Half. And next.'

'I promise, Bartlett.'

'Kiss *that*, Angel arse. Go on kiss it!'

Remembering with a shiver Bartlett's previous order to kiss, he did as he was told.

'May I go now, Bartlett?'

'Yes. But remember...'

'Yes, Bartlett! I will, Bartlett.'

'And tell *nobody* about this interview. Ever.'

'Of course not, Bartlett.'

'Go on. Say it. With your lips on the Bible.'

So there was to be no tightening-up. Just kissing the Bible. The relief was enormous. He did as he was told and scurried out.

Back in Libe, Ellerman was waiting by his Cell 'Seen Bartlett? It's all right, he told me he was seeing you.'

'What did you say, Ellerman? Why did you have to say anything?'

Ellerman smiled but did not answer.

'Has he made *you* swear on the Bible too?'

'So that's what he did? Should be safe enough with you, AC.'

'Didn't you have to swear too?'

'Dear old AC, you've been in Ansell's almost five Halfs and you still continue to amaze us. Of course he didn't make me. Why should I tell anyone?'

'You might.'

'Not now,' Ellerman said, patting Angus' shoulder paternally. 'Not now Bartlett's apologised to me.'

On the last evening of the Half, pushing his way through Junior Election in Corridor, Angus saw a small card on the Housemaster's notice-board:

J.G. St J. Bartlett will succeed A.A.D. Tarrant
as Head of Ansell's in the Summer Half

iv

Ellerman always seemed first with news. They were unpacking when he hurried into Big Dorm. 'Have you heard? "Grandpa" died suddenly in the holiday.'

Baker said, 'Not surprised, he always looked about a hundred.' 'Grandpa' Ebsworth was an elderly bachelor recalled by the wartime staff shortage from a comfortable and well-earned retirement. An experienced, undemanding teacher who had no trouble with discipline, he rarely needed to raise his voice.

Baker said, 'I wonder who'll be our new Div Pro?' By a curious and antiquated system their whole Election was still shared a Division, although Baker, Ellerman and Angus were obviously considerably brighter than the rest.

'I know that too! Bartlett told me.'

As new Head of House, Bartlett had taken over Tarrant's Warmer, Jeffrey, the quiet self-contained boy with a shy, almost sleepy smile, whose niceness, efficiency conferred a sort of dignity which had, to some extent, curbed even Tarrant's passion for getting him to tighten-up on the slightest pretext. However, this had not diminished Ellerman's almost patronising interest in the older boy. 'It's a new Beak. He's called Ellins who's been invalided out of the army, like Craigie. He was in the Guards.'

Mawsom, with his customary neat efficiency, had pulled out the slim book which, despite paper-rationing, was still produced anew each Half and gave names and addresses of everyone teaching or being taught at Cranchester. 'S S Ellins, BA, MM – that's the Military Medal, isn't it?'

Notting said, 'Cranchester must be hard up. It means he wasn't even an officer – otherwise it'd've been the MC.'

This, coupled with the fact that Ellins was far from confident, was unfortunate. He was nervy, almost twitchy and had the flaw, fatal in a young schoolmaster, of letting things get out-of-hand then, suddenly, reacting ferociously. Almost always he selected as a culprit one of those in the Division who had been least to blame. It was a curiosity of the Cranchester system that those teaching did not beat their pupils – only the High Master, the Senior Master or a Housemaster could do that. By the end of his first fortnight half a dozen of his Division had been unjustly beaten by their Housemasters, including Mawsom.

None of the Division knew that he had then been taken aside and told that his approach 'would not do' for Cranchester and that it would be better for him to resolve his own disciplinary matters rather than invoke the sanctions of Housemasters so frequently. Although after that things apparently settled down to an uneasy truce, it became a competition to discover how he could be teased and bated to a point where he became almost incoherent with fury, without ever giving him cause enough to hand out serious punishment.

In fact he was a promising and enthusiastic teacher and, with sounder advice, he would have enjoyed what he was doing. As it was, Atkinson, a loutish boy from Tortellier's, took it upon himself to devise original ways of tormenting Ellins. The most ingenious stemmed from the fact that, on the first day, Ellins made a plan of the room and, where each of them sat, he wrote the appropriate name. After about a week Atkinson suggested they should all change places, but answer to the name of the boy who was in that seat according to the plan.

I bet he can't remember faces,' he argued. Atkinson was tall, rather bigger and considerably older than the rest affecting, with those who taught him, a disarmingly amiable manner. Without being academically stupid, he was either slow, or uninterested, or both. He had been in the Division longer than anyone else and had, somehow, acquired the sort or 'seniority' which can only happen in a school. Although the majority of the Division were on the whole keen to learn, they accepted Atkinson's ploy without demur.

After a few more days they moved round again and then they repeated the tease. It was a month before Ellins became suspicious. Thus it was established that nobody took him seriously.

He said, one morning, 'It seems to me that you are not sitting in the correct place, Atkinson. Nor you, Tredgold, nor you, Angus.' Sheepishly they moved back to their 'planned' seats.

Atkinson had not finished. As they waited for Ellins the following day, he said, 'Browning, you can fake anyone's writing, can't you?'

'Pretty well, Atkinson.' Browning was small, clever and pleasantly impish.

'Bet you can't manage Ellins!'

'It's easy.' At the corner of his exercise book he wrote: '*Extremely well written, Browning.*' Even the phrasing – using Browning's name was typical of Ellins' marking.

'Why not do another plan, Browning...? We'll sit where he puts us and we'll just change some of the names on his plan.'

It led to several days of further confusion, but the tide of opinion had begun to turn. As they ambled back to Ansell's for lunch Mawsom said to Angus, 'I wish Atkinson'd lay off. Ellins can be jolly interesting.'

Snider said. 'It's not just Atkinson. We all do it. Even AC rags him.'

Angus felt ashamed. Snider was right. So was Mawsom. As though to make up for his lack of co-operation he said, 'Do you think he's right? I mean about the most important invention of the nineteenth century?'

'Like Atkinson, I felt that it was a bloody stupid suggestion when he first made it. Then he explained ...and I thought he might be right.'

Snider said, 'I expect it's the first time sewage pipes have ever featured in a history teaching at Cranchester.'

In the face of initially ribald and hostile disagreement, Ellins had maintained that the invention of the earthenware drainpipe had contributed more to the immediate health and happiness of millions than any other nineteenth-century invention of its time. Patiently and logically he had fielded the incredulous 'What about's ...' from Atkinson and others until he had reduced the opposition to silence.

Baker said, 'I still think electricity was more important. Though Ellins was jolly convincing.'

※

Angus wanted to find a time when he could talk alone with Mawsom; somehow they had drifted apart. There was no longer the easy intimacy of the previous year and he sensed a sort of wariness on Mawsom's part – and on his own. They met quite by accident at Roman Gate on the turn of Marathon. Mawsom had his shoe off. 'Blister,' he said economically.

Angus said, 'I'll walk back with you if you like. I only came out to get out.'

Marathon was not much used in the Summer Half. They walked on the old Roman road, larks rose from the sheep-cropped downland turf each side of them.

Angus took a deep breath: 'Can I ask you something?'

Mawsom looked at him warily. 'I you like. I can't promise an answer.'

'Do you masturbate?' Having said it, the rest was easier. He went on quickly, sensing that Mawsom would not want to answer. 'What I mean is – I do. I can't seem to help it. I know what everyone says. I keep promising I won't, but then...well I do. I'm sure that something's wrong with me.'

Mawsom wouldn't look at him. After a while, his eyes fixed ahead, he said, 'You don't change much, AC. You asked about tasselling with a cricket match in earshot! Now...'

'There isn't anyone here.'

'I mean that only you, AC, would ask about it at all.' He paused: 'It's probably this place Cranchester...Ansell's.'

'*Do* you, Mawsom?' He heard Mawsom draw a deep breath. After a pause, he continued, 'Some days I can't seem to stop. One Saturday it...I...' he dropped into a whisper '...five times!' And, almost hopefully, 'Is it ever like that with you, Mawsom?'

'Sometimes.' Then quickly, gruffly, 'Pretty often actually.'

'What about everyone else? We could ask Brinton.' Brinton was one of the Chaplains.

'Do you want your arse tanned black and blue? You know what would happen if anyone else knew. It's something we'll get over I expect. Like measles.' Mawsom did not sound optimistic.

'Hope you're right.' Angus paused. 'Worst of all, it's...well...' he was now muttering, ashamed. Then plucking up courage, '...it's nice...enjoyable when...' He could not continue. 'But I've really been making an effort. Lots of runs and baths and things. All last week...not once.'

'There you are, AC, you'll get over it long before the rest of us.'

'Now it's something worse, Mawsom.'

'Worse?'

'Like this morning...when I woke. It must've happened again whilst I was asleep. I didn't know anything about it. Mawsom, I really do think

I've got something seriously wrong with me, some sort of sex madness.' He stopped walking because, once again, the familiar rising panic tightened his chest to breathlessness.

With immense relief in his voice, Mawsom said suddenly, 'I don't think so...I mean I'm the same. I've never told anyone till now. We mustn't. I know what you mean about five or six times in a day and about not doing it for days and then when you're asleep it makes a disgusting mess. Do you know what I do, AC? I only wear pyjama top and sleep on a towel now, just in case. So's I can sort of accidentally drop it in Tosher in the morning.'

Angus said, 'You don't think it is...you know, that disease...called...VD?'

Mawsom offered no reassurance and they walked on in the same apprehension and guilt although, somehow, each of them found comfort in the fact that at least he knew he was not entirely alone in his dilemma.

※

Towards the end of May, Angus played for the House XI. It happened by accident. Early on in the Half he had been gratified to discover that his limited cricketing ability had somehow matured. It was if, suddenly, the years of daily practice in the bumpy net at home with his father and the manic sessions with his grandfather (whose enthusiasm for the game in his northern fastness was regarded as eccentricity by his neighbours) seemed to have come to fruition. To his delight he found that he could now do what he had never quite been able to manage before. He could pitch a ball with remarkable accuracy. His slow left-handers were not particularly difficult, but they were very well pitched; in the nets batsmen got themselves out to him.

He had begun to find unexpected satisfaction in simply going by himself to a net behind Ansell's when it was not otherwise in use and bowling at a single stump. He used an old playing card to mark where he wanted to pitch the ball and moved it each time he hit it. It was a measure of his modesty that it did not occur to him he should put himself forward for any trials.

One day, about a week after his conversation with Mawsom, he was amusing himself by trying to pitch the ball on a florin. When he turned from gathering the half-dozen scuffed cricket balls at the wicket, he noticed Harrington watching. Harrington was Captain of the Ansell's side, which was not, for Ansell's, very strong. He said, 'How often do you hit the coin, AC?'

'I haven't hit it yet, Harrington!'

'Perhaps you ought to use something bigger to aim at.'

'I usually use this.' He drew out a grubby playing card.

'How often do you hit that?'

'Almost every time, Harrington.'

Harrington was sceptical. The first ball missed. The second hit it. Angus moved the card and clipped it with the next two. He moved it and, just missing it with the first two, landed satisfactorily in the centre with the third. Harrington was impressed. 'Can you spin it?'

'Not really enough! People think I'm going to because I'm left-handed,' Angus said with a laugh. 'Couldn't fool anyone really good – like Maunder, or Singleton. Or Ellerman.'

'It'll be worth some wickets. Do you bat?'

Angus shook his head. 'I can stay in a bit, but it's mainly luck.'

'What's your fielding like?'

Angus said without affectation, 'I think that's my best thing. My grandfather said you'd always get a game if you were a good fielder.'

The following Tuesday, Harrington asked him to stand in during the House fielding practice. It went well, he took several difficult catches. Although he had hoped against hope, to his disappointment he was not selected for the following day. As usual he was scorer.

It was a convention in Ansell's that the scorer, like the players, should wear white and thus it came about that late in the afternoon, with about an hour to go, Ansell's were in the field when Bartlett, running to stop a boundary, turned his ankle. Twelfth Man had absented himself briefly from the immediate vicinity. When Bartlett came off he said, 'Harrington says you're to go out as you're on the spot. I'll finish scoring until Twelfth Man comes out to relieve you.'

'What about gully, AC?' Seeing Angus hesitate, Harrington said, 'Over there.' Fielding for his grandfather had not included the subtleties of field placings. He was not in the least nervous; it was like singing in the choir. He knew that he had a good eye and quick reactions.

As they crossed over, Ellerman said, 'This is a great day, AC.' It was not meant unkindly.

Nothing happened during that over. There came a change of bowling. Time was running out. The ball was given to a tall boy with flopping hair called Arthur. He fluctuated between the Cranchester First XI and Second. He was fast but erratic. The first ball went wide to leg. The second, on the off, was cut very late by Gower, Captain of the Cranchester XI, who moved a couple of paces up the wicket and turned to watch the ball reach the boundary. Angus stopped it. Neatly, without any fuss and very quickly he scooped it in his hands and returned it with unnerving accuracy to the wicket keeper. Although Gower was safely in his crease, the fielding was rewarded by some desultory clapping. Much the same thing happened on the last ball of the over, except that it was bouncing and Gower, taking no chances made the first run and turned to find that, once again, Angus had returned the ball speedily and with deadly accuracy.

Nothing could stop the match from being a draw and there were four overs left. Arthur continued to bowl, Gower continued to try to find the gully boundary when the right ball came, which it did two or three times an over. Angus managed to cut it off, each time. The last couple of overs were, to the amusement of all present, a sort of duel between Angus who looked almost diminutive in the distance and the tall, elegant Gower at the wicket.

Arthur sprinted up and hurled the last ball of the match in a final wild effort. It was a little short, but Gower cut it away, confident it was well out of Angus' reach. However, as Arthur had begun his run some instinct prompted Angus to move very deep; his heel was almost on the white boundary line. Calmly he took half a pace forward and without ostentation held the ball securely in both hands above his head. Gower, as amused as anyone else, joined the applause, clapping one hand against his bat and waiting for Angus to come up so that they could walk in together.

He said, with a hand on Angus' shoulder, 'That was bloody mar-vellous fielding! Gully's a stinking position.' To Harrington he added, 'Where'd you find him? New frog?'

'Oh no! AC just hides his light under a bushel. Last year we thought he was so wet he'd probably float away.'

'If he does, float him over to us in the Orangery. We'd've thrashed you if we'd had a few fielders like him.'

At supper Ellerman said, 'I never knew you could field like that.'

Suppressing his euphoria, Angus said, 'Actually neither did I. It's the first time I've actually fielded in a match.'

Turning to Mawsom, Ellerman said dramatically, 'Is AC pulling my leg?'

Mawsom said, with a mock-solemn shake of the head, 'I shouldn't think so. AC doesn't go in for jokes.'

※

On the first of June, Atkinson played into Ellins' hands. It was Friday. The weather outside was warm, almost hot, and the last Division of the day. Ellins said, 'You don't look as though you're going to work very hard. We'll have a general session. You can ask any question you like.'

'Does it have to be History?'

'Not necessarily, Atkinson. Though I may not know the answer.'

'May I ask a question then, sir?'

Ellins took off glasses and polished them. Giving Atkinson a shrewd glance and said without irony, 'I'd be glad for you to do so.'

With deceptive mildness Atkinson said, 'Please, sir, could you tell me the meaning of something I've read.' As if they sensed Atkinson was leading Ellins on, tension gripped them all.

'I'll certainly try.'

'It's a word, sir. It's not in the dictionary, sir.'

'Go ahead!'

'Mastibation, sir.'

They had not expected such daring. There was absolute quietness. Not a paper rustled. The proverbial pin dropping would have sounded like thunder. An inquisitive bee coming in through the open window sounded loud as an enemy bomber. Atkinson himself realised that he had gone too far; his cockiness oozed from him. No eye was on Ellins, each of them looked ahead. They expected an explosion, or an embarrassed avoidance. Ellins polished his thick glasses again and replaced them. 'Write the word on the board please Atkinson.' The words hung in the stillness.

'Sir?'

'I said, write it up on the board.' Again very quietly but distinctly.

Atkinson looked round, but there was no glance or smirk of support. Slowly, reluctantly, he moved to the hoard and picked up the chalk.

'WRITE IT UP, Atkinson.' Never loud but unmistakably authoritative. Suffused with embarrassment, Atkinson did so. The chalk broke more than once.

'It does not surprise me that you could not find the word in a dictionary, Atkinson. If you erase the first "i" and replace it with "u" you'll be more successful.' Ellins' tone was silky. Atkinson's legendary deficiency at spelling encouraged a giggle which momentarily eased the tension. Atkinson began to move back to his seat. 'No. Stay there, Atkinson. We may need the benefit of your hand again.'

Ellins looked deliberately round the entire Division. It took a long time. Nobody held his eye. He turned back to Atkinson, took the heavy dictionary from his desk, and opened it. *Masturbation* Atkinson, signifies stimulation, specifically *self-stimulation, of the sexual organ*. He closed the dictionary. Since we are all male here – do you know what I mean by *male*, Atkinson? Good. I shall confine my remarks to masturbation as it concerns males, although females can also practise it. I trust you know the difference between male and female, Atkinson? Good. That's a start.'

It seemed as though nobody breathed.

'Since the rest of the division has such a deep interest in the desks, which are singularly uninspiring, Baker, perhaps you will come up to the board and ensure that the others are in no danger of misunderstanding what I am about to say by drawing the male sexual organ. As scarlet as Atkinson, Baker sheepishly stood in front of the board and drew on it.

'Larger Baker, much larger. Do make sure that everyone can see it. Perhaps I ought to ask Snider to help you. I gather you're good at Biology, Snider. Or Congleton? Thank you, Baker, I glad you're so artistic and well informed, unlike poor Atkinson here. Atkinson, do you know what that is?'

'Yes, sir.'

'Tell us.'

Atkinson stood speechless.

With exaggerated, quiet politeness, Ellins said, 'Since you recognise it, please be so good as to tell us all what you call yours, Atkinson.'

Head down, Atkinson whispered, 'My prick, sir!'

The tension forced a brief, slightly hysterical laugh. 'Thank you, Atkinson. What you call a "prick" (in the best Shakespearian tradition I may add) Atkinson, biologists call "penis". Have you ever heard that word?'

'Yes, sir,' almost a whisper.

'Good. Write it up.'

The chalk squeaked in the silence.

'No, Atkinson. This time it's an "i" not a "u". You really must get these terms right otherwise you'll never he able to look anything up in the dictionary. Masturbation with a U and penis with an I. Repeat that after me.'

'Masturbation with a U and penis with an I, sir.' This time the laugh was more prolonged.

'Well done, Atkinson! The rest of the Division seem to appreciate your progress. Now Atkinson, the male sperm is secreted from the testicles through the penis. That's what happens. It's called "ejaculation".'

Atkinson said nothing at all.

'When you are sexually roused, Atkinson, blood causes the penis to swell so that it will "tumesce" and become "erect". Tell us the Cranchester term for that, Atkinson.' There was a pause. Ellins said sharply, 'Atkinson?'

'Horny, sir.' He did not lift his head.

'Is that correct, Notting? Notting? Ah. I see you nod. Now tell us what the correct expression is?'

'Erect, sir.'

'Thank you. What was the other word I used? Angus?'

'T...tumesce, sir?'

'Very good. Full marks. Now listen carefully, Atkinson. After the onset of puberty, if the adolescent becomes sexually stimulated so that his penis is fully erect, or tumescent, he often finds it very difficult to resist fondling it (or even persuading someone else to do so, Atkinson) until he ejaculates.

Of course the biological reason for all this experimentation, it is sometimes suggested, is that later in life he will use his sexual organs so that he and a female partner may consummate their marriage and propagate the species. Procreation, Atkinson, is specifically given as a reason for marriage in the church service.' With quiet deliberation Ellins put down the chalk. 'You may well find, Atkinson, that in adolescence, reference to the sexual act tends to cause giggling and similar behaviour. Indeed mere reference to it can cause the penis to become erect, so that sometimes it may even be an embarrassment for somebody of your age to stand up.' He paused, 'Or even to turn round from the blackboard, Atkinson?'

They could see Atkinson's neck suffuse with blushing. Ellins said gently, 'Don't worry. Everyone here understands. Now, before you go and sit down, Atkinson, since you did not know what the word *masturbate* meant, please tell us what word you did use. Others may have similar ignorance.'

Atkinson said mulishly, still turned to the blackboard, 'I don't understand, sir.'

'Oh dear? How old are you, Atkinson?'

'Nearly sixteen, sir.'

'Yes, the oldest in the form. What I mean is this, Atkinson, if at your age and physical maturity you have never in your life masturbated, then you fall into a very rare category. Probably about two per cent of the population.'

There was absolute silence and then Ellins added, still very quietly, 'So please tell us what your phrase is for this activity.'

No reply.

'Am I to understand, Atkinson, that you've never done what I've described?' There was a long pause. 'Well then, Atkinson, what about telling me the term you may have heard others use at Cranchester?'

Clenching his hands, his eyes fixed on his shoes, Atkinson said thickly, 'Wanking...sir.'

'Ah! Not unique to Cranchester. Thank you, Atkinson. If I explain, in your terms, that it is not unusual, at your age, that when you feel "horny" you "wank" and that's what's called "masturbation", do you now understand what the word means?'

'Yes, sir.'

'Well done, Atkinson, now you may resume your seat. You too, Baker.'

The ensuing silence went on and on until at last Ellins broke it: 'Now listen, all of you. I'm not putting up with this nonsense any longer. I know very well why Atkinson asked the question. But he only did it because he had you for an audience and you thought he had me for a victim. I have little doubt that, like him, each one of you knew pretty well what the word meant and if there is one of you sitting here who really was totally ignorant of what I was talking about, then I apologise.' He waited: 'Right, I take it from the general silence that you're not a unique collection of biological specimens, but a perfectly normal set of grubby-minded youths who tried to roast me. Instead I've called your bluff. As a penalty, I shall expect a good deal more work from you than you've let me have up till now. Mind you, if anyone tries anything like this again, I'll make sure his Housemaster "tans his arse" (That, incidentally, is the charmingly explicit Cranchester expression, I gather?) so thoroughly that he'll not be able to sit down in this, or any other Div Room for a week.' They knew Ellins was not angry. Tension had eased almost tangibly.

Ellins banged his hands together to remove the chalk dust and, leaning over his desk, said in a friendly tone, 'As a matter of fact I don't know that I've explained things very well, I'm not really much of a scientist. However, since we've broached this whole subject, and I am your Div Pro (who is, I am told, responsible for your training in Divinity and Moral Precepts, according to my brief from the Headmaster) perhaps I ought to offer some advice which may help some of you.

'Quite a lot of you will have found that you have nocturnal emissions From time to time. Probably you'd call them "wet dreams". Some people find this very frightening, especially the first time it happens. They've no need. It's quite usual. It used to trouble celibate mediaeval monks who believed they had been visited and seduced by devils in their sleep. That's nonsense, of course. It's part of growing up and often it's worst for those who, for religious or other reasons, deliberately try to avoid masturbation at all costs. Anyway, the best advice I can give you about your sexuality is to suggest that each of you should come to terms with it and come to terms with yourself. Above all, don't believe the Victorian horror stories. There's no need to go around as if carrying a guilty secret. You're not unique. Nor are you going mad. It's the same for everyone. I was damned miserable when I was your age because nobody ever explained what was happening to me and I thought I was headlong for hellfire.'

He added gently, 'I wouldn't wish that on anyone, even you, Atkinson, and you've been a real thorn in the flesh.'

Atkinson looked at him darkly, unsmiling, his influence over them melting away as Ellins talked. He now held them all in the palm of his hand, their relief at his explanation earned their total respect; at last somebody had talked about 'it' openly, in their language. It was as if a refreshing wind had blown through the room.

'One thing more before you go. You'd be quite wrong to go away thinking I was encouraging you – I'm certainly not – and I'd probably get the sack if anyone got impression I was! I've just tried to give you the main facts to relieve your minds and take away some of the darkness which worried me. I'm not making your own personal decisions for you. I am neither condemning or approving. You must do that for yourselves.

'A final point, there may be some of you who'd welcome some advice on one particular topic but dare not ask. It's this. In a place like Cranchester, there's likely to be a good deal of sexual involvement with somebody else.' Once again nobody in the room wanted to breathe. Ellins continued, 'Mutual masturbation is not unusual, nor even, necessarily, psychologically damaging according to some recent medical opinion. In fact, a good many doctors reckon it must be expected in closed societies. However, anyone who gets caught at Cranchester and similar schools will discover that authority will be rigorous in punishing and totally unsympathetic. Perhaps it's because we're all frightened. Perhaps Authority is right. Nonetheless, any sexual liaison, especially between an older and a younger boy, however scientifically explicable, will almost certainly result in expulsion of the older boy and probably of the younger as well.' Ellins paused: 'So if anyone you know is worried because he is caught up in something he can't handle, then he may find it helps to talk it over in confidence. I suggest the Chaplain. Your Housemaster perhaps? Even me if you wish,' he added as an afterthought.

He looked at his watch. 'A few minutes early. Probably the only lesson you'll ever remember! Please read the section about Disraeli and the Suez Canal question before you turn up next time. All right, you may go.'

He swept out to a spontaneous chorus of 'Thank you, sir.'

Baker's diagram was still on the blackboard although no longer the focus of any reaction – no snigger, nudging, nor even embarrassed aversion of eyes. Somebody took a board-rubber and, without fuss, erased the drawing as he passed. Some sort or demon had been cast out of each of them.

Because they were early, they walked back to Ansell's slowly in one loose group. Notting, although not by nature particularly perceptive, said, 'It's just like the sun coming out. Remember what Maunder said? And Tarrant? Typical of Atkinson to use that oik word.'

Ellerman said, 'Well, *we* wouldn't know about *that,* Notting!' and as Notting coloured up, 'Even if Ellins is right and it's all quite natural, it still makes you unfit.'

Snider said, 'I don't think Ansell's will agree with Ellins!'

'It helps to know everyone's like we are,' Mawsom contributed.

'Except AC.' Notting, having been snubbed by Ellerman, could not resist the dig.

'I think it was bloody *mar-vellous,*' Snider said, so unexpectedly using the phrase, that everyone laughed. '*No*. I mean it. Who'd've thought a Cranchester Div Pro would speak out like that!'

'Atkinson didn't like it!'

Mawsom said, 'Atkinson got what he deserved.' There was general agreement. He dropped back to join Angus. 'Ellins answered all the questions I couldn't answer up on Marathon, didn't he?'

'And some I didn't ask! You know, Mawsom, at the end, if he hadn't told us about nocturnal…'

'Emissions…yes?'

'I think I might actually have asked him.'

'Thank God you didn't, Angus, it'd've been all round Cranchester. Even The Digger would've heard! You know sometimes I think you're not safe to be out alone,' Mawsom said lightly. 'We're bloody lucky to have him as Div Pro. God! If only somebody could have said all that last year!'

'Anyway, it's been said now,' Angus concluded. Then added, 'I've never heard that word, you know the one Atkinson used.'

Mawsom said, 'You wouldn't, especially in Ansell's, unless it was Notting! It is an oik word.'

'Typical of Atkinson,' Angus agreed. 'Anyhow, it's a fine day and I've got a fielding practice with the House Eleven.'

'Better watch out, AC, you'll be a Tassel if you're not careful and none of us will be able to speak to you!'

'You don't get Tasselled just for fielding.'

'Well, what about your bowling?'

'Just because *you* can't hit it, doesn't mean that people like Bartlett and Ellerman and Gower wouldn't thrash it out of sight. Anyhow, I'd just like to get in the side especially for the Old Ansell's match.'

'What would you do if the opening batsman was on forty-nine and sent you a catch in the gully?'

'Catch it of course!'

'Even if it's Singleton?' Mawsom teased gently, revealing the trap he had set.

'Perhaps Singleton would've *meant* me to catch it,' Angus replied with exaggerated demureness, obviously accepting the implication in good part.

Mawsom said, 'My God, AC, you *are* coming on! Six months ago you wouldn't even have seen the point of my remark.'

As he drifted off to sleep, he rejoiced again at Ellins' lucid frankness. *As if the sun had come out*. Yes! Just like that, putting fear and guilt in proportion And Ansell's no longer seemed quite so dark and threatening.

✻

Harrington picked the team for the Old Ansell's Match. Two days before it was to be played, Angus found him crossing off the names of Singleton and Maunder, substituting two others. 'They can't get time off from the Army,' Harrington explained. 'Dennison's bloody marvellous. He was Captain of the Eleven when we were Junior Election.' Angus felt disappointed and depressed; however on the evening before the match they had a torrential thunderstorm which continued for most of the night.

It was still raining the following morning and all cricket was cancelled; it left a curiously flat feeling which lasted for some days.

A week later Ansell's played Pettifer's, favourites to win the Cricket Cup. Ellerman scored a hundred and one impeccable runs, not out; Harrington eighty. Ashton took six wickets including the hat-trick. Angus held three exceptionally difficult catches. They won by twenty-five runs.

On Tassel Night Harrington said to Angus, 'Shall I see you?'

In bed Harrington made no move to reciprocate Angus' ministrations. Although, because he was physically excited, he was mildly disappointed, Angus was not entirely displeased that Harrington, unlike Bartlett (or even Ellerman) observed the convention. It was as it should be. Harrington said kindly, 'You played well today, AC. Good catches. After a pause he asked, 'What about Warming for me till Brownlow's back in action?' Brownlow, a lithe, athletic boy in the Junior Election had painfully twisted an ankle during a Colt's match and was in Nurs'ry 'Ten bob a week, but you'll have to tighten-up if you don't have my OTC kit looking like new. Brownlow's hopeless at it,' Harrington continued without heat.

'Of course, Harrington. I should like to.' He was absurdly pleased to have been asked.

In the dark on the way back to Big Dorm he stumbled into somebody in the semi-darkness. His eyes accustomed themselves to the gloom and he could see it was Jeffrey of the Junior Election. 'Anything wrong?'

'Thanks...but...no...'

Obviously there was. With sudden insight Angus said, 'Were you with Bartlett?'

'Yes. I'm his Warmer.'

Angus said quietly. 'I was too, one Tassel Night. Bartlett leaves this Half.'

'That's weeks away.'

'But Tassel Night's over.'

'It's not just Tassel Night, Angus.'

Angus did not know what other comfort he could offer, but said lamely, in a whisper, 'If you want to talk about it, you can. To me. I shan't say anything.' Instinctively he put an arm round the other's shoulders 'Don't let it upset you. It doesn't mean much. And you were Tarrant's Warmer after all.'

Jeffrey said, 'Oh that was different. I don't mind tightening-up! It happened all the time at my Private. Tarrant was all right really. With Bartlett it's well, different. Disgusting.'

He felt Jeffrey shiver. Angus hugged him and said, 'Yes. I know.' They stood in the dark outside Big Dorm.

'He'd half kill me if he knew I'd said anything to you, Angus.'

Remembering how terrifying Bartlett had been the Half before, he whispered, 'Of course he won't know, I promise.' Then, 'If you want to talk, I'll he up on Marathon tomorrow afternoon.' He gave the thin shoulders another comforting squeeze.

'Thanks, Angus.'

Jeffrey did not appear on Marathon. However Angus came face to face with him in Big Change. 'Hullo...' he began, until Jeffrey's imploring face stopped him. Later, after Tosher, Jeffrey slipped into Angus' Manger.

'Bartlett's just given me six-up.'

'What for?'

'Not Warming properly he said...I think he suspects I was talking to you last night. It'll be a Praefaectors' next time, he said.'

'I see.'

'Perhaps I was making a bit of a fuss last night.' Jeffrey slipped away.

During the course of the next few days they did not exchange a word, although he was conscious of Jeffrey's frightened face and occasional covert, anxious, glances. Then, one night as they went upstairs Jeffrey whispered as he hurried past Angus, 'I'm doing Marathon tomorrow,' and vanished.

The following afternoon he waited until Jeffrey had been gone some ten or fifteen minutes before he departed himself. He caught up with him at Roman Gate, the remotest part of the course. There was nobody else in sight or hearing. They could see at least half a mile in all directions, but the younger boy looked pathetically scared. 'Last night, after...after we...did things, he made me swear on the Bible that I'd talk to nobody.'

'You *can* tell me.'

In his running kit, Jeffrey looked even younger; it did not occur to

Angus that he himself would have seemed scarcely older to a casual observer of the pair of them.

Jeffrey looked at him longingly, 'I can't, Angus, because I've sworn on the Bible. Unless I told the Chaplain? Or Digger? What would happen then, Angus?'

The magnitude of the suggestion took Angus' breath away. 'There'd be one hell of a row!'

'Would my people get to hear? I couldn't face that.'

'I don't know.' As he said it, he was conscious that for some unexplained reason he wanted to avoid The Digger knowing. He amended his reply: 'Probably they would have to know.' He said it not so much because he really believed it, but because, treacherously, he felt instinctively that it might deter Jeffrey from undertaking such a dramatic course which could involve them all in the end. After some minutes' silence, Angus said, 'What was wrong when you had to go off to Nurs'ry last Christmas?'

Puzzled at the change of subject, Jeffrey answered, 'Nobody was ever quite sure. I had a high temperature all the time and I think they were a bit worried it might be polly...you know...infantile paralysis. Luckily it wasn't. Why?'

'If you were in Nurs'ry, Bartlett wouldn't matter. He won't he back next Half.'

They had walked slowly to the end of Roman Road, where the track dropped down back into view of part of the school as they came to the river.

Jeffrey caught hold of his hand and said, 'Yes. Thanks, Angus. Thanks a lot.' He gave his sleepy smile and looked almost cheerful. 'Should I go on ahead. Just in case...I mean I don't want Bartlett to think I've been talking to you.'

'Of course. Good idea. Go on. I've got a stone in my shoe anyhow.'

He sat by the river for some ten minutes and then trotted slowly back. There was no sign of Jeffrey. Bartlett came out of Small Change as though he had been waiting.

'What are you doing?'

'Just done Marathon, Bartlett.'

'You've been talking to Jeffrey, haven't you?'

With a calmness he did not feel and the tightness rising in his chest, he equivocated, 'Why on earth should I? When do you mean, Bartlett?'

'I mean just now. Out on Marathon!'

'Did *Jeffrey tell you that*?' He made it sound incredulous.

'You were the only two out on Marathon from Ansell's today.'

'Were we? Well, he must've gone some time before me.'

'You took a long time on Marathon.'

How did Bartlett know? He must have been watching him leave. 'I got a stone. It gave me this blister,' he held up his foot as proof.

Bartlett seemed mollified. 'What I told you last Half still stands as far as you're concerned. If you've said anything...'

'You made me swear *on the Bible*, Bartlett.' He dreaded a direct question.

However, Bartlett relaxed His mood changed. 'No, AC. Of course. You're somebody who keeps his word. Anyway, I was pissed on cider that night.'

'Yes, Bartlett.'

'Anyhow, AC, you know enough about Ansell's to know that you should stick to your own Election. Young Jeffrey's showing too much *side* – he's nothing more than a little tart, AC – so keep clear.'

Did Bartlett remember that it was what he'd called Angus that Tassel Night? He remembered how Ellerman had used the phrase about Dermott-Powell – and Maunder about the impertinent Ellerman. He did not believe Bartlett but said sycophantically, 'Yes, of course, Bartlett.'

'You'll do, AC.' As he left, Bartlett added lightly, 'Still a good time before you can cover-up, AC. Unless or course you get Tasselled for cricket.' It was intended as a joke but Angus found he resented it. He not only feared Bartlett, he hated him.

Jeffrey sought him out in his Manger that night with a face of such desperation that Angus was frightened for him. He said at once, 'Look here, Bartlett doesn't know we met on Marathon. Unless you've told him,' he added as an afterthought. Jeffrey shook his head and relief flooded the younger boy so visibly that it was like a light coming on.

He said, 'Thanks,' gripping Angus' hand in both his. 'Thanks very much, Angus.'

He dropped his voice even lower, 'I've just been given six-up because tonight I wouldn't...' Angus nodded in the half-light. Jeffrey said, 'You know, don't you? Without me telling.'

He caught the other's arm, 'I wouldn't either...I pretended I'd eaten too much...you know...might puke. Now you'd better get to bed, or you really will catch something.'

The following evening, Mawsom said, 'Have you heard? Ellerman's Warming for Bartlett the rest or this Half.'

'What about Jeffrey?'

'He's ill again. Gone to Nurs'ry.'

Notting laughed heavily, 'Shagged out!' He turned to Angus, 'I'm surprised he didn't ask you, AC! You still look like the Junior Election and you seemed to be quite a buddy of Jeffrey.'

'What do you mean?' He felt his hearth thud. 'Well, he was in your Manger last night.'

'He was asking me about a Latin Prose.' The lie was out, clear and convincing before he had even thought of it. Notting said with scorn, 'If anyone in the Junior Election had asked me about a Latin Prose I'd have booted his arse for him.'

Snider, who had listened quietly without speaking said pointedly, 'That, Notting, is precisely the difference between you and AC.'

At first Notting thought it some sort of compliment to himself, then he reddened. 'Oh shag off, Snider!'

Snider said, 'I heard that Jeffrey might have polio and has gone home.'

Notting paled. 'Christ! That's bloody infectious. What about the rest of us?'

Snider said, 'What about *him*, Notting? Perhaps he's already in an iron lung.'

A couple of days later Angus found an envelope addressed to him on the letter board.

Dear Angus,
They can't decide what's wrong with me. They thought it might be polio.... The Doctor told my people it could

be the climate. I haven't told them. Don't say anything. Thanks for not letting on about our talk on Marathon. And thanks for your help.

It was signed childishly, '**Love from David**' with '**JEFFREY**' written as an afterthought in capitals and a slightly different ink. Angus wondered how he had been able to convince them that he was ill. Perhaps he really was ill? Next Half, with Bartlett safely out of the way, he would be able to find out. It occurred to him for the first time that he had enjoyed Jeffrey's dependence: it had made him conscious of his seniority. He felt a wave of affection for the sleepy-eyed, scared boy who had gripped his hand so gratefully three nights before.

However, a little later in the Half, they heard Jeffrey would not return. There was a rumour that he had changed schools because of delicate health. Nobody took much notice. Jeffrey's presence had made little lasting impression and he was not missed, except by Angus, who realised with surprise that he had been looking forward to pursuing a new friendship.

※

Brownlow returned to Ansell's with a slight limp. Harrington held out two new notes, 'Two weeks, AC. If Browning can't match your standard with my OTC kit, he's going to have a sore arse.' They both laughed and Brownlow, who was standing with them, joined in. He did not seem perturbed.

Angus said awkwardly, 'It really doesn't matter about the pound, Harrington.'

'In Ansell's only the Junior Election Warm for nothing. Unless you take it, I'll give you six-up.'

'Oh, in that case I'll take it, Harrington. Thanks.' He pocketed the notes. He had rather enjoyed Warming for Harrington, it had been like the old days – except for Tassel Night of course and that had been the only exception. He had found a security which, he realised, he had missed since Singleton's departure. Before he reached the door, Harrington said, 'By the way, Angus, if you want to use this study, if I'm not here, you're welcome' He turned to Brownlow. 'If AC feels like a cup of tea, you can make it for him, young Brownlow.'

Brownlow said demurely, 'Of course, Harrington.' It was all very friendly.

'Thanks. Thanks very much, Harrington,' he said as Harrington left them. It was like being awarded the VC.

Brownlow was looking rather despairingly at the toecaps of Harrington's OTC boots gleaming like a mirror 'I say, Angus, I'll never get them up like that!'

Still euphoric in the aftermath of Harrington's magnanimity, he said, 'Tell you what, Brownlow. When I'm in here, I don't mind doing his boots – at least until you've got the knack. Don't let on. Otherwise we'll both be tightening-up.'

' Would you really? You mean it? I say, *thanks* Angus!'

' Oh, one other thing, *everyone* in Ansell's calls me AC – unless I'm tightening-up to them. And I'm *not* tightening-up to you!'

Brownlow grinned: 'Cup of tea, AC?'

V

One evening almost a fortnight later Angus was summoned to Big Study. His heart in his mouth he climbed the stair. Bartlett was there with Ellerman, and Snider. 'Are you in the same form as Atkinson?'

'Yes, Bartlett.'

'Is it true that Ellins told you how to toss yourselves off?'

There was silence. Although Angus had never heard the term before, it was obvious the others had.

Snider said, 'Atkinson pretended he didn't know what the word "masturbate" meant and Ellins explained.'

Bartlett said forcefully, 'Did he tell you how it was done?'

'Well, I suppose, in a way, he did,' Snider admitted reluctantly. 'But he wasn't telling us to do it.'

Angus said, 'He was sort of helping everyone to understand things and punishing Atkinson at the same time.'

'Helping?'

'Well he said it was something that we should all understand and that it happens to everyone and so we shouldn't let it worry us,' he concluded all in one breath.

'Anything else!'

Snider said pointedly, 'He said if we were doing it with anyone else and were worried, we should see the Chaplain.'

Bartlett retorted sharply, 'If anyone in Ansell's goes off to the Chaplain, we'll tan his arse till it looks like rump steak. The Chaplain is a nosy sod. Ansell's Men don't go to the Chaplain! Understand?'

'Yes, Bartlett.'

'Come to *me* if there's anything like that worrying you.' Angus thought fleetingly of Jeffrey. 'As for what Ellins said – bloody well forget about it.'

'Yes, Bartlett.'

'It does *not* happen to everyone, not in Ansell's! If any of you is caught after this, then it'll be a Praefaectors' with twelve-up. Got that? Snider? Angus? Make sure the others know.'

'Yes, Bartlett.'

'Yes, Bartlett.'

'Oh, I want a word with you, Angus.'

When the others had gone he said, 'You weren't thinking of going to see the Chaplain, I suppose?'

'No, Bartlett, of course not, why should I?' Angus' surprise was convincingly obvious.

'No reason, except that you and the Chaplain probably have a halo each.' But the sarcasm was lost on Angus.

'Yes, Bartlett.'

✽

To the awe of the rest of Ansell's they were summoned to appear before The Digger that evening. Vividly, they remembered the first night they had been there in the sober study. He did not ask them to sit. 'I am extremely sorry to hear that you have all been subject to unpleasant and, I have to say, pernicious, even wicked instruction. I refer, in case there should be any misunderstanding, to your recent "lesson" from Mr Ellins.

I believe I have been correctly informed when I say that he spoke to you at length on the subject of self-stimulation, that is masturbation. Am I correct?'

'Yes, sir.' A subdued chorus.

'I do not intend to question you as to what he said. I asked Ellerman to answer my questions, on behalf of you all, not a task to be envied at your age I am sure. I believe he represented truthfully and even objectively the circumstances. I would like you to have my assurance that you will not again be subject to such regrettable misinformation. When you arrived here in Ansell's, I told you that there was no problem about which I could not be approached. None of you has approached me. If I may for a moment refer to an old unpleasantness, I must say that Dermott-Powell's beastliness has obviously shadowed your Election; though perhaps I now can see some excuse for him were he ever as perversely instructed as you have been. If so, you know very well where such unsavoury instruction led Dermott-Powell. It is clear to me that *Mister* Ellins sought to curry favour with you, by suggesting that this decadent and unnecessary vice is usual, even acceptable and, perhaps by implication even commendable at your age. You have my assurance that it is not. It represents loathsome conduct that is corruptingly self-indulgent. No boy at Cranchester, certainly no Ansell's Man should delude himself into thinking that such beastliness is, nor could ever be, anything but sinful. I assure you that those who cannot conquer these wholly base and perverse urges are lost souls.'

The Digger's eyes rested on each in turn and seemed to burn into them. 'As I should have told you when you are a little older and being prepared for Confirmation, you each have to fight a battle with yourselves. You will find that a healthy life, plenty of exercise and the avoidance of suggestive talk will provide you with most helpful safeguards. Some of you may find you are more frequently troubled, I should say more "tempted" than others. I can only say that it is my experience that such thoughts do not, *unbidden*, trouble those who are unlikely to succumb to them. Self-stimulation is, as I have told you already, a disgusting and degrading habit; those who cannot suppress it do not deserve to be here at Cranchester, let alone Ansell's. Over the last twenty years I am glad to be able to say that Ansell's has set an example which some other Houses may envy but seem, sadly, unable to emulate.

'One further thing. I believe *Mister* Ellins may have also led you to believe that you might, in the normal course of things expect, ah, "nocturnal emissions". I cannot agree. This has never been a problem for the boy with a healthy mind and a faith in prayer. If any of you should suffer in this way, far from dismissing it, you should take it as a warning – and take steps to see it does not happen again. Too many blankets, too little exercise, too much loose talk, lies at the root of such promptings. I can reassure you that, despite the fact *Mister* Ellins may have poured scorn on such simple remedies, you will discover that early bedtimes, early rising and regular cold bathing will provide a regime under which such temptations will simply and rapidly disappear. Finally, I suppose in the circumstances I shall have to say that I trust, despite this man's wrongheaded "advice", nothing he may have said has led any of you to experiment along the lines his talk may have suggested?'

As he stopped speaking, they stood very still, quite silent.

Quickly Ellerman stepped forward and said very clearly, 'I think I can give you our word, sir, that Mr Ellins' lesson has not altered the personal conduct of anyone in Ansell's in any way. I'm quite sure Mr Ellins' lesson has not made any of us, er, "experiment".' They realised that he was picking his words with almost pedantic deliberation so as to avoid an outright lie, whilst still implying that something disgraceful had taken place in the Div Room.

'I'm glad to hear it – not *relieved* to hear it, you note, for I should expect nothing less of Ansell's Men. I shall now see each one of you alone. You first, Angus.'

The others stood in alphabetical order waiting. At last Ellerman said somewhat defensively, 'Well, did Ellins' lessons lead us to experiment?'

Snider answered quietly, 'Only because we didn't need to "experiment". We already knew.'

Ellerman retorted impatiently, 'Digger wanted reassurance, not confessions!'

Angus reappeared. Baker went through the door.

For no particular reason, they waited in Libe until The Digger had finished with them all. Snider took longer. Eventually Ellerman remarked, 'I hope he hasn't been a silly sod.'

As if on cue Snider appeared. It looked as though he might have been spouting. He was certainty upset. 'What's up?' Mawsom asked.

'What happened, Snider?'

Through tight lips, Snider said whitely, 'The Digger gave me eight-up and it bloody well hurts.

'What for?'

'He asked if I'd ever indulged in "this degrading and unnecessary vice"!' Snider closed his mouth.

'You mean you...?'

'I told him the truth. He said in other circumstances, it would have been twelve and he'd've written to my Father, suggesting that perhaps Ansell's was not for me after all.'

Ellerman said, 'Bloody bad luck! Poor old Snider!' But you are an ass. Anyone could see that The Digger wanted to believe that all Ansell's Men are like dear old AC here. He'd've had a seizure if everyone had told the truth.' They all laughed.

The group broke up and Mawsom said confidentially to Angus, 'Snider's got more guts than me. The Digger asked me the same question.' He added with a mocking bitterness, 'It just shows that dishonesty's the best policy. You were bloody lucky he didn't ask you, AC. There's an advantage in looking small and innocent.' They had walked out into the evening air outside the battered fag door. It was warm and scented by a long-forgotten plantation of stock.

'Actually, Mawsom, he did ask me!'

'Well, he still let you off with a warning against being led astray. Blamed it on Ellins, I suppose! Whereas great hairy Snider was expected to know better!'

Angus muttered, shamefacedly, 'I gave the same answer as you.'

'Oh!' There was a pause. Then in a different, almost incredulous tone, Mawsom added, 'Three cheers for you, AC. You're showing a bit of common-sense at last.' Nonetheless the revealing pause had told Angus quite clearly that it had never occurred to Mawsom that Angus would tell anything less than the truth. Despite his own evasion and the light tone and the carefree air of camaraderie, Mawsom was disappointed in him. This recognition fetched from the back of his mind, where he sought to suppress it, the uncomfortable, nagging, certainty that, despite his timidity and incapacitating terror of physical punishment, the previous year he would have faced The Digger's wrath rather than lie.

In an attempt to excuse his conduct to himself, he sought to take comfort in remembering Ellerman's affectionately dismissive sympathy for Snider although, even as he smiled at the recollection, he made a discovery that took him unawares and astonished him. For the first time since he had come to Ansell's, he found he admired the gawky Snider with his inconvenient, almost painful determination not to evade moral issues, more than the graceful and charismatic Ellerman.

He was too immature (and it was too dimly perceived) for him to be able precisely to put his finger on what really occasioned him most cause for unease; an elusive, perhaps instinctive, suspicion that were he to persevere in such heretical choices as Snider's, it must inevitably bring him into conflict with what Ansell's demanded of him. It was, he acknowledged fleetingly, his reluctance to sacrifice his new, hardly won, acceptance by his peers which persuaded him to emulate Ellerman less, rather than more, critically as reason, logic and his almost stifled integrity too feebly urged.

※

The following morning there was an air of suppressed excitement when they reached their Div Room. Nobody was seated; Atkinson stood near the door, Angus heard him say, 'My father wrote to the High Master and my Housemaster.'

'What for, Atkinson?' Snider asked.

'Because a man like that ought not to talk like that to a Div in a place like Cranchester.'

'How did your father know? You must have told him?'

'Well, it just came out of a letter home. And then Old Barnyard had me in. Then I had to go with him to see the High Master.'

Somebody else asked, 'What did you tell him?'

'I just told him what happened?'

Snider said evenly, 'Including the question you asked him?'

'I said I came across the word in a book!' There was a hostile silence. 'Which I jolly well did!' Atkinson ended defensively.

'If it was in a book, why couldn't you spell it and find it in a dictionary? You knew what it meant! We all did.'

Atkinson looked stubborn. 'I wasn't sure!' He sensed that somehow he had lost the advantage.

Notting said, 'Anyhow a chap like that shouldn't be teaching at Cranchester. He wasn't even a Guards *officer* – only Sergeant or something.'

Across the muted murmur of reluctant agreement, Griffiths, a quiet boy from Orangery called out 'Oh, but he *was* an officer.'

'Couldn't be with the Military Medal.'

'He got that at Dunquerque. He was a TA volunteer sergeant then.' After a pause he said, 'Actually, he was commissioned in the field – during the evacuation.'

Notting shuffled: 'How were we supposed to know that?'

Griffiths went on, 'I don't suppose you knew he was on the First Commando raid either? Captain, acting Major. That's where he nearly lost his sight.'

Guiltily, they found their customary places. A big, jolly, boy with the unfortunate name of Batty said conversationally, 'You know, Atkinson, writing to your people makes you a bit of a turd.'

'If you think...'

At that moment there were steps in the corridor outside. When the door opened, Craigie the master who had once congratulated Angus on his singing, came in, still limping slightly and put books on the desk.

'I have to tell you that for the rest of the Half I shall be your "Div Pro". Mr Ellins is, unhappily, no longer teaching at Cranchester. I expect you knew he was recommended for the VC at Dunquerque?' After a significant silence, he said quietly, 'You will open your books and tell me where you have reached.' He looked up: 'Ah...Angus?'

Later Snider said, 'Batty's right. Atkinson's a turd.'

Ellerman added, 'You must admit, Ellins did seem to have some weird ideas. I mean, you don't get pushed out of Cranchester for nothing.'

'Perhaps *he* left *Cranchester*? Anyway, what you said to The Digger wouldn't have helped his cause.'

When Mawsom and Angus were alone, they were both silent for a long while.

'I'd begun to like Ellins.'

'Me too.'

'Do you think he was right. About everything?'

'I don't know.'

'The Digger was quite…frightening.'

'I know. What most makes me think that Ellins was well…wrong is that he made everything seem so much easier to explain and understand. Everyone else – like my old headmaster and The Digger make it all…darker. And even the rest of us feel like that – well, except for you, AC, but then you're a freak!'

Eventually Angus said, 'Mawsom, The Digger doesn't know about Tassel Night, does he?'

'What do you suppose?'

'Now, I suppose not.'

'What do you mean, "now"?'

'Well, last year I might've thought he did – if I'd thought about it at all.'

Mawsom said nothing for a while. They were by the river, flipping stones into the water. 'Ellerman's right in a way. The Digger knows we expect him to expect things to happen a certain way because he's just as pleased to *believe* things are going the way he wants, as he would be if they really were.'

'Don't you think he suspects anything at all?'

'It's possible The Digger knows more than he says, but as long as things are "officially" all right, he accepts it. That's why Ellerman was right – about Snider – The Digger didn't want to hear Snider telling the truth.'

Angus said, 'Actually, Mawsom, inside me, I think I feel The Digger must have been right about…everything…too…'

'I know. That's what makes it worse.'

'It's mainly because it does make it worse, that I feel he was right.'

If, as Notting had put it, the sun had come out on the day of Ellins' lesson, then now it had gone in for good. Everything seemed bleaker than ever. As they were about to leave, Angus said, 'Do you remember when we bathed in that place by the barrow? On Field Day? Last year?'

The inconsequential nature of the question halted Mawsom, 'Yes. Why?'

'Well I looked it up on a map and that stream flows into the Crann and the same water comes past here.'

'So what?'

'Nothing really.'

Mawsom banged Angus lightly on the skull with his knuckle 'Come on, AC, just wake up. The river's got nothing at all to do with what happens here.'

'No. Except...'

'Except what?'

'Well, you remember how the pebbles and the sand there were white?'

Mawsom said with exasperated patience as though humouring a deficient child, 'Yes, Angus. I *do* remember the sand. And the pebbles And that they were white. And I remember Father Time.'

'I was just thinking,' Angus said, 'that here the pebbles are all dark brown or black. Even the sand here is sort of brown and muddy.'

'So?'

'It's just that it's exactly the same water.' Even he did not really understand the point he was trying to make.

To bring Angus' philosophising to an end, Mawsom let fall a large flat stone which splashed them both. Uninhibited retaliation and counter-retaliation followed. Thus, unintentionally, they became absorbed and, when, panting, wet and exhausted, they eventually finished their boisterous game. Perhaps, without realising it, they had moved back into uncomplicated childhood for the last time, and then out of it forever.

✳

Five days before the end of Half, Ansell's played the House Match Final against the Tuskers (as Oliphant's was familiarly known). Angus, at deep square leg, was tested by a spectacular chance. Fielder-Jones, had scored seventy-six without fault. Ashton let fly a really bad, short ball that deserved to be thumped. It rose shoulder-high from the wicket, but Fielder-Jones, an elegant attacking batsman, hooked it hard, easily and gracefully, slightly topping it. Angus saw it leave the bat; then it seemed to vanish into darkness and the background of trees. He moved to his left and forward with confidence born of twenty-nine catches well taken already that season. He saw the ball again where he had anticipated and relaxed.

Suddenly, unexpectedly, it dipped sharply and swerved. He flung himself along the ground, felt his left arm scrape the hard turf and the ball diddle insecurely in the top joints of his fingers. Desperately, as he rolled, he clamped his right hand over his left. His momentum left him panting and breathless, his back to the field, the ball clasped to his chest and he became conscious of applause and cheers. Rising shakily on one knee, he could see Fielder-Jones already walking back to the pavilion.

Ansell's crowded round. Ellerman said, 'I thought you'd lost that one, AC!'

Hartington thumped him on the back. 'Bloody marvellous, AC. Ashton never deserved that wicket. Bloody awful ball!'

Ashton grinned: 'Not at all. I bowled for that catch. I knew AC would get it. He always does,' inviting the good-natured jeering he anticipated his remark would call forth.

Snider was not playing, but had walked round the boundary. 'Congratulations, AC. You must have glue on your fingers!' But Angus had turned back for the next batsman who was already taking guard. Ansell's won the match by nine runs.

※

At the end of supper Harrington banged on High Table with his tankard and called out, 'Angus!'

Notting hissed, 'Go on! It's you, AC.'

Angus stumbled to his feet and somehow found himself standing behind High Table facing Harrington. There was a good deal of ribald comment.

Harrington held up his hand. 'If anyone had told me last year that I'd be Tasselling AC for cricket this year, I'd've given them a dozen-up for *side*. I don't—' Interrupted by a burst of laughter he began again, 'I don't think anyone, except perhaps the Good Lord himself would've thought he'd be the second in his Election to be Tasselled.' More cheers and laughter. 'Anyhow he's taken more catches this season than anyone else in our records. If he'd dropped Fielder-Jones, the Tuskers would have won.' Tremendous cheering. Angus felt a coldness near his heart. He could imagine the remarks from Notting and others had Fielder-Jones not been dismissed. 'So, even though it's not Tassel Night...'

Then Angus felt the coveted cap whisked onto his head, the equally coveted Tassel in his fingers and Harrington shaking his other hand and everyone cheering. Cheering him! When he rejoined the others and they were leaving the room, Mawsom said, 'You looked stunned You must've been expecting it.'

'No!' Angus paused: 'I don't deserve it.'

'Of course you do! Thirty catches. It's bloody marvellous to get Tasselled for fielding.'

'I didn't mean that.' He seemed about to say something, then changed his mind. 'It's not even Tassel Night,' he ended lamely.

'Well, who cares about that! You won the match for us today! Of course you deserve it. Anyhow, it's been pretty obvious Harrington wanted to Tassel you before he left.'

'Obvious? How?'

'Come on, AC! Which of the rest of us has use of a Praefaector's study?'

Angus thought: 'Well, Ellerman,' but Mawsom's expression said, 'There you are then!' Angus said, hotly, 'If you think Harrington's like Bartlett...'

'Of course not!

'Anyhow, it was because I did some Warming for him when Brownlow was out of action.'

'Why did he ask *you*? It's not just because you're his Cricket Find of the Season. He obviously likes you.'

'He's been very decent to me. I never had to tighten-up to him.'

'That's what I mean. Anyhow, you need somebody to keep an eye on you now Singleton's gone,' Mawsom said with kindly amusement.

Angus flushed. 'I...'

'I'm not getting at you, AC. It's just that you bring out the protective instinct in decent Praefaectors, like Harrington and Singleton. You deserved your Tassel. Even Notting says so. You might look a bit more cheerful. I dread to think what you'd have been like if you'd *dropped* Fielder-Jones! Anyhow, at least you can cover-up now.'

'So I can.' Angus brightened; he had forgotten about the privilege. 'Thanks, Mawsom. Goodnight.'

He did not stay in his Manger. Slipping on his dressing-gown after Tosher, he went to Harrington's study. Brownlow, looking sunburned and cheerful, was Warming, even though he was only lying on top of the sheet on Harrington's bed because the weather was so hot. 'Congratulations, AC, what a catch! Bloody *mar*-vellous.'

'Thanks.'

Harrington's voice behind then said mildly, 'Listen Brownlow, he's *Angus* to the Junior Election. You deserve six-up for *side*, don't you think so?'

'No, I told him to...' Angus realised that it was intended as a joke. Then he said, 'Yes! Better still a dozen! But seriously, Harrington, I told him everyone calls me AC, didn't I, Brownlow?'

Brownlow, not at all abashed, nodded.

Harrington said, 'You can cut along now, Brownlow.'

'Goodnight, Harrington. Goodnight...AC. It was the best catch I've ever seen. It was...*angelic*.' He slid out of the door quickly.

Harrington laughed. 'It certainly was miraculous.' He looked at Angus hard. 'What's up, AC? You look as if you're expecting the world to end.'

'About this, Harrington,' he held out the Tassel.

'Yes?' Puzzled.

'It's just that...'

'Spit it out.'

'I don't deserve it.' He had said it.

Had he set out to astonish Harrington he could not have found a better way. 'Surely I'm the best judge of that. Don't you want to be Tasselled?'

'Oh yes, Harrington, more than anything.'

Harrington said, 'I suppose it's that turd Notting! What's he been telling you? That nobody ever gets Tasselled for fielding? Listen, AC. You've taken thirty catches this season. It's a record.'

'Notting hasn't been saying anything.'

Harrington continued as if he had not heard him, 'If you hadn't caught Fielder-Jones today, we'd never have won that match. He was set for a century.'

'That's the point, Harrington. I don't think *I did* catch him.'

'Oh! I see! Then who did? Your double? I say, AC, you haven't a touch of the sun by any chance?'

'I mean, I think I put it down, Harrington.' He paused. 'As I fell.' He stopped again. 'Then when I got up, Fielder-Jones was already walking. It was all so quick. And everyone was clapping.... And I wanted...' He ran out of words and waited.

Harrington stood up from the side of the bed and went to the window. At last he said, 'Well *I* thought you caught it. Fielder-Jones thought you caught it. Both the umpires thought you caught it.' He stopped and then said very distinctly, 'Are you quite certain, absolutely *sure*, you put it down, AC?'

Angus was silent. At last he said, 'I...*think* it went down.' Harrington said nothing. Angus waited, then, 'Maybe I'm wrong.' He paused and sighed, as he felt prompted by conscience to say, 'But maybe I'm not...'

Harrington said. 'If you insist, I'll try and do something. Of course. I don't see how we can replay the match. Fielder has left already. He had to report to the army by Sunday – that's why the match couldn't be played next week. Anyway, it doesn't affect the Tassel. You'd still get that for twenty-nine catches.'

They stood in silence. Harrington took him by both shoulders as Singleton had so often done. 'Now look at me, AC. Are you absolutely certain that you *didn't* hold that catch? Can you truthfully tell me you are *sure*...one hundred per cent sure?'

Angus saw himself getting up from the grass, heard again the applause, saw Fielder-Jones already walking from the crease. If only Fielder-Jones had stayed there and the umpires had asked him! He imagined he could still feel the impact of the ball on the top of his fingers as he dived for it. Had he *imagined* that, as the ball had rolled down his arm, it had just touched the grass as he scooped it to his chest with his right hand? Harrington was looking at him hard.

At last, turning away slightly, Angus drew a deep breath and muttered, 'Well, perhaps not a hundred per cent certain, Harrington.'

'Forget about it then, AC. After all, you didn't appeal, Fielder-Jones "walked". Umpires are there to sort things out.' He squeezed Angus' shoulder and walked him across to the window. 'You're the only chap in the entire School, let alone Ansell's, who would have doubts about taking credit for a magnificent catch like that. And think about the other twenty-nine.' With his arm still round Angus, he continued, 'It doesn't always help to have too much of a conscience, AC. You'll find there are plenty of times in cricket when you're victim of a bad umpiring decision, when you should have been awarded a wicket, when you were not LBW.' Harrington turned him and, holding him by both shoulders, grinned: 'When it comes to the House Match Final,' he tweaked Angus' nose affectionately, 'nobody remembers the losers.'

'Thanks, Harrington.' He spoke neutrally.

'Keep up your bowling. You'll be important to Ansell's as a bowler in the future. And as a fielder of course. You'll probably catch me out in the Old Ansell's match next year. *I* shan't walk, until you appeal *and* the Umpire raises his finger!'

Angus knew Harrington was pleased he had not pressed his confession. He tried to convince himself it was not his fault. He really had tried. Had tried hard enough?

On the Tuesday there was a postcard for him. signed jauntily 'Aunty S'.

> *Sorry about the Old Ansell's Match. Bumped into Fielder-Jones (the Tuskers). Hear Ansell's won the House match because of your catch and that you got Tasselled. Bloody marvellous, A.C. See you on the pitch next year.*

There was no address and only a very blurred postmark. Angus was glad he could not reply; Singleton's congratulations only exacerbated his unease. Worst of all was the knowledge that he would be ashamed to discuss the outcome with Singleton.

That afternoon he put his Tassel in his pocket when he went on Marathon. It was a bleak sunless day, the wind cut him coldly, so near the end of Half that he was the only runner. Leaning on the parapet of the bridge across the Crann, he held the cherished symbol over the water; in the end, he could not bring himself to cast it away. After all, Harrington said he would still have been Tasselled for twenty-nine catches; however, he also knew he had already taken twenty-nine by the end of the semi-final against Orangery and had not been Tasselled then.

Back in Ansell's, he re-read the card. Singleton's evident pleasure choked him with conflicting emotion. Finally, because it so pricked his conscience, he tore it up and flushed it down the lavatory. Although, after the immediate relief this afforded, he discovered that his action, like his abortive dramatic gesture at the bridge, somehow only compounded his sense of guilt. The truth was that he was unwilling to fall back into the obscurity from which Tasselling had rescued him.

During the short remainder of the Half, the glittering Tassel (carefully pinned to the left-hand side of his Manger as tradition decreed) seemed, at one and the same time, both a symbol of the success he had achieved as an Ansell's Man and a finger admonishing him for the price he had paid although, deep down, he knew how much he relished being a 'Blood'.

Chapter Seven

One quite extraordinary feature of those years now strikes me very forcibly. War was raging. Castonians we knew well left to fight, to be killed. There were food shortages, blackout restrictions, even firewatching duties from time to time, but I now realise that war did not really impinge on daily life. It seemed as if news of it came from somewhere else, somewhere outside and quite unrelated.

Cranchester was a world apart and, discrete within this world, was Ansell's, another world, even smaller, tighter, more secretive and much, much darker and looming than air raids, or the threat of invasion. For us, as for our Housemaster, Ansell's *was* Cranchester, the realm, the universe. Ansell's was self-sufficient, entirely enveloping; Moloch-like, all-consuming, it was jealous of any other loyalty, jealous even (perhaps especially) of home and family ties.

Like all Public Schools, Cranchester then, even in peacetime, was completely and utterly distanced from home, not only by physical miles, but also emotionally. They were irreconcilable worlds which hardly ever met, let alone mixed. A train journey at the beginning and end of each Half was all that connected most children to the outside world, the real world. However, perversely, for an Ansell's Man home was unreal too; Ansell's was *our* real world.

I have never calculated it before, but I now realise that, for five impressionable years, Ansell's was all that counted for more than eight months of the twelve – forty months out of sixty between the ages of thirteen and eighteen! Parents simply did not visit Cranchester in those days, except on very special occasions like 'Orations' ('cancelled for the duration') as our Speech Day was called, unless a boy was seriously ill, dying, or being expelled. Visiting, watching matches, wasn't 'the done thing'. Ownership of cars was by no means universal and anyway, on the outbreak of war, petrol was severely rationed.

There was no telephone available to ordinary Castonians in the School, let alone in Ansell's; I doubt even The Digger had one when I was first there. The nearest public phone was in Cranchester; in those days, to use the telephone was an adventure – a science-fiction facility for emergencies only.

Our parents received no individual subject reports from the hand of those who taught us. Div Pros signified academic progress to our Housemaster who summarised it his end-of-term letter – meticulously handwritten by The Digger, of course. Years later I found, in Father's desk, several of mine which must have been sent to him whilst he was serving outside the UK. Obliquely, they tell a story more concisely than I ever could: (Those from my first year seem to be missing; I recall Mother telling me that, until he died in the summer holiday before I began my fourth Half, she had sent them on to Grandfather who, I gathered much later, had paid my fees.)

> *Academically, he has not shown quite the same sharpness as in his first year.*
> *Another academically uninspiring Half.*
> *...academically very disappointing; much more effort expected next Half.*
> *...a welcome improvement in Maths and Science.*
> *...his Greek preparation needs his full attention next Half.*
> *I am relieved to hear that, during recent weeks, he has bucked up his ideas However, I am sorry to have to tell you that this welcome improvement did not manifest itself until after he was beaten in consequence of numerous written complaints (and despite my warnings) of 'persistent inattention' in class and, on half-a-dozen occasions, 'showing up' shamefully skimped Latin preparation. <u>He is better than this!</u>*

> *His academic work is much improved all-round. Keep it up.*
> *He came easily first, in a very good Division. Well done.*

Other than a blur of fishing or sailing, I remember nothing at all of holidays. Fathers, uncles, elder brothers and cousins were almost always absent somewhere on Active Service. Much more vivid, is the memory of that nauseous deadening in the pit of the stomach as the moment of return to Cranchester began, increasingly, to cloud even the brightest remaining days. For us, home and holidays were a Technicolor dream-world from which we awoke to the grey reality of Ansell's.

Letters?

Oh yes, letters were written and posted. To home. From home. After Mother died, I came across all mine, every one of them, all neatly sorted by date, still in their envelopes, with a dried sprig of white heather in a chocolate box complete with faded colour picture of Loch Maree on the lid. Brief, factual, scrawled.

> Match results: *Beat Pettifer's by three wickets.* Accounts of school entertainment: *On Saturday we saw* **In Which We Serve**. *Not bad. But the projector broke down .... twice!!!* The usual schoolboy comments on food: *Semolina five days UGH*!!! Pleas for *some extra pocket money* <u>PLEASE</u>.

Achievements were occasionally mentioned self-effacingly: '*If you like, you could let Father know, when you write to him in where-I-mustn't-say, that I was Tasselled for cricket* and, later, *Our Div Pro sent up my Latin Prose to the High Master because, by a fluke, I got full marks!*

Letters home, you see, contained what we understood our parents expected; what, instinctively, we knew they yearned to hear: that Cranchester really was 'the best school', Ansell's certainly 'the best House'. We divined that they wanted us to confirm their choice. So we obliged. Mine, certainly, contain nothing at all of our real lives. Nothing even as innocently gossipy as Jennings might have written home. Despite knowing all I do, I can find no single word or phrase which implies anything less innocuous than life at Greyfriars as serialised in *The Magnet* — not the vestige of an inadvertent hint at our grubby, deceitful, claustrophobic lives. Nothing unguarded enough to arouse even the slightest suspicion of the surreptitious, passionate, liaisons which alone instilled some warmth into the drabness of those middle years as they crawled by. Liaisons which, I now suspect, also relieved pent-up adolescent sexuality which might otherwise have manifested in brutal physical bullying.

So, you ask, what were all those beatings, if not 'brutal physical bullying'? It's difficult to explain, but they were so disciplined – 'ceremonial' is the only word for it – that perhaps, in some obscure way, they offered expiation for both beaten and beater. I now realise how they provided a ritualised safety-valve for the highly charged sexual urgency which gradually tautened the atmosphere in Ansell's to fiddle-string tightness as the Half progressed; ninth week was always worst. After each Praefaectors' came that euphoric, almost tangible, slackening of tension which expressed itself in our sincere, but unvoiced, sympathy for the victim; he had been our scapegoat – 'Now, it can't be *me*.' Until the next time! A Praefaectors' expressed 'Official', rather than personal, individual, disapproval, which is presumably why each Praefaector had to be involved. I now understand why Maunder, idiosyncratically (but individually and personally) tossing the switch out of the window on the last night of his reign, had provided me with such reassuring perspective.

Recently, on *Radio 4*, I heard a professed Christian justifying himself to the 'politically correct' woman hectoring him, by pleading that, on discovering his ten year-old son had been shoplifting, he had caned the boy 'out of love'. How odd it is that I can recall no occasion when I was conscious of genuine hate behind such a beating.

A Praefaectors' was, clearly, public expression of disapproval, but now, and I find I surprise – even dismay – myself here, after this lapse of time, I begin to wonder whether it too was not also public expression of affection, administered 'out of love' – a ' family' punishment, more in sorrow than in anger? After all, whatever we had done, however guilty we were, there remained the comforting assurance of knowing we still belonged – still remained 'Ansell's Men'.

ii

'Do you still recognise me, Singleton?'

'Of course!'

In Lodge they shook hands almost formally. Angus picked up the cricket bag, pleased to be walking beside the dapper figure in khaki with new pips and glinting cap badge. Singleton realised that somehow, foolishly, he had been expecting Angus to look as he had looked two years before. The hair with the white flash was, however, just as prominent. Angus was not tall even now, but he was taller. The face was recognisably the same but more drawn, the eyes too, although they now held a cautious, almost shielded look and were darkly set. Something, which at that moment he could not exactly define, that had previously characterised Angus seemed to have vanished; he looked…guarded? Was that the word he sought?

'My Manger's about halfway along Big Dorm now.' When Angus smiled, Singleton thought, 'It's still there – the same old Angus!' They walked and he cast two or three covert glances, but the guarded look had returned. There was some important quality lacking. As they turned into the high-walled alley, he realised that what he missed was the naivety, the spontaneous frankness which had made Angus so appealing. They arrived at Door, it was opened by a junior boy who held it politely for them. Angus strode through, paying no attention. Singleton thanked him courteously. Despite the *en fête occasion*, Singleton felt dispirited. Angus' vulnerability seemed to have been succeeded by a brash confidence that was thoroughly unattractive. Was it almost arrogance? Perhaps it had been a mistake to have returned for the OA Match?

Angus too had had second thoughts. As the day of the Match approached, he had realised, with something of a shock, that he was looking forward to meeting Singleton far less than he had anticipated. The previous summer he had felt genuine disappointment on learning that Singleton would not be there. Now, this year, he had been almost ashamed to find he secretly hoped military duties might again interfere. He had, he realised, hardly given Singleton a thought during the last two Halfs. He thought to himself with a shock, 'I've grown out of Singleton.' He had, however, dutifully replied to the occasional cards or letters which arrived, despite the moment when he realised he felt awkward and too embarrassed to conclude with 'Love Christopher', as he still concluded his letters home. Instead, he began to sign his increasingly perfunctory replies to Singleton, 'Yours sincerely, Christopher Angus,' or even merely 'Angus' on the last few occasions.

Singleton's letters had become an embarrassment in themselves. Notting, it seemed, had an eagle-eye for their arrival and took spiteful pleasure in saying when others were around, 'I *say*, AC, here's *another* from your affectionate "Aunty".' It caused considerable amusement amongst those who had known Singleton, but it was also Notting's sly, malicious, way of spreading old gossip amongst those who were newly joined. Even Mawsom, whom he had once regarded as an ally, enjoyed the joke. What Angus did not comprehend and what Singleton's sentimentality refused to acknowledge, was the simple fact that even an 'AC' had to grow up.

Only the day before he had been reading the card with the names of the OA cricketers when Notting, like the bad penny of myth, had turned up. One of the Junior Election was at the board too. Noticing this, Notting said in a voice shiny with insincerity, 'Oh, I see your Auntie's able to play this year, AC.' The smaller boy raised an eyebrow and slipped off grinning at Notting.

Changing the subject quickly, Angus had said, 'Is it true they've not asked Bartlett?'

'Yes! He's not allowed back. Not surprising I suppose. Pity though. I dare say he'd find Simonsen less shockable than Jeffrey, don't you?' They were now alone, but Angus felt his ears burn. Notting continued pointedly, 'I dare say you'll be telling Aunty all about Simonsen.'

'What's that supposed to mean, Notting?'

'For Christ's sake, AC, Simonsen sees more of your Manger than his own!'

'We just like chatting.' The quick response betrayed him.

'At that time of night? Anyway you never seem to be *talking*. I wasn't born yesterday, AC. Not that anyone cares. Lucky for you Harlow's such a slack Head of House.'

Seeking ammunition for retaliation, Angus said, 'What about you and Brownlow for that matter?'

'I don't deny that Harlow being slack suits me and everyone else. But we don't have to face Aunty Singleton. I just wondered how he will receive the news that Angel Arse has slipped from grace! Anyway, don't forget Simonsen's Harlow's Warmer, so you and he are treading a thinner line than anyone else.'

Notting pushed off. Angus was forced to acknowledge to himself that he did not want Singleton to know about Simonsen. He wouldn't mention him. However, despite his resolution, the matter was taken out of his hands.

The match, largely uneventful in itself, resulted in an honourable draw. Angus had been was put on to bowl towards the end of the game, until Maunder, hitting three spectacular successive sixes, made his second over his last. However, deep in the gully, he held two difficult catches. Singleton scored a respectable forty-three before being run out, amidst good-humoured banter on the part of Old Ansell's, not least Singleton himself, by a swift return from Angus. Even so, the OA Match was somehow not as much fun as he had anticipated when, the previous year, he had been looking forward to it.

The Match Supper was quite jolly, a good deal was drunk, rather like Tassel Night. When it was over, Angus took Singleton up to Big Dorm; he had made up a bed on the floor for himself. Singleton sat heavily on the proper bed. Angus left him for Tosher, dressing-gowned as befitting his Tasselled status. A younger boy passed and looked in. Singleton thought, 'How extraordinary to have to walk around stark naked till you had proved you were a man!' Then it occurred to him how even more extraordinary it was that neither he, any of his contemporaries, nor any of the present Ansell's Men, would have had it any different – until, that is, he had left and returned.

He became aware that the small boy, evidently back from Tosher, had now entered the Manger. When Angus returned, he was dismayed to find Simonsen sitting beside Singleton on the bed, talking animatedly.

'Hello, AC! Singleton says you were his Warmer.' Simonsen had known that perfectly well already. Angus could tell from the lift of the eyebrow that Simonsen was teasing.

'That's right. I wasn't very good.'

'Did he have to tighten-up to you, Singleton? Very often I mean?'

Angus, sure that Singleton's reluctance to beat was known to Simonsen, said quickly, 'Oh about average!'

Simonsen smiled impishly. 'Do you want to see me tonight, Singleton? AC can vouch for me!'

Singleton gave a brief smile. 'Thanks. But I'm a bit tired. Too long at the wicket. And I've got a fair old journey tomorrow, starting early.' His courteous voice gave nothing away.

'Oh well! Pity! There wouldn't have been any need for a tip – since you're a friend of AC!' Simonsen grinned again and vanished. Almost at once Angus heard him talking to Tarrant at the far end of Big Dorm. He drew the curtain across his Manger; Singleton was still sitting on the bed.

'Who was that?'

Angus could not quite meet Singleton's eye. 'Oh, that's Simonsen – Junior Election.' He stopped. 'You don't want to take him too seriously.'

'What about you? Do you take him seriously?'

'He's Harlow's Warmer. Harlow's Head of House.'

'Do you see a lot of him, Christopher?'

'You forget I'm a Tassel now!' he snapped, but the use of his Christian name made him immediately regret his brusqueness and lured him to confide. 'Well, practically every night's Tassel Night this Half. If that's what you want to know.' Angus still did not look straight at Singleton.

'Is that what *you* want?'

Angus said quickly, 'Harlow's pretty slack.' He hurried on, 'Everyone's the same.' He paused and added, with an attempt at a man-of-the-world manner, 'Simonsen's good fun. And no harm's done. That's what, Ellins our Div Pro last year, told us.' He smiled in a bright, brittle, way which disturbed Singleton. 'If you know what I mean.'

Singleton held his eye and said evenly, 'Yes. I think I do.' He paused. 'It doesn't seem quite like you, AC.' He knew it was a blunder as soon as the words were out.

Detecting a censure which, to do Singleton justice, was not intended, Angus retorted, 'Well, I've changed, Singleton. I was fearfully wet that first year! He managed to put a more matter-of-fact tone into his voice. 'You remember how pathetic I was when I had to tighten-up for that Praefaectors'?'

'Yes. You hated it.' Deliberately Singleton added, 'You were very frightened.' Relenting as Angus flinched, he added, 'No wonder.' Then, almost as if to himself, 'It was *barbarous*.'

Angus felt himself colour up. 'Well, I didn't understand then. Tightening-up doesn't mean anything and it's usually deserved anyhow.' He drew breath and said in a curiously blank tone, 'They probably thought I deserved it!' Was he implying that it was Singleton's fault for not having made him tighten-up? They looked at each other, almost with hostility. Then relenting, 'Well, Praefaectors don't use it unless…they *think* it's deserved,' he finished unconvincingly. 'Unless they're Tarrant!'

'And when you're a Praefaector?'

'*If* I am.' Angus paused, then said almost too loudly, 'It's necessary in a place like Cranchester.'

'Is it?'

Feeling uncomfortable and vulnerable, Angus retreated a little. 'Well, sometimes. Especially bullying and things. Anyhow, it doesn't really count… . It's soon over. It doesn't hurt much.' Sensing Singleton's disapproval at his response, he said with a renewed brashness which came over as cockiness, 'Last Half I had to go to Big Study thirteen times! It was the record – just!'

'What for?'

'Nothing important. Not like bullying…or anything. Only one or two cuts at a time. He glanced at Singleton: 'All our Election were the same. In the end we had a sort of sweepstake – who had to tighten-up most without getting a Praefaectors'. That disqualified you. Notting and I were the only ones left to fight it out by the end. I won. Ellerman got least. Ellerman doesn't really count, of course, because he's in the XV. It's like being a Praefaector. So he doesn't have to tighten-up much, unless the Praefaectors are really ratty – like they were last Half.'

Singleton was looking away from him, out through the darkness and Angus was extremely glad he had managed to change the subject and that at last they had drifted away from Simonsen. Nevertheless he wavered.

229

What if he relied on their former intimacy? Told Singleton all about it? He was surprised and mortified to discover he craved Singleton's understanding...and absolution?

※

Simonsen had arrived at the beginning of the School year, small, shy and faunlike, with secret eyes and the habit of moving close to anyone with whom he talked. Vulnerable, appealing, he seemed utterly cowed into obscurity; during the first weeks he hardly opened his mouth, until a naturally spontaneous (but until then, unrecognised and unexploited) sensuality offered him escape: he accepted the role proffered because it ensured the affectionate protection his timid nature craved. He found the best way to avoid trouble, especially painful visits to Big Study, was to rely on elfin brightness, a melting smile and in being 'obliging'. By the end of the Lent Half he had 'obliged' several of the Praefaectors; timidity had been replaced by an eager, if taut, self-confidence, which any discerning visitor to Ansell's would have found disturbing.

Angus, almost unique in Ansell's, had remained virtually unaware of Simonsen until shortly after the beginning of the Summer Half. He had been selected for the Fourth XI to play in a match at a village some twenty miles away. Simonsen had been co-opted as scorer by Harlow, a mediocre cricketer, who captained the side. The team had travelled in a country bus because petrol rationing left no option. In a way the rambling journey through country lanes was part of the charm of the fixture. They won the match by a single run, scored as it happened by Angus, the tenth batsman. On the return journey, the bus became full. Simonsen, sitting at the front, gave his seat to a rosy-cheeked country woman with a basket. He came to the back and a lurch of the bus precipitated him onto Angus' lap. 'You don't mind if I sit on you, do you, AC? No standing passengers allowed!'

As the elderly vehicle rattled along the worn and narrow country lanes, the bumping proximity of his own personal passenger aroused Angus so insistently that he sweated with embarrassment in case Simonsen should notice. They lurched fiercely into a corner. Simonsen grabbed Angus' hands and pulled them round his waist. Laughing he said, 'You'd better hang on to me tight, AC, or I shall shove my head through the window!'

Angus realised at once that, far from being unaware of Angus' embarrassment, Simon had deliberately provoked it, and now drew attention to the fact that his own arousal was indisputably more pronounced than that of Angus.

They exchanged no further word on the bus, but Angus was unsurprised when, that night, after Warming for Harlow, Simonsen slipped silently into his bed. They did not speak. There was no need. He reciprocated Simonsen's expert touch immediately and, just as spontaneously, found himself aroused to the remembered heightened excitement with Ellerman, but now culminating in the climax he had first experienced the night he had failed to tassel Ashton. However, now he relished orgasm with no hint of panic or guilt. Perhaps Ellins' lesson had liberated him, and repelling Bartlett's sinister attentions given him confidence? In fact, the truth was much simpler: Simonsen was uncomplicated fun, and it was quite evident that Simonsen found him fun too. Their mutual unsophisticated enjoyment of each other, quite uncluttered by intense emotions, was unashamedly sensual.

Two nights later the same silent assignment was repeated and again a few nights later. Angus felt no guilt, only blissful release; Simonsen glowed in the approval of his sporting hero. Under Harlow's benign leadership, Ansell's went on its self-indulgent way. Nobody, it seemed, objected to their growing intimacy; perhaps nobody noticed, for Angus and Simonsen took care never to flaunt it publicly in the face of the decorum imposed by Ansell's custom. Angus enjoyed the younger boy's admiration; it was his first taste of hero-worship.

About a week before the OA match, Simonsen said, 'Who's David?' Angus looked blank. 'I found this letter in the Virgil crib you lent me.' Angus took the letter.

'Oh, Yes. Jeffrey. He was in Ansell's.' He had forgotten all about Jeffrey.
'He's not on the boards!'
'A Junior Election who left!'
'Did he get sacked?'
'Good Lord no! He was always getting ill. He went to another school where it was healthier or something.'

'Why did he write to you?'

'I gave him some help. He was not really an Ansell's Man. He got across the Head of House. Chap called Bartlett.'

Simonsen looked alert: 'What was Bartlett like, AC?' and, as Angus said nothing, 'Come on, AC. I've heard one or two things.'

Reluctant to speak ill of the absent, Angus said, 'He was a bloody marvellous rugger player.'

'That wasn't what I heard about him!'

'Oh?'

Simonsen said with a knowing giggle, 'I heard he was too randy, even for Ansell's and that he was almost sacked in his last Half.'

'I never heard that.'

'Everyone says you're always the last to hear anything, AC. Anyhow, I heard that he's been banned from returning for OA matches. Was it because of Jeffrey?'

'I don't know.' It was possible, Angus thought, that once Jeffrey was at home he had said something. Had The Digger refused to take action until the last weeks of the Half had passed? Or had something been said much later, after Bartlett had left? It was typical that Simonsen should know Bartlett was not allowed back as an Old Ansell's Man and that he, Angus, should not know.

*

Now, for a brief instant in his Manger, Angus was filled with his old trust in Singleton and he thought of confiding in him completely. Emotionally, his liaison with Simonsen was undemanding; it was sheer sensual pleasure – lust – which provided the strongest bond. This shameful knowledge made him hesitate. How could he tell Singleton that?

He sensed that Singleton's gentle advice might help him unravel the fearful tangle of his own thoughts and desires. If, at that instant, he could have convinced himself that Singleton would understand... . However, now, at the critical moment he felt that they were no longer close enough for him to be able to believe that Singleton could do anything but despise him for such unashamedly carnal enjoyment. Thus, on the very brink of confiding, he stepped back. He even, momentarily, considered revisiting the shabby Priest Street Chapel, with its shadowed Confessional and no-longer anonymous darkness beyond the grille. The moment came and went and was gone for ever.

So Angus talked brightly and quickly. He could hear the brittle tone in his own voice rattling on of unimportant matters like cricket and rugger results. He spoke animatedly in order to quieten the uncertainties and self-disgust which somehow threatened to surface. He was conscious of playing a part.

Singleton perceived that Angus was determined to stay with trivia, reluctant (or unable?) to recapture their former intimacy. He found himself responding in a similar vein, regaling Angus with anecdotes from his training. They talked quietly. Outside the Manger they could hear the murmur of similar conversations, surreptitious movement, occasional half-laughter. All the time he suspected that Angus was wanting to confess (and wanting not to confess) the uncomfortable truth which underlay the superficial gossip they exchanged.

The great clock above Lodge struck midnight. Singleton said, 'I suppose we'd better get some sleep. There's a very early train. I must get that. We're getting ready for something special. I think it may be...' He stopped himself and paused. More than ever, he wanted to ask how things were; how they really were. But he could not penetrate the defensive barrier that Angus had erected. If only they had been back in the old study, he suspected the barrier between them, whatever it was, would have dissolved. Or was the barrier not so much between him and Angus, as between a child he remembered with such affection and the guarded, spiky, cocky, youth here with him now? He had lost the key which might have unlocked their former easy relationship.

In the forefront of Singleton's mind was the memory of Simonsen's alert, humorous flirtatiousness. Nothing much changed at Ansell's! And Angus did not want to talk about Simonsen. 'Are you going to be okay on the floor there?'

Angus nodded. In unconscious imitation of Simonsen's pertness, he said lightly, 'I don't think we'd both fit into my bed now.' It rang hollow.

Singleton set a small travelling alarm clock. 'Mustn't be late up!'

They had been using a precious nightlight. Angus scrambled into the bed on the hard floor and snuffed it.

'Goodnight, Christopher.' He used Angus' Christian name deliberately, wanting to suggest that they should walk to the station in the morning; even more, he wanted Angus to suggest it. Flickers of sleep began to bring moments of oblivion. Apropos nothing at all, he said, 'Were you Confirmed? We had the most ancient Bishop I've ever seen. What about you?' And paused. No reply except for deep breathing. He called again without result. Drifting off to sleep, he recognised sadly that, even as they did so, they were also drifting even further apart from each other.

Angus was far from asleep. He was as aware as Singleton of the unasked questions and enquiries which still hung in the air. Fortunately, in the dark he could pretend to be asleep. Relief that Confirmation had not been previously mentioned flooded into him. Had the topic come up earlier, he would never have been able to maintain his evasion and Angus knew that, paradoxically, what he least wanted to discuss with Singleton was what he most needed to discuss.

It would have been difficult enough to admit the nature of Simonsen's attraction, but to admit what he had found out about himself during the preparation for Confirmation would be impossible. He recalled how he had boasted to Singleton that he had conquered his fear of tightening-up. It had been on the tip of his tongue to go further, to try to explain, however inadequately, why he had sought to appease his conscience and relieve his burden of guilt by committing trifling disciplinary offences in the desperate hope that the punishments he invited would purge him of sins, unguessed at by Praefaectors, known only to himself. Perhaps the treacherous intimacy conferred by darkness and their close physical proximity in the small dark Manger lulled him and, for a second time that evening, he was momentarily overcome by an urge to confide in Singleton completely, to tell him everything. However the gradual onset of sleep dissipated his initial impulse so that it was not even as strong as that which, earlier, had almost impelled him to tell Singleton the truth about Simonsen. Drowsily, he reasoned that confessions should be kept to their proper place although, curiously enough, his lustful intimacy with Simonsen had never bred guilt enough to send him back to visit the tiny Chapel in the Cranchester back street.

He wondered idly whether Singleton knew of it, dark, dilapidated, squeezed between two disused grain-merchant's stores. Had Singleton ever seen it? Had he been inside it? He wished that enough of their old intimacy remained to have enabled him to ask.

iii

The first Confirmation Class had taken place on the second Sunday evening of the Autumn Half. They sat in The Digger's clinically neat, dimly illuminated study for an hour, listening and occasionally discussing uncontroversial topics. Session by session, they covered The Catechism point by point. Occasionally, discussion was quite interesting, although Snider seemed to have curiously little to say.

In November, the topic was the Sacrament of Confession. They sat, contributing nothing, as The Digger explained the part it played in the Roman Catholic faith. He told them that it was also a voluntary element in the Anglican rites. 'Although some claim it to be a little "High".'

It was the first time Angus had ever heard the phrase. Ellerman, always to be relied upon to ask the necessary question, said, 'What happens, Sir, if the person confessing can't remember all his sins?' The Digger looked at him gravely, 'If he really cannot remember, I daresay those he has genuinely forgotten will be forgiven. Provided the intention was to remember. However,' he paused impressively, 'deliberately to fail to mention all the sins that could be remembered is a grave sin. It would constitute abuse of the Confessional, invalidate the Confession and nullify any absolution given. You see, Ellerman, Confession in the Roman church and, indeed, in ours, is a Sacrament and may not be defiled. Just as the bread and wine – the Communion Sacrament – may not be defiled.' They sat unspeaking. Angus thought, 'I could not do that. There are some things I could never tell anyone.' It flashed into his mind that he would not have felt like that in his first year.

The Digger closed the service book he had been holding. 'I suppose

I ought to end by reminding you that I always expect Ansell's Men to make their Confession before Confirmation. It is of course voluntary. Nevertheless, I would hesitate to put forward any candidate who could not make his Confession. It allows the Confirmand to start with a clean sheet. Though I have no doubt that as Ansell's Men you have clearer consciences than most. Any questions?'

The long silence was once again rescued by Ellerman. He said courteously, 'Should we make an appointment, with the Chaplain? For confession I mean, sir?'

'The Chaplain.' He looked hard at Ellerman. 'I should not say this perhaps, however there is in Cranchester, as in any school, an unfortunate tendency for gossip to spread. Not that I suggest the Chaplain would ever deliberately betray anything he heard under the seal of the Confessional. Nonetheless, he is human. No, Ellerman, I think Ansell's business is the business of the Housemaster of Ansell's. It may be an old-fashioned view, but then I am happy to be considered old-fashioned. You perhaps forget, Ellerman, that I am Ordained in Holy Orders, just as the Chaplain is. It is always the custom for me to hear the Confession of Ansell's Confirmands, just as it is my pleasant task to prepare you for full membership of the Church.' He paused: 'So, Ellerman, you can ask *me* for a time, when you feel like doing so. I shall of course expect each of you to approach me before Confirmation. I could not otherwise see my way to presenting you to the Bishop. There are no more questions?' He waited. 'Good. Let us meet the same time next week.'

Back in Din Room Baker said, 'Christ! Confession. *And* to The Digger Not me. I'm not going to be Confirmed!'

Notting said, 'Then The Digger'll guess why.'

'Come on, Baker! We don't have to confess everything. If people did that, he'd hardly have any Ansell's Men left,' Notting put in. 'I'm going to say I've lied and sworn. You know, in a vague way. Been unkind. Selfish. All that sort of thing. I bet he'll believe it.'

'He said it doesn't count unless you confess everything,' Angus muttered uneasily.

'I don't expect God'll strike me dead, AC!'

'No? Look what happened to Snider when he told The Digger.'

'That wasn't God, it was The Digger. Anyway it wasn't *"Under the Seal of the Confessional"*,' Mawsom intoned.

'Do you think that'll make much difference to what The Digger thinks of you?'

Notting said forcefully, 'We don't all have Snider's nasty habits!' He dropped his eyes. 'That's why Snider's not fit.'

'You're a bloody hypocrite, Notting! You're no different from me, or the rest of us.'

'Oh, yes I am. So is Mawsom and Angus and Baker,' Notting said with loud stubbornness.

'Why don't they say so then?'

'You just accepted what that chap Ellins told you. It's a disgusting habit easily cured if you want.'

They knew Notting was lying, but they looked agreement.

Snider said, 'I shan't make a confession to The Digger.' He concluded with startlingly uncharacteristic venom, 'He's a dirty-minded old sod!'

'Well you won't be presented for Confirmation,' Ellerman said.

'In that case I'd rather not be.'

'Don't be an ass, Snider. It's all a load of superstition. Just tell The Digger what he wants to hear and get Confirmed,' Baker said placatingly. Snider looked mulish. 'If you don't,' Baker reasoned, 'you're finished as far as Ansell's is concerned. You'll never be a Praefaector.'

'Who wants to be a Praefaector!'

Baker said, 'I bloody well do. I can't wait to tan a few arses!'

Notting laughed: 'Me too! I think I'm going to go for Tarrant's record when I'm a Praefaector! Ansell's is going soft under that ass Harlow.'

Snider said, 'What about Tassel Nights? Are you confessing that?'

'Oh come off it! That doesn't even come into it.'

'Why not?'

'It's just a tradition. Letting off steam. I bet The Digger knows about Tassel Night anyhow.'

Ellerman said intently, 'If you do decide to tell The Digger all your nasty little secrets, Snider, I'd advise you to forget about Tassel Night. Anyhow, you aren't a Tassel! You can't even cover-up yet!'

Snider went a bright red and walked quickly away.

Later Angus said to Mawsom, 'What are you going to say to The Digger?'

'Not what Snider might say! I want to stay at Cranchester! I say, AC, are you going to do something bloody stupid?'

'What do you mean?'

'You're just the sort of chap who really will tell the truth. Even Snider won't do that when it comes to it. At least I hope not. But you! You just might, AC.'

Uncomfortable, Angus muttered, 'I didn't last time.'

'No. That's true! I must admit you surprised me there. But this is a bit more serious. And anyway you have an advantage.'

'Oh?'

'Well you never seem to be really worried by sex and all that.' He buffeted him on the shoulder. 'One cross you don't have to bear, AC. It must be fine to be a saint. The rest of us aren't.' Then quietly, 'Though, we all are, as far as The Digger is concerned.'

'What about on Marathon that day?'

'Well, yes.... But even then, you actually talked about it to me. I'd never have dared...even to you. You'll see, The Digger'll never suspect you. I bet he doesn't even mention it.'

Angus found he could not admit even to Mawsom that he had as much fear of talking to The Digger as they did. In the ensuing weeks he practised rigorous self-restraint, although not always successfully. In his darker moments, before sleeping, or after waking early in the morning, he felt the march of time taking him towards a confrontation with The Digger which must, he knew, involve ignominious disgrace. After their initial discussion the others seemed unconcerned: they would, Angus realised, fulfil The Digger's expectations. Even Snider would acquiesce.

Just before supper on Tassel Night, Ellerman said to Angus, 'Your first time as a Tassel, AC!' Angus nodded. 'Why don't you ask Brownlow to see you? He's no longer a Warmer.'

'I wasn't sure I'd bother, Ellerman.'

'Thinking of The Digger's confessions, AC!'

Angus flushed, but said nothing.

'It's up to you of course, but we all thought you'd grown up a bit. There's nothing wrong with Ansell's traditions.'

They met in Corridor. Brownlow said, 'Hullo, AC.'

Angus said quickly, 'Shall I see you tonight, Brownlow?'

Brownlow grinned: 'Okay, AC.'

When, after the singing and the bread-throwing, the lights in Big Dorm were turned off, Brownlow entered his Manger. He said quietly, 'I hoped it would be you who'd ask.'

Although it was clear that Harrington had been a good instructor, Angus found to his huge embarrassment that he could not respond. 'I don't think I'm ready.' He remembered Ashton's shame and his own unsympathetic response.

Brownlow was different. 'Perhaps it's not the right night for you, Angus.'

Angus heard himself begin to say, 'Sorry,' although he bit back the words. He was, after all, a Tassel. At the same time he became aware that if he was not ready Brownlow certainly was. 'Pity you're not a Tassel, Brownlow.'

'You're telling me.' His voice in no way implied that he expected Angus to contravene Ansell's extraordinary code of conduct. He giggled: 'I've got the Eiffel Tower.'

It made Angus snort a laugh. Brownlow touched Angus again and as if, switched on, he responded at once: 'You too now, it seems!'

Thankfully Angus rejoiced in the fact that after all he had avoided Ashton's humiliation. So Tassel Night undid all his good resolutions and, during the last days of the Half, he found himself unwilling to submit to the self-imposed restraint of the previous month. The fact that imminent Christmas holidays distanced any necessity of having to discuss Confirmation with The Digger contributed to his fall from grace.

※

Ten days into the Lent Half the entire Election had to tighten-up for Henderson. He was not Head of House – that was Harlow. But Henderson was such driving force as there was. 'You're a bloody disgrace,' he said. They were in Big Study. 'You contribute almost nothing. Except you,

Ellerman. You at least are a credit to Ansell's. The rest of you are a "shower".' It was a word that had become popular, spilling over from army slang. 'With the exception of Ellerman, you'll all get three-up. You first, Angus.'

Having shaken hands they trooped out. 'Bloody unfair,' Notting complained. 'Still, Henderson's no great shakes with a switch!'

Snider said, 'It was quite unjustified. They're just picking on our Election. They always have. Ever since Dermott-Powell! Even The Digger looks at us with suspicion.'

Baker said, 'Nobody looks at Ellerman with suspicion.'

'I think we ought to *earn* tightening-up!' They all looked at Snider questioningly 'I mean, if they are going to make us tighten-up, let's bloody well earn it!'

'How?'

'Oh, by being "tedious".' It was Ansell's slang for being subversive. There were many small ways in which the discontented could achieve it.

Mawsom said, 'We'll just have to tighten-up even more!'

'If we're clever, nobody'll know it's us.'

Ellerman said, 'Why not have a sweepstake? If we all put in ten bob, it can go to whoever has to tighten-up most. A sort of insurance!'

'What if we get a Praefaectors'?'

'Oh that can't count. That disqualifies.'

In this way, the Praefaectors were quietly harried. Football boots went missing. Notting discovered that the most effective and annoying irritation was to fray a football lace so that the unfortunate owner broke it just as he was pulling it tight. Notices vanished from Corridor. Books went missing to turn up in unexpected places. Although they were not caught, the irritable tension led to an unusually large number of visits to Big Study for everyone in Ansell's. Angus, no longer frightened, found that his punishments, when they came, eased his conscience about other matters.

The date of Confirmation drew closer. Ellerman was the first to see The Digger. He seemed unscarred by the experience. 'I went to that tiny room at the far end of Chapel,' he said. 'Couldn't even see The Digger in the dark.'

'What did you have to do?'

'Oh, say The Lord's Prayer several times.' Despite further resolutions, Angus found that such self-restraint as he had practised during the previous Half now seemed an impossibility. Twice he was brusque with Praefaectors; on the second occasion got six-up from Harlow.

'You're showing too far much *side* for your own good, Angus. If you're not careful, you'll find yourself meeting all the Praefaectors. As you did once before.' The memory of that brought his heart to his mouth and sobered him.

After the second Confirmation class of the Half, The Digger stopped him as he was leaving Private. 'I'm sure that you haven't much to say, Angus, but should we make an appointment in Chapel sometime soon?'

'Yes, Sir! I wanted to do it next month. As near to Confirmation as possible.' The Digger nodded.

※

It was sheer chance which led him to St Anne's. He had gone into Cranchester and, day-dreaming, found himself in an unfamiliar cobbled back street. It was lined by some dusty houses on one side and by a number of storehouses and small warehouse on the other. In the middle was a small straggly circular garden, much overgrown which, evidently, the sun rarely reached; the railings had been taken early in the war for scrap and the street bowed out on each side of it. On one side, set back, was a small, dark house. An almost illegible sign at the dilapidated gate said *THE CURACY*. Opposite, on the other pavement was a small, equally dark church looking as if, to their resentment, it had squeezed itself reluctantly between the tall buildings either side of it. The heavy door within the pillared porch was open. A shabby notice board (headed in faded gold letters **The Chapel of St. Anne, Priest Street)** held a list of services: **Sung Eucharist**...**Evensong**: he glanced idly down. **Confession**: *Father Dunsley will hear Confession Daily 5.00 p.m. or by appointment.*

Perhaps he could confess here? Anything rather than face The Digger! He went to the door, with no real intention of entering. However, once inside, his breath was caught by the unfamiliar waft of incense. For an instant he felt his old choking panic. Then it cleared. His eyes accustomed themselves to the dimness. He could see two booths to the right. He glanced at his wristwatch. It was four-thirty. Filled with curiosity and conscious that nobody but himself was present, he stole towards the confessionals; two small, curtained boxes. Hesitating, he opened a curtained door; just room enough to kneel. He could just make out a narrow grille at the back. How would it feel to say what he would have to say, kneeling there? He looked around. Nobody. Quietly, he knelt and felt the door swing closed behind him. There was a card pinned to the ledge in front of him. In the near darkness he could just make out the words. Would he ever have the courage to face The Digger like this? How would he feel in a few weeks time in the Cranchester Chapel?

Unthinking he began softly to read the words aloud. 'Father I have sinned and am heartily sorry.' He continued to the end. In capital letters it said *Here the truly Penitent shall number each of his separate sins, that none may be left out.* Beside it was a sort of checklist. He had never expected that. It meant there could be no excuse for omitting anything — even the lust which possessed him so frequently. How would it feel to Confess?

He heard himself whisper, 'I have sworn; I have taken the Lord's name in vain; I have cheated;' he paused; 'I have disobeyed my parents; I have disobeyed my teachers;' he went on rehearsing as many as he could, trying to remember. 'I have stolen.' That sounded so terrible — there seemed no formula to discriminate, no way of saying that what he had stolen had been some sweets he had 'borrowed' from Mawsom — it was all the same if he had robbed a Bank. Nonetheless, even there, alone, he could not bring himself to admit aloud, even to himself, the full course of his degradation, until clenching his hands and squeezing his eyes tight, he said quickly, 'And I have committed impure actions, I have...masturbated.' At last he had said it, though knew he would never be able to say it to The Digger.

'Once or many times, my son?' The voice came out of the darkness.
   Horrified, he felt frozen to the hard floor.
   'My son, don't be afraid to tell me.' All the time, there in the darkness,

the priest had been waiting, listening. He wanted to go, to run away, but he could not move. He muttered, 'Many times Father. I have tried...'

'Have you spilled seed?'

He breathed deep: 'Yes, Father.'

'More than once?'

'More than once!'

'By yourself, or were others concerned?'

'By myself.' He fell silent. 'And also with...' Brownlow! Ellerman! '...others.'

'Have you been with women, my child?'

'With women?'

'Have you had sexual knowledge of women?'

A sin he had not committed! 'Oh no, Father! Never.' He wondered why he said 'Father'. There was silence.

'Do you truly repent?'

'Yes, Father.'

'Is this your first Confession?'

'Yes, Father.'

'How old are you?'

'Fifteen, Father.'

'Prayer will help you to contain those thoughts which prompt the actions which you have confessed and for which you are heartily sorry. You are granted forgiveness. I absolve you in the name of the Father and the Son and the Holy Ghost. Say slowly before you leave this church The Lord's Prayer. And remember, always, Confession is a full and blessed sacrament.'

'Thank you Father. *Thank* you!'

'Do not thank me. Give your thanks to God'

Five minutes later he was outside in the dingy street. Although dusk was approaching it seemed to him that it was lighter than it had been for weeks. He had been relieved of the immense guilt with which his despicable lack of self-control had burdened him! The slate had been wiped clean! He could face The Digger with a clear conscience. His shameful past had been forgiven, would not have to be included in his Confession to The Digger. He felt as if he wanted to dance and sing there in the street. It was so simple. So easy! Painless. Confession was a Sacrament – he could understand that now. That night Ellerman said, 'What's up, AC? Have you won a prize or something? I haven't ever seen you looking so cheerful.'

After Curfew, Angus was given two-up in Big Study for throwing a sponge in Tosher. It seemed a mild penalty for so much forgiveness. The following night in his Manger he fell from grace once more. And the next night. He made his second Confession a week after the first. Once again, came the welcome Absolution; the anonymous voice in the darkness expunging all his fear and his guilt. Now that he went every seven or eight days, the tally of sins seemed to be so slight — really only the one; on that first occasion he had needed to expiate the sins of fifteen years. Forgiveness from the grille never seemed recriminatory. So it was that, although Angus did not consciously admit it, confessional visits to St Anne's insidiously began to provide permanent *carte blanche*, enabling him to abandon even the vestiges of self-restraint.

His own session with The Digger came late one afternoon after an earlier visit to St Anne's. His conscience was so clear that, in order to say something, he swore loudly twice in Ansell's and deliberately pushed one of the Junior Election down the last two stairs so that the boy cut his lip. (Henderson who had, unfortunately, overseen the incident, gave him four-up after Curfew. 'Remember what we said before about you getting above yourself, Angus?')

'Yes, Henderson. Thank you, Henderson.'

He had not meant to cause Garner any damage. It was just that he thought a minor unkindness would be a sin acceptable to The Digger. He was right; The Digger heard his Confession and was satisfied.

It was not the same with Snider. He returned very quietly. Notting asked, 'What's up, Snider? You don't mean that you told The Digger the truth?'

Snider said, 'No. He didn't believe me. He said that he had long felt me to be untrustworthy and that he had not forgotten that I alone of the Ansell's Men had been influenced by Ellins.'

'What did you do?'

'I stuck to what I'd told him...that since then I'd not...' He stopped and coloured. Of course he had.

'Good for you!'

'It doesn't do any good. I'm not to be confirmed.'

'NOT! Why?'

'He thinks I am an unworthy candidate. He says he thinks I lied in my confession. He's right, of course.'

Baker said expressively, 'Ker-rist! If only he knew.'

Snider continued miserably, 'He said he hoped he'd see fit to think better of me another year.'

Notting said, 'I wouldn't give much for your chances of becoming a Praefaector, Snider.'

Ellerman snapped, 'That's a typically oikish thing to say. Trust you, Notting.'

'I only...' Notting's face was flushed.

'Sometimes we wish you'd "only" shut up,' Mawsom added with uncharacteristic asperity. 'Snider's no worse a candidate for Confirmation than the rest of us.'

Baker said, 'Except Angel Arse of course.'

It was Angus' turn to blush and he walked away from the group.

※

The afternoon before the Confirmation service he paid another visit to Priest Street. He was halfway along the shelterless road from Lodge when with a splitting crack of thunder it began to rain torrentially. He decided to continue, but the rain did not abate. By the time he reached St Anne's, he was soaked to the skin. As he knelt he could feel the water running from him and hear it drumming down on the roof of the tiny church.

He went through his catalogue, smaller, but unvaried. 'I have lied; I have taken the Lord's name in vain; I have had impure thoughts; I have committed impure actions; I have spilled my own seed.' As he specified them, he felt again the welcome relief, imagining his sins oozing out of him just as the water was oozing from his clothes.

When he reached the door of the church it was still torrenting down. He found a figure beside him. 'You are soaked to the skin and you'll catch your death if you go back in this downpour.'

It had to be the priest he had never met. The priest who had heard all his sordid sins. He recognised the voice although the other gave no indication that he knew who Angus was, despite the fact that there had been only the two of them in the church.

'Come to the Curacy and let's get you dry.' The priest put up a large umbrella. Angus could feel his teeth beginning to chatter. They ran across to the dark house. In a dark room with many books a large wood fire burned brightly.

'I'll fetch you a bath towel and dressing-gown and you can take off those wet things in front of the fire.'

Angus did as he was told, relishing the warmth on his skin. He heard the door open behind him and turned round. Long past the brief stage in his fourth Half of being embarrassed by his own nakedness, it never crossed his mind that he should wait until Father Dunsley returned with the towel before stripping off his sodden clothes. Wrapping himself in the huge gaudy towel he sat on the leather padded seat around the top of an iron fender similar to that around that in The Digger's study, allowing warmth from the flames to glow into his back.

'Perhaps you'd like some tea?'

Father Dunsley poured tea. Then they toasted crumpets on a rickety fork, sitting side by side, feet in the hearth, without speaking. After a time Father Dunsley said, 'What is your name? May I know?'

'Of course, sir. Angus.'

'Ah! Not a usual Christian name in these parts.'

'Oh I'm sorry, sir! My Christian name is Christopher.'

'Christopher. Well, Christopher, may I be allowed to say something?'

'Of course, sir.'

'If ever you need advice, outside the Confessional, you know where I live.'

'Yes, sir. Thank you, sir.'

After a pause: '*Do* you need advice, Christopher?'

He turned his head and was aware that Father Dunsley was looking at him as if asking something more. 'Perhaps…sometimes.' He felt almost hypnotised.

'Well, you know where to find it.' Angus sensed there was more to come: 'At your age, you may find it hard at times, to balance the…uh…urgencies of your body with the teachings of religion and school.' There was a pause. Then the priest said intensely, 'That's hard at *any* age, Christopher. Lapses are only to be expected. That is why God forgives.' He looked intently at Angus: 'Do you understand what I am saying?'

Despite demands of common courtesy, lulled by the warmth, the tea and the sheer release of tension after making his Confession, Angus could scarcely keep his eyes open. Father Dunsley's voice receded. He was a younger Angus, back in Ansell's with Ellerman stroking first his thigh and then.... To his horror his body responded to the unmistakably familiar day-dream in the equally familiar way. He shook himself and still only half-awake, stood up groggily finding himself close to Father Dunsley, who also stood up, perhaps to steady him. Pulling the bath-towel tight around him in a vain attempt at concealment, he was mortified to discover, too late, that it merely served to reveal his predicament so explicitly that the priest could not possibly be unaware of his excited state.

The relief when he realised he must still be dreaming! For it was unthinkable that Father Dunsley himself should be similarly aroused beneath the silky roughness of the cassock pressing against him.

A voice – briefly he was reminded of Dawes and Bartlett – choked, distant, scarcely recognisable as that which dispensed Absolution from behind the grille and the not-altogether-pleasant mustiness of tobacco mixed with incense emanating from shabby vestments dispelled at last drowsiness, jolting him back to the gloomy room, the rustle of subsiding logs in the dying fire and the startlingly white cups and saucers...

'I dare say your clothes will have dried off a bit by now, Christopher.' They stepped out from the guarded hearth chatting politely. By not the slightest inflection of his voice, now restored to its normal pitch, nor any tell-tale gesture, did Father Dunsley hint that he had saved Angus from falling into the fire – if that was indeed what he had done – let alone give grounds for inferring that even the slightest intimacy had occurred, which, Angus dozily thought to himself, was hardly surprising if he were dreaming it. Relishing the still-considerable warmth on his back, he shrugged off the towel and, slowly began to dress again.

Minutes ticked loudly by.

What if it had not been a dream? If the hand on his thigh had really been Father Dunsley? The possibility conjured up neither fear nor loathing, just weary acceptance. If it had happened, it had happened. Did he really mind? Perhaps it was always like this? Everywhere? That you never grew out of this sort of thing, as you grew out of nappies and toys? That the time would inevitably come when, he too would be unable to tear his eyes away from the sight of a naked boy putting on still-damp clothes in the glow of a dying fire? He didn't find Father Dunsley's prurience frightening, so much as simply quite funny. Funny and…'tedious'…was the Ansell's word which sprang unexpectedly to mind.

He had felt so relaxed and so warm that perhaps it really had been a fleeting dream. After all, he might well have fallen into the fire had not Father Dunsley caught him. Had Father Dunsley 'caught' him? Or held him? He could remember nothing distinctly. Between being on the verge of nodding off and suddenly standing up, hastily clutching the towel to himself, he could be absolutely sure of nothing more definite than, for that one brief moment, the texture of the priest's cassock pressing on his skin; that was all. Was this enough to convince himself that it had not been a dream yet, at the same time, too little to prove he had been definitely mistaken?

The rain had stopped. Warm and almost dry again, he bade a courteous, even grateful, farewell.

'Don't forget, Christopher, You are welcome at the Curacy any time…if you need advice.' *Or anything else?* It was the intensity of the priest's voice which implied the question. Or was it a plea? For the first time that afternoon, Angus felt fearful. He had not been dreaming.

The instant he stepped into the narrow still-glistening street, he found he was unbelievably glad to be quit of the dark, tobacco-scented Curacy and knew also he would never again willingly visit the shabby little chapel. He drew a deep, clean, breath as if expelling the last lingering tang of incense and tobacco. Although conscious that Father Dunsley was still watching him, he did not wave, nor even turn his head. As soon as he rounded the corner, he began running back to Ansell's, at first trotting slowly but then, like an escaping prisoner who, deciding that familiar limitations imposed by the constraints of captivity are far preferable to the vulnerability of freedom, he sprinted pell-mell.

❋

Despite the fact that he was to be Confirmed the next day, Angus found that memory of the incident in the Curacy aroused a desire which he could not quench, try as he would. When he eventually succumbed, guilt suffused him utterly. How, in that state of sin, could he possibly stand in Chapel with the others? Fire and brimstone would strike him dead! He went hot and cold with terror before dropping off at last into an uneasy sleep just before midnight.

In his dream he saw Father Dunsley and could hear the calm voice saying, 'If you need advice, Christopher... . If you ever need advice, Christopher.' They were sitting again on the fender in front of the fire, although somehow it widened and became a great roaring inferno which scorched him and all the time the voice insisted, '*If you need advice, Christopher.*' He even seemed to smell the tobacco-and-incense-scented cassock and to feel the priest touch him. 'It's hard to balance the urgencies of the body *at any age*, Christopher...'

He awoke with a start into the first light of dawn and realised, with disgust, that once again in his sleep he had been unable to avoid the consequences of his ungovernable sexuality. He recalled Ellins' advice, but could no longer find comfort in it. He was depraved. Father Dunsley's lapse – if indeed he had not dreamed it in his diseased imagination – must have been his fault. There could be little doubt now that in Chapel he would be struck by a great brand of fire. Short of running away there was no way he could avoid his fate: there was no way in which he could make another Confession before the Confirmation ceremony. For one wild moment he considered there and then, going to seek the proffered advice from Father Dunsley. At four in the morning? He took himself to Tosher and quietly ran a lukewarm bath. It was almost five when he returned and he slept fitfully until the seven o'clock bell, when he rose feeling hollow-eyed, nauseous with foreboding. At breakfast, which he did not really want, Notting grinned and said, 'If I didn't know you, AC, I'd say you looked shagged out.'

Snider said irritably, 'Shut up, for God's sake, Notting. You've got a mind like an open sewer.'

'At least I'm *allowed* to get Confirmed, Snider.' There was silence on the table. Snider got up and, without another word, left the room.

Mawsom said, 'You'd no need to say that!'

'Why not? It's true, isn't it? Of course The Digger wouldn't let him get confirmed! I don't care what anybody says. With a name like that he's bound to be a bloody Yid!'

In his invective Notting's voice had risen and they noticed Harlow at the nearby Top Table, looking their way. Notting coloured and shut up.

At the end of the meal, after Grace, Harlow stepped down. 'Notting, we heard what you said. You know very well Snider is not Jewish. Even if he were, it wouldn't bloody matter. He's an Ansell's Man. We're not like those bastards in Tortellier's who made Newman's life hell.'

'No, Harlow. I'm sorry.'

'You'll go, now, and apologise to Snider without reservation.'

'Yes, Harlow.'

'And make sure you tell him from me that he can cover-up. Do you know you've probably created a record, Notting?'

'Oh? What's that, Harlow?'

'Getting Confirmed and a Praefaectors' on the same day, Notting. We'll see you after Curfew.'

'Yes, Harlow.'

The small white card in Corridor read bluntly:

Notting will be beaten by the Praefaectors for being a confirmed turd.

Reeling like a man walking to his execution, Angus went with the others to Chapel. The sun was bright. Birds sang. He noticed none of it. He was going to meet his God and God would punish him.

At the porch, breathlessness engulfed him again, worse than ever before. It attacked him the moment he with the other Castonians came through the door into the soft luminosity of sunbeams coloured by the old glass. His chest was so taut that he could scarcely breathe, that he must faint, that he must die there on the flagstones. He felt cold, although sweat beaded his forehead. Yet he could not retreat. As the service wound its way, moments of blissful relaxation were superseded by far more intense moments of choking tightness. He expected to die. That was it; he would not come out of Chapel alive. His burden of sin and deception was too great for the mere laying on of hands to absolve him. His head would scald the Bishop's fingers. Had there been no press of people, he would have fled even then.

The others in his pew began to move and, all of a sudden, there he was, as they had rehearsed it, kneeling by the altar rail. Baker next to him. He knew, while he waited, kneeling, head bowed as if his neck were on the block, that the moment the Bishop's hand touched him he would die A bolt from God would stop his heart. And then he came into a great calmness. Nothing mattered any more.

The muttered words.
The touch on the head.
And then…
Nothing?
No blinding flash?
No thunderbolt?

The Bishop did not falter, but moved on. Angus heard the muttered words again, as Baker was Confirmed. He felt sudden blissful release from all the nightmare tension as though, lanced by the touch of the hands, some repellent foulness oozed from an internal bubo. The Digger had not perceived. The Bishop had not perceived. God had not perceived.

There was no retribution. Only marvellous peace.

When he rose and walked back down the aisle to his own pew, although he kept his eyes modestly on the stone flags, inside he glowed with intoxicating knowledge. He walked as if on air. Purged at last and finally reborn! Paralysing lightning had not struck. The worries and fears which had plagued him for months were irrelevant. Not even God had minded.

The efficacy of the visits to St Anne's were proved beyond any doubt. Or was that just mere superstition? Anyhow, now it felt as if all his visits to the dark confessional had been somehow rolled together and superseded forever. Now he had heavenly acquiescence. Whatever The Digger may have implied, Angus now knew that, however sinful his conduct, he was not irredeemable. Despite Father Dunsley (or was it because of Father Dunsley?) he knew he could always clean the page by a visit to the dowdy confessional. That was the assurance he needed. The laying-on of hands had confirmed the efficacy of all those absolutions. As they all left the Cranchester Chapel, he experienced a lightness of heart that, he assumed, must be what the Bishop in his address had meant by exultation.

The following Half, the sense of release and uncomplicated sensuality which he experienced with Simonsen seemed somehow to grow from, or be part and parcel of, the same exultation. By the simple act of laying on hands, the Bishop had lifted from him any possibility of permanent guilt, had freed him from the necessity of making any merely moral decisions about his actions. He had not, since then, felt the need even to consider revisiting the musty confessional. That Sunday morning in the Cranchester Chapel had told him what he ought to have known all along: God readily forgave conduct, such as his with Simonsen if, indeed, God ever noticed it.

Thus it had been an unwelcome discovery to find that now, at this stage, Singleton's presence had caused him to waver in his newfound confidence. He did not want to discuss the matter because Aunty Singleton would be very stuffy about it. So Angus lay and breathed deeply as if asleep until, in the end, he did sleep.

※

Angus awoke early, just after five. The bed on the floor was hard. Singleton was still sleeping. Angus dozed again. Singleton stirred, but did not wake. Angus remembered with a start that he did not want to walk with him to the train. He did not want to risk the chance of being betrayed into the sort of dangerous confidentiality which had so nearly swept over him the previous night. Singleton might ask him again about Simonsen. Or even Confirmation.

Getting up quietly he walked silently to Tosher. The Cranchester clock struck half-past five. Forty minutes and Singleton would have gone. He turned himself a bath. The water was, unusually at this early hour, very hot. He got in and dozed. He heard Singleton enter. Or was it somebody else? He did not stir. Whoever it was departed. He quietly turned on the hot tap once more. He did not want to meet Singleton again, it made him too uncomfortable but nevertheless he was ashamed at his cowardice. When he was quite sure Singleton had gone, Angus went back to the Manger and quietly made up his bed. He heard a slight movement and found Simonsen standing beside him. Simonsen grinned knowingly. 'Tarrant left early – for the train.'

'So did Singleton!'

'Tarrant tipped me.'

'It's the usual thing,' Angus said sharply.

'Not for the usual thing,' Simonsen whispered. 'Were you here with Tarrant? Do you remember him?'

'I should say so. We had a reign of terror when he was Head of House. The whole of the Junior Election had to tighten-up for him on the twelfth day of their first Half.'

'That explains it.'

'Explains what?'

'Why he got me to cut along to Big Study first.' Unselfconsciously Simonsen stepped from his pyjamas and turned round.

'Tarrant did that?'

'Oh I didn't mind tightening-up. Well, not much.' He paused. 'Well, actually it hurt like hell,' he added confidentially. 'But he made it worthwhile.' Simonsen held up two notes.

For the first time in his life Angus said, 'Christ!' Then added dazedly. 'Ten pounds!' He found he was shaken at the thought of Tarrant paying Simonsen to tighten-up; it made him feel slightly sick.

'It's only six-thirty,' Simonsen said. 'We might as well keep warm in your bed.'

'I wouldn't let on how much Tarrant tipped you.'

'Why not?'

'Well people might think...things.'

Simonsen said with pert complacency, 'So what! Harlow won't do anything about it.'

Angus found he could not despise Simonsen for his mercenary amorality; perhaps part of him secretly admired it. They enjoyed their uninhibited, uncomplicated concupiscence with mutual gratification. It was quite evident that tightening-up to Tarrant had diminished Simonsen's ardour in no way at all.

※

The early train struggled itself away from Cranchester station through a bright dawn. Singleton seated in the corner of a grimy compartment, stared through the anti-shatter net glued smearily over the window. After a while, taking out a pad, he started to write a letter.

My Dear Christopher,

I'm beginning this letter in the train. I can still just see the tip of the Church. Thanks for the bed last night. The match was fun, but I have the feeling that I shan't be at the game next year. Things change. I don't know, Christopher, when I shall finish this letter. Nor even if I shall finish it. And if I do finish it, I may well not post it. If I do post it, you may not want to read it – although you won't realise that until you have read it.

He stopped writing. Sad and angry he stared sightlessly out of the window. Was it just because Angus was no longer the serious, shy, apprehensive small boy he had idealised? 'I had to go to Big Study thirteen times last Half! It was a record!' Or anger at his own sloppy romantic sentimentality? Or was it because Angus reminded him uncomfortably of something he too had lost? His own fall from grace at a similar age? Perhaps it was a mixture of all three reasons. Recollecting Angus' brash remarks about Simonsen and life in Ansell's, he winced. He did not really want to remember himself at Angus' age, let alone any details which, he realised with dismay, was even more disconcerting than his total inability to recall any image of himself in those years.

He said aloud in the empty compartment, 'Bloody *mar*-vellous! Two years after leaving and I expect everything to stay the same!' To his confusion he sensed tears at the back of his eyes. He opened his wallet and took from the back compartment the snapshot Angus had left for him on his last morning at Ansell's. The writing on the back was still clear. With sudden bitterness he wanted to write: 'I thought you ought to have this photograph back because you've changed from the Christopher Angus here and you can see it's for the worse. I'd rather we did not meet again.' However he could not bring himself to do that. Instead he wrote,

When we met at the Match, you asked me if I could still recognise you. Last evening however, I felt that I didn't really recognise the Christopher Angus in this picture.

He read what he had said. 'Pompous ass!' Could he ever really send something like that? 'I don't claim to have been the soul of virtue myself...' That was worse, even more fatuous. Instead he wrote:

I wonder about Simonsen. Do you really know what you're in for? There's always somebody like him around. (Remember Dermott-Powell?) What I really mean, Christopher, is that I don't think Simonsen's your sort of person.

He considered adding, 'and if you're not careful Ansell's will crucify you.' He looked at the last sentence. It seemed stuffier and even more pompous than before.

Minute by minute the chattering train jerked him away from Cranchester and Ansell's and, he recognised, away from the last threads of a former self which had, until then, still retained some powerful hold on him. Perhaps he was jealous of Simonsen. Was that it? An unwelcome solution, but an explicable one.

He looked again at the snapshot and with the quick enlightenment of complete objectivity, he knew it was not as simple as that. The boy in the photograph had seemed to possess something which, instinctively, he, Singleton, had sought to cherish; something which he had imagined (foolishly, it now seemed) he might preserve for ever. The Angus he had met yesterday was no longer the boy in the photograph, but someone very different; somebody who now stood as conclusively on the same side of a great invisible divide as Singleton himself. In that enlightened moment of his new maturity, Singleton knew it must always be like that;

it always had been. Whatever precious quality he divined in the photograph, he could never have preserved it and rescue had never even been a possibility. The words he was directing so resentfully towards Angus were pathetic camouflage, a cry of frustration; nothing more nor less than a futile, childlike, tantrum. He saw that now. Nevertheless, despite the feeling that he might never post it, he continued with the letter throughout the journey and during the following weeks, because merely writing it seemed to help him exorcise some sort of personal demon: in a curious way, it kept him close to the Angus he wanted to remember.

iv

The following night, about an hour after everyone was asleep, Angus, lying on his back, woke to find Simonsen, naked, sliding in beside him, he pretended to be asleep but was immediately roused to expectant hardness.

'Old Prinners at the Choir School showed us how he liked it done to him. Want me to show you?'

'Didn't know you were a Chorister.'

'Can't sing for toffee, but the Choir School has non-singers as well. Do you?'

'I don't mind.... Yes.'

'Togs off then.' Sliding off his pyjamas, Angus shivered when a small, rather cold hand felt gently between legs, and then shivered again, but this time not from cold as, with well-tutored skill the fingers were drawn very lightly and extremely slowly from the back of his scrotum, over his testicles along the shaft, lingering at the, by now excitingly-sensitive, tip, before pulling back his foreskin until it was stretched so painfully tight onto his urgently thrusting tumescence that it could not, of its own accord immediately, retract over the swollen, exquisitely tender, head of his penis. Once. Twice. The third time, hard as he tried, Angus could contain himself no longer, ejaculating with such explosive completeness that he wondered whether he might have injured himself.

'I did that to Tarrant. After Big Study. That's really why I got the second fiver.' There was an expectant pause: 'Come on, Angus. Your turn.... Bet I can hold out longer than you! No, much slower.' Simonsen managed to hold out until Angus touched him for the fifth time when he too gave a stifled gasp of repletion. They repeated their mutual gratification thirty minutes later.

Angus woke still sleepy and exhausted, lethargically shuffled along to Tosher.

'*Another* tiring night, AC?' Notting leered.

Catching sight of Simonsen in the mirror, Angus gave him a conspiratorial lift of his eyebrows.

Three weeks before the end of the Half, Harlow came up to him and said quietly, 'Can I have a word with you in my study, AC?'

To his surprise, he found Simonsen there already, no longer the elf-like, mischievously sensuous, little Ansell's tart. The younger boy was plainly terrified. He looked pleadingly at Angus.

'Harlow made me tell him. About us.'

Angus felt his heart turn over. He said nothing.

Harlow said with a curious, precise primness, 'Is Simonsen right?'

Unable to look at Simonsen, or Harlow, Angus remained mute. 'Come on, Angus, it's bloody serious.'

Angus wanted to say, 'Well, what about everyone else in Ansell's?' However he realised that the less he said the better. Harlow said, 'It's not a matter of tightening-up for the Praefaectors. The Digger'll have to know.'

'The Digger!'

'Tell him, Simonsen.'

Simonsen stood, miserably mute, then blurted out, 'I think I've got VD.'

'He's got a rash. You know, down here.' The dawning enormity of the situation took Angus by the throat although he managed a puzzled shrug, as if to say what's that to do with me. 'Simonsen's been in your bed virtually every night, I gather.'

Curiously calm and with a quickness which surprised even himself, Angus said, 'He's your Warmer. You know what I mean. What about

Tassel Night?' Harlow turned noticeably pale. Finding within himself an alien toughness, born of fright, which he had never previously exploited Angus added, 'We'll deny it if you do tell The Digger, won't we, Simonsen?'

Simonsen, the picture of misery, made a half-nod and muttered, 'Harlow, you promised me you'd not say anything about Angus.'

Now realising his own predicament, Harlow was thoroughly alarmed. 'The Digger would never believe you. I'm Head of House.'

Gaining courage from Angus' determination, Simonsen said huskily, 'I wouldn't tell The Digger about Angus.'

With an unattractive sureness, Angus said, 'I bet they'd believe *us*. Because *you're* older.' His tone implied 'because everyone knows I don't lie'.

Harlow tried to call his bluff. 'We'll see!'

Reckless with fear, Angus said, 'It'd be worse for you, Harlow. As Head of House. If I am going to get sacked, I'll write to the *News of the World*. Like that chap at Eton.' A notorious scandal, made much of by some sections of the press, had been the source of a good deal of gossip and speculation. They stood looking across at each other defiantly.

Harlow said, 'Christ, what a mess!'

Simonsen had unconsciously moved towards Angus, as if for protection. Angus said, 'If they started asking questions, I wonder what they'd think of Ansell's? You're Head of House.'

Gratified to find that now he was not in the least frightened, he also knew he had won the argument. 'Anyway, Simonsen's rash might go tomorrow.'

Harlow had an unhealthy, raw-pastry colour. He turned to Simonsen. 'You'll just have to keep your mouth shut. Can you do that?' He shook Simonsen till his teeth literally chattered.

'I'll try Harlow. But if it is VD and they ask me how it could have happened? What shall I say?' None of them really knew much about VD, nor how it was caught, but they had seen the posters.

'Act dumb. Just pretend you're too young to understand what they're talking about.' Suddenly Harlow was struck by a new idea. 'Anyway, I think you can catch it from seats in public lavatories. Get permission today to go into Cranchester – use the one there. Then you can tell them about that if you have to.'

Early the following morning Simonsen appeared in Angus' Manger before he was awake and shook him. He whispered in a low, urgent, tone, 'The spots are worse. I'll have to go to the Flanders' Mare.' Angus gazed at him sleepily. The rash certainly looked very angry and seemed to be spreading in blotches. Simonsen said, 'I'm sorry I told Harlow. I promise I won't mention you, AC, I *promise*.'

Despite his own fear, Angus felt sorry for Simonsen. 'It's probably just a rash,' he said gently, although more than ever convinced that he was wrong. Simonsen vanished. For a few moments Angus lay in bed, thinking of what he had said to Harlow. He had been fighting back as Notting or Baker fought back when they were cornered. Snider would not have behaved like that. Ellerman would! For the hundredth time he wished that he'd had nothing to do with Simonsen. He wished that he had Singleton to turn to for advice.

That evening after Curfew he knocked at Harlow's study. Harlow looked up and said, 'I've heard nothing.' He was looking worried. 'I always thought you owned up to things, AC.'

Angus flushed: 'What about Tassel Night?'

'Tassel Night's quite different. You know that.' His voice changed to scathing contempt as he added, 'Or are you going to tell me that you're actually in love with that little tart Simonsen!'

'Of course not,' Angus said it quickly, equally scathing, but as he experienced a stab of treachery at the abandonment of his hero-worshipper. 'It's just that he's, well, fun.'

Harlow gave him a hard look. 'So our precious AC is just as randy as the rest of us! I admit you had *me* fooled. Let me offer you some advice, in case you're still here next Half. Tassel Night's a tradition that doesn't do any harm, even if it wouldn't look very good in *The News of the World*. However, the way you two have been going on is a bloody disgrace. You both deserve a Praefaectors' and would probably get one if it weren't so close to the end of Half. That's bad enough. But *falling in love* with the Junior Election – that's bloody perverted. Ansell's won't stand for that sort of crap...you ought to know that,' and, taking Angus by surprise, he added, 'I don't reckon you and Singleton would've lasted the Summer Half if he'd stayed on.'

'Singleton didn't... Singleton wasn't...'

Harlow cut him short. 'That wasn't how it looked, I can tell you! It's a great pity that oaf Dawes wasn't around a bit more before he got sacked, he'd've put things in perspective for you and tanned your arse whilst doing it!'

Angus said fiercely, 'I really would write to the papers.'

Harlow said, 'I know you would *now*. Who'd've thought Ansell's would succeed even with you? Get out!'

There was no news after lunch. However in the middle of supper The Digger entered still in his gown, an event so unusual that there was an immediate hush. He spoke briefly to Harlow. Angus guessed it must be about Simonsen. He closed his eyes and waited.

'I have news that I'm afraid will cloud the rest of the Half for some of you. You will all know Simonsen went to The Nurs'ry today. A few minutes ago the School Doctor telephoned to tell me that he expects that others will follow Simonsen because he was very infectious.' There was a terrible ominous pause as if the world held its breath. He cleared his throat: 'Hmmmm, I find this extremely embarrassing.' The Digger coughed. Angus, hanging on his words, kept his eyes on his plate and clenched his fists; he wished he could leave. This really was the end of the world.

'Simonsen has developed... *German* measles.' The Digger paused; 'It really is most unpatriotic of him!'

The astonished silence was broken suddenly by an incredulous voice: 'Christ! The Digger's cracked a joke!' followed by an ear-splitting roar of laughter and clapping. Angus felt almost hysterical with relief. The Digger, pretending not to notice, disappeared in a swirl of gown.

Ellerman shouted out, 'It's gone to his head! You know, D-Day and all that! It was certainly outside the memory of anyone in Ansell's that The Digger had ever risked more than a relieved frown.

German Measles proved highly contagious. The following day Harlow went to Nurs'ry followed by others who, like Simonsen, went home early as it was so near the end of Half. By an ironic quirk, Angus escaped altogether. Ten days later he received a letter with a London postmark. He did not recognise the writing, but it was from Simonsen.

Dear AC,

I expect you heard it was only German Measles. What a relief! They've sent me home as I'm not out of quarantine till almost the end of Half. Why don't you come and stay here on your way home? Ask your people. My mother says its okay by her, if you don't mind us having to share a double-bed because she's having other people here that night. I said we wouldn't mind!! !!! Do come. We could see the new film. We'll expect you on the 20th unless you write to say you can't come.

Yours,
Simon (SIMONSEN)
P.S. Tell your people we've got a shelter which is the safest in London!

It would be easy for him to refuse; Simonsen's betrayal of him to Harlow had caused him to wonder whether he should not take the opportunity to end their liaison. Nevertheless, despite the small voice chiming in his ear warning him that the lax Harlow would not be in charge the following Half, anticipation of Simonsen's practised, uninhibited, sensuality was far too seductive after ten days' deprivation. He wrote for permission to stay overnight in London with a schoolfriend.

Two days before the Half ended, The Digger made another appearance halfway through supper. He looked old and drawn. He said, 'You all know Simonsen went home to convalesce from German Measles. I have just received a telegram from his father.' He shifted uncomfortably. 'It saddens me very much to tell you that their house was destroyed by a direct hit from a Flying Bomb. Simonsen, his mother and an elderly relation were all killed instantly. Mr Simonsen was at his office and escaped. It'll be mentioned in Chapel tomorrow of course but it must be a particular sadness and shock to all of us who knew him. I always found him a cheerful and lively fellow. I know he was popular with all of you. He'll be missed. In his year with us, he'd made himself a real Ansell's Man.' Obviously overcome, The Digger left them. The meal finished in silence.

After the shock of the announcement, Angus found that somehow he could not grieve. Part of him knew he should; however another, secret, unattractive, part was relieved that Simonsen's death destroyed a bond which he knew he could not have broken of his own volition. For a moment, before he managed to repress the notion, it occurred to him that he was glad things had turned out as they had done and then, once again, was ashamed of his treachery.

Notting sidled up and, with clear reference to The Digger's speech, said, 'I expect you especially will miss Simonsen next Half, AC.' The sneering innuendo was blatant. They were alone in Big Dorm. Outrage at Notting's insensitivity, resentment at his innumerable teasing persecutions, the shock of Simonsen's death and, above all, deep-down guilt at his relief that Simonsen would never return, boiled over. With Simonsen back next half, he would have been playing with fire. Now that a doodlebug had removed the temptation and his own relief betrayed the devotion of his sensuous little acolyte, Notting had touched the rawest of spots.

He struck out with all his force. Angus felt his tormentor's nose crush against his fist and he was revolted to find blood on his knuckles. He turned and went without a word to Tosher, washed his hand and locked himself in one of the lavatory cubicles. He slumped down, ashamed that the power of his lust for Simonsen had caused him to descend to physical violence. Never before had he struck anyone really hard, in anger. The tears he shed were not for Simonsen's pathetic death under London rubble, nor even genuine regret for his own shoddy, discreditable, self-deceptions of the past year; they were indulgent tears of self-pity and mortification.

Eventually he went back to Big Dorm. Notting was explaining to anyone who would listen how he had dashed in, slipped on the shiny floor and crashed into a partition. Nobody doubted his story. As Angus passed,

Notting looked up, but never by so much as a flicker of the eye did he betray the truth.

Angus was unable to sleep. Each time he closed his eyes he saw with shocking vividness a great pile of smoking rubble. It was so real that he imagined he could, even smell the dust. However what frightened him most, was the fact that, try as he might, he could no longer conjure up Simonsen's elfin face at all.

Chapter Eight

I have before me the House photograph taken a day or two after the OA match that Half. Immaculate Praefaectors flank The Digger and The Flanders' Mare. Here we are in our gangling years – sheepish in the middle row, except for strikingly good-looking Ellerman, nothing in our bland faces to betray fears or lusts – with neatly brushed hair; Angus' white patch catches the sun. I've seen similar, recent photographs: sons, grandsons, nephews of friends and relations, all away at schools like Cranchester. It is uncanny; there *we* are, the same boys with different faces. Put their faces into our photographs, ours into theirs and who would know there were fifty years between them? The Junior Election sit cross-legged at the front. In the centre, Simonsen stares out, cherubic, innocent and, wary – as if something, or someone, beyond the photographer awaits him. A Praefaectors' in Big Study? Is it merely an old man's foolishness to wonder whether little Simonsen has a premonition of smoking ruins, even glimpsed the shadow of that hoary old labourer with hourglass and scythe who waits so patiently for us all?

Truth? Frankness? They are all very well now, but looking back at us in those middle years in Ansell's is hardly edifying. Did we really behave like that? I have to confess, yes, we did. Did I? Can I recognise myself? Identify myself? Of course I can, but I do not want to do so. So, once more, I could well have stopped here, cast aside my pen. Couldn't I? No, of course not! Oh how ineffectually I attempt to delude myself.

Even after all these years, the sequel remains etched so sharply on my mind that I can still recall all these scenes in uncompromising detail, conversations word for word. You think I exaggerate? That memory dims and blurs like eyesight? Distortion of old age?

Perhaps only those who experienced those war years away at school know how vividly these images can still remain. Even now I sometimes wake up suddenly, sweating: I am in my Manger early on Monday morning and I haven't yet completed the Latin prose due in to the Div Pro at nine o'clock. But far, far, worse I forgot to Warm for Bartlett last night. I actually cringe down in bed – until pricked awake by involuntary tears of relief, I come to full consciousness and find it is only the familiar half-waking nightmare. Even as I write this down, the sheer bliss of knowing that it all lies behind me a lifetime ago and that I cannot ever be back there again, makes me shut my eyes in gratitude.

ii

He did not discover the letter awaiting him in the rack until the day after the Half had started. It had obviously arrived towards the end of the long summer holiday. The envelope was grubby, partially disfigured by several post-office stampings. It had been opened and re-sealed by heavy brown tape over which a rough rubber stamp had printed **Passed by Censor**. *From Lt. C. A. Singleton, On Active Service.* The censors had blotted out regimental details. Then, with a jolt, he noticed it was addressed to *Christopher Angus* **Singleton**, *Ansell's, Cranchester, Wiltshire*. 'Singleton' had been squeezed in by a different, thick-nibbed pen and a different hand. Bloody Notting! How typical of Notting not to tell him the letter was there, so that all Ansell's would see and be reminded about him and Singleton. He knew it was his own sensitivity to such teasing which fuelled Notting's spiteful humour, but that only made him even angrier. He had hoped, evidently in vain, that it had ended. Between clenched teeth he said viciously, 'Notting's a sod!'

Although there was nobody about, he put the letter in his pocket surreptitiously. During the previous year, as gratitude towards Singleton had given way to hot embarrassment at the memory of his own hero-worship, Notting's constant pinpricks had caused him more and more secret agony. He, Angus, was all right now. He was on his own. He did not need Singleton any longer. He had tried to make that clear to Singleton on the night of the OA Match although he discerned that Singleton was in some way disappointed by their meeting. Despite his anger at Notting, he could not suppress the flicker of shame as he recalled the way he had avoided walking to the station with Singleton the following morning. Under his breath he said, 'Why the hell did he have to put his name on the back when he wrote?' Neither Notting, nor the rest of the Election, would ever let him forget Singleton's affection for him. Each letter made him a hostage to fortune; he simply *had* to get to the rack first each day.

However, another, almost submerged, part of him was secretly pleased that Singleton had written; he wanted to hear from Singleton, but for nobody else to know. It was a measure of his own ambivalent uncertainty that he could not yet acknowledge that he was developing both a private and a public attitude to Singleton. Because of the conflicting state of his emotions he did not read the letter, nor even open it until after Curfew, when he was alone in his Manger. He looked again at the franking. Singleton, he realised, must have gone across with the D-Day landing. Perhaps it would be an account of the fighting. When he opened the envelope a snapshot fell out. Idly he picked it up and turned it over. A small boy grinned back at him.

With genuine shock he realised it was himself. How on earth did Singleton have that? He looked at it again and felt himself flush as he remembered the circumstance. *He* had given *that* to Singleton? He turned it over and read the words on the back...and written *that*! Fiery embarrassment burned him, in order to dissipate it he turned over several sheets without really looking at them. Eventually a phrase caught his eye: *'If you think we'd still be on speaking terms after you've read this, you can post the photograph back. I hope you'll want to.'*

Conscious of a curiously empty sensation, he found he did not really want to read the letter; however he knew he must. Reluctantly he turned back the pages. Obviously they had not all been written at the same time. And so he came to the beginning.

Dear Christopher,

I am beginning this letter on the train.

Doggedly Angus read on. He wanted to stop, but as if hypnotised he read on. Anger, disappointment and frustration brought tears to his eyes. How dare Singleton! *HE WAS NOT LIKE THAT*! What bloody right had Singleton? He clenched his hands but, despite mounting fury, he still could not restrain himself from reading on although, at the same time, railing inwardly. *Bloody AUNTY* Singleton. So Aunty Singleton didn't approve of Tassel Night? Who the Hell cared? It was just that Singleton didn't *dare*. Anyway, what the hell did it matter to *Aunty Singleton* if he and Simonsen.... Of course, Singleton was jealous! That was it! After all, hadn't Singleton hinted on that first OA match night, that even with Angus he'd wanted to? Why hadn't he? Why hadn't Singleton introduced him to the pleasures of Tassel Night? When he, Angus, was a Praefaector he'd make bloody sure...

Fury got the better of him. Although there were still some pages to go, like a spoiled child in a paroxysm of temper he tore the letter once, several times, many times, into smaller and smaller pieces. To his chagrin he found he was unable to bring himself to do the same with the snapshot. After he had ripped it savagely once, it seemed somehow as if he were destroying himself; he stuffed the pieces out of sight in the back of his writing case. The tiny fragments of the letter he flushed angrily down the lavatory. He would ignore it. He would pretend Singleton had never written.

That night he caught sight of the anthology Singleton had given to him on his departure. He had scarcely opened it since then. He flipped it open at the inscription on the flyleaf:

Father, what you buy me I like best.

Father? *Aunty* Bloody-Singleton! Savagely, he tore out the flyleaf and screwed it up. The next day he dumped the mutilated volume in the dustbins.

Nevertheless, as time passed, he was niggled by a feeling that for him not to reply at all was another example of the cowardice he had demonstrated over Simonsen's tragic death. He scribbled two rambling, hysterically self-justifying replies which offended even his almost dormant integrity. Finally he wrote something which, in its cold, curt, rudeness was less a letter, than an acknowledgement of a correspondence he did not intend to continue. In a cold anger he walked all the way into Cranchester to post it.

When, during the following days, he remembered what he had written, he swept the recollection hastily from his mind and suppressed twinges of a conscience, refuelling his indignation with remembered phrases from Singleton's hateful letter. His self-justification and self-deception were a striking tribute to the success with which Ansell's was shaping him. He strove to repress entirely any recognition that his intemperate anger was in part aroused by the knowledge that he was deliberately misrepresenting Singleton in order to avoid facing himself with the unwelcome truths implied by Singleton's admonition. Nonetheless, however hard he tried, he found that he was unable wholly to convince an inconveniently persistent flicker of conscience that Singleton's sermonising really was 'inexcusable'.

During unguarded moments, embers of his former self-honesty and integrity flared into life. At such uncomfortable times, he did his best to avoid acknowledging that what had really hurt him most was the loss of Singleton's good opinion. He could not satisfactorily banish the knowledge deep within himself that still, somehow, he valued Singleton's approval more highly than the approval of his Ansell's contemporaries. This insecurity served only to stoke his anger ever more furiously. What bloody right had 'Aunty Singleton' to tell *him* what to do? Bloody Aunty Singleton expected him to remain forever the pathetic little wet who would cry on his shoulder. Yet a secret bit of him still missed the shoulder.

Because he had torn it up, Angus could not amend his hasty and emotional perusal of Singleton's letter. Possibly, had he been able to indulge in a more reflective reading, he might have perceived that Singleton's words were prompted neither by anger nor priggishness, but by a concern which is only possible where there exists that degree of love which is beyond destruction. Perhaps he would have pondered sporadic, unconnected paragraphs that were sometimes almost repetitive. Perhaps he would have needed to be older too: indeed, even Singleton had not realised how much he had inadvertently revealed. Certainly it would have needed a more skilled and experienced pen than Singleton's to have avoided sounding sentimentally pompous and censorious.

※

For reasons which Angus could not entirely rationalise, he had continued in the Choir, now as an undistinguished Tenor. Occasionally, when on a Sunday or a special occasion there was a solo, he experienced a fleeting nostalgic pang. He was secretly glad that nobody else had done the anthem he and Dermott-Powell had sung. However, the following Monday, perhaps because the organist was playing a piece by Mendelssohn which reminded him of their duet, he was listening with only half an ear to the short morning service. It was the first of October. Outside, the air was clear and sharply bright. A shaft of light fell through a blue pane of glass and across the hair of the boy in front of him, giving him a curious piebald look. The High Master from his stall had read the Lesson.

Then he began to speak and Angus was jerked from the reverie that had led him to miss the opening words: '...Singleton died from the wounds received. He was commanding a squadron during the advance of Caen, when they ran into a very strong German armoured group. Singleton's tank received a direct hit.' In the hush that such announcements always engendered, the High Master continued, 'Singleton was a Castonian who was, perhaps, not much known outside his own House, Ansell's. Moreover although of course only a subaltern, he was Acting Major, in command of a crack tank squadron. He met his death in an action for which, you will all be proud to know, he has been recommended for a Bar to the MC awarded for gallant leadership during the Normandy landings which was, sadly, Gazetted only yesterday.'

Because he was at the end of a choir stall, Angus found that the rest of the row had left him. A few boys were still shuffling out of the Chapel doors when he finally moved down the aisle as if in a dream.

Singleton killed in action.

That possibility had never crossed his mind, just as it had never crossed his mind that little Simonsen would be in danger from doodlebugs. However, there *was* a difference, Simonsen's death was like a car accident – nobody could have forecast it. With Singleton, he ought to have known that it might happen. Singleton's letter had come from France, from the battlefield, yet even that had never impressed on him the fact that Singleton was really doing anything dangerous. He remembered the skull-and-crossbones cap-badge.

He walked out into brittle October air. *Singleton is dead*. He had been dead for the past weeks and he, Angus, had not known. Somehow he felt cheated; he *ought* to have known: he had read of those who had premonitions about the death of those close to them. Perhaps was it because their closeness had vanished that there had been no intimation: Singleton had posted that letter and then been killed. They could never now meet again. He thought of his own reply and was surprised that he should now feel such a gap. Had he been deluding himself? Had he not meant the bitter words he had written back? Had Singleton ever received his reply? Perhaps it had not yet reached him in the confusion of battle. What happened to letters like that? Would it be sent back to him? Had he even put on his address? Certainly not on the envelope. So somebody would open it and read it...or would it be sent with his other effects, to Singleton's mother and father? All at once, he hoped that whatever had happened, it would not now be sent to them. Somehow, he felt, he had betrayed himself in it.

Despite his resentment at what Singleton had written, he was suddenly, dreadfully, far more troubled by the notion that Singleton had received his reply and died before Angus could apologise. Or even, having received Angus' reply, had deliberately gone out to his death. He collected himself with a start. 'Singleton, ought to have apologised to me,' he argued through clenched teeth. But did not convince himself. Fortunately the Div Pro was even later than he and so his delayed arrival aroused no comment. Throughout the lesson and the rest of the day, he found himself increasingly troubled by the fear that it might have been his reply that had driven Singleton to his death. Then, later, he was even more troubled by the thought that if it had, was it possible he was more awed by his own power than saddened by Singleton's death?

Mawsom came into his Manger before lights were put out. 'Sorry about Singleton!'

'It was bad luck, wasn't it? Especially in view of the MC.' His voice gave nothing away.

'Didn't you get a letter from him recently?'

'Letter? Oh! Yes, as a matter of fact I did. Bit boring. More of a sermon than a letter! Expect he was going to be a parson like his father.'

'I thought you'd be more upset.'

'Did you?'

'Well, you owe him a good deal for your first two Halfs.'

'Do I?'

'You told me you did.'

'That was a long time ago. I think it'd've been better if he'd been more like the other Praefaectors.' Angus busied himself with his hairbrush.

Mawsom said quietly, 'Is that what you really think, AC?'

'Yes,' came indistinctly from behind the brush.

'God! You've changed.' Mawsom got up. 'Sometimes you sound like Ellerman – or Notting.' That stung.

'When we were Junior Election, I was bloody wet.'

'Perhaps. But you were also a bloody sight nicer.' Mawsom vanished to his own Manger.

In the dark, Mawsom's words circled round and round in his head. Bloody *side* on Mawsom's part! However, it was no use; the doubts he had more or less managed to suppress on receipt of Singleton's letter emerged more dramatically now Singleton was dead. And he, Angus, had driven him to sacrifice his life. Nevertheless, although appalled by his own callousness, he found that repeating remembered phrases from the hateful letter still served to dissipate his sympathy and stoke his petulance. 'I can *never* forgive him for writing as he did.' At the same time, images from the past flittered into his memory that contrasted uncomfortably with the Singleton he had sought to construct for himself on the basis of the too-truthful letter.

During the following days he sought his own company, which was not difficult, because nobody, it seemed, sought his. Perhaps they mistook the reasons for his melancholy. Ellerman came up to him and said, 'Sorry about Singleton.'

'Yes. Bad luck for him, wasn't it?' He did not want to think about Singleton. However, the more he wanted to forget, the more he remembered and the more he wished that he had not put forward a show of such indifference to Mawsom. He noticed that Mawsom, almost pointedly, avoided his company, never even suggesting that they should run Marathon.

At the end of the month there came another letter. He found it when he returned from watching Cranchester sweep to victory; three marvellous tries had been scored by Ellerman. He had hoped that either Snider or Mawsom would walk back with him but somehow, after the final applause he found they had slipped away. He picked up the blue envelope and, glancing at it, was at once coldly furious that it was addressed

Christopher Angus Singleton

Bloody Notting again! Then he realised his anger was unjustified, for he could see that there was no alteration, but he did not recognise the writing. Could it be a joke? For some reason he thought of Dermott-Powell. The postmark was somewhere in Kent. When he opened it the address meant nothing, the handwriting painfully neat.

Convalescent Hospital,
Erdridge,
Kent.

Dear Master Angus,

> I hope you won't mind me writing, but I was Captain (sorry, Major) Singleton's Batman. I'm sure you'll of heard of his death long since. We was in the leading tank and when it was hit I was wounded. He got me out and then went back to keep firing. He went on firing the gun even after they hit the tank the second time and he was badly wounded. I saw him in the dressing station just before he died. I was lucky and only lost a leg.

He was a good officer. Everyone in the Squadron thought a lot of him. Very friendly if you know what I mean, not like officers are supposed to be at all. I expect you know he thought a lot of you which is why I wrote. He had your photograph in that leather case and I once said that anyone could see you two was brothers. At first I think he was going to tell me off, for being nosey you know, but after a bit he said, He's the nicest kid I know, Johnson, serious like. So I know you was close – some brothers are and some aren't. I had a brother who was a great pal but he died with the scarlet fever when he must've been about your age judging from the photo. [Johnson, Angus realised could not know the photograph had been taken three years before.] I hope you don't mind me telling you that. But what I really wanted to say is that I hope you got that letter from him. I knew that he'd been writing you quite a long letter. Always at odd moments when we weren't on the move. When I was packing up his kit afterwards, I realised he hadn't posted it. So I posted it for him. I hope it arrived. Perhaps I ought to have kept it till I got back here on leave. I put the photograph in seeing he was so fond of it. Hope I did right because I noticed he hadn't signed it, although of course I didn't read it.

Excuse if this isn't a very good letter. It's the longest I ever wrote. I liked Mr Singleton and we all did.

We was all very glad about the M.C. Should've been a V.C. but those all go to the P.B.I. if you'll excuse the word.

All very best wishes, yours sincerely,
Edward Johnson (22345876)

Singleton had not sent it!
Singleton had *not* posted the letter.
He stood unmoving, as though stunned by a blow from a great hammer.

He felt he had been within some sort of shell which had now been broken, restoring to him vistas and perspectives he had forgotten. Suddenly, Singleton was there, in front of him, nodding a greeting, no longer the unjust, hateful letter-writer his imagination had conjured up, the deserving recipient of his own hysterical reply. He was the Singleton with whom he had last talked as a friend and mentor on a stile on a bright summer morning.

He read the letter again. One or two Ansell's Men looked at him curiously as they passed. Eventually, suddenly, he came to a decision. He took writing paper and envelope into Din Room. Because it was strictly forbidden, except for meals, he knew that nobody would dream of seeking him there. He looked at the names on the walls. Singleton's was there; it looked no different. Would they add MC? No, that would be in Chapel. It was not quite silent; diffused sounds from the kitchen intruded and occasionally, in a curiously muffled way, sounds from the boys' side of Ansell's seemed to increase the isolation. He had never been in there without the rest of the House, or Praefaectors, being present.

> Dear Mr Johnson,
>
> It was kind of you to write. Thank you also for posting the letter and the photograph to me. I shall miss him a lot. He was always very decent to me. I am so sorry to hear about your leg. Thanks for writing.
>
> Yours sincerely,

He could understand how Johnson might have mistaken Angus for a Christian name. Wouldn't it be ungenerous to embarrass the batman by drawing attention to the misunderstanding? After a long pause, he signed it carefully, Christopher *Angus Singleton*'. Because it was, in a way, intended as an apology and also a tribute, he felt Singleton would have understood the deception. He posted the letter in the shabby wooden box by Door.

Clad in muddy jersey and shorts, he started out on Marathon. Already it was growing dark. However, as the ground rose, it seemed that the sky became marginally lighter. He drew great breaths, feeling cold air cleansing his lungs so deep that it seemed his chest must burst.

On Roman Road, he walked. He felt almost euphoric. Singleton might have written the letter, *but he had not posted it*. Had he ever really intended to send it? The various additional paragraphs had not been dated; Angus remembered, dimly, that the last addition had been written in August. Not for the first time, he wished he had kept it. He took out Johnson's letter and read it again, for there was still light enough.

He forced himself to look at the Angus seen by Singleton at the OA match the previous Half but through the eyes of the boy in the embarrassing photograph he had torn up and he did not enjoy what he saw. Almost at once, his mind began the self-justification which had become second nature to him. 'What right had Singleton' until, inside his head Mawsom's voice surfaced, ' …you were a bloody sight nicer.' He would not excuse himself. Not any more.

Because he felt flattered – no, more than flattered, cherished, even loved – he did not notice the bitter wind. Singleton had allowed Johnson to go on thinking he, Angus, was his brother, despite what he had written. It came to him at that moment that it must have been Johnson who had added 'Singleton' to the address of the humiliating letter, the alteration which had so angered him at the time. Angus was ashamed at the memory of his burning hatred for Notting, whom he had assumed to be the culprit. Furthermore, with his new perception he could now admit to himself the truth of the matter – nobody had teased him about Singleton during the Half nor, if he were honest had they teased him very much during the previous year. He had chosen to imagine a persecution for the convenience of his conscience. It was as if he had been viewing everything through the wrong end of a telescope.

It was not the wind that chilled him, but remembrance of his own shameful reply to Singleton's letter – until he realised that Johnson could not have posted it until after Singleton's death; he had posted his savage reply to a dead man. After momentary relief the chill returned, deeper. Had Johnson read his reply? It was nearly dark but he re-read the batman's letter again, the writing was large and black, and he was reassured. Surely it could never have been written had his own reply arrived and been opened.

It was as if he had been stripped and forced to gaze upon his own soul. It had been necessary for him to know what Singleton had thought, however unpalatable, but far more important was the knowledge that Singleton had not actually posted the letter. Might he have still done so, had he lived? No, Singleton would not have posted it, ever: perhaps it was Corporal Johnson's letter which offered him such assurance.

With extraordinary vividness he recalled the little chapel in the back street of Cranchester, the musty Confessional. It must have been almost a year ago that he had first poured out his fall from Grace. He remembered (having knelt penitently afterwards in a hard pew) stepping from the incensed air and burning tapers into the dark street where nobody could see him, feeling that he had been released from some hideous burden. Now, admitting to himself that Singleton had not been unjustified in what he had written, he felt the same release. Would he once again be able to make a new, a different, beginning? He could no longer hide from himself the fact that he had used his subsequent Confessions to license uninhibited, unrestrained conduct.

Angus is the nicest kid I know.

The wind had strengthened; it flapped the thick paper. Perhaps he relaxed his grip, for all at once it was snatched from his fingers. Briefly the pale rectangle flattened against a gorse-bush. He made no move to recover it and the sheet danced free again, bowling off into the darkness. In his imagination he could hear the brittle page clicking as it darted and jumped across the rough pasture of the downs, ink dissolving in pools and streams and the spitting rain. It seemed right to let it go; after all he had destroyed Singleton's letter. He had not even read the final pages. Had Singleton ever intended to sign it? He would never know for sure.

He could no longer hide from himself that the delusion of it being his curt reply which sent Singleton to his death seemed utterly odious now. Had he wanted to believe that he'd had such a hold on Singleton's affection that one bitter letter...? What despicable arrogance! Worse than arrogance. He remembered Dermott-Powell. He remembered Ellerman boasting of Bartlett's apology. He remembered what Maunder had called

Ellerman that last evening. Congratulating himself on his power over Singleton; he, Angus, had become a tart. He wasn't like that. He was *NOT LIKE THAT*.

In the dark he began to trot downhill. The path steepened, his pace increased. Until now he had shown no grief at the news of Singleton's death. His hitherto impenetrable self-deception had allowed him to show none, for it could never have survived such honesty. Above all, he felt bitterly ashamed at his own sickening vanity. At first he pretended the tears on his cheeks were the result of sleet and cold stinging his eyes. However he knew the pretence for another shabby betrayal and, by the time he stumbled across the ford into the main Cranchester bounds, he had acknowledged them for what they were – tears for Singleton's death in a burning tank. But also perhaps for the unblemished frankness of a small boy smiling guilelessly in the holiday snapshot which he had mutilated in guilty denial. Uneasily he sensed that even this acute private grief, sincere though it was, did not discharge in full the obligation he had so subtly contracted.

iii

'What the Hell is a *non dies* anyhow?'

'It's a day that doesn't count,' Snider said. 'They don't happen very often. The last one was for the Coronation and before that The Armistice at the end of the Great War.'

'Oh.' Notting sounded unconvinced.

'It's a sort of holiday?' Angus said. 'We can do what we like?'

'But must be back by Curfew. For the bonfire,' Snider added.

Notting said, 'I'm going to do something today that I shall always remember. Something I shall tell my children about.'

'That limits your choice, Notting. If you're going to be able to tell your children about it, I mean,' Baker muttered slyly.

Notting opened his mouth, then thought better of it. He reddened. 'Shut up, Baker!'

'I haven't said anything.'

'Well don't then.'

'I was only going to suggest you should spend the day reading *Oliver Twist.*' Baker smiled in the confidence that Notting would not understand. He walked off.

'What's that mean?' Notting stormed after him.

'What on earth was all that about?'

Mawsom looked at Angus sideways. '*Oliver Twist.*'

'Stop being so bloody intellectual, Mawsom.'

Mawsom said patiently, 'Oliver Twist's real name was Brownlow.'

The liaison between Notting and Brownlow had been much noted since the beginning of the year. Mawsom said, 'Didn't you get on quite well with Brownlow last year, Angus?'

Angus forced himself to look at Mawsom. He said, 'I saw him on Tassel Night a couple of times.'

'Before Simonsen,' Mawsom said pointedly.

'Before Simonsen,' Angus acknowledged as though it were a confession. In doing so he acknowledged the gradual return of the friendship between himself and Mawsom.

Mawsom said, 'If Brownlow would listen, you could tell him that he's going too near the line.'

'I'm not a Praefaector.'

Mawsom said, 'I expect he'd be most likely to listen to you.'

'Perhaps. Though I've hardly spoken to him this year.'

'Notting's bad news for him.'

'Notting's sometimes misjudged.' He thought guiltily of his unjustified condemnation of Notting for adding 'Singleton' to Corporal Johnson's letter.

'He's never stopped getting at you about Singleton!' Mawsom said. Then, emollient, 'I say, Angus, an uncle of mine, Godfather actually, who lives not too far from Salisbury, has asked if he can take me out. There are celebrations in the village…bonfire and all that. What are you doing?'

'I haven't thought.'

After a pause, Mawsom said diffidently, 'I'm sure you could come if you want. The Digger's like a dog with two tails. Anyone'd think he'd won the war himself.'

'I'd love to come,' Angus said warmly. It seemed as though Mawsom too was offering to re-establish their old intimacy. 'I'd like to very much!'

'It's overnight. We'll miss the bonfire here.'

Angus said, 'I don't feel like celebrating Victory at Ansell's. It's been bloody awful this Half. You'd think we'd lost the war!'

Mawsom said sympathetically, 'I know. Everyone's been edgy.'

The onset of obvious victory in Europe had somehow swamped Ansell's with a sort of depressed sourness. Harding, a boy in the Election below them had been given a Praefaectors' for nothing more than failing to turn up to a Colts practice to which, he protested, he'd never been summoned, having been selected as a last-minute replacement for the first choice who'd been carted off to Nurs'ry. There was an air of savagery.

'I'm not even good at cricket this year!' Angus was finding it difficult even to hold his place in the House side. His bowling was spectacularly unsuccessful and even his fielding seemed to have lost its edge. 'I think they'll play Winterson instead of me.' Winterson had come in the Autumn Election with a reputation as a very promising batsman from his Private.

'Oh, that's just Ashton twisting your tail. They'd never drop a Tassel.'

'No?'

'Well, it's not likely.' Mawsom did not sound as though he believed what he said.

'I can't even seem to take to a catch properly.'

'Well, forget about it and spend tomorrow at Bowerford with me.'

'Thanks. I'd really like that. To be away from Ansell's, I'll feel like a prisoner of war being released.' He immediately looked round in case anyone should think he was casting a slur on Ansell's which, inadvertently, he was. 'I'll ask The Digger before Curfew.' No objection was raised. So it happened that they spent VE Day and the night, away from Cranchester. They were driven back in time for morning chapel. Mawsom's uncle had influence and petrol.

※

There was an air of debauched somnolence about Cranchester when they returned. Everyone looked tired and subdued and, at lunch, the air persisted. There was little conversation. Notting hardly spoke a word. After Curfew, in Big Dorm, Angus said, 'I say, Mawsom, have you seen Brownlow's arse?'

'Why should I be interested in his arse?' Mawsom raised his eyebrows and gave him a mock quizzical look.

'Whose arse are we discussing?' Ellerman had joined them.

'Brownlow's apparently,' said Mawsom, looking across at Angus.

'What about Brownlow's arse, AC? If it's not a delicate matter?'

'It looks as though...'

'We polished it for him last night,' Ellerman said. 'Used two whole tins of Cherry Blossom Dark Tan. And Dubbined his balls.' He laughed.

'Who did? And why?'

'Oh! The whole of Ansell's, Mawsom. If it hadn't been a *non dies* they'd've got a Praefaectors'.'

Mawsom said, 'Ansell's are like a lot of bloody savages after a few pints of cider.'

'They deserved it!'

'They?'

'Brownlow and Notting?'

'You mean you Cherry Blossomed Notting too?'

Ellerman smiled: 'Yes *and* we shaved him.' Seeing Angus' incomprehension, 'Not his *head*! The joke is that it means he can't cover-up until it grows again.'

He nudged Angus and they were in time to see Notting slip into his Manger.

'So it wasn't like Tassel Night?'

'Oh yes. Afterwards. Later. Early on Botting said Notting had been jumping the gun and that, anyway, Brownlow wasn't a Tassel. He made Notting put the first of the boot polish on Brownlow's arse. Then, whilst the Junior Election held Notting down, Brownlow had to lather him up for the shaving and make the first stroke with the razor.' Ellerman said, 'You missed something. Tassel black; arse, appropriately, Dark Tan. Great value.'

Mawsom said flatly, 'It sounds it!'

'Actually, Brownlow took it very well.'

'Don't suppose he had much choice, did he?'

Ellerman said meaningfully, 'Well, he's become a regular little tart, hasn't he, Angus?'

'If that's your opinion, Ellerman.' Angus refused to be drawn. When he had gone, Angus said, 'I don't much like Notting, but I'm very glad we were with your uncle.'

Mawsom said, fastidiously, 'This boot polish thing. Only oiks do that.'

'I think it happened at OTC Camp last year, in Wales. Some Grammar School lot were there at the same time as Cranchester. Notting's been going on and on about how they did it to one of their NCOs. That's probably what gave everyone the idea, so it serves him right, I suppose.' Angus said thoughtfully, 'I bet he never tells his children!'

'Perhaps the Peace is going to be worse than the War,' Mawsom said softly and vanished.

※

Whatever had happened on VE night, had not happened 'officially'. In Ansell's, except for Notting and Brownlow, there was no outward sign that anything had taken place beyond what Cranchester, in its staid way, would have approved. Nonetheless, in the following days and weeks it became obvious that not only in Ansell's, but in other Houses too, that VE Day had been time-out-of-time. Quite evidently, scores had been settled. It was as though the end of the war had released everyone from some sort of truce. Moreover, whether it was the brighter light of early summer, or something more than that, it seemed as though, almost overnight, Cranchester, Houses, Masters, even the boys themselves, all looked somehow suddenly shabbier, coarsened.

Snider had always been the most observant of their Election. On a fine afternoon, Angus came upon him sitting on a long-abandoned horse-roller watching the Colts Game. They stood for some time without talking. Eventually Snider said, 'You weren't here on VE night, were you?'

'No! I heard it was...rough.'

'It was incredible.' Snider paused and said shamefacedly, 'Me too. Even you'd've been the same had you been here, AC. It was...like an infection.'

'I'm sure I should've been just the same.' Snider, he thought, must have noticed his behaviour in the previous year although, he now realised, he had not noticed Snider. He had been too immersed in himself and Simonsen ever to bother about others.

'I was reading about the recapture of Paris,' Snider went on. 'You know, everyone had been co-operating in the French underground, right till the liberation. Then they all split up into rival groups, Communists and so on. They settled old grudges. Even killed each other.' He paused. 'It was a bit like that here…everyone was getting his own back on Notting. For things he's said. As if he was a collaborator, the enemy.'

'Bad luck on Brownlow then!'

'With Brownlow it was more of a rag. Although that too was like France – I can't explain it except to say they cut off all the hair of the women who'd had German boyfriends – when they started on him. I mean, he didn't like it, but I think he knew Ansell's didn't really mean it. He wasn't scared because he knew it was a bit of a rag. Notting was. Notting knew he was hated.'

'Notting's got a sharp tongue.'

Snider said, 'Yes, so's Baker, but I reckon if we'd been in Paris, Notting would have been strung up from a lamp post. Like Mussolini. Nobody really likes Notting.' He paused, 'I think that's why he's been told he can't cover-up until his hair grows again. And he's keeping quiet.' Notting had barely exchanged a word since VE Day.

By chance, after nets, Angus found himself alone in Change except for Brownlow towelling himself vigorously. 'I expect you heard about VE night! Cherry Blossom doesn't come off very easily.' Brownlow grinned. 'My own fault I suppose for getting caught up with Notting.' He did not seem at all abashed. 'We all got tight as ticks on some cider that The Digger got from somewhere in Dorset. Even little Weston.' (Weston, a small dark cherubic child was the most timid of the Junior Election.) 'He did the dance of the Seven Veils on the table.' Brownlow laughed. 'He can't remember anything about it now. Just as well. I don't know where he picked up the song he was singing. As for the gestures! By the time he passed out and got carried to bed, he was wearing only his socks!'

'I'm glad you didn't mind too much.'

'Well, it was only my arse they Cherry Blossomed. They just Dubbined the rest.' He gave a secret grin: 'As a matter of fact, Angus, I got an Eiffel Tower while they were doing it, so Botting said that, as it was VE night, they might as well carry on and finish me off.' He flung down the damp towel, 'Anyway it's not much use "minding" in Ansell's, is it?' Brownlow looked at him quizzically. 'You'd never last you first Half if you did. Was it like that when you came, AC?'

'I think it's always been like that.'

'Probably why Ansell's is such a bloody good House.' It seemed to Angus that, although a year junior, Brownlow had come to terms with Ansell's far more completely and successfully than he himself.

He said, 'It doesn't agree with everyone.'

'You mean Jeffrey?'

In fact Angus had not meant anyone in particular except possibly himself.

'He wasn't really the sort for Ansell's. We were at the same Private,' Brownlow added by way of explanation.

I didn't know. However, even Jeffrey lasted out the year.'

Brownlow nodded: 'I suppose you're right. He talked to you, didn't he? Jeffrey? Did you tell him to go to Nurs'ry?'

'Perhaps.'

'Good for you, AC. I wouldn't have lasted if I'd Warmed for Bartlett,' although his tone indicated that he knew he would have survived.

'I know I wouldn't've.'

Brownlow gave him a sharp look. 'Well, you certainly made up for lost time with Simonsen last year! Is it true he'd invited you to stay with him and his people in London, before...you know...the doodle-bug?'

Angus was glad that Brownlow took himself off without waiting for a reply.

iv

The Old Ansell's Match was the following day. After lunch, Ashton sought him out. 'I'm sorry to have to tell you, AC, that I'm dropping you from the House XI tomorrow. What's happened to your fielding? You dropped two dollies against the Tuskers.'

Angus flushed: 'They weren't exactly sitters, Ashton. Right down in the gully.'

'Two years ago, you'd've snapped 'em up.'

Angus knew he was right but said, 'I'd rather expected to play. Especially as I'm a Tassel.'

Ashton said, 'I can't ever remember us dropping a Tassel before, but young Winterson has now scored three half-centuries for Cranchester Colts. To be frank you're a bloody shambles this season. You can't even bowl a decent length any longer, your fielding's gone absolutely to pot and you never could bat anyway.'

'Is this your master stroke as Captain?'

Ashton, not yet a Praefaector, was sensitive to such gibes. 'That's nothing to do with it.' He got very red. 'You show a bloody sight too much *side*, Angus. Ever since Harrington Tasselled you because you let him pat your arse, you've thought you could play cricket!'

'It was because of my fielding! My catching.' He found he had clenched his fist.

'Was it? If I'd been Fielder-Jones I'd never have left the crease until the umpire had signalled.'

'You bowled a bloody awful ball and I saved your bacon.'

'You know, AC, I've always thought you put it down. When you stood up, you certainly *looked* as though you had, I was facing you. Then I couldn't really believe Angel Arse would lie!'

'You were keen enough to claim the wicket!'

'Oh, all's fair in love and a House match. Anyhow, you might still get on because you'll be Twelfth Man.'

Twelfth Man! All the OAs would know he'd been dropped for loss of form, not because of injury.

'No, I bloody shan't!'

'Yes, you bloody will, Angus. Or you can explain to Botting…'

'He may be Head of House, but he makes me sick,' Angus retorted fiercely. 'Neither he, nor you, can make me sit there tomorrow, scoring.'

'You needn't score, little Weston's volunteered, but *you* are Twelfth Man. *And* you'll be there. All day, whether needed as a sub or not. You might even have to sub for OAs.'

Angus hoped that others would feel his loss of place to be unjust. When he had played for the House as a surprise choice and the youngest in the side that first Summer Half, somehow he had known that everyone was pleased – glad he should be encouraged. Now, however, he sensed that everyone approved Ashton's decision and the crowning of Winterson as the new, young, golden boy. It was as though he had run out of their sympathy. Or had he exhausted it, the previous year?

In bed, he reflected that, although he had re-established himself with Mawsom, he was no longer…he vaguely remembered there a Latin phrase *persona* something…and stuck. As he lay dozing, it came to him, the apposite word slid in sideways, as it so often did just before he fell asleep – *mascot* that was it. In those first couple of years he had been Ansell's mascot. Now taller, brasher and as often insensitively crude as most other Castonians of his age, he no longer warranted the affectionate protection his naivety had once invited.

Nevertheless, he had no real intention of defying Ashton. Despite his truculence, disobedience had never really been a possibility. What a waste of a day! For, on the Saturday of the Old Castonian games against their former Houses, there was no Early School before breakfast (an unpopular pre-war discipline, which had been reinstated immediately hostilities ceased) nor Morning School. His fielding had been bad. How on earth had he ever taken all those catches in his first year? Did Ashton really know about the Fielder-Jones catch? Or was it a guess? He was both glad and sorry he had never told Singleton about it.

Then he remembered the letter that had come ten days before. It was still light enough to read, so he pulled the envelope from his writing pad and looked again at the thin scholarly writing. He drew out the sheets.

The Rectory Lower Chalke Wiltshire.

31st May. 1945

Dear Angus,

Although we have never met, I trust you will excuse me writing, like this, unannounced. But I feel that I know quite a lot about you, because Christopher often spoke of you during his last year at Cranchester and after his death last year, when his diary was returned to us with his few other possessions, your name often featured in that too.

As you will have heard, he was killed on active service and buried many hundreds of miles away. Nevertheless, we, his family, are holding a simple Memorial Service here. Some money had been left to him by an uncle and we feel that we should like him to be commemorated by a small stained-glass window. We know from things he said and wrote that is what he would have wished. He was very fond of the church here and we shall dedicate the window at the service.

I wonder if you would care to be present at the service? Although I do not think Christopher would have wished for any 'official' Ansell's, or Cranchester, representation – I am not sure how much he enjoyed it until his final year – I know he would have liked you to be present, because it is evident that he was very fond of you. My wife and I had always hoped that he might have had a sister, or brother, but that was not to be. Nevertheless, from what he said in his diary he evidently thought of you as he would have done a younger brother.

I realise that it may be difficult for you to get permission to be away and would quite understand. Moreover you may now find that Christopher is somebody whom you now can barely remember. I know what school friendships are. Nevertheless we would so very much like to meet the 'Christopher Angus' with whom our son once felt such kinship and, even if you cannot come to the service, we shall always be happy to see you if ever you could find a moment to come all this way. With the war drawing to its close in the Far East and the families of our friends and parishioners, who were Christopher's contemporaries, re-uniting, we are, as you may imagine, even more conscious of our loss.

This letter needs no reply. Just turn up if you would like to do so. The church is next to the Rectory. You would be most welcome to stay for lunch or supper – or both! The date is Saturday, 16th at 3.00 p.m.

*Yours sincerely,
Charles Singleton.*

For the first time since the evening of Marathon, he found tears in his eyes. Until the letter, he realised he had not even known Singleton's name was also Christopher. The ethos of Ansell's had conditioned him to think of him all the time as 'Singleton'; 'Aunty Singleton' at most. Tomorrow was the sixteenth and, with no School, there would be ample time to cycle there and back. If he was not scoring, then he would surely never be missed, provided everyone was fit and well. Moreover, it did not matter if he were. He owed Singleton this epilogue.

He found he could not stuff the letter back into the pocket of his writing case. Impatiently he emptied it. Some torn card was the cause. In the fading light he put the odds and ends back with the Singleton's invitation and was about to crumple two torn triangles of thin card when he stopped. It was the photograph Corporal Johnson had enclosed which he had torn but not been able to bring himself to destroy. He had entirely forgotten its presence until that instant. The tear he noted, had missed him altogether, merely cutting across the blurred background. He glanced across at the mirror and then back to the snapshot. He was still recognisable – just. Had he really looked as young as that when he first came to Ansell's? He turned the pieces over; despite the tear, the smudged, round, childish hand was still legible:

Last year – on Skye…. . The dog's called <u>Hairy</u> Lauder and that's half my cousin, Rory. I'm the one in the kilt! <u>Don't</u> EVER tell anyone in Ansell's about the kilt!!!!!!! *A.C.*

Until, today, perhaps until this moment, he would been unable to read what he had written without squirming but now, as if he had turned a corner and, for the last time, was glancing back on a landscape he would never revisit, he felt no embarrassment. Only understanding and gratitude to the Singleton who had so affectionately, even dangerously, tolerated the naivety and woeful incompetence of the kid in the faded kilt whom Angus too could now regard, as if from a great distance, with amused affection. Even the previous summer he had been able to wear that old kilt – just. This year it would certainly be too small. Perhaps this perspective was what was meant by growing up? Without quite knowing why he did so, he placed the torn pieces of the snapshot in the envelope and tucked both into his inside pocket.

As on Field Day, morning Curfew on Match day was seven a.m. He had intended to go into breakfast. Notting changed his mind for him. 'I see you're not playing today,' he said loudly, standing in front of the board in Corridor.

Angus registered a note in The Digger's neat precise hand:

W.W. Ashton. Acting Head of House until further notice.

Mawsom had joined him and said, 'What's happened to Botting then, I wonder?'

'Sacked I expect!'

'Don't be an ass, Notting! We'd've heard. Anyhow, he was here yesterday.'

Angus said, 'He didn't take Curfew last night.'

'All the Praefaectors were Din Room with The Digger,' Notting said. 'Ask McCallum.'

McCallum, the Junior Praefaector, was approaching from the stairs. Mawsom said, 'What's up with Botting? Is he ill? Will he be away long?'

McCallum said shortly, 'He's had to go home.'

'What for?' Notting was heavily suspicious. 'Do you know?'

'Not really. The Digger said not to ask about it.'

'Probably financial trouble at home,' Mawsom said. 'Wasn't his Father caught in that big insurance loss? Anyway, the really interesting thing is Ashton. I mean he wasn't even a Praefaector, yet now he's Head of House.'

'Only until Botting gets back. I expect it's because Ashton's Captain of Cricket and it's the Cricket Half,' Angus said, but Mawsom drifted off unconvinced.

Notting said, 'You'd think Cranchester might let him stay on till end of Half, even if his people have gone broke!' As he turned to go, he remarked smarmily to Angus, 'If they Tassel Winterson, will you have to give up yours, AC?' It was clear that Notting intended to keep on throughout the meal, so letting him get well ahead, Angus slipped away.

*

Although he did not use it very often, he still had the bicycle bequeathed him by Dermott-Powell which, by dint of heavy padlock and the surreptitious use of a long abandoned wash-house, he had managed to preserve intact. Whereas it had once been big for him, he had now grown into it, but it was creaky and stiff with disuse. Nevertheless it would do.

Having pumped the tyres and heightened both saddle and handlebars, he pushed it along a shrubby path out of sight of any of the buildings and eventually onto the road well away from Lodge. His heart was beating fast as he jumped on pedalling as quickly as he could.

What would happen if one of the living-out beaks happened to see him? Then he remembered there was no School for anyone that morning because of the cricket matches. He did not need to use the map for the first five miles or so, because he was very familiar with the lanes. As soon as he turned from the Cranchester road, he felt safer and, at the second crossroads, he stopped and removed his jacket, folding it into the dusty leather saddlebag. He took off his tie and collar, carefully placing the studs in a corner of his wallet. There was a faded blue scarf in the saddlebag. His own? Dermott-Powell's? He could not remember. Perhaps it belonged to somebody to whom he had loaned the machine. It did not matter. He wound it round his neck, It might help to conceal his identity, although anyone meeting him, cycling in waistcoat and striped trousers could hardly have mistaken him for anyone but a Castonian. Nevertheless, the scarf was somehow a symbol, like a cockleshell in a mediaeval pilgrim's hat; in a way, it was a pilgrimage he was undertaking.

Already it was almost uncomfortably warm and he was glad when the road took its way through wooded lanes. Villages were awake but not bustling. Because it was Saturday they still had a sleepy air. No children walked to school; even the occasional postman seemed later. By nine o'clock he was wishing he had not missed breakfast. As if to tantalise him, he came up to a small cottage set back in an ordered wilderness of hollyhocks. An almost overgrown sign said: **Bed and Breakfast**; there was a smell of bacon in the air. Could one get Breakfast without Bed? Probably not. What decided the matter was the wobble on his front wheel. He looked down. The tyre was flat to the rim. The elderly rubber had split. He knew there was a dubious puncture outfit in the saddlebag, but suspected that its tube of glue had long since dried hard.

As he considered the matter a country voice above him said, 'Flat tyre?' Looking up, he saw an elderly man looking down from a low ladder where he was doing something to an apple tree which was still partly in blossom.

'Afraid so. I don't know whether I can patch it.' Once again he smelled the aroma of bacon. He said, 'Would I be able to get breakfast? In the house?' He pointed to the sign.

'Well, the wife don't usually. Except for guests. But, since she's cook'n...'

'I missed breakfast.'

The old man had come through the gate. He too was wearing a collarless shirt, with a small scarf and a much worn waistcoat. He said, 'Have you raan away from school?'

'Good heavens no!' He stopped. In a way he had. 'I'm going back tonight. I'm just visiting. Going to a church service in fact. A Memorial Service.'

'Someone killed in the war?'

'Yes. In France. Last September.'

'We 'aad th'Grandson killed. On D-Day. You'd best come in.'

Angus followed.

'I'll ask Bella,' the gardener said and Angus could hear voices inside. Minutes later a short ample woman appeared in the dark doorway.

'In you come, m'dear.' Angus thought, so people really do say it like that. 'The visitor's 'aavin'er breakfast in bed. On'oliday. Won't take me a minute to do one for you.'

He sat at the open window. A large tabby-cat dozing on the sill in the sun, briefly opened one green eye. No vehicle passed on the road outside. Bella, setting his place, was welcoming without being talkative. There was a brown, much-ironed, tablecloth, bread on a board, with a worn horn-handled knife and butter which had been patted into a small block leaving a design which, he noticed with a slight pang, was a thistle. Bacon, two eggs and a large pot of tea in a thick woollen cosy appeared. The spout, he noted, was surmounted by a neat little metal device to compensate for a chip that would have otherwise rendered it useless. He realised her husband must have fashioned it. She reappeared with a hot-water jug, 'Will – that is my husband says there's not much as can be done with thaat tyre. It's pretty well rotten. Farr'tergo?'

'Lower Chalke. She raised her eyebrows. 'My, thaas'a good way, that is.' She vanished again. So that was the end of his attempt to pay last respects to Singleton. He would not be able to walk back in time for the beginning of the OA match. He dawdled over the last of the meal; both the honey and marmalade were home-made, the date pencilled on the pot in comfortable round hand. With a shock he realised that the marmalade had been made before the war had started. She had carefully eked out her store; he felt curiously privileged to be allowed to taste it. He said, 'I like the marmalade. It's very good. I see you made it before the war.'

She smiled, pleased, 'The last year. Af'er thaat we couldn't get oranges. We're promised some this year. That's why I've begun on the last half-dozen jars. Big jars, min' you, they were Will's mother's.'

'You must've made a lot!'

'Always five dozen of marmalade. During the war we allowed ourselves one pot each month. So with whaat I already 'aad in store it just lasted out.'

He was intrigued by the careful way the couple had planned it. He had never thought like that about something as ordinary as marmalade. It suggested touching intimacy, an undemanding completeness. Like the extraordinary sense of security he had felt when they were hoarding and burning fir-cones in Singleton's study. He remembered how they had always known exactly how many cones and pieces of coal there remained and how they had rationed the fires so that they would last the Half.

'Will says you'c'n borrow a tyre if you like. Or wheel I should say.'

Angus looked up.

'He reckons that front wheel on my ol' bike'll just about do you. It's the same he says. It'll get you to the Church. Memorial Services i'it? Brother?'

He remembered Johnson's letter – ' Christopher Angus Singleton' – it seemed somehow disloyal to deny it. He nodded.

Her face saddened: 'Y'd not want to miss thaat.'

'I'd like to be there. If at all possible.'

'You'm borrow the wheel then.'

'I'll bring it back when I return.'

'It don't matter today. Otherwise you'll not get home.' She smiled mischievously. 'Truth to tell, I haven't rid that bike uv mine this paast twenty month. I reck'ns I'm paast bicyclin', 'cept in'mergency.'

It had been assumed that he would accept, because when he got outside the wheels had been changed over.

'Please tell me how much I owe you for breakfast.'

Bella said, 'One and seven-pence. Used to be one and four-pence before the war.' He handed over a florin and she counted the change from an old stone jam-jar. He divined that it would be quite wrong to think of leaving a tip. Instead he shook hands with them both and promised to return the wheel in due course. They stood, the one behind the other at the gate to see him off, for all the world as though they had known him all his life. He cycled on quietly through the lanes. At one-thirty he came across a wooden signpost: **Lower Chalke 3**. It evidently had been recently re-erected (after wartime dismantling 'in order to confuse enemy parachutists') for the soil at its foot was new-turned.

He did not want to be early. He felt, somehow, it would be right to arrive only just in time. He was, in any case, too late to impose himself on the Singletons for lunch, moreover he did not want to have to converse politely. It seemed a day for saying nothing. Within a quarter of a mile there came a steep dip and the road forded a shallow stream. On the other side was a shabby public house with a bench outside. Below an almost faded picture on a faded brown board, once-white letters proclaimed **THE TABBY CAT**. Perhaps it was owned by the cat at the bed-and-breakfast? It was the sort of day when anything was possible – for no reason at all the name seemed propitious. In smaller lettering above the door he read, *Prop. Albert Poore, Lic. to sell Spirits, Beer and Tobacco.*. Propping up the cycle he entered. It was extremely dark inside and it took him some time to become accustomed to the gloom. There was a pungent smell of beer; his feet scuffed a layer of sawdust.

'Order, sir?'

A deep voice from the dark startled him. He could make out, at last, a very wide man in an apron which looped round his neck. He was almost bald. Two massive arms lay on the dark counter, deep tanned almost to the same colour.

'Could I have something to eat, please?'

'Yesssir. Thaat you may. Have to if I'm to keep my licence. Being an inn.' Seeing Angus' puzzlement, he went on, 'Inns have to supply refreshment for bonney fidey travellers. And you,' he glanced at the thick white dust on Angus' shoes and waistcoat, 'look bonney fidey to me. Bread? Cheese? Pickles?' Angus nodded. 'And to drink, sir?'

He would not have cider, he thought. It always made him muzzy at Ansell's. Out here it would probably mean he would never get to Little Chalke. 'Ginger beer, please. A pint.'

He ate and drank outside. No other customers arrived. No traffic passed. Perhaps he was the only person who had come that way the whole year. In the distance a church clock struck twice, the chimes lingering in the air. Otherwise there was only the song of unseen small birds who flittered amongst the trees and hedgerow the other side of the road and the curiously ever-changing, restless note of water running through the ford, where the surface was so placid that the water appeared to be still. Only occasional stones breaking the surface gave notice that there was quite a swift current.

Then he took up the bicycle and walked up the short hill above The Tabby Cat. There was no wind. The road wound ahead of him past stubby copses and fields nodding with ripening grain. In the distance he could see the slim tower of a church. He knew it was Lower Chalke. When he came to the first houses he took his jacket and tie and collar from his saddlebag. He used the scarf to dust his shoes and then shook it in the still-warm air. The clock struck a third quarter with a mellow musicality that was entirely in tune with the day.

There must have been about twenty people in the church and he slid into one of the pews at the back. Two or three other groups came in after him. Some were village people, soberly dressed older men in stiff suits and creaking boots, their wives in carefully stored hats. There were also those who might have been relations. One or two young men had the look of being uneasy out of uniform and there were three in uniform. One in the coarse battledress of a non-commissioned airman, the other in immaculate service dress, with three pips and the familiar skull and cross-bones bade on the cap under his arm. In an aisle position at the front, was a figure in bright blue hospital uniform. Angus could see the arm of a crutch propped on the pew-back.

It was a short, simple, service. They sang two hymns, led by a small choir of scrubbed village boys, in cassocks mostly a little too big, and a motley collection of surplices which had obviously been a good-deal mended. Then a prayer by the tall, stooped, clergyman with benign silvering hair: 'That's how Singleton would have looked had he reached the same age!' Angus thought with a start Briefly, he wondered how he himself would age; he recalled the old man who had watched him and Mawsom bathing on that first Field Day.

They sang the Twenty-third Psalm. For some inexplicable reason, the choir instilled the music with a feeling which can only occur when unsophisticated singers divine a special meaning in the words and intuitively understand a tune they love. It was neither loud nor dramatic nor, perhaps, even perfectly in harmony, but it was very beautiful. The small congregation, sensing this, gradually stopped singing themselves and listened. Treble notes with the slight huskiness of untrained voices, the words softened by the warmth of West Country vowels, reached into the corners of the small church. The sound seemed exactly in keeping with mellow stones which looked as if they had melted into each other over the centuries, with the slight creak from the organ loft, with the warm light falling through the deep yellow of the window behind the altar, and with the shimmering column of dust motes which rose and fell in the beam of hot sun that warmed a patch on the pew-shelf in front of Angus.

After that, they all moved to the back of the church. In a side aisle was a small window with a panel of stained glass. It showed a sower broadcasting seed, the border decorated by alternating ears of wheat and thistles. At the sower's feet, a scroll:

and some fell by the wayside

Stepping forward Mr Singleton said, 'I would like to thank all of you so much for joining me and my wife here. It's made more bearable what must be for us all a sorrowful occasion, just as your sympathy has been one of the things that has most encouraged us to feel that perhaps Christopher's death and the deaths of others like him helps to achieve a purpose which we cannot always understand. A purpose which was perhaps more clearly discerned by those who re-dedicated this church when already three hundred and fifty years old, to three men from this village who never returned from the First Crusade, in the belief that by commemorating them, it would help to sanctify their deaths and, although buried far away, reunite them for ever with those they loved and who loved them.

'The earliest memorial in this church, as you know, is the brass of William Gournay, who died in the Holy Land. We all pray that this window here will be a memorial to what our descendants will come to know as the Last Crusade. I hope you find it as significant as we do, that this window is not new, but comes from a tiny church in the City of London with the same name and almost as old as ours. It was totally destroyed by bombing – except for this one small window which was dug from the rubble miraculously intact.'

There was a brief silence. Then, Singleton's parents moved quietly, hand in hand, to the door of the church. Those present followed them slowly, reading the discreetly cut letters on the unobtrusive stone plaque beneath the window:

In Loving and Grateful Memory of Christopher Singleton.

Born 16th June 1924.

Baptised in this Church.

Died in action outside Caen, where he is buried,

11th September, 1944.

&

And all those who, like him, lie far from Home.

Singleton had been killed on the very day the Half began. And he realised something else. Today would have been Singleton's birthday. Until that moment it had never occurred to him that he ought to have written immediately to Singleton's parents when he had first heard news of his death.

He was the last to come out into the sun. Mrs. Singleton said, 'It is Christopher Angus, isn't it? You gave Christopher a snap once. Now of course you're a good deal taller. You won't mind us calling you Christopher, will you?' He sensed she was talking to stop herself from having to think.

'Of course. Please do.'

'You'll stay to supper?'

'Thank you very much. But I must get back. I've come by bicycle.'

Her husband moved across. 'Goodness, that's quite a ride. Christopher did it once. Missed getting back for Curfew – by ten minutes. I'm afraid he'd have had to "tighten-up" for that, don't you?'

'I'm sure I'll have plenty of time, sir.'

'Anyhow there's tea,' Mrs. Singleton said. 'You'll have time for that.'

'Thank you.'

※

Tea was set out in the enormous garden beneath a majestic chestnut tree. 'It saves us having a summer house,' Mrs. Singleton said, as he was offered a cup of tea and a plate of fresh sandwiches kept moist by a liberal sprinkling of parsley. 'Please stay till the end – after the others go,' she added sotto voce. 'I know Charles wants a word with you. I think there's something of Christopher's he feels you ought to have.' Tea lazed on. He knew nobody else and nobody seemed to notice that he joined none of the groups. He was content to sit on an abandoned log helping himself to another sandwich, or a slice of cake, from time to time.

All of a sudden he found the soldier in the bright blue uniform beside him, crutch under his arm, balancing a cup of tea. He was wearing darkened glasses. Realisation dawned. 'Corporal.... No, I see it's now Sergeant? Johnson? Congratulations. Thank you so much for sending on the letter. And the photograph.'

'He must have looked very like you, sir. When he was your age that is. Best officer we ever had, sir.'

'I'm not...' Angus began, but then took in the significance of the thick, dark lenses and stopped. Why embarrass this man who, he now noticed, wore the ribbon of the Military Medal? Eventually Sergeant Johnson, limped away, having shaken Angus' hand and he was joined eventually by a large, elderly Golden Labrador. He said, 'Hullo Sheba,' before looking at the tag. It troubled him that, although obviously Singleton had told him the dog's name, he had no recollection at all of the occasion.

Mr Singleton's voice said, 'Sheba's getting on. She always seemed to know when Christopher was coming back from school. She'd wait by the gate. We always knew he'd be turning up, even if he hadn't told us. Or on leave for that matter. Odd thing is she did it today for the first time since we heard the news. You're honoured, she doesn't usually make the first approach to strangers. They say that dogs know things we don't. Or is it just that they sense it from our preparations?'

'I'm afraid I've never thought very much about that, sir.'

'I expect my wife told you that we thought there was something we'd like you to have. If you want it. One of Christopher's books. In fact the only one to come back with his kit – there was that and his diary and some clothes. There wasn't much else.' He paused. 'The tank caught fire, you see.'

'They didn't say much in Chapel, but his batman, Lance Corporal...that's Sergeant...Johnson wrote, because he'd posted on a letter addressed to me that Sing...that is, Christopher, had left...I knew he'd gone back after the tank was hit and went on firing.'

Mr Singleton looked intently up into the chestnut tree. 'Yes. Had he not returned to the tank after getting Johnson out, it would have been his twenty-first birthday today.'

They stood for a long time in silence. Eventually Angus said, 'I noticed that on the plaque, there was no mention of rank, or his MC, I wondered...I mean we were told that the award and the Bar were Gazetted. Corporal Johnson said it should have been a VC.'

'Both my wife and I thought that medals...decorations...didn't seem right somehow. Not in the church. They sent it to us of course.' He stopped. 'We don't look at it.' They were moving towards the house. 'If you'd come into the study for a moment.' He smiled briefly: 'Or do I sound like your Housemaster?'

'No, sir. It's never called study in Ansell's. Just Private.'

'Of course! I'd forgotten. One forgets a lot. Although I find as I get older that it's the good things I forget. What I remember most are times I would most prefer to forget.'

They entered the house and turned into a long untidy drawing room with French windows giving out onto the lawn. He followed the clergyman who suddenly seemed old, even frail, into another very large room, walls lined by books, many of them in worn leather bindings. In a bay window looking out onto the garden there was a fine polished table upon which were a few sheets of paper neatly arranged, together with a large, fat, old-fashioned fountain pen and a glass inkwell. Despite its tidiness, it was comfortable; at the fireplace were two chairs, the heavy leather softened by decades of use. A reassuring place to be, like Singleton's room at Ansell's had become – welcoming – unlike the dark study of the Priest Street Curacy.

It was cool too. Book-lined walls and the chestnut-tree combined to diffuse the light into a sort of greenish amber. Mr Singleton led the way to the window and indicated that Angus should sit on the window seat. He himself sat the other end of the curve so that they faced each other. Scent from the flowers drifted in through the opened French windows. Angus did not know what to say.

Suddenly, quietly, the old man began to speak 'He was very attached to you, wasn't he? I expect you know that.... How do you think of him? Now, now you're older?' He looked grey, anxious. 'I wondered, after I had written, whether I was being too naive. I wished I had not written. I wondered—' He hesitated. 'Would you have wanted to meet him again had he been alive? Had this been his birthday party for instance?'

Angus looked across into the troubled eyes. He said, 'Oh yes, sir.'

'Good.' The other drew breath. 'Good. I had wondered. I hoped, but I also wondered. I'm a Castonian. A long time ago. At Ansell's. We thought it the best House. Now – looking back – I wonder sometimes.'

Angus said, 'I've seen your name, sir. You were Head of House?'

'I believe I was. It was a very long time ago. Things change. But some things don't change. One hears ...'

Meeting the level gaze, Angus felt an assurance he had never felt before. As if vouchsafed a revelation, he divined what was in the old man's mind. 'Sing...your son...Christopher...was very kind to me. I was, well, pretty wet in my first three Halfs. I don't think I'd've lasted without his encouragement. If he hadn't been there.... Well...in your letter, sir, you said something about having hoped to have a brother for Christopher. Well, he *was* one to *me*. He made life bearable.' He paused. 'Did you know, sir, Corporal Johnson assumed I was Christopher's brother. Even this afternoon. I didn't tell him. It seemed better to leave it. Hope you and Mrs Singleton wouldn't've minded.'

'I'm very glad, Christopher. You put my mind at ease.'

Emboldened Angus went on, 'Mr Singleton, sir, you don't have to worry. He wasn't like...I mean he disapproved of some things in Ansell's...things that didn't bother others. For instance, he didn't approve of t—' He couldn't mention tasselling! 'Of tightening-up...and that sort of thing,' he ended lamely. Then, although he did not know why, he felt impelled to say, 'Sir, Christopher always behaved entirely as you and Mrs Singleton would have wanted. *Always*.' Pausing, he added in a low voice, 'Mind you he might not've wanted to meet me again. I...I think he felt I'd let him down after he left.' He looked out into the, garden where Sheba wandered disconsolately and sensed the old clergyman beside him. A very gentle hand took his.

'Oh no. I'm quite sure you didn't, Christopher. Recognising we've made mistakes is *quite* different. We all make mistakes. You. Christopher. Me. But it's admitting them to ourselves, that's the hard part. The most important part too.' They stayed side by side looking out into the sun and the garden; he put his arm on Angus' shoulder and it was, he noticed, trembling. 'I'm glad you put my mind at rest about Christopher.... My wife and I were never sure that Cranchester was right for him.'

Angus said firmly, 'Well I think it was. He was very important...to me. And everyone else in a sort of way. I don't know how to explain it, except to say that otherwise there'd have been no obvious alternative to the way everyone else did things.'

Mr Singleton had moved to the table and picked up a battered book, the pages were filled with familiar handwriting. 'This came back to us with his other odds and ends. There wasn't much.' Mr Singleton paused and his voice quavered, 'His diary, his wallet, a book of poems. And his watch...smashed...burned. Not much after twenty-one years. He kept his diary up to date. I think you ought to read this. It's about you.'

Embarrassed, Angus read the rather blotchy hand:

Not much of a pen. We move at first light, within the hour. I've had that letter to Christopher very much in mind. I've added so much that it's got out of hand. I've looked at the beginning and tried to imagine what I'd have done if I'd got a letter like that at his age in Ansell's! I'd've written a very short letter back! <u>Especially</u> if what was said were true! I can't send it.

I know it's not really my business any longer, but I want it to be my business. It'll work out in the end because of that marvellous frankness he had. That <u>must</u> turn up trumps in the end. I wonder if I'll go back one day and find him a Praefaector? (Will Ansell's ever be ready to have somebody like that as Head of House?) No pompous letters. I'll destroy it when I'm finally reunited with my kit. Next Ansell's match, I'll tell AC how near I was to handing out unsolicited advice for which he'd have given me a well-deserved raspberry! We've just had the signal to move.

He turned to the next page. It was blank.

Mr Singleton said, 'He was killed, it seems, later on that morning. The letter must've been destroyed in the tank. It wasn't with his kit.'

Angus hardly heard him. Now he knew for certain that Singleton had not intended to send it. 'Thank you very much for showing me, sir.'

'This is yours, I think.' Mr Singleton held out an envelope, much postmarked and dirtied. 'It arrived after Christopher's death, I imagine, and they sent it on to us.'

Angus took it slowly.

'I did not open it, of course. Before I met you and before you told me what you did just now about Christopher, I thought.... Well sometimes schoolboy letters are better not read by parents. If you understand me.'

Angus nodded, remembering Simonsen's last letter.

'In your case it would have been all right, as I now see.'

Somewhere, a clock was striking. Angus said, 'I really must get back. I'm afraid I didn't really ask permission to be out.'

'My dear boy, I'll telephone.'

'No please don't, it's not necessary. I've still got time to get back before supper. It's the Old Ansell's Match today.'

'I hope you didn't give up the game because...I know you were Tasselled. Christopher mentioned it on his last leave. He hoped to bat against your bowling this year.'

'I'm afraid they didn't play me. I seem to have lost form.'

'Oh, I am sorry.' He said almost absently, 'Cricket's such a marvellous game.' The focusing on Angus again, 'It'll come back. However, before you go, my wife and I would like you to have this.' It was a dark green leather-covered book, even more battered than the diary, on very thin paper. 'Christopher kept it with him – even in the tank usually. It was a present. He asked for it. The only sort of present that he had any hope of keeping by him while he was training, he told us.' Angus could not read the worn spine, so he turned over the first page. **The Poems of Gerard Manley Hopkins.** In spidery black ink was inscribed: To Christopher, on his 18th Birthday, from Mother and Father, with our love. God bless June 16th 1942.

'But surely you and Mrs Singleton...?'

'No, Christopher. We think he'd like you to have it. He wrote some notes in it. We'd like you to have it as a memento. That is, if you'd like to.'

Angus nodded, too overcome to speak clearly. They walked across the lawn to the gate.

'Goodbye, Christopher. Thank you so much for coming. Come and see us again. It has made all the difference. I'm sure Christopher would have wanted you to be here with us today.'

'Thank you for asking me, sir. And for tea.' He wheeled the bicycle along the path through the churchyard.

At the church porch he stopped, took the returned, unopened, letter from his pocket and, after momentary hesitation, forced himself to read it.

Dear Singleton,

I got your letter. I don't think Ansell's is anything to do with you now. I've torn the picture up. I look bloody pathetic. I was bloody wet that first year at Ansell's and you ought to have tanned my arse. Simonsen was killed by a flying bomb, if that makes you feel any better. I'm glad you'll not be at the Ansell's Match next year.

C. Angus.'

He cringed. As a further penance he made himself read it again. Then he tore it into tiny, tiny, pieces, which he scattered to the gravel path where it mixed with the remains of confetti from a whole succession of post-war weddings.

On a sudden impulse, he stepped through the porch. Inside the tiny church it was utterly quiet. A shaft of sunlight pierced the stained-glass window, bathing the white memorial panel in rosy light. Reaching into his pocket, he looked for the last time at a photograph of a slight, serious, kilted boy who gazed out with such smiling ingenuousness and who now seemed so utterly remote from himself. Fleetingly, dimly, he had an inkling of why Singleton had cherished the snapshot. *If you think we'd still be on speaking terms after you've read this, you can always post the photograph back. I hope you'll want to.*

In Loving and Grateful memory of Christopher Singleton.

The mason had not yet quite finished his final pointing and there was still a thin slot between stone and mortar. With a pencil he wrote on one of the torn pieces, Happy Birthday. AC. Gently, he slipped the pieces of photograph into the gap and, with the aid of a safety-pin he found in the back of his lapel, he pushed it out of sight. He did it without embarrassment, without sentimentality. He was discharging a further instalment of debt he had admitted for the first time that evening on Marathon when the wind had blown away L/Cpl. Johnson's letter.

❋

When he reached the cottage he found that, by some miracle, his own wheel was ready. Another worn but serviceable tyre had been found and every attempt at repayment was refused. He arrived back at Cranchester unnoticed. Boys' supper was over and he could hear the aftermath of the Old Ansell's Match in full swing in Din Room. When he reached for Hopkins' poems, he found that Bella had placed a pot of home-made marmalade in his saddlebag. It said 'January 1939' and she had added, 'The last jar'. Her kindness brought tears to his eyes.

He went quietly up to Big Dorm. There was nobody there except Brownlow making up a bed on the floor. He said, 'Harrington's bagged my bed!' Angus said, 'I daresay he'll share it with you.'

'That's what I thought.' Brownlow grinned perkily. 'I could do with a fiver. You going to bed?'

'I'm very tired.'

'Ashton was looking for you. Needed as a sub for Old Ansell's. Somebody called Maunder was delayed, turned up with about a minute to go.'

'Thanks for telling me. Goodnight.'

He had a lukewarm bath and returned to his Manger. Brownlow had gone. Before he got into bed he took up the battered copy of Hopkins, unsurprised at where it fell open. Once again Singleton had lightly marked the second and third stanza.

> What the heart is! which, like carriers let fly—
> Doff darkness, homing nature knows the rest—
> To its own fine function, wild and self-instressed,
> Falls light as ten years long taught how to and why.
>
> Mannerly hearted! more than handsome face—
> Beauty's bearing or muse of mounting vein,
> All, in this case, bathed in high hallowing grace.

He read the whole poem again, for the first time since his first year. He spoke half-aloud the puzzling line inscribed in the anthology he had destroyed in his anger at the truths in the letter which, he now knew, Singleton had never intended to post.

{Father, what you buy me, I like best} AC!

As he spoke the words to himself, he realised that, although still not understanding the poem in its entirety, he once again felt enormously pleased, even proud that here too Singleton had bracketed the line and pencilled *AC!* He divined, if obscurely, the tenderness behind the impulse which had led Singleton to emphasise especially that one word on the flyleaf he had so savagely torn out of the anthology. He was no longer embarrassed, even when tears pricked the back of his eyes.

※

After breakfast the following morning, Ashton came up to him. 'We were looking for you yesterday, Angus. Twelfth Man.' He knew Ashton was feeling his way, but making no accusation, for it would have been quite possible for Angus to have been present, but remain entirely in the background. 'We thought you were going to have to sub for Maunder.'

'I know.'

'So you were here?'

It would have been easy enough to say 'yes', but he was not going to do so.

'Actually no, Ashton. I cut the match. I had a previous engagement. 'Brownlow told me about Maunder when I got back last night.'

'Did you have The Digger's permission?'

'No. I didn't decide to go...until the last minute.'

'I warned you.

Angus said nothing.

'Have you seen the notice in Corridor?'

'Why?'

'You've got a Praefaectors'. For cutting the Old Ansell's match. You're a bloody fool, AC.'

The old choking at first prevented Angus from speaking. He said, with an enormous effort at dignity, 'Then I'd better have a look.'

Brownlow was at the board. He said, 'It's a bloody shame, AC. They didn't need you.'

The Praefaectors gave him twelve, as hard as they could make them. He bit his lip as a precaution against making any sound at all. They hurt a good deal. He felt neither frightened nor humiliated, although he had to swallow as he stood up, because his throat was dry. It was, however, he felt another part-repayment of a debt of honour. He said, 'Thank you, Ashton,' with such disdainful courtesy that the Praefaectors were more uneasy than himself.

'We don't care for giving twelve-up to somebody of your seniority. However, cutting the Old Ansell's match is a very bad example to the Junior Election.'

Angus said gravely, 'I'm sure you've done what you feel is necessary. I should not wish to be treated differently from Arkell, for instance.'

'Why Arkell?'

'Arkell was given six-up on Tuesday, four-up on Thursday and another three-up tonight, just before me.'

'He's a little tick!'

'I can't disagree. He is also half your size; half your weight and, because he's had a pretty rum Private School, he doesn't know much better yet.'

'Are you showing *side*, Angus?' This came from Carstairs, a boy who played every game well, but was not clever.

'I was asked why I mentioned Arkell.'

Ashton diplomatically changed the subject: 'Anyway, where the Hell were you, AC?'

'I was in church.'

It was received in an astonished pool of silence.

'Any more *side*, Angus, and we'll create a record by giving you another dozen-up,' Carstairs began menacingly.

'It's the truth. I was in church.'

Ashton, recognising that there was more to it than Carstairs could perceive, said, 'Bloody long service! You never put in an appearance all day.'

'The church was forty miles away.'

'Do you mean to say you've cycled *eighty* miles today?'

'That's right.'

'But that'd take about four hours each way!'

'About that.'

An elegant Praefaector called Hemming said, puzzled, 'What was it? A wedding? Why on earth didn't you get permission?'

'I'd still have missed the match. As a matter of fact it was a Memorial Service. For somebody who was killed in Normandy.'

There was an awkward silence. Looking very uncomfortable, Ashton said, 'Why the Hell didn't you tell us, AC? It could have made all the difference.'

'You didn't ask me where I'd been, Ashton. Anyway it was none of your business and you wanted an excuse to have me beaten. He added woodenly, 'I'd still've been cutting the match, wouldn't I?'

Ashton said magnanimously, 'Well, we're very sorry. Was it a close relation?'

'Not a relation at all.' They were all watching him. 'I expect you remember Acting Major Singleton. MC and Bar?' In the split second before he revealed the name, he saw realisation begin to dawn in Ashton's eyes. 'Singleton's father wrote asking me to go to a Memorial Service which dedicated a window.'

There could be no question but that now the room was stunned into guilty silence.

Carstairs said, 'Christ, Angus! Why on earth didn't you tell us? The Digger'd've given permission. Probably gone himself and taken you in his car.'

Ashton added, 'After all, you *were* representing Ansell's.'

As composed as he had been that afternoon with Mr Singleton, Angus said remotely, quietly, with huge dignity, 'The Digger was not invited. I was there as myself. As a friend of Singleton's. I was certainly *not* representing Ansell's.' Into the silence he continued distinctly, 'I don't think that the Singletons wanted Ansell's there. I do know that *Aunty*'— he deliberately emphasised the word—'Singleton would not have wished it.' After a pause, he added, 'I take it I have your permission to leave,

Ashton? In the circumstances, I don't think I want to shake hands with any of you.' He walked quietly from Big Study.

They heard the door to Big Dorm close. Hemming said, astonished, 'Do you know, I think he meant that Singleton wouldn't have wanted anything to do with Ansell's.'

Carstairs exploded. 'Who the *hell* does he think he is?'

A lanky Praefaector called Leather said, 'Silly little sod. I'm glad I tanned his arse.'

Ashton said, tensely, 'Are you? Well I'm not. I'm ashamed.' He looked round, 'Sometimes, quite often in fact, we all behave like barbarians. Remember VE night?'

'Brownlow's a tart!'

'Notting's a turd,' Carstairs added vindictively.

'So's Angus.' That was Leather.

Ashton said, 'No, Angus is not. He may be an oddity, but he's not a turd. Or a tart. Our treatment of him tonight was pretty shameful.'

'*He cut the bloody match,*' '*He's still in love with bloody Singleton,*' Carstairs and Leather said simultaneously.

'*So I should bloody hope,*' Ashton articulated savagely. 'I just hope that one day somebody still loves me enough to think *my* memorial service a bloody sight more important than a bloody cricket match!' He looked round. Suddenly quiet, despondent, 'Sometimes, Ansell's Men make me sick...I certainly make myself sick.' He went out shutting the door with enormous restraint.

✻

Mawsom and Snider sought out Angus on the following afternoon.

'Is it true Ashton apologised for the Praefaectors'?'

'Not really...well, sort of.'

'It's all round Ansell's and most of the School.'

'I've said nothing about it.'

'Did you really go to Singleton's Memorial Service?'

'Yes.'

'I thought you'd gone off him after that letter,' Mawsom prompted.

'He never meant to send it. His batman posted it. After his death.' Angus stopped, took a breath and added, 'Anyhow, Mawsom, he would have been right to send it.'

Snider said, 'You really liked him, didn't you?'

After a pause, Angus replied simply, 'I think I loved him.'

'My, my, AC. First Singleton, then Simonsen! You're a dark horse.'

Snider said, 'Mind you, Simonsen had a passion for everyone!'

'Singleton wasn't like Simonsen. *At all.*'

'We all thought he had a passion for you. Singleton, I mean.'

'I never knew anything about Tassel Night until I was Dawes' Warmer.'

'Didn't you really stay with Singleton all his last night?' Mawsom asked. 'We all thought you did.'

'Yes. I went off to sleep. So did Singleton. In the same bed. If The Digger had found us, we'd both have been sacked. I don't expect you to believe it was all quite innocent.'

'You're about the only member of Ansell's I would believe if they told me that.' Snider added thoughtfully, 'Singleton was a bit of a Puritan, wasn't he?'

'I suppose so.'

'And what about you, AC?' Mawsom asked mildly.

'I don't think I'm a Puritan at all.'

Snider said, 'You certainly seemed to be kicking over the traces with Simonsen. If Harlow hadn't been such a feeble Head of House, you'd have been for it.'

'Simonsen had Harlow under his thumb too,' Mawsom interpolated.

Angus, curiously unembarrassed, thought to himself, 'I must have been quite mad with Simonsen.' It seemed hardly possible to recognise himself as the Angus of the previous summer.

'Anyhow, AC seems to be back on track for a halo. I wish I were. What do you think of little Garner, Mawsom?'

'Probably the same as you, Snider.'

'You probably *feel* the same as me. Sometimes I wonder if I'm just a sex maniac. He walked past me to Tosher last night and the Eiffel Tower wasn't in it. Yet during the holidays,' Snider admitted, 'I feel so bloody ashamed when I remember what we all get up to. Garner's going to be as big and hairy as us in a year's time. It's not like girls. I mean you can't marry him or anything.'

They had forgotten Angus was still there, he said quietly, 'Singleton told me that once you've left, it all looks very different.'

'Probably did to him,' Mawsom said. 'But look what happens on the night of the Old Ansell's match. Some Old Ansell's.... You heard about Tarrant last time? Seems he taught even Brownlow some new tricks.'

Angus nodded. 'Perhaps it'll be up to us to change it all.'

Snider laughed: 'Some chance!'

Mawsom put in, almost as if challenging himself, 'The trouble is that, in a way, we don't really *want* to change it any longer – if we ever really did. After all, it doesn't seem to do anyone much harm in the end.'

Fleetingly, Angus thought of Jeffrey but he said nothing. At that moment, because the tone had become serious enough to open a door they did not wish to enter, Snider broke into a mock American accent with a popular catch phrase from a fashionable film, 'If yuh don't like the heat, keep outa da kitchen.'

V

'It's bloody stupid to have a Field Day when the war's over!'

'It's still happening in the Far East,' Mawsom said unprovocatively.

'Well, in that case,' Ellerman went on, 'it'll be a fat lot of use practising a platoon attack in Wiltshire as preparation for Malaya or Burma!'

Baker said limply, 'Now I've got three stripes, I shall enjoy Field Day for once.'

'Doing nothing very much if we know you, Baker.'

'Exactly!' Baker smiled benignly. 'I shall be looking after stores and shall stay in the three-tonner all day. I hope it pours with rain on the rest of you.'

In the event, it was a very bright hot day. About the middle of the morning Angus was leading his section by a circuitous route towards a small wood. They were stopped by an officer wearing the armband of Official Umpire who appeared unexpectedly from a clump of gorse.

'This platoon?'

'Cranchester. Under-Officer Angus.'

'I'm very sorry, but you've just walked through a minefield.'

Angus looked at the talc over his map. 'We were given this at the briefing. The minefield isn't shown.'

The umpire took Angus' map and looked at it. He was apologetic. 'Bad luck. To tell the truth, whoever planned this exercise made a bit of a cock-up. I'm afraid I can't really let you through.'

'Of course not, sir, but it's a bit unfair.'

'Tell you what! I'll let some of you through. Say half. You can draw lots.'

Angus and six others were deemed dead.

Transport was, miraculously, waiting. However, the driver said, 'I can't take you all. It's only a fifteen-hundredweight. Five of you, no more.'

Angus said, 'I'll walk. RV at Avebury at the end of the exercise, don't we?' The officer nodded and vanished back into the gorse. The truck bumped away. Angus walked off down the dusty road. It had grown very hot. He consulted his map and took an ill-defined footpath across the Downs. All of a sudden he knew where he was. He recognised the 'sleeping-dog' of West Kennet Long Barrow ahead of him and he could see the great stones poking like teeth from the main part of the mound. He climbed up and sat on the top. Should he eat his packed lunch here? Glancing at his watch, he saw it was still not midday. He decided to wait and have lunch instead on the top of Silbury Hill. He was very conscious of the fact that three summers before he and Mawsom had been up here on another Field Day. He wouldn't mind a bathe in that stream.

He walked steadily down the rough track across the prehistoric downland kicking up flint and chalk as he did. He thought of himself and Mawsom as he reached the shady path by the river and their bathing place where two boys of about eleven were splashing and laughing. His presence did not daunt them in the least. One waved.

He waved back. 'Wouldn't mind joining you. What's the water like?'

'Just right. It's deep enough to swim.' They both demonstrated, making about three strokes before grounding. 'Come and try it.'

'If I got in there'd be hardly enough room for anyone else,' he half-joked, surprised to find he was saddened that he had grown past being able to join in. 'I bathed here once.' He was about to add, 'When I was about your age'. Instead, he said, 'I must get on,' and waved farewell. The splashing and laughter rang in his ears all the way to the main road.

As on that previous occasion, the peace and softness of the Wiltshire countryside had begun to expunge all thoughts of Cranchester and Ansell's. After he had puffed hotly to the top of Silbury, he felt quite liberated. He ate some of his rather dry sandwiches in the hollow at the top and, when he had finished taking off his battledress top, he made a pillow for his head. He wondered if, the war now over, the woman in the Post Office would make tea for him.

He must have slept for some time. He awoke with a start, feeling he was not alone. Turning his head slightly, he saw at first only sandals and brown legs. A boy stood, arms akimbo, gazing down on him. For a moment he thought he was dreaming and that it was the phantom of Mawsom or himself on the previous occasion, for the child wore blue games shorts and a striped jersey. Then, fully awake he realised it was a total stranger.

'Gosh! You gave me a shock. When I climbed up and saw you, I thought you must be dead.'

Angus sat up on one elbow. 'No such luck I'm afraid.'

'Are you a parachutist?'

'No, just on an exercise. I expect you heard the thunder-flashes earlier on. That's if you've been around here.'

The boy nodded. 'What regiment?'

'Cranchester OTC. We're on Field Day.'

'We've got the day off too. Instead of VE Day when we had a service in the Cathedral.'

'You're from the Choir School?'

'Yes. Second Treble actually. Probably First when Aitcheson leaves.'

Angus was amused at the way the boy, settling beside in the grass beside him and, hugging his knees to himself, assumed that everyone would know Aitcheson. 'I say, if you're throwing this away, I wouldn't mind eating it.'

'Go ahead. It's a bit hard by now. Cranchester packed lunches are pretty indigestible.'

'So're ours. But ours're feeble too. I ate mine before we bathed.'

'Was that you? In the stream this morning?'

The boy looked at him. 'You're the soldier! Ransom and I thought that if the war had still been on you might have been a spy. Because of what you've got on your sleeve.'

The archaic elaborate red and gold braiding of an Under-Officer in Cranchester OTC was indeed almost Ruritanian. Accepting the spirit of such charmingly contorted reasoning, Angus agreed: 'You can never be too careful.'

'You didn't look Japanese, so we knew you were all right.'

Angus felt a sudden lightness of spirit. 'I'm glad I didn't look Japanese.' He was immensely cheered by the uncritical, uncomplicated response of his companion, who showed no inclination to go. He said, 'What's happened to...Ransom...is it?'

'He said he's got a slow puncture and wanted to set off back after the bathe. We're not supposed to split up really, but nobody'll notice. And I wanted to see what was up here. I say, what's your name?'

'Angus.'

'Mine's Christopher. Do you have a watch?'

Despite an inclination to say,' Mine's Christopher too,' he felt that to explain Angus was his surname might be taken as some sort of rebuke. He murmured, 'It's after two-thirty, I must get on to Avebury.'

'If we go down that side and get my bike, I could walk with you.' Having discovered a companion in uniform, even if only a cadet, his chatty new friend was unwilling to let him escape. Truth to tell, Angus was rather enjoying himself. There was something utterly engaging about such hero-worshipping curiosity; a memory of himself accompanying Officer Cadet Singleton to the station three years before floated into his mind. 'Lots of Choristers go to Cranchester. What House are you?' Angus remembered the knowing Dermott-Powell, so very different from this artlessly gossiping child sliding down the grassy slope on his haunches beside him. He said, 'Ansell's.'

'Oh. That's the best House isn't it?'

'Of course! How do you know?'

'Mr Prinsep. Latin and Harmony. He was there.'

They trailed through tall grass and cow parsley on the faint path that led to Avebury which grew so thick and tall that, on occasion, it completely obscured his small companion and entangled itself in the bicycle. In the end Angus pushed the cycle whilst its owner went ahead armed with a stick, enthusiastically striking down the nettles in their path calling back, 'It must be like this fighting the Japanese, in the jungle!'

At last they came out into the Avebury circle. The remembered chill seemed to strike him again.

'I say, Angus, these stones are a bit spooky aren't they!'

'They are a bit. Tell you what, let's see if they have any lemonade at the Post Office. They did last time I was here.' Once again he thought of himself and Mawsom.

A small, new notice in the window said **TEAS**. It was dark and cool inside. The postmistress was the same. 'You told me to come back when the war ended,' Angus said. 'So here I am! There were two of us. You said we couldn't buy the guide book.'

The woman looked at him. After a long moment she said, 'Of course. You've grown, but you've still got the silver patch in your hair. This your brother? You were about his size last time.'

'I'm a *friend*.' It was obvious that a friend rated far higher than any mere brother.

'Oh, I beg your pardon! In that case it'll have to be a particularly special tea.'

They were given scones with strawberry jam, rough thick brown bread and some lemon-curd tarts. When he tried to pay she refused.

Angus said, 'You did that last time!'

'Well I'm doing it this time. You know why?'

Angus shook his head.

It's the first tea I've done since the war ended. We only just started again. Haven't been able to get a permit before today. Rationing and all that. And I'd told myself the first customer gets tea free. A sort of celebration that the war's over.'

'That's jolly decent of you,' the boy said grandly. She laughed.

Angus said, 'It is. Thank you very much.'

They went out into the sun. A hidden church clock chimed. 'Gosh! I must go. I promised Ransom that I'd meet him just outside the Close, so's everyone could see us cycle in together.'

'Won't he have been waiting quite some time?'

'Oh, he won't mind. He'll have been at Carker's – that's the pet shop. Ransom's potty about animals, I expect that's why he wanted to get back. Carker's is out of bounds because he lets us have his spare mice and the Matron says they're vermin.'

He rode off through the stones. 'Thanks, Angus.' Turning to wave he very nearly fell off.

Spare mice!

With his departure it seemed as though a bit of the sun had gone in. He had not noticed the lorry drawn up in the car park of the Red Lion. He wandered across. Turner, of Jonquil's, whom he knew slightly, said 'Who was that, then, Angus?'

'Don't know really. Some kid I met on the top of Silbury. One of the Cathedral choristers I gather.'

A dark-haired boy from Pettifer's, whom Angus disliked, made suggestive kissing noises with his lips. 'Oooh, pretty little choirboys is it? And we all thought you lot in Ansell's were pure as driven snow.' Everything was soured, he was back in the atmosphere and environment of Cranchester. However Angus knew better than to rise to the bait, so he ignored the remark.

※

During the rest of the Half, there were moments when Angus was to recall the slight figure in striped jersey and baggy shorts, sitting in the Silbury grass, arms hugging his drawn-up knees. It perfectly symbolised an entire world no longer available to him – one that, until now, he had never thought to regret, seeing it rather as the world to grow up and away from. Now, all at once it seemed attractive; an uncomplicated, bright world where, as in a well focused photograph, black and white were sharp-edged, distinct, unmistakably different. It was a lost world which haunted him each time he remembered the creased, fading, torn snapshot which had so unexpectedly – so uncomfortably – tumbled out of the envelope nine months before and which he had stuffed into Singleton's memorial.

The three-tonner broke down three times, so they arrived back late. Angus found that he had missed a presentation to the Flanders' Mare. He was not sorry. He had never found her very sympathetic; a rather cold woman with a long, hardly smiling face, and glasses. She was leaving unexpectedly to look after an elderly relation who had been taken suddenly and seriously ill. She was not popular and so, smitten by conscience, Ansell's had subscribed to an extravagantly handsome leaving present. In the middle of a short speech of thanks, she had broken down and wept copiously to the embarrassment of everyone present.

Later that evening, after Curfew, Baker said, 'I don't know so much about looking after relations! I think she's in pod!'

Shocked silence.

'Oh, come on, Baker!'

'She must be about ninety!'

Baker said doggedly, 'Well, she looks a jolly sight fatter than she used to. Like my sister about five months before she had her baby, Anyway, she's only thirty-seven. I overheard her talking to the High Master's wife once, after Chapel.'

'That's as good as ninety!'

'It's always more dangerous to have a child late,' Snider said with what they recognised to be medical precision.

'Do you think she's secretly married The Digger?'

A ribald voice added, 'Perhaps they eloped to Gretna to celebrate VE Day!' There was general laughter.

Baker said, 'I don't think she's *married* at all. That's why she'd have to leave.'

Mawsom said, 'I think it's bloody bad form to talk about the Flanders' Mare in this way. The poor woman was frightfully upset when she thanked us. Must be fairly awful going back to spend the rest of your life looking after an invalid.'

Baker stuck his lip out obstinately. 'I bet I'm right!'

Notting, who had joined them late, said loudly, 'Balls! Where'd she ever find someone to father it? She looks like a bloody horse in glasses.'

It was typical of Notting – coarse, pithy – but even Mawsom was disinclined to dispute the matter further.

vi

Angus was lying beside Snider on the grass. Cranchester were out in 'The Middle', batting. Ellerman, hazed by heat, had already scored fifty. It was a hot, cloudless afternoon. After a while Snider dozed off to sleep, his glasses folded on a book by his head. Idly, Angus picked them up. He wondered what it would be like to have to use specs. He slipped them on his nose. As if by magic Ellerman sprang into focus, sharp, clear. He took the spectacles off. He could see the batsman, knew it was Ellerman, but the heat-haze had returned and blurred him. Once again he donned Snider's glasses. Ellerman was again sharp and Angus could follow quite easily the pace of the quick bowler. There was no heat haze.

Leaving Snider asleep, he took the glasses and moved over to the nets where the next two batsmen were getting their eye in. One of them, a Tusker he knew quite well, said, 'Hello, Angus.'

'Shall I toss a few down, Hammet?'

'What about your togs?'

It was a rigorous rule that Castonians should wear whites even for nets, now that the war was over.

Angus said, 'If I put your sweater on, no one'll take too much notice. It's too hot to come across from Pavilion.'

'Never seen you wearing glasses before, Angus.'

As he came up to bowl, Angus was conscious that for the first time in the season he could see the batsman's boots sharp and crisp on the sharply defined blades of grass. With his third ball, he just clipped the stumps. Hammet said, 'I can't see why Ansell's don't bowl you. Is it true you've been dropped?'

Angus said unemotionally, 'Off form.'

Hammet said, 'Daiches has just walked out of Pavilion. You'd better make this the last, otherwise you'll be done for Improper Dress.' He struck the ball sharply and slightly edged it. It proved a low, difficult, catch. Without haste or awkwardness, Angus pushed himself forward and caught it cleanly. 'I'm surprised they don't play you just for your fielding,' Hammet observed.

Angus took off the jersey and Snider's glasses, put on his jacket and walked off in the opposite direction to Daiches, the Cranchester Captain.

Snider was awake. 'Have you seen my glasses?'

'Yes. I tried 'em out.'

'You'll ruin your eyes! You should never do that.'

'Don't think so. Not just this once. You're not a doctor yet, Snider.'

The following day he missed Chapel to see the School Doctor in Nurs'ry and, three days later, found himself sitting in the darkened room of the optician in Cranchester, staring at the illuminated letters as a benign elderly man shuffled lenses.

'Have you ever worn glasses before, sir?'

'No. I didn't think I needed them.'

'Eyes change, sir. Especially at your age. You'll probably find that when you're twenty-one you'll no longer need them. Funny things, eyes.'

Angus came out. He had not realised it was the far end of the same street as the dark chapel. Abreast of it, the faint aroma of incense touched his nostrils and, in an instant, he felt the tight, breathless choking return. The events of the previous year pressed on him. Across the road was the dark house where for moment he had been the object of (almost invited?) Father Dunsley's attentions. Overcome by fear and shame he ran.

A fortnight later he collected wire-rimmed spectacles from the optician. 'You'll be able to play games in those without too much risk, sir.' This time he avoided Priest Street by making a long detour.

A couple of days afterwards, largely on account of injury to other players, Angus was reinstated in the Ansell's team and, because the injuries affected bowling strength, he was put on to bowl to enable Ashton, who wanted to change ends, to take a couple of overs' rest.

Pettifer's were well in control and looked like winning the game handsomely. Ansell's resigned itself to seeing Angus hit hard to the boundary. His first over gave away no runs and had Pettifer's batsmen in difficulty, so he was given a second over. He dismissed both batsmen, taking a fine catch from the second himself. He could see the white line and the toe of the bat clearly and crisply, felt confident he could put the ball wherever he chose. Pettifer's lost their nerve when he took three further wickets. His final figures were seven wickets for nineteen runs and included three fine catches from his own bowling. Ansell's won without difficulty.

Ashton said, 'Bloody *mar-vellous*, AC. What's come over you?'

Angus tapped the wire rims.

'I've never seen you wearing them before.'

'I found out by accident that I couldn't really see. Not as well as I can with these.'

'You kidding, AC?'

'No, I'm not, Ashton. It was why I'd been dropping catches too.'

Brownlow, standing near enough to overhear, said, 'Magic spectacles! Like that chap in America. He said he'd been given magic spectacles. Started some religion or other.'

'Mormons,' Ashton said with a condescending air. 'They can have lots of wives too, you'll be interested to hear, Brownlow.'

Ellerman, who until then had remained silent, said thoughtfully 'A pity it's so late in the season, AC. Next year you'll get Trialled for the Eleven if you can still bowl like that.'

They drifted back. Angus, slightly apart, recalled his delight and surprise at his selection for the Ansell's side that first time two years before. Now it seemed to have happened all over again and somehow the new ability to focus sharply seemed to go hand in hand with the clarity with which he could see himself. He felt elevated, light in heart as if dancing on air and, although, during the remaining matches of the season, Ansell's quicker bowlers did most of the damage to the opposition and slaughtered Orangery in the Final, Angus' tally of fine catches confirmed his returned confidence. Perhaps, with a couple of seasons ahead of him, he would represent Cranchester one day, even join Ellerman out in 'The Middle' for, with glasses, his batting had also improved immeasurably. He enjoyed the day-dream, but more than that, it was as if he really had come safely out again into sunshine and warmth from the dark shadow of that 'hideous wood' around which he had floundered so shamefully since his first year.

※

The day before the end of Half, Ellerman came up conspiratorially to Angus and Mawsom as they stood looking at last notices in Corridor. 'Come into my study a moment.'

Snider and Notting were also there and Baker squeezed in his ample frame into the tiny space. Notting said, 'What's up, Ellerman? Have they picked you for England or something?'

'Baker was quite right about the Flanders' Mare. She's preggers. It's due some time in the holiday.'

'I told you,' Baker said. 'You all thought I was making it up.'

'Oh, all right, wonderboy! Most of us haven't your intimate knowledge of these things.'

When the laughter died away, Mawsom said, 'You look as if there's something else.'

You'll never guess who the father is?'

Notting said, 'What about AC!' The renewed laughter in the tiny room was almost overpowering.

In order to stop it, Angus said, 'You don't know. You're making it up.'

'No.' Ellerman was not smiling. 'It's even more bloody unbelievable.'

Baker said, 'You don't mean that it *is* The Digger!'

'Come on, Ellerman. Who is it, you reckon?'

'I don't reckon. *I know*. Absolutely! For certain. Who's Head of House?'

'Ashton! I can't believe...'

'You're off your head, Ellerman...'

'You must be joking...'

'No, you bloody dimwits.... I mean why did Ashton take over from *Botting*? That's why he left when he did. The Flanders' Mare had to go before she got too noticeable, but obviously she couldn't go at the same time as Botting. It's all been stage-managed by The Digger.'

'You're trying to tell us that Botting was screwing the Flanders' Mare?' Notting was coarse with disbelief and sounded more repelled than anything else. 'Bloody hell, she could have been his mother!'

'Just how did you discover this amazing news, Ellerman?'

Ellerman shuffled, a little shamefaced. 'I happened to have to go over to Private – about something to do with home. When I went in the draught blew some papers off the desk. Digger wasn't there, so I gathered them up and couldn't help seeing the letter. I'm not making it up, Snider. It really was an accident.'

'Huh! Some "accident", Ellerman.'

Mawsom said, 'No wonder The Digger's been looking so grim these last weeks.'

Notting sneered: 'It's bloody disgusting! She's an old hag. It's bloody unnatural.'

'She's only in her thirties. And, if it comes to being "unnatural", what about Tassel Night?' Snider put in quietly.

'For Christ's sake, Snider, that's no different from any other place like Cranchester.'

'I dare say the outside world would think you and Brownlow more "unnatural" than Botting and Miss Horsefall.'

'It's a million times different,' Notting said explosively. 'Brownlow's only while we're here...as Ellins said it's all perfectly natural – shut up like prisoners in Ansell's, with no girls. The Flanders' Mare was old enough to know better. At least when I'm thirty-seven I hope I shan't still want to be tossed off by small boys.'

His coarse logic silenced them until Snider, not to be defeated, murmured, 'Well, I suppose Botting and the Flanders' Mare were also prisoners in Ansell's.'

'Come off it, Snider, Notting's right. It isn't the same. Even if Notting's way of expressing it is more suited to an oik school than Ansell's,' Ellerman added crushingly.

Notting flushed deeply as he always did when it was implied that he was not quite the right social level either for Ansell's or Cranchester. It was, they had discovered, the surest way to shut him up.

Mawsom and Angus went outside. They were joined by Snider. 'Do you think Ellerman's telling the truth?'

Mawsom said, 'I'm sure he is. Now I've got used to the idea, it doesn't seem quite so impossible. I mean nobody would ever know if one of the Praefaectors left his study and went up to the top floor after Lights Out.'

There was a considerable silence. Snider said, 'I feel sorry for her. I can't help thinking how lonely she must have been. Probably thought it was a sort of last chance.'

'Of course,' Mawsom suggested, 'it's possible that it's happened before – with other Praefaectors – only she, well, took precautions.'

'I just wouldn't have thought it of Botting,' Angus said. 'I mean he seemed like everyone else.'

'He was. That's what makes it so...alarming.'

'I do believe you had your eye on her, Snider?' Mawsom attempted to lighten the tone.

Snider retorted with a touch of asperity, 'I mean that, we're all cooped up here and, according to a book I read, we're more sexually active than at any other time of our lives. It's like having unexploded bombs around.'

'You seem to get hold of all sorts of books that would give The Digger a fit. I suppose it's under cover of doing Biology.'

'As a matter of fact, Mawsom, I'm going to read medicine at Oxford!'

Thoughtfully, Mawsom continued, 'I suppose Tassel Night's a sort of safety valve.'

Snider said, 'Or perhaps schools like this are wrong. But I s'pose you could be right about Tassel Night.'

'No need to blush, AC.'

'I wasn't. At least I didn't mean to be. I was just thinking about what you and Mawsom were saying. Tassel Nights probably are a good thing. At least, with Ashton in charge, it's only once a Half.' In fact he was thinking most about Botting and the Flanders' Mare. He said suddenly, 'I say, wasn't Botting up in the sick room with some bug or other? In January?'

'You could be right, AC.'

'Actually I'm a bit like Snider, I can't help feeling...well, sorry for them both. I mean what happens to them now?'

'I expect Botting'll go up to Cambridge. His people will probably send an allowance to her. Provided she keeps quiet.' Mawsom tried to make it sound a reasonable arrangement, but failed.

'Do you think she's got any relations? What do you do if you're unmarried, with a baby?' There was genuine compassion behind Snider's question that they would have preferred to be able to ignore.

'Go and live somewhere under another name?' It was all Angus could think of.

Snider said, 'People are bound to know, with ration cards and insurance cards and all that.'

'Get it adopted.'

'Unless, of course, Botting marries her.'

Mawsom said with quiet authority, 'I'm sure it was to avoid anything like that that his people took him away.'

'It's the poor wot gets the blame', Angus recognised a line from one of the less reputable Tassel Night songs. However, it was clear from Snider's tone that he did not make light of it.

'I wonder if those people who think that the Public Schools should take girls will expect places like Cranchester to have a maternity unit?' Mawsom offered as if to end the topic by moving towards a joke.

Angus said thoughtfully, 'I suppose that at least Tassel Night doesn't have lasting repercussions. Not like a baby, I mean.'

'According to my book, I'm not so sure you're right about no repercussions, AC. In fact it says in a book I was...' Snider got no further.

'We've heard about enough of your dirty books,' Mawsom barked, his usual equanimity deserting him. 'For Christ's sake, let's drop the whole subject. This bloody Half ends tomorrow. Thank God nothing else can happen before then.'

Breakfast was always later on the day they were to catch the London train. Afterwards Ansell's stood round the walls of Libe, Praefaectors their backs to the fireplace. All jackets buttoned correctly (one button undone in third year, two in fourth – Praefaectors' silver buttons all undone; all arms folded – except the Praefaectors. Sun cascaded through the barred windows on the right so that those standing opposite had to screw up their eyes against the glare. Ashton came in very rapidly closely followed by The Digger and called List very brusquely. The Digger wished the usual good fortune to those leaving, thanking them for their contribution. He ended.

He paused and, unusually, did not leave – a break with tradition. Ellerman whispered, '*Botting!*'

'The war is virtually ended. I have been Housemaster for a good many years. I think perhaps I ought to tell you that I shall be retiring from Ansell's at Christmas. It has been a difficult decision to make. My successor will be Mr Craigie. I have written to your parents. Have a very happy holiday.' He vanished.

Stunned disbelief.

Ashton, shouting, protested defensively, 'The Digger only bloody told *me* when I went through to fetch him! He's been asked to advise on setting up education in Germany. That's why he's going at Christmas. Cranchester's agreed to "second" him for the best part of next year.'

Everybody spoke.

Everyone except Angus.

Animated, shocked conversation washed round him. He heard it, but was not of it – detached by his own thoughts from the sober, regretful, almost awed tones of his companions. 'The Digger going!' A God-given sign, consecrating his unspoken vow to uphold Singleton's values, crystallising his emotional, ill-defined yearning to expiate the dark years once and for all.

'It's the End of an Era!' Baker was booming complacently, with all the conviction of the middle-aged golf-club-pundit utterly certain that he has said something original and profound. His loudness momentarily penetrated Angus' introspection.

Baker was right! 'The End of an Era.' Thank God. A chance to begin again, to make a fresh start. It was as if the sun had once again burst out after an interminable winter of darkness, as once it had seemed to do in the wake of Ellins' lucid, matter-of-fact explanation of their adolescent lusts and fears. Intoxicated with relief, he recalled other rare, but marvellous, out-of-time moments; evenings of fir-cone fires; the breakfast provided by Bella; tea at the Singletons, the quiet church, the vicarage study; himself and Mawsom at Avebury. Unbidden, came an image of a boy sitting, hugging his knees on Silbury Hill – that too had been out-of-time.

'The End Of An Era!' club bore in embryo Baker reiterated, literally wagging his finger.

'A new Housemaster.' Craigie, he knew instinctively, would see things very differently. It was a God-sent opportunity to make the break, to liberate himself completely from Ansell's, to repay, finally, his debt of honour to Singleton's memory. By conquering himself he could secure salvation.

'The Digger?'

'Going?'

Voices ebbed and flowed, indignant, regretful, even resentful at The Digger's abandonment of them. Angus, conscious of the words, repeated them in his own mind with the very different intonation of sheer elation.

'…So we'll make next Half The Digger's last Half, the best there's ever been in Ansell's…' Ashton had never had such an attentive audience.

Angus was filled with such rejoicing that that could hardly restrain himself from shouting, 'Only one more Half with The Digger? Bloody *mar*-vellous.'

'…We'll win everything! Every bloody thing.'

He had nothing in common with cheering, stamping Ansell's Men applauding Aston's peroration. In the New Year, a New Start. *Only one More Half!* and at last, he would be free!

1945-1946

Fall

O the mind, mind has mountains; cliffs of fall
Frightful sheer, no man fathomed. Hold them cheap
May who ne'er hung there.

Gerard Manley Hopkins
Sonnets (65)

Chapter Nine

Redemption. How tempting to leave you to imagine for yourself the happy ending which so providentially offers itself, as it always does in the archetypal school story. Redemption?

As I write these words, late winter afternoon fades into darkness. It is cold. For a few minutes there will be a marvellous sky against a rolling landscape which opens out before my window.

Is this the landscape of old age?

Let me pursue the metaphor. I know what this open, familiar, panorama I see before me will bring, because I know what it has brought in the past and I can detect, many miles away, the first tell-tale signs of sun or storm, of dawn or night. By contrast it seems to me that the landscape of my schooldays was different, more like Devonshire, where secret narrow lanes and high banks make it impossible to predict what might be around the next corner – menacing dark copse, or a breathtaking seascape; innumerable grey days and sudden, unexpected cloudy squalls, then suddenly, as if vouchsafed by some divine lottery, stunning idyllic, interludes of sun and small, unbelievably soft clouds.

Even after three or four years at Ansell's there were still unbearable tensions; one was always waiting for something to happen. When it did, in my memory, it was rarely what had been anticipated. As a junior member of the House this sense of foreboding terrified me. Each day, on awakening, there was an instant of sickening dread which clutched at the heart. It happens even now and – have I told you this before? – I wake suddenly, back in Ansell's, drenched in beads of perspiration.

You never knew what it would be. Perhaps it was good — you had been unexpectedly selected for a match away from Cranchester. Perhaps bad — summarily losing a team place so dearly cherished. Or some work handed in, neither much better nor much worse than usual, would be inexplicably deemed particularly unsatisfactory — worst of all, 'slack'. That would mean facing the Div Pro. Possibly it would be necessary to show it up to the Housemaster, always a savagely painful interview in the case of The Digger.

Most often one had, quite unwittingly, offended against some arcane aspect of the Cranchester code or, even more venal, against the code of Ansell's. On one occasion I did both. I had a loose button. It caught on the pew in Chapel and wrenched itself off as I rose from my knees. I put it in my pocket. On the way out of Chapel, Sanderson (fancy recalling his name after all this time) a Praefaector in Tortellier's noticed. I can hear him now. 'Only Classics [those in the Classical Sixth Form] may wear two buttons. Let Tennant know.'

Tennant was Head of House and I let him know before Late School. He said, 'I know. Mansell (Head of Tortellier's) has already told me Sanderson said you should report yourself. You should have told me at lunch-time. You'll get two-up for the button and another two-up for not telling me earlier. At Curfew, in Big Study.'

ii

September

Ellerman said, 'Do you all realise that we shall be part of a new era?'

Notting did not notice Angus standing behind him. 'With Craigie it'll not be much of an era. He'll probably make AC Head of House and insist on Praefaectors wearing halos.'

Everyone laughed. Ellerman said, 'No offence, AC.' Notting reddened and continued hastily, 'If I were Head of House, I'd give each of the new Election six-up on the eleventh night and tan their arses once a week thereafter. The new Election's so wet it's probably dripping! Have you seen Orton? It's sickening the way he looks at Watson.'

Snider said, 'You're just jealous! You wish you were Watson!'

'If I were, I wouldn't let everyone know…. He can't keep his eyes off Orton.'

Snider said, 'The same can be said of half Cranchester.'

'Anyhow, I wouldn't stand for it if I were Head of Ansell's.'

'Well, you never will be, thank God, Ellerman'll be Head of House after Ashton. Everyone knows that.'

Ellerman said smoothly, 'It's difficult to know what Craigie's likely to do. Ashton's been Head of House for Hell of a long time…because of Botting.'

'Anyhow,' Notting persisted with unpleasant intensity, 'I think new Elections ought to have their arses tanned a damn sight more than it's done nowadays.'

Into the pause Snider asked, with quiet mock-scientific enquiry, 'I've always meant to ask, if it's true that the first time you had to tighten-up you peed yourself in Big Study so that the rug had to be binned, Notting?'

Notting turned purpley-red; controlling himself with difficulty he spat, 'You'd believe anything, Snider! Don't forget that you're the only one in Ansell's who was beaten by the Housemaster for tossing himself off!'

Snider's sallow skin paled. Eventually he said quietly, 'At least I told the truth. A fault you don't have, Notting,' and walked out.

Into the silence Baker said gleefully, 'Game, set and match to Snider, I think!' Notting looked as though he would explode, then he too strode away.

There was a lull and Mawsom began placatingly, 'Actually Notting's quite shrewd, although he's a turd.'

'What do you mean?'

'You could be Craigie's man, Angus. He's always had his eye on you, ever since he took over our Division after Ellins.'

'Bloody nonsense, Mawsom.'

'No it isn't, is it, Baker?'

Baker grinned. 'When Craigie took over the Div, yours was the only name he knew.'

'That's only because he noticed me in the choir. He spoke to me after the duet with Dermott-Powell.' Notting, recovered from the wounds received in his encounter with Snider, had sidled back. He added, 'Well, after all, he is ordained and we know all about clergymen and choirboys from the *News of the World*.'

Mawsom said casually, 'You have a very nasty mind, Notting.'

Ellerman added in a deceptively suave tone, 'Because, being an oik at heart, my dear Notting, you can't be expected to know any better.'

Notting flushed darkly.

'Furthermore, Notting,' Ellerman went on, 'as you have obviously forgotten, The Digger was a clergyman too.'

'I was only saying...'

Mawsom, peacemaking, cut him short. 'It's odd how one forgets The Digger has a dog-collar.' It was a frequent comment amongst them.

'That's because The Digger's a bloody good Housemaster. That's what makes you forget. We're never likely to forget it with Craigie. Which is why he'll be a disaster for Ansell's if we aren't careful,' Ellerman said forcefully. 'It'll be up to us to make sure he isn't. This time next year we'll be Senior Election. We'll have a Housemaster to train as well as a new Election.'

'I heard a rumour today that Ashton's staying on an extra Half to see Craigie in,' Baker said.

From the way Ellerman stopped suddenly it was clear that this was something he had not yet heard, but he recovered himself.

Angus said, 'It'll probably be Watson. After all, he's Ashton's year.'

'Watson?' Ellerman exclaimed. The utter scorn in his voice was echoed by the others.

'*Watson!*'

Angus said mildly, 'He seems nice enough to me.'

Ellerman retorted, 'It's not enough to be *nice* as Head of House. Harlow was *nice enough* if you remember. And Ansell's was a bloody shambles.'

'Not really,' Mawsom began.

'Not really? Come on, Mawsom!'

'Well you seemed to enjoy it! So did Notting if I remember rightly. Even AC.'

'That's what I mean,' Ellerman snapped. 'We were allowed to get away with blue murder. If you remember, Carstairs spent a weekend in London and it was never discovered. I'm not having that when I'm ...' He stopped.

'Head of House?' Mawsom finished delicately and Ellerman coloured up; he had not intended to give himself away.

Angus said, 'Don't see why you need be embarrassed, Ellerman, it has to be you at some stage.'

Mawsom persisted: 'I don't think we should underestimate Craigie. We admit he's very different from The Digger. I think he could go for Watson.'

'My God!' Ellerman threw up his hands dramatically. 'Watson's one of those who don't even believe in tightening-up. You never heard such a load of crap as he argued in that debate about corporal punishment last year! Ansell's will go downhill if we have him at the top. Look at Jonquil's!'

Ellerman had a point. Jonquil's had abolished all beating and all fagging on the first day of the Half. The liberal intentions of the Head of House had not been justified by any corresponding upsurge in morale. Three of Jonquil's Praefaectors resigned in a dramatic gesture; the remaining two were well-intentioned, but quite ineffective.

Baker said, 'Well, what can you expect! Loopy Longhurst probably votes Labour!' Jonquil's benign, but entirely disregarded, Housemaster, a notable Greek scholar had, for years, allowed his most senior boys to rule themselves as they wished.

Notting said, 'Did you hear they burned all the switches!'

'Tell us something new, Notting!'

Mawsom said, 'Must've be fun for the Junior Election!'

'They don't have "Juniors" or "Seniors" in Jonquil's any longer. Strawson made a speech on the first night of the Half. He said that any sort of hierarchy was all nonsense and that the youngest of the new Election had just as much right to have a say as he himself. They run it by a sort of parliament now,' Mawsom ended, 'or try to run it.'

'Sounds rather a good idea to me,' Angus said mildly.

'*You* would think so, AC,' Notting threw out. 'But could even you see Ansell's being run like that?'

'No, not really. I wasn't being serious.'

'And,' Ellerman added, 'as we can all see, under that system Jonquil's doesn't *run* at all – in fact it hardly moves. We'd be as bad with Watson and Craigie.'

'It'll just have to be you, Ellerman,' Notting said.

'However,' Mawsom demurred, 'we seem to forget that Watson's a Praefaector already, so are one or two others. Even you are not a Praefaector yet, Ellerman.'

'Nor was Ashton when he was first appointed, I seem to remember,' Snider interposed.

October

Within a month of the start of the Half, a notice went up in Corridor announcing that Ellerman had been promoted Praefaector. Although not entirely unexpected it was none the less sensational.

'After all,' Baker explained to anyone willing to listen, 'there's never been anyone made Praefaector whilst still in Little Study.'

'That's only because there's a Big Study out of action since mice got at the wiring.'

Brownlow had joined the group round the fire in Libe: 'Wasn't there somebody called Maunder?'

'Could be. He was Head of House when we arrived,' Mawsom said. 'I never heard he was a Praefaector early.'

Notting sniggered, 'I wonder who'll be first to tighten-up for Ellerman and when?'

Baker said, 'It'll be Arkell!'

Mawsom said, 'Well, it won't be Lawson!' There was a laugh of agreement at the implication.

In the event, it was Lawson.

'Who'd've believed it!' Snider remarked. 'What was it all about?'

'Something to do with missing a tackle in the Colt's match against Pettifer's.'

'Lawson's Captain of Colts!'

'Ellerman reckons he missed an easy tackle.'

Mawsom said, 'It wasn't that he missed. He just didn't bother.'

Angus said, 'I'm not surprised. The game was virtually over and Ansell's were twenty-nine points ahead! What's more, that Pettifer's man weighs about four times as much as Lawson.'

'Ellerman says no Ansell's Man ever funks a tackle, no matter what the score.'

'Lawson doesn't seem too upset. Probably regards it as an honour to be Ellerman's first victim.'

Snider interrupted almost primly, 'Technically, I don't think Ellerman had to be a Praefaector to punish for a rugger offence. As Ansell's Captain of Rugger, he could have done it anyway.'

'I never thought of that. What if he'd decided to beat Watson for cutting a tackle!' Notting teased. 'I mean earlier in the Half, before he was a Praefaector himself. That would have been fun.'

Although, by proposing this absurdity, Notting was merely trying to amuse, Snider said patiently, 'You seem to forget that because of his asthma Watson does not play rugger.'

Baker said, 'Let's hope to God that Craigie *doesn't* have a brainstorm and make Watson Head of House after Ashton leaves.'

The following day Ansell's beat Jonquil's by seventy-nine points to nil and came away from the match barely muddied. Ellerman said later, 'A bloody disgrace! Why they even bother to field a team I don't know!'

As they went into Little Change, Notting laughed, 'I hear Jonquil's abolished Tassels for Rugger now. That's why the whole side were wearing Colours socks.'

'In that case I'm only sorry,' Ellerman retorted, 'that we couldn't have got a century against them.'

During a similar conversation at supper, Snider asked with tongue-in-cheek puzzlement, 'Why should abolishing fagging and tightening-up be blamed for a weak rugger side?' He had the irritating habit of posing questions which were difficult to answer.

Notting said, with exasperation, 'Because, my dear Snider, if you don't have discipline, then you can't expect to play rugger well.'

'Ah, I see! And I always thought,' Snider continued provocatively, getting up for Grace, 'that games were played for pleasure not discipline. I hadn't realised that, apparently, nobody actually enjoys playing them.'

Infuriatingly there was not time to reply before Grace was read and Snider slipped away immediately afterwards without having to admit that, deep down, even he disapproved of the new regime at Jonquil's.

November

In November, Angus decided, at the last moment, to run The Marathon. Unlike every other sport, it was an open event so, although it was mainly the senior part of the school who participated, the best of the younger runners also took part. For some reason lost in the mists of time it had become a tradition that Ansell's never entered a team, in consequence very few Ansell's Men even took part. News of Angus' entry was greeted good-humouredly as another acceptable, almost expected, eccentricity.

It had rained for several days and, on the afternoon of the race, udders of cloud poured torrential cold drops from a heavy, leaden sky with monotonous continuity. It was therefore perhaps a smaller entry than usual; nonetheless there were over two hundred runners and a sparse collection of watchers under umbrellas. The starting gun went off in a flat, echoless manner, as though the wetness had got into that too. The conditions were atrocious, the worst within Cranchester memory.

Angus was thoroughly familiar with the course. During the last year or two he had run it every day, though Ansell's indifference to the event meant he had never previously considered entering the race. His decision to run was, unconsciously, part of his shrugging off Ansell's. He did not set out to compete. It never occurred to him that he might be better than anyone else. He had never even thought about that. Though excitement buoyed him up, he set out merely to re-complete the race. He positioned himself on the outside, farthest from the starter and determined to start quickly, with a sprint; the path up to Roman Gate was narrow and, in the rain would, he knew, be very muddy. So he shot off into the lead by twenty yards before the route narrowed through a stone wall; he could hear the squelching patter of shoes behind him. As he went through the wall a voice said, 'Who on earth is that? He'll burn out before Roman.' If there was an answering reply, he did not hear it.

His heart had been pounding much faster than usual at the start, however, now out there in front, in the rain, he felt just as he always felt on Marathon, free, exhilarated. The mud was cold and the rain teemed; he could feel goose-pimples on his arms and accelerated his pace to heighten body heat. The steep track was as slippery as if it had been oiled; to his mild surprise, he found that he was not yet being challenged. The land rose, cloud clothed the bushes and walls on either side of him in ragged drifts of mist. At a turn in the path, he glanced back and could only just make out dimly running figures. He was astonished: 'They must be at least fifty yards behind.' It was perhaps at that moment he first thought of trying to win. Very slightly he increased his pace again, running easily, his breath coming evenly, fuming the cold, damp, air ahead of him as he expelled it. By the time he reached Roman Gate he could not hear any sound behind him. He swung through. A group of shrouded figures peered at him. A voice said, 'Who is it?'

He grunted through his teeth, 'Angus, Ansell's' and, conscious of a stir of surprise, added, 'Seventy-nine,' although he supposed they could read the number pinned to his shirt. One of the voices called through the mist behind him, 'Keep it up. You've got a good time so far.'

Along Roman Road the even ground relieved the strain on his calf muscles and he lengthened his stride. Taking deep breaths of cold air, he turned his face to the clouds and relished even colder rain drilling into his face. A first gust of breeze lifted the mist for an instant and he glanced back Who was closest? He risked another look. Nobody at all between him and Roman Gate? He couldn't believe it. He was hundreds of yards ahead of the field. Before he could look again, mist closed down and he was once more alone in a white world. He quickened pace and almost ran into the steward at the turn at the end of Roman Road.

'Sorry! *Who?*'

'Angus, Ansell's. Seventy-nine.'

He vanished again into the mist as the route began the first of the treacherously narrow and rocky downhill sections. There were pools of water in the dips. The stones were slimy and awkward, but he trod on them lightly, almost as if flying. The astonished puzzlement in the voices of the stewards had amused him, flattered him too and he felt himself responding to it. There came the wire fence. He had to clamber through. Two figures crouching beneath umbrellas peered at him intently.

'Is that *Angus*?'

'Yes, sir. Seventy-nine.'

Another anonymous voice said, 'Ansell's never do the Marathon.'

'I'm the only entry,' Angus grunted before slipping again into the gloom. It seemed definitely darker. The ground was now heavy and boggy. The pools of water now disguised peaty dips. He had to choose his route, by hopping from tussock to tussock. Over confident, he misjudged, slipped, and fell face-forward in a pool of obnoxious-looking (and tasting) black water. Spluttering, he got up, shook himself and ran on. He laughed. He felt elated.

The ground underfoot hardened and the long gentler downhill stretch to the ford began. Despite the mist, he knew exactly where he was, the ground under his feet was familiar terrain. He had never felt better and quickened pace yet again, now running really hard. Eventually, as the ground dropped below the mist, he could see the ford and the bridge lined, even in the rain, by spectators. Although the finish lay some half-mile beyond it, the bridge was the favourite grandstand because the route lay through the water. Today, after all the rain, the river was running strongly. He came down the last of the hill with long strides. There was a buzz of interest. Various voices asking, 'Who is it?' He heard Mawsom, probably the only Ansell's Man in the crowd, say 'Blood-dy Hell! *It's AC!*'

'Who?'

'Angus, Ansell's.'

'Oh, is that the chap with the white patch in his hair?'

'What? Yes. It *is* AC. He looks as though he's been wading through the marsh. *Come **on,** AC!*'

To a crescendo of cheers, clapping, and remarks about his mud-streaked condition, Angus sped down into the ford. The current was much stronger than he had expected, the water splashed against his knees and soaked him through his shorts. It was very cold too, it took his breath away. At the middle, more than waist high, it tried to tug him off his feet, but he waded on encouraged by cheers from the bridge. When he emerged the lower half of his body was as conspicuously clean as the upper half was black with mud. His nearest challenger was just coming into sight below the hanging mist when he emerged on the far bank and headed strongly to the finish – by tradition, on Old Fifteen – where there was a taped funnel. He virtually sprinted in, to the same surprised repetitions of his name.

'Who?'

'Angus?'

'Who the Hell's "Angus"?'

'Ansell's. Grey hair. Bit of a bowler.'

It was not until almost five minutes later that the next man entered the funnel, by which time Angus, having received various congratulations, was making his way back. There was no Ansell's Man at the finish. He arrived back at Door and made his way to Small Change, where, as a Tassel, he could rely on hot water. A scattering of Ansell's Men were sitting around in various stages of undress. Ellerman had deliberately insisted on holding a compulsory House practice game, though it was, they all knew, quite unnecessary and no other House ever did on the afternoon of The Marathon. The place was heavy with steam.

Baker asked, 'Is it true you ran The Marathon, AC?'

Stripping off his sodden shirt Angus nodded. Ellerman said, 'Always the individual, AC.' There was no animosity. Angus had never become a rugger player of even moderate ability.

'Must've been a bloody awful day for it,' shouted the un-Tasselled Baker from Big Change.

Angus said, 'There's mist up the top. And the ford was high. And cold! I almost got swept away.'

'You ought to grow a bit,' came from the other side.

'And you, Baker, ought to grow a bit *less*,' came Ellerman's voice from the steam. 'I hope you didn't make an ass of yourself by coming last, AC,' he concluded.

'I didn't.'

Sitting in the hot water, it occurred to Angus that although Ansell's was interested only in winning, it was typical of their lack of interest in the race that nobody even asked him who won it. Part of him had hoped somebody would ask how he had done; he was not going to volunteer the information. He had been immersed for about seven minutes when, from Big Change, he heard one of the Junior Election clatter in and throw football boots into a corner and say breathlessly,

'I say, did you know Ansell's won The Marathon?'

There was a muttered consultation. Baker on the other side called, 'I say, Angus, you didn't actually *win* the bloody thing, did you?'

Ellerman called out, 'Orton!' A slight boy, looking very pink in the steam, stood in the doorway.

'Did you say Angus won the Marathon?'

'Y-y-yes, Ellerman.'

'Did he win it easily?' Ellerman looked across, grinning, at Angus who had his back to the door. 'Yes. By four minutes twenty-eight seconds. They said it's a new record.'

'Were you there?'

'Yes, Ellerman.'

'Have you congratulated Angus?'

'No, Ellerman.'

'Do you know who he is?'

'I think so, Ellerman. Isn't he the one they call AC with white in his hair?'

Ellerman climbed out of the bath. 'He is indeed! Wouldn't you like to congratulate him?'

'Yes, Ellerman, when I see him I shall.'

'What about now?' Stepping quickly up to Orton, Ellerman lifted him over Angus' head and dropped him in the muddy water. Orton rose spluttering, not quite sure whether to be frightened or to laugh. 'You're looking at Angus,' Ellerman said.

'I say, Angus, umm, well done!' Orton said in a hesitant voice. Then a bit less nervously 'Bloody *mar-vellous*, Angus!' to raucous cheers of 'Well done', aimed perhaps as much at Orton for using the Ansell's phrase, as at Angus.

'Now you'd better get back to Big Change, before you have to tighten-up for being in Little Plunge,' Ellerman teased.

Orton scuttled out to a great burst of laughter from his contemporaries who had crowded into the doorway to watch the proceedings.

Ellerman said, 'You are a *very* dark horse, AC. Have you been training to win?'

Angus thought: 'No, I just found I was at the front and I felt like running. I expect the track got very slippery. So I'd've had the best of the conditions up in front.'

'I can't see what you see in running,' Baker said, coming in from Big Plunge, 'but, well done.'

'When you run, my dear old Baker, you look like a mobile jelly!' came Mawsom's voice.

Angus mused aloud, 'I don't know why I run. Perhaps it's just a chance to be by myself.'

Notting, who had remained almost unnoticed, called, 'I suppose we're not good enough for you, AC.'

Ellerman turned: 'Notting, you really are a turd! Trust you to assume that AC means it as an insult to you.'

'I didn't mean that, I was joking.'

'A joke from you is like a kick in the pills from anyone else.'

Notting was silent for a long minute, then he said, 'Well, I was going to congratulate AC if you hadn't butted in.'

'A pity you never learned to play rugger, AC,' Ellerman said. 'You've obviously got stamina and must have quite a turn of speed.'

'I suppose that, when I came to Ansell's, I was so bad that it didn't seem possible to catch up with everyone else.' Angus climbed out and grabbed a towel which was already damp. 'I'd just never played it before.'

'And you were scared of getting hurt?' Notting interrogated tauntingly.

Angus turned round and looked at him. 'You're probably right, Notting. If you're not very good, you get hurt more.' Admitting the spiteful point took the wind from Notting's sails. He could think of no reply.

Ellerman came to the rescue: 'Well, come to that, AC, none of us enjoys getting done over – so I can see your point. So can Notting, if he tells the truth. It explains why you were bloody useless on the line your first half. Why didn't you say you'd never played?'

' Would it have made any difference?'

Most other Ansell's Men quietly congratulated Angus on his victory. Even Ashton recognised his success with a private word. At the weekend, Mawsom said, 'Did you notice, AC, that your win was never mentioned by The Digger at Curfew, or Lunch?'

Angus grinned: 'Of course. He doesn't approve of Ansell's competing in The Marathon, Just as he doesn't approve of Ansell's Men joining Cranchester Scouts!'

'I wonder why.'

'He says that running is purely selfish, according to Ellerman, "Not a team game, Ellerman." ' Snider mimicked.

'I think the truth of the matter is that I'm not really a team man.'

'My dear old AC! It's taken you four years to recognise what we knew within the first four hours.'

'I wish I were. It has its advantages.'

After a silence, Mawsom said, 'In the end, the disadvantages might prove to be more important.'

'Not at Cranchester. In Ansell's.'

'No, not in Ansell's.'

※

Ten days after his win, Angus was loping over the course in the late afternoon when he came to a small lonely figure at Roman Gate. It was Orton. 'Gosh! I'm glad somebody came. I didn't know which way you go. They said the Roman Road and it goes both ways.'

Angus said, 'You turn left here.'

'Whew, I'd just decided to go right.'

'I'll show you the route if you like. You should always do Marathon first few times with somebody who knows how. Didn't your Nanny tell you?'

'I shan't be able to keep up.'

'I'm just trotting.'

At the beginning of the rocky downward track Angus said, 'You blown?'

The other nodded. 'A bit.'

'We'll take a rest.'

'If you tell me which way, you can go on if you want.' Orton spoke between panting breaths.

'I'll wait.'

'I used to be a good runner at my Private. I'd like to win The Marathon one day. Like you.'

'You'll probably break my record,' Angus suggested kindly. They set off down the hill. 'How do you like Ansell's?'

'It's good. The best House. I'd hate to be in Jonquil's or Pettifer's.'

Angus looked at Orton sideways. It was clear that he believed what he said. Angus thought, I expect I'd've said the same. Though *I* wouldn't've meant it. Briefly he recalled himself and Mawsom running the same track all those years before.

'Watson's very decent,' Orton said. 'I've forgotten to Warm heaps of times and he's only made me tighten-up once. I think he quite likes me,' he said naively, and added matter-of-factly, 'most people do. So it's not so bad. Not like Arkell. I'd hate to be him.'

Trotting slowly beside the younger boy Angus wondered, 'Ought I to tell him that it's not all as it seems. That one day Ansell's will pounce?' Perhaps all would work out. Orton was not naive – like himself at the same stage. He said, 'You'd better go over the bridge? Or do you want to try the ford?'

'Oh, the ford!'

'It's quite deep. I'd better go first.' Not halfway across, he stopped. 'I'd go over the bridge if I were you.'

'No fear!' Orton plunged in. By time he reached Angus, he was up to his chest, the current was strong and, at that moment, a surge swept his feet from him. He clutched at Angus and they both fell and were washed to the further side. There was no danger, but they were both very wet.

'I'm sorry,' Orton said through chattering teeth.

'Doesn't matter.'

'I knew I'd be getting out of my depth,' Orton said, 'but it was quite exciting. I might have been swept away for miles! To the sea. You probably saved my life, Angus.'

'I doubt it. Too shallow on the far side of the bridge.'

In the steam of Little Change, he once again reflected on how unlike himself at the same age was confident, assured, little Orton. He had no intention of embarking on a Singleton-like mission to protect Orton. No need. He recalled the boy's words at the ford: *I knew I'd be getting out of my depth, but it was quite exciting.* Orton was undoubtedly the sort of chap who would always find it exciting to get out of his depth. Orton would manage everything in his stride, like Ellerman, or Mawsom, or Brownlow, or almost anyone in fact – except himself. Yes, Orton would manage better than most, especially if he basked in the warmth of Watson's approbation.

December

Tassel Night had been deliberately placed as late as possible, on the last night of the Half as it happened. It was timed to coincide with The Digger's final night and great celebration was expected. It was rumoured that there was even to be a toast in champagne. Underneath the excitement however, was an air of lawlessness, of recognition that an 'Era Was Ending'. Most evenings had seen three or four visiting Big Study, mainly the Junior Election. It did not seem to matter. It was, Angus remembered, rather as though everyone was throwing restraint away and taking off masks. He remembered, fleetingly, Maunder's last evening all those summers before.

When it came, the night lived up to expectations. The Digger unexpectedly brought in a visitor.

'It's Maunder!'

It was Maunder, very dapper in Service Dress and, breaking precedent, he sat at the top table on The Digger's right hand. Baker said, 'He got special leave. The Digger wanted him to be present and Ashton wrote to ask him.'

It went on for a long time. The dinner was, by standards of rationing, magnificent. Someone had presented enough brace of pheasant for the entire House. Instead of the usual cider, there was wine; champagne, just a glass each and then claret. Unused to it, several of them clearly drank more than they should. When The Digger rose after Ashton's short, but vociferously cheered, introduction and presentation on behalf of them all, there was only as much silence as could be expected in the circumstances.

'When I rise as now I do, to reply to the toast "Ansell's and the School", I am, I realise, coming to end of a very long and important part of my life. I became Housemaster of Ansell's on an autumn day in 1925. I had been a beak for five years. I was not expecting to be Housemaster for many years more. The then High Master called me to see him. He said, 'I am giving you Ansell's. It is a very bad House as you will find out. I shall expect you to make it a very good one.' Now that I leave, I hope the High Master is not having to say that to my successor.' There was a great roar of laughter and cheering. 'I am sure, in fact, that it is by far the best House at Cranchester [more riotous cheers] and before you think I'm showing *side* and being immodest, I hasten to say that the credit is not mine, but yours. Yours, and those who have been Ansell's Men before you. So I'm particularly pleased to have here with us tonight one of the most distinguished Heads of House I have had the good fortune to see in Ansell's – and I may tell you the standard is high. Some of you will remember Eliot Maunder because you were here in his time. It is due to Maunder and other Heads of House like him, that we are a House to be envied. I have been fortunate in having exemplary Praefaectors and, as those of you who are observant will know, the House takes its tone from its Praefaectors.

'In my time at Cranchester, I have observed that no House with good Praefaectors has ever been a bad House. I am only sorry that we can see for ourselves what happens when a House does have bad Praefaectors. I think we showed what we think of that sort of House on the rugger field. [Riotous cheers and cries of 'United Soviet Republic of Jonquil's'.]

'I do not intend to speak at length. I do not intend to rehearse all our triumphs on the games field. ['Shame!'] However, I do wish to thank you all most sincerely for the very handsome silver coffee set with which you have presented me. I shall use it often and it will remind me of you. As you know, I'll be away for most of next year, on government business. However, on my return from secondment, the High Master has asked me to become Under Master. So I shall always be happy to see Ansell's Men who care to visit me at Town House – the traditional residence of the Under Master – for a cup of coffee.'

More cheers.

'And I shall always expect to see Ansell's in House Match Finals!'

Louder cheers.

'Thank you all – Ansell's Men past and present – for twenty memorable and happy years.'

Before the chattering could take over, Maunder leapt to his feet and held up a hand for silence.

'I just want to propose a toast. I'm the only one who can do it, since I can't be given a dozen-up!' He lifted his glass. 'Ansell's Men, pray be upstanding. Here's to Cranchester's finest Housemaster. The Digger!'

Encouraged by Maunder's use of the nickname, there was a great shout as they rose, 'THE DIGGER! DIG-GER! DIG-GER! DIG-GER!' which continued until, ushering Maunder before him into Private, The Digger vanished from sight.

From somewhere, the usual cider was now produced and, unwisely, many of those who had drunk wine moved on to the cider. The High Table seemed to have acquired a decanter of port. Tasselling for rugger proceeded and Brownlow's engaging popularity was recognised by riotous cheering. The Junior Election were knocked off their bench, Orton the last, looking pink and sparkling in contrast to one or two of the others who had clearly had more than enough to drink.

At the conclusion Ashton stood up and said, 'The Praefaectors have decided that the member of the new Election with the best singing voice must sing a forfeit song – *The Lincolnshire Poacher*. So let's vote on the best voice.' He knew well enough what the answer would be but, in the time-honoured formula which had been revived by Ashton, he said formally, 'Which Ansell's Man has the best singing voice?'

In unison came the shout, 'Orton! OR-TON!'

Angus thought, 'Thank God they didn't do this with us!'

Orton seemed totally unabashed. He climbed onto the table.

'Go ON!'

'*When I was bound apprentice. In good old Lincolnshire.*'

'Forfeit!'

Ashton said, 'It should be "famous". Pay a forfeit and start again.'

Grinning, Orton took off his jacket.

When I was bound apprentice. In famous Leicestershire.'

'LINCOLNSHIRE!' came the shout.

'Come on, another forfeit!'

Laughing, Orton took off his tie and collar.

'When I was bound apprentice. In famous Lincolnshire,

'Right well...'

'Forfeits Forfeits!'

Ashton said, 'That'll cost you your shirt, Orton.' Cheers.

'I say, AC, I feel a bit pissed! I'm going outside,' Mawsom said.

'I'll join you.'

Angus extricated himself and found Mawsom already at Door drawing deep breaths. 'That's better.'

They walked for a while in Yard. Shouts cries and laughter erupted behind them. Angus said, 'Orton's too tight to get it correct!'

'I don't think he was even trying to get it right,' Mawsom said. 'He knows better than to spoil the game.'

They arrived back just as Orton divested himself of his last garment, to whistles and cheers. He finished the song without any further mistake.

Ashton said, 'Well done, Orton. Have this!' This was a glass of port. Stark naked, flushed but triumphant, Orton lifted the glass and looking towards Private said, 'The Digger!' It got a terrific reception, with cheers and laughter before he was allowed to retire and dress himself.

'Which of us would have had the nerve to do that in our first Half?' Angus muttered.

'Dermott-Powell perhaps? I think we were all too frightened. But I suppose this is a very different sort of night.'

As they drifted away, a boy came up to Angus and said, 'Mayer can't see you, Angus. He's drunk too much!' Angus had forgotten Mayer. He said, 'Thanks, Ferguson. Tell him it doesn't matter.'

He fell asleep as soon as his head touched the pillow. Almost immediately, it seemed, he was awoken by the bell. It was still dark. With difficulty he looked at his watch. Three o'clock?

'Fire alarm.'

The lights did not work. There was a banging of shutting windows. Comparatively silent and orderly, they filed out down the stairs and stood under the chestnut tree. Ashton read List by torchlight. There were two or three absentees and Praefaectors had to go to fetch the sleepers. Eventually it dawned on everyone that it was only a practice. Then The Digger's absence was noted.

They heard Ashton say, 'Still those two missing!'

Carstairs appeared, 'I say, Ashton, I've found this in the fuse cupboard. Somebody's hoaxed us!'

Ashton said, 'It'll be a Praefaectors', end of Half or not!'

Ansell's were getting cold.

'Did you read it, Carstairs?'

'No, too dark. What's it say?'

'*Goodbye to the Fuhrer and his S.S. – from Jonquil's!*'

'Bloody Jonquil's!'

'That shower!'

'Ansell's can get back into bed,' Ashton said. The lights came on. 'And nobody mentions this to The Digger.'

As they climbed the stairs to Big Dorm, they came face to face with Watson. He said, 'What the Hell's going on?'

Ashton behind them called out, 'Is that you, Watson? We had a fire practice. Where were you?'

'I'm afraid I was still fast asleep. You can't hear the bell in my study.'

As they walked up Big Dorm, Ellerman said quietly, but distinctly, 'You'll have noticed that Orton was the other one missing.'

'Well, he was in his Manger when we came in just now. I saw him fast asleep there, the curtain was drawn back.'

'He was not there when the fire bell went. I heard Carstairs tell Ashton. He said he'd checked Big Dorm.'

Snider said, 'So what? It's Tassel Night, isn't it?' They had reached Mawsom's Manger.

'It's nothing to do with Tassel Night. Right from the beginning of the Half, Watson has...'

'Right from the beginning of Half, Notting, you've been as jealous as hell of Watson,' Snider said.

Unexpectedly Ellerman backed Notting: 'I don't always agree with Notting, but he's right this time. I think...' He paused. They encouraged him by their silence. 'I think it's different with Watson.'

'In what way?' Snider said

'I think Watson's in love with Orton!'

'Oh come off it, Ellerman!' Angus sounded quite shocked.

Snider began, 'Well, what about you and Lawson and what about Tassel Nights?'

Ellerman cut in, 'For Christ's sake, Snider! That's different.' He went on without embarrassment, 'That's just sex. We've all bloody well got to grow up, even in this monastery! It doesn't mean anything more. But you can't have the Senior Election behaving like Watson! Mooning around and holding hands with the Junior Election!'

'Rubbish!'

Ellerman said patiently, 'I wasn't exaggerating, Snider. I saw them. I went on a training run-around and came back by Roman Gate. And there they were. Orton and Watson. Watson had his arm round Orton.'

'Perhaps Orton'd hurt himself. Twisted an ankle or something.'

Ellerman gave Angus a withering look: 'It didn't look like that, I can tell you!'

'What did they do when they saw you?'

'I took good care they didn't see me. When Watson came into Change it was a good deal later than Orton. I was just leaving. I think they didn't want anyone to know they'd met!'

Mawsom said, 'Well it's end of Half anyhow.'

'It's the end of Ansell's as we know it,' Ellerman added.

iii

January

From the first day of the Half, it seemed like a new era. Immediately after Curfew, all Praefaectors went to Private. It was a short meeting. Ellerman said on his return, 'He's going to have one each week. He said we must keep him "in the picture".' Ellerman put the phrase in inverted commas as though to hold it up for comment.

'Anything else?'

'He gave us all Madeira.'

'Can you imagine The Digger doing that!'

Ellerman said, 'The Digger had no need. I think Craigie's a bit wary of us. Trying to butter up the Praefaectors. After all Ansell's has been here a damn sight longer than he has.'

At that moment Ashton entered Big Dorm. He called out, 'The Housemaster.' Craigie walked in. He stopped at each Manger and his visit took quite a long time. 'Where's the Junior Election, Ashton?'

'Oh! I expect they'll be Warming, sir.'

'I see. You'll need to explain all this to me.' When he came to Ellerman's Manger he said, 'Good evening, Ellerman. I've much admired your efforts for Cranchester. That run of yours. Where did you learn that? Are you, by chance, related to L E Meacher?'

Taken off guard, Ellerman stuttered, 'Yes. Yes, sir, he was my uncle.'

'I thought he might be. I once saw him play. He was past his best, but he scored one try – with a run just like yours. Against us, I'm afraid. Left us all grabbing air.'

He turned across to Angus. 'I watched you finish The Marathon. Do you run for a club? In the vacation?'

Angus said, 'I'm afraid I live a long way from any clubs, sir. The nearest would be Glasgow, I dare say. That's about a hundred miles.'

'I was surprised that there was no supporting team from Ansell's.'

'It's not the Ansell's custom to put in a team,' Angus said.

'Oh, why's that?'

'I don't know, sir.'

Craigie turned to Ashton. 'Do you know, Ashton?'

'Not really, sir. I think The Dig...I mean Mr Jowling, felt it wasn't a team game. We weren't banned from entering. It's just that we don't bother.'

'Well let's hope we bother next time,' Craigie said evenly. 'Perhaps Angus could encourage a team to train.' He passed on.

His progress through Big Dorm took about half an hour. He went through Tosher and looked in on Warmers in the studies.

Angus said, 'Well, I suppose he was bound to make an inspection on his first night.'

'He's going to come round Big Dorm every night so he told us.'

'Every night!' That was Notting. 'Bloody Hell. If he takes that long we'll never get to sleep.'

'The Digger never did that.'

Snider said, 'Yes he did. At first if you remember.'

'Oh, but that was only to look in and about twice each week.'

'I expect the novelty of being Housemaster will wear off.'

It did not wear off. Craigie came round each evening. Notting complained to Ashton, 'I like my sleep. Can't you hurry him up?'

Baker said, 'He's poking his nose in too much.'

Ashton temporised. 'I don't know. I think he just wants to find out what's going on.'

Ellerman said, 'The best Housemasters know that, without spending all their time sloping around on the boys' side of the House.'

✳

In the third week, Ellerman rather obviously drew his Manger curtain and settled himself to sleep. He did not respond when Craigie looked in and, as the days passed, others followed his example. It was difficult to know how much of this came from a genuine desire to get off to sleep and how much was a subtle expression of disapproval. By the end of the month, virtually the whole of Big Dorm was silent by the time Craigie came in and he took to walking through quickly and in to Tosher. Ten days later he had reverted to The Digger's habit of merely coming to the door and calling out 'goodnight'. It was tacitly accepted that Big Dorm had notched a victory but it had to be Notting who said vigorously, 'We're bringing him into line!'

Ellerman said, sitting, on the end of Notting's bed with two or three others after the official visit, 'Don't be too sure. I don't think he's very keen on some things. Warming for instance. And "this covering-up business", that's what he called it at our meeting. He asked what we thought…'

'And?' Snider said.

'Oh, Ashton and the rest of us pointed out that it didn't do any harm. That it's what has always happened in Ansell's. I don't think he'll do anything about it – unless the Praefaectors want it to stop.'

'He may find that he gets to know more than he wants,' Baker said.

Notting said, 'Tassel Night, for instance?'

'He's not likely to hear about *that*,' Mawsom interjected.

'It doesn't do any harm anyway,' Baker said. 'I'd be bloody well fed up if he tried to abolish that, just as I've been Tasselled!'

There was a general laugh. Snider observed, 'I don't suppose it'll even occur to him to enquire! Especially as Ashton will head him off.'

Ellerman said, 'I must hand it to Ashton. He really handles Craigie very well, you know. He doesn't oppose him, he says nothing and then sort of brings him round.'

'God knows what'll happen next Half!'

'You'll have to handle him just as carefully, Ellerman.'

Snider said, '*If* it is Ellerman. I still reckon it'll be Watson. Craigie's always talking to him. Or it could be Carstairs. He couldn't ask any of the others!'

Ellerman said, 'I'm not sure he's very keen on games players. He's not like The Digger.'

※

Ellerman was a shrewder observer than any of them realised. The first obvious confrontation came about because of a rugger match. Ansell's had been drawn to play the Orangery. Their opponents were strong and dogged, though not particularly skilful. By half-time there had been no score. They were playing on a distant pitch in thin rain, watched by only a handful of spectators, one of whom was Craigie. Shortly after the game was re-started there was a scrummage. Carstairs, always hot tempered and irritated by poor support, tried harder and harder. Finally, he was brought down fairly, but roughly, as he was gathering speed with the ball in his hands. Jumping up, he lashed out with a fist at his opponent and broke his nose. There was blood everywhere. In a miserable hush Carstairs was sent off. Nobody could recall such an incident before. As if believing that they were being unfairly penalised, Ansell's put in an uninhibited display of toughness and roughness, which brought a try.

There was further pressure in a bad-tempered mêlée and two more Ansell's Men were sent off, together with an Orangery player. One of those sent off was Brownlow, usually very even-tempered. Ansell's won, but knew that they had put up a remarkably unlovely display.

At Curfew, Craigie said, 'I wish to see the three of the Ansell's team who were sent off this afternoon, immediately after List. I would like the Captain of Ansell's rugger to be there.'

Carstairs followed him out, Garner went after him. As Brownlow passed, Angus said, 'Bad luck. Don't suppose it'll be too bad.'

In Big Dorm, some time later, Ellerman stormed up to the senior end. He said explosively, 'Jesus Christ! What a turd!'

Baker said, 'Who?'

'Bloody Craigie of course!'

'What happened?'

Ellerman nodded to the other end. Brownlow and Garner had come in through the door. 'Ask them!' Brownlow seemed less chirpy than usual. Garner Major glowered. 'What happened, Brownlow?'

'Eight-up apiece!'

'*WHAT!*'

Shocked silence.

'Just for being sent off?' Notting said. 'The man's a maniac!'

'Anyhow,' Baker said, 'at least it wasn't The Digger.'

Garner said, 'Don't go away with the thought that Craigie doesn't know what he's doing. Whuuh!'

Ellerman said by way of explanation, 'He got a Blue for golf!'

'What about Carstairs!'

'That's just it. He said he'd've beaten Carstairs too, had he not been a Praefaector and that it was his example that was responsible for the other two.'

'What happened then!'

'Carstairs demanded to be beaten the same as the others, or that none of them should be. Craigie said he had no intention of beating a Praefaector. He said Carstairs' punishment was thinking about the fact that he's put others in the wrong. And then...'

'And then?'

'Carstairs lost his wool.'

'He didn't hit Craigie...?'

'No! This is Ansell's.'

'Well, what did he do?'

'He said, "In that case, Mr Craigie, sir, I resign. I don't wish to remain one of *your* Praefaectors, sir."'

'Good for him.'

'So Craigie had to ask him not to?'

'Craigie accepted it.'

'No!'

'Ker-rist!

'What happened next?'

'Craigie said, since you're no longer a Praefaector, Carstairs, 'I shall now also beat you for disgraceful conduct on the games field and if you're ever sent off again for violent conduct, I'll see you never play for Ansell's or Cranchester any more. He gave him a dozen-up!'

There was silence.

Mawsom said, 'Were you there all the time?'

'Yes. I had to stand there. I thought he was going to beat me!'

'He didn't?'

'No. But he said that as Captain I could have controlled our side to avoid "The Incident" and that he expected me to make a better job of it next match.' Ellerman did not add that Craigie had held him back and when the rest were gone stressed that he thought Ellerman was more concerned with his own personal performance than the play of the team.

Brownlow said, 'So Carstairs is no longer a Praefaector?'

'That's right!'

'Perhaps Craigie will ask him again in a few days?'

Notting said, 'I don't suppose Carstairs will accept.'

Snider said, 'Of course he will!'

Mawsom said, 'Where's Carstairs going to sleep?'

'In his study of course!' Angus began. Then he stopped.

Baker said, 'He won't have a Big Study tomorrow, if he's no longer a Praefaector.'

There was a silence. Ellerman said a little shamefacedly, 'Ashton's told Carstairs to change with me tomorrow – as I'm the only Praefaector without a Big Study. Carstairs'll have my Manger.'

Snider said very quietly, 'So every cloud has a silver lining? I don't like Carstairs, but it's bloody hard on him,' he murmured. 'Couldn't you leave it least till end of Half to change over? I mean he might be made Praefaector again.'

Ellerman looked up, paused, and said, 'If so, he'll be junior Praefaector, so I'll have the last of the Big Studies anyway.'

He went to his own Manger. Mawsom raised his eyebrows. There was no further comment. Two minutes later Craigie came in. When he said 'goodnight' he was met by studied silence. That too became the custom.

In the next House Match Ansell's played with exaggerated gentleness. It caused much amusement, for news had spread and everyone wanted to see how Craigie would take it. Craigie stood, unmoved, on the touchline. Ansell's played, in consequence, very badly, although Ellerman's skill kept them just ahead for they were far better than Oliphant's. However, in the last minute, one of Oliphant's forwards snatched an awkwardly bouncing ball, gathered it, ran past a lethargic Ansell's defence to score between the posts. The conversion sailed through the posts as the whistle blew, putting Ansell's out of the Final for the first time in seven years. It was a savage if appropriate punishment. Ellerman was livid, as were all the senior members of the side.

Hoist by their own petard, they were further mortified when, at Curfew, Craigie said, with ironic gentleness, 'I was so pleased that Ansell's decided to play like little gentlemen today. I'm sorry we lost, but I'm sure you would agree that the better side won.'

'Better bloody side, my arse!' Ellerman exploded. 'We were playing with them!'

Mawsom added, 'Do you think Craigie really meant what he said? I don't. I think he was twisting our tails for playing in a sulk. If so, I think he's won that round.'

Baker and others who had played disagreed. Angus said nothing. He had however been watching Craigie's face and knew Mawsom was right.

February

Midway through the Half, Snider came fleetingly to prominence. It happened because the Cranchester Literary Society held a debate on Capital Punishment. It was not until the notices came round that Ansell's realised he was proposing abolition.

Notting, as always, was the first to be vociferous. 'It's typical of you, Snider. What would you do if somebody broke in and murdered your sister, or your mother?'

Snider said, 'I should be heartbroken and furiously angry. That's why I ought not to be responsible for vengeance. The State should never allow judicial killing.'

Ashton came upon them discussing the matter. 'I hope you're not going Communist on us, Snider! It's bad enough getting knocked out of the Final.'

'I'm merely defending the motion.'

'Well everyone's asking whether we're going the same way as Jonquil's!'

Snider said, '*Capital* punishment is hanging and all that!'

'I know that! Do you agree with *corporal* punishment?'

Snider said, 'I don't know. I think I oughtn't to, but how could you run a place like this without it?'

'Exactly! Well it's the same with capital punishment.'

'No it isn't. If you beat somebody and you're wrong, you can apologise. Like you did last summer to AC.' And, seeing Ashton about to protest,

'If you kill somebody, you can't apologise because even you, Ashton, can't bring them back to life.'

Notting said, 'An eye for an eye and a tooth for a tooth.'

Snider retorted, 'That's the *Old* Testament.'

'So what, it's the Bible!'

Snider said carefully. 'In the *New* Testament, there's something about turning the other cheek. I seem to recall Notting, once upon a time that it was you accusing me of being Jewish.' Snider went off.

'What's he mean by that?'

Angus said, 'I think he means that Jews recognise only the Old Testament.'

Notting glared in a frustrated way. 'Does he mean *I'm* Jewish! Bloody cheek, I'm a damn sight more English than him. He's too clever for his own good. Anyhow he'll get slaughtered.'

※

In this he was wrong. The meeting of the Literary Society coincided with one of the rare films projected by the newly formed Film Club, so only about sixty turned up to the debate. On the whole they constituted those at Cranchester who considered themselves the intelligentsia. It was a vigorous, even passionate, discussion. Snider carried the motion by thirty-eight to twenty, with two abstentions.

'Jammy, Snider. If it'd been on a normal Saturday with most of Cranchester, you'd never have stood a chance,' Baker said, back in Ansell's.

'I stand by the result,' Snider smiled modestly; 'Cranchester shows more sense than we thought.'

There the matter might have died except for an accident. The Secretary of the Society, newly elected and full of zeal, sent a note of the result to *The Cranchester Gazette*, a sleepy local paper where it would normally have aroused no interest, as few of the School and nobody in Ansell's ever read it. However, by chance it caught the eye of a local 'stringer' who sent a few lines to a popular Fleet Street paper where a paragraph appeared in a gossip column.

Change is even sweeping even our great Public Schools. In a recent debate at Cranchester, the boys voted by a substantial majority to abolish hanging. One of the Houses of this, the most traditional of schools, has already abolished beating and fagging. Shall we soon see co-education at Cranchester?'

The day it appeared, Snider was summoned to Big Study. Ashton said, 'It's not a beating matter, but you should bloody well be more careful. Craigie's been rung up by some oik from the *Daily Mirror* wanting to speak to you.'

Pale, but determined, Snider said, 'I didn't know it was going to be in the papers.' Then, stubbornly, 'Even if I had, I'd still have said what I said.'

'You make us sound like a gang of bolshies, Snider.'

'I make us sound civilised. Anyway, why don't you write and tell them it was only small numbers who voted?'

'Craigie said we mustn't get in touch with the newspapers. We don't want reporters down here. Remember that business at Eton in the *News of the World* a couple of years ago?'

It was an irrelevant point, but Snider nodded. 'Well, I'm sorry if it's upset Craigie, or the High Master, or Ansell's. I wasn't to know. Anyhow, next season we're going to have a similar debate – in November. It'll give you a chance to have your say.'

Ashton said, 'I shall, I hope, be six months into my National Service by then.'

'May I push off, Ashton?'

'Yes. But no calls to the *Daily Mirror*.'

By the following week Fleet Street had become more interested in a particularly complex society scandal and Cranchester slipped from the pages as suddenly as it had arrived.

March

Angus was dawdling back from Morning School on the first day of March. The weather was mild and the pale blue sky gave a promise of Spring.

There was even a flitter of sun. However, it was damp under foot. He was overtaken by Jamieson, a tall dark boy in Pettifer's who shared several of his Divisions. 'Congratulations, Angus.'

Angus turned questioningly, blankly: 'Congratulations? On what?'

'Yes, on.... Do you mean to say you don't know? You really are in a world of your own these days, Angus. I should go and look in Lodge if I were you. And...congratulations.'

Angus turned and went back to Lodge. There were lines of glass-fronted notice boards. He wondered if perhaps he had been given Colours for Cross Country; he had run regularly for Cranchester since The Marathon, but hardly enough matches for Colours. You did not get Capped for Cross Country – it was, in Cranchester terms, a Division Two sport. He could see nothing. As he left, convinced that Jardine, who had a quirkish sense of humour, had set out to tease him, he glanced idly at the High Master's Board.

Greystoke Essay Prize, 1946
'The Language of the Poet'
C. Angus* (Ansell's Hall)
Proxime Accessit: R. F. Leighton (The Doctor's)
* In the opinion of the Judges, this was an outstanding entry.

He could hardly believe his eyes. His decision to enter had been made hesitantly. The Greystoke was worth £100. *One hundred pound*s! He walked across Great Quad as if treading on feathers. He would tell nobody in Ansell's. He was willing to bet with himself that nobody had noticed. And he was right.

The talk at lunch revolved round the rugger. Out of the competition for the Cup, they were still in the Plate and due to play Pettifer's. If they won they would probably meet Jonquil's in the Plate Final. Notting was saying, 'If we do meet them in the Plate, we score a century against them.'

They trounced Pettifer's by forty-five points to nil. At Curfew, Craigie congratulated the side; it was met with stony silence. 'There is also one more success. Angus has won The Greystoke Essay Prize. As far as I can make out, it is the first time we have had the Greystoke Prize-winner for a hundred years.' He went out as polite clapping greeted the news. Angus blushed.

Baker said, 'What the Hell's The Greystoke?'

Snider said, coincident with a small silence in the hubbub which always greeted the end of List, 'It's worth a hundred quid. That's what it is.'

There was a whistle of surprise. In the following days Angus was shyly congratulated by several people in the Junior Elections, to whom the value of The Greystoke was clearly far more significant than the prize itself.

'I say, Angus, how long was it? Your essay!'

'I don't know, Orton, five or six thousand words.'

Orton widened his eyes. 'How many pages is that?'

Angus told him.

'That's about ten pounds a page,' Orton said triumphantly.

'I hadn't thought of it that way!'

'Anyhow, well done, Angus. Bloody *mar*-vellous!' Orton grinned the Ansell's phrase and disappeared.

Ellerman said, 'What on earth did you write about? I've looked on the High Master's Board and it says something about poetic language.'

'The title was "The language of the poet".'

'You're getting as bad as Snider, AC, I can't see what there is to say about poetic language. I suppose you were talking about all this modern stuff. *The Dead Land* and all that.'

'*The Waste Land*,' Angus corrected gently. 'No, in fact I was writing about somebody who died in the last century. He was a Jesuit priest.'

Ellerman laughed with genuine amusement 'I might have guessed.' He turned to Mawsom and Snider who had joined them. 'Guess what! AC wrote his essay on some poet who was a monk!'

Snider said, 'Hopkins?'

Angus nodded.

Mawsom came into his Manger. 'That battered old book in your study. That's Hopkins, isn't it?'

'Uhuh.'

'I was looking through it. It's got Singleton's name.'

'His parents gave it to me. It came back.'

Mawsom said, 'I wondered. Odd stuff. I couldn't understand most of the bits I read. There's that one about the hawk. I liked that.'

'*Windhover*, I wrote about it a bit. Not very well. He tried to invent a new sort of poetic language. That's why you found it so hard to read.'

'I wonder, AC.'

'Wonder what?'

'Are *you* going to become a priest?'

For a moment Angus thought of the dark house in Priest Street; it was as if a cold draught fingered his scalp. He said, 'No. I don't think so. Nor a monk – as Ellerman seems to think.'

'I just wondered,' Mawsom said. 'It's just that you seem to be out of touch with the rest of us. I don't mean anything bad.' He paused: 'I rather envy you as a matter of fact, but you seem to be...on your own.' As Angus looked questioningly, he said, 'But come to think of it, you always have been. Well, most of the time, except...' He came to a stop.

'Simonsen?' He could say it now without heat, no longer associating himself with the person he had been during those months.

'You were more one of our Election that year than any other. Now you're off on your own again. First The Marathon. Now The Greystoke. What's next?'

'Do you want to know?'

'If you like?'

'I'm going to try for a Balliol Scholarship.'

'My God, AC, why Balliol? What's wrong with The House? Or Teddy Hall. An Ansell's Man at Balliol! They'll think it the Millennium.'

'Well, Hopkins went there. How's that for a reason?'

Mawsom laughed, delighted. It fitted in with his picture of the sort of reason Angus would choose.

'Singleton had a place there.'

'I should have guessed.'

'And it's about time we had a Balliol Scholar,' Angus continued mildly. 'We forget that Ansell's Hall originally housed all the Queensmen in Cranchester.'

Mawsom looked thoughtful. 'I wonder what The Digger had against them. There's never been one since we've arrived.'

'I've heard he said he'd prefer somebody who could hold his own on the rugger field. God knows how he accepted me!'

'What about your father and godfather?'

'Perhaps.'

'Anyhow. Good luck.'

'What for?'

'Balliol.'

'That's not until next December!'

'I know. Good luck all the same!'

Angus got a message to go through to Private to see Craigie the following day. He went, with trepidation, after lunch. The study was different. It was lined with books and it looked less tidy, more used. There was a grand piano. A cheerful fire burned.

'Have some coffee, Angus. I thought I'd like to congratulate you personally on The Greystoke.'

'Thank you, sir.'

'Here is your essay. I took the liberty of reading it. Very good indeed. What made you think of Hopkins?'

'I was given a book of his poems, sir. I'd been looking through them. Then I saw the title for The Greystoke. I wrote most of it at home during the Christmas vac.'

'Time well spent. You may not realise of course that Hopkins was, amongst other things, trying out linguistic ideas he got from reading Anglo-Saxon and Welsh.'

'I've not done any of that.'

'Of course not.' Craigie paused: 'Could you make anything of *The Wreck of the Deutschland*?'

Angus drew breath. 'Not all of it, sir. I found it difficult. But the language is...is magnificent – where I can understand it.'

'It's a difficult poem. Are you by any chance Roman Catholic?' He smiled. 'As your Housemaster I ought to know, shouldn't I?'

'No, sir, I'm not.'

'Well that makes it even more difficult.'

Angus ventured, 'That wasn't the most difficult. There are some sonnets. Towards the end.' He paused. 'I expect it sounds silly, but...I found them frightening.'

'Oh no! That's not silly. Not silly at all.

> *O the mind, mind has mountains; cliffs of fall*
> *Frightful sheer, no man fathomed. Hold them cheap*
> *May who ne'er hung there.*

Craigie paused for a long time. 'Who knows what Hopkins was thinking about when he wrote that? He was a man in mental agony. I've always wondered...' Craigie stopped and smiled. 'We must talk about him when there's more time.'

Angus said, ' "To What Serves Mortal Beauty" – I don't quite understand it all. It seems an odd poem for a priest to write.'

Craigie said, 'Odd? Perhaps. Or is it just honest?'

A silence hung between them. 'What about a university place? Any thoughts?'

'I thought I'd try for an Award. At Balliol.'

Craigie said, 'By all means. You should have a good chance, not least because one of the Fellows was The Greystoke judge. It seems appropriate, with its Scottish connection. I'll drop a note to the Master in due course, I've met him once or twice.' Best of all there was no surprise in his tone. 'And we must talk a bit more about Hopkins. Have you come across this chap?' He handed over a thin volume in wartime paper. 'Dylan Thomas. He too uses English in an interesting way.'

'Oh thank you, sir. I'll let you have it back when...'

'No, no it's yours.'

The flyleaf read C. Angus – Greystoke Prize 1946. Congratulations. It was signed **George Craigie.**

'Thank you very much, sir.' He was a little embarrassed by the gift, glad to make his escape, but could not be certain why. He felt that somehow he was getting drawn into to some sort of commitment and preferred to remain in his cocoon.

※

It was a fine, warm afternoon. On his daily Marathon, Angus had reached the stretch leading to Roman Gate, when he was conscious that somebody was sitting on the wall. For a moment he thought it was Orton, until he realised it was somebody, bigger, older, dressed in ordinary clothes. He wondered if it were Watson. As he came up to Roman Gate he saw with astonishment that it was Craigie.

'I thought perhaps I'd see you, Angus. Can you spare a moment, or are you timing your run?'

'Oh no, sir. I quite like the Dylan Thomas. "Fern Hill" is a marvellous poem.'

'I'm glad. However, it wasn't about poetry I wanted to talk. I just wanted to have a word with you. Away from eyes and ears. It's quite unofficial.'

Angus felt his chest tighten and his heart thump.

He's going to ask about Tassel Night!

'What I wanted to ask you is this; will you take over as Head of House at the end of this Half?'

Literally, his knees felt weak and he had to sit. 'Me, sir?' It was all he could think of saying.

'Yes, Angus, you. It'd be a tough job, because I think Ansell's is ready for some changes. Or should I say, needs some changes it may not be ready for. I think you're the man to do it.' He paused: 'Otherwise I wouldn't ask.'

'I don't know what to say, sir. It's such a shock.'

'I mean it to be a compliment!'

'Of course, sir. It's just that I'd never even considered—' He lapsed into silence.

'Perhaps that's what makes you the most obvious candidate in my eyes. Anyhow, it's taken you off-balance. Think it over. Keep it to yourself. I'm afraid I must ask you not to consult anyone else – even Mawsom. Tell me tomorrow after lunch, before you go out to the Jonquil's match. I hope you'll accept. You'd better go on now or you'll catch cold.'

Angus began to run again. His legs had stiffened slightly. Head of House! Him! There was a sense of exultation. Then, as the path turned down he began to think more clearly and exultation left him. Notting! Carstairs, who would still be there! Watson would not show any animosity, but what about Ellerman? *Ellerman was the obvious choice*. How could he overcome that?

Every so often a spurt of confidence and excitement decided him to accept. At other times he knew he did not want to do it. It would cost him too much. He sensed that Craigie saw him as somebody who could implement a new, different philosophy in Ansell's. He was not sure that he could. Even as he formulated the notion, he became aware that it was truer to say that he did not want to involve himself any further with Ansell's, or with anyone in Ansell's. Craigie was far more perceptive than any of them supposed; somehow Craigie had known the only person he might consult was Mawsom.

He went to sleep late and awoke early. As the hours ticked past, the idea of himself as Head of House had seemed more and more fantastical. *Ellerman was the obvious choice*. He was basking in Ellerman's affability at the moment – the first time since his first summer there – and he enjoyed it. Nevertheless he knew how easily Ellerman could make things virtually impossible for him. Surely Craigie must be able to see that?

There was nobody about when he went through to Private after lunch. He knocked.

'Angus? Come in, sit down. Coffee?'

'Thank you, sir.'

They discussed possible scores in the Plate Match. Angus said, 'We're determined to do better than last time!'

'Oh dear,' Craigie smiled wryly and put down his cup. 'Have you thought it over, Angus? Got used to the idea a bit.'

'Yes, sir.'

'Splendid!' Craigie looked relieved.

'I meant, yes I have thought it over and,' he swallowed, 'I'm the wrong person for the job, sir. I couldn't manage it.'

He knew at once Craigie was disappointed in him, very deeply disappointed, though nothing more than 'Ah' was said.

'I'm sorry, sir.'

'So am I, Angus. So am I. Very, very sorry.' His words hung between them. 'You're quite sure? Don't be modest!'

'I'm quite sure, sir. I wouldn't be the right chap, sir.'

'You understand that nobody must ever know I asked you?'

'Oh. Of course, sir. It's just that...I know Ansell's.'

'Better than me?'

'Well in a way, sir. I don't mean to be rude. But really, sir, your best bet is Ellerman. Everyone does as he suggests. I'd have difficulties where he wouldn't.'

'I take your suggestion, Angus. Of course there would be difficulties, but I believe you would do it much better than anyone else – especially Ellerman. Would you like time to reconsider your decision?' He waited. 'Well, I won't press you. Thank you for coming to see me. I respect your decision, even though I think it's the wrong one for Ansell's. We'll meet again on the touchline. All this must remain confidential, absolutely confidential.'

'Of course, sir. I understand.'

At the door Angus turned. Craigie was standing with hands behind his back, looking stiffly out of the window. Almost, Angus changed his mind, he even opened his mouth. 'No, Ellerman *was* the man.' Certainly, Ansell's needed changing, but he did not want to do it, to be involved. He had begun to find his own way, to do without Ansell's. He left the room without speaking.

In the Plate Final, Ansell's accumulated 101 points. Each member of the side scored. Cool, machine-like, Ellerman converted every try. In the end, even Jonquil's began to enjoy such a historic defeat.

Tassel Night followed. Despite the Plate victory, it was a restrained affair compared with all the others they could recall. Craigie sat with the Praefaectors, but as far apart from them in spirit as if they had been in different rooms. It was clear that there was little conversation. Ansell's blamed Craigie for the fact that they would not be in the Final the following week; that was the underlying resentment not far below the surface. Carstairs, no longer on the Top Table, drank a great deal of cider. He became loud; his truculent, over-exaggerated, laugh dominated the room, accentuated by the unusually subdued volume of the rest. The meal came to an end more quickly than usual.

Ashton rose. He proposed 'Ansell's and the School'. In its response 'Ansell's' was heavily stressed. There was absolute silence as Craigie rose.

'It seems to be the custom to say a few words. As this is my first occasion, I think I shall be brief. First let me congratulate the footballers on their record victory this afternoon.' It was usual to greet such announcements with cheers; Ansell's preserved mulish silence. Perhaps Craigie assumed it was always that way. He continued, 'I must take this chance to thank Ashton and his Praefaectors. As Head of House he has done a fine job and guided me past several pit-falls. I wish him every success in the future.' This at least received vigorous clapping.

Craigie went on. 'It seems to me, therefore, that this is the right moment to announce his successor.' There was now a definite stir of interest, for it had always been The Digger's custom to put up a small white card on Corridor. 'You'll all be pleased to hear that your new Head of House is to be Watson.' He looked towards Watson. Snider whispered, 'Told you so!' The silence was beginning to unnerve Craigie; he concluded quickly, 'I'm sure that you'll help him to keep the House running well.' He looked round. Then he left.

As the door shut there was an immediate outburst of excited conversation. Carstairs could be heard saying, 'Christ! What an anus that man is!' Watson looked uneasy, but Ashton took charge. As he stood, the chant 'Ashton! Ashton! Ashton!' was taken up. With consummate skill Ashton overcame the tension and raucous good humour began to take over. He spoke for a long time. Almost everyone was mentioned in one way or another. With Craigie absent, things were back to normal.

Angus, a little out of it all, lost in thought, saw Orton looking at him. He smiled across abstractedly. Had he been right to reject Craigie's offer? What if Craigie had announced 'Angus' – not even a Praefaector? For the first time in many months, he thought of Singleton. Although something told him that Singleton would have urged him to accept the responsibility, he was glad that he was out of it. He did not envy Watson.

When it came to Tasselling, Ellerman said, 'Ansell's has never broken the century before, in the rugger. Nor has any other House at Cranchester. Therefore, I've decided that Tassels shall be awarded to all those in today's side who haven't already got them! For a bloody marvellous season, even though we missed the Cup!' The cheers were deafening.

Mawsom nudged him. 'I reckon he did that to cock a snook at Craigie.' This had not occurred to Angus but, looking round and listening, he could see that it was exactly how Ansell's interpreted it.

He had made no arrangement with anyone. It was a deliberate decision. He lay in the dark looking at the lighter square of the window. Aware of a movement of his curtain, he said quietly, 'Who's there?'

'Orton.'

'What on earth do you want?'

'I thought, when you looked across, you wanted to see me...'

'What about Watson?'

'He's with Craigie and Ashton. He said he'd not be back till long after I'd be asleep.'

'You'll get cold if you don't cut along.'

Orton seemed not to hear. 'I expect it's good fun when you're a Tassel, isn't it, Angus?'

'It used to be. But it was all a bit dull tonight.'

'Oh yes! When Craigie was there.' Orton hesitated and continued in a different tone. 'I meant afterwards. *When you're a Tassel?*'

He thought again about telling Orton to cut along. However virtuous his intentions may have been, he welcomed Orton's unscheduled presence in his Manger and now in his bed. It was after all the Ansell's custom and one with which Orton was evidentially entirely comfortable.

However, once or twice during the days which followed, he found he rather despised himself — not for any lapse in morality, but solely because of his failure to adhere to his initial resolve. Next Half it really would be different.

iv

May

Summer Half began in a spell of magnificent weather. Watson settled in to his new elevation. On the surface, nothing seemed very much different from the previous Half. However undercurrents of resentment at Craigie's way of doing things cranked up tension. In all fairness, although his was very little different from the way his predecessor had worked, or the ways of other Housemasters, each small difference was noticed by the senior elections, commented on and, in this way, seemed magnified.

At the beginning of the Half he revived his initial custom of saying 'Goodnight' individually in Big Dorm, but it was not a success. Almost always everyone was asleep. Or apparently so. Then he ceased to appear altogether. At first it was thought it was intermittent and that he was otherwise engaged, but at the end of a week when he had not appeared, it was clear that he was not going to bother any longer.

According to Ellerman, he had said as much at one of the weekly meetings which were an innovation that continued. 'Told us you were a sullen lot!' Ellerman reported grinning. Watson told him The Digger only made occasional visits and that perhaps you weren't used to a regular appearance.'

'What did Craigie say to that?'

'He said something I didn't quite understand…about it being early days yet. And, oh yes – he's going to make sure we get a Queensman from the Scholarship!'

Notting said, 'If Ansell's is to be the home of eggheads that is THE END.'

'He wants a musician.'

'What! He must be mad! If it's a creep like Chauntrey, he'll not survive in Ansell's.' Chauntrey, a thin, heavily bespectacled eccentric in Oliphant's, was a Cranchester byword for magnificent disorganisation.

The submerged hostility towards Craigie was paralleled by the senior members of Ansell's subversive censoriousness at Watson's partiality for Orton. They chose to affect the attitude that, like Caesar's wife, Ansell's

Head of House should be above suspicion. Had he not been elevated to what was regarded as an undeserved position, the liaison would have gone more or less unremarked.

Snider said, 'I can't see why you're so vindictive about it, Ellerman. Have you forgotten Maunder? Head of House when we were Junior Election? Remember?'

Ellerman had the grace to flush slightly. 'That was totally different.'

'I wonder what the rest of Maunder's Election thought about him and you?'

Mawsom said, 'It was different because Maunder was so obviously best bet for Head of House and everyone liked him. Watson's nice enough, but he's just a bit wet. And,' Mawsom added shrewdly, 'you thought it ought to be you, Ellerman.'

'Craigie'd hardly choose someone who wasn't in the Senior Election!' Ellerman snapped.

Mawsom pressed on, 'Anyhow, Orton and Watson seem pretty harmless.'

Baker said, 'Everyone in the House is talking about it.'

'Only because we are.'

Ellerman insisted, 'You can't have the Head of House falling in love with kids like Orton – it's bloody bad for House discipline. Bloody bad for Orton too. He'll have a Hell of a time when Watson goes.'

Snider said, 'You didn't, Ellerman. I seem to remember Bartlett took over where Maunder left off.'

Mawsom said, placatingly, 'Let's forget about the past.'

Notting could not refrain from saying, 'Well, it's a bloody disgrace…it's worse than Singleton and AC…'

Mawsom turned on him: 'If it's like Singleton and AC, then you can be pretty sure it doesn't amount to anything more than a sort of mutual hero-worship.'

'Forget about Singleton and AC. I can assure you that Watson and Orton can hardly bear to be out of each other's company. I'm surprised you haven't noticed, Mawsom.' Ellerman spoke flatly. 'In fact, it's been noticed in other Houses. Did you know they've been seen several afternoons in Crondall's?'

Mawsom looked up: 'No, I hadn't heard that.'

'Well, it's true enough.'

'I suppose that does make it a bit public. I hadn't really noticed.'

'Well, if you keep your eyes open, you'll be surprised.'

'I know somebody who won't ever notice!'

There was a chorus of 'AC'.

Baker laughed: 'He's even more remote than usual. One day he'll float away.'

Mawsom said, 'He never was with us very much.'

'Except when Simonsen was around,' came from Notting.

Snider said, 'You know, I think he's sort of dedicated himself to Singleton's memory.'

'Balls! He hasn't even mentioned Singleton for years.'

Mawsom said, 'What Snider means is that AC is sort of following in Singleton's footsteps. As a matter of fact, last Half, I thought he might be taking Orton under his wing – doing a Singleton. Now I think he's just detached. I don't think he's interested enough in Ansell's to bother to notice anything.'

'He's not being vague about cricket,' Ellerman said. 'He's had two damn good trials for the Eleven and I think he'll be in the side any moment now. You remember he got those frightful wire-rimmed glasses last year? Well, they've given him eyes like a sparrow-hawk. I think he'll get in as eleventh man, for fielding, although his bowling is damn good too.'

※

A week later, Angus played his first game for the Cranchester Eleven, against Sherborne. He was not called on to bowl, but took two fine catches far in the deep. The following week he took two more, one exceptionally difficult, looking into the sun. He was not called on to bat and, before he could be called on to bowl, the opposition collapsed to the two opening fast bowlers.

The Free Foresters' match was played on a gloriously hot Saturday towards the end of May. Cranchester batted first and raised a respectable total before declaring a few runs short of three hundred. Ellerman scored seventy-two fine runs, before being stumped. Three other batsmen reached their half-centuries.

Free Foresters began slowly, but impenetrably. They did not look like ever getting out. Half an hour before tea, Castleton threw the ball to Angus and set the field. Angus was very nervous.

The first three balls were poor and pitched short, but they were treated with undeserved respect. A very slight breeze had come up, blowing behind his arm. In the second over, he was hit for a six and then a four and finally for two. In the next over he was hit for three consecutive sixes, despite the field spread out on the boundary. At the end of the over, Angus went to Castleton. 'I expect you were going to take me off, sorry!' Then diffidently, 'I think it's the wrong end for me. I ought to be bowling into the wind.' He spoke with quiet confidence.

Castleton was tempted to cut him off, but he was a good Captain and he had been impressed with Angus in the nets. He said, 'We'll see! But I'm afraid they got hold of you that time.'

After the tea interval the faster of the opening bowlers and the boy from Oliphant's who bowled quick left-arm cutters began the attack, but the batsmen had the bit between their teeth. The score ran along at a good rate. There was another change of bowler, to no avail, and then another. It seemed possible that Cranchester might lose the game without taking a wicket.

The sun was distinctly lower and the great gold pavilion clock had struck six. Less than an hour to go. The breeze was a little more noticeable. Castleton tossed Angus the ball. 'You can't do much harm at this stage, try it into the wind.' Angus grinned.

The field spread deep and the opening batsman lengthened his grip on the bat. The first ball was a little full and was hit hard, but straight to a fielder. It was worth only two. The second ball was well pitched and carefully played. He was an experienced batsman, canny enough to realise that the bowler he had caned for sixes was now a different proposition, especially as there was a dusty worn patch on the wicket, where the opening bowler had continued his run-through. Carefully, Angus altered his length and the ball, hitting the worn patch, moved sharply into the wicket, where it was efficiently smothered.

In the following over no run was scored, the batsman watching for a ball to force away, could not find one. A round of applause for a maiden over. The scoring rate had slowed at the other end too; the left-hander had come back.

On the third ball of the fourth over, Angus put the ball onto the edge of the worn patch once again and it moved sharply, the other way. The batsman had already made up his mind to score, tried to cut it, but the movement of the ball unsighted him enough to cause him to edge it, to be taken cleanly in the slips with a great cheer from the pavilion. It was the first Free Forester wicket to fall.

The new batsman took guard. Angus gave him precisely the same ball. The batsman, who had been waiting some two hours, was not expecting it. Castleton, in slips took a carbon copy catch. There was another great burst of clapping.

Castleton handed the ball back. 'You're on your hat-trick, Angus!'

The next batsman took careful guard. The ball hung a little in the wind, pitched perfectly and was smothered. There was a subdued chorus of 'Bad luck, Angus.' The final ball of the over was skilfully hurried away to a four. More runs were scored at the other end.

With the first delivery of his new over, Angus took the wicket of the new batsman. The ball went through quickly and clipped the leg stump. The next batsman got off the mark to a quick two, followed by a single. The other opening batsman, within four of his century, was very cautious and took a single. Angus' next ball took the wicket of the new batsman, who came well forward and was stumped. His successor was just as expertly stumped on the next ball.

A large crowd had gathered as news spread through the school. 'Angus is slaughtering Free Foresters.' Ansell's emptied. There was a great deal of applause when the opener got his century.

'On the hat-trick again, Angus,' Castleton remarked softly.

The well-set opener faced him. Angus floated the ball against the wind. It was carefully watched and stopped. No score. No hat trick. It turned into another maiden over.

Castleton said, as he handed the ball for the next over, 'I don't know whether you've noticed, Angus, but they're nearly up to our score and there are only about three more overs.' On the last ball Angus took another wicket.

They scored five runs at the other end. When Angus took the ball for the last over, Free Foresters needed three runs to tie and four to win. They had plenty of wickets in hand. The first ball, beautifully pitched, was hit firmly away, but was well fielded. The batsman hit the second hard and high, but there was no fielder in place to take the catch; they ran two. On the third ball, the batsman tried to force it off his legs and was caught easily by Angus.

The new batsman looked round, adjusted his cap and watched carefully. Once again Angus put the ball on the worn patch and it spurted between bat and pads. Middle stump! There was an enormous, enthusiastic cheer. Although it would hardly be possible to win, for even if each of the following balls took wickets, it would make only eight in all. No, the real excitement now, lay in seeing whether Angus would get his hat-trick. He came up smoothly to the wicket and flighted the ball into the breeze so that it dropped just a little short. The batsman came forward and hit it very hard. It soared away towards the boundary where Ellerman waited. The ball was swooping. Going very hard, Ellerman ran forward and, with his hands above his head, held it, caught his foot, fell – and dropped the ball. The clapping for the hat-trick which had begun, trickled away. The opening batsman, sensing winning runs, shouted, 'Yes.' They crossed and began to run again. Angus had turned away, biting his lip in disappointment.

'*GET OUT OF THE WAY, ANGUS!*'

Instinctively, he stepped to the right. There came a sharp crack, one of the bails struck his hand: the oncoming batsman was well out of the crease. There was another tremendous cheer and clapping from the pavilion. Ellerman, recovering the ball, had thrown down the wicket, virtually from the boundary. It was a fabulous run-out, destined to go down in Cranchester history. He came up to Angus. 'Bloody sorry, Angus. About your hat-trick. I just couldn't hold it.'

Laughing, Angus said, 'It doesn't matter. What a throw! Bloody *marvellous*.'

The final ball of the game was something of an anticlimax. It moved stodgily from the wicket and rapped the batsman's pads. Angus did not appeal. Castleton did. The match tied.

Angus walked in with Ellerman and they were joined by the Free Foresters' undefeated opener, who said to Ellerman, 'That's the finest run-out I've ever seen! A fantastic throw!'

Ellerman said, 'I spoiled his hat-trick though!' and clapped Angus affectionately on the shoulder.

As they approached the pavilion both sides lined up, together with a number of spectators, applauding. Angus and Ellerman allowed the batsman to go first. Angus started to clap too, until Ellerman whispered, 'They're clapping you as well, you ass!' Angus looked round. Most of Ansell's seemed to be there. As he came up the steps onto the veranda, Castleton stepped forward.

'Oh Angus, I think that this is the moment you get Capped.'

Angus was lost for words. Stupidly, it had never occurred to him that he might be Capped-on-the-field. In the end he said lamely, 'But it's only my third match for Cranchester.'

There was a good-natured laugh from all those who heard him. Castleton said, 'Well you may never get eight wickets again! Certainly not against Free Foresters! So I should accept it now if I were you.' He put the coveted white cap with the blue rings on Angus' head. There was more applause. He felt enormous pride, almost as though he would, literally, burst. He walked back to Ansell's oblivious to Orton's almost possessive excitement beside him, explaining how it was he who had roused Ansell's to the growing drama. Everything was justified by this moment, everything had been worthwhile; the fears, the self-doubt, the misery of the past years were all expunged completely in this moment.

He was a little late into Curfew. The whole of Ansell's clapped as he entered. Was there a self-congratulatory element in it, as if Ansell's were saying, 'Look! *We* can make a useful Castonian even of Angus?'

※

Fine weather continued. The date of the OA match approached, there was an increased tautness in Ansell's and Snider remarked, 'I don't think Craigie will altogether approve of the arrangements.'

As the days slipped past and nothing seemed changed from previous year, Angus wondered if Craigie knew he had handled matters the wrong way the previous Half and was deliberately avoiding a new cause for confrontation. In the event the OA match was an anti-climax. At midday there was a torrential thunderstorm, so prolonged and fierce that within minutes all the cricket pitches were under water. It continued to rain for the next hour and it became clear that there would be no more play. A lengthy lunch took the place of the usual evening meal.

Unexpectedly, despite the weather, it turned out to be a thoroughly good-humoured affair. Craigie entertained both sides to sherry before lunch and coffee afterwards. Old Ansell's lingered and many of them stayed until tea, but by five o'clock all but two had taken themselves off. The last two shared a taxi to the station to catch the six o'clock train. Mawsom and Snider, squeezed into Angus' study, reflected on the day.

Mawsom said, 'I think it's just as well nobody stayed the night, especially as Bartlett was playing. I reckon Craigie would have had a fit.'

'If he'd found out what went on.'

Angus said, 'It'd be difficult not to find out – on Match Night.'

'The Digger never did.'

Mawsom mused, 'I've always wondered about that. I think he knew enough not to look for trouble.'

Snider agreed, adding, 'Well, Craigie's bound to find out next year. He's always snooping about the place.'

Mawsom disagreed thoughtfully: 'By next year, I reckon either Craigie'll have learned his job – or he'll go off his head!'

'What do you mean?'

'What I mean, AC, is that although *you* would never notice I suppose, Craigie definitely twitches. He knows he's not much liked.'

'I quite like him.'

'You would! What I mean is that he's trying to change everything overnight at Ansell's.'

'Not before it's time perhaps?' Snider said provocatively.

Mawsom did not disagree. 'Possibly, but there are ways of doing it. Craigie won't manage it – especially with Watson as Head of House. After all, who takes any notice of either of them?'

'If Craigie'd any sense, he'd have made Ellerman Head of House. At least Ellerman could carry Ansell's with him.'

'Ellerman's not for any changes at all,' Mawsom reasoned.

'That's why it would have worked out better,' Angus said. 'I haven't noticed any changes. Which ones?'

There was silence because Angus was right. Eventually Snider said, 'Well everyone *thinks* Craigie wants changes. Queensmen in Ansell's for instance. And he suggested to the Praefaectors that perhaps they ought to try punishments other than tightening-up. Nor is he very keen on Warming.'

'I didn't know that.'

'My dear old AC, we've not even been sure that you're on this planet just recently. Too much cricket's gone to your brain.'

'It makes life much easier – not to know what's happening in Ansell's.'

'Well,' Mawsom concluded, 'good luck to you if you can keep your head down. Something's going to happen.'

'What do you mean by that?'

'I don't know exactly, but I do know that all this tension is bound to lead to an explosion. Don't you agree, Snider?'

'I think Mawsom's right.'

'It's always been like that at Ansell's. Ever since we came,' Angus reflected soberly. 'I've never known what was going to happen next. When we were Junior Election, I used to wake up in the morning, feeling almost sick as if I were in the condemned cell.'

'I think it'll be about...' Snider stopped.

Mawsom said, 'Well don't keep us in suspense.'

'I think it'll be something to do with Watson...and Orton.'

There was silence.

Angus said, 'Why should it? That sort of thing's always happening at Cranchester. Who's going to notice?'

'That's just the point, AC. With those two everybody *does* notice.'

'Only because Carstairs keeps making remarks about them.'

'It's more than that now. It really is.' Snider turned to Mawsom. 'Ellerman was quite right about Crondall's – I've bumped into them twice this week.'

Angus said, 'I think Orton's a bit lonely – Watson's somebody he can talk to.' He remembered how he had felt at the same age.

'He's heading for trouble. The Praefaectors are gunning for him.'

Angus said, 'Lucky Watson'll look after him.'

Mawsom added distantly, 'Eventually he'll not be able to.'

Angus changed the subject: 'Look at the weather now.'

The skies had cleared; it was a magnificent evening and the damp ground was steaming in the fading sun. The following day, Sunday, was scorching hot again.

June

'Angus! *ANGUS*! *WAKE UP*!'

It was still dark, though light enough in the bright moon to make out Notting shaking him. He replied muzzily, 'What?'

'God! AC, you sleep like the dead. *GET UP! FIRE PRACTICE!*'

Angus felt for his dressing-gown and shoved his feet into his shoes. The rest of Big Dorm were on the move. He found himself next to Brownlow, who whispered, 'Let's hope this isn't another hoax by Jonquil's.' The voice of a Praefaector called, 'Shut up, Brownlow! No talking.'

In a quiet whisper Angus said, 'Craigie's keen on fire practice.'

From behind him, a voice said, sotto voce, 'The Digger managed a whole war without them!'

Outside the moon was bright and the night warm. They stood in a disciplined line. Craigie emerged from the shadows of the House. 'Somebody should read List, should they not?' he asked courteously. Ellerman was closest and he said, 'The Head of House does it, sir. He's not down yet.'

'Well, I think you should start then, Ellerman, he's probably shutting doors or windows.'

Ellerman read List and sleepy voices responded. When he came to the end, he read again, 'Watson?' There was no response. He cleared his throat. 'Orton?' The ensuing silence was broken by a half-suppressed snigger that set off a spluttering laugh which went along the line like a fuse.

Craigie's next remark was unfortunately phrased. He said, 'Has anyone any idea what Watson and Orton are up to?' The night was broken by a raucous guffaw of suggestive laughter. Craigie snapped, too sharply, too loudly, 'I can't see anything funny in the fact that, if there was a real fire, Orton and Watson would be burned in their beds.'

A clear, but unidentifiable voice from the darkness rang out, 'In Watson's bed.' There was communal in-drawing of breath, then utter silence. All Ansell's realised the anonymous heckler, seduced by darkness, had gone too far.

Craigie, suddenly alert to the implication, said smoothly, 'The rest of you will stay here. Lambourne, please keep them reasonably quiet. Ellerman, you and the others come with me, we'd better search the House.'

Ellerman returned twenty minutes later. 'Right, you can get back into bed now. Without too much noise.'

'What about Watson, Ellerman?'

'None of your business!'

He could not so easily put off his own Election.

'Come on, Ellerman.'

'Were they asleep?'

'Did Craigie catch them?'

Ellerman said quietly, 'Not a sign of either of them. Watson's bed had obviously been Warmed. Orton's is undisturbed. Craigie reckons that Orton's run away for some reason and that Watson's gone after him.'

'What do you reckon?'

'I reckon they went for a walk?'

'At *this* time of night!'

Ellerman said slowly, 'They've done it before. Several times. I've heard them pass my door.'

There was an air of unsuppressed excitement in Big Dorm when Craigie appeared. 'If anyone knows of anything that may have made Orton unhappy, he should let me know.' There was no response. 'Well, if any of you can think of anything, please see me first thing tomorrow morning. Goodnight.' He turned out the light.

This time there came a chorus of 'goodnights' and a good deal of animated chatter and moving about after he went, but eventually everyone dropped off to sleep.

※

'Angus! Angus!' For the second time he was dragged out of his sleep. But this voice was whispering. The moon showed fully in his window. He guessed it was long after midnight.

'What is it now?'

'Shh. It's me. Orton.'

'Orton! Where the devil have you been? Craigie's...'

'I've seen Craigie.... He was waiting by Door, when we came back.'

'We? You and Watson?'

'Yes.'

'Where the hell were you?'

'We went for a walk...up to Roman Gate...we've done it several times...it's so warm these nights. Just to talk.'

Angus thought of himself and Singleton lighting fires. Would they have gone for a walk in the summer had Singleton stayed on? 'You're bloody fools leaving the House. Why not talk in Watson's study?'

'I just like ... well, being away from Ansell's sometimes. So does Watson. What'll happen, Angus?'

'I don't know. If it had been The Digger...' He stopped. What would The Digger have done? he wondered. As he did so, he realised it could never have happened like that with The Digger. For a start, Watson would never have been Head of House. 'I reckon The Digger would've given you a dozen each. Sacked Watson as Head of House...if you'd only been out for a walk that is...'

Orton had begun to sniff. He said unevenly, 'It's not Watson's fault. It's mine. It wouldn't be fair to sack him as Head of House, because of me.'

Angus could think of nothing to say. At last he asked, 'What did Craigie say?'

'He told us to come and see him before breakfast.'

'Well, perhaps it'll not be too bad.'

Orton said, 'I expect everyone else'll be pleased.'

'Why on earth should they?'

'Ansell's doesn't think I should spend so much time with Watson,' Orton said with a touch of defiance. 'But he's the only person I can ever talk to. Except you, Angus.'

'You'll find everyone stands by you in a row like this. Of course there's bound to be some sort of punishment. It'll seem worse for Watson because he…'s older.' He had been about to say 'should have known better'. He added, 'I don't suppose it'll be anything worse than tightening-up for you.'

'Will they write to my people?' There was a touch of panic.

'Shouldn't think so. After all, you've only been found outside after Curfew. Or is there something else?' Orton said nothing, but he looked away. Eventually his fears somewhat allayed, Orton went off to bed, a small, pathetic figure. Angus fell fast asleep as soon as his head touched the pillow and was not awoken again until the rising bell.

❃

Speculation was rife at breakfast. Baker revealed that Craigie had held a long session with the Praefaectors before sending them to bed. Everyone seemed to know that Watson and Orton had run into Craigie on their way back.

Snider said, 'A walk is pretty harmless. It was bad luck that Craigie should have chosen last night for a practice Fire Alarm.'

'Oh! You haven't heard then?'

'Heard what?'

'Craigie didn't ring the fire bell!'

'Who did?'

'That's what Craigie wants to know. Nobody's admitted it.'

Mawsom put down his cup. He said, 'I wonder…'

'Wonder what?'

'Whether the fire bell was deliberately aimed at drawing attention to the absence of Orton and Watson of course,' Baker deduced excitedly. 'Autumn Half, the same thing happened on Tassel Night.'

'The Digger's bell didn't ring then. That was Jonquil's.'

Angus said, 'Why should anyone want Craigie to find out about Orton and Watson?'

'Oh come on, AC! All the Praefaectors are up in arms about Watson and most of the Junior Elections are fed up with Orton. It could be anyone.'

Snider said, 'What about Carstairs? After all, he's been very anti-Watson, hates Craigie after that rugger business and it'd give Craigie one in the eye to find his Head of House in bed with somebody in the Junior Election.'

Mawsom said, 'What's more, Carstairs could easily see that Orton wasn't in his bed in Big Dorm.'

'I can't see even Carstairs doing something like this,' Angus said. The thought of it being deliberate made him strangely angry; he had been moved by Orton's distress and could imagine how Watson felt. Nobody had seen either of the victims that morning. The Praefaectors had another session with Craigie before Chapel. At lunch time there was a neatly typed white card on the board in Corridor:

M.R. Ellerman is appointed Head of House

Watson did not appear again. Orton did. He looked pale and isolated. Although his Election made no attempt to ostracise him, he was silent and withdrawn. At the end of lunch Craigie rose. He said, 'I should like to see the Praefaectors and the next Senior Election immediately in Private.'

Notting said, needlessly, 'That's us.'

There were not seats enough for them all, so they stood in the study, Craigie in front of the fireplace. 'I felt that I should tell you all, as the most senior men in the House, that Watson is leaving Cranchester today. I stress he is not expelled. I've talked to him a lot this morning and he feels that he cannot really face going on. He said,' Craigie cleared his throat, 'that he felt you were all antagonistic towards him.' There was no movement. 'However, I was not born yesterday. Last night, when we did not know where he was, I talked with the Praefaectors. I asked them frankly for the reason for certain comments made last night at the Fire List.

'Although I am encouraged that Ansell's did not applaud the liaison between Watson and Orton, I have every reason to believe that it was not really an older boy exploiting a younger one. Indeed, I think it was more a case of a lonely younger boy's hero-worship and an older boy feeling sorry for him. I urged Watson to stay here until the end of this Half but, as he clearly could not remain Head of House, he prefers not to do so. He will leave by the evening train and I shall not trouble the High Master with the matter unless the matter wanders beyond Ansell's.

'Orton is more difficult. I have thought about it a good deal. I think perhaps he needs guidance more than anything. You may not know, but his father was killed in the war, as was his elder brother to whom he was particularly attached. I have told Orton that I am writing to his people, and I've made it quite clear to him why I think his relationship with Watson was ill-advised and of its dangers. I have been as explicit as it is possible to be in a letter to a widow, although I think he may have been fortunate in that Watson's attachment seems to me to have been platonic.'

Ellerman said, 'May I ask you, sir, what you've done to Orton? What his punishment has been?'

'I haven't *done* anything to him, Ellerman, if that's what you mean. I have done nothing – except writing to his uncle and mother of course. I do not intend, for instance, to beat him.'

Carstairs said, 'Won't that give others the wrong idea? I mean if he gets away with it?'

Craigie said coolly, 'I don't think he's "got away" with anything. He is very small, very miserable, very frightened and, above all, very lonely. I have emphasised that in future he'll make his friendships amongst his own age-group.'

'I see, sir, Thank you, sir.'

They trooped out into Libe. Carstairs said, 'Bloody Hell! Poor old Watson gets the boot and that little tart Orton gets off scot-free.'

Snider objected, 'Well, if you call a letter home telling them what's been going on is "nothing"! I'd rather have a dozen-up from Craigie! Anyway, Watson didn't get the boot.'

There was a buzz of disagreement. Angus thought, 'Now that he's going, it's "poor Old Watson".' However, he said nothing. The rest drifted off, but Ellerman hung back with his own Election.

Mawsom said, 'Congratulations on your promotion.'

'Thanks, Mawsom. I'd rather it hadn't come about this way.'

'What happened last night?'

Ellerman looked over Mawsom's head, then met his gaze: 'We told Craigie exactly what had been going on.' After the silence encouraged him, Ellerman said, 'The Praefaectors made it clear they don't approve of love affairs between Praefaectors and little boys in Ansell's and that Watson and Orton ought to be booted out.'

'A bit harsh?'

'Is it, Snider? I don't think so. Nor do the other Praefaectors.'

Angus said, 'Well, Watson has chosen to go – he's not been sacked.'

Ellerman nodded, 'But as for that little tart Orton...'

Angus said, 'I think I agree with Craigie. Orton wanted somebody to talk with and they were only up walking at Roman Gate.'

'How do you know that?'

'Orton told me that. Last night. After Craigie had caught them.'

'They weren't at Roman Gate that previous fire-alarm, I can tell you,' Ellerman interrupted. 'They were in bed.'

Angus continued levelly, 'That was Tassel Night and anyway they wouldn't have been the first to be caught in bed would they, Ellerman?'

Baker said, 'The point is, Orton stays and Watson goes! It seems bloody unfair.'

'I agree. Craigie's been taken in by all Orton's twee-ness! If you ask me, Craigie doesn't blame Watson, he envies him,' Ellerman ended decisively.

There was another card in Corridor.

J.P.P. Orton will be beaten by the Praefaectors after Curfew, for being a tart.

It was signed 'M.R.E. Ellerman'.

Angus had feared something of the sort would happen; he felt sick and helpless. To clear Ansell's from his mind he changed and went on Marathon. Hardly anyone ran it during the summer. It was warm, he was running fiercely, punishing himself all the way up to Roman Gate. High up, he relaxed. He could smell the scent of the heathery peat land. Larks sprang up, the sky was blue. He could not even see the school. He felt himself relax into a lope as he began the downhill stretch. As he approached the ford, he became aware of a lone spectator on the bridge. It was Orton, gazing despondently down into the water. He slowed and stopped. Orton looked up. He had obviously not been running for he was in School Dress. Angus guessed that, although undoubtedly gated, Orton was slipping into Cranchester. He looked very small and dark-eyed. Angus said amiably, 'Hello.'

'I'm surprised you're still allowed to talk to me. What did Craigie say to you all?'

'Nothing bad. He said he thought that you needed somebody to talk to.'

Orton blinked.

'And he said he wasn't going to beat you.'

'Have you seen the card in Corridor?'

'Yes, bad luck. But once it's over, everything'll be all right.'

'Oh yes! How would you know?'

'It's happened to me twice. That's how I know. In my second Half the first time!'

'You, Angus! What for?'

'Showing *side*.'

Orton looked at him with new interest. 'It was all right afterwards?'

'Yes. It was as if I'd suddenly become a real member of Ansell's. But it was a bloody painful entrance fee!'

Orton said with naive confidentiality, 'I'm a dreadful coward about being beaten. I made a frightful scene when it happened at my Private.' He looked down: 'I spouted...a lot.'

'Bite your lip and whatever happens don't spout till you get outside.' On the spur of the moment, he said, 'If you feel really frightful afterwards, you can always sneak into my Manger and talk it out. Somebody let me do that.'

'He's writing to my people.'

'I know.'

'They'll be very cut up.' Orton paused, then hesitantly, sheepishly, 'We...I...didn't tell him...everything – about me and Watson.'

'Better not to,' Angus said. 'It'll soon blow over. Where'r' you going?'

Orton looked round: 'Cranchester,' he said defiantly. 'I'm going to say goodbye to Watson, he's been very decent. His train's at six. Do you think there'll be anyone else there?'

'I shouldn't think so.'

'Do you think Watson'll mind? I haven't seen him since.'

Angus was feeling a little cold. He looked down at Orton. He said, 'No, I'm sure he won't. I expect I'd've done the same in your place.'

✻

Orton was not present at Curfew.

Brownlow burst through the door into Big Dorm, 'I say! Have you heard? Orton's bunked! Cut his Praefaectors' and run off!' Speculation was rife and continued with animation until the Praefaector in Big Dorm for that week arrived.

'I say, Livingstone, is it true? Has Orton bunked?'

'Get to bed, the lot of you.'

'Come on, tell us.'

Livingstone, a good-natured, rather weak Praefaector, looked round carefully and grinned. 'All right! Don't let anyone know it was me. Yes, Orton's pushed off. He's probably somewhere in London by now.' He paused and they sensed there was more. 'He got on the train with Watson according to the porter at Cranchester.'

Livingstone's Warmer, a small, dark, intelligent, sparkling boy called Jardine, said, 'I say, Livingstone, is that what's called an elopement?'

It took Livingstone by surprise and he could not restrain his laughter, 'No! I think it's called a scandal!'

'You know, I don't really blame Orton,' Angus said quietly.

Mawsom said, 'Nor me. I don't think Ellerman should have carded him for a Praefaectors'. After all, Craigie had dealt with it.'

'I wonder if Craigie knew about the Praefaectors'?'

'Probably not until now.'

'I met Orton on Bridge. He was going to see off Watson. I suppose he must've decided to get the train too, on the spur of the moment. He didn't have any luggage with him.'

Mawsom said, 'Well, that photograph of his people in the leather case has gone from his Manger.'

It occurred to Angus that Orton might have been deciding what he should do when they met. Had their conversation decided him? Had anything he said persuaded him to get on the train with Watson? Or had Watson persuaded him when he heard about the Praefaectors'?

On balance, Angus thought, Orton had made the right decision; he wondered what would be Craigie's reaction when he discovered that Ellerman had decided to take the matter of punishment into his own hands. He wondered too, who it was who had rung the fire alarm. Above all, he wondered how he would have coped had he accepted the appointment as Head of House. Might Watson and Orton still have been with them?

July

They sat in a temporary hut-like room belonging to the CCF. A youthful major pointed with a cane to the big map. They looked at the maps on their knees. Nobody had bothered to open the windows and, in consequence, it was very warm, although there was damp misty rain outside. Angus felt himself dozing off more than once. 'Your CO tells us that you've all been commanding various platoons in your Cadet force and that today he wants to try the up-and-coming contenders. He also said also that you're a bit bored with the usual OTC exercises, so here's something different for you. For the purpose of this exercise, this installation here, at Bunker Hill is the site of some very new and very secret radar equipment. Your task is to guard it. Now, out on Salisbury Plain, we've got a couple of units of chaps who are finishing off their time, before demob. They've seen service. We've made up a unit of about a dozen, all young officers as it happens, and they're going to try to get through you and destroy the radar. We'll tell 'em that the radar is to be moved by ten a.m. Tuesday and it'll be there, in trucks from some time in the afternoon on Monday. Now, there are three times as many of you as there are of them, so you should be able to stop them. Oh, one other thing. They'll be anxious to get past you without even being suspected because they won't want you to know which way the attack is coming in. They'll not want to risk you waking everyone with a rifle shot. Any questions? Yes?'

'How do we know when we've killed an enemy — or they've killed us?'

'That's always tricky on these jobs. On the whole, if you're seen by the other chap first, then he is reckoned to have got you. No Umpires today. You're all potential Officers and Gentlemen, so it's on trust. Like scoring at tennis.'

They arrived at Bunker Hill two mornings later. There was a small flat parking area where the trucks would arrive. It was surrounded with a wire-mesh fence. Bastable, Senior Under-Officer, said, 'If they manage to tie a thunder-flash onto this fence, it counts as success.'

'Can't they throw it?'

'That's not allowed.'

They reconnoitred the area. On one side, a grass slope ran down to a wide, shallow, river. On another was a quiet road lined by trees and hedges. A third side had a mane of bushes and thickets so closely set as to be almost impenetrable. It was decided to have a small force up at the enclosure; an outlying cordon in hastily dug slit trenches and, finally, at the river, two outposts, with another two on the road and two more at the toe of the wood which forked down two small valleys. The 'radar trucks' arrived. They ate lunch and then a sort of tea meal. Nothing stirred.

It would be an all-night job. It was so difficult to get through the wood, even by daylight, that it was decided the two outposts should stay there permanently. Angus was appointed to the farthest. He was given a Verey pistol.

Bastable said, 'We're probably not meant to have them, Angus, take this one, with a red flare, and you, Eagleton, take this with the green flare, only fire them if you're certain you've seen the enemy, then we can tell which side of the wood they're coming.'

Angus and Eagleton set off, with the pistols, a groundsheet-cape, a blanket and some rations for an evening meal. The wood was already quiet as they forced their way through the tangle of branches and thorns. It was also quite dark. Eagleton said, 'I don't think I'm going to enjoy sitting out there alone all night. We could combine. Who'd know.'

Angus said, 'If they want us to play their games properly, we'd better do as they ask.'

Eagleton looked at him sideways. 'Typical Ansell's!' Eagleton was Jonquil's, Angus said nothing. Irritated Eagleton said, 'We all thought Ansell's preferred going off in pairs.'

Angus did not rise at the reference to Watson but, looking at the map, said without expression, 'I think our routes diverge here,' and turned off.

He had been well instructed. 'Keep in the wood, in the shadow. Find a big tree, put your back to it and sit still. Remember in the dark, you can't be seen unless you move. It's always the mover who's seen. Don't give yourself away until you're certain of a kill. Then fire your Verey pistol.'

He found an ideal tree. The ground was damp. He took off his steel helmet, which had been issued complete with camouflage net and sat on it while he smeared his face and hands with mud as instructed. As it grew dark, he began to fancy he could see moving shapes and figures. He heard noises too. He was frightened. When it was quite dark, he ate the first of his iron rations.

He was astonished at how slowly time passed. He crouched, sitting on the helmet, hardly daring to move. Listening he could hear a shuffling, creaking, sound. Should he investigate? No, that would make a noise. Twice he was sure that a figure was creeping up towards him unaware of his presence. He held his breath and, each time, the figure resolved itself into a bush, or a thick branch. Even if he did hear a noise, he would not want to leave the comfortable safety of the tree.

It got cold despite the blanket, but he dared not move. One o'clock, two o'clock, three. He could just make out the luminous dial of his watch. Suddenly he was sure he could hear something. A shuffle. It stopped. He strained his eyes. Something wavered in front of him. An arm? A branch. He listened. Nothing. Then he heard it again. Was it a man or some woodland animal? Could he hear stifled breathing? Ahead of him a sort of hump shifted, but there was now a slight breeze and he was sure it was the same bush. A twig snapped somewhere. He listened, tense. He strained his eyes into the darkness. Then he was sure he could see something that had not been there before. He tightened his hold on the Verey pistol.

It grew clearer and clearer – a man, crawling, moving his shoulder. He raised the pistol. All at once it resolved another bush; he could make out individual branches. Surely it had not been as close as that before? He had not previously been able to see such detail. A moving bush? Was it growing lighter? A distinct greyness began to filter through the trees. Dawn! It *was* getting lighter. He could have cried out in relief. Slowly he stood up, his back still against the tree. It was now getting light quite fast. He put the Verey pistol beside his helmet and arched his back, flexing his fingers; it was agony stretching his cramped legs.

A gloved hand filled his mouth, pulled back his head, something pressed into his spine. A quiet, authoritative, voice said, 'You're a dead man!' It was so terrifying, so unexpected. For a moment everything went black. It is even possible he momentarily fainted, he could not breathe; in that instant he was back in bed with Ellerman, discovered by Maunder. 'No shouting from dead men.' The glove removed itself.

Angus was trembling all over. 'God! I nearly died of fright. I think my heart stopped!' He turned to look at his assailant. The other, wearing a parachute jacket with Captain's pips and a khaki wool cap, whites of eyes showed starkly in the blackened face. The voice said, laughing, 'I just don't believe it! I've caught AC again!'

Angus still did not recognise the face, but the voice really was familiar. He said incredulously, 'Maunder? Is that you?'

'Quite right!'

They stood looking at each other in silence. Maunder glanced at his watch. 'We've got half an hour before our plan goes into operation. As there's nobody else near, we can spend it in polite conversation. Do you smoke?'

Angus shook his head.

'Silly of me to ask, AC.'

'I didn't know you were a Captain.'

'Only Acting, now. I was Acting Major for a short while. What are you doing?'

'Recovering from the fright of my life.'

Maunder said, 'Pity about the OA Match. I was looking forward to knocking you off a length. I hear you got Capped-on-the-Field after the Free Foresters'.'

Angus said, 'It probably doesn't fit in with the Angus you remember.'

Sitting on a tree, hand cupped round his chin, elbow on knee, Maunder said, 'Well, I reckoned you'd probably do something interesting if you survived your first year.' As a memory occurred to him, he looked quizzically at Angus: 'I seem to remember you did.'

Angus said sheepishly, 'I think mine was the last but one arse you tanned.'

'Will Ellerman be Head of House next year?'

'He is already?'

'Oh! I'd heard Craigie went potty and appointed Watson. I can hardly remember him at all – quiet chap with glasses?'

Angus said, 'Well, there was a row. Watson was sacked as Head of House. In fact he's left.'

Maunder looked sideways at Angus and said, 'For the usual thing?'

'I suppose so.' Angus hesitated, but Maunder was an Ansell's Man after all. He related the saga. Maunder listened in silence. He said, eventually, 'I suppose Craigie hadn't much choice but to get rid of Watson as Head of House, especially in view of the fact that everyone knew.'

'What do you think The Digger would've done?'

'For a start, he'd've made sure the Praefaectors knew there was going to be a fire practice.'

'That's the odd thing. The fire practice wasn't Craigie's idea. Nobody knows who set off the alarm. I think it was Carstairs – he's had a grudge against almost everyone since being demoted. And everyone thought Orton and Watson were just too public.'

'Craigie didn't punish Orton?'

'No, that's why Ellerman carded him for a Praefaectors'.'

'Craigie forbad it?'

'Orton bunked. Went off with Watson – same train. Nobody realised till Curfew. We think there's a great row going on in the background, with Orton's people and Watson's. Craigie looks worried.'

Maunder said, 'I'm not surprised. He ought to have demoted Watson, given Orton a dozen-up and kept it all "in house". I bet The Digger would've done.'

'Like he did with Bartlett and the Flanders' Mare.'

'I heard about that. I'd forgotten she was even female! So things are a bit tricky?'

'We think Craigie's out to change Ansell's.'

'Well he'll not manage that very easily,' Maunder said. 'I can't see Ellerman as a reformer.'

'No, I don't think he cares for Craigie, even though he's Head of House. We all felt Watson would've gone along with changes, except that none of us would really have listened to him.' As he said it, he thought, perhaps that's why Watson sought Orton's company – perhaps Watson was as lonely as Orton? The idea had never occurred to him before.

'It sounds as though Ansell's is going to the dogs. Perhaps he ought to have put you in charge, AC.'

'Why me?'

'Oh. I don't know. Perhaps you'd've got your own way by asking and smiling at people. As a matter of fact, it may surprise you, that Tarrant always said that he thought you'd end up as Head of House. The rest of us were never quite sure whether or not he was joking.'

'I'm sure he was.' It was on the tip of his tongue say he had been asked. Had it been Singleton sitting there he knew he would have broken his promise to Craigie.

'Maybe. Know when he said it first? After your Praefaectors'. Everyone thought you'd run away rather than face it.' Maunder paused. 'You really only got it because Singleton so disapproved of tightening-up.'

'I know that now,' Angus said. 'I think I really knew it at the time. Thank God I've grown up a bit since then. You helped me there!'

Maunder said, 'By the way, I was very sorry to hear about Singleton. Is it true he got a Bar to his MC? Somebody said there was a memorial service somewhere for him.'

'Yes, to both. At his home. In the parish church. I went, because his father wrote to ask me.'

'Good for you, AC. Tell me, how did you twist The Digger's arm? He never approved of Singleton really.'

'I didn't ask. I just went. And got a Praefaectors' – for cutting the OA match as Twelfth Man!'

'Well done, AC.' Maunder looked again at his watch. 'I ought to move now. I reckon we'll manage to do our stuff in the next forty minutes. You can amble up at your ease when you hear the racket.'

'Cheers, Maunder.'

'Are you going to be at Ansell's for the OA Match next year?'

'Yes.'

'See you at the wicket, if not before. I hope Craigie can come to terms with Ansell's. If he doesn't, it'll break him.' Maunder vanished into the undergrowth. Forty minutes later there was an outbreak of firing and some shouting. Then silence.

'At least they didn't manage to plant the bomb,' Angus thought as he set off. Somehow with Maunder it had seemed so certain that Cranchester would be defeated. He had hardly gone three hundred yards when there came a loud explosion. He reached the top as the invaders were celebrating their victory.

They were taken back to Cranchester via Salisbury where they stopped for a few hours. Angus wandered the streets feeling conspicuously grubby in his uniform, although nobody seemed to notice. About three o'clock he found himself in the Cathedral Close and stood looking up to the steeple. There were very few people, only a slow trickle, mainly elderly women, passed. Evensong was shortly to begin.

As he was about to enter his progress was arrested by a familiar voice. 'Good afternoon, Angus.'

'Oh, good afternoon, sir.'

Craigie said, 'You look a little worse for wear after your Night Op.'

'Yes, sir. They got through to the radar. Not much sleep.'

'I know what it feels like. Now you're here, you should stay for Evensong.' Craigie paused. 'You would have enjoyed singing in a Cathedral as a Chorister.'

'Yes, I think I would have done. I expect it takes a bit of getting used to.'

'Choristers seem to take it in their stride.' Craigie stopped for a moment. 'Angus, may I ask you something? Come out into the Close a moment.'

They moved back into the sun.

'I gather that Orton was to be beaten by the Praefaectors. Do you think that's why he went off?'

Angus remembered his conversation on the bridge. At last he said, 'It may have helped to persuade him. I think...' He stopped.

'Go on.'

'Well, I think he believed he was going to be very lonely, without Watson there.' He stopped again and said, 'I must've been the last Ansell's Man to see him. He was on Bridge when I came back from Marathon. I talked with him for a bit. I don't think he was running away then. He said he was going to the station to say "goodbye" to Watson.' He looked at Craigie. 'Is he coming back?'

'No.' Craigie seemed serious. 'He doesn't want to. I don't think Ansell's want him back. I don't think it would be in his own best interests, do you?'

Angus did not answer. They stood in the warm sun.

Craigie said, 'What puzzles me is who set off the fire alarm.'

'Nobody seems to know, sir. It was bad luck on those two really.'

'Or deliberate and malicious,' Craigie continued. 'I'm not making excuses for Watson and Orton; I disapprove of that sort of thing very much. However, I have a feeling that my attention was deliberately drawn to it. If I'm right, Angus, then there are wicked people in the House.'

It was on the tip of his tongue to offer his suspicion of Carstairs, when Craigie said, 'I'm forgetting, this is a day off. I should not have spoken.'

Angus knew that he meant 'I should not have spoken this way, in view of the fact that you are not Head of House.'

He said doggedly, 'I think things will work better under Ellerman.'

'I hope so. Angus. I certainly hope so. I must not be late, I have an appointment. You'll be glad to know that I told them to leave the hot water on all day today at Ansell's, so that you'll get a hot bath when you get back.'

Craigie vanished and Angus pushed the door open. He sat in the back row of seats. Choristers processed into the nave led by the gleaming Cross held high. He felt a great tranquillity. Light fell through the windows and lay in long slices across the stones, slashing the choir pews and the figures on the tombs. He could see, in corners of the cathedral, tattered banners of regimental colours. A solo voice lifted him with its sweetness. He remembered that he had once made that sort of sound himself, piercing in its intensity. Perhaps it was the boy who had found him on top of Silbury Hill the previous Field Day? First Treble now, as he had so engagingly predicted?

He stayed throughout the service, kneeling and rising with the few others, entirely at ease. He wished he could sit there forever. As the procession left, he cursorily scanned the faces, but the robes and the frilled collars so disguised them that even if the boy were there, he was unrecognisable. Anyway, perhaps it had been some other cathedral.

He remembered Mawsom asking him if he would become a priest and his unequivocal 'no'. Now, there in the cathedral with the voices of the choir still lingering in the tracery of the ceiling, with the candles and the robed figures, he was not so sure. He thought of the old cloister there, of monks who had once paced the stone flags and the quiet, secluded gardens. 'Yes, yes! This is what I want. This calm, this beauty, this passionless state of being.' Had Hopkins felt like that? Had Singleton felt like that? Uplifted by the singing and the calm of the great building, almost intoxicated by tiredness and lack of sleep, he felt that he must dedicate himself in Singleton's place. It would be a fitting vocation. It was the only way ahead.

Still in this elevated state he was almost last to leave. The light had moved a little from the great window. It was noticeably darker. He passed the machinery of the great clock in momentary wonder and went out into the porch. A clergyman came from the brightness of the Close outside into the gloom. He could not make out the face distinctly against the dazzling light of the open door but, for an instant, their eyes met in instinctive mutual, momentary, awareness. Then, as he stifled his own reaction and, seeing the glaze suddenly shielding the eyes of the other, he knew that this response too was mutual. Within seconds they had passed without backward or sideways glance. He had not been mistaken; Father Dunsley had recognised him.

※

There was a new notice in Corridor. Angus and the rest of the Election were to be Praefaectors the following Half. It was hardly a surprise, but he still felt inordinately pleased with a secret, but satisfying, pride. In that traumatic first Half, it had never seemed possible that he would one day be a Praefaector. Notting came up, tapped the notice and said heavily, 'We'll soon have Ansell's back to what it ought to be. No more of Craigie's half-baked experiments – he'll've seen the light after Watson.'

Chapter Ten

Could I have excused myself from going on with this history, even at this late stage? Although I set out to tell the truth, to reveal what really happened, I was still prevaricating until a third coincidence convinced me that these were not coincidences. Random chance played no part at all in making me face what I have always tried to forget; fate dropped an envelope through my door.

I paid it no particular attention when I gathered up my letters on the way to breakfast and opened it without even giving it a glance. It was an invitation attached to a photocopied notice:

Ansell's Gaudy
1941 Election
Toast
'Ansell's & The School'
Proposed
Sir Michael Ellerman

We're the last all-Digger Election and it'll be our last chance to eat in Din. Room before it's all renovated. Half will have ended, so we can sleep in our old studies – by permission of the retiring Housemaster (remember Ashton?)

An almost illegible hand has scrawled in ball-point. *Saw you're back in UK. Do come. You always were an elusive bugger, AC! P.S. Nightcap in Big Study!!!.* The signature is indecipherable.

No more evasion or procrastination. I must face up not merely to my part in unwittingly precipitating the dreadful climax, though that is terrible enough, but face up to *my* responsibility. I must acknowledge also that (although not alone in maintaining this long silence) my cowardice, in saying nothing at the time, promoted despicable injustice by cravenly condoning the shameful aftermath.

I shall not be present for a *Nightcap in Big Study*.

❋

Big Study!

Overpowering, far more vivid than I welcome, like the posed photograph of a scene in a play, there returns that moment in Big Study, during my last year.

We are all Praefaectors.

It is autumn, just before Evening School.

A damp, misty smell of leaves drifts through the open window from the fine chestnut tree ripe with conkers outside and mixes with the scent of coal fire and toasting bread. The large square table is covered by a not-very-clean tartan cloth. On it are two piles of books, the fat Lexicon, the great Bible in its shabby binding, a pot of home-made jam in a chipped saucer with roses on the rim and an old breadboard with a bread-knife, its split bone handle whipped together by string. On a wooden tray, a motley collection of cups and non-matching saucers. The big brown earthenware teapot sits on its cracked wood-framed tile. Rubber tubing supplements the badly chipped spout in a vain attempt to make it pour predictably; the lid (from a different pot of floral design) is slightly too small. From one side of the fireplace juts a small cast-iron hob on which the enormous squat, blackened kettle hums gently, emitting, every so often, a wisp of steam from spout or lid.

As I record the tranquil domesticity of this scene, I am almost entirely engulfed by nostalgia. I now believe that moment of that autumn teatime was the last of our innocence.

Perhaps, if you read what follows, you will object that those present were far from 'innocent' even then. I understand the reason for this. However, until that moment, although we were all seventeen or eighteen years-old, we were still capable of innocence. We may have been – at times, certainly were – thoughtless, deceitful, crude, frequently lustful, even cruel and unscrupulous, but never all at once. Not all the time. Until that afternoon we were not totally submerged.

He stands in front of the fire.

The rest of us have turned from the window. He might have been asking which of wanted toast – as he did in almost the same breath – turning his attention back to the grimy but utilitarian toasting-fork.

'We must destroy him.'

No hiss of indrawn breath, no bubble of subversive agreement, certainly no protest. It was as if he merely articulated something tacitly agreed already. There was not even the air of a difficult and tortured decision having been finally reached at that instant. *That* was when we crossed the line.

Ellerman's statement crystallised, I suppose, an unvoiced acceptance that had been formulated gradually over the course of the previous months. Or was it years? Had we been directed imperceptibly towards making that decision from the very first day we set foot in Ansell's?

One thing for sure, Ellerman's quiet, undemonstrative declaration marked the moment when we finally and completely evacuated the world of the schoolboy for... . For what?

Throughout my life I have sought vainly, time after time, to persuade myself that I have paid enough and owe no further obligation. I do not ask you to excuse, let alone condone, what happened. The reason I write is not to seek forgiveness, if forgiveness is possible, but because I feel final expiation lies in asking you to try at least to understand, how and why those distant events happened; how it came about that, early one autumn evening in Big Study we accepted, unquestioningly, a decision made for us by the people we had educated ourselves to become.

Perhaps I still yearn for the easy absolution of that dark, musty, little Confessional? Can I find some vestige of excuse after all? Can I plead that it was 'bad luck'? Or that Fate took a hand, deciding long, long, before we were born that, like Hardy's iceberg converging on the *Titanic*, our destinies 'were bent' by 'paths coincident' waiting only 'till The Spinner of the Years said *Now*'?

No. That will no longer do.

Reflecting across this span of time, there is only one word precise enough which comes to mind, but it is so unfashionable and prissy that perhaps you will smile. It does not make me smile, even after all these years. At that moment we stepped quite deliberately from a world where the tatters of innocence were still possible into…what?

Corruption?

Oh yes, certainly we were corrupt. We had been slowly, insidiously, subtly corrupted since the first minutes of the first hour we arrived in Ansell's. That is part of it. But it seems to me now, as an old man, that the only appropriate word for what we finally embraced that fading autumn afternoon is wickedness.

ii

Despite his vows to the contrary, Ansell's took hold of him as soon as they returned. He found — they all found — that their new status as Praefaectors meant more to them than they cared to show. Ellerman was used to it of course. However, Notting and Baker, even Mawsom and Snider now seemed more conscious of their responsibility to see that Ansell's was the Ansell's of old. Even Angus found, on reflection, that he was, marginally, more hostile towards Craigie than he had been previously. Collectively they wore a cloak of conservatism which, during the intervening months of the holiday, seemed to have become more precious.

Nevertheless he determined to keep Ansell's and Cranchester at arm's length. The previous year he had been able successfully to distance himself with the beginnings of a fastidiousness that was almost priggish. He found that, as Junior Praefaector, he had been allocated the room which he had first entered as Singleton's Warmer, it was, he supposed with a shrug of acceptance, inevitable. Nonetheless, it pulled the past closer to him.

It had changed hardly at all, perhaps it was a little dingier. He knelt by the fireplace. The loose board was still there beneath the torn fringe of linoleum. He scrabbled around inside with his hand. There were still some fir cones and fragments of coal. Had the other occupants used the store-place? His hand encountered something cold. A bottle. He drew out a small flask-like bottle, the sort bought on railway stations. He opened it and sniffed. The aroma was still there, despite the emptiness. The label said **Gordon's Gin** and looked both familiar and unfamiliar. It had obviously been there a long time; he realised it was a thicker, glossier, pre-war label. Who had been the secret drinker? Had Singleton known the bottle lay there? He reached further and dragged out a handful of cones and dry, brittle twigs. One had three small stunted cones all coming from the same stem. Sharply, immediately, he remembered picking it up himself in his first winter. Somehow it had escaped the fires he and Singleton had lighted. Awed by the way chance worked, he did not put it back, but placed it as a sort of mascot on the black iron over-mantel.

Autumn warmth flowed in through the windows. He sat on the bed slowly unpacking, placing clothes in the battered chest of drawers. He put up two pictures on the already waiting nails. They had come from the loft at home. One showed a landscape with a spire in the distance. It was not a good reproduction. In tiny writing he saw the name of the artist 'John Constable'. On the other side in small printed capitals it said *Salisbury Cathedral*. The second picture was not a reproduction, but a copy done by a student. A soldier of a past age, on horseback, was being offered a glass of ale at a decrepit inn. The thatch was bare and the countryside stretched away bleakly in the distance. There was a buxom girl and two or three grubby children. For no reason at all, Angus had decided it was Dutch. He put over his bed the green tartan blanket that he had brought from home for the purpose and the room looked clothed. Finally, he took two or three armfuls of books and placed them in the dusty, waiting, shelves. Then he selected some for Big Study; it was the custom that the Praefaectors should each contribute to a small working library.

He weighed the battered copy of Hopkins in his hand. It opened as it usually did at 'The Handsome Heart: At a Gracious Answer'. Without any embarrassment now, he glanced at the pencilled *AC?* He was glad he had made his peace with the ghost of Singleton, although it was as if the Angus and the Singleton of that time were two people whom he had once known – people who now had nothing to do with him. He read the lines as he had done many times before and, once again, was moved by the purity of the poet's sentiment. Although he would have confessed it to nobody, he still felt strangely flattered, elated that Singleton had pencilled in his initials by those particular lines. He cast his thoughts back to the previous Lent Half but, remembering Orton's appearance on Tassel Night, quickly dismissed them. That had been the final occasion. He had made no Tassel Night assignation in the Summer Half. That was all behind him. It gave him a sense of superiority. Others could do what they liked. He put the volume on the mantelpiece next to the cones and the copy of Dylan Thomas poems Craigie had given him for winning The Greystoke.

It did not occur to him that he had, unconsciously, placed them side by side, nor did it occur to him that he was perhaps, also unconsciously, making a vow (for he would have denied that) to follow a path Singleton had mapped out, but he would do it all more wisely. For an instant he remembered the intensity of some moments of their relationship, innocent though it had been. That sort of intensity must be avoided. He would be pleasant to his Warmer, kindly but not sloppy. He hoped for somebody down-to-earth, like Orton, or chirpy as Brownlow had been in his first year. He would follow Singleton's example on Tassel Night.

Although he would not have admitted it before, nor would he ever to Ellerman, or even Mawsom, he now felt his relationship with Singleton was something which he, as a Praefaector, would not have approved. For a moment or two he wondered what Maunder had thought about it – had really and truly thought about it? Had Maunder understood, he wondered fleetingly, how much he, Angus, had really needed Singleton's 'auntying' in order to survive those early Halfs? Beneath all the formality and the grand manner, was it possible Maunder could have been as perceptive as that? Not for the first time he recalled Maunder flipping the switch out of the window and laughing, almost as if in relief.

The sense of unreality, of a wheel coming full circle, was even stronger that evening in Big Study. They sat in fading light, after Curfew, waiting for the Junior Election to present themselves for Inspection. Except for Ellerman, it was a new experience. Each of them remembered – clearly and distinctly, what they had felt when they had been the new Election and now here they were sitting as Maunder, Tarrant and all the others had been sitting that unforgettable evening when they themselves were new. At the time it had never occurred to Angus that, for most of those Praefaectors, the situation had been as novel for them as for the new Election and that the Praefaectors were probably as nervous as they themselves had been. He suddenly realised he had left his glasses in his study, but there came a knock on the door.

Ellerman said, 'Come.'

A voice outside said, 'Go on. I stay outside.' Six timid figures in pyjamas shuffled in to stand in a sheepish line. Maunder stood up and looked at them. The other Praefaectors lounged back, as Ansell's Praefaectors always did on such an occasion.

'I'm Ellerman, as Jardine should have told you. This is where you come when you're to be beaten with this. It's called a switch.' He waved it. 'Did Jardine tell you what to do? Come on, speak up!'

A boy at the end of the row swallowed and said, 'Yes, Ellerman.'

'Well go on, show us.'

Uncertainly the boy moved to the chair and placed himself across the arms.

'Your hands are in the wrong place.' The boy altered the position of his hands.

'Didn't Jardine tell you how to tighten your arse?'

There was a complete silence, then, 'I think so and I've forgotten, Maunder.' He was very obviously trying not to let their Nanny down.

It became clear, as Ellerman made the other five perform the ceremony that Jardine had entirely omitted this important detail about tightening-up.

'Come in, Jardine.'

The door opened and Jardine, usually rather ebullient, looked anxious, his dark hair accentuating his unusually pale face.

'Did you tell them how to tighten their arses?'

He looked round and passed his tongue over his lips. 'I...I...might have forgotten, Ellerman, I'm sorry.'

'Well you can damn well show them now. Take off your dressing-gown.'

Confused, and nervous, Jardine first of all placed his own hands incorrectly.

'Tighten that arse Jardine!'

Jardine pressed his feet against the bar of the chair. Maunder was still holding the switch. Without fuss or exertion he delivered seven hard cuts. Jardine, not expecting it, gasped at the first and then kept silent.

'Right you can get up now, Jardine. That's one for each of the new Election you failed to Nanny properly. And one extra because I'm not allowed to beat the member of the new Election who tried to cover for your forgetfulness by lying. You ought to know by now that I'll not have slackness while I'm Head of House. Tell your Election that.'

'Yes, Ellerman. Thank you, Ellerman.'

'Off with those pyjamas and let the new Election see what happens when they forget. Or lie.' For Jardine, who had never before had to tighten-up with anyone present other than the Praefaector beating him, it was almost the last straw. 'If you're going to spout, remember it's another two.' Ellerman turned to the new Election. 'I never overlap, even with a dozen-up, do I, Jardine?'

Scarlet with embarrassment, Jardine shook his head.

They shook hands. 'You can cut along now.' Fumbling to draw up his pyjamas and clutching his dressing-gown, Jardine shut the door.

The new Election stood even more silent than they had already been, if that were possible. They stared straight ahead. Angus' eye travelled to a boy at the end of the row. 'He reminds me of someone. One of us I suppose. One of us must've looked like that when we were the new Election. Ellerman?' Certainly there seemed something familiar about him but, without his glasses, he could not be sure. He had the younger Ellerman's good looks, but was much slighter, more finely drawn probably, Angus thought, he was less of a games-player than Ellerman had been at that age.

At the near end of the line was a tall bronzed boy. It must be Arnold-

Ferguson, Angus realised. They had heard about him. He had been stranded in Australia, with his mother, at the beginning of the war and was coming to Cranchester almost a year later than he would otherwise have done. Ellerman pointed to him: 'Inspection, Arnold-Ferguson, up there on the table. For God's sake take off your pyjamas first. Then get up on the table and stand on the Bible.'

It occurred to Angus that they were almost the same words as had been used to them five years before. The whole thing was a cherished ritual. The same words, the same procedure — everything passed on from Head of House to Head of House — not in writing, but by oral tradition. 'Come on, Arnold-Ferguson. Turn round, we want to see what you've got.' There was dutiful laughter from the assembled Praefaectors at the time-honoured crudity.

Arnold-Ferguson turned round awkwardly, he had reddened. It was not only with embarrassment, for there was a touch of asperity when he said, 'Fer Christ's sake! D'yer mean ter say yer have ter look at me dongo? Prap's y'd like ter measure it next.' It sounded comic rather than impertinent. Everyone laughed, even some of the new Election. Encouraged by this Arnold-Ferguson went on, 'That reminds me, Jardine told me I'd get permission to cover-up with all this hair.' The Australian twang was even more pronounced.

Ellerman said, 'Not, usually, in your first Half, but we'll see. I hear you play rugger.'

'A bit.'

'For the Australian National Schools?'

'Yeah. It's because I'm quick on me pins. And I don't mind tackling the big buggers.' He grinned.

Ellerman said, 'Well you'll be all right, if you watch your language. Otherwise you'll get your arse tanned.'

'I don't suppose that'll worry me. Me last school was run by Christian Brothers and you'd grown a leather arse after the first term with them. They even used a bloody hurley-stick.' He looked round, 'It's a sort of Irish hockey stick and it was never less than half a dozen. Usually twice that. One poor bugger had to go to the San afterwards.'

There was more laughter. The inspection was getting out of hand.

'Okay you can get down.' It only took a moment before the tension and the formality returned for the others had been thoroughly cowed by Jardine's harsh punishment.

The boy at the end of the row was last. He looked a little pale but he stood on the table quickly enough and without embarrassment. 'Turn round, Carleton.' The boy did so. The impression that Carleton was somebody he knew again touched Angus. He remembered very clearly, Ellerman on the same occasion. However, Carleton, he realised was tense and far more timid than Ellerman had been.

The usual questions were asked: 'What punishments are given in Ansell's?'

'You get beaten, Ellerman.'

'What's our name for that?'

'Umm. Tightening-up?' There was a tinge of anxiety. Ellerman nodded.

Then as if suddenly his mind was switched back to their own inspection, Ellerman said, 'You don't have any hair, Carleton, do you?'

'No, Ellerman, I don't think so.'

'If you'd said "yes" we'd have had to get out the magnifying glass!'

The Praefaectors laughed dutifully.

'Yes, Ellerman.'

'What's this?' He used the tip of his switch.

'My tassel, Ellerman.'

'And this?'

'It's...my bottom, Ellerman.'

'It's your *arse*, in Ansell's, Carleton. Go on, say it.'

'Arse, Ellerman.'

'Say it, don't whisper it. You aren't ashamed of it, are you?'

'No, Ellerman.'

'I hope you're not proud of it either!'

'Oh no, Ellerman.'

'Well then, say ARSE.'

'ARSE, sir...I mean, Ellerman.'

Angus found that he was becoming agitated, for a reason he could not divine. It seemed to him that Ellerman was making a dead set at Carleton.

'Again.'

'ARSE, Ellerman.'

When the boy said it, it sounded different and seemed to make Ellerman's pronunciation of the word more obscene. 'You sang in the Cathedral?'

'I was Head Chorister, Ellerman.' It was a statement of fact, not a boast.

'Why've you come to Ansell's so young?'

'It's because of the Music Scholarship, Ellerman.'

'Well, we're more interested in Rugger. You're the first Queensman in Ansell's for about twenty years, so don't put on *side* or we'll tan your arse black and blue.'

'No, Ellerman.'

It was about to end when Notting said from deep in a chair, 'I say, Ellerman, there's something we've forgotten to ask them.'

Ellerman looked blank. 'Go ahead.'

Notting said, 'Just before you go, Carleton, have you been shown how to masturbate?' and grinned across at Angus in reference to the similar question Tarrant had asked him during his inspection. However, from Notting's lips it seemed particularly gross.

Still standing on the table, Carleton looked round, his eyes slightly wide. He said, 'Jardine didn't show us...' then stopped, remembering what had happened to Jardine already for forgetting to instruct them.

'We're very relieved to hear he didn't,' Notting interrupted, amongst sniggers from the other Praefaectors. Angus noted that although Carleton and several others looked completely mystified, Arnold-Foster and Davidson looked hard at their feet.

Carleton thought a moment, then his face cleared and he said, with the pleased relief of somebody who has remembered the answer, 'I'm very sorry, Ellerman, I'm not much good at geometry, but—'

'Never mind, go on, Carleton,' Ellerman encouraged with a wink at the other Praefaectors.

'Is it something to do with the erection...?' Then, as Baker began to giggle uncontrollably, 'Sorry Ellerman, I mean *construction*...'

'Well, thank God for that,' Ellerman said, stuffing his handkerchief into his mouth to stop himself laughing.

Thoroughly unnerved Carleton, repeated, 'I mean construction' and blundered on, 'of a circumcised circle?'

The roar of laughter pricked the bubble of embarrassment that Notting's question had inflated. Baker gave guffaw after guffaw and the others joined in. Even the New Election smiled, although except for Arnold-Ferguson and Davidson, it was evident that they had no understanding of the joke. Carleton looked relieved, scared and puzzled all at once. Still laughing, Ellerman said eventually, 'All right, you can all go. Oh, just a minute. You'll be Warmers for the following Monitors. Arnold-Ferguson, Notting; Crichton to Baker; Elveston to Mawsom; Rimer to Snider; Carleton to Angus; Davidson to me. You can all cut along now.'

They trailed gratefully out. There was more laughter. Notting said ecstatically. 'Erection! Construction! I though he was going to tell us he had an Eiffel Tower!' Collapsing in paroxysms onto the chair, 'It sounds as if Carleton's just the man for you, AC.'

Snider, still chuckling, said, 'It was a pretty gross question, Notting.'

'I don't see why. Angus was asked the same sort of thing.'

Angus said, 'I don't think it was quite the same.' He was short with Notting because he was puzzled. He had assumed, as soon as the New Election had appeared, that Ellerman would choose Carleton for his own Warmer. He hoped Carleton would not prove a complication. He was the first of the Praefaectors to leave.

After Angus shut the door, Mawsom said, still grinning, 'I must say, Ellerman, we all thought that you'd be appropriating Carleton.'

Baker said, 'He'll be the toast of Cranchester. A pity to waste him on AC.'

'It's a pity that somebody as young as that should come to Ansell's at all.' Snider's tone of voice invited no reply.

Ellerman said shortly, 'As a matter of fact, it was Craigie's idea that he should Warm for Angus.'

'I thought he didn't approve?'

'Of Warming, no. But he said that he wanted Angus to keep an eye on Carleton.'

Baker added quickly, 'Most of Cranchester will do that.'

Mawsom said, 'Craigie seems to be taking a lot of interest in the running of our side of the House.'

Ellerman continued as if he had not heard, 'Craigie also said that Carleton has a fine voice and, as Angus himself used to "have something of a voice", he'd be a help.'

Baker interrupted: 'I don't think that you need to be a singer to want to help somebody who looks like Carleton,' and beamed when they all laughed.

Ellerman cut him off: 'Anyway, I'm sure that AC will be able to preserve the innocent reputation of Ansell's as far as Craigie's concerned. Although I seem to remember that the late-lamented Dermott-Powell was a chorister – so we might be in for some surprises. Anyhow, there are only six in the new Election so somebody's got to have Carleton.'

'Or everybody will have him.' Because it was Notting there was no laughter and he coloured up.

'Even after all this time, Notting, you're a bloody oik at heart,' Ellerman said. 'I should think that you and that awful Aussie'll get on fine.' He went out closing the door in a marked manner.

Mawsom sighed. 'You ask to get your arse kicked, Notting. The trouble is that you can't resist putting into words what everyone else thinks but reckons is too obvious to be worth comment.'

Notting muttered, 'Ellerman's jealous as hell about Carleton. And he's got it in for Craigie.'

Snider gathered up his books. 'Rubbish. He's no more against Craigie than anyone else. After all, none of us wants Ansell's to turn into a kindergarten.'

When he reached his room Angus found Carleton in his bed. He said, 'It didn't matter tonight, after Inspection.'

'Jardine said that he'd kick the daylights out of any of us who forget in the first ten days. His...arse...was.... Outside Big Study, I think that Jardine...' he began and stopped lamely, realising he might have already said too much to a Praefaector.

'Spouted? It's all right, it doesn't count as long as it's not in Big Study.'

'It's true, you know, that Ellerman never hit the same place twice!'

'I expect that's what comes of playing racquets.'

After a silence, Carleton said, 'I thought that your name – Angus – was a Christian name? You should have told me, I'm sorry.'

Something in Carleton's voice made Angus turn from where he was hanging his dressing-gown and he looked faintly puzzled. 'Told you? We *never* use Christian names in Ansell's.'

'I *thought* you'd probably forgotten me.' Carleton sounded a little disappointed.

'Forgotten you?'

'We've met before. Once.' Angus thought back to the recent holiday as Carleton continued, 'On Silbury Hill.'

Enlightenment flooded as he reached for his spectacles, 'Of course! Christopher. Second Treble?'

Looking happier, Carleton nodded. 'Yes, Christopher Carleton,' and, diffidently, 'First Treble actually.'

It explained the feeling of familiarity that Angus had already experienced. Constrained by the totally familiar surroundings of Ansell's it had never crossed his mind that it was his erstwhile companion of that hot Field Day. Now, however, now he could see it very clearly.

'I expect I've grown.' In fact he had grown very little.

'I'm sure that's it. I'm sorry. It just never occurred to me. How on earth did you end up at Ansell's?'

'Oh I got the Music Scholarship. When they asked if I'd any preference for a House I remembered you said Ansell's was the best House. Mr Craigie came over to meet me last term...I mean Half.... He said I'd be the first Queensman in Ansell's for a long time.'

It must have been the afternoon Angus had seen Craigie at the Cathedral after the Field Day Night Op.

'I told Mr Craigie I'd met you. I said I though I'd seen you in Evensong that afternoon. I expect that's why I'm your Warmer. I say—' he faltered a little '—do you hit people as hard as Ellerman?'

Angus said, with an attempt at lightness, 'Probably. I haven't tried yet. So you'd better watch out.'

'Oh I never forget things,' Carleton said with unboastful assurance. 'You can't if you're Head Chorister, you know,' he confided.

'I think it might be best if nobody knew we'd met before. Ansell's is odd like that.'

'That's what Mr Craigie said. He said schools like Cranchester and Houses like Ansell's are very...something beginning with "h" I think?'

'Hierarchical?'

'Yes. That's it. I don't know what it means really. That's why I didn't say anything in Big Study just now,' he grinned.

Angus shut his eyes. He could imagine how it would have been if Carleton had sung out a cheerful greeting in this artless manner. However, at the same time, he knew that it ought to be allowable, without anyone else turning a hair. Carleton, naturally responsive and friendly, expected everyone else to be the same. Outside Cranchester Angus would have been pleased to be greeted enthusiastically by Carleton. Inside – it would be an embarrassment. No, worse than that, it would be positively hazardous for them both. However, Carleton also had commonsense it seemed, for he said, 'It's easy for me to call you Angus. I suppose you'd better call me Carleton. Except in here of course – then nobody'd ever know.'

Angus felt the situation was being taken out of his hands. He said almost helplessly, 'Yes, I think you're right. Anyhow, you'd better cut along to Big Dorm now.'

Carleton put on a serious face and said primly, 'Yes, Angus,' and then grinned again. He suddenly added seriously, 'Actually, I'm glad it's you. I...' he hesitated. Angus raised his eyebrows encouragingly. Carleton muttered, 'Well, I didn't think I was going to much like Ansell's I mean...when I first saw it.' He stopped, then added in a quiet, even voice, 'It's a bit frightening. Do you think I'm being wet?'

Angus shook his head. 'No!' he said. 'Don't tell anyone, but when I was here first, I was terrified...most of the time.'

'Now you're a Praefaector.' Carleton seemed reassured. 'Goodnight, Angus.'

'Goodnight, Carleton.'

❋

For a long time after Carleton had vanished Angus sat on his bed. Had he been like that himself once? What most alarmed him was the realisation that Carleton simply and wholly trusted him. Their meeting at Silbury convinced the younger boy that there was a bond that could give him assurance and Angus did not see how he could avoid honouring it, even if wished to do so. As he ruminated, he realised that he did not mind at all. It was up to him to justify the trust. The wheel had indeed come full circle. Here, sitting on the bed that had been Singleton's, in what had been Singleton's room, it seemed that somehow he had inherited an awkward but, he divined, not impossibly burdensome, legacy. With the dark years behind him, perhaps he could now undertake the responsibility at least as successfully as Singleton. Perhaps better? Perhaps he could, at the very least, ensure that Carleton would not make the mistakes he himself had made. At least he would not require Carleton to perform on Tassel Night although he might, at some time, have to answer Carleton's questions when he heard about it from others. He was more than ever glad that he had so successfully waged the battle with himself in the past year.

As the days passed, his attitude shifted almost imperceptibly till he found he was not sorry to have the younger boy's companionship for a few minutes each evening. He was aware too that, increasingly, just as he himself had done, Carleton found the room a welcome oasis and refuge. Nonetheless, the boy grew less and less ebullient than he had been on the first evening and, in Ansell's during the day, often looked tense and drawn. About a fortnight after the beginning of the Half, Angus said, 'Have you settled in?'

Carleton looked at him. 'I think so, Angus.' His voice was flat.

Angus sat on the bed. 'Listen to me. It is tough. There's a lot you won't like. I told you I was scared stiff during most of my first Half.'

Carleton looked at him. 'It's difficult to believe that now.

'Well, I'm telling you the truth.' He paused, wondering if there was anything he could do to help, then he said, 'If you want a quiet place to work any time I'm not here, you can use this room.'

Carleton's face literally lit up, his grey eyes wide. 'You mean it? Oh thanks, Angus!' He said suddenly, confidentially, 'This is about the only place I like being in the whole School. This and Chapel.'

Carleton's joy gave Angus a surge of pure pleasure. He nodded. 'I know. What are you going to sing in Chapel? I heard that you and that chap from Pettifer's are doing an Anthem some time.'

'Yes. It's true. His name's Robertson – they call him Marm, short for marmalade – Robertson's marmalade.' He gave his nice grin. 'I've sung it before of course. It's by Mendelssohn. "I waited for the Lord".'

Angus thought, 'I might have known it would be that.' It almost had to be. Something about the realisation almost frightened him. 'Have you ever heard it? – someone told me it was once sung in Chapel here. About five years ago. Were you here then?'

Angus said, 'It was in my first Half.' He wondered whether to say any more, but then he added, 'As a matter of fact, I was one of the singers.'

'You were? That's amazing. The coincidence I mean. Who was the other?'

'Another Ansell's Man. A Chorister too I think. Dermott-Powell.'

'Oh yes! I've seen his name in the Head Chorister's book.'

'He left some time ago.'

'I suppose he must've done. I mean after all he was in that film, wasn't he?'

Angus looked blank: 'What film?'

'Didn't you know? Old Prinsep told us. Said it wasn't a very good film, but that Dermott-Powell *was* very good. It was called something like *Easter Holiday*. I'm surprised Ansell's didn't go to see it.'

'Dermott-Powell wasn't very popular. So you'd best not to mention him, but I'm surprised no one noticed his name.'

'Oh he sort of changed the spelling – he's called "Diarmid Powell" now instead of hyphens and things. Mr Prinsep says it's his stage name.' Pleased to have been able to repair Angus' ignorance and cheered by the offer of the study, Carleton looked far more animated. 'Mr Craigie says you had a very fine voice – better than mine.'

'That's to stop you showing *side*, I expect. Anyhow, it's time you cut along.'

Carleton gone, Angus again thought of the coincidences. He and Singleton and now, he Carleton, sharing the same Christian name, each of them sharing this small room. Had Singleton sung in the choir? Would

Carleton in his turn inhabit this room as a Praefaector? For the third time it seemed as if some giant wheel was slowly, inevitably, swinging round. He recalled an illustration in a history book. *The Wheel of Fortune* – that was it. A giant wheel with peasants, kings and popes clinging on as they rose on one side, only to be hurled down into the pit on the other. He shivered. Had what had happened to him also happened to Singleton before that? Would the same things happen to Carleton? Somehow it seemed so predictable, so inevitable. He shook himself. Of course there would be differences. There could not be an exact repetition. Nevertheless the speculations worried him obscurely.

Although the easy, comfortable, intimacy which Carleton had so spontaneously initiated that summer day in Wiltshire inevitably dictated the tenor of their relationship at Ansell's, Angus was aware that there were still tensions. It was as if there was, in the back of the younger boy's mind, a shadow. He often looked very tired and, during October, on a couple of occasions omitted to Warm. It did not matter to Angus – indeed the whole concept of having somebody to 'wait' on him, so to speak, had faintly embarrassed him at the beginning of the Half, though he had not confessed it, even to Mawsom. He accepted Carleton's apologies and did not mind in the least; Carleton required as much sleep as possible.

iii

Ellerman caught up with Angus as he drifted back towards Ansell's one evening after Late School. 'I'm glad I caught you, AC. There's something I wanted to mention. As Head of House.'

'Fine, go ahead.'

'Is it true that Carleton's forgotten to Warm for you twice?'

The question took Angus unprepared. 'Possibly, I haven't really noticed,' he prevaricated quickly. 'He's very small and a bit young. Gets tired out.'

'No doubt. However I don't have to remind you that, as a Praefaector, it's up to you to see the Junior Election don't get away with any slackness.'

'When I think Carleton's slack, I'll take the appropriate action.' Angus put an edge to his voice.

'Well, as long as you're not going soft like Aunty Singleton.' Angus did not reply and Ellerman, sensing he had drawn blood, said, 'I daresay you'll recall that all his Nannying didn't do much for you.'

'I'm *not* Nannying Carleton.'

'Well, he's the only one in the new Election who hasn't had to tighten-up yet.'

'Are you suggesting to me that I ought to beat him just for that, Ellerman?'

Ellerman said, 'Don't be an ass, AC. We both know that a new Election always needs shaping up. Otherwise they get damned slack. We've had quite enough slackness in Ansell's for one year.'

'If I think Carleton deserves to tighten-up to me, then he will,' Angus said with more asperity than he intended. 'As it happens, Ellerman, he hasn't deserved it yet.'

'Well, if I were you, I'd make sure he does deserve it some time soon. I seem to remember that you didn't much enjoy your own awakening at the hands of the assembled Praefaectors!'

Angus tensed at the old memory and had to swallow hard before he replied, 'I deserved what I got. Showing *side*. If Carleton's slack or anything like that I'll tan his arse.' He was ashamed that the phrase rose so glibly to his lips, but that very fact seemed to satisfy Ellerman. All the same Angus knew that somehow he had betrayed himself.

That night Carleton forgot to Warm for the third time.

They came face to face in Corridor the next morning.

'Where were you last night, Carleton?'

Carleton dropped his eyes. 'I went to sleep, Angus. I'm sorry.' He looked up anxiously.

'That's the third time.' He felt his heart thudding. He said, 'Wait for me outside Big Study after Curfew,' without looking directly at Carleton.

'Yes, Angus.' Their eyes met. Was there an expression almost of relief on Carleton's face?

They had neither of them noticed Ellerman, who said quietly as he passed, 'About time you got your arse tanned, Carleton, you're getting a slack little sod.' Carleton vanished. 'My word, AC, you sounded quite fierce!'

Angus retorted with some heat, 'I feel quite fierce.' It was true. He was angry with Carleton for putting him in a situation he did not relish. Furthermore, he suspected that Carleton had been lying; he did not believe he had really forgotten. Above all he bitterly resented that Carleton appeared to be taking advantage of his good nature.

Big Study was empty when they arrived after Curfew. Convention dictated that other Praefaectors did not enter until after the beating. Carleton was standing outside in his pyjamas and dressing-gown, with hollow eyes, not at all nonchalant. He seemed very small. Angus ignored what he saw – in fact he was angrier at what he was going to have to do than about the offence itself. They went in. He shut the door. Ellerman, or somebody else, had left the switch prominently on the table.

'You'll get three-up. One for each time you've cut Warming.'

'Yes, Angus.'

Angus could see Carleton was fearful, but he refused to let himself be moved and in fact it made him angrier. He said, 'You'll get another if you spout.' He made his voice cold and hard; Carleton's lip trembled. He found that now, provoked into action, he did not mind if he reduced Carleton to tears. The bloody child had forced him into this. Then conventions and formality took over, making it easier than he had expected as he heard himself say, ' Get over The Chair.' Then perfunctorily, 'Tighten that arse, Carleton, or it'll be one more.'

Carleton whispered, 'Yes, Angus,' but in truth his feet were already against the bar. Angus could see the whitening knuckles. Automatically he picked up the switch and swished it experimentally. A moment of panic. How did you do it? How did you actually hit somebody? Suppose he missed? Suppose it was too gentle? What would Ellerman say then?

Well, whatever else, he wouldn't be too gentle. Once again, anger at Carleton for putting him in this situation and anger at himself for caving in to Ellerman's pressure took over. He flexed his wrist, drew back his arm and brought the switch down far harder than Carleton anticipated. The boy writhed, winced sharply. He saw it cut into the tight-drawn cotton and found the expected fastidious distaste for what he was doing, swamped by curious exaltation, a feeling of complete power, a fierce desire to hurt. He'd make damn sure Carleton never forgot to Warm again.

He drew his arm back again, higher and brought it down even harder.

Without warning the switch was wrenched from his hand, there was a sharp explosion and something fluttered and tinkled round them in the total darkness.

His eyes accustomed themselves to the firelight. Carleton was still there waiting, tense. There was silence, it seemed, for a very long time, but it could have been only for fractions of a second. Carleton asked very timidly, 'What happened, Angus?'

'I h-hhit the b-bloody light,' Angus stammered. 'I've smashed it to bits.' The anger and the savagery had left him; with shocked revulsion he realised he had, momentarily, enjoyed the idea of inflicting pain on Carleton. The realisation disgusted him. He felt weak and found he was actually trembling.

'I hhhit the li-li-light instead of your…your…your arse!' He found it difficult to suppress a desire to giggle helplessly.

'May I stand up, Angus? Until you get another lamp?'

Angus bit his lip to stop laughing and muttered, 'There's a standard lamp by the fire.' Competently, Carleton moved across and switched it on. He came back and placed himself across The Chair as before.

'Get up, you ass.' Angus was hiccupping with the effort to suppress a desire both to apologise to Carleton and to laugh out loud.

'You said three, Angus.'

'I c-cc-an't…even if I wanted to, which I don't.' He felt laughter boiling up in him again uncontrollably 'I've broken the bloody switch.' He could contain himself no longer and tears rolled down his face. Speechless, he held up the two pieces he had taken from the floor. 'P-p-please get up from that bloody chair, Christopher. Here you'd better have one piece. As a m…mm…memento.'

Infected by Angus' laughter, Carleton too began giggling, until they both stood shaking with almost hysterical silent mirth. Angus put his hands on Carleton's shoulders, still incapacitated by the guffaws he suppressed with difficulty, he said, 'I broke the bloody switch on … on … on …'

He could not finish, but Carleton said, 'On…m-my…ARSE!' Getting the word out, finally released the last vestiges of restraint, their relief was such that they clung to each for support.

'I'm sorry, Christopher,' Angus said, during a calmer moment, 'I hit you much harder than I should. I'm so sorry.'

'It doesn't matter. But I'm glad it was only one,' Carleton said, also quieter. Then timidly,' Shall I clear up the glass?' For some reason that set them both off again.

'We'll both do it,' and Angus dropped to his knees, as laughter shook them both.

Glass lay everywhere. The bulb had exploded. Thin fragments seemed to have got everywhere, even in the chairs. There were also slivers of the green glass shade. Whilst they were thus engaged, Ellerman came in accompanied by Mawsom.

'I thought Carleton was tightening-up to you, AC, but it sounds more like *ITMA*,' Ellerman began. Angus stood up. 'He *was* tightening-up. Only, I'm afraid that I smashed the light, broke the shade and the switch. Look!'

Astonished, Ellerman inspected the ruined switch. He said, 'Bloody Hell, AC! You can't even tan an arse without causing chaos.' The broken switch was too much, even for Ellerman, he turned helplessly to Mawsom and they both started to laugh, which set Angus and Carleton off again.

'Only AC could do it,' Mawsom gasped. 'Did you manage to score on Carleton at all? Show us, Carleton.' Carleton obliged.

'If that was the first one,' Ellerman said between convulsions, 'it's just as well you didn't finish. He'd've probably sliced you in half, Carleton. You'd better cut along now.'

Carleton said, 'Thank you,' and held out his hand to Angus. As they shook hands solemnly, laughter threatened to bubble up again in all of them and Carleton fled, stuffing his hand into his mouth, whilst Ellerman flung himself down on the ancient sofa by the window, convulsed by sobs almost of hysteria.

Mawsom said, 'For God's sake, Angus. It's painful to have to laugh so much!' He was off again.

'Where's the rest of the switch?' he managed.

'I gave it to Carleton...' Angus was convulsed with another paroxysm of laughter, 'as a sou...sou...sou...venir.' He put his hands on the table and shook.

When finally it subsided, Ellerman said, 'We'll have to get another switch. And *you* can pay for it, AC.' Hysterical laughter threatened again. Angus left them before it died as Notting entered, mystified at the commotion. As he shut the door behind him, Angus heard Ellerman say, 'You'll never believe this, Notting, but AC broke the switch tanning Carleton's arse.'

Carleton was Warming when he got back. Angus said, 'You needn't have bothered. After Big Study.'

Carleton said, 'I don't want to have to tighten-up again. It really did hurt. It's the first time I've ever had my arse tanned.' He used the Ansell's slang quite unselfconsciously.

'I'd have thought at the Choir School...' Angus began.

'Not really. Never with a switch. Old Prinsep used a slipper sometimes for dormitory ragging. He liked using his hand usually. It didn't really hurt. Anyway, I was all right because I was quite a favourite of his.'

'Well, please, don't forget to Warm again.'

'Oh, I didn't really forget...' Carleton began, then reddened.

Angus said, 'I suppose you relied on thinking I'd never tell you to tighten-up.' His voice had acquired an edge.

'Oh no! I had to make you. My Election said I'd get a Praefaectors' if I didn't get my arse tanned by you. That's what happened to someone once. A long time ago.'

'You mean you *deliberately* didn't Warm?'

Carleton said, 'Well, yes. You see, I was the only one in the Election who hadn't had to tighten-up. I thought I'd rather it was you than.... A Praefaectors' sounds beastly,' he said, looking away. 'Probably I'd have spouted.' He paused: 'They all said you didn't really agree with tightening-up anyway, so I thought.... Well, I was wrong; I jolly well did feel it!' He felt himself gingerly.

As Carleton spoke, Angus remembered his own Election and the gathering resentment of Ansell's at Singleton's humanity. Singleton, he realised, would not have been as suggestible to Ellerman's persuasion as he himself had been. Perhaps Carleton was right, and what had happened was for the best. 'Well, I'm not...'

He was about to say, 'I'm not going to do it again, however many times you forget to Warm,' but sensed that it was not what Carleton wanted to hear. Instead he concluded, 'I'm not going to bust a switch on you next time! It's too damned expensive. Now you'd better cut back to Big Dorm.'

Carleton said, 'I think it'll be all right now. With my own Election I mean. Thanks.' He swung his legs over the edge of the bed.

'Yes, I'm sure it will be.' And he was sure. 'I'm really sorry I tanned you so hard. I didn't mean it like that.'

With unnervingly ingenious intuition Carleton said, 'It was probably because you didn't really want to tan my arse at all.' Angus felt as though the other could see deep into the working of his mind. After a brief pause, Carleton went on, 'After that first one, I knew you meant it and…and, well I was a bit scared.' Then added, with a return of the friendly smile, 'When there was that bang and the light went out'—Carleton's grin broadened—'I thought you'd been struck by a thunderbolt. End of the world. You know – Vengeance of the Gods!'

They both laughed. Angus said, 'Hey, don't move,' put his fingers in Carleton's hair and carefully extracted something which he held out. 'That,' he said, 'is glass from the light bulb.'

Carleton pushed his head forward. 'Is there any more there?'

'No. It seems to be clear. I say, I hope Notting doesn't go and flop down in that chair as he usually does. Otherwise he'll get glass in the arse.' They both dissolved again in convulsions of barely stifled laughter.

By Chapel next day it was all round Cranchester that Angus had broken a switch on one of the new Election. The blurring of details by Ansell's in general and Carleton in particular had two unexpected repercussions. In the first place, Angus was astonished to discover it was widely believed he had broken the switch at the culmination of a beating of almost legendary ferocity and, even more surprising, it accorded him almost as much status as his bowling performance against Free Foresters the previous Half.

The second repercussion arose from the first. A week later Ellerman said, 'By the way, Angus, Craigie's heard the rumour about you beating Carleton.'

Angus was not sure how to respond. He would have preferred Craigie to have remained in ignorance. 'What does he say?'

'That you probably don't know your own strength and that I should try to discourage such a savage beating.' Angus coloured. 'I hope you told him it was only one?' Ellerman ignored the question and continued, 'He asked me if there was a limit and I told him half a dozen. Do you know what he said?'

Angus shook his head.

'He said he'd heard you gave Carleton at least a dozen-up!'

'Perhaps I'd better go and tell him the truth.'

'Best leave well alone.' Ellerman's voice took on a touch of exasperation. 'However, you're to blame for the book!'

'What book?'

'We must now keep a punishment-book – and, if anyone has to tighten-up, it's to be recorded. Who gave it and how many, etc.'

Angus shrugged, 'Probably a good idea.'

'It's a bloody bad idea!' Ellerman exploded savagely and Angus realised he had been repressing his feelings. 'It's a first step to cutting it out.'

Angus said mildly, 'Then perhaps Craigie ought to know that I gave Carleton one cut and smashed the switch and the light.'

'That'll make it worse. Do you know what else he told me, Angus? He told me that it was illegal to raise a "cane" higher than the shoulder!' Ellerman almost spat it out. 'As if we're some oik Grammar School. Trust you to cock everything up, AC.'

'Don't blame me! You practically ordered me to tan Carleton's arse. Shall we tell him that?'

Ellerman looked furious. 'I might've guessed that you'd do something bloody stupid!'

His tone angered Angus and, with a spurt of annoyance, he retorted, 'As far as I'm concerned, if Craigie does cut it out so much the better. That's the last time Carleton tightens up for me.' And added meaningfully, 'Or anyone else.'

Ellerman looked at him coolly. 'I very much hope you don't mean that. Singleton really was a disaster for you, AC.' He went on slowly, meaningfully, 'I very much hope you'll do what is necessary if Carleton steps out of line again.' He stopped and, in a more informal manner, 'Actually, you'd better be careful over Carleton.' He paused fractionally and then said pointedly, 'Remember what happened to Watson and Orton.'

With a sudden flash of insight, Angus said softly, almost to himself, 'It was you! *You* rang the fire bell that night, didn't you, Ellerman? You knew Watson and Orton would be absent.' He was thinking aloud.

Ellerman said too quickly to be convincing, 'Lots of people knew they were out.'

'You rang the fire bell so that Craigie would discover it.' He heard himself say very calmly, 'If you were ever to card Carleton for a Praefaectors', Ellerman, I should refuse to participate and explain to Craigie about the switch and the light. I might also suggest he should ask you who set the Watson and Orton fire alarm.'

Ellerman looked back with unwinking, expressionless, eyes. Eventually he said softly, 'I shouldn't let your imagination run away with you, AC.'

'Then you'd better lay off young Carleton.'

❈

The Praefaectors were all in Big Study when there came a knock at the door. Ellerman said, 'Come.' Carleton stood in the threshold. 'It's all right, Carleton,' Ellerman said meaningfully at Angus who had opened his mouth to protest. 'Close the door. I just wanted to ask you something.'

'Yes, Ellerman?' The apprehension was still there. He looked at Angus who gave him a wink of encouragement.

'Come over here, please, Carleton.'

Carleton moved over by the fire.

Ellerman said kindly, 'I just wondered why you go over to Private every evening.'

To Angus' surprise, Carleton blushed: 'Not every evening, Ellerman.'

'Well, most evenings then.' Carleton said nothing more. 'Do you have Specials?' It was the name for Private Tuition.

Carleton blushed more deeply. 'Not exactly, Ellerman.' He halted, and then suddenly stumbled on, 'I'd rather not say, if you don't mind – Mr Craigie said I'd better not.'

Ellerman said with deceptive mildness, 'Oh that's all right. As long as there's nothing wrong.'

'Nothing at all,' Carleton said breathlessly, 'Please may I go? I should be Warming for Angus.' He was obviously flustered.

'Cut along. Goodnight.'

'Goodnight, Ellerman.'

The door shut to a questioning silence. Eventually Angus said, 'What was all that about, Ellerman?'

'Oh just an idea. He's been looking a bit anxious lately. I wondered if he'd got into some sort of trouble because I'd seen him go through several times to Private. Perhaps he'll tell you, Angus.'

Puzzled by Ellerman's sudden solicitous interest in Carleton and vaguely disturbed, Angus said, 'If I bother to ask.' He left Big Study almost at once.

When Angus got to his room Carleton, pale but composed, looked up warily. 'When I got to Big Study and you were all there I thought I was going to have to tighten-up to all of you.'

'I wondered what you'd been up to when I saw you in the doorway.'

There was a pause and Carleton said, 'They've replaced the light: shall I have to pay for it?'

'If anyone pays it'll have to be me. After all, I broke it.'

'You wouldn't have done if I hadn't failed to Warm.'

'Then, we may have to share the cost.'

Carleton said, 'It's got quite cold this evening.'

On the spur of the moment Angus said, 'Let's have a fire,' and when Carleton glanced at the empty grate, he prised back the loose board and brought out the remaining wood, cones and coal. 'It looks as though we'll have to replenish stocks.' He stopped, conscious that he had said 'we'. Once more the sensation that he was inevitably following a course of action which was predetermined by what had happened before was overwhelming.

'Gosh, is that a secret store?' Carleton made it sound like treasure trove. 'Or does everyone have one?'

It had never occurred to Angus that it might be commonplace. He said, 'In my first Half, the Praefaector who had this room used to keep wood there.'

'Was that Singleton?'

'How did you know?' He asked the question sharply.

Carleton said uncomfortably, 'Oh somebody said something. That you Warmed for him. I asked, you see. I thought I'd like to know. Like a family tree, sort of.'

'He was killed in the last year of the war.'

Surprisingly Carleton said, 'I know. I found his name on the war memorial. He got an MC.'

'That's right and Bar.' The fire was by now burning brightly.

'This was his study?' Carleton seemed insatiably inquisitive.

'Yes. That's how I know about the secret store.' He laughed. 'These cones could even be some of those I gathered when I was Junior Election.'

'I could get some too. Shall I? In case we have another fire one night.'

'If you'd like to, but...' Angus stopped.

'Oh, I shan't tell anyone else.' Somehow Carleton had divined what was in his mind. They sat on the side of the bed companionably.

Then, hardly knowing why he bothered, Angus asked as casually as possible, 'I say Christopher, why do you go? Over to Private I mean?'

Carleton drew up his legs and looked at his fingers in embarrassment. 'Well, I'd rather not talk about it, Angus...if you don't mind. Mr Craigie...' He looked pleadingly at Angus. 'I'll probably tell you sometime. If you'll promise not to tell anyone else. Even Ellerman.'

Conscious of the boy's unease, Angus said quickly, 'Of course you mustn't tell me, unless you want to. It doesn't matter at all. But if you ever want to, I'll keep it quiet.' Silently he cursed Ellerman for suggesting that he should try to find out.

Carleton's engaging vivacity returned. 'Thanks for the fire, Angus.' It had begun to die. 'I'd better get back to Big Dorm. I'm feeling a bit tired.' At the door he said, 'Anyhow, it's just as well you didn't need to give me six-up in Big Study.' He grinned: 'Ansell's might run out of light shades,' and vanished.

iv

The notes soared up into the Evensong dimness of Chapel. He was far more moved than he had been when he sang it himself. Then, he had been lost in it too, but lost in the cool technical way of the good performer who is completely involved in a work; now, it swept him with an emotional intensity that astonished him. Had he really been able to sing those notes once upon a time? With that same piercing purity of tone? Had Craigie meant what he said, when he told Carleton that Angus had the better voice? The glorious notes wound themselves into him: *I waited for the Lord.... And he heard my complaint.* On the verge of tears although, in the gloom, nobody else noticed, he looked up the aisle where Carleton stood unselfconscious of both his beauty and his voice, totally immersed, silver sound flowing effortlessly from him.

Somehow, imperceptibly, during the passing weeks the nature of their relationship had undergone a subtle transformation. Carleton had become his charge, his responsibility. He was aware also that he had moved a step nearer an area he wished to avoid. Had Singleton felt like this when he himself had sung in Chapel? Certainly he had not been conscious of it at the time; he could remember only that Singleton had seemed rock-like and infinitely assuring amongst a great deal of uncertainty.

Angus floated out into the darkness, the memory of the music still in his ears, the words hovering on his lips. Idiotically, he found he regretted that he could no longer make those sounds — he had never felt like that before. Indeed he no longer even sang in the Choir. Perhaps he would rejoin — as a Tenor or Baritone.

He was still in this mood when, much later, he entered his study. Carleton blinked sleepily. Angus said, 'You sang well. Bloody *mar*-vellous!' The words were out before he realised that he was using the same Ansell's sporting phrase as Singleton had used to him.

'I'm sorry, Angus, I must've fallen asleep.'

'Doesn't matter. You sang it far better than I did.'

Carleton said, 'If I did, it's because I've sung it before in the Cathedral.'

'I know that, but tonight it was still bloody marvellous.' He remembered

Singleton saying, 'I thought you'd crack the roof,' so he added, 'Roof-cracking!'

'I wish I'd heard you sing it!'

Angus looked down at the boy in bed and was filled with affectionate warmth. 'I sang the other part, Dermott-Powell sang your line.'

'We'd've sung it together if we'd been in the same Election.'

'Dermott-Powell's voice was just about to go.'

'Mine ought to last about a year they say, so I daresay you'll get fed up with it in Chapel,' he grinned. Angus thought fleetingly of Dermott-Powell. However, together with the timid apprehensiveness which was so evident outside Angus' study, there was a frankness and disarming naivety about Carleton that Dermott-Powell had never possessed. It was this which made Carleton most endearing. He wanted to hug Carleton.

Carleton pushed back the sheets and sat up as a preliminary to getting out of the bed, exposing the skin of his stomach where there was a gap in his pyjamas. Perhaps subconsciously recalling Singleton's gesture on the night of his own solo, almost automatically Angus placed his hand as Singleton had placed his all those years before and, uncannily, just as Angus had done in identical circumstances, Carleton placed his own hand on top of Angus', finger for finger. Suddenly, realising what was happening, Angus tried to draw away, but Carleton put his other hand there too and, with a sort of sleepy stretch, pushed Angus' hand down the smooth skin until, with a confusion of disbelief, dread and, deep down, excitement, Angus felt his fingers halted by Carleton's small stiff arousal. He was as uncertain whether Carleton's gesture had been altogether accidental, as he was certain of his own immediate, urgent tumescence.

Carleton said, matter-of-factly, 'I say Angus, does this happen to you sometimes. Going all stiff I mean? In bed? Or in the bath?' He asked without embarrassment, with the earnest, almost scientific, enquiry of a child who questions the only adult he knows he can wholly respect and trust with a particularly delicate confidence.

Momentarily lost for words in his own panic, Angus was, providentially, directed by Carleton's ingenuousness. Casually disengaging his hand, he managed to reply in an affectionate but objective tone which almost matched Carleton's. 'It's called an erection, actually. It happens now and then to everyone. Nothing at all to worry about.'

'I'm not worried.' Carleton put his feet on the floor, stood up and stretched again. Yawning, he said, 'It's just that I just heard some of my Division talking about it today.' He stopped and grinned, 'Not Ansell's Men!'

'Oh, Ansell's Men don't worry about what others say,' Angus answered with helpfully conventional chauvinism. He was pleased to move to less treacherous ground. He turned towards his bookshelf. 'How do you like it at Ansell's, now you've settled in?' It was a rhetorical question.

'Not much!'

His imperception had been such that it was the last thing he expected to hear. Looking closely at Carleton he could see lashes beaded with tears and the lip trembled. So he said quickly, pretending not to have noticed, 'Oh, after a bit you'll find we're not so bad.' He spoke with artificial brightness.

'It's...it's ...' Not knowing the word for impersonal, Carleton stammered, 'It's so different from home,' and burst into tears.

' He's homesick!' The revelation washed over Angus. Perhaps that's why he's looked so tense? He said quietly, 'Come on, talk about home if you like. It sometimes helps.' Carleton clung to him fiercely and Angus remembered how in different circumstances he once had clung to Singleton. He was only thankful that Carleton was not hysterical as he himself had been.

Then, like a summer shower, as suddenly as it had occurred, the moment passed and Carleton was recovering his composure. Angus could still feel the dampness of tears on his own pyjamas. Slipping an arm round the slight shoulders he gave a reassuring hug. 'Better?' He felt Carleton nod. At the same time he became aware that the boy still pressing himself to Angus was once again sexually roused. Angus was aware too of his own swift hardening. So, taking Carleton by both shoulders, he pushed him gently to arms' length and said reassuringly, 'You're okay? Breathe in deeply.'

Carleton took two or three deep breaths. 'I'm all right now, Angus. Thanks. I'm very sorry. I've never done that before. You must think me pretty wet.'

'We've all felt like that. Singing a solo is tough on the nerves, even if you've done it before. I'll not tell anyone,' he added, answering the question before it was asked. Something prompted him to say, 'Perhaps when you're a Praefaector, you can do the same for somebody in the Junior Election.'

Carleton laughed; as always, it lighted up his whole face, 'I don't think I'll ever be a Praefaector like you or Ellerman.'

Completely in control once more, Angus said, 'I'll tell you a secret, we all knew Ellerman would be Head of House but nobody ever thought I'd be a Praefaector! This year we're so hard-up they had to have even me,' he added with comic self-mockery. 'You'd better cut along now, or we shall both die of pneumonia.'

Carleton hurried off.

Angus' own sexual excitement was now entirely abated. He had refused to succumb. He did not want it associated with Carleton. Carleton would be as dismayed by overt sexuality as he would have been with Singleton. 'Carleton is not Dermott-Powell. Or Ellerman. Or Simonsen. Or me.' Carleton was different. How vulnerable he was. Angus glowed with a sense of purpose. Carleton must be sheltered – preserved, like a precious relic. That would be his task. He was filled with the confidence of crusading zeal. Perhaps obscurely he felt that he would also be restoring a part of himself that he had too long forgotten – a quality which quite unknown to him, Singleton had cherished so passionately.

He shivered. He was cold. He climbed into bed.

All his rationalising and crusading idealism proved to be of little avail, for he had been exceptionally aroused during those minutes with Carleton. Hardly had he fallen into a deep and heavy sleep than he was overtaken by an orgasm of such totality that his body was convulsed by the spasm; lights danced before his eyes. Projected suddenly back into wakefulness and genuinely alarmed by the intensity, he even wondered miserably whether he might have suffered a heart attack.

When he realised what had occurred, he feared it would demolish the restraint he had so carefully exercised during the previous year as completely as if he had never attempted it, and leave in its place insistent lust frightening in its urgency. Self-imposed, his comparative abstinence was nothing more than a temporary damming up of insupportable pressures which, now released, must sweep him along. Exhausted by disappointment and self-loathing, he felt almost too lethargic to remove the unwelcome evidence of what, he recognised with consuming despair, must be irredeemable decadence.

※

Subsequently Angus began to come to terms with himself and with reality, although it turned out to be a complex and long-drawn-out process. He was relieved to be confirmed in his supposition that Carleton had not the slightest inkling of his near fall from grace and, with a spark of shame, realised the boy was protected by his apparent total incomprehension of sexuality as much as his own hard-won self-discipline. He should, he knew, distance himself from Carleton. He made attempts to do so, but they were half-hearted for he had begun increasingly to look forward to the few minutes' chatter each evening. Often he would deliberately lengthen it, by appearing earlier than had been his custom, absenting himself from the customary gossipy, toast-making sessions in Big Study. On other occasions, overcome by guilt, he sought to make up for this indulgence by appearing very late and packing a sleepy Carleton off immediately. Carleton seemed to notice no inconsistency and he, for his own part, eventually shrugged off the last remaining vestiges of reticence. Inside the study their intimacy was as complete as if they had known each other all their lives; door shut, Ansell's did not exist.

Alert to the hazards such intimacy conferred, and particularly to his own vulnerability, Angus knew he must avoid creating a situation where he would be unable to contain the impulses which so often seemed to engulf him. However, as the days passed, he occasionally doubted whether, even if he found himself incapable of restraint, there was anything which could blur Carleton's entrancing innocence. Fortunately a small, fragile thread continued to insist that such lines of thought, however seductive, must inevitably betray him. It forced him to acknowledge that, when Tassel Night came, to argue it would be doing Carleton no kindness to keep him in ignorance of the Ansell's tradition, would be selfish casuistry entirely convenient to his own lustful inclinations.

However, it did nothing to quell the other persistent subtle voice whispering persuasively, 'Why not be selfish occasionally? After all, something of the sort is only to be expected in such a close, intense community.' Fragments of Ellins' lecture, conveniently out of context and distorted by Ansell's gossip, came quickly into his mind to support such argument. *At least Tassel Night's a safety valve*, a 'control'. '*It's safest to formalise sex*,' he remembered Ellerman saying. Then he recalled Snider's quietly retorting, 'That was a utilitarian argument for licensing brothels.'

So it was that his dilemma grew. As the days passed, Angus found himself tugged both ways. The urgency of physical desire, which disgusted him once the phase had passed, was always succeeded by white-hot determination that he would never exploit Carleton's wide-eyed trust and devotion. Paradoxically, the intimacy encouraged by Warming, although beset by temptations, helped to defuse other tensions. He knew he would have found it insupportable had Carleton been Ellerman's Warmer for instance.

Nonetheless, he returned more than once to the treacherous, convenient but entirely unproven notion that Carleton was less hesitant than he himself had been. At such moments as these he found himself anticipating the allowed licence of Tassel Night, for he suspected that he would be unable to emulate Singleton's self-restraint and, furthermore, that he might not wish to try. As passage of time began to blunt memory of the panic which had submerged him on the night of Carleton's solo, these subversive notions gained a more insidious grip on his imagination. Ansell's was right to allow them all to come to terms with their sexuality. Tassel Night conferred a moment of guiltless license, to which a blind eye was turned. No – not a blind eye. The convenient thing about Tassel Night was that it attracted no eye at all. It was accepted by everyone, so went quite unremarked. Perhaps, had it involved only those who were Praefaectors and Tassels (or even those who could cover-up) Angus would have been more easily won over, without any qualms. The seditious voices were alluring: 'Forget your piddling scruples. The junior Election don't mind at all! Did you, when it finally happened?' Nonetheless, however strongly part of him embraced the spurious validity of such persuasions, he remained uncomfortable by the fact that each new Election was expected to participate as a matter of course.

Thus Angus' conscience, which had always remained to sting him however deeply he submerged it, proved to be his most unrelenting and inconvenient adversary. Not least, it forced him to recognise that, for all his crusading determination to preserve Carleton's innocence, the unwholesome truth was more mixed and muddy. For all his exemplary promises, some part of him craved for more than a chaste, fraternal relationship. At such moments, realising the younger boy admired him even more passionately and uninhibitedly than he had admired Singleton, Angus' baser instincts implied that Carleton would be a willing, even an eager, participant. He himself would have submitted without hesitation, indeed enthusiastically, to any suggestion made by Singleton. After all, he told himself brutally, he had accepted, without demur, the gross initiation of Dawes – whom he had positively disliked. Better himself, whom Carleton admired, than a Dawes or a Bartlett after he'd left.

Thus it was, throughout this continuous muddled, tainted, catechism, Angus strove fiercely to maintain his altruistic campaign to look after Carleton. It was a measure of the romantic idealism and the remaining vestiges of his own innocence, that it never crossed his mind that he might salvage his own integrity in the struggle to do so.

Several times he was tempted to return to St Anne's in Priest Street where he could cleanse himself by admitting his inclinations at the grille in the dark Confessional. Except that too was tainted now; remembering the roughness of that tobacco-tainted cassock, he could never again unburden himself to Father Dunsley.

In rational moments, however, he knew it would make no difference; he no longer believed Confession to be a Sacrament as The Digger had insisted. Instead, he was drawn with increasing frequency to Hopkins, as though the poems held somewhere a key to his tortured self-debate. The sonnets particularly took on new, almost revelatory meanings. Whether he was working, running Marathon, or in Chapel, he found himself constantly reciting diverse lines to himself until words and lines ran together, forming one continuous monologue. *I cast for comfort I can no more get...My own heart let me have more pity on...I wake and feel the fell of dark, not day. What hours, O what black hours we have spent this night...*

Once, during a long, boring Sunday Sermon, he became conscious of a pew neighbour eyeing him curiously and he found he was saying softly, but distinctly, *I am gall, I am heartburn, God's most deep decree / Bitter would have me taste: my taste was me.* Embarrassed, he turned the other way where his eye fell on Carleton in the choir. Immediately other lines came to him, *To what serves mortal beauty – dangerous does set dancing blood.* The phrases swam round and round in his head.

Back in his study he read Sonnet 65 and re-read it, although he had long since committed the lines to memory;

> *O the mind, mind has mountains; cliffs of fall*
> *Frightful sheer; no man fathomed.*

How much more he could have said now, had he been preparing The Greystoke! He recalled something he had entirely forgotten until that moment – Craigie had quoted those same lines, before saying, 'Who knows what Hopkins was thinking about when he wrote that?'

> *Hold them cheap*
> *May who ne'er hung there.*

Now he himself 'hung there'. He still did not know why Hopkins had written those lines, but felt sure he knew how Hopkins felt when he wrote it – as he, Angus, felt, isolated, alone, at the edge of some precipitous chasm whose depths possessed a terrible, fascinating magnetism.

One week slipped into another, Angus found, when Carleton was in his room, that he was inclined to engineer a light-hearted excuse to touch him casually, light-heartedly, gently to tug an ear, or a lock of hair. Or contrive a situation where Carleton had to brush against him accidentally. Sometimes he imagined that Carleton recognised the pretence and did not object in the least. The construction he put upon this at such moments allowed him to encourage himself to believe that more explicit physical contact, when it came, as inevitably it must — or so it seemed to him at such moments of self-deception — would be welcomed.

Afterwards, sickened by these lapses into imagination and sensuality, overcome by remorse, he swung violently to the other extreme. No! He would *not* be like Dawes! Or Bartlett! Or Maunder! Or like himself and Simonsen. Especially not that. So, in Chapel the following morning he prayed with passionate fervour to be offered a solution, a release, or at very least, to be given strength to suppress that part of his nature of which, kneeling there in the dim light from the stained glass, he was so bitterly and sincerely ashamed. On these occasions the words accompanying Mendelssohn's music seemed to offer hope.

> *I waited for the Lord*
> *And He heard my complaint.*

Although he prayed fervently that the Lord would 'hear his complaint', day followed day and there was no diminution of the struggle. It seemed that his own battle, like Hopkins', involved a struggle against a treacherous, relentless adversary lodged entirely within himself. In Chapel, it all seemed so easy, victory seemed within his grasp; he departed buoyed with confidence. Away from Chapel, moments of naked lust prompted him so fiercely that he could even relish the prospect of his eventual failure.

V

Not long after Carleton's solo, Snider spoke once again in favour of abolition of capital punishment. On this occasion however, the debate was well advertised and so Great Hall was packed. The forces of conservatism, chagrined by the previous result, turned out in strength. Most of the school was present. Even the local press were there. It began and ended in an atmosphere of suppressed tension. Snider spoke well. He was eloquent, factual and uncomfortably scientific about the technicality of hanging. Cranchester was not in a mood to listen. He carried on, through a barrage of cat-calls. Twice the meeting was called to order by the Chairman.

In contrast, his opponent, a tall, thin-faced boy called Cherryson, from The Doctor's, who had an unsuspected streak of the demagogue in him, was cheered almost every sentence. The debate veered wildly off course. Half those who spoke defended corporal punishment as well as capital punishment; in vain Snider and his supporters tried to interrupt on points of fact. Snider's summing-up was hardly heard. The vote was taken.

Under the impact of the excitement of the moment, most of those who had been persuaded by Snider on the previous occasion deserted the cause. He got nine votes. There were more than three hundred and fifty against. When the result was announced, a great cheer went up and it continued time after time. Despite this, there was no animosity towards Snider. He was seen in the light of the gallant loser, the eccentric who had battled against fearful odds. In its way Ansell's was quite proud of him.

Angus was one of the few who did not attend. On his return Mawsom said, 'You know Ellerman voted for Snider!'

'Ellerman did? But he was furious with Snider last time.'

'I know, but he said he was damned if he was going to vote for some damned fascist from The Doctor's when there was an Ansell's Man around.'

Angus laughed: 'I suppose I might have worked that out. It always seems to be Ansell's versus the rest of Cranchester. What about you?'

Mawsom looked sheepish. 'I didn't vote.'

As might have been predicted the national press was entirely uninterested in this reversal of the previous verdict.

※

Angus was getting up for breakfast when Ellerman put his head in the door. 'I want to see all Praefaectors in Big Study before breakfast.' He vanished. It had to be something important for Ellerman to carry his own message. The rest were already there, still tying ties. Notting was lacing up his shoes.

'What's up, Ellerman?'

Ellerman shut the door. 'I found this under my door when I got up this morning.' He waved a blue envelope. 'Listen, *Dear Ellerman, I've had about enough of bloody Ansell's. I'm not coming back unless I'm allowed to cover-up and unless you tell that sadist Notting to lay off. I thought the*

Christian Brothers were bad enough, but bloody Notting's tanned my arse every day this week and I'm buggered if I'll Warm his bloody bed for him. I'm staying at The White Hart until I hear from you. If I don't hear, I'm getting the London train. It's signed Arnold-Ferguson, though you could guess that from the language.'

Notting said viciously, 'Sidey little sod! I was going to suggest a Praefaectors', even though it's his first Half!'

'Why?'

'Last night he told me I could Warm my own bloody bed! I'd tanned his arse for not getting it warm enough two nights ago. Then he didn't Warm the next night, so I tanned it again. Hard.'

Baker said, 'Serves him right.'

Ellerman asked, with deceptive quietness, 'Just how many times did you get him to tighten-up this last week Notting?'

Notting stopped a moment, then mumbled, 'It must've been every day.'

'And you gave him?'

'Half a dozen each time.'

'What with AC breaking the place up and you behaving like something out of *Tom Brown's Schooldays*, I wonder if I'm in a madhouse. You know that Craigie's down on excessive punishment at the moment.'

Notting grinned. 'Don't worry, I only put the first one in the book.'

Ellerman said forcefully, 'Then I suggest that you put the rest in now Arnold-Ferguson's bound to tell Craigie.'

'Hell! I hadn't thought of that.'

'And,' said Ellerman, 'if anyone else has been omitting to sign up – as we all have – then I suggest we do it now. In chronological order, before I tell Craigie.'

Snider said, 'Well, couldn't we get him back before anyone knows?'

'After all,' Baker added, 'he's a damn good rugger player.'

Ellerman stared at him, 'If you think, Baker, that I'm prepared to let a Aussie oik like that dictate terms, you've got another think coming.'

'Craigie'll stop him when he sees that letter.'

'This letter will not have been seen by me, officially, until after the London train leaves. Craigie's not going to see it at all. I'll simply tell Craigie he's gone. The letter was addressed to me after all.'

So it was that Arnold-Ferguson vanished.

✵

At lunch a few days later, Craigie said he wanted to talk with the Praefaectors immediately after lunch and asked them to join him for coffee. They sat uncomfortably in the comfortable study. The extent of Craigie's library was impressive. The great black grand piano polished to mirror-like sheen even more so.

'Yesterday I had an uncomfortable meeting in London with the Arnold-Ferguson family. The boy told me, in front of his parents, a number of things which I must say I found it hard to believe. He told me for instance that he'd been beaten every day in his last week for failing to get your bed warm enough, Notting.' Notting kept his eyes to the floor. 'Imagine my further dismay when I examined the punishment book and found that it was true. As far as I can see, Notting, you dealt him forty-two cuts last week. I notice that you also beat several other boys in the House. I think that is irresponsible. Here and now, Notting, I am withdrawing from you, the right to beat anyone at all. If you think they need it, you can send them to me.'

Notting looked stunned.

Ellerman, interpolated, smoothly, tactfully, 'If I might suggest, sir, perhaps Notting could refer to me before getting anyone to tighten-up.'

Craigie said acidly, 'I have already decided what shall happen, thank you. I would have been more impressed with your suggestion, Ellerman, had you noticed that Notting was behaving like a savage before Arnold-Ferguson set off from Cranchester. Moreover, I told you, Ellerman, some time ago, that I expected you to ensure the punishment book to be kept up-to-date. It is clear to me that many of the entries so far were done all at once, in a hurry. Probably on Sunday when you realised Arnold-Ferguson had gone – and why he had gone. Is there any one of you who thinks he is able to keep discipline without beating?' He looked round. 'How very disappointing. I may as well tell you that I am seriously thinking of moving Ansell's into the twentieth century and forbidding Praefaectors to beat anyone. I'll give you my decision at the end of the Half. Meantime, as from now, if anyone does so without entering it in the book *at the time*, he will cease to be a Praefaector.'

Ellerman said, 'I'm sorry, sir. The book was my fault. I ought to have insisted.'

'Yes, Ellerman, you ought. Thank you for your apology. There's something else. According to Arnold-Ferguson, the Praefaectors "Inspect" all the new Election, usually on the first or second night of the Half. Is that correct?'

'They all come into Big Study. We need to make sure we know who they are, sir.'

'Then it seems a little extreme to make them stand naked on the table, to make sure who they are, Ellerman. Most beaks, for instance, have to manage it, even when Castonians are fully clothed. I think you might have been somewhat surprised, not to say indignant, had I insisted I got you all to do the same when I came into Ansell's.'

'It's always happened, sir. It's only a bit of fun really.'

'Was it fun for you Ellerman, when you'd been here one day? Or you, Angus?'

Angus felt himself grow hot. He muttered, 'Not much, sir.'

Craigie went on in even tones, 'I am against this sort of initiation ceremony, or indeed initiation ceremonies of any sort. As far as I am concerned, every new boy is just as much a member of the House as anyone else. May I also say that I think the custom of not allowing boys to "cover-up" as I understand the term is, seems to me positively barbaric. I gather, incidentally, that Lyman, who is quite senior, may still not "cover-up" because he has Jewish antecedents.'

'No, sir, it's nothing to do with…'

'He thinks it is, Ellerman. That is nasty. I've just fought a war to end that sort of discrimination. I don't blame any of you personally for a custom which has been long-established. However, we shall end it. That was the last "Inspection" and Lyman must be given permission to "cover-up" at once. As from the beginning of next Half, I shall be obliged if you, Ellerman, will give everyone permission to "cover-up", including the Junior Election. Or would you prefer me to give it?'

Ellerman said woodenly, 'No, sir, It's all right. I'll give it.'

He looked towards the door.

Interpreting his glance, Craigie said coolly, 'I'm so sorry, but I must keep you even longer.' He paused and went over to the window. 'I've been wondering when I should broach this, but I suppose it might as well be now.' He paused and turned to them. 'Last term, you'll remember, Watson and Orton left us. Watson was leaving anyway. Orton hasn't come back. He's at another school and he seems to be happy. Happier than he was here.'

There was a pause.

'His uncle wrote to me – the father's dead as you know and his uncle's his guardian. It was not a nice letter to receive. He had talked to the boy during the holiday and he learned a number of things that, not surprisingly, much disturbed him and which, I may say, very greatly trouble me. He is very understanding. He was himself at Cranchester – but not an Ansell's Man – a very long time ago and agreed to let me sort the matter out. From what his nephew said – of course the boy was very upset and emotional when he set off, nor did the uncle wish to go into details in a letter – he gathered that the boy may have been deliberately corrupted; initiated into wholly unacceptable institutional sexual practices.'

They had all guessed what was coming, but that made it no less stunning. Into the silence, Ellerman said, 'We all realised that Watson…'

Craigie interrupted brusquely. 'Oh no, Ellerman, I'm afraid I don't think it was all Watson. In fact it seems to his uncle that young Orton retains genuine affection and respect for Watson. At the same time as I was up in town to see the Arnold-Fergusons, I met Watson, at my Club, by arrangement. He was reticent and very loyal to Ansell's, but I received the impression there may be certain let us call them "traditions" connected with Tassel Night for instance…'

'Watson obviously has an axe to grind, sir.'

'I realise that – however, before you tell me Watson's completely untrustworthy, I should say that he did not deny what Orton's uncle implied, nor seek to excuse himself.' Craigie looked round. 'Of course, neither Watson nor Orton would give any names. Although Orton's uncle did say the boy told him that the only people he felt he could talk to, apart from his own Election, were Watson, and Angus too, I was glad to hear.' He waited. 'However, in view of Watson's confession I shall assume that whoever else was responsible for such unsavoury conduct has now left.'

There was a visible relaxation of tension.

'I'm sure you'll agree that such "traditions", were they found to exist of course, would be utterly repugnant to me. To us all, I assume? For that reason I think it best that there shall be no more Tassel Nights – at least for the time being.'

Ellerman stood up and said quietly, very firmly, 'Sir, I'm afraid you can't do that.'

'Oh, I'm afraid I can, Ellerman. And I do.'

'Please reconsider it, sir. Tassel Night's enjoyed by everyone.'

Craigie looked straight at Ellerman. 'From what Orton's uncle and Watson told me, I can, unfortunately, believe that Tassel Night is "enjoyed" as you put it, by some people and I am very sorry indeed that it should be so. However, I wonder whether the Junior Election enjoys it as much as you do? I have already considered the matter very fully, Ellerman, and I repeat, there will be no Tassel Nights in future. To the outside world this may seem the best House at Cranchester, but I must tell you all, that to me it seems that each time I turn over a stone, I find too much I dislike to be able to agree with the world at large. Take this custom of "Warming" for instance. It seems to me it is something which could be, shall we say, "misinterpreted". It could even be thought to encourage sexual immorality. I shall certainly think about stopping it; I was inclined to forbid it at the start of this Half. I'll tell you whether it is to continue next Half. Have any of you any questions?'

Notting said, foolishly and belligerently, 'You're trying to ruin Ansell's! We shan't let you.'

Visibly, Craigie stopped himself from making a quick, angry answer. He drew a deep breath, with evident restraint, he said courteously, 'Considering that you, Notting, gave a new boy, in his pyjamas, forty-two cuts over seven days and there was, apparently not one Praefaector in Ansell's who even noticed your sadistic behaviour, I'm not sure there is much left to ruin.' His voice became noticeably sharp. 'That's all, gentlemen. Thank you. You may go.'

They left in silence. Outside, in Din Room, they stood demoralised, without speaking. Ellerman said, 'Some of us have a practice. We'll all meet in Big Study for tea.' They understood his tone.

Angus ran Marathon, his feet scuffing up fallen brown and yellow leaves. He was not surprised at Craigie's ultimatum but he was surprised to discover that he resented Craigie's interference and, at that moment, saw Craigie through Notting's eyes. Craigie would ruin Ansell's He was resentful of that and, in his resentment, it was easy to quell the awkward little voice that whispered to him that Craigie was entirely justified. He ran hard up the hill; instead of keeping to the path, strode through dying bracken which whipped at his legs and brought up minute beaded lines of blood where the sharp fronds lacerated his calves.

Anger and resentment of Craigie stemmed, he knew, from a sense of guilt. He remembered how Orton had presented himself at his Manger. Was it possible that he, Angus, was the 'corrupter' in question? Was that what Orton had meant? Or had Orton's uncle surmised more than intended? No, Orton had named him as one of his saviours. Thank God, there had been no other names. He guessed from the tone of Craigie's words, that the Housemaster did not really believe all those responsible had left Ansell's at the end of the previous Half. It was intended as a warning for the future. He came to the ford and splashed through it.

'Craigie's is making a typically silly fuss!' However, he could not even convince himself. He was glad Craigie had not asked them individually; The Digger would certainly have done so. On reflection, he realised Craigie appeared to believe Tassel Night concerned only the new Election and Praefaectors. He had not been a Praefaector on Tassel Night the previous Half; Craigie would have absolved him of possible complicity. He felt a thump of guilty relief. It did not occur to him until much later that abolition of Tassel Night would resolve his dilemma over Carleton.

❋

It was a very warm autumn, and they had opened the window. Last leaves still clung to the chestnut tree. However a fire burned, battered toasting-forks stood round it like soldiers weapons during a lull in the fighting. They were drinking tea from the array on a battered tea tray.

Snider said, 'Well, there's nothing we can do about it. Anyhow, perhaps Craigie's right. After all we've just won a war and we ought to look forward, not back to the past.'

Baker said, 'It's bloody nonsense, Snider, and you know it. He's a red!'

'Why the hell Watson and Orton couldn't have shut up—' Baker began.

Angus said quietly, 'Perhaps Orton would have stayed if he hadn't been facing a Praefaectors.' That silenced them.

Notting said acidly, 'We might have known you'd back Craigie. He'd have probably been idiotic enough to make you Head of House if you weren't so feeble.'

As a matter of fact, I think Craigie's wrong. But I can't see there's much we can do about it,' Snider said.

'We must destroy him!'

They turned. He stood in front of the fire. 'Anyone else for toast?'

Snider asked, with withering false politeness, 'Precisely how are you going to do that, my dear Ellerman? Even you, Ellerman, can't be proposing the perfect murder!'

Ellerman buttered his toast carefully. 'Nothing so melodramatic. He must be persuaded to resign.' There was an incredulous silence.

Baker said, 'Why should he?'

'Because,' Ellerman said, 'he has a weakness. A flaw if you like. Haven't you spotted it yet?'

They looked at him blankly. 'And,' Ellerman continued, 'I shall use it.'

'What about Tassel Night?' Notting interrupted impatiently.

'Even if we don't have one this Half, *officially*,' Ellerman emphasised the word heavily, 'it will be back *officially* next Half. I promise.'

'How can you be sure of that, Ellerman?' Mawsom said quietly. 'You make it sound like a declaration of war.'

'Would you disagree if it were?'

Mawsom said nothing more. Notting closed the window. 'Well, you can count on me.'

Snider shrugged his shoulders, 'If you hadn't been so heavy-handed, Notting, we'd never be in this mess.'

'Craigie ought not to be at Cranchester, let alone Housemaster of Ansell's.' It was a statement of fact, not an opinion. The misty smell of an October evening began to drown the tang of toasted bread. Ellerman continued authoritatively, 'A showdown would have come some time. It may as well be now.' He sounded utterly confident.

Mawsom said slowly, 'Exactly what's in your mind, Ellerman?'

Ellerman turned to Angus and said, 'Did you ever ask Carleton?'

'Ask him what?' Angus sounded completely mystified.

'Why he keeps visiting Craigie after Curfew?'

'Oh that. Yes I did ask, but he wouldn't say. I didn't like to press him. He seemed too embarrassed.'

Baker said petulantly, 'For God's sake, Ellerman! What's this got to do with your mysterious plan?'

'Isn't that obvious?'

'It's not to me!'

Ellerman said with elaborate patience, 'Carleton's been going over to Private almost every evening, before Tosher and Warming.' He held up one finger. Then he added a second: 'In his dressing-gown. He put up a third finger: 'Did that ever happen with The Digger?' He held up a fourth: 'Craigie's a bachelor and a clergyman.'

'So was The Digger,' snapped Snider.

'But,' Ellerman continued with elaborate patience, 'The Digger never invited pretty little boys to Private each evening. Craigie's all music and painting. Moreover, when he first came to Cranchester he ran the Scouts and we read about scoutmasters and little boys in the *News of the World* every week.'

Snider laughed. 'What *bollocks*, Ellerman. We don't have beaks like that in a place like Cranchester!'

Ellerman said with unemotional authority, 'There are people like that everywhere.' Angus thought of Father Dunsley. 'There's even been some sort of scandal at the Cathedral recently. Or haven't you heard?'

Angus said, 'Of course we've heard, but that doesn't give us the right to accuse Craigie. It's idiotic to think of him like that.'

Mawsom nodded in emphatic agreement.

'In that case,' Ellerman said, 'why wouldn't Carleton tell even Angus what he gets up to? And you said he was embarrassed, AC.'

Angus said, 'There's bound to be a simple explanation.'

'Then *why* wouldn't Carleton tell *you*? He seems to think you're some kind of God,' Ellerman insisted, an edge to his voice for the first time.

Was it possible that this really was the reason for Carleton's unusual reticence? 'Balls!' It was so unusual for Angus that they all knew Ellerman had pinked him.

'Well, let's have your suggestion then?'

Baker said placatingly. 'Do you really think that's what happens, Ellerman?'

'What other explanation is there? Why do you think Craigie refused to punish that pretty little tart Orton, after as good as sacking Watson?'

'He wanted Orton's pretty little arse to himself!' Notting burst out. 'What if Carleton won't tell us?' Notting asked.

'Oh he will,' Ellerman said easily. 'At least, he'll tell us enough for us to frighten Craigie off.'

'Carleton'd never put up with that sort of thing,' Angus said agitatedly.

Ellerman lifted his eyebrows at the others, implying, 'What did I tell you,' and said, 'Come on, AC. Just because Carleton *looks* as if butter wouldn't melt.... You've been around Cranchester long enough to know better than that.'

Angus said rapidly, 'If Craigie really is doing what you say, then I agree the sooner he goes the better. I'm quite sure it's not at Carleton's wish, he's just a very small boy who ought to be at his Private still.' He had spoken with some passion.

'All right! All right! Only don't make an ass of yourself as Singleton did over you. I'd not be as understanding as Maunder.'

With barely suppressed fury, Angus said evenly, 'I seem to remember Maunder understood you well enough. Me too.'

For the first time Ellerman faltered and, momentarily, refused to meet Angus' gaze; the others were aware he had been put off his stroke by an undercurrent they could not interpret. He recovered himself and said, smiling, 'Exactly, *I* knew what I was doing as far as Maunder was concerned.' His tone implied that Carleton knew very well how far he could go with both Craigie and Angus.

'Well, I didn't at Carleton's age.'

'Never a truer word. However, it's hardly conceivable that Ansell's should get two ACs in one century. Nor two Singletons for that matter.' He was not angry, but condescending. He put a hand on Angus' shoulder.

Angus thrust it away. 'At least Singleton gave me time to find out about Ansell's in my own way!'

Taken aback by Angus' vehemence and realising that he had strayed from his own main line of argument, Ellerman said soothingly, 'You have to admit that, at Carleton's age, you were so wet we practically had to wring you out.' Angus bit his lip, recognising the justice of the jibe. 'You owe Ansell's something. It's the only House in Cranchester worth a fig. It's made you. It's even made you a Praefaector.' There was a general laugh. 'And, despite everything, you enjoy the traditions as much as anyone else now you're at the top. Including Tassel Night.'

Angus' fury died as quickly as it had arisen. 'All right, Ellerman you've made your point.'

'That's why we're damned if Craigie's going to transform it into a kindergarten.'

At the door Angus turned. 'I don't disagree. Though I'm hanged if I ask Carleton again.'

✳

When he had gone there was an audible relaxing of tension.

Mawsom said, 'You shouldn't tease AC like that! If you're right, Ellerman, there's bound to be a Hell of a row and that won't do Ansell's much good.'

'If we handle this properly, nobody except us'll ever know. We promise Craigie that we'll keep quiet if he resigns and leaves Cranchester.'

'Do you think he'll accept those terms?'

'He'll have to,' Ellerman said, 'if he wants to go on teaching somewhere else and stay out of jug.'

'If he's what you say, he shouldn't be teaching anywhere…' Snider began.

Ellerman interrupted him disdainfully: 'Who cares what he does, or who with, as long as he gets out of Ansell's? Agreed?'

'It's probably blackmail,' Mawsom said. 'Mind you, justifiable I suppose. Anyway it all depends on what Carleton says.'

'Even Angus can't find that out!'

'In that case, we'll have to persuade the little tart to tell us the truth.'

'Oh come on, Ellerman! Carleton's hardly a tart. We can't accuse him of that. He hardly dares open his mouth to anyone but Angus.'

Ellerman said, 'I reckon he'd've been mixed up in that Cathedral business, after all he was there last Half. Anyone who looks like him must be a tart, or soon will be one at any rate.'

'Well, you'd probably know all about that, Ellerman.' Snider snapped.

Imperturbably Ellerman said, 'Yes. And it shouldn't have been allowed to happen. I don't intend to allow it to happen while I'm Head of House. But at the moment I'm more interested in these visits to Private. Carleton's going to be Craigie's downfall. After Craigie's gone, I daresay a Praefaectors' will give Carleton a clearer view of what Ansell's thinks of pretty little tarts. And it won't be in the punishment book, because we won't have a punishment book.'

'What about Angus?' Baker said suddenly. 'He's always rather taken Craigie's side in our discussions.'

Ellerman said shrewdly, 'At the moment, dear old AC has girded himself with Aunty Singleton's armour. He sees himself on a white charger with a sacred mission to rescue pretty, innocent-looking Carletons from growing up and especially from filthy sex! So he won't be **v**ery pleased with Craigie.'

'If,' Snider interrupted, 'there really is anything in your theory about Craigie.'

Notting said, 'Of course Ellerman's right, Snider. It's obvious!'

'Well, it wasn't very obvious to anyone except Ellerman until half an hour ago,' Snider persisted doggedly. 'However, if you're right, Ellerman, and I must say you're pretty convincing, then we're all with you.'

'As for Tassel Night,' Ellerman concluded, 'it'll be back officially next Half, as I've already said. What's more, there'll be no nonsense about abolishing Warming or covering-up either. The next Housemaster will find Ansell's just as it was under The Digger. As we've always been.'

※

Ellerman's bombshell about Carleton's visits to Private exacerbated Angus' personal confusion. Despite his public scepticism, he was unnerved by Ellerman's belief that Carleton was being seduced by Craigie and, even more, by the inference that Carleton might not have be an unwilling participant. Or was he implying that Carleton invited seduction? He recalled Dermott-Powell's knowingness, the evidently practised fingers of Simonsen; Carleton too had been at the Choir School.

At the same time as Angus strove to hold at bay an everyday world where events and developments at Ansell's impinged with increasing urgency, he struggled against the demands of a sexuality he had believed to be tamed the previous Half but which reawakened, every so often blazed unpredictably, uncontrollably. Carleton personified both platonic idealism and carnal temptation. Moreover the corrupting notion against which he had been unable to close his mind, namely that, even if not inviting physical intimacy Carleton might be, at the very least, compliant with somebody he trusted, suggested to Angus that Craigie might be precisely such a person.

His continual, tortured, self-analysis had gone virtually unnoticed by his contemporaries, which served to increase his own sense of isolation. He set himself to achieve punishing times on Marathon, running to the point of exhaustion. There were nights he slept badly and, not surprisingly, there were occasions when he was morose.

Mawsom, always the most perceptive of his contemporaries, was the only one to recognise he had something on his mind, but all attempts to talk were rebuffed. One evening he mentioned it casually to Ellerman who merely raised an eyebrow and said, 'I'm surprised you haven't worked it out.'

'Worked what out?'

'What's on Angus mind? It's Carleton of course.'

'AC? You can't be serious!'

'I'm perfectly serious. Wasn't he a bit odd when we discussed that business about Carleton going to Private the other day?'

'I thought it was merely that he didn't believe you. He hardly seems to take any notice of Carleton about the place. It's not like Watson and Orton.'

'Not everyone makes a complete ass of themselves like those two. Anyhow, can you offer a better explanation?'

'I just thought it was AC being AC. He's been worse since he won the Greystoke and decided to try for Balliol. One of the Elephants told me he mutters to himself in Chapel. I suppose he always has thought too much for his own good...' Mawsom tailed off. After Ellerman's explanation, his own must sound very unconvincing, even to himself.

※

Angus and Mawsom clattered into Small Change. They had completed Marathon in a good time. Only Ellerman was there. 'Shall you win it this year too, AC?'

'Shouldn't think so. I was very lucky last time. It was so wet that the track got too muddy for anyone to catch me before Roman Gate. It's much later in the Half this year. I don't know why.'

'Are you encouraging the Junior Election to run?'

Angus paused: 'Should I?'

'I just thought Carleton might be a cross-country man,' Ellerman said pointedly. 'He's a hopeless footballer,' and, lightening his tone, added, 'A bit like you, AC. I'm sure he'd run if *you* suggested it.'

Angus plunged into the bath. Ellerman, on the point of leaving, said with affected casualness, 'That reminds me, has Carleton told you yet what he's up to in Private?'

Angus retorted abruptly, 'No! I don't intend to ask him again.'

Ellerman said distantly, 'I notice he hasn't had to tighten-up for you since the time you smashed the lamp.'

Angus keeping his voice even, wondered whether Ellerman were implying that Carleton ought to tighten-up if he refused to tell. 'As it happens, I now realise that the only reason he didn't Warm for me that time was because his Election told him that if he didn't tighten-up for me it would be a Praefaectors' on some other excuse. Was that your brilliant idea, I wonder, to hint that and "sic" them onto him?'

Ellerman flushed. 'I had nothing to do with it. If you let Carleton make an ass of himself, he'll have to take the consequences. I thought you'd learned that lesson a long time back.' He vanished through the steam.

Angus hurled a loofah into the grimy water. 'I don't know what Ellerman's on about? I haven't tanned Carleton's arse because he hasn't deserved it!' He appealed to Mawsom, 'What about you with Elveston?'

Mawsom said, 'Only about three times. Ellerman resents Craigie interfering in the matter of Warmers.'

The outside door banged behind Ellerman. After a while, Mawsom said, 'There's something you've never understood, AC, about Ansell's that is.'

'I've never understood Ansell's. Full stop!'

Mawsom persisted, 'As long as it's just sex and you're a Praefaector, nobody will take much notice – if it's not too obvious. If it's Tassel Night, nobody cares.' He paused and added half to himself. 'In fact, you might say that if you're a Praefaector or a Tassel, it's expected of you really.' He continued more vigorously, 'However Ansell's won't stand for anything more. Affection is out; Orton and Watson went too far for Ansell's. They were too fond of each other. Ellerman reckons they were in love – you know that?'

Angus grunted.

It was difficult for Mawsom to judge whether in agreement or dissent. 'What's more, whether or not Ellerman's on the warpath, it's only a matter of time before even your timid little Carleton puts a foot wrong and then Ellerman will expect you to take action again.'

'Which I shan't do!'

Mawsom said with a patient sigh, 'Exactly. So Big Study will take it out of your hands – as they took it out of Singleton's.'

'For God's sake let's forget about me and Singleton. Even on Tassel Night Singleton didn't...'

'Of course he didn't,' Mawsom interrupted. 'Everyone realised that, which only made it worse. Ansell's couldn't even write it off as randy old Singleton having a whale of a time after years of self-restraint! That would have been all right. As it was, Singleton thumbed his nose at Ansell's' customs. That's why you got a Praefaectors'. Your showing *side* was merely Maunder's excuse. If you aren't careful you'll cause the same sort of thing to happen to Carleton.'

Angus knew that Mawsom's analysis was correct. He said fiercely and meaningfully, 'If anything like that were to happen, I shouldn't keep quiet. I'd go to Craigie.'

Mawsom seemed not to have heard; he said thoughtfully, 'You know, AC, I suppose at the back of it all – you and Singleton I mean – there was a sort of fear...'

'I wasn't afraid of Singleton!'

'No I don't mean that. It's never occurred to me before now, and I'm not quite sure what I mean. I suppose it's just that if there's something or somebody who is still, well, innocent, the rest of us are afraid – ashamed of ourselves I suppose – and want to destroy it. Probably we want them to be like us, because we know we either don't want to be, or can't be like them even if we wish.' Mawsom was speaking aloud, as if to himself. 'Perhaps that accounts for Orton and Watson too,' he concluded, musing.

Angus had the uncomfortable feeling that he was almost an eavesdropper. He said abruptly, 'Orton wasn't innocent – certainly as far as Tassel Night was concerned!'

'You think he wasn't.'

'I *know* he wasn't,' Angus said unguardedly in a tone that denied contradiction.

Mawsom looked sharply across, 'Oh! I see.'

'And so,' persisted Angus, 'how the hell can Ellerman think Orton and Watson are like me and Singleton? Or,' he added quickly, 'me and Carleton, for that matter.'

Mawsom thought a while before replying, 'What you and Singleton had in common with Watson and Orton was that in both cases you valued your loyalty to each other more than your loyalty to Ansell's.' Mawsom paused then, genuinely surprised by his own perception, said with astonishment, 'I suppose you could say Ansell's is simply very jealous of rivals?' Lulled by the warm water, he continued in the same speculative vein, 'Now The Digger's gone, Craigie's looking for changes. Ellerman is not Maunder. What's more, Ellerman envies you. Or he's frightened of you.'

'You mean because of Carleton?'

'No, not really. I mean because of what you represent.'

Angus flicked back to an earlier remark. 'Did you really mean what you said about everyone wanting to destroy innocence, Mawsom?'

Emerging from his daydream, Mawsom said, surprised, 'Did I say that? I was probably talking nonsense, I almost dozed off.' He sounded as if he wished he could convince himself more strongly.

Angus said, 'Another thing, in my case the Praefaectors' didn't really work, did it? I mean it pushed me and Singleton closer if anything.'

'Yes, everyone realised that afterwards and I'd swear Maunder thought he'd gone too far. The real joke was that, in the end, it only needed that horny oaf Dawes to set you properly on the road to salvation, Ansell's style.' They were lying at opposite ends of the big tiled bath, talking through the drifting steam. Mawsom returned to his earlier theme: 'Ellerman has always envied you. I meant that.' He laughed. 'Do you know, AC, I even wondered whether you were blackmailing him during our second Autumn Half. He seemed to me to be very cautious of you.' Mawsom must have sensed the tension there in Big Study, when Ellerman had thought him about to reveal how Maunder had demolished him so contemptuously after he had beaten them both on his last evening. 'Anyhow, Ellerman now reckons he's got the upper hand because of Carleton. That means Carleton is very vulnerable.'

'I'd see Craigie if…'

'That would hardly make Carleton any more popular. You'd do better just to let things take their course.'

Angus pulled at his lip, obstinate.

Mawsom sat up and said quite gently but with great maturity, 'We all have to grow up, AC, Carleton will manage well enough without your cotton wool. After all, you won't be around to sort things out forever. What's more, the time will come when he won't want you to. Be realistic. For all Singleton's guidance, it didn't stop you and Simonsen. In the end you got fed up with Singleton, didn't you? As a matter of fact,' Mawsom went on, 'most of Ansell's thought Simonsen was the best thing that had happened to you, AC. It made you almost human.'

Angus said with self-sneering bitterness, 'You mean everyone was glad Angel Child was a Fallen Angel!'

Quietly, guiltily, Mawsom said, 'I suppose I do.'

'You're saying that Carleton's like I was at first?'

'I don't know. He hardly says anything except to you. Most of the time he looks scared stiff. Perhaps the real danger is that *you* think he's like you were.'

'Do you think Ellerman's right about Craigie?'

Mawsom considered: 'I don't know. I'm not sure. At first I thought Ellerman was going potty. The more I've thought about it.... After all, it *was* odd about Orton, wasn't it? The Digger would have had a fit – certainly given him a dozen-up, yet there was a lot he didn't seem to notice. Craigie notices a lot, but he wasn't thinking of punishing Orton because he's Junior Election.' The water was cooling. They climbed out onto the duckboards and grabbed towels. Mawsom said, 'He *is* interfering far too much in the day-by-day running of Ansell's. I don't reckon Ansell's customs are really as bad as all that. Do you?'

Angus did not reply. He wished he were able to say that he had grown out of Ansell's and its customs. He could have done so the previous Half. Now? He was no longer quite so sure.

※

On November 5th he stood at his study window after Curfew. Carleton came in. He said, 'Oh! Hello Angus! Here already?'

'I've not been to Tosher yet. I was watching the fireworks in Cranchester. You can see them from here.' Together they stood in companionable silence as rockets cut the dark night sky. About every four minutes there was a huge star-shell which burst into hundreds of crackers which they could hear exploding high in the air. They lost track of time till Carleton shivered suddenly.

'Hey! You're supposed to be Warming my bed!'

Carleton scrambled in. However, when Angus arrived back from Tosher there was a fire blazing.

Carleton said, 'I hope you didn't mind, I've collected quite a store of cones and things.'

'I suppose we ought to have a fire on Bonfire Night,' Angus replied amiably. 'Hang on, I even think I've got some toffee.'

They sat on the side of the bed chewing solidly at some tough sweet which effectively silenced conversation for a time. Carleton moved to put some more cones on the blaze. He looked very young in the firelight. When he came back to the bed he sat as close to Angus as he could.

'I say Angus, what *is* your Christian name? I mean I shan't use it if you don't want, but I'd like to know.'

'It won't be too difficult to remember. It's the same as yours.'

'I don't believe it!'

'No I'm not. Cross my heart and hope to die, if I'm telling you a lie,' and they both laughed as he cited the childish rhyme.

'Can I use it sometimes? In the holidays?'

Angus laughed, 'Well, as I shan't see you in the holidays and they'd scalp you if you used it in Ansell's...'

'We might meet in the holidays... . It's why I asked really. I think my mother's going to invite you to stay. Before Christmas. Will you come? I suppose I ought to have asked earlier. The first time she suggested it, I thought she was just being polite. You know what mothers are like...they don't understand about schools.'

He realised that Carleton was not joking, and then that he wanted to go very much, to be with Carleton away from Ansell's and Cranchester where they could resume the carefree chance, uncomplicated companionship of Silbury. At the end of the Summer Half – he would be no longer a Castonian – he'd arrange for Carleton to visit them in Scotland. Nobody in the family would wonder at it. He'd explain how Carleton had never been to Scotland and that his father was abroad, something to do with India and Independence. They would fish and sail the awkward boat on the loch.

It was so possible, so real, above all, so desirable, that he was lost in the daydream and had not responded to Carleton's question. Hastily he said, 'Well, if she writes, I'll see.' He tried deliberately to restrain himself from sounding too enthusiastic, although he was not sure why. Perhaps he felt that Ellerman might somehow find out. He knew his tone disappointed Carleton; he could see the boy wondering if he had ventured too far. So he went on warmly, 'I'd love to come, of course. But I live in Scotland, so it could be a bit difficult.' He gave Carleton's shoulder a reassuring squeeze.

Carleton's face brightened. 'Oh that's all right. You could come on your way home, couldn't you? You pass through London.'

For some reason he had assumed Carleton lived in the country. 'Yes I do. And I often stay in London on the way home. It's very kind of your mother.'

'Good! I've a special reason for asking you. But it's a secret.'

For the first time in years Angus thought of the invitation to visit the Simonsens. Carleton was not Simonsen, nor would be, and now there was no war, no flying bombs. The room, noticeably warmed by the blaze, encouraged intimacy.

'I say, Angus.'

'Yes?'

'Do you still want to know about my visits to Private?'

Angus felt his chest tighten. He said carefully, 'Only if you're sure you want to tell me.' He still had his arm on the younger boy's shoulder.

'Do you absolutely *promise* not to tell anyone else? Even Ellerman?'

'Of course, if that's what you want. Of course I'll promise.'

'Cross your heart?'

'Cross my heart!

And Carleton told him.

vi

They were drinking tea. Ellerman looked at the clock. He said, 'We're expecting Carleton.'

'Why?

'It's time he told us all about Craigie.'

'AC'll go through the roof!'

'He won't know, until we've done with Master Carleton. Don't forget it's AC's week in Big Dorm. That's why I've chosen tonight.'

Notting said, 'What's it to be, an unofficial Praefaectors'?'

'Don't be a bigger ass than you can help, Notting. Have you forgotten Craigie's bloody book?'

Carefully he placed the huge, heavy Bible with its worn binding, in the middle of the table.

Mawsom said, 'What's that for?'

'It's the dock,' Ellerman grinned. 'I think Carleton will feel more like telling us the truth if he's up there on God's Word.'

There came a timid knock. In a friendly voice Ellerman called out, 'Come.'

'Crichton said the Praefaectors wanted to see me.' Carleton glanced round.

'That's right, we do. Come in and shut the door. Do you know why you're here?'

Carleton, his dressing-gown tied untidily round him, small and scared, said indistinctly, 'No, Ellerman. It isn't for a Praefaectors'?'

'Why? Have you done anything to deserve one?'

'I don't think so, Ellerman.'

'Good. Let's keep it that way. All you have to do is tell the truth.'

Carleton looked puzzled.

'You've just come from Mr Craigie? From Private?'

Mechanically Carleton said, 'Yes, Ellerman.'

Ellerman continued, still in a friendly tone, 'Would you care to tell us what you've been up to?'

Carleton's face fell: 'If you don't mind, Ellerman, I'd rather not.'

Ellerman's voice hardened. 'I'm sorry you feel like that. You see that Lexicon and that Bible?'

'On the table, Ellerman?'

'Yes. You can take off your dressing-gown and get up there and stand on them.'

Carleton hesitated, unsure as to whether it was some sort of joke, but remembered the Inspection.

'I said, stand on it.' Ellerman picked up the switch. Carleton scrambled onto the table; gingerly he stepped onto the Bible and the Lexicon perched precariously above it. It made him look even more diminutive.

'What we want to know Carleton, is,' Ellerman said sharply, 'are—you—a—little—tart?' He spaced the words.

Now very frightened, Carleton shook his head as if trying to speak and managed to say at last, 'I don't think I understand, Ellerman? Do you mean a jam tart?' he asked in desperation, panic-stricken and puzzled.

Mawsom exploded with suppressed laughter but turned it into a cough.

'You've been here long enough to learn. Unless of course you knew already,' Ellerman continued, ignoring Mawsom.

'I don't understand you, Ellerman. Really.' Carleton cast round for aid and support.

'Angus isn't here to help you out. And he won't be. He's in Big Dorm.' Then suddenly he dropped his hectoring manner and smiled again. He asked amiably, 'By the way, is it true that one of the masters at the Cathedral was sacked last summer?'

Deceived by the return of the friendly tone, Carleton nodded, 'Oh, Mr Prinsep! Yes.'

'Why was that?'

Carleton said politely, 'The Dean told us we shouldn't discuss it with just anyone.'

'Well, it's all right to tell us. After all, we're not "just anyone" are we? We're Ansell's, like you.'

Carleton's face cleared at once. 'S'pose not. Well, the Dean said that Mr Prinsep had to go away because he wasn't very well. It sounded,' Carleton said confidentially, 'as if the Dean thought he'd gone a bit mental. We all agreed.'

'Do you know what the Dean meant?'

'I think so. The Dean asked us all lots of questions like had we been in Mr Prinsep's rooms after lights-out, and things like that!'

'Had you?'

Without hesitation Carleton said, 'Oh yes – well, most of us – heaps of times.'

'Including you?'

'Oh yes, of course.' He was cheerfully unembarrassed.

'Did the Dean say anything else?'

'He asked us whether Mr Prinsep had ever been,' Carleton struggled to find the word, ' "familiar" with us,' he ended triumphantly.

'Did you know what that meant?'

'Yes, well, only after he explained,' Carleton said with a strict regard for honesty. 'You see Mr Prinsep used to tickle us sometimes.'

'What do you mean?'

Carleton giggled and said confidentially, 'Well, he'd, you know, tickle your bottom…' then correcting himself quickly, 'I mean your arse,' and down here of course, your tassel.'

'Why did you let him?'

As though the question had never occurred to him before, Carleton said, 'I suppose we all thought that because he was a master it must be all right. Everybody at the school knew about it. The Choristers I mean. It's what he'd always done and some of them had to tickle him back.' Then laughing, 'His was enormous. Anyhow,' he added thoughtfully, 'it didn't seem to matter very much.'

'You didn't think there was anything odd in his behaviour?'

'Not really. At least, not until the Dean started fussing about it. Deans always make a fuss about everything,' he added almost condescendingly. 'I suppose he was going mental – Mr Prinsep, I mean, not the Dean.'

With the air of a successful prosecuting barrister, Ellerman said, 'Now you understand what a tart is?'

'Oh, you mean Mr Prinsep?' Carleton said with an air of revelation to half-stifled laughter from Baker.

'No,' Ellerman snapped. 'I mean pretty little choirboys who get into other people's beds.'

His performance was wasted for it was clear the accusation went over Carleton's head. 'Oh, I didn't get into his bed, only Treadgold did that. Can I get down now, please, Ellerman?'

'You can go after you've told us why you go to Private.' His initial fear having left him, Carleton revealed a stubborn courage. He closed his lips firmly. Ellerman said, 'We'll have to see about that then, won't we?' From the chair at the far end of the table he picked up Carleton's dressing-gown and drew out the crimson cord.

'Do you see this, Carleton?'

Wide-eyed, Carleton nodded.

'Well, I'm putting it over this beam.' Ellerman pointed to the beam in the ceiling above the table which ran from wall-to-wall, supporting two trusses from the long sloping ceiling. Ellerman tossed it over the beam. In one hand he held a loop and in the other the two ends. Standing on the table slightly behind Carleton, Ellerman said, 'I have made a hangman's knot and I'm going to put it over your head.'

There was a movement and Snider protested, 'I say, Ellerman, steady on!'

Ellerman in fact did nothing of the sort. Unseen by Carleton, he winked and put a finger to his lips, indicating that there was no question of hangman's knot. Instead he slipped a harmless open loop round Carleton's neck, held it together with his fingers, pretending to fuss with the non-existent knot. 'You can feel that, can't you, Carleton?'

Carleton nodded frantically; he looked terrified once more.

'Unless you tell us, I shall haul on the rope and you'll choke.' Ellerman said it in such a matter-of-fact way that it was utterly believable. They could all see that the rope hung harmlessly over the beam in a loop, closed only by Ellerman's hands. Notting grinned at Mawsom, who glanced uneasily across at Snider, half-risen in protest.

'Now, Carleton, tell us exactly what happens when you go to Private. We already know as a matter of fact, so you needn't be too embarrassed.'

Despite his terror, unexpected toughness in Carleton made him almost foolishly obstinate in the face of threat. 'If you already know, why ask me?'

Notting said savagely, 'We want to hear it from you, you little tart.'

Certain that Angus had said nothing, he stammered, 'Well you w-won't!'

Ellerman slightly raised his hand and, to ease his neck, Carleton stood on tiptoe and said defiantly, a little hysterically, 'I shan't tell you! Even if you choke me to death! If you do, they'll put you all in prison.' It was so exactly like a line from a boy's book that even Ellerman had to smile.

Imperceptibly the tide had somehow turned: Ellerman's bluff had been called. Except perhaps for Notting, they were not bullies at heart. Carleton's game refusal to be intimidated won their respect. Even Ellerman could see that and was no longer angry, though he made one last attempt. Putting on a gruffness he no longer felt, he said, with mock exasperation, 'For Christ's sake, Carleton! You don't seem to mind telling us about Prinsep stroking your tassel and you stroking his, so I can't see why you're afraid to admit it's just the same with Craigie!'

Carleton opened his eyes very wide. His jaw fell open as if it lacked all muscular control. Whatever reaction they had anticipated – tears, denials, guilty silence, even defiant justification would have found them unsurprised – they were totally unprepared for Carleton begin to giggle helplessly.

'I say, has anyone seen young Carleton?' Angus stood in the open doorway.

His question pricked their balloon of justification. They were immediately embarrassed. Mawsom and Snider felt more than that – they were ashamed they had acquiesced in Ellerman's charade.

Silenced by disbelief, Angus took in the scene. Sensing salvation, Carleton said eagerly, 'Now you can ask Angus,' and stepped instinctively towards his deliverer.

Loose in its elderly binding, the great Bible squirted sideways, unbalancing Ellerman, pitching Carleton from the table. The cord whipped loosely over the beam, checked only momentarily by Ellerman's involuntary grab.

Angus reached Carleton and caught him fractionally before he had stopped falling. He said furiously, 'For God's sake, let go, Ellerman, or you'll choke the poor little beggar!' Almost maternally, he gathered the boy and gently placed him on the table. 'He's banged his head and knocked himself out. What the Hell's going on?'

'More like he's "Fainted in the Strong Arms of His Gallant Protector". How very romantic! AC to the rescue in the nick of time!' Notting concluded by blowing a rasping blast on an imaginary trumpet.

Snider turned from the table. 'Perhaps it's time for you to shut up, Notting, Carleton's dead.'

Chapter Eleven

Nobody moves.
Nobody speaks.

Tableau in a Victorian melodrama: Ellerman, half-kneeling on the floor. Notting, hand still holding his imaginary trumpet; Mawsom, backs of both hands to his mouth; Baker, half-risen from the chair, goggling through his pebble-lenses; Angus, one arm still cradling Carleton's legs; central to it all, reminiscent of a picture by Rembrandt, Snider — tall, thin and dark, his long fingers touching the delicate yet-to-fill-out groove in the nape of a slender, absurdly childish neck, which hypnotises them all with its obscene comic-cuts angle.

ii

Inside the room silence flowed on and on. No sounds from the rest of the House outside. The clock ticked as it had ticked unnoticed for millions of ticks before; now it seemed a loud, unnatural, intrusive.

Angus knew for certain that Snider was wrong. He said confidently, 'Of course he's not dead. He can't be. He looks alive enough, doesn't he?' The small hands and the delicate flushed face assured him. Quietly he called, 'Carleton. Christopher? *Christopher*! Until at last he was forced to recognise the grey eyes held a blankness that would never acknowledge him again.

A hoarse, unrecognisable voice grated, 'Artificial respiration!'

'It'll be no good, Ellerman,' Snider insisted with quiet but utterly impressive authority. His neck's broken. The cord must've snagged on something as he fell. Or someone, Ellerman.' He explained it gently as if to a small child.

Notting began to weep hysterically. 'What do we do now? It was all your idea, Ellerman. It's all your fault.'

'*SHUT UP*, Notting!' Assessing the situation rapidly, Ellerman spoke loudly and carefully in his normal authoritative voice. 'Remember this, all of you. *This* is what happened. *Angus opened the door, just as Carleton fell.*' He paused significantly, '*And we were all outside, with Angus, looking for Carleton.*'

Snider said, 'We can't say that!'

'Why not? It was an accident, wasn't it? Will it do any good to explain that we were getting Carleton to tell us what his Housemaster – our Housemaster – was up to? Do we want this to feature in the *News of the World?* Is that what you want, Snider? Or you, Mawsom?' Ellerman concluded urgently, shrewdly recognising that Mawsom was Snider's most likely ally.

Baker said, sotto voce, 'Angus mightn't go along with it.'

Notting said querulously, 'I don't think he's heard us. What's wrong with him?'

Ellerman turned and answered witheringly, 'For Christ's sake, Notting! Don't you notice anything? Angus was in love with Carleton. That's what's wrong with him.' The savage scorn in his voice forced them to pay attention.

Mawsom said, 'Then why should he tell your story?'

'Because he won't want anything to come out.'

'To come out?'

'About him and Carleton.'

'Perhaps there isn't anything to come out.'

Ellerman retorted sharply, 'That's not what it'll look like. *If we stick to our story.*'

'Somebody'd better get Craigie.'

'Angus! *ANGUS*! Christopher ANGUS.'

It was the unheard-of use of his Christian name which brought Angus back to them. He looked blankly at Ellerman.

'Listen, AC. *IT—WAS—AN—ACCIDENT*. Do you understand?'

Angus nodded blindly, as though hypnotised he repeated, 'Yes, Ellerman, It—was—an—accident.'

'Don't forget *we came in with you and saw Carleton fall as you opened the door.* Do you understand?' Angus nodded again wordlessly, like a puppet.

'Now, go and get Craigie,' Ellerman said. 'Just tell him there's been an accident. Don't say anything else. Get him here Do you understand?' He shook Angus' arm.

Once again Angus nodded.

'Okay? Then get going. Angus? *GET GOING, ANGUS!*'

Angus left the room still without speaking. Baker asked, 'Why send him, Ellerman?'

'It's important we all get our story straight. Get the room straight. We're all in this. Empty the tea-pot and those cups. Pick up The Chair. Remember, we were coming in through the door.' They did not meet his gaze. He jerked them back to attention, 'Well, was it an accident or not? Did we mean to kill him? What about you, Mawsom? Is that what you intended?'

'Of course not. But you were bloody criminal with his dressing-gown cord.'

'You tried to stop me?' There was no ignoring the irony. 'Put that down just here, Mawsom.'

Snider said wearily, 'I don't think this is the moment to argue, do you?' He looked at the table. They all looked at the table. 'Ellerman's probably right. It's an accident and we don't want complications.'

'But if Angus—'

'I've told you, Angus will do as he's told. Leave that to me. When Craigie gets here, let *me* do the talking.'

Mawsom said, 'I still think Angus…'

Ellerman rounded on him, furious. 'He'll do what he's told. After all, if he'd got Carleton to confess the truth about those visits to Private, as we'd asked him to, it would never have happened.'

Was Ellerman implying that it was Angus' fault, Mawsom wondered? That Carleton deserved what had happened because he was stubborn? For a brief moment, it seemed that Snider was about to object, but the moment passed as the enormity of what had happened clarified itself. Consequences filled their imagination like a nightmare. One by one they dropped their eyes from the table with its terrible burden. Nobody contradicted Ellerman.

❋

As if hypnotised Angus went down the stairs, through Libe and into Din Room. He could hear a piano very faintly. He knocked.

'Come on in, Carleton! I expect you've come back for your music.'

'It's me, sir, Angus.'

Craigie turned and took in what he saw. 'Angus? Whatever's the matter? Here, sit down.'

'Ellerman wants you to come to Big Study. There's been an accident.' His voice was devoid of expression. He could hear the fire burning. 'It's Christopher Carleton.'

'Carleton's hurt?' Craigie got up, concerned.

Angus heard a flat voice that seemed not to be his own say, 'Carleton's dead.'

Craigie ran through the door. Still like a robot, Angus followed. He did not really want to go back into Big Study ever again; when he arrived Craigie was at the centre of the silent group. It was uncanny, only a yard away, through another door, most of Ansell's was blissfully asleep.

As Angus entered, Craigie turned round. 'Notting, please will you go at once to the High Master with a message I shall give you.' He wrote rapidly on a page from a notebook. 'Baker, please tell Matron I need to see her. I shall have to inform the School Doctor and Inspector Simmons.' He stopped. He was grey and drawn and made no attempt to disguise the tears in his eyes. 'You say, Ellerman, that you opened the door and found Carleton standing on the Bible?'

Ellerman said in a whisper, 'I expect it was because otherwise the cord wouldn't reach. Then, sir,' he gulped, 'when he saw us, his foot slipped, Angus almost got to him before he hit the table.'

'We must touch nothing,' Craigie said. 'I think we should not stay in here.'

'I'll wait with him until the doctor comes,' Angus said mechanically. He found he could not remove his gaze from the table.

Craigie said with understanding, 'It's very right of you to offer, Angus. Much appreciated. But you look as though you should go and sit in Private for a while. Perhaps most of you should. None of us should be in here. The police...I take it you've touched nothing.'

'Only...Carlton, sir, Angus put him on the table and we moved the cord from his neck in case...but...'

Snider was the most composed. He said with touching authority,' I'll wait *outside*, sir, if you like. Just in case anyone blunders in. I don't think Angus should, sir, he looks...'

'I'll stay with you,' Mawsom offered.

They all moved towards the door except for Craigie who spoke in a detached, clear voice. 'Have you noticed Carleton's hands? He would have been the finest pianist Cranchester ever had.'

They were puzzled. Was he addressing them? Or Angus? Or merely talking to himself? The tears in his eyes embarrassed them, dry-eyed as they were themselves and, in some curious way, they resented it. He said very quietly to Angus, 'Come along, I'm afraid Christopher, Carleton doesn't need either of us any more.'

Angus felt the terrible tightness in his chest grip him as it had not done for years. It was as if his lungs had become paralysed. He could not breathe. He made a step towards the door, the floor came up to meet...Snider caught him.

iii

click-click-clickclickclickclick-click-click-click
An old, brittle, film, projects itself unevenly, unpredictably: rapid jerky runs of blurred, out-of-focus, scenes; juddering slow-motion distorted sequences of jammed celluloid; a break; suddenly, unexpectedly, one frame, one place, one scene, so clear and sharp-edged that it seems to be happening now.

Hushed voices seep and whisper like incoming tide...'I say, have you heard something happened last night in Big Study?' Wonder, disbelief, fear Above all fear.

> 'Little Carleton's dead.' Death stalks among the
> Mangers, almost visible, almost tangible, a subtle,
> ubiquitous presence.

Nobody spoke normally, in fact hardly anyone spoke at all, there was none of the usual bustling noises. Only sounds that usually passed unnoticed – a bed creaking, a shoe dropped, hair being brushed, a Manger curtain swishing back on its big brass rings.

Nobody asked Angus. It seemed tacitly agreed that they should not. They asked Ellerman and Mawsom and Baker.

'Is it true that Carleton killed himself because he was going to get a Praefaectors'?'

'It is not true, Jardine. If you go round saying that sort of thing, *you'll* be getting a Praefaectors'. But it is true he's dead. We came into Big Study and found him.'

Breakfast, eaten in similar silence. Neither reverence nor sorrow. Fear. Everyone touched by Carleton's mortality.

Craigie addressed them all after breakfast. 'You'll have heard, I dare say, of the tragic events last night. There'll have to be a proper Inquest in due course. We believe it was an accident. If any one of you has any reason at all to believe Christopher Carleton was unhappy, you must let me know.'

Every conversation in the School seemed hollow, as if at the back of it was a different conversation that they wanted to have and dared not.

> 'Carleton hanged himself in Ansell's?'
> 'Remember that kid Orton who ran away from Ansell's?'
> 'Then that new Aussie in Ansell's bunked this Half,'
> 'Carleton was miserably unhappy in Ansell's'
> '…badly bullied in Ansell's…'
> 'Frequently beaten in Ansell's.'
> 'Buggered nightly in Ansell's.'
> 'Not surprised that Ansell's kid Carleton hanged himself'

It bound Ansell's together even more closely. Indignation fired them. There grew a conspiracy between the most junior and most senior. They closed ranks even tighter against the outside world, yet each was conscious of his own individuality, of his own isolation.

> Lunch, eaten virtually in silence.
> Craigie leaves.
> Ellerman stands.

'Listen Ansell's. There are some damn silly rumours going round Cranchester. *We* all know that Carleton was perfectly happy. What happened last night was an idiotic, tragic accident. Just tell that to anyone who asks. At the Inquest they'll find that's the truth.'

The rest of the House filed away leaving only the Praefaectors. Angus had eaten nothing. As if conscious of the others for the first time since he had opened the door to Big Study, he turned on Ellerman and said, 'You say it was an accident. It looked to me as though you were hanging him.'

'It was a try-on,' Ellerman said, 'a joke. He wouldn't tell us what he was doing with Craigie every night. He wouldn't tell you. We knew of course, but we wanted to have it from Carleton. When he saw you, his foot slipped.'

'Obviously we can't tell Craigie that,' Notting butted in.

'If it's what happened, I don't see why not.' He looked at them viciously, 'You bloody well killed him. The lot of you!'

'We can't tell Craigie because of what Craigie was doing to Carleton. Angus, for God's sake! Craigie had his hand up Carleton's arse.'

'*WHAT*!' Angus' utter astonishment took them by surprise. 'Did Carleton tell you that?'

Baker said, 'Carleton, was a little tart, he obviously didn't mind what Craigie was doing to him. In fact he began to laugh when we told him we knew perfectly well that—'

Ellerman interrupted: 'He didn't deny it. He was just going to tell when you appeared. I might say that if you think he was a little innocent, you're mistaken. That Choir school? You ought to hear about what the masters got up to there.'

Mawsom said, 'That's by the way, Ellerman. After all Carleton didn't actually say Craigie had done anything to him.'

Ellerman said, 'It was only a matter of time before he told us everything. It's a pity you didn't ask him again, Angus.'

Flatly, dully, Angus said, ' Oh yes I did. He told me.'

They looked at him but did not move.

'When was this?'

'About ten days ago.'

'You didn't tell us!'

'I promised him I wouldn't tell anyone, especially you, Ellerman.... He begged me not to tell *you*.'

Ellerman flushed. 'I'm not surprised he didn't he want anyone to know.'

Angus said distantly, '...Because he was too embarrassed.'

'Well, he wasn't too embarrassed to tell us that a master at the Cathedral fiddled with 'em all and got them to tassel him.'

'It was quite different with Craigie.'

'How, different, AC? It'd still be indecent assault.'

'Hardly, Ellerman.' Angus still spoke very remotely. 'Carleton had to practise his music for at least an hour each day. He was embarrassed about it because we're all such fine rugger players here.' Angus' voice took on a different timbre: 'Since there's nobody else in Ansell's who's even looked at a piano, or a violin, or any other musical instrument, he thought you'd despise him for it. There's not even an old piano in Ansell's, let alone a decent one, so he went to Private each evening to use Craigie's piano. Out of sight. It's a very good one, Carleton said. Steinway,' he added almost irrelevantly. He had their attention. 'Carleton was a very fine pianist. He was due to play an important solo, with a national orchestra. Not here at Cranchester. In London. Just before Christmas. At some big concert for refugee children. Next Half he was going to have to go up to London each Saturday, because there's nobody here good enough to teach him.'

Baker exclaimed, 'Christ!'

Angus ploughed on relentlessly, 'He even asked me to go to it, the Concert. He didn't want anyone else except Craigie to know. He knew Ansell's wouldn't approve of piano-playing.' He looked at them all. There was no question of even Ellerman disbelieving him, although he could not know that it was because it explained, as nothing else could, Carleton's extraordinary giggling reaction to Ellerman's final question.

Ellerman realised, within seconds, what was happening in the minds of Snider and Mawsom and Baker – even Notting. He was losing them. Before their understanding hardened into unshakable conviction and they sided with Angus once and for all, he interpolated smoothly, 'I'm sure that you're right, AC, I expect Carleton did go to Private for music practice. But why always in pyjamas?'

'Because it was late and because Carleton had to be ready to go to bed, Ellerman, at the same time as the rest of his Election, otherwise you'd no doubt have had me getting him to tighten-up every evening for being late Warming.'

Ellerman said easily, 'Well, the fact they played the piano together doesn't change my opinion.'

'Not *together*, Ellerman.' Angus was scathing. 'Craigie wasn't even in the room usually.'

Ellerman overrode him. 'How do you know? As far as I'm concerned, music was Craigie's cover. Remember this,' he looked meaningfully at the others, ' Carleton never denied our accusations…'

'That was only because…' Snider began.

Ellerman cut him short and rushed ahead. 'And anyway, Carleton's death *was an accident*. Anybody deny that?' He looked back at Snider as if inviting him to speak now. Snider remained silent. 'What's more, it would be damned odd if we were to change the statement I made to Inspector Simmons today.'

Angus said, 'I've not made any statement yet. When I do it'll be the truth.'

Rattled, Ellerman snapped shakily, 'If you'd bloody told us what Carleton told you, none of this need ever have happened. It's no use blaming us. You're to blame most of all. If you hadn't been so besotted with your precious little Carleton, he'd be alive now…. If you'd been a *proper* Praefaector, Angus, instead of a product of Aunty Singleton's nursery school…. If you hadn't chosen to open the bloody door at that moment, your precious little Carleton wouldn't have rushed to the arms of his guardian Angel Arse!'

It stung Angus out of his numbness and put him very close to tears. He shouted, 'Wouldn't it? Would he still be alive? You won't believe the truth, even now I've told you. Would it have made any difference at all, if I'd told you last week? Would you have believed me then?'

'Shut up, Angus, you're shouting! Somebody'll hear.'

'Let them,' but he lowered his voice. 'You're the ones who've got to worry, not me. You killed him, Ellerman, as good as. You put the cord round his neck, didn't you?' He paused, and said intensely, 'Perhaps if you hadn't been holding it when he fell, his neck wouldn't have...' He moved quickly to the door. 'If any of you think I'm going to tell lies at the Inquest, you've got another thought coming.' Very quietly he said, 'You killed Carleton – all of you.'

When he had gone, Baker said uneasily, 'We'd much better tell Craigie the truth now. After all he's right, the whole thing was your idea, Ellerman. You did put the cord...'

'And you watched me *without objecting*, Baker,' Ellerman said coldly. 'Listen, all of you. *It was an accident.* None of us intended him to come to harm. Just to scare him into telling us the truth about Craigie. We're telling the truth.' Her kept his voice low, but intense. 'Remember, we wouldn't have done it if Angus had told us what Carleton told him last week. All we've done is to put us *outside* the door, rather than inside. And I spoke for all of us. If you, Baker, want to change the story and leave us open to manslaughter – or something of the sort – then go ahead. It'll be prison for *you* because you're already eighteen.' Implicating them all, he frightened them very much.

'What about Angus?'

'Perhaps they won't need him at the Inquest,' Mawsom suggested hopefully. 'After all, if they've got Ellerman's statement...'

'I think they will need him,' Ellerman corrected. 'They'll have to. They'll want to know if Carleton was unhappy and Angus is the obvious person to tell them. Craigie knows that. In fact he told me that he thought both Angus and I would have to give evidence.'

'Then we're done for!' Notting, already sounding panic-stricken again.

Ellerman looked at him with a twitch of what might have been contempt. 'No, we aren't, Notting. Unless you lose your nerve; you look as though you're about to pee the carpet again.' That shut Notting up. 'If we all stick to our version, it's five to one. We all know how Angus felt about Carleton. He's very upset now. Not rational. Leave Angus to me.'

'The Coroner doesn't know all that,' Mawsom objected.

'I've already pointed it out to Craigie who was here when he fainted. And,' Ellerman added determinedly, 'if I have to tell the Coroner about Angus and Carleton, I would. It could be a relevant factor.' He sensed their disapproval, but also he sensed their fear. 'And I *would* do it if the alternative was a manslaughter charge. because *I* know, we all know Carleton's death was an accident?'

Nobody argued with him because, despite the fact that events were not yet twenty-four hours old, Carleton's death was already beginning to merge into the perspective of the Half and of Ansell's.

Baker said, 'There's no doubt Craigie'll insist on doing things his way next Half.'

Mawsom said shrewdly, 'Whatever we say, I bet he suspects that he hasn't heard the full story. He's bound to wonder why Carleton should have gone to Big Study. And why it was empty at that time.'

'Perhaps Angus…?'

'No! He hasn't had a chance. If you remember he passed out last night and was put to bed. However, Mawsom's right, Craigie would know that no boy in the Junior Election would go there by himself.'

'Unless he wanted to hang himself on one of those beams,' Ellerman said pointedly.

Snider said, 'That would mean a verdict of suicide!'

'Suicide would be a better verdict than manslaughter,' Ellerman said flatly.

'For Ansell's? For Carleton's parents?' Snider enquired sarcastically.

'No, Snider, for us. For each one of us. For you especially, if you want to be a doctor as you say.' It shut Snider up.

They left the room and went out into weak afternoon sun.

Grey light. Shabby walls. Lethargy. Listlessness.

'I wondered if you were all right, AC?'

'Oh yes.'

'I'm so very sorry. We all are. I don't think we've been very helpful to you.' After a silence which Angus made no attempt to fill, Mawsom said awkwardly 'I mean we know that you and Carleton…' He came to a halt.

Angus said tonelessly, 'I think I was in love with Carleton.'

'No. Well, yes. Not like Watson and Orton.'

'Who knows? Perhaps it would have ended up very like Watson, I don't know.'

'And Carleton?'

'I don't know. It wasn't something we'd ever've discussed.'

'No, I'm sure that's true, AC. You know, it really was an accident. A terrible accident. Ellerman thought…wanted to believe…that is, we thought that Craigie was messing around with Carleton and we wanted to get the truth. It was a pure accident.'

'I didn't think *you* intended it, Mawsom.' After a bit he said, 'I read somewhere that fathers often want their sons to live out their own ambitions. If I have a son, I'd want him to be like Carleton. I suppose that sounds bloody wet.'

'I expect we'd all feel the same.'

'I wouldn't send my son to Ansell's.'

'Perhaps there has to be an equivalent of Ansell's for everyone – somewhere along the line.'

Angus looked at him and said nothing; he could not disagree.

'What do you feel about the Inquest, now?'

'Now?'

'I mean what'll you say?'

'I shall tell them exactly what I saw when I opened the door.'

'I see. Goodnight, AC.'

When he had gone, Angus wondered whether Mawsom was attempting to persuade him to change his mind.

Black windows. Dim light from Corridor seeping through glass fanlight above door. Dozing.

'How do you feel about the Inquest tomorrow, AC?'

'I don't feel anything at all about it, Ellerman.'

'What are you going to say?'

'I shall tell them what I saw when I opened the door.'

Ellerman strolled across to the window and looked out into the impenetrable blackness. 'That's a pity.'

'For you?'

'Not really. For you too, but for Carleton mainly.'

'Carleton's dead.'

'Yes. It would be a pity if everyone got the impression that he'd taken his own life because you couldn't keep your hands off him. Or that he was such a little tart that you were jealous and he was waiting to tighten-up for it in Big Study.'

'That's not true.' Angus stood up. 'You know it's not true. Neither of those things.'

'All *I* know is that we found Carleton hanging himself. We *all* found him, Angus. As to why he was doing it, that's a matter of conjecture. Of course, if a great big hairy Praefaector had been making unwelcome advances that might seem a good reason to. So of course he'd cook up a different story.'

'That's what you intend to say, is it?'

'It's what the Coroner might think.'

'No.'

'Are you sure?'

Angus was not sure.

'Look here, AC, Carleton had you wound round his little finger. He was a tart – no, wait. You didn't hear what he told us about Prinsep, that chap at the Cathedral. He told us the Choristers didn't care what Prinsep did with them. In and out of his bed like rabbits in a burrow.'

'I don't believe it. Not Christopher.' He recalled Carleton saying he was one of Prinsep's favourites. What had that meant?

Ellerman shrugged. 'Hmm, so it was "Christopher" was it? All right. What about you and Carleton then?'

'What about us?'

'Did you ever touch him?'

Angus hesitated fractionally before saying, 'Not in the way you mean.'

'What way *do* I mean, AC? Are you admitting that you touched him in some *other* way? In what *way*?' Getting no reply, 'How would you answer that sort of question tomorrow?'

'They won't ask questions like that.'

'They could do. Coroners can be very nosey. Especially if they think there's a newspaper in the court,' Ellerman insisted. 'He just might – if he thought that Carleton killed himself because of what you were doing to him.' Ellerman let the meaning sink in.

'I never...'

'*Touched* him...? At all?' He sensed Angus' hesitation again. 'After all, the Coroner was probably at somewhere like Cranchester himself. Now, I know you, AC – we all do and have done from the beginning – but the Coroner doesn't. If someone else, questioned by the Coroner, happened to give the erroneous impression that you, a senior boy were, well, romantically "keen" on Carleton...pressing unwelcome attentions on him...'

'*Someone else* being you?'

'Carleton was often quite late in your room. Later than the other Warmers. *I* don't know what went on, of course. Nor do the others. So we have to guess.'

'Nothing *went on*.'

'Of course not, AC. That's why you're the chap to speak to the Coroner. You're the chap who saw Carleton's foot slip as you opened the door. Some silly dare, perhaps? You nearly saved him – we can all vouch for that. You would have saved him if anyone could've, you were so quick off the mark. Brilliant effort. We were behind you and saw you reach him just too late.'

'I would never have let anything happen between me and Carleton. Even *you* must believe that.'

'As a matter of fact I think I do. But I'll bet you thought about it.'

Ellerman had assessed him more shrewdly than Angus could have suspected, 'I read recently that, in the Catholic Church, a sins counts as a sin even if it only happens in the imagination.'

'I'm not a Catholic, Ellerman.'

'I know you're not – that poet you're keen on wasn't either until he became one at University. Wouldn't surprise me if you went the same way.'

When he had gone, Angus felt sick and dazed. Ellerman was not bluffing.

Faceless boys. Faceless masters. Weak December sun. Whispering voices. Soft organ. Coughs. Snuffling. Turning loud pages.

Was he to blame? Would tragedy really have been averted if he had told Ellerman about the music? If he hadn't opened the door at that precise moment?

> *I waited for the Lord*
> *And He heard my complaint.*

An even more terrible thought struck him. Was this the way his prayers had been answered? Had God played some despicable game with him? He had prayed in here, morning after morning that he might be protected from the lust which Carleton roused in him. Now he was protected. For ever. Carleton was dead. His prayers. All those glib, worthless, Confessions at Priest Street? Was this his ultimate penance? After all, it had been the great Bible on which Carleton stood that had been the ultimate instrument of his death.

God had heard his complaint. In order to save Angus, God had killed Carleton. As He had killed Simonsen. As He had Singleton. This was the way 'God' responded to prayers and confessions – unpredictably, maliciously. Ellerman was right, though for the wrong reasons. It *was* his fault. Final proof of his culpability? Angus himself had precipitated Carleton's death by opening the door at that critical moment. God had chosen the moment for him to do so.

However, he now knew, it was Ellerman who had interrogated Carleton. He could have done nothing to stop that. Unless of course…unless he had accepted Craigie's invitation to be Head of House. He had forgotten about that. Every way he looked at it, he himself was to blame for Carleton's death. When he rose to leave with the others, he found his legs so trembly that they could scarcely support him.

✷

Small room, panelled dark. High windows spreading little light. Wall-bracket lamps contributing a mellow glow. Quiet, hushed. Formalities proceed slowly, quietly. Coroner, small turnip-shaped, Pickwickian, half-moon, gold-rimmed, glasses, questioning expertly, patiently, with sympathy and, occasionally, with unexpected acuity. Craigie distinguished, anguished, low-voiced but clear.

'You can think of no reason that this boy might take his own life?'

'None whatever.'

'Have you any suggestion at all as to why he might be by himself in this particular room which, you say, was the province of senior boys?'

'I have no suggestion at all.' There was a pause and a consultation.

Mr Pickwick said with gentle determination, 'I think we must try to ascertain the state of mind of this boy. I would like to hear from the Head of House, Mr Ellerman. And from Mr Angus. I'll begin with Mr Angus.'

Preliminaries.

What was a Praefaector? Matters of that sort. The Coroner said kindly, 'Do I gather that Carleton was your, er, "fag"? It probably isn't the Cranchester term but you'll know what I mean.' Angus nodded.

'So you saw him quite often?'

'Oh yes. Every evening at least. Usually every morning too.'

'On that evening?'

'Well, I hadn't seen him yet. I wanted him to do something for me. I couldn't find him…'

'Until you opened the door of the Praefaectors' study?'

'Yes.'
'And Carleton was standing on the table?'
'Yes. He was.'
'On this old family Bible?'
'Yes, sir.'
'Can you tell us in your own words?'

>Looking out into the room.
>Ellerman.
>Their eyes lock, hold.
>Moment of decision.
>Moment of destiny.

'I know it's distressing, Mr Angus, but please tell us what happened.'
'Carleton was on the table. Standing on a book. Books. The big Bible that's always there. There was this cord round his neck and round the beam.' He hesitated.
'His dressing-gown cord in fact?'
'Yes, sir, 'he hesitated, caught Ellerman's eye. 'Well...then...then he saw me. His foot slipped. At least, it was the Bible which slipped. It's loose in its cover. I managed to get across to him before he hit the floor. But the rope the cord must have...' His voice dribbled to a stop.
Gently the Coroner came to his rescue.
'Yes of course. We've heard from the doctor. His neck was broken. I'm only sorry that your splendidly prompt action was of no avail.'
Angus nodded, unable for the moment to speak.
'Can you answer another question or two?'
He nodded again.
'Did you have any reason at all to feel that young Carleton might be considering taking his own life?'
'*NO!*' It came out very loudly. 'I'm sure he didn't mean to do that, quite sure.'
'I'm sorry to persist, but if there was any unhappiness...any bullying for instance?'
Angus heard himself say, 'We don't stand for that sort of thing in

Ansell's. I'm quite certain he was not being bullied. I would've known. He would have told me if there'd been anything like that.'

'Thank you, Mr Angus. I can see it's been particularly harrowing for you. I may add here, that I am informed that letters home mentioned your name many times, as somebody whose understanding and kindness he very much appreciated as a new boy. I hope that this may be of some small consolation to you.'

Ellerman was called. He answered quietly, convincingly.

'You are Head of the House?'

'Yes, sir.'

'Are you quite sure that there was nothing which could have caused Carleton to contemplate taking his own life?'

'No, sir, nothing like bullying, if that's what you mean. As Angus has said, sir, we don't stand for bullying in Ansell's. I may say, sir, that Angus in particular is respected by us all for his friendliness and courtesy to those who are his junior.' Ellerman caught Angus' eye – *Debt acknowledged and repaid* – Angus dropped his. So this was the payback. 'However, sir…'

'Do you mean that you've thought of something else?'

'Well, not really, sir. It's only just occurred to me. It's just an idea.'

'If you think it may help, please tell us.'

Angus thought, Christ! He's going to tell them about Craigie!

Ellerman said carefully, 'Well, sir, earlier in the Half – that is the term – there was a debate in the School. Most people went. It was about Capital Punishment. There was a lot of talk about whether it was justified, lots of technical stuff – whether it was a quick death, you know. That sort of thing. It occurs to me that perhaps Carleton was, well, trying an experiment which went wrong…when Angus opened the door, he moved suddenly and the Bible slipped from beneath his feet. Its covers are loose. I mean he might have been startled, because, after all, he wasn't supposed even to be in Big Study. That's all, sir. It's probably a bit silly.'

With his striking good looks, Ellerman waited, deferential, modest, graceful, neat, in no way betraying that he knew perfectly well he had given a brilliant performance.

The Coroner said firmly, 'Not at all. It's a very sensible suggestion indeed, presented with, if I may say without embarrassing you, Mr

Ellerman, the modesty and deference both to this Court and the dead boy which we have come to expect from those who so splendidly exemplify the very best of our great Public Schools like Cranchester. I have to say that a similar tragedy occurred only a fortnight ago and was widely reported in the papers.'

The air of tension had dissolved from the courtroom. Ellerman's explanation was like a lifebelt to a drowning man. It was now possible to see an alternative to suicide. Shortly afterwards a verdict of Accidental Death was reached. The Coroner gave a rider to the effect that in his opinion neither the Cranchester nor any individual was to blame in any way. It was, he felt, a terrible accident, a tragic end to the young life of a gifted musician and popular pupil.

As they left the Court, Ellerman said, 'Well done, Angus.'

Angus did not reply.

Ellerman added, 'The verdict is right, you know. It was an accident.'

The High Master approached. He said, 'You both stood up remarkably well on such a very sad and nerve-wracking occasion. Ellerman, that was a very timely suggestion of yours. It would have been truly terrible for Carleton's parents had they returned a different verdict.'

In Ansell's the verdict was received with relief and Ellerman's part in it gratefully recognised. However, spirits were in no way raised. The House was a gloomy and hollow place echoing with rumours that the High Master might send the whole House home early.

Crumpling three cards into the grate. Balliol inviting him for examination this very morning: Memorial Service, Chapel: Funeral, small, private St. Peter and St. Paul, two o'clock.

A bright December day, as they went in, it clouded over during the service. Ansell's seemed cocooned in a special misery of its own, regarded with sympathy by the rest of the school. The fine music and the prayers washed over their bowed heads like an unfelt sea. To Angus it seemed a dream. He registered only the address, given by Craigie, who spoke remotely from the pulpit, changed, elevated somehow by his clerical bands.

'I have been asked to say some words and I do so with the saddest of hearts, because Christopher was somebody who ought to be living. It seems very hard to understand how tragedies like this can come about. He had not been at Ansell's very long. However, he had been with us long enough for us to know him and to value him. His musical gift was great, perhaps very great. Sadly, we shall never know for sure. It was his candour, his honesty and his sincerity which immediately communicated itself to us. We can therefore imagine how much more he will be missed by his parents, his relations and all those who had known him, valued him and loved him so much longer. Before I conclude these few and utterly inadequate words, I want to say two things more. First, to say how much we endorse the finding that Christopher's death was accidental. We who knew him did not need the verdict, because we know that nothing would ever have induced him to take his own life. The second and last thing I wish to say is that I shall always remember him, earlier this Half, in this place, singing "I waited for the Lord".'

Craigie stepped down. Nobody else moved. All they could hear was the soft sound of his footsteps until the organ sounded an uncertain note and they began the last hymn.

The High Master recited a prayer slowly, gently, and they all knelt in silence for what seemed a long time, but could only have been minutes. Faintly the organ notes roused them again. All except Ansell's Men were going back to classes. The High Master had indeed decreed that Ansell's should leave for a lengthened holiday on the midday train, although the Praefaectors would stay to attend the funeral.

As he stood up and began to shuffle towards the cold air outside, so softly that at first he thought he imagined it, Angus realised the organ was playing the introduction to 'I waited for the Lord'. He should have anticipated that, but he had not and he found it upset him more than he could have explained.

He would not return to Ansell's for lunch. He thought about going to

Cranchester, where he would need to be for the funeral at two. Already, however, taxis taking the rest of Ansell's to the train were appearing. So he turned the other way and walked, turning off down the road he had once ridden on his way to the Singletons. After about half a mile there was a turning and a small, not very clean pub. Inside, it was extremely dark, however there was a warm fire. It was totally forbidden for Castonians to visit pubs, The Harrow, in particular, had been the reason for several expulsions. He did not care.

He ordered cheese and bread and a large tankard of bitter. He was not used to beer, the hops caught the back of his throat. He pushed it to one side. The bread was palatable, the cheese excellent. He chewed monotonously, looking into the flames with unseeing eyes. He could not forget the organ music, it wound in and out of his head like a thread of hot wire. When he finished the bread and cheese, he left the beer and wandered out. It had become even more overcast. He walked briskly back, past Lodge until he came to the Church. He pushed through the lych-gate, up a mossy path. His eyes could not ignore the newly dug grave by the far wall to his right.

At the back, the, darkest corner, taking no notice of trickle of people taking their places in old pews damp with condensation. He does not acknowledge the other Praefaectors when they arrive, nor even Craigie. They let him be.

It was short, barely more than committal, entirely without music because of the Memorial Service that morning in Chapel. From the back, he had an impression of muttering voices, anonymous hunched backs, of a clergyman he did not know reciting the comfortable but useless words of the Burial Service, which he had never heard before. He was conscious of the box glinting at the front of the altar-rail which he did not want to see. He had feared that he and the other Praefaectors might be called on to carry it, but in the event it seemed it was to be handled by professional men in black. He shut his eyes tight, as the procession passed him on its slow way, pallbearers, a single woman, Craigie, the other Praefaectors and only moved himself when he knew it was safely outside. Then he followed.

A little after three o'clock but already a luminous dimness invests misty air, tingeing each globule of moisture, making the encroaching darkness almost tangible, draining depth of colour from everything – hawthorn hanging over the wall, faded, yellowing stone of the wall itself, the grass. Even the clothes of the mourners seem to be losing their intense blackness. Faces, pale blobs pierced by the dark holes of eyes and mouth.

They stood beside the grave. The bright soil, demurely awaiting its return to the hole, alone seemed to have retained its colour. A robin, beady-eyed, inquiring, scavenged the new earth. It hopped irreverently here and there, stopping occasionally, head on one side, looking, listening, as if deciding, almost obscenely, that what was taking place did not matter, was of no consequence at all.

The grave-shaft cut harshly into close-cropped turf carving out the block of darkness below. It was spanned by two unplaned boards, which supported the small coffin, handles and plaque shining in the last of the light. The cords through the handles were lifted, the boards silently removed and the box lowered so gently it seemed as if the universe held its breath. At the bottom it quietly came to rest, palely gleaming. The words of the Committal hung in the cold air with the breath which spoke them.

The loneliness of it gripped Angus then, for the first time; numbed by the futility of it all, he could remember only the way Carleton had clung to him that night after his solo – was it only a few weeks ago, days ago in truth? – lonely, seeking the assurance, friendship and affection which Ansell's denied. Once again, he imagined he could feel the boy's body pressing against him; the memory was so powerful that, opening his eyes, he was almost surprised that it was not so.

A hollow drumming. First nodules of earth fell on the yellow box at the bottom of the black shaft. He wanted to weep but found he could not.

He stood a long, long, time. Eventually he lifted his eyes. It was very nearly dark. The others had gone. He had not heard them depart, the last spadeful of earth had been turned. It was the cessation of 'huisshing' shovels which had disturbed him. Where there had been a shaft, there was now a neat dark mound. Cold dampness was eating through the soles of his shoes. When at last he turned away, he found he was not alone.

'You must be Angus?' Unspeaking, he nodded.

'Christopher told me about you. In his letters. He said you made it all better. He was very homesick. I think he hated it.'

'I know, he told me. I told him it's always a bit like that at first.'

'You don't think...'

'No,' quickly reassuring them both. 'No, it was all right now. He wouldn't have missed the concert. He was living for that...' He realised what he'd said, but she understood.

'Thank you so much, for your kindness to him. It helped him. It helped me to know there was somebody he could talk to and trust. I never really wanted.... And his father...his father.... They haven't been able to get in touch with him yet...he's...he's...'

Angus had never seen an adult cry and it embarrassed him. 'I'm so sorry.' It was inadequate. What else could he say?

'You'll have to be going back...'

'What about you?'

'Mr Craigie kindly said I could stay. I couldn't bear that. Not now that Christopher's...' She broke down again. Angus wanted to comfort her by putting an arm round her, but somehow he could not bring himself to do so. 'I'm getting a train.'

'I'll walk with you to the station.'

'Oh no. I'd rather be alone. If you don't mind.'

They stood awkwardly. He could not even make out the features of her face now.

She held out a small hand. 'Thank you. I hope it won't embarrass you, when I say Christopher thought a lot of you. He wanted me to ask you to stay for the Concert.'

Angus nodded.

'You were his hero, you know. I think he saw you as a sort of elder brother. You don't mind me saying that?'

'Oh no. I'd've liked that.' He wanted to say something more, but did not know what to say. Or how to say anything at all. Until, all at once Johnson's letter sprang to mind.

'Mrs Carleton, Christopher was the nicest kid I know.' He blurted it out. The pale oval of her face turned towards him. She squeezed his hand. He could bear it no longer. He moved away in the darkness and walked quickly back along the uneven path to the lych-gate and out onto the road.

He made his way back to Ansell's, unable to push Carleton's mother from his mind. He imagined her rattling away from Cranchester with the tiny handkerchief she had clutched at throughout the afternoon pressed to her eyes, travelling further, minute by minute, from the grave near the wall still observed by the perky robin, beady, alive, entirely unconcerned.

Ansell's virtually empty. A hollow, dark-eyed, empty skull. Ellerman's voice faintly. Smell of burning toast.

He retreated and walked out of Door into the night. Elsewhere, lights were on all over Cranchester. The School went on as if nothing had happened. There were still some days of the Half to run. Tomorrow, Angus reflected, would have been Tassel Night. The banned Tassel Night. Praefaectors alone inhabited the shell of Ansell's – their seats reserved for the midday train. Except for Ellerman. He had elected to remain behind to play for Cranchester in the important Marlborough Match. It was a decision which the High Master appreciated enough to send Ellerman a personal note. As he wandered outside he looked back. Light flooded from Big Study.

Automatically he turned towards Marathon. He walked quickly, breathing misty air deep into his lungs. Unsuitably clad, hands deep into his pockets, he felt the mud splashing his shoes and trousers. At Roman Gate he stopped. The higher land was above the mist, the clear sky bright with stars and moon. He imagined he was familiar with every stone underfoot and continued to walk fiercely down towards the ford and across the narrow bridge. Mist enveloped him again, his suit felt soggily permeated. In Big Study somebody had now drawn the curtains badly and shafts of light flecked the chestnut tree. He climbed the stairs and slipped along to his study, ignoring the murmur of voices behind the door with the dinted handle.

Slowly he shed his wet clothes, pulled a towel from the drawer and padded into Tosher. There was plenty of hot water because there had been nobody to use it earlier. He filled the bath and lay numbed, not by cold, but by a total inability to think of anything apart from the warmth of the water. He could feel nothing else.

The door rattled. Mawsom said, 'Is that you, AC?'

'Yes.'

'There'll be supper in if you feel like it.'

'Shan't bother.'

'Craigie wants to see us all. At eight o'clock.' In one way he hoped Mawsom would have stayed, would have offered some consolation, but the outer door banged shut. He stayed where he was until the water was too cool for pleasure. What could Craigie have to say? Nothing of consequence. Nothing more was left to say. He was wrong on both counts.

Six leather-seated upright chairs from Craigie's own dining room in front of his desk. The great, black, shiny grand piano accusingly silent.

'Before you sit down, may I say how grateful I was for the support of Ansell's this morning at the Memorial Service and to all of you for your support this afternoon at the funeral. It has been a terrible day. I thought the House behaved with great sensitivity and sang most beautifully. Christopher's mother asked me to tell you how much they appreciated what you did for him. Also,' he took his glasses off and polished them, 'they want you all to know how happy he was here.'

For one dreadful moment it seemed as though Craigie might break down altogether. 'They know from his letters home that suggestions at the inquest that he might have been bullied were quite unfounded. I must say that, after the Arnold-Ferguson business, I am particularly pleased to hear that. She asked me to thank you, Ellerman, as Head of House. And you, Angus—' Angus looked at his feet, hoping Craigie would stop '—for looking after him. It seems that in his last letter he said you had been "very decent". High praise.' Craigie smiled bleakly.

Angus knew he would be able to hold out little longer but, as if in answer to a prayer, Craigie stopped. He blew his nose, and put away his handkerchief. He said, 'Now for another matter. First of all perhaps you will all take a glass of wine.' He indicated some Madeira already poured, on a silver tray. Mawsom, being nearest, offered it round. Ellerman refused.

They sat, awkwardly holding the small glasses.

'Ellerman came to see me on very serious matter today. It would seem that, prior to Christopher Carleton's death, there had been considerable speculation as to why he should have come through to Private so frequently at night. I believe that the fact he did so, attired for bed, encouraged the supposition that I had been behaving with him in a highly improper way.'

Nobody moved. They were frozen, staring into their glasses, except for Ellerman who looked doggedly at Craigie. The directness of Craigie and the even tone of his voice shocked them. Ellerman's theory seemed, now, utterly untenable.

'I have to say that, with such suspicions, it was only right and proper, not to say courageous, for Ellerman to see me before talking with the High Master. If I may do so, Ellerman, I shall relate the substance of what you said, unless you wish to do so yourself?'

Ellerman said stonily, 'No, sir.'

'Very well, gentlemen.' Craigie referred to a sheet of paper on his desk. 'The Head of House says that you, the Praefaectors, believe I had been systematically interfering with Carleton sexually. That is what you said, Ellerman?'

Momentarily Angus was reminded of Ellins trying to discomfit Atkinson in that early classroom. Ellerman did not drop his eyes. 'I did say that, yes, sir.'

'Specifically you alleged that I have been fondling his penis and testicles on more than one occasion when he was here for music, and persuading him to do the same to me. Is that what you and the Praefaectors allege, Ellerman? I wish everyone to be quite clear about the charges.'

'Yes, sir. That was what I said.'

Angus, at the extreme end of the row, could see the frigid, expressionless faces of the others.

'I am sorry to be so specific, but it is necessary that you must all know what was said on your behalf, in case any of you disagree.'

Nobody moved or spoke. Angus remembered the Coroners Court. He could not go back on that story.

'You are quite certain that there is no other specific allegation?' Craigie paused looking directly at Ellerman. 'Buggery for instance?'

There was a shocked expelling of breath.

'Oh no, sir! Of course not.'

'In a case like this, Notting, there can be no "of course" about it. Fellatio perhaps?' He paused and looked at them. 'Well, I suppose I should be relieved that I can read from your faces that oral sex, at least, is unfamiliar to you.'

Craigie glanced back at the note before he took a sip from his glass and continued in the same even tone. 'As I have already indicated, I am indebted to you, Ellerman, for your courage in coming to me. It could not have been easy. I also surmise, gentlemen, from what Ellerman said, that it must have been Carleton himself who revealed these regrettable circumstances. Indeed, it is clear that such intimacy could have been specified only by either Carleton or myself and of course it would be most unlikely that I should boast about such conduct, for the behaviour Ellerman outlined constitutes indictable offences. Ellerman also pointed out that your suspicions were confirmed by my conduct in Big Study. He refers to the fact that emotion overcame me – for which I do not apologise. If I was moved to tears, I would have hoped I was not alone.

'Of course the one person who could have clarified this situation for us was buried this afternoon.' Craigie took more wine. 'I wonder what you expect me to say? After all, if I am guilty, as I am assured you all suppose, I will also deny it. Of course, if I *were* guilty then perhaps Christopher Carleton's death could have been brought about by his unhappiness at such unwholesome attentions from an adult on whom he relied. And trusted. Such conduct might well have that effect on a child who was sexually unaware. I wonder if that is what you intend to imply? Ellerman?'

'I did not say that, sir.'

'No, I agree. However you certainly implied it. If I am not guilty, then we can only wonder at the imagination and motive of Carleton and at how he came to invent such a story. It would suggest that he was perhaps mentally disturbed. Or that he was knowledgeable about perversion and that his true nature utterly belied an exterior which seemed frank, ingenuous and, as I'm sure you are all aware in a school like Cranchester, remarkably beautiful. However, as literature reminds us that

> *Though all things foul would wear the brows of grace,*
> *Yet Grace must still look so*

'Shakespeare puts it so well. And after all, it was the fairest of Angels who was cast from Heaven.'

There was a long silence.

'Of course there is another possibility. One which surely can hardly be contemplated in a school like Cranchester. However, in reviewing all the possibilities, however distasteful it deserves to be examined too. It is that this unsavoury tale is a fabrication, not by Christopher Carleton, but by yourselves for reasons which I suppose it might be possible for an astute investigator to deduce and that Carleton's terrible death was a fateful chance which came at an opportune moment for you. Alternatively, the astute investigator, Ellerman, might make deductions that would place you, Ellerman – and the rest of you Praefaectors – under suspicion. Suspicion that you, Ellerman, and all the rest of you, were directly involved in Carleton's death. Certainly under suspicion that the true circumstances of Carleton's death differ in some very important respects from the version offered to, and accepted by, the Coroner. If that is the case, it would of course imply a depravity and depth of corruption which no worthwhile community would countenance. Don't you agree, Ellerman?'

Looking directly back at Craigie, Ellerman said, 'I would agree, sir. *If* that were the case. Which it's not. Sir.'

'Perhaps, Ellerman, you will take round the decanter. Oh, have none of you touched your glasses? I will have a little if I may, Ellerman.'

They could hear Ellerman's feet as he moved across the carpet, the coal rustle in the fire and the sharp sound of Craigie placing his glass on the desk.

'Well, gentlemen, that is the situation as it would appear to me. Ellerman is anxious for the sake of Ansell's and the school that there should be no breath of scandal. In some ways I agree with him – as of course I would if I were guilty. That being so, we shall all need to make some sacrifices.'

They stirred uneasily, Ellerman's face clouded.

'If I were not guilty (and I am certainly not guilty) you will agree that I would be most anxious to remove any whisper of such allegations. With Carleton dead, and if as he was, as you apparently all aver, the accuser, I therefore have no alternative but to ask the High Master for a formal hearing, a rigorous investigation by a first class KC, and who will insist that there is sworn testimony (that is on oath) before a Justice of the Peace from you, Ellerman, Mawsom, Snider, Baker, Notting, Angus – from each one of you, recording the details of Carleton's specific allegations as accurately as you can recall them. You can all understand that, I expect.'

Colourless, but unflinching, Ellerman did not drop his gaze. He said respectfully, 'Of course, sir.'

'Because we would all wish to discover the truth, would we not, Ellerman? If it were discovered that any one of us had not told the truth in front of the Coroner, we could be held in contempt of court, couldn't we, Ellerman? Angus? Or would it be perjury, Ellerman?'

Ellerman mumbled incoherently, 'Dunnosir.'

Notting made a small noise, as if he were about to speak, but Ellerman, recovering control, looked round quickly, quellingly, 'I mean I suppose it would, sir, if anyone had lied, but Angus and I didn't.'

Notting closed his mouth.

Though he sat bolt upright, Angus felt quite limp. He was both fascinated and repelled by Ellerman's doggedness and determination. What did Ellerman really believe? Sworn statements! He knew that he would be unable to stick to his statement at the Coroner's Court if he had to write it down and sign it. He suspected Ellerman knew it too although, after his moment's uncertainty, Ellerman seemed once more unshakeable. Angus wanted to get up and end it all, confessing to Craigie that it was a pack of lies. Throwing themselves on his mercy. He glanced round. Mawsom and Snider caught his eyes momentarily, but looked away.

Craigie's eyes came to him. What he thought he read there took him aback. It was almost as if Craigie knew what he might say, was willing him to stay silent. 'Although I can well believe you, Ellerman, were responsible in some way for his death, after lengthy consideration I have come to the conclusion that you did not in fact murder him.'

There was a gasp. Ellerman had gone white.

'If that had been the case, I like to believe that there is certainly at least one of you here before me who would have come forward with the truth.' Angus knew Craigie meant him. 'I'm only sorry to have to say I don't think there would be more than one. I have my own theories as to what really happened. I surmise Big Study tried to put Christopher Carleton under some sort of pressure. Some sort of trial. Some perverse form of bullying that perhaps frightened him so much that he took his own life. Because I can't believe that was your intention, and only because of that, I have decided to sacrifice my right to clear my name.

'Of course, if I were guilty, as you all say you believe, then this is obviously just a ruse on my part to escape justice. In that case, the fact that you let me escape is the sacrifice which, I suggest, you will be willing to make for the sake of Ansell's.

'However, if I am not guilty, that requires another sacrifice, the sacrifice of Christopher Carleton's reputation, because, if I am not guilty, we must all accept that he told you wicked and shocking lies which could have put me in prison, had he been here to repeat them. It would also mean that Ellerman, Angus and I perjured ourselves in court when we gave them a quite different impression of him. It would mean that I was either a credulous fool, or a complete hypocrite with my address in Chapel this morning.

'Now because each one of you came to know something of Carleton, only you will know whether what you know refutes, or confirms, the spiteful, mischievous and corrupt little liar that such false allegations would prove him to be. If you choose to believe I am in fact innocent, Ellerman, that would have to be your judgement on Carleton. And yours, Mawsom, and yours, Baker, and yours, Snider, and yours, Notting. And,' Craigie gently cleared his throat, 'yours too, Angus.'

'However, I came to know him too, although perhaps in a different context. Not in the Biblical sense, Ellerman, if you understand my reference. Let me tell you how I found Christopher Carleton. A boy of rare talent, of absolute honesty, generosity of spirit and, most valuable of all perhaps, possessed of genuine and endearing innocence. That is how I shall always remember him and I am not willing to sacrifice his reputation, gentlemen.' He stopped for a very long moment and, for the first time, Ellerman was looking away, out of the window.

'You will therefore appreciate that if I remember Christopher Carleton, as I found him, and if I am, as I assure you I am, in no way guilty of the obscene conduct you allege, I have to view the allegations Ellerman has advanced on your behalf quite differently. I have to regard you as malicious, evil, spineless young men who destroyed more than a little boy whom you should have protected; you have destroyed your own souls.'

Angus felt his throat dry. Nobody moved a muscle. They stayed like that. Eventually Ellerman moved. He looked back at Craigie.

Craigie said in the same quiet tone, 'Of course, believing me guilty as Ellerman assures me you all do, you will be unconcerned by these words of mine.' He looked at each of them in turn. If you have clear consciences you will dismiss them as the contemptible device of a corrupt schoolmaster attempting to escape the consequences of his despicable actions. Your own integrity is of course your salvation,' adding with velvet voice, 'or your own damnation of course.' The clock ticked loudly. 'It is my belief that you will never, throughout your lives, free yourselves from what you have done. Or allowed to be done in your name. It is what you deserve.'

He stood up. Slowly, the tension drained. Notting was licking his lips, trying to catch Ellerman's eye. Baker polished his heavy spectacles. Mawsom and Snider gazed fixedly into the glasses they did not sip. Angus felt numb. He did not want to think into himself.

With a quick decisive movement, Ellerman stood up and moved to the desk. He and Craigie were barely a yard apart. The colour had come back into his face. They stood like two opponents, two fencers, two chess-players, alert but relaxed, each sure of his ground.

'What is to happen now, sir?' He might have been asking about a cancelled House match. No visitor entering at that moment would have been able to guess what had just passed.

'Do please sit down, Ellerman. Or would you like some Madeira? No? I'll tell you what is going to happen.' He poured himself another glass. 'In view of what you have said, Ellerman, and what I have said, it must be clear to each one of you that either you cannot stay as Praefaectors, in Ansell's, at Cranchester—' There was a communal indrawing of breath. '—Or, Ellerman, I cannot stay as Housemaster. Ah, do I see that this solves a problem for you, Ellerman?'

Ellerman made no response.

'Of course, if I were guilty, as I am told you all believe,' he cast his eye round, 'then who could trust me with another Carleton? On the other hand,' his voice took on an edge which had been entirely absent until then, 'as I am not guilty, I must make it equally clear that I would wish to have nothing at all to do with any of you. Or with a House such as Ansell's. Does that confirm my guilt? Is it cowardly? Would not a guiltless man stay loyally soldiering on? Even if he felt the House deserved to be razed to the ground like the monastery which once stood where the School now stands? If, when I wept in Big Study the other night at Christopher Carleton's death, it was, in your eyes, proof of my guilt, so be it. However, I can assure each one of you of this: there is no danger at all that I shall weep for Ansell's. Nor for any of you.'

With a change of tone, 'I have taken the following steps. After Ellerman came to see me today and after I had thought about the matter, I went to see the High Master. As you would expect, if I were guilty, I did not reveal too much. I did not explain, nor give him all my reasons, so you will no doubt draw your own conclusions to suit your own consciences. I asked for permission to give up Ansell's. And to leave Cranchester. When he demurred, I insisted. I suspect he thought I was being rather weak, cowardly. I told him that after such a tragedy I could not live with myself. I expect that will be true of us all in various ways, don't you? I have little doubt, from the High Master's response, he feels that if I am feeble enough to throw in the sponge because a boy dies, then Cranchester would probably be better off without me. He has arranged that Mr Jowling, now back from his secondment, will take over until a permanent appointment can be made in time for the Autumn Half. He will be once again your Housemaster from the beginning of next Half.'

Ellerman's jaw tightened. Relief? Victory? Did it seem like victory to the others? Angus could not tell from their faces. As for himself, he felt that any victory belonged to Craigie. Yet Ellerman had achieved what he had intended.

'If you have finished with your wine, please leave the glasses on the tray.' They stood up, awkwardly. 'Oh Angus, I'd be much obliged if you would take that tray through to my pantry there, as you pass.' They shuffled towards the door. Should they say goodbye? Shake hands?

Ellerman, polite, now unruffled, said, 'Good evening, sir. Thank you for the wine,' despite the fact he had drunk none himself.

Angus put the tray in the small pantry cupboard and trod soundlessly back into the study. He wanted to say something, anything. Craigie stood, his back to the room, gazing into the fire.

Angus said, rapidly, incoherently, 'You're not the only one who'll remember Carleton as you said you'll remember him...' He ran out of words.

Without turning round Craigie said, 'Have you ever thought, Angus, how strange it is that, at a Christian school, we can so rarely bring ourselves to use Christian names? Have you ever thought that, Angus?' He did not turn from the fire.

Angus fled.

He could still hear the others talking through in Libe. Ellerman's voice was loudly confident, as though convincing himself most of all, 'Of course he must have done it. Why else would he give up the House? He thought I'd go to the High Master. Anyway, the main thing is he's going. That's what's important! I told you Tassel Night would be back next Half.'

Mawsom asked, 'What would you have done, Ellerman? If Craigie had insisted on a proper investigation? After all, Carleton never actually said anything at all.'

'You'll never know now, my dear old Mawsom.'

He heard Notting say, 'I think you would've carried it off somehow. We'd've backed you up.'

'Would you, Notting? I think you'd have cracked, as soon as you were faced with a policeman. Probably wet yourself again.'

'In a full enquiry,' Snider questioned, 'would Angus've backed you up?' I wondered for a moment in there, if he was going to say something.'

'Dear old AC,' he heard Ellerman begin with patronising certainty, 'would have told the same story as the rest of us. I think I can guarantee that.'

The far door opened and closed. He could hear no more. Angus thought, 'No! I wouldn't have backed him up! Not this time. Not again.' It expressed wish more than a certainty. He regretted bitterly that he had not spoken out in there in Craigie's room. Then he recalled the look Craigie had given him. In that he had not deluded himself. Why had Craigie not wanted him to speak, even then?

He was awed by the fact that Craigie was willing to forgo the investigation that would certainly have cleared him completely of Ellerman's allegations and condemned them all utterly. Angus had no doubt of that. Could it be that Craigie was not concerned to prove his own innocence because he knew that by doing so they would all perjure themselves more deeply, less forgettably? Craigie was content to leave them to cope as best they could with the ragged edges of their self-deception, which would, anyway, haunt them for the rest of their lives. How could anyone in his position, so unjustly charged, remain so calm, so utterly non-vindictive. All at once, he perceived the contempt for them all that must underlie it; with deadened heart, he acknowledged that it was his own failure to reveal all the facts in that musty Coroner's Courtroom which had led to this squalid final betrayal, for that is what it was.

He could not blot his cowardice from his mind. Betrayal of Craigie and all Craigie stood for; betrayal of Singleton and all Singleton stood for; betrayal of Carleton who had trusted him so completely. It was all part of the price he had paid for becoming 'a real Ansell's Man': Praefaectors' beating in his second Half; Maunder's discovery of himself and Ellerman in their squalid ecstasy; kindly, humane Singleton burned alive in a tank; affectionate, erotic, Simonsen crushed beneath London rubble. His own ultimate, continuing penance and final payment – the last instalment, of Ansell's membership fee – Carleton's broken body in Big Study.

Table.
Scattered Bible.
Childish neck at an obscene comic-cuts angle.
click-click-click...click......click.... Click.

iv

Angus pushed open the door into Libe. The fire was long dead. He wondered irrelevantly who would clear it now that the House had gone home? He sat where he had sat during his first Half, on the bench polished by dozens of other Ansell's Men. Where Carleton had sat only a few evenings before and where, next year, somebody else would sit. On the stairs he could hear the others in Big Study. Somebody asked, 'Where's AC?' and heard Snider say, 'In case you haven't noticed, he's not been in here since...' and there was an awkward pause.

Mawsom said uncertainly, 'I expect he'll be okay next Half, after the vac.'

To avoid the open door, he kept to the banister and walked quietly to his study. Methodically, he began his packing, placing clothes and books neatly in the black trunk. There would be time enough tomorrow for all that but he did not wish to be idle and to have time to think. He came across a thin blue exercise book on his desk which he did not recognise.

C. Carleton – Latin Prose – Ansell's.

The letters were elaborately ornate and coloured. He remembered Carleton's pleasure at being told he could use the study. Inside was Carleton's copy of his Election photograph. Angus gazed at it, remembering his own; Carleton gazed back, an apprehensive newcomer as he himself had once been.

Until that morning and the Memorial Service, there had been times when he felt Carleton was still near him. Once or twice, as he woke, he had half-expected Carleton to turn up, round a corner, telling him that it had all been a hoax. The finality of the funeral and the sound of backfill rattling on that dreadful box had changed that. Carleton was now just a face in an old photograph. Even the deliberate brutality of putting it like that failed to move him. Perhaps that was what frightened him most, for it confirmed what he had suspected there in the winter churchyard. He could no longer feel anything at all.

On impulse he opened the secret cavity, by the fireplace and scooped out all the cones, wood and coal lumps that remained, stretching his arm as far as it would reach. In the farthest recesses he found another cone which he fancied that he might have gathered in his first year. He piled some of the fuel behind the bars of the thin black battered grate and lit a fire. He tore the exercise book to pieces and fed the flames. Then he did the same with the photograph, testing himself to find out how much the destruction of these last links hurt. It made no impact. He tore off the covers and disengaged the pages of the Dylan Thomas Craigie had given him for winning The Greystoke and fed them in bunches to the flames. In the distance he heard footsteps of the others coming to bed. He switched out his light. He heard Mawsom next door. After a while Mawsom knocked gently. Feigning a sleepy voice, Angus muttered something unintelligible.

'Sorry,' he heard Mawsom say quietly. 'I didn't mean to disturb you, Nothing important. I'll tell you tomorrow.'

Mawsom's door closed. After some time, he heard Mawsom get into bed. All the time he had been slowly feeding cones to the fire. He felt wide awake. He switched on the light again and resumed packing, now with more purpose. He did not hurry, but at last he had packed almost everything, even the shabby old green tartan blanket that had turned the trunk into a convenient extra seat. It would be sent home with all the other school trunks at the end of Half. Last of all, he placed his small overnight case on the bed and put inside it his pyjamas and his washing kit. He knew that it was too late now to go to bed. Or too early.

There was still the battered volume of Hopkins on the mantelpiece.

He opened it at '*To Mortal Beauty*'. Deliberately he tore out the page and burned it in the dwindling flames. Then slowly, methodically he added the other pages one by one, until he was left with one sheet and the covers. He broke the boards and added them to the small pyre. For a time he held back '*The Handsome Heart*'. The pencilled initials, C.A., in Singleton's hand seemed to interchange themselves and change back again – *C.A .AC CA ACCA ACCA AC CA A CC AC*.

Eventually he committed that too. By then the fire had almost died to nothing and this last page did not burst into flame, but slowly, gradually, charred brown and writhed as though it had life of its own, *CA ACCA CAA CC AC*, until finally it lay complete and unbroken, but entirely burned, a fragile black rectangle. The lines of print shone silver and, by some quirk, Singleton's pencilled 'C' stood out larger and bolder than anything else.

Christopher Singleton. Christopher Angus. Christopher Carleton.

Putting his forehead on the hard ledge of the mantel, Angus was overtaken by the grief he had been unable to feel at the graveside. Even now, no tears came to his eyes, but in his heart and imagination he wept as he had wept once, a long time before in that same room. He did not know how long he stayed like that.

Eventually he sat down. Perhaps he even slept a while. Outside he heard the clock strike in Great Quad. The window seemed not so black. It might not be very long now before one of the others rose early to finish packing Snider, or Notting, or Ellerman, or even Mawsom next door. He did not want to meet them. Again. Ever. He bent down to the grate and, with his forefinger, gently crumbled the blackened page until it merged anonymously with the rest of the ashes.

Picking up the overnight case, he walked carefully, quietly, down the stairs and out of Ansell's. It was still extremely dark. The flagstones in Great Quad were rimed with ice. No light shone in Lodge. It did not occur to him to avoid it, as he could so easily have done. When he trod the road he was conscious that he had no difficulty in discerning its especial blackness against the grey fringe of frosty hedges. The station too was in darkness except for a feeble platform lamp and a distant signal which glowed redly in the greying air.

He sat, chilled, alone, on a scarred bench, feeling loose within the clothes he wore as though he had somehow grown smaller. Perhaps he dozed again. Far away, he heard the lumbering approach of the first, slow, stopping-train. His eyes played tricks. For minutes at a time, it seemed much lighter, with the cold flat light of a December morning then, as he tried to peer into the gloom it would become darker again. Eventually the locomotive snuffled lethargically into the station and his consciousness.

The train, unlit because of some temporary fault in the circuit, settled darkly at the platform, dribbling steam and waiting for the signal to drop. He had no difficulty in finding an empty compartment. Perhaps he was the only passenger. Perhaps it was not a real train at all, but some funereal phantom come to take him into oblivion. He closed his eyes. For a moment he saw Carleton on Silbury clasping his knees and talking animatedly; this image was immediately replaced by the picture of the small, anxious figure in pyjamas slightly too large, stepping forward from the old Bible in Big Study, so certain of rescue as Angus opened the door.

The memory was too much to bear. All at once he thought he could smell again the new-turned clay in the graveyard, scent so strong that it seemed to fill the compartment. It grew overpowering. He imagined the small wooden box pressed down to the bottom of the shaft by the column of earth on its lid, imagined granules of soil pressing on his own eyelids and the damp, musty, taste on his own lips and tongue. He gagged, could not breathe, the familiar tightness far more terrifying than he had ever known before, so that he cried out aloud, gasping for air, as if the earth pressed on his own chest and each spadeful of soil drummed down upon him as it had drummed on Carleton's coffin.

The carriages jolted; lights came on suddenly; the nightmare receded. His breathing began again; he found his face cold, but soaked with perspiration. Sluggishly, laboriously, the train reluctantly began to haul itself away from Cranchester. He tried again to conjure up Carleton's face but, as with Simonsen and Singleton, he could not remember it any longer. The dim, flickering lights of the compartment blurred and multiplied in his eyes as he swayed to the gathering motion. Uninvited, unwanted, a single haunting phrase of music slid into his mind and forced itself onto his lips, *And he heard my complaint*, but the tone of voice in which he murmured the familiar words utterly belied their original meaning.

The night sky had faded a little in anticipation of daylight. Through a square of still splinter-netted window the squat tower of St Peter and St Paul, with its curious stumpy little spire, pointed accusingly up at the heavy December sky from the dark earth beneath.

Retribution

A**ngus** never returned to Ansell's. He brought forward his National Service, extended it for three years and served with Intelligence in Malaya and Aden (where he won an MC). You would often have seen his Sunday column on world affairs, which became essential reading both in the House of Commons and internationally and you saw him on television frequently. Though he never took up the Balliol Scholarship offered on the evidence of his Greystoke Essay (submitted in his absence by the High Master of Cranchester) he was the enthusiastic choice for the Mastership of a new graduate college at Oxford specialising in international relations, founded by a stunningly generous donation from Oil International. He adamantly refused to allow his name to go forward.

Baker stayed until the summer; was finally Tasselled for cricket because he was a member of the Ansell's side which won the House Cup for the fourth year running although he never had to bat or bowl the entire season. He won a Science Scholarship to a famous Cambridge College, has held innumerable visiting professorships and received various honorary degrees. He will make a notable President of the Royal Society in the not too distant future.

Dermott-Powell created an entertainingly notorious scandal when he vanished from an illustrious London boys' day school, at the same time as the Director of Music and disappeared until, a few years later, under different names, they burst to stardom playing father and son in a musical Hollywood spectacular, where his good looks and auburn hair broke hearts of both sexes. You have almost certainly laughed with them, sung with them, danced with them (and on seeing his most recent film, cried with them). Their private life was a source of endless speculation for gossip columnists.

Ellerman captained the Eleven (also the Fifteen) and was a notable Head of School. After representing the Army in both Rugger and Cricket (and playing several times for the MCC) during his National Service, he got triple blues at Oxford for both sports; took a double First in Greats; won the most spectacular All Souls Fellowship of his decade and then, having been capped for England, in both Cricket and Rugger, threw it all up to help found a new university in a Middle Eastern sheikdom, where his inevitable involvement with the discovery of oil brought, just as inevitably, a knighthood as Chairmanship of Oil International. Heading the new Commission on Sport in Education means that, at the very least, a seat in the Lords will follow.

Mawsom is still a solicitor in a large West Country market town. He, his wife and four delightful-looking children, featured some years ago in *Country Life* when, unexpectedly, he inherited Bowerford, his godfather's beautiful, small, country house with its famous rose garden, about forty miles from Cranchester. He took over as Head of Ansell's on Ellerman's elevation to Head of School and stayed on a further term after the summer. The names of all four sons appear in Ansell's Lists.

Notting avoided National Service because an expensive Harley Street consultant certified a heart murmur or something similar. He made a great deal of money soon after he left, discovering that he could understand the Commodities Market without trying. Subsequently his thrusting abrasiveness gained him wary respect in the City. He has been a Cabinet Minister, for he is still a leading authority on Overseas Investment. No world financial crisis these days seems complete without some comment or quotation from him. It is rumoured that, although politically ambitious, he has had to watch his back.

Snider was also Tasselled for cricket, for he too was in the side (none of their opponents ever scored treble figures) that summer. He never married, but became perhaps the world's finest paediatric surgeon, renowned for the remarkable work with children terribly injured in accidents in his exclusive Swiss clinic, until he threw it up in order to operate sixteen hours a day in a ruined hospital, on children maimed in a remote, civil war-ravaged African state.

※

For only the second (and perhaps last) occasion, I take out from that grubby, much re-addressed envelope tucked away amongst all those other school photographs, an unheaded sheet of thick, yellowing, writing paper, the folds already slightly brittle:

Christopher's father and I would like you to have this. With all our thanks for what you did for Christopher. Margaret Carleton

On that one and only return visit, there were three things I deliberately did not do. I saw, but avoided reading, an unobtrusive commemorative oak plaque at one side of the Roll of Honour in Ansell's. I did not seek out a small marble rectangle in Chapel Cloister. Above all, I did not push open the lych-gate of the small but perfect church of St Peter and St Paul, nor walk across mossy turf to a spot where the faded snapshot accompanying her sad little note shows the mellow briar-draped wall now shelters a grey stone slab with its restrained inscription:

HERE LIES
Christopher Carleton
Music Scholar of Cranchester School
Who Died Accidentally on November 30th 1946
Aged Twelve Years, Eleven Months and Five Days
Safe in the Loving Memory
of his Mother and Father
and Friends at Ansell's
I waited for the Lord